J.R. VAINEO

The Onyx Prince

The Journals of Ravier, Volume III

JRV Books, LLC
UNLOCK YOUR POTENTIAL

*To the one who has talked me out of a dark pit
so many times, I've lost count.
You know who you are, and I thank you.*

Contents

III   At the Precise Moment

IV   To Become a Legend

Acknowledgement

Special thanks to some people who made this book possible.

J. VaineoHurst, for always being a listening ear; encouraging the continuation of the story, even when it was hard; and being an all-round good guy. Life is better with a partner. I'm glad it's you.

M. Gray, for being an amazing editor. Ever so patient with all questions and concerns. She's a super editor. Up there with the greats! I can never thank her enough for being tougher on my writing, making me grow as a writer. There are still things I'm stubborn to change. It's definitely been a team effort.

T. Barber, of Dissect Designs, for crafting absolutely stunning book covers. His work is that final, breathtaking detail that brings the story to life before the first page is even read. Each project has been a blast to work on.

I want to thank **my readers** as well. Y'all are great! Books are worthless, without a fan base. I'm glad you're along for the ride.

Here's to living an incredible life. Cheers!

Summation of Volume I:

« Kings of Muraine »

Tyler Malik Ravier grieves the loss of his father, Lance. It has been a year since his death. The new reality has set in, and it's crushing Tyler. He wonders how he'll be able to bear it. Over dinner that night, his mother, Amira, gives him the gift Lance had intended on giving the year before: the black-and-gold diver's watch. Tyler has no sooner set it to the current time, that night of his fourteenth birthday, when he finds himself falling fast asleep. His senses are starting to sharpen.

He startles awake, when a creature screeches in the night. After he spots darting lights passing the forest edge, near his home, he knows he must go investigate what it is. With that one decision everything begins to change for Tyler.

Two strangers have arrived from another world: Muraine. To his shock, Tyler learns that Muraine is where his father was from. The land of Paragon, specifically. Talok and Ryco have brought him LanSoren's dragon-horse, Awngeleik. Still young and brash, she's in grave danger on Muraine. The Vitiosyn King, Zymarc, demands that she be given over. But these Paragonians refuse to do so. Tyler doesn't understand *why* they refuse. At first, he doesn't care much either. He's simply consumed with the anger that his father never confessed the truth to him, while living. And, now, Tyler's given the task of finding his father's hidden belongings, while also tending to Awngeleik. What could go wrong?

Much, it seems. Tyler discovers that his hated classmate *and* nearest neighbor, Gemma Galloway, somehow plays a part in all this. She's desperate for a chance to make up for her unkind actions of the prior year. Gemma wants to change. Tyler doesn't believe that she can. Yet, her knowledge of things he's ignorant of, things to do with Muraine and his father's last words, make Tyler hesitate in pushing her away completely. Then there's the plight of Gemma procuring pictures of Awngeleik, swimming in the lake surrounded by forest, near Tyler's home. He must hide Awngeleik's existence. He must steal those pictures. He must destroy the evidence. No one else must ever know about the dragon-horse.

What started out as a task of stealing and lying and sneaking around, however, leads Tyler into the beginnings of a truce. A friendship with Gemma Galloway. She tells Tyler of a particular person she imagined, when she was a child. His name was Soren. Tyler recalls the two strangers calling his father by the name LanSoren. He thinks his father may have been this *Soren* Gemma's talking about. Then Tyler discovers Soren's full name: Soren of the Monel. There's a painting of him, hidden away in Lance's study. Soren's face is blacked-out in the image, and a phrase—*'Thirteen. You're done.'*—is painted in red over it. Also featured in the painting with Soren is Adair Tomatsu Galloway, Gemma's great-grandfather.

More truth starts unfolding, when two King's Guard of Talok's come to check on Tyler. Musgrae and Ben tell Tyler that the portal's been broken for six months on Muraine. Somehow, only days have passed on Earth. It baffles the lot of them. The two guards also seem distressed over the news that a star creature—a Vardiya, which Tyler and his mother caught at the lake—has died. They also don't much like the fact that a beast was hunting Awngeleik, just moments before their visit. Neither Tyler nor Gemma saw it. But they felt it. Tyler sensed the power coursing in its body too. He craved whatever it had to give, yet he had no idea why. These feelings of his, he keeps to himself long after the incident. The beast had almost happened upon where Tyler and Gemma were hidden. There to distract it was Tyler's unseen—and unknown—protector. The two creatures ran off, leaving Tyler and Gemma free to get Awngeleik to safety. They relay all of that to Musgrae and Ben.

Even after traveling to Muraine, to The Eye of Paragon, still, no one has an answer for Tyler and Gemma. Nor an answer for whom the unseen protector could be. Also in question is the matter to do with his father's sister, Miriam. Tyler's never met her, yet she sends birthday cards every year, without fail. Despite this, he's told by Talok that she died many years ago. And why does no one know the real cause of LanSoren's death? Things just aren't lining up.

It's a whirlwind of events, shortly after they make it to Muraine. Tyler helps to save a Keeper of Memories from dying. But not without consequence. He's able to make a quick recovery, and is then given a special coat his father helped to design with a Vaegon woman named Madeleine. King Talok recognizes the coat's design as the Sleeping Dragon. Gemma, as well, is fitted with new clothes. The two of them are quickly fitting in, with the habitants of Eyo'el; even a sad girl, who's possibly lost both of her parents in the attack earlier that morning, makes fast friends with them.

Both Tyler and Gemma have been cleared to stay for two days by Zepharre, and Talok's other advisers, while the Paragonians celebrate their yearly festival, the Withrasyn-Vaegon Festival. This year's different in Eyo'el, however. With their King ReNovak, Gyronawv and the Onyx Warriors are there to perform in the celebration. The last time they were a part of it was centuries ago. Back when Zymarc was a young Onyx Warrior, the favored one of ReNovak, *before* he became the feared King of Vitiosus. It seems, his power is growing. Yet he honors the Rules of Engagement. He gives the Paragonians one last festival, one last chance to hand over the dragon-horse. But war is brewing.

The first night of the festival concludes, after Siveyra Gyronawv—Warrior of the Nyxane—summons Soren of the Monel. Tyler's quick to regret his taunting request of King ReNovak to have Soren summoned. The Sorsryn of Old is more powerful than most. And he's on the hunt for Gemma Galloway. He's obsessed with her, really, and none are sure as to why. What is so different about the Galloway family? Sure, Adair was Soren's apprentice long ago. But was that all? Is there something different about Gemma? In fact, different about all the Galloways in Gemma's lineage?

Tyler has little time to think on the many questions piling up. In the early-morning hours of the celebration's second day, the Vitiosyns strike. It's chaos, during the mad dash to escape the Castle of Sosha. They wish to escape the city, but it's too late. They're forced to stay, to take shelter in the bunkers below the city.

Before heading to the bunkers, Talok commands his King's Guard to protect Tyler and Gemma. He means to create a ceasefire, by offering himself in place of Awngeleik. Against the others' wishes, Talok abandons them to head for more dangerous ground: the forefront of the attack. An Emerald Sorsryn, by the name of Rozeth, takes the Paragonian King there. Hours pass. Khyra, the City Architect, is wounded badly. But Madeleine suffers a bleaker outcome. She nearly dies from her injuries. Members of the King's Guard, Quall and Kent, relay the awful truth that she will most definitely have to relearn everything. Only Tyler's whispered commands to her—to forget the past, forget the pain—save Madeleine from losing everything. But she loses eight years of her memories. What mystery she had about her aura is gone too. Bright and happy, but confused, it seems that Madeleine will survive the worst. But will Talok? He manages to arrange for the Vitiosyns to call a ceasefire. His consequence is to be marked for death. His death will come slowly. At the end of twenty-two days, King Talok of Paragon will die, unless Awngeleik is relinquished to Zymarc.

Tyler is brave to some, and stupid to others, for breaking the Rules of Engagement. With the Paragonians behind him, and the Vitiosyn line in front, he steps onto the forbidden space of ground and demands that Talok be given over to him. The Paragonians have lost out on being named the Onyx Victor. It is a title the Vitiosyns have won, instead. But there's still time to think of a plan, time to save Talok, and opportunities to keep Awngeleik hidden. It's all because Siveyra Gyron was able to procure the twenty-two days for them.

The Onyx Sorsryns are neutral. Their allegiance must be won. Their prospective ally's worth must be proven. And the Vitiosyns have proven their worth, with the work of a spy placed among the Paragonians. Gyron has no choice, but to side with the Vitiosyns. Though he's fallen for a Greyvon ally of Paragon, Rorka of Pariah, there's nothing he can do but obey a new master. And that new master is Zymarc of Vitiosus, by proxy of King ReNovak, who has mysteriously skipped out on giving the verdict in Eyo'el. No one's seen him since the night of the festival. Where could he have gone?

Tensions rise, when the spy's identity is revealed. Tyler duels this spy, this traitor to his heart, as a means to make Zymarc and his Vitiosyns leave for a time. What starts out as a duel is interrupted by the Greyvon Alpha, Jasper. He missed the festival. Now, the commotion of his arrival in Eyo'el is enough to stop Tyler and the Vitiosyn spy from killing each other. During this pause in the fight, something shocks Tyler. He's taken back through time to see his father. Lance is tending to the Arkivara of Trauvo, a place where memories are kept, when he notices Tyler there with him. He hardly believes it.

There's much conversation. Tyler gets some answers. He also gets to hear his father's goodbye. Against his will, Tyler is thrust back into the present. Someone follows him through. As the city of Eyo'el starts coming back into focus, Tyler sees Talok, still looking defeated. Zymarc gazes on, in victory. Then there's Alpha Jasper appearing fearful, as the intruder behind him fades into focus. It is Soren of the Monel, elated to have found his way to the present time. Seeing the ill intent in Soren's gaze, Tyler is certain he means to kill someone. But whom? Find out, in **Hunt the Dragon Within**.

Summation of Volume II:

« Hunt the Dragon Within »

Tyler Malik Ravier is thrust back to the present. Soren of the Monel has followed him through, managing to get hold of the twin daggers while he was at it. Tyler finds himself defenseless for the first part of the scuffle of trying to wear Soren down. Alpha Jasper has been put in some kind of containment prison, initially unable to assist in stopping Soren. Ironically, it's King Zymarc of Vitiosus who does most of the beginning work in keeping Soren from going too far, to stop the Sorshrynak from breaking laws of time too badly.

After great effort, and additional assistance from various characters on both sides of the war between Vitiosyns and Paragonians, Siveyra Paydinn uses his Book of Time to put Soren back where he belongs in the past. As promised, the Vitiosyns leave Paragon, with the assurance to return to discuss agreements. Before their departure, however, Zymarc reclaims allegiance of Deezalo's Hammer, by surviving an attack from Alpha Jasper while he's in beast form. That weapon is also the one thing able to break through Soren's barrier, to free those trapped inside.

Only the City Architect of Paragon, Khyra, was able to pass through the barrier, in order to distract Soren. Later on, when Tyler finds out that the food stores have been poisoned, and the people in the city of Eyo'el are going to starve to death or die from depletion of magic in their systems, he turns to Khyra for aid. They fail the first time, in lifting the poison. They die together, in limbo. That place between life and death. Tyler's never gone there with another, until Khyra. Something causes time to revert. Tyler hears a dark voice—not that of the Vardiya, Aysivak, who loaned him the power he'll have at age eighteen. Rather, a different voice. Then Aysivak fades in, talking to Tyler, telling him not to use any of his three chances, next time. Get it right the first time.

Before Tyler leaves Paragon with the others, he discovers that Awngeleik has two hearts—a dragon heart and a horse heart. Also, he and Talok attempt to send Gemma Galloway home through the portal. When they get to that spot in the forest, they find King ReNovak there, waiting. He has even drawn the portal waters together. Tyler senses something amiss. The same feeling he got when the beast lurked near his home on Earth overcomes him. In reaction, Tyler activates the place of in-between, and he asks Aysivak to break the portal. Only restore it when it's safe for him and Gemma to go home.

Talok is livid over it, but he doesn't know for sure that Tyler did anything. Much later, he does find out, and his blood craving increases. Talok's hunger starts out slow. It progresses as time goes on. He only has twenty-two days, before the Geldryn device on his wrist is set to kill him.

Ben went to Yharss-Rawshuen, after Tyler gave him the gloves that were hidden away with the twin daggers behind the Windmill painting. It was a parting gift, or so Tyler thought. Later, in the city of Grevagg, home to winged creatures, Darklyres of RawZend, it's apparent that his father, LanSoren, anticipated this gift being given to someone, a person who could later find Tyler at the right time. The gloves and daggers are like beacons to each other, if you know what to look for.

Tyler and his friend are quickly caught up in a race against time to save King Talok of Paragon. The device of old is slowly changing Talok. Though Tyler and the team are desperate to find a way to free him of it, Tyler also stays alert to anything that could tell him who his father's killer is. No one seems to know who killed LanSoren of Trauvo. It is a truth Tyler will look for always, until he finds it.

The group of them goes on a journey across the landscape of Muraine, meeting many new faces and encountering new species along the way. In the end, Tyler's wits and beginning power are able to procure more days for Talok. It gives them the time they need to carry out the means to save the King of Paragon. There isn't any surety that they can save King Talok, but a mysterious Darklyre of Clan Jhire, Arsyn, holds the answer. What is it? Tyler, Gemma, and the Paragonians will soon learn what it is, and that knowledge will lead to the hardest decisions any of them have had to make. Join Tyler in his many struggles held within the pages of **The Onyx Prince**.

Prologue: Legends of Two Sorsryns

Winter's Vondaen has fallen from Zymarc's grasp. I now stoop down, to pick it up, and give it back to Zymarc, before making my request of: "Add thirteen days to the device."

Azabahk chortles out a scoff-like sound. "You could've ended King Zymarc, yet days of thirteen are all you ask, devil-born tyke."

Zymarc counteroffers with, "Eleven days."

I div to Ryco, asking, *"Is that enough?"*

He subtly shakes his head.

"No," I reply, to Zymarc. "Thirteen days. Or we're done." Just to make him understand the seriousness of my request, I aim the dagger tip to my own throat, and add, "You'll be giving my cousin those thirteen days, or you'll be watching me shove this dagger into my throat. Your choice."

I know the bet that I'm the hole in Zymarc's armor is risky. But, for whatever reason, he doesn't seem to want me dead. Quite the opposite. Very much alive, and apprenticed to him. To what end, I've no idea.

Zymarc scratches at his throat. Then he sheathes Winter's Vondaen. "Done," he says. "Bring him here."

I lower the dagger.

Ryco and Rozeth drag a resisting Talok toward Zymarc. He's almost to him, when a ruckus sounds within the wide hall outside.

Unconcerned with the approaching noise, Zymarc steps forward. "Did I mention," he says, in innocence, "that I brought a certain old Von-dog with me? Turns out, he couldn't stay away. He had to try to save his son. I confess, I've starved him for nearly two days, to work up his appetite. And he's *very* hungry."

The space surrounding Talok's wrist darkens, and Zymarc manipulates the device. But we can't tell what he does. Zymarc concludes his work. The shadow fades, and as it does, Quall, Musgrae, and Eli are chased into the room by Merlynite. He's in that vicious, metal-beast form. Behind him are Mekka and Jasper, in Von form, trying to corner their turned comrade. All of them are beaten down, or bloodied up, save for Mekka and Merlynite. The two Vons go at each other. Darklyres and Vitiosyns flee to their own spaces of safety in the library.

Jasper roars, and the room shakes. Books fall off shelves, and turn into birds. They head right for Jasper. As they pelt against him, he takes on his metal fur, and eyes likened to hot coals. He's bigger than Mekka now, yet nowhere near as quick.

Frightened by this form of Jasper's, the birds fly off. When they land on various surfaces, they change back into books.

"Jasper," I call out, "there's a Soren statue. Monel's spell-book too."

Jasper rushes that way, taking giant leaps; Zymarc goes to cut him off. He manages to dive over a desk, and kick Jasper down.

Jasper rolls, shifting into human form. He's bruised and bleeding. His chest hammers out each breath, as he weakly calls to Mekka, "You have to kill Merlynite. He's born of the same generation as me. He seeks to claim the title. He seeks to drain me till I'm dead."

"Please, Alpha!" Mekka growls, in sorrow. "I can't kill him!"

"Then Musgrae," says Jasper desperately. "Musgrae, you do it."

Jasper closes his eyes. His hair starts turning white. His breaths get even shorter. Zymarc watches, in fascination. He seems honored to be here, witnessing the death of a great Von.

Musgrae's crouched down, hiding from Merlynite, as are most within the room. A few Vitiosyns and Darklyres have been made fodder for Merlynite, and their blood has splattered all over, staining Soren's library.

Hiding up on the rafters are King Aygor, and the surviving Darklyres. They shoot magic and arrows down, ensuring that the wards—still held at knifepoint—are safe from the Greyvons. Yet, they do not hit a single Vitiosyn.

I go crouch down by Musgrae, and give him an encouraging nod. "Go on," I whisper. "Merlynite doesn't know what he's doing. He's a pawn, slowly killing his alpha. He would want someone to take him down. And he couldn't have a more noble death, than by your hand, Mooz. Restore his honor, back to a Von."

"What of those answers you want from him?" queries Musgrae, sounding gruff. "Gemma told us about who you think he is. You may never get answers for why he was there, hunting you near your home."

"It's all right," I reply, "I can live with that. Save Jasper."

Musgrae nudges my shoulder, as he stands up. He grips his blade tightly, before making the rush frontward. He and Mekka move as partners. Musgrae lines up his blade. He's ready.

Mekka senses this. The hair on his spine stands up slightly. He heightens the severity of the dog fight with Merlynite. It takes a while of maneuvering, but Mekka gets an opening, and Musgrae takes it, cutting deeply into Merlynite's chest. Almost the entire blade is swallowed up by Von flesh. And that Von yelps from the sharp pain. His metal fur changes back to that scruffy coat of Vons.

Unexpected tears stream down my face. Then more flow, as Mekka bites into Merlynite's throat, and holds him down. He suffocates his former comrade, till the old Von-dog stops his struggling. He lies still.

Musgrae pulls the bloodied blade out.

Mekka lets go, his snout covered in blood too.

They appear more defeated than Merlynite does now, even as he bleeds out upon one of the old, pink rugs, staining it back to red. He's gone.

Hardly do I believe it. The beast that hunted Gemma and me, back on Earth, is dead. Yet I've no answers, for why he hunted us in the first place. Did he have a master, who wasn't Jasper? Was Zymarc already his master? Or was it something else, driving him? I may never know. And, now, I must let go. For what is coming, will call for every measure of strength within me. It's time to discover what aura I am.

Do I hold the strength of dyns? Or the cunning of Vons? Is it arrogance to think that I could be an aura of both, the way the Onyx Prince, Setharyn, was? Unlike him, I've no mark of Vardiyas upon my forehead. Therefore,

I must choose an aura, and I choose the dragon aura. I decide to hunt the dragon within. But I quickly realize that I already have. I've already been bold and strong, in the way a dragon would be. Further, I must cultivate, what has begun. I must become bolder and stronger. For the only way to defeat Zymarc may be to overpower him. Outsmarting him seems unlikely. In fact? Near impossible. He has set his pieces down perfectly, for whatever goal he seeks. So, what good would Von aura do, for me? I am not a Von, though some say I am equal to them.

Zymarc moves his focus off Merlynite, lying lifeless in the middle of Soren's Library. The Vitiosyn's gaze stops searching, when he spots me. He divs, *"This day, I shall never forget, Ravier. The day I gave you a false sense of hope, then broke your spirit. For, while you were asking for what you thought you wanted, secretly, I had already planned to take away what you needed. Answers. And now? Certain ones you shall never have. Yet, I will let you live. But the others, with you? Only the spirits know their fate."*

Brokenly, I reply, in Mensa-div, *"Come what may, I'll not let you succeed. I'll learn the truth of what you're really planning. And I will stop you."*

His div echoes, *"Yes! Stop me! I want to be stopped, by the Son of LanSoren."*

For the briefest of moments, his appearance flickers to resemble Soren of the Monel. Then he's back to being the King of Vitiosyns. Zymarc . . .

The one I must now find a way to break, in order to defeat Vitiosus forever.

I

Ignite the Memories

"Ease my burden,
for it numbers in the thousands.
Give me hope, for I've near lost it."

1

What Must Break

Grevagg! It's a city I'll never forget. The capital city of Clan RawZend, where Darklyres gather every year for their Grand Clan Gathering. So many moments I've experienced here will forever be burned into my mind. But these many minutes spent in Soren's Library, surrounded by Darklyres and Vitiosyns alike, will take the highest stage. This moment of hopelessness . . . it rises above all else that has happened.

I, Tyler Malik Ravier, age fourteen, had the chance to end Zymarc of Vitiosus. I had that tip of my dagger, NeiSator, right on his throat. My friend, Gemma Galloway, helped get me that opportunity. But I chose another path. The one with the surety to add more days to my cousin's life. I spared Zymarc, for him: King Talok of Paragon. The cost was great. I may never know the truth of how my father, Lance, died.

I've no idea how to go forward. Sure, I'm of the dragon aura. Strong and brave and stubborn. But that does not tell me what to do, when desperate.

Merlynite of Vondurheil is dead. He was draining Alpha Jasper of life. The one who had to stop it from happening, the one who had to take the kill strike, was Musgrae of Bethsaide: Fourth of the King's Guard. He's retreated to being with the other guards. His face is blank. With each passing breath, though, it darkens further with hatred. No longer does he resemble that human tank on two legs, teasing Kent of Dysarda about his Vaegon ancestry. No. There's only malice in his eyes. That fearsome demeanor of Greyvons has entered his features. In this moment, I fear he could kill one of those Gatroes—the six-limbed, hairless beasts—with his bare hands.

Zymarc strolls around the library for a few paces, then stops by the dried-up stone fountain. He looks to Jasper in pity. "It didn't have to be this way, Alpha Jasper. I hope these Paragonians *and* that Equidyn are worth all you've lost."

Jasper opens his eyes. His white hair slowly returns to a peppered-gray color. "Take what you came for, and leave this place, Vitiosyn. You've won this day, and it is enough. You are enough, Onyx. I am sick of your voice."

"Say it again," says Zymarc, in a tone like silk.

Jasper yells out, "You've won!" He crumples to the floor. Then he strokes Merlynite's whiskered snout and wipes away the tears of his fallen comrade, tears most likely shed during the final moments.

Mekka growls at his alpha, but he does not attack.

Zymarc laughs, and that black, metal mask covering the lower portion of his face makes the sound more chilling. He quiets down. Yet the invisible rope of emotion draws tighter around the room. Around the lot of us, afraid this may be it. We may not be leaving Grevagg with all our members intact.

Arsyn of Jhire is poised to strike. His gaze makes him look nervous. He keeps eyeing Skylin, who looks sick. Sick to her stomach, she can't even tear her gaze from Merlynite's lifeless body.

Talok breaks the silence, declaring, "This is not our surrender. We, Paragonians, do not surrender, *will not* surrender to you." He draws out his weapon of a long-blade.

"What of your ally, the Vons?" queries Arsyn, starting to sweat.

Still in Von form, Mekka confirms, "No weak-willed are here, though my alpha has briefly lost his senses. Even if I should have to challenge for the title, I will not let Vons bow down in defeat."

Desperately, I contemplate how to stop this madman, Zymarc. Death, he does not fear. In fact, he hurts it: Sivondel. I think back to first seeing the King Vitiosyn. The way he took hold of Belzara from afar, with the use of twin snakes, all while we hid Awngeleik from his notice on the road to Eyo'el. He even manipulated a Siveyra into doing his work of punishing Belzara for her misconduct.

How's he doing it? I wonder. *Vitiosus? Metimoran magic?* (those answers seem too simple) *And why fear Jasper that day in Paragon but be absent of fear now?* I conclude that it doesn't make any sense, without knowing why. Without knowing what drives him. What he's really after. And how he's changed. For he has changed. But so have I.

"Are you challenging me, dear Talok?" queries Zymarc, drawing out Winter's Vondaen. He takes a step toward my cousin.

My cousin tenses, standing ready.

Caleiso suddenly enters the room, smiling. "King Zymarc," she says. "I have it. I have the Shield of Shylen. Had to kill some sentinels to get it, but I've got it. We can go." She has in her grasp a large shield forged of three metals. She stands just inside the doorway of the library.

Zymarc glances about, calmly saying, "That simply leaves the blade, Veldakryn. Where is it, King Aygor?" Zymarc looks up at Aygor, still on the rafters, as magic crackles and sparks in the grasp of the Darklyrian King.

Before Aygorinaith can muster a response, Prince-General Azabahk points to someone else on the rafters. "One up there has it. That young sentinel, yonder." His Deathasyn grin emerges, as he focuses on Seqwhyett.

King Aygor wrenches the named blade from Seqwhyett, his former ward, and glides down. Once his footing is firmly planted on the marble floor, he throws down Veldakryn. Still sheathed, it lands with a clatter at Zymarc's feet.

Caleiso, after strapping the shield to her back, moves to pick the named weapon up. She unsheathes the blade to inspect it closely. She gives a nod to Zymarc. "It is the true Veldakryn, my Lord-King Zymarc."

As soon as Caleiso has sheathed the dark blade, the King of RawZend demands, "Release my wards. They are mere children."

Caleiso approaches King Aygor. "Oh, but not all of them are children, are they? That dark-haired girl is my age. Thirteen." She points at Keturah.

Ketty panics. She tries to spot an opening to run, to distance herself from the Vitiosyns. Tears stream down her cheeks. There's no opening. And we're too far away to help her quickly enough.

Caleiso remarks, "Keturah is her name, I do believe."

I clench my jaw tight. Teeth-cracking tight. The muscles of my face and neck ache. How I hate this one before me.

Caleiso's gaze is searching. It stops on me. *"Hello again,"* she divs, with a grin. *"How fares the search to save your cousin? Do you really think adding days to the Geldryn device will save him? He is marked for death. Fate will have him. You cannot stop what has already started."*

My blood boils. I hate her even more.

"Thirteen?" queries Zymarc. "Old enough for her to be a pawn of war. We'll be taking that one, to ensure your cooperation . . . unless you wish to resist, and for all your wards to be slaughtered today, King Aygor?"

"A duel," Ryco suddenly voices. As he positions himself by Talok, he looks to me and then to Zymarc. He concludes, saying, "Between Tyler and Caleiso. You'll recall that they never finished their duel. It is evident they want a rematch. Let the young Sorsivytes decide the outcome of today."

Zymarc's caught off guard. He mulls over his decision, running his fingers along the mask.

Caleiso draws out Veldakryn. "I accept those terms, my king." She's staring at me hungrily. She widens her grin, and all her teeth slowly grow pointed, sharp like Deathasyn teeth.

Zymarc flinches. "What terms? You've not even heard their terms. Nor have we stated ours."

"It is clear to me," she says. "They will want the Darklyres left out of it, as they did with Lemara and his Laykonians."

I rip my daggers off my belt, and yell, "No!" I rush her, until I'm a mere arm's length away. I've NeiSator pointed at her. Its tip is inches from her face. I'm so angry. My outstretched arm shakes. "If I win today, Caleiso, you die. I will get to end you. That is my term. Talok!" I shout, not turning to look at him. "Have I your permission to do this?"

Caleiso's mouth is agape. She closes it, and swallows hard.

Zymarc bellows out a cruel laugh.

I shiver inside, but I dare not look at him. Dare not give away that I *do* fear him. Fear how much he knows. Afraid that this is *exactly* what he wants.

Is it? I wonder, lowering my raised weapon. *How is it that he always gets something he wants? It's maddening! Now he and I possibly want the same thing. For Caleiso to be destroyed. Why would he want her destroyed, though? Hasn't she faithfully served him?*

"Yes, Tyler," my cousin quietly answers. "If you win, you may end her. She deserves no less, for the plot to starve our people. Set the score in our favor."

Soft footsteps pad along the bare floor. Claws click on the marble. Jasper comes into view, in Von form. "Do not lose," he says. He goes to the doorway and sits back on his haunches. He wraps his bushy tail round his legs. His fierce, green eyes have dulled. The hidden storm is hidden no longer. It's simply not there. The sorrow set deep in his heart can't help but show through.

Mekka treks his way to the opposite side of the doorway and takes a similar stance. The two Vons look on as blinking, breathing statues. Aside from that, they do not move.

Zymarc poses his questions of, "What is your term, Caleiso? What will you demand, if you should win against Tyler?"

"I demand the girl, Keturah of RawZend." Caleiso spits out her next words. "She will occupy Krina quite well. Surely one of them is bound to—"

Interrupting her, Zymarc says, "We'll not keep this Keturah. Merely use her as a means of motivation for King Aygor to let us take our leave today, without hindrance. He must agree to that term, before you and Tyler begin."

Keturah, having found her chance, takes off through a gap between the Vitiosyns, who are huddled together to keep the King's Wards trapped.

Azabahk closes in. He catches Ketty by the wrist.

Screaming, she struggles to free herself. She's unsuccessful. "Don't let them take me," she pleads. "I don't wish to go."

"Hush, Ketty!" Deamond, beside Arsyn, speaks out. "If it is a binding spell, you'll survive. They'll have to return you. It is the way of magic."

Ketty quiets down, yet provides a constant stream of sounds—soft sobs, as well as quiet, sporadic breaths.

Aygorinaith keeps calm, asking Zymarc, "How will I know no harm will come to her? And how can I trust that you'll return her, if I let you leave this day? A binding spell of promise is not enough for me to agree. Give me further details."

Zymarc replies, "I will entrust her to King ReNovak, once I've safely made it home. He will keep her in Oniva. You, or a sentinel, may go get her during The Sodon."

After Azabahk hands off Keturah to another Vitiosyn male, he offers Zymarc a paper.

Accepting it, Zymarc lays it on the seat of the fountain, and leans down to sign it. Straightening his posture, he then offers his quill to Aygorinaith. "Do you wish to sign now, or after my Prime-Warrior, Caleiso, has won the duel?"

Zymarc flashes me a look, and divs, *"Good luck winning, Ravier. Do you see the weapons she wields? Veldakryn and the named shield."*

"Do you see what I wield?" I div, in return.

My grip on the daggers tightens, as the Darklyrian King bends down to read the document.

"Are you satisfied with its wording?" queries Zymarc, before continuing a div with me, *"I've seen what they do. They're no match for Veldakryn and the shield, Ravier. Back down. Convince this king to agree to the terms. That way no one else dies today."*

King Aygor replies, "Whether Tyler wins or not, I don't see that I have much choice in signing. What good will come to me, if this Caleiso should die? You'll still be here, threatening the city of Grevagg." Aygor reaches to sign the paper. The quill scratches marks on it. His signature finished, Aygor sets the quill on top of the document.

"King Aygor?" Ketty's voice quivers. "Are they really going to take me prisoner? Are you truly going to let them?"

"You'll be all right, Keturah," King Aygor reassures. "Don't protest too much. Be strong. I'll come for you soon."

Zymarc folds the document up and leaves it on the fountain. But he takes the quill, to slip it into an inner coat pocket. "Has anyone anything else to add, before the duel begins?"

Talok indicates to Caleiso. "Only offensive weapons for this duel. As there is no shield of equal strength among us, or likely to be nearby, you must take it off, girl. Take off the Shield of Shylen. Or concede the win to my cousin. Your choice." He still holds his long-blade in hand.

Caleiso steals a glimpse at Zymarc.

His Vitiosyn-red eyes flicker with amusement, as he looks to my cousin. "Come, come, Caleiso. Stop dawdling. The King of Paragon gave you an order. You should listen to him. Take off your shield. Or"—he pauses, his features turning serious—"keep it on, and fight Tyler *and* his cousin." He focuses on her.

Following a loud, forceful huff, Caleiso reluctantly removes the shield. She gives it to Azabahk.

"Wise choice," says Talok, his expression equally as stern as his voice. He sheathes his long-blade, then circles around the room to stand beside Jasper.

I div to Zymarc, *"How about now? Have you got a bet on me or her?"*

Zymarc shrugs at me, before stuffing his hands into his coat pockets.

"That's my move," I div.

Zymarc takes on Soren's appearance, then he removes the mask. With a flick of his wrist, he discards the metal piece. He goes to sit beside Merlynite. Once he has sat down, he nonchalantly pets the fallen Von on the head.

Azabahk startles at the sight. "My lord-king, what are you doing?"

Mekka starts his low growl, no longer like a living statue by the doorway.

Zymarc looks up. "His spirit still lingers," he says, whilst continuing to pet Merlynite. "A life that's lived as long as he, simply does not fade in an instant. Therefore, I'm telling him what's happening, and what will happen. I want him to carry a message to the spirits and Vardiyas. For Vons do not go to The Kievas. They join the elements. Also, I'm telling him that his son still lives. Droediin. He'll not be dying anytime soon. But it is possible you might be, Caleiso." He looks at her. "I will not save you, if Tyler should defeat you. May that knowledge give you the strength to win." Zymarc eases to his feet. He stands tall, proudly gazing on at Caleiso. "All I have taught you, you must use now."

Caleiso smiles at him, then she directs a scowling gaze at me. The smile diminishes. The blade forged of black metal starts to absorb the light around it, while in her grasp. It lights with fire, then that fire turns black. By the crackling sounds of flame, I know it isn't smoke that licks at the blade's cutting edges. Rather, a type of fire I've not encountered.

Suddenly, I wish my daggers were greater in my hold. That their magic would be revealed, for I know they must be great weapons to have been wielded by Soren, himself. An idea creeps to the surface.

Upward, I glance to the high windows dispersed around the circular library. It is the midday; nowhere near the time of dusk. I toss NeiSator to Ryco and then approach this soul I've hated from that second day of being here on Muraine. It was weeks ago. But it might as well have been an hour ago, for the amount of abhorrence I have for her in my heart.

Confused, Ryco looks over the dagger and then to me. "You're sure you only want one, Tyler?"

"Positive," I reply. Taking a sharp breath, I stare RotaSyn down. I try to focus the hate I feel into the dagger colored of red, yellow, and white. The waking-dagger. Authority, malice, and justice, all in one. It is in my right hand.

A voice speaks out from the metal, as if carried on a gentle wind. It's of neither a woman nor a man. Yet I cannot understand what it says. It stops speaking. The windows of Soren's Library shatter, letting the outside air in. The blade transitions to the dull-yellow color. The handle conforms even more to my grip. I cannot let go of it. It refuses my rejection. And I accept it as it is. The metal of it turns golden; flames to match set fire to the blade.

A second time, I aim one of my daggers at my foe. I walk forward. One foot in front of the other, I circle her. I speak out, "RotaSyn of Dawn's Light, I bid your help to defeat this one before me: Caleiso of Vitiosus."

A voice replies from the blade, "Ravier, I am yours to wield however you wish. But know that you are young, and I am not. Infinite downfalls have I witnessed, while you have not. Countless deeds, deciding the fate of wars, have I and a master done. But you and I are at our beginning. So let us begin. Should this Caleiso be worthy of a downfall, I shall strike her down to the soul, and her life essence shall bleed out to feed Death. Fate is thirsty. Let us quench it. Let our moment be written in the pages of time. I am ready, always ready."

I lower his tip, pointing it to the floor. I stop going forward, and wait for the call of commencement.

Caleiso hisses out a spiteful breath. She tightens her grip on Veldakryn's hilt.

I simply give her my crooked grin.

"Begin," my cousin calls out in a strong voice.

I run at her. She sprints to me. Our weapons clash. The sound is as a crashing wave on rocks. Sparks fly to the sides of us, crackling on the floor as if it is made of hot oil rather than cold marble. Yet nothing lights on fire—only my decision is ignited, and Caleiso's, not to be the one meeting with defeat.

It's as if only we are in the room, such focus have the two of us on being the victor of today.

Though she's on two feet, she snakes around in that feral way. Her blows are blunted by my coat of the Sleeping Dragon. Its fabric refuses to yield to her, to give in to the sharp edges of Veldakryn.

I strike; she counters. She lashes out; I dodge. No blood has been spilled yet. I take off. Skirting around the corner of a desk, I shove it toward her. It hits her hip, and she's thrown off balance. I leap on top of the surface of that desk, then dive down for an attack while she's still on the ground. She rolls away, then kicks me in the head. It hurts. But it doesn't stop me from catching hold of her foot with my left hand. I drag her closer to me. I'm able to stand up. She thrashes, landing her boot heel on the back of my knee.

Pain sears in my leg. But I keep going.

She keeps going.

We won't give up.

Then she gets herself into a position where I must study her movements. She's taunting me to run after her. I won't fall for it. Not a chance. She then casts magic, throwing sparks then fire then ice spikes at me. I cut through them with RotaSyn. The spells absorb into the blade.

Caleiso pants for breath, at the end. She seems depleted of ideas. Her teeth are no longer sharp and pointed.

Ten feet separate us.

I startle a bit, almost drop the dagger, as RotaSyn speaks out, "From that moment of our first meeting, Ravier, when you plucked me from the back of that painting in your home, I've waited for this moment. The moment when we truly are the other's. For it was not at the beginning, nor that day in Eyo'el, fighting against Soren. I slowed down for you, then. Now, I am as I always was. Equipped for whatever comes."

I look from the blade to Caleiso.

She's caught her breath, standing ready for anything. "Your talking blade doesn't scare me," she says.

"But it should, Caleiso of Vosh-Perida," says RotaSyn. His edges flicker with brighter fire. He grows to be an even better blade. More weightless in my grasp. It is no different than if *nothing* were in my hand, slowing my movements.

Caleiso's unsettled, taking a tiny step back. She holds up Veldakryn enough to guard her front side. "This was the weapon of the mighty Veldar, heir of Jhire, former Keeper to The Kievas. So known was he, a trace of him lies within all the land. Even a foreigners' city was named after him. You cannot wipe out all memory of him, he who tamed death. Tamed death with this *very* blade, so the legends tell."

Skylin risks telling me, in div, *"Veldakryn had a weakness, though, in the legends. His power was strongest on the darkest night. He was fashioned for night. Not day. Wield the day, Tyler. That blade obeys you."* She gives me an encouraging look, seeming proud to witness this duel.

Confidence rises up, as does a wild idea.

Soren's Statue is in sight. His look of wanting is directed right at me. I'm in line with him, in line for a shot. I can't help but wonder if I can give my weapon a form. I've thrown RotaSyn before giving it a second thought.

I speak the words, summoning from the past: "Invitios-el-RotaSyn!"

The waking-dagger plunges into the statue's chest. Soren's chest.

Caleiso comes at me with renewed vigor.

I've no weapon. Only quick dodging saves me.

Caleiso shouts, "Ventus!"

Her gale-storm is fearsome, for it isn't simply wind. Rather, it's a disarming wind. My coat takes off with it, leaving me absent of its protection. It splats against the bookcase behind me. The force makes the case teeter. My coat falls to a faded rug. I bolt forward, fully knowing that birds are about to flap about the room in chaos. And they do.

They head for Caleiso, for she is the reason for their disturbance in the first place. She shrieks, as they pelt against her. Next, they come for me. They've almost reached me.

Soren's statue-eyes awaken, glowing green. The dagger exits through his statue. It comes back to me like a boomerang. I catch my dagger. The birds cower away; they head back to their bookcase, and return to book form.

I whirl around, to begin dueling Caleiso again. She's tired. So am I. But we continue until, well . . . how to describe it? Until the world seems to turn upside down. Caleiso and I tumble to the floor. She glances about in confusion, feeling her way around. I do much the same.

I catch sight of the statue in time to watch a figure step out from it. He's tall and tan and thin. His skin shimmers like aged metal. Slicked back, white feathers cover his head, and his eyes glow akin to fire. Light emits from him. A soft light. The kind that could be sustained forever, for it never falters by flickering.

He slowly smiles at me. The world stops spinning.

"Ravier hath summoned RotaSyn," he says, with a strong voice. If dawn had a voice, it'd be his voice. "I hath answered from across the distance. Answered the call of my last master. You, Ravier, are he."

Caleiso's found her footing. She lunges up to attack me.

RotaSyn is quick to act, dashing to my side. He takes a ghostly appearance as thin fog. My movements match all his subsequent ones. I let him lead. Let him show me how to fight this one before me. I find that I'm somehow able to keep up. To speed up, in fact. I'm faster than I've ever been.

Blood is quickly spilled from slashes to Caleiso's arms and legs. She cries out.

So do I. My heartbeat sounds in my ears. I start to hear nothing but my heart pounding as if it'll explode.

Voices swirl around.

I collapse. My vision blurs. I blink hard, trying to clear my focus. It doesn't work.

It's like that day I saved Nyrim of the memory overwhelm. So many feelings do I sense. This time, however, it's excruciating.

Still blinded, I force myself to stand.

A joyful voice shouts nearby, "Denizens of Jextoran! We have won the war. It is over. It is done. Our Nerosh of the Mettos has seen to it."

Sounding curious, a whispering voice asks the first speaker, "Was it truly necessary to mention me, Highness? And did you see where RotaSyn went? He was standing right here beside me a second ago."

Answering him is a dark voice (in fact, the same voice as when Khyra and I died, and time rewound), saying, "Oh, you know how he is, Master Nerosh. He went to check on one of our future masters, to study him. It's what he does. He learns how they are. That way, when they find us, he's ready for them. Indeed, ready to teach them. Always will they be vastly younger than us, and inexperienced."

Nerosh asks, "NeiSator, do you mean to tell me that I die? How lovely to tell me that bit of news, whilst complaining over your future masters being young and inept. Does this mean you will always prefer me to the ones who doth come after?"

"Not telling," replies NeiSator. "But this I will tell. RotaSyn is meddling, not just with time, but with another world. Want me to tell a future master? There's merely one, who can do anything about the meddling, about the harm RotaSyn could do to one of the inept masters."

"Another world?" queries Nerosh, outraged. "That RotaSyn! I've warned him and warned him *not* to do such things. Foolhardy soul of dagger."

NeiSator adds in, "Well, he did have a good reason this time. The future master has much to learn. And he's about to have the lesson handed to him. Want me to tell of that?"

"Yes," says Nerosh. "Tell me at once."

Their voices fade, while I'm still attempting to regain my sight. Currently, it's pitch-black to me. It's getting too quiet. My heartbeat is starting to slow. And not in the good sort of way. It's hard to breathe.

I manage to rasp out words. "RotaSyn, you've got to go back home to Nerosh. Please," I beg him.

He doesn't answer.

Screams start swirling in my head. Of women. Of children. Of warriors. Creatures too. Beasts, even. Yet, silent I remain. And sightless. It's becoming so cold.

Someone calls my name. To my disturbance, it's Zymarc calling out to me.

He strolls into sight. He's the only thing I see. He doesn't look like Soren anymore. Nor the Vitiosyn. Rather, something else. Like a dying, decaying beast on two legs. His welted skin renews itself only to be burned away by whatever surrounds us in this moment.

His voice untouched by pain, Zymarc says to me, "The way to cut the flow from the past is to bleed yourself of magic. Any summoned ones feed off bits of the summoner. Cut off your excess in one sudden moment, and they must go back. They've not a chance to bleed you dry of magic, ending in your death and their continuation. Even if that is not this RotaSyn's intent, it's what he's doing."

"Is that how my father died?" I rasp out. "He summoned someone too strong for him, while he was trying to kill you?"

Zymarc doesn't answer. He simply looks away.

I press harder, willing this Vitiosyn to reply. "He's dead because of you, isn't he?"

That makes him angry enough to scowl in my direction. Yet, silent he remains on the matter, the only matter that truly makes me go forward, come what may.

Seemingly an eternity passes, before he says something. "Call your other dagger to you. Cut deep into your arm. Bleed yourself of some magic. You'll lose the duel, but at least you'll live."

He turns and walks away. He fades from sight.

I scream in anger. Then I summon NeiSator to my left grasp. I plunge the tip into my right arm. More screams echo out. My screams. I tremble. NeiSator slips from my grip. My sight starts to return. RotaSyn's figure is drawn violently back to Soren's Statue. He vanishes. The waking-dagger creeps its way to being closer to me. I take hold of both daggers and struggle to my feet.

Caleiso holds Veldakryn with both hands.

We battle again. Only, I'm bleeding blood and magic now. I can't sustain the strength it takes to defeat her.

She sees my struggle. At last, she kicks me down.

I lie there, bleeding and defeated.

"Say it!" she shouts, pointing Veldakryn's tip at my throat.

Hatred in my heart, I tell her, "I have lost to you, Caleiso of Vitiosus."

She sheathes her weapon, then offers to help me stand.

By my own last bit of strength, I stand without her aid.

Caleiso still offers her left hand to me. "It is how you part ways on Earth, is it not?"

My mouth twitches in disgust. I give a slight bow. Then I force my way to Keturah. My blood leaves a spotted trail, the whole way. Sickened, I reach for her hand. "I tried my best, Keturah. But I've lost. You've no choice but to go. You must go with them."

When she backs away, I start choking up. I hate that I must forcefully take hold of her hand. "Please, Ketty," I beg. "They'll kill us all, if you don't go quietly. Be as brave as you were that day the beast nearly killed you. We were watching. The lot of us, Paragonians. If any of King Aygor's Wards can face this fate, being made all the stronger for it, it is you, Keturah of RawZend."

Ketty nods dejectedly. Though she snivels in fear, she lets me lead her to Caleiso.

We pass Aygorinaith, along the way.

"I will come for you, Ketty," he whispers in heartbreak. He briefly cups her face, before retreating to his other wards.

Caleiso takes hold of the girl, and she binds her wrists with rope.

I turn away.

Skylin shifts on her feet to move in my direction, but her father holds her back.

I find that I can't go forward without collapsing.

No one else comes toward me. No one except for Zymarc. It is by his mercy we are held captive rather than being slaughtered.

I look down, for I cannot bear to see his reaction at hearing my question of, "Who else are you taking captive, King Zymarc of Vitiosus?"

His footsteps getting closer, Zymarc states, "Grawllik, Son of RaeZorgin. I've an interrogation to perform on him, for he has been to the Monel. And I've not been for quite some time. I wish to know if it is as I remember it."

"Anyone else?" I ask quietly.

Zymarc sighs, sounding a little resigned. "No, Ravier. Your efforts of today have saved all the rest."

I just nod. I refuse to look up.

Zymarc sighs again, now frustrated. "But," he adds, "if you don't look at me, before I go, I will let the girl witness horrific atrocities, from this day forward, until she is reclaimed."

I clench my jaw. My breaths sound as hisses. I'm so mad. Today? So full of hate.

Zymarc commands, "Look . . . at . . . me, Ravier."

Swallowing hard, I do as he demands.

He no longer looks as a decaying beast. He has the metal mask back on. His crimson-red eyes consider me. His head is bare, only sporting the marks of what I assume he considers to be his crown. He has hold of my coat by the collar. The Sleeping Dragon. "As you gave back Winter's Vondaen, so I give this coat back to you for a fight well played." He holds it out.

I go to take it. But then Zymarc Mensa-divs, *"You really are quite something, Ravier. If I were younger, if I were still an Onyx, I do believe I'd pledge myself to you. But I'm not an Onyx. I'm a Vitiosyn, through and through. An abomination to the nations of this world. I've accepted my fate. Will you accept yours?"*

My cousin comes to me, then. He's there with Ben and Gemma to heal me, to let me lean on them. King Aygor has spread his wings. All his wards fit in his wide, feathered embrace. Sonya wails. All the wards cry, except for Dea. She stands alone, outside of Aygor's embrace. She lifts her head high, as if to defy what she feels inside.

I reply, in div, *"I can't, if I don't know what it is."*

Once healed, I reach for my coat again. As soon as my fingertips brush against its fabric, I quickly snatch it from his grasp. I stuff my arms into the sleeves. As I'm doing so, I realize that Merlynite is at my feet, still lifeless. I sink to the floor to bury my fingers, then my face, in his fur. I inhale that smell of Greyvons. That strong odor of their blood. I begin to weep silently.

I lift myself up enough to whisper, "Just leave, Zymarc. Leave the city of Grevagg."

"Very well, Ravier," he says. "King Aygor, if you would, please lead us on the safest path out of the city."

No other words are said.

I listen, as many footsteps pace for the exit of the library and then down the long hallway of the palace.

Keturah's whimpers wrench my heart near in half. When her screams echo from the palace entrance, desperate screams for Aygor to protect her, I'm swallowed up by a sick feeling in my heart. I brave a look over my shoulder.

Arsyn has released Skylin, so that she can come to me. Many of the King's Guard have crowded closer to me. Ben now hugs Gemma close, as she softly cries.

I ask Arsyn, "Isn't there something we can do?"

He shakes his head forlornly.

Dea speaks up, saying, "That is a magical contract that has been signed. King Aygor has a piece—enchanted paper. And that abhorrent creature has the other—an enchanted quill. They're of the same set. Whatever's written on that document isn't easily broken. Though I wish that Vitiosyn's head was."

Jasper and Mekka have left their stations by the doorway, both in human form now.

Siege strides past them, to observe the hallway passage. "Shouldn't we be leaving too? And, Quall, where's Warren? Did something horrible happen to him?"

Arsyn, previously staring at the floor, looks up. "Are you mad? Do you want to give him the chance to change his mind? No. We need to give them a head start. Make sure they don't follow your trail. You all hold quite a lot of things he desires. He simply hasn't placed what all those things are, yet."

"He's hiding," Quall replies to Siege. "He said something about having the Kyanite Spear of Guyheiz, and that it could be something Zymarc's after."

"Warren will be fine," Ryco assures him.

"But I'm not too sure about us and our present situation," states Talok. "Also, what of that device, Arsyn? My Uncle LanSoren said you know how to free me of it."

"You're out of time," Ryco says, "for withholding that knowledge."

Arsyn looks as horrible as I feel inside, as he replies, "It's you, Parasogyn. You are one-quarter Sylvadyn and Withrasyn, in addition to half Vaegon. Your blood is valuable to Talok. There aren't any Sylvadyn Parasogyns who are also of a similar race to your young king. It must be you, to forfeit your life in trade for his. I have the spell here." Arsyn gives a worn leather pamphlet to Ryco. "There's a catch, though."

Kneeling on the floor beside Merlynite, Jasper states weakly, "They will need the Blades of Neutrality from King ReNovak—Enyxar and Aevimeis."

Talok sends a great scowl at Jasper. "You knew of this?" he shouts. "And said nothing!"

Ryco begins paging through the pamphlet.

"I didn't have the spell," Jasper replies firmly, as he stands up. "Without the words, knowledge of the ritual is useless. I thought the Geldryn had destroyed that book ages ago. I believed that it was lost forever. But Soren must've saved it, brought it here." Jasper takes in the library, seemingly for the first time. "If only he had remained a scholar rather than become a mass killer."

Eli's near speechless. "Does Ryco truly have to die? That's not a win at all."

"Does that mean you'll miss me, Kirjan?" Ryco grins wickedly, never taking his gaze off the pamphlet.

"This is no time for your banter," says Quall, as he starts to button up his coat. "Is this the only solution you've uncovered, while here? I knew I should've come with. What a mess all this is." He glances to Ryco.

Ryco closes the pamphlet. "We are King's Guard, Quallendeis. The life of the king matters more. It's why we exist."

"My word!" Quall exclaims, undoing the top button he's just fastened. "You never use my given name. You've already made up your mind, haven't you?"

"Yes," replies Ryco, tucking the pamphlet away. "And you can thank Tyler for buying us enough time to carry it out, for it must happen on the Plateau of MarcKand. It's quite the journey. We'll only have time to stop half a day in Vondurheil. A full day at home, to resupply. One night at The Sodon. Then a dragon's flight to the Monel."

Siege counts all the days on his hands. "Seventeen days left. Fifteen, to get there. We'll have two extra, if we travel especially fast."

Musgrae adds, "You have to plan for things going awry. We'll *barely* get there in time."

"Collect anything important," Kent says. "We need to be ready to run, and soon."

"What a day this has turned into," says Musgrae, before suggesting, "Shouldn't some of us go after them? It doesn't feel right, letting them go quietly like this."

Siege grins. "Oh, it won't be quiet. Dragons are growing restless."

Skylin offers to help me up, as no else seems to notice I'm still at Merlynite's side. Before I accept her help, however, I div some words to Merlynite, one drawn-out farewell of: *"I understand. If it was you, who hunted me back home, Merlynite, you who wished to steal Awngeleik from me, I forgive you. I forgive you for only doing what you thought was necessary to save your son. Goodbye, old Von."* I pet his shoulder one last time, and bid him a restful end.

Skylin pulls me up. She hugs me tight. Even presses her wings against my sides. It warms me.

We trail back to the others, as Ben says something about, "Grawllik mentioned that dragons have taken over the Monel as well. They might pose a problem for us."

Aygorinaith abruptly rushes into the library. "Quick!" he exclaims, as he starts shooing us into the wide hallway. "You must leave the city. And I beg that you take my wards with you. I can't have them with me. It's too dangerous at present, and I must convince the Darklyres to flee to Clan Ayzaga. It being at the foothills of where Rubidyns live will protect us from the Vitiosyns following us there. I've sent word to King Rentwar, asking if we are welcome to dine with him. To negotiate new terms."

Dea shouts, "Calm yourself, King Aygor! You're not thinking right."

Aygorinaith whirls around and goes to grip her by the shoulders. "You don't understand, Dea!" He shakes her. "You're half the Shield of Shylen. I disenchanted that shield years ago. I put half the enchantment on your wings, and half with the most mundane of objects here in the palace. Once that mad king attempts to use the shield, and it doesn't work, he'll be coming back with questions. I don't want to be here for that."

In shock, Dea pushes away, trying to process the news.

Like a rant, Aygor continues, "And I must get Keturah back, before he learns the truth. I'm amazed he didn't notice that something wasn't right about it. It must be his obsession with that Sorsivyte, Tyler. I confess I've not ever seen a soul look at another living thing in such a way as that. It's disconcerting. At any rate, I'm hoping King Rentwar will aid me. There is no one else to strike fear into this Vitiosyn, Zymarc. He's not even fearful of the Greyvon Alpha. How are we to intimidate him, without Rubidyns backing us?"

King Aygor then turns his attention to Jasper. "Also, I would ask you, Greyvon, before you depart . . . Will you care if I seal up your fallen brother here in the library? Or do you wish to take him now for burial? Either way, I must ensure that no further harm comes to Soren's Library, during my absence."

Coming out of the shadows, SynKievas states, "A Time Guard spell should do the trick."

Jasper replies, "We will come back for him, if ever it is safe to do so."

"Then I must stay, and cast the spell straightaway," says King Aygor. "SynKievas and Arsyn, go with them. Help give my wards safe passage. Seqwhyett and I will be heading up the trek to Ayzaga, prior to meeting with Rentwar. And, Dea"—he turns to her again—"you know the way through the Fleishyn Forest. Make the path clear. Go as quickly as you can."

Dea takes the lead, and we run after her, exiting Soren's Library.

2

Flee with the Shield

Once outside the Palace of Grevagg, it's loud chaos in the city. Many Darklyres are swiftly packing up food and their belongings.

Several sentinels restrain armed Darklyres to prevent them from taking flight. The ones held back shout curses, begging to be free to go after the Vitiosyns. They're furious.

Arsyn and SynKievas yell commands, and the Darklyres blocking our path move out of the way.

We stumble up the hill, then tear our way to the start of the Fleishyn Forest.

"Yo!" Warren exclaims, rushing from where he stood to come join us in the sprint. "I was getting worried. Was about to start heading for home. Warn everyone. Thought you all might've died."

Ryco shouts above the noise, "Not dead yet! But we're to head for home. Quall said you have the spear. Now's a good time to use it, War."

Warren grimaces. "Not a good idea, actually. Not until we're past this twistin' forest."

Ryco runs faster, grabs Dea by the arm (she's not stopped her full sprint forward). He pulls her to a halt. Her heart beats so hard, her pulse is visible on her neck.

"Hold a moment," says Ryco, out of breath. "This one. She can make the path straight, Warren. The forest obeys her. Use that spear to take us to where we started three days ago. And, tell me, where *ever* did you get that Spear of Guyheiz?"

Tapping his chin, Warren thinks a moment. "I've never practiced magic with a Darklyre, Ryke. To be fair, I thought they'd gone extinct, until we happened upon them yesterday."

Ryco remarks, "It won't be much different than partnering your magic with mine."

"Uh-huh. Sure. No different at all." Warren exaggerates the nod of his head. "As for where I got the spear, it was in King Lemara's armory. It's what I took for my reward. They hadn't any idea of its special importance. Must've been something Vayohl brought with her, centuries ago. Go figure."

Ryco tugs Deamond toward Warren. "Warren, meet Deamond of RawZend. The one who lured us here, with her shifting of the forest maze."

Warren recoils his outstretched hand and states, "Impressive."

"Tell me what to do," says Dea, on edge. Her black, stiffened wings have feathers poking out, making them appear prickly rather than the usual softness.

When Warren takes out the silver, white, and cobalt-blue spear, it grows to full size. It's as long as Quall is tall. Warren tosses the spear, and it floats, moving to encircle the lot of us.

"Take my hand," Warren instructs Dea, as he grips the spear one-handed.

Ryco asks, "Is it true that spear is thrice as fast as the one you enchanted years ago? If so, please be sure to control the velocity. We don't want our things ripped away from us—including our skin—to be left behind for scavengers."

Warren aims his attention to Ryco. "That was one time. My rookie year. You were ill-tempered, that day. It was your own fault, Ryke. Rookie had to do something to stand up for himself. What better way than to strip *Third Guard* of all dignity, while showing my mad enchantment skills by making a running spear? You respected me after that, didn'tcha?"

"Missed you too, War." Ryco grins like a charmer. "Now start us for home."

Dea grips Warren's free hand, then she closes her eyes. Her stiffened wings relax to appearing soft once more. "Do you see the way?"

Warren looks ahead. He slowly nods. "Yeah, got it. Hold tight. It'll be the ride of your life."

He throws the spear, and it soars, whistling like a bottle rocket.

Skylin comes to grip my arm. She huddles close, whispering, "I've never been farther west than the Fleishyn Forest. What's it like?"

"Lots of color," I reply. "Grand trees, which soar higher than any I've seen. Dyns that sleep under glowing coals. There's a sentient castle too. He'd do anything for the people of Paragon."

Sonya says, "Sounds lovely. I wish Ketty was with us to see it."

The sensation of being pulled forward starts out slow, getting faster. All goes white. We hear the air rushing toward us, but we don't feel the force of it.

Then it hits us. We're not pushed back. Instead, it's as if we're leaning against a wall while gale winds hit us from the front. Regardless of how it feels, we have to bear through it.

When we eventually slow down, Warren shouts, "Get your feet ready. We're comin' to a stop."

The wind turns to a breeze.

I start falling forward, disoriented beyond words.

Skylin grabs around my waist to keep me from falling.

We finish the stop where the Fleishyn Forest meets the northern part of the Metsundai.

Deamond collapses on the ground. She gasps, as her black wings alter to a gunmetal color; they take on the appearance of metal too.

SynKievas and Arsyn dash to her side.

"What's happening to her?" queries Sonya, in concern.

Arsyn replies, "Her distance from the other enchanted object is weakening the shield's power. Her body will soon adjust. For now, she needs rest."

Quall wipes off sweat that's beaded on his face. "We all do."

"Three days' journey, skipped," says Siege. "Yet one day for rest."

Gemma adds, "Gives us four extra days. Think we can spend two days in Paragon?"

"We'll see," replies Talok, coming to my side.

Kent winces in pain, as he eases down to sit on the ground. "I think my knee's blown."

Quall and Ben are there instantly, checking Kent's knee joints.

"He won't be able to put weight on this," states Ben, his face clouding over with a multitude of emotions. His features are drawn tight.

Nyrim asks, "Where did your EquiNeins go off to? You didn't walk all the way to Grevagg, did you?"

Rozeth's brows rise. "It'd be ambitious, if you had."

"We lost them in the forest," Eli grumbles. "All its shifting and twisting. It's a wonder we weren't all separated from each other. Ty and Gem too. You broke my streak. Never had such trouble tracking nothing but the two's you. I hope you're pleased with yourselves."

"Stop your whining, Eli," Ryco says. "We don't care about your winning streak."

Eli's about to give his retort; he decides against it, firmly clamping his mouth shut instead. Then his eyes brighten. "Want me to start collecting food for dinner? I learned quite a lot of what's edible in the Metsundai."

"So did Talok," Musgrae comments with a straight face.

Pressing a hand to his knee, Kent grimaces. "Here we go."

Quall strides forward, shock on his face. "You're volunteering to help with camp rather than being commanded? Are you feeling all right, Eli?"

Skylin still clings to my arm, watching the scene before us.

My cousin sends me a look of teasing, then pats me on the back. He approaches Eli, to swipe a hand through the Kirjan's miraculously perfect, styled hair, which is perfect no longer.

Eli's stiff shoulders lift, yet he accepts the restyling of his hair without complaint. Not even a cry of frustration escapes him. Only an icy stare directed at Musgrae.

But Musgrae looks away to Mekka and Jasper, then focuses on the ground.

Siege queries, "Are any of us all right, after everything that's happened? I'm certainly not." He sinks to the ground to sit and rest and think.

SynKievas and Warren get Dea situated, helping her lean back against a fallen tree.

Then there's Arsyn, who goes over to Kent. He shoos Ben away. "Rest a while with your friends. Let me see what I can do for this meek one."

Skylin and I decide to go sit with Dea. Grateful for our company, she grins somewhat as Sonya and the young wards gather round behind her.

Ben straightens to his full height, massaging the muscles of his arms. He glances around, unsure of what to do with himself. But not for long, because Gemma marches right up to him and cups his face. She kisses him. He wraps his arms round her waist and pulls her close.

That's when Eli's control breaks. He shrieks, "Ben, what . . . what are you doing? I . . . I thought you said—" He blinks as if dust has just been blown in his face.

Ben pulls away to speak. "What I said was: it's unlikely that Ravier would be all right with it. But Gemma said it does not bother him. And I *confirmed* that it doesn't bother him. The one bothered by it, is you, Kirjan."

Eli has his hands lifted to the height of his waist, palms facing up. Both dangle there, unsure, twitching out in the open air. Then his fists ball up. He quickly straightens his arms, as he exclaims, "Just . . . just break my heart, Galloway!" He wheels around on his heel, to stomp away.

Gemma rushes to him, before he's gone far. She playfully pecks him on the cheek. Giggles ensue from her.

"Little Witch Charm," Eli grumbles, folding his arms in defensiveness.

"Come on, Kirjan." Musgrae sighs. "Let's go collect some wood. Start a fire."

Eli states, "I'll start the *fire* by myself."

Midstride, Musgrae stops and then laughs loudly.

Warren proclaims, "That's what he said."

Mekka adds, "Before the *fire* consumed him."

"Not like that!" Eli shouts, stomping off.

Their banter does the trick. For a moment, we forget our problems. Too soon, dinner is ready, and we're gathered round the campfire in solemn silence.

Ryco's the first to say something. "Ben, did you happen to collect any plant and herb specimens, while on your travels?"

Ben sets his bowl of soup down on a large stone, then unhooks a pouch from his belt. He digs through it. "Right here," he says, giving Ryco a plain box made of wood.

Ryco pulls the tiny specimens out, and they resize themselves. They're not any vegetation that we came across during our journey. They're more spindly and spiked, as if adapted for droughts.

"They're in perfect condition," Ryco remarks quietly. "Still look as though you dug them up yesterday. Will you add them to what I've collected?" Ryco offers to Ben a black-stone box with some gold engraving etched into it.

Ben's contentment fades. He eyes the box, before accepting it. "Ryco, were you"—he pauses to look over at the Second Guard—"planning to ask someone to wed you?"

Ryco replies, "Actually . . . I was hoping you would. But it's not fair to expect that, now. No. I'll be the one asking her. Her, being Khyra." Ryco blankly stares into the fire, gulping down more of his soup.

Ben starts adding his specimen collection to Ryco's proposal box.

The news has stunned several in the group.

"Isn't she still your ward?" queries Musgrae, dumbfounded.

"In two days, she'll be sixteen," is Ryco's report. "At which point, she belongs to no one except for whom she chooses. I wish she was older. That I was younger. That Paragon wasn't in the middle of a war. That her parents had actually raised her. Instead, they left her to my care. My mother was meant to be her primary guardian. Not me. Then my mother died. And I couldn't bear letting Khyra's talents go to waste. She's gifted in magic. Always has been. They wanted her to be a master of Gendras. But they never wanted her to learn Death Magic. *Make her the best she can be,* they said. But never would they consider letting me teach her Black Magic. Never would they let me teach her spells that would actually make her a threat to an Onyx on a battlefield."

After a time, Ben says, "I don't love her anymore. Not that way, Ryco."

"Of course you do," Ryco argues. "You've loved her since the first time you saw her. And it's only gotten worse, over the past few years. You just don't want to forgive her for all the rejection. But let me tell you how it was. The first four times you asked Khyra to be yours, she was too naïve to know what you were asking. She had to ask me to tell *her* what *you* were asking. I didn't know how to explain it. I thought I'd be overstepping. That sort of explanation should be given by her parents. Sadly, they never held still long enough to raise the girl into a woman. I did that. Got her to apply to be the City Architect of Eyo'el. A position higher than my own, I might add. Eventually, I recruited Madeleine to explain certain things to Khyra."

"And the other times?" queries Ben, practically glaring at Ryco.

He replies, "The next three were during her secret engagement to Talok. While many Sorsryns of nobility knew of the engagement, Paragonian citizens were kept in the dark. She couldn't consider your offer. She was busy keeping Talok from having to accept one of the dozens of offers the Sorsryn Clans sent us. She's been waiting for you to ask again, for a year."

Ben takes in a sharp breath. "Why didn't she ask me, then?"

Ryco sighs heavily. He finishes his soup, then sets his bowl down. "Khyra's only ever wanted to please her parents. She was never good enough, however. Eva and Dhavin always found fault in something she did or didn't do. *And* they hold to the old traditions."

Quall clarifies, "Withrasyn women were expected to wait for an offer."

Kent adds, "And Vaegon women had to wait for their parents to procure a match."

Ryco continues, "Imagine how it would crush Khyra, if they chastised her for boldly taking charge of her own life. Breaking tradition, only because she wants to be happy. And tradition won't allow for it. In their concern to follow the old ways, they'd crush their daughter's heart. Khyra won't risk that. She'll simply wait."

Skylin, who's sitting beside me, quietly poses the question: "Does she have to marry soon?"

Ryco shakes his head. "No. But her being a wife to one of the King's Guard affords her certain protections. And her being my widow will potentially provide more. But I'd rather keep that part to myself."

"Of course," says Arsyn. "No more questions for now, Skylin. Help Aygor's Wards clear the dishes, and repack what you can. We should turn in for the night, as soon as we are able. SynKievas and I will keep the first watch. Deamond and you, second. It'll be dark soon."

I look over to Talok, expecting that paleness to have returned. It hasn't, and I'm a little worried. It seems to me, a false sign that his health is returning. I won't buy into it. Not without a clear explanation as to why.

Arsyn's setting out bedrolls, while Dea is nearby, helping Ryco set up a small canvas canopy for shelter overhead.

Unfolding the blankets that Siege handed to me, I ask, "Arsyn, what can you tell me about the Shield of Shylen?"

"It's one of the ancient, defensive weapons of the Silverian Clan. It's what King Aygor used—in fact, what the kings of RawZend have always used—to shield RawZend from outside view. During events, the King of RawZend would deactivate the shield so that Darklyres could enter."

Assisting with the bedrolls, SynKievas adds, "The Fleishyn Forest doesn't usually shift, until the device is inactive. Never knew the device was actually the Shield of Shylen, though. It's news to me."

Arsyn continues our conversation. "The shield protects against many things. I've seen the way you've been watching your cousin, as if he'll sprout horns. The answer for why he's faring better has to do with the shield. Now Deamond, apparently."

SynKievas whispers, "The farther we get from the shield's other half, the worse your cousin will get. You might want someone in your group to start considering ways for restraining the young king."

"We know how that Geldryn device is changing him," Arsyn adds quietly.

We finish setting up the temporary sleeping quarters. Then I head for Warren. He and Ryco are talking in hushed tones, as they filter some of the Metsundai's water into flexible, leather canteens. In the dusk light, Ryco's eyes have started their citrine-yellow glow.

I swallow hard, barely believing that I might never see those eyes again after two weeks' time.

"Gemma's already started crying over me," says Ryco. "Don't you start too."

"Not a chance," I state. "But I want you to know, in case you've not suspected it already, the Shield of Shylen is why Talok seems better."

"Warren and I were just discussing that. Did Arsyn confirm it?"

I nod.

Warren starts capping the canteens. "We've got to figure out a way to keep Talok from starving, while also preventing him from drinking anyone's blood. As funny as it was when Eli was bitten, it can't happen again. And we've nothing left of the antivenom."

"I know," says Ryco, in defeat.

I ask, "You and Rozeth know how to restrain a Sorshrynak, right? Are there other kinds of restraints, which could suit Talok's situation?"

"Possibly," he says. "However, Rozeth's memory might be better than mine. She continued her training in the ways of Dezarin, while I had to learn other things after becoming a King's Guard."

Warren hands me one of the full canteens. "Let's go find her."

As we trek back to camp, we keep a lookout for Rozeth. When we find her, Nyrim's beside her, watching her put out the embers of the fire. Before Ryco says a word, she jolts upright and whirls to face him. Her tousled, raven-black hair frames her sad face.

Ryco brushes a wisp of it back behind one of her ears. "Rozeth," he starts.

But she bursts out, "Will you go to the place where your mother rests?"

"It's a spell of Dei-Athos-Kree, Rozeth," he replies. "I will go where Deathasyns go when they die."

"No!" Rozeth shouts, clenching her hands into tight fists. "That will not do. An apprentice to Dezarin, go to that horrible place of torture? I can't let this happen."

"I enjoy pain." Ryco smiles like a devil.

Rozeth pummels her fists on his chest. "Stop it, Ryco! Can't you let me be sad over your impending sacrifice?"

"So long as you don't cry." Ryco presses his palms on the back of Rozeth's hands to keep her close to him.

She leans against his chest, and he hugs her.

"I will be all right, Rozeth," he says. "I can handle hordes of Deathasyns, seeking to destroy me down there. I'm good at running. Good at fighting. Not so good at loving."

Rozeth snivels in heartbreak. "Evie didn't think so."

Ryco's lips quiver, yet he holds his composure. He takes in a deep, calming breath. "We need your help with something else that could quickly become a problem."

"What is it?" Rozeth pulls away.

"Restraints for Talok," I state.

Warren adds, "We're worried 'bout his blood craving. Zeekryn's not here, to make an antivenom. And we've not any venom left, to make some. Talok's either going to starve, or die from blood consumption."

Rozeth paces about, deep in thought.

"Well?" Ryco asks, after a time.

She replies, "All I can think of are ones too detrimental to his health. What of making a muzzle for him? It'd stop him from biting anyone."

"He's got to eat, though," Warren argues.

The sound of small, timid steps comes from behind a nearby tree, and Sonya is soon revealed. "I may know of a way," she says, sounding helpful. "It's not ideal, but it could aid Talok."

"We're open to suggestions," says Ryco softly.

Sonya shivers, then she hugs her wings close to her body. "It makes

Ketty feel nauseated, but it's edible. Things like burnt feathers, mashed beetles, mossy wood. To get the most nutrients, you have to cook them like you would a soup until it's nearly a paste."

Nyrim covers his mouth, about to gag. I'm not far behind him.

"Ketty called it Soup of Ashes," says Sonya. "I know it sounds horrid, but it's worked for me for the past few years, when young Darklyres are to attempt survival in the wilderness on their own."

Ryco starts chuckling. "Talok's going to *love* that." He looks to Warren. "Promise to help me force-feed him, if we have to?"

Holding back a delighted smile, Warren bobs his head up and down.

Rozeth simply inquires, "Is there anything you need me for, before that set day in the Monel?"

Ryco turns serious. "Not that I can think of."

"Then I must be away," says Rozeth, in restlessness. "I must find Dezarin. Bring him to the Plateau of MarcKand; ensure that you are not sent to where Deathasyns go. It's a dismal gift, after all our years together. Yet I must do something for you, Ryco of Paragon."

She starts to walk away, but Ryco grabs her by the wrist and yanks her back to kiss her firmly on the mouth. A sob escapes her. She starts clawing into his neck, kissing him back.

I turn away, and motion for Sonya to head away with me. In silence, Warren and Nyrim follow behind us. We drop off the water canteens by a pile of other supplies outside the canopy.

Dea gives sleeping assignments to all the King's Wards, including Sonya.

"May we have a bedtime story, Dea?" one of the littlest of the boys asks.

"I'm too tired to think of one, darling," says Dea, through a yawn.

I dig out *The Dark Prince* and toss it to Dea. Flinching, she still catches the book.

"Now, you don't have to think of one," I state, before collapsing on a bed near Gemma. I listen to the children gather round Dea for story time.

Opening the small book, she begins, "There once was a shrouded prince, in a shadowed land. Its forest was so dark, all light there was consumed.

Only the footsteps of the prince lit up, like stars upon the blackened ground. Behind him, his steps remained lit. But the path in front was sheer night. He thought, *If I had wings, I could fly over. See the sky. Find my way home.* But he didn't have any wings. He didn't have anyone with him who had wings, either."

A different boy interrupts, saying, "We could've helped him, Dea. We all have wings."

"That we do," says Dea, trying not to laugh. She goes on, "He was all alone, searching for the way home. You see, he had lost his way. Chased out of the circle of six pillars. Though he knew not by what. He couldn't remember. All he remembered was that the circle was of color. Of hope. The last time he had been happy, together with those he loved. And now? He couldn't even remember their faces. The faces of the ones he loved."

A little girl starts sniffling. "This is a sad story, Dea. I don't want to listen anymore."

"Vards!" Dea exclaims. "Stop interrupting me. The story isn't over yet." She starts reading again. "He went on, endlessly, crossing over his lighted footsteps, trying to find the right path. Then he saw something in the distance. And he stopped. It was of color. He couldn't remember which color. But he knew it was of color. That's all that mattered. It was something different, amidst all the darkness and crisscrossing lighted footsteps. He followed it."

"How does someone forget a color?" an older boy asks. "That's stupid! You can't forget colors."

"It's not stupid," says Sonya. "But you should shut up, before Dea threatens to steal our voices away, and we end up muted tomorrow."

"Not a bad idea," whispers Arsyn from somewhere nearby.

Skylin says to her father, "Don't you dare do that to me."

Dea asks the children, "Do you want me to finish this story, or not?"

"Finish!" all the wards cry in unison.

Dea reads more of the story:

It would dash away, turning this way then that. It'd stop again, to let him catch up. Each time it stopped, it let him get closer and closer. At last, he saw that it was a girl with colored hair.

She smiled at him.

He didn't smile back.

Instead, he asked her, "Who are you?"

She didn't answer. Just smiled at him again.

He asked two more times. He was about to ask a fourth time. He thought, Can't she hear me? Why won't she answer? Doesn't she know who I am?

It was then that the girl spoke, "I am not a commoner, Dark Prince, that I must answer when you ask."

He was speechless. Why had she called him Dark Prince? Was it that he wandered in a colorless land? Was it that he was unkind in his questioning of her?

He didn't know. He didn't ask. And she didn't tell him. But she led him, and her lighted steps were the same color as her hair. Purple! He remembered a color.

When the girl came to a stop, he had recalled a great many things. The faces of his loved ones. His own face. His name: The Dark Prince. He remembered his purpose. Why he was called that. Like a piece of black canvas waiting to be filled, he waited for the pillars to light. For their power to fill him, give him the strength to color the land again. No more night, unless his father wished it. No more shadows to hide in, unless it was to burst out from them to give a friend a delightful surprise.

He looked up. The girl had brought him to the circle of six pillars. They each glowed with their own color. Six colors. He went to stand in the center of the circle, and wait. The girl waited with him, and said. "Soon, they will ignite. No more night."

And so they waited for the lighting of the pillars, together, hopeful to see the faces of their loved ones again, very soon.

The end.

The book closes.

A little girl wails, "Wait! I want to see the pretty pictures again."

Dea shushes the girl, saying, "Quiet. Do you want a Gatro to hear you? Come find you? And *eat* you?"

It's suddenly very quiet. A soft wind blows against the shelter, making the canvas stir. Then Dea leaps up and roars playfully. Sonya and the children erupt in fits of squealing laughter. I sit up to watch the lot of them being chased about by Dea, or tickled by Skylin.

Dea stops when she realizes someone's watching her, and *only* her. I glance behind. Ryco's leaning against a tree. Arms crossed over his chest, he gazes intently at Dea. It's not a look I've ever seen on his face. A look of sorrowful longing. Even perhaps of wanting something he can't have.

He startles as soon as he knows he's been seen. He looks away. Ambling in to find a bed, he takes the one near me. "Since you have an awareness for excitement, Ravier, wake me if there is any, will you?"

I reply, "Sure thing."

The night's uneventful as far as I can tell. I wake to the sounds of snickering and playful whispers.

Nyrim, with knees drawn to his chest, sits on the end of Ryco's bedroll beside Warren. "Aren't they adorable, how they've piled on Dea? I can't even see her under them all. *Is* she truly in that pile?"

Ryco starts to wake up. A tired chuckle escapes him.

Warren adds, "I'm tempted to blast them with a little puff of wind, see if they burst into a cloud of feathers."

"You do," says Kent, about to walk past the bedrolls, "and Gemma will go rogue. She and Ben, for the past hour, have been working on a large enough breakfast to feed the Paragonian Sovereignty."

Standing near Kent, Musgrae states in sarcasm, "Right. Breakfast. Sure that's what they're doing?"

"Yeah," Kent replies, taking a moment to rest his injured knee. "They're teaching Talok the finer points of cooking. Not that it matters. He won't be tasting it. Any day now, he'll be served up that Soup of Ashes Warren told us about."

Musgrae clicks his tongue. "Poor Talok. He'll be as delighted over *it*, as I am with eating off of silver. Not one bit happy."

Ryco, still groggy, says, "We don't need 'happy Talok.' We need 'living Talok.' If it keeps him alive, I'll *happily* force it down his throat."

Warren says, "Well, let's wait for him to show signs of being sick, before we resort to that."

Fully awake all of a sudden, Ryco glances at me. "Now that you're up, Ravier, shall we begin the day?"

I plant my face into the blankets and groan as loud as I can. Next thing I know, the King's Guard are pulling me out of bed, and dragging me away from its warmth. They throw clean clothes at me.

Siege runs off with my Sleeping Dragon coat, presumably to clean it.

Warren flicks his hand, and cold water dumps on me from up above.

Ryco scrubs my head with soap, then my face, before stepping back. "Again, Warren," he says.

Musgrae grabs me, keeps me from running away.

Kent's there for moral support, saying, "If you hold still, it'll all be over sooner."

Warren snaps his fingers, and more water plummets down upon me.

When Musgrae releases me, I ask, "You satisfied?"

Ryco begins dressing. "Not until we do the same to the last Paragonian out of bed tomorrow."

Eli's the next day. Then Musgrae and Siege. Somehow, Talok's escaped the corporal punishment.

Throughout our journey in the Metsundai, we found no sign of the horses left behind in there, nor the ones lost in the Fleishyn Forest. After the three days, we get to the edge of the Metsundai that's closest to Vondurheil.

Arsyn queries, "Will we be safe to fly over, and follow you, Greyvon? The wards can't keep a fast pace, on foot."

Jasper, in Von form, replies, "Fit as many upon my back as you are able. The others on Mekka. The rest of you must keep pace on the sands. Doesn't matter if you have to slow to a walk. You must keep moving, or be swallowed up by the desert."

"Such a comforting thought," Gemma remarks.

I ask, "Will your knee hold up, Kent?"

He nods. "It has had time and magic enough to heal."

The older Darklyres take to the sky. Dea is much improved, after the initial shock of being separated from the other half of the shield.

The rest of us begin the trek on sand, and it's seemingly endless without our horses there to gallop upon it. Talok's about to start dragging his feet, but I push him forward.

The sunlight beats down, glaring on the sands, and making it near unbearable to look at. Arsyn and SynKievas take turns picking up those of us who can't keep going.

I'm about to signal for my break, but Jasper slows his pace to match mine. "There's room for you, Ravier. Get on."

When I do, I start sensing every tight muscle, sore bruise, as well as a thirst that drives me mad.

Jasper starts down a steep sand dune that gives way to a cave entrance. We wind around a corner. Mekka looks up at the Darklyres flying overhead, and nods at them. They start their descent. As soon as the sand fades into hard-packed dirt, they land and then run downhill.

Very quickly, the temperatures turn frigid near the cave opening. All the King's Wards shiver, then tuck their wings close to themselves. They look like overgrown bats or birds, with heads of small children that bobble as the pace of the Vons jostles them around. They're adorable.

We arrive at the bottom: the start of Vondurheil. How I've missed it. Missed the demon-horse. Even more, though, I wonder how Rorka has been faring. I ask Mekka, "Do you think Awngeleik knows we've come back for her?"

Mekka howls a bit, then barks, announcing our arrival.

Jasper stops. The others do the same. The group catches their breath, and I climb down from Jasper to wait.

That returning screech of Awngeleik makes my heart pound in excitement. Any minute now, I'll see her again. My dad's Equidyn.

3

Unfinished Dealings

Now farther into Vondurheil, Gemma ambles her way toward Jasper. She pets him on the shoulder, while we wait for Awngeleik to appear at the top of the first hill.

She quietly says, "We're sorry for everything that's happened, Jasper."

Talok, who's helping the Darklyre children down from Jasper's back, adds, "Merlynite will be missed. If we have a chance, we'll hold a ceremony for him in Eyo'el. And we will try to get Droediin back, see if we can't rid him of Zymarc's control."

Musgrae's brown eyes sadden. He's silent, as he sets his blade in front of Jasper. They each meet the other's gaze.

"Any blade," says Musgrae, "that's pierced the heart of an old Von belongs to you, Alpha Jasper. Now that you are home, take it. It's served me well for nine years. But I can't bear wielding it anymore."

Jasper shifts to human form. The smoke surrounding him dissipates. He gives Musgrae his own blade colored of cobalt-blue. It's not Winter's Vondaen. But it still looks to be a mighty weapon. "This was mine"—Jasper grips Musgrae by the shoulder—"when I was barely past the age of a Vonsai. A VonGuard to Shena. It's when Merlynite and I began our friendship, as well as protectors to the matriarch. Born of the same generation. In the same VonGuard—together, The VonGuards of Midnight. He and I are the last of that generation. Last to have seen

40

the Battle of Queens. Last who suffered watching the Rubidyn-Greyvon alliance crumble."

I ask, "Is that why Merlynite could drain you of life, back in the library?"

Jasper nods his confirmation. "He knows my heart, my weaknesses, my faults. Near everything about me, he knows. Or, rather, he knew. We carved out Vondurheil together, with other old Vons. It took centuries to make it as it is now. Though some were mere pups when the War of Ichors Von had ended, they helped build Vondurheil with as much fervor as the battle-hardened. Never would I have thought our friendship would end as it did. I had wished for old age to take us." Jasper looks down, and his face tightens in grief.

Quall comes forward. "What do you wish for us to do?"

"Let me rest here," replies Jasper, sounding old, "while all of you return to your home, then make for Oniva, for The Sodon. I'll meet you there."

"That's fine, Jasper," Quall states. "Shall we continue on? Resupply for the journey? Capture an illustrious Equidyn? I don't think she's going to play easy to get."

"You mean to take her to Paragon?" queries Mekka, who's become the perch for all the young Darklyre children.

With their wings still wrapped tight round their little bodies, the children resemble penguins—some black, some brown, others tan—all fluffed out and plump. Their faces are pink from the cold. If anything could be killed by cuteness, it'd be the sight of Darklyre children, trying to keep warm, atop a massive Von's furry back.

While rummaging through various supplies in his pouches and pockets, Ben replies, "Awngeleik would never forgive us for leaving her again."

Mekka grins. But on his Von face, it's more of a growl absent of sound. "No doubt, that's true," he says. "Rorka's likely ready for a break."

"Break?" Jasper exclaims, regaining some strength behind his voice. "She's the one escorting them home. You, her, and her Theocktras. Go get her. Tell her the news."

Mekka asks, "Did you send word, telling her of Droediin and Merlynite?"

"Of Droediin, yes," replies Jasper. "But not of Merlynite. Such news should be told in person."

Mekka lets his head hang lower than his shoulders. He turns, and starts toward the hill.

Jasper's mouth twitches. "Mekka," he says. "Vonsai have never seen Darklyre children. Best to leave them here, for now."

Mekka plants his butt down firmly on the snow, sweeping some flakes into the air with his bushy tail.

The Darklyre children shriek as they slide off him all unexpectedly and land piled on top of each other.

A little girl wails, "Dea! I'm cold! And what's this horrid white stuff? I hate it." She grabs a fistful of snow and smacks a boy's face with it.

"Frozen rain, dear," replies Dea, glancing at Warren.

He's biting down on his lower lip, struggling to hold back his one-liner.

Jasper shifts to Von form again. When he starts forward, clumped-together snow crunches beneath his paws.

Mekka trots off. He's almost to the top of the hill, where one can view the rest of Vondurheil.

A bird lands atop one of Jasper's furry shoulder blades. Then it flutters around his head.

"Galloway," he says, stopping short, "would you read the letter sent to me?"

Nearest to the alpha, Gemma jogs to catch the bird. It turns into a folded piece of parchment. Smoothing it open, she reads, "To Jasper of the Greyvons. From Aygorinaith of RawZend."

In interest, the Darklyres crowd closer to Gemma.

She continues, "I wish to thank all of you for leaving Monel's spell-book. It means a great deal to me. You easily could've taken it, but didn't. It shows your character to be of Vardiyas: good of heart.

"Now, to another matter, as I don't have long before I must depart for Ayzaga, there is something I thought you should know. By the time I returned to Soren's Library, your fallen comrade's body had vanished. Seqwhyett, Litreez, and I searched for what may have happened to it.

As we were leaving, we spotted a small trail of his blood leading down the hall. It hadn't been there, upon our return. Merely upon our last departure from the library. By the time we entered the grand hall, where the golden statues are, his trail had vanished. I can't tell you how sorry I am to have lost him. The least I could do is save you the journey of coming to get him, when he isn't here.

"Best wishes for safe travels, and may the Vardiyas light your path. –King Aygor." Gemma folds the letter up, as her face scrunches with confusion.

Bewildered, Siege asks, "What could've happened to his body?"

Reaching for his blade hilt, Arsyn states, "Nekrosis. Reanimation. Will that pose any threat to us, do you think, Alpha Jasper?"

Jasper mutters to himself, "Is that why I've no wish to leave home?" Jasper quickly looks to Mekka. He shouts, "Mekka, stop! Merlynite's here." Jasper starts sprinting, his paws kicking up loose snow.

Mekka's already to the top of the hill. He glances back.

Something dark breaks over the crest of the hill and approaches him. This figure on two legs shoots bursting fire on the ground where Mekka has stopped. Mekka yelps. The ground beneath him gives way. He tumbles back down the hill, chunks of hard snow crashing along with him. What fur of his that's caught fire is put out by the time he stops rolling. He gets up to shake himself; soot and snow fly off. He takes the metal battleform of Vons, and growls low, vibrating the ground.

We're all on high alert, readying ourselves to scatter.

Merlynite stands on the hilltop clothed much like Jasper in human form, with his leather clothes and accentuating fur trim. Even from here, we see his eyes glowing blood-red. A smaller figure, cloaked in midnight-blue, comes to stand beside Merlynite. This one leads Awngeleik forward. Her wings are tied up, and her legs are shackled. She's been muzzled too. Muzzled by what appears to be of Geldryn make, jeweled brass and bronze.

The figure removes the hood. It's Zymarc, calling down through a metal mask, "We thank you for the head start, Paragonians. Gave Caleiso time to double back and perform her best trick yet. What do you think of your Merlynite? Isn't he striking, reanimated? Should have twice the strength he had before."

Mekka roars in anger, and the ground quakes. Loose snow ripples up into the air. It's akin to rising fog. The air gets colder. Each inhale stings.

Zymarc laughs. "Now he's an abomination, I know. There's only one way to kill him, in his present state. Take off his head. Can't be reanimated, after that. And, if one of you doesn't do it, Merlynite will succeed in bringing me the head of the alpha. Jasper, you'll look lovely, mounted on one of my walls back home."

Awngeleik violently struggles against her restraints. She can't run. Can't fly. Barely, can she move her head. She's restrained to taking small steps. There's no hope of her freeing herself. So she just screeches in despair. The muffled sound of her pricks at me like dull needles. The feeling drives me mad.

Merlynite leaps from the top of the hill, shifting to battleform, midair. When he lands, his strides take him far. Very quickly, he's near us. The Darklyre children scream, then cower in fear. The older Lyres go to guard them. They won't be helping us stop Merlynite. Their duty lies in protecting King Aygor's Wards.

Behind me, Skylin pleads, "Father, let me help them. I can't watch this. I've got to do something."

Gemma crowds close to me, holding me back. "Wait," she says.

From all around us, a rumbling begins.

"Clear the way!" Zymarc shouts, rushing down the hill as fast as Awngeleik's short, quick steps can take her.

Merlynite and Mekka rush the other, snarling, biting, and clawing. Their Von blood splatters on the snow around them. The fight is horrifying. Much worse than in the library, where they had not the room to gain momentum. There's no furniture here to get in their way. No comrades nearby to lessen the blows. They can be one hundred percent Greyvon: vicious, cunning, and precise.

Jasper guards us, watching his two Vons. In defeat, he looks to Zymarc and Awngeleik.

A Greyvon catches his attention, then our attention. One, colored the same as a fiery-red sunset. She runs the rest of the way into view on the hilltop. It has to be Rorka. Why else would Soren have called her a sunset? A mass group of Vons is behind her. Greyvons come from seemingly every direction, except for the entrance into Vondurheil.

Surrounded, Zymarc's looking around in alarm.

Rorka shouts, "I knew that beast was *not* our Merlynite, from the second you had him step foot in Vondurheil. And, again, when news of Droediin came to me, but not of him. Why else would I occupy him with so much talk? I was merely waiting for Jasper to return home. I could feel him getting nearer. Now it is you, Vitiosyn, who will lose."

Zymarc calls out, "Even when I lose, Greyvon, I still win something." He rips the muzzle off Awngeleik, and burns away her shackles. "If you kill me, Equidyn, you will be free. No more masters. No more chains. Come kill me." Zymarc finishes his descent down the hill, sprinting.

All Vonsai let loose, running after him. They yap and growl and roar. It's deafening.

"Move, move, move!" Eli shouts, pushing against many of us. "They'll trample us all!"

It's chaos, trying to keep watch of Zymarc, with the Greyvons running about recklessly.

"Awngeleik!" I shout. "Don't kill him. It's what he wants."

With all the noise, it's unlikely she heard me. I spot her, taking her demon form. That's when all Vons get out of her way.

I try to link my thoughts with hers, to Mensa-div, *"Don't kill him. Not like this."*

Something pushes back, and my head hurts. My thoughts spiral. I stumble a bit.

Gemma shakes me by the shoulders. "Tyler! She's blocking all of us. You have to go after her." She points to where Zymarc slips past the chaos of Vons.

Awngeleik follows him. Like a silvery black creature of death, she's bent on killing him.

Seeing the Spear of Guyheiz made small and clipped to Warren's belt, I rush to snatch hold of it.

"Yo!" he shouts, stopping my hands. "You can't use that yet. It's still charging. It'll blow up in your hands, if you use it right now."

I let go, and just run to the place where Awngeleik headed.

"Tyler!" Warren shouts. "Where you going?"

The Paragonians yell after me. But their noise fades very quickly. I'm past the line of chaos, and running down the other side of the hill. I spot the remnants of snapped ropes that restrained Awngeleik and head in that direction. I follow Zymarc and Awngeleik's tracks. Twisting, winding, clawing my way farther. I run, until my lungs burn fiercely from the cold air. Then I run harder. The colored wind of blue, green, and gray pushes me forward. It seems to be helping. But then it starts sweeping the tracks away. They lead toward the forests of Vondurheil.

The trail's gone by the time I reach the trees colored of blue glass, with silver quills on their branches.

I stop to listen. It's quiet. The wind has ceased. Steam must be seeping off my skin and through my clothes; it emits out into the air like smoke.

My footsteps crunch loudly in the snow, and I cringe. *I must not let them know I'm here. But how?* I wonder, *What if she's killed him already, and she now hunts me? The other master. Does she want to be free that badly? I never asked to be her master.*

Taking more brave steps in the eerie quiet, I spot blood that's trailed around in an odd pattern. It's as if Awngeleik bit into him, then whirled him around a bit. But their foot trail isn't there. Only the blood.

Something drips on my face. When I wipe it away, blood's smeared on my hand. More drizzles down from above. I look up. It collects at the tree's quill tips, then drips down again, splattering the snow with red.

Fighting off dread, I muse, *Of course they'd be up in the trees.*

More steps, I take in agony, thinking, *What if, with one strike, she's freed herself? Freed Zymarc too, so he can become ruler over the elements?*

Timidly, I look behind. She's not there. Yet I feel *something* calling to me. Calling for me to trust. I lift one hand, and pretend to strum strings in the air. My footsteps are swept away. The snow's made blank. I lift my other hand and do the same, softly speaking, "Ventus."

A quiet wind blows through the forest, dampening the sound of my footsteps. I go forward more bravely. I stop the strumming and lower my hand, confident that my tracks will fade, that the wind will continue. I'm not wrong.

Studying every detail around, I search for more signs of them. I listen too. For their breaths, their heartbeats. Movement. I see it, ahead. Frost falling from some trees. One of those trees has been gouged near the base, a bit of its translucent, bluish bark spread out broken on the ground.

I follow the gouge mark with my gaze, looking up. There she is. Silvery black and terrifying, though her back is to me.

She balances on a tree limb, while Zymarc's throat is trapped in her biting jaws. He's pressed against the tree trunk. Still alive, he has his hands up in surrender. Yet he doesn't seem happy over his impending death.

I approach, whispering, "Awngeleik, don't do this. Can't you see it? He wants to die."

She releases his neck, and he takes a deep inhale through his black mask of inferior size to the one that was damaged that day in Paragon.

Zymarc rasps out, "He is the other master, Awngeleik. Once you're done with me, take him too. Then you shall be free. Then you can bring your best master back. LanSoren. He would never chain you, would he? Not like those Paragonians. Not like me."

"He's lying!" I shout, my heart feeling as if it's breaking inside my chest. "You can't bring him back." My throat burns. I cough.

Zymarc continues, "Can't you feel him here, Awngeleik? Can't you smell him? His body went through here, after his death. You know it to be true, Equidyn. Take the two, and the third might be revealed to you."

I take a few frenzied steps forward and cry out, "He's a killer. Don't listen to him. Listen to me. LanSoren would never wish for you to become some kind of slayer. He would want you to heal, not wound. To restore, not destroy. Don't be a demon of death, but a demon of light." I sink to the ground of wet snow, and beg with a whisper, "No more dark, no more night. Choose the light." Tears in my eyes, I look up at her.

Her body transitions to appear as blackish smoke. Slowly, it's as if she turns around to face me, without doing any of the movements for it. Her front side's now visible where her back once was. Those piercing eyes colored of white stare into my soul. Quickly, the demon form fades, and she's herself again. Standing farther out on a tree limb, she bends her head down to get a better look at me.

She snorts playfully, blinking those blue snake-eyes at me. I smile.

Zymarc lowers his hands. His clothing's torn and bloodied in several places. Hatred seeps into his crimson-red eyes, as he draws out Winter's Vondaen. He's about to strike Awngeleik. He doesn't have to deal a mortal blow to get his way. Only has to anger Awngeleik.

Rushing closer, I shout, "Get down, Awngeleik!"

I reach for her, trying to will Zymarc to miss. I feel him push back with his mind. Thrown off balance, I collapse in the snow. A shout of terror escapes from me. When I regain my footing, Zymarc's swinging arm has stopped midair. He's fighting against something. Sweat beads on his brow. More blood oozes from his wounds to fall on the snow below.

Doubly afraid, I wonder what's holding him back. It certainly isn't me. Sure footsteps approach.

"Sleep," speaks a feminine voice, behind me, "slumbering deep in the heart of the dark. Krim-Karasa-dim-drim."

Fear sinks into Zymarc's eyes. He looks to the narrator. He tries to move. But his tensed-up limbs only shake.

Gemma walks past me, her movements having purpose. She has her right hand lifted, aimed at Zymarc. "Light of night," she speaks, "bright on the right of Kyanite asleep. Harin-nae-Varin."

Awngeleik jumps down to glide to a stop beside me. I put my hand on her scaly shoulder, bidding her to stay with me.

Zymarc spits out, "You will regret this, girl." He moves his swinging hand slightly forward.

Gemma pushes back, speaking more words of: "To sleep, so deep you'll reap of the dragon's keep fast asleep. Din-drim-Delaysarin."

Zymarc says, "Wait until I plot a way to get him alone. No cousin, no Equidyn, no Galloway. Just Ravier. His heart will be mine. No one to save him from himself."

Gemma speaks more, "To summoning a slumbering Rubidyn to the sleeping dyns'hyn el Ravieras-Savak." She snaps her fingers, then briefly shuts her eyes.

Zymarc stops struggling. The red of his eyes dims. He goes limp, then falls from the tree. He lands with a thud in the snow. He groggily lifts his head, trying to stay awake. "You won't keep me asleep for long, Galloway."

"We don't need long," she replies. "We just need long enough. Still think I'm no threat to you, Vitiosyn?"

Zymarc softly chuckles, before drifting to sleep. His head plops against the cold ground.

"Quick," I rasp out. "We need to bind him. Have any enchanted rope?"

"No," Gemma replies. "And I haven't learned magical bindings either. Only the knots and tying."

Someone rushes into the forest, calling my name.

"Skylin?" I call back, my gaze searching for her.

She darts into view. Once to me, she grabs my arm tight. "Tyler, you're all right! I'm so relieved. They've managed to subdue that Merlynite. He's injured quite a few, though. Even my father. Mind-controlled the Vonsai. Made them start attacking everyone. Only I saw where you went off to, during the chaos. We should go. Talok's worried sick. And I'm worried for Father." She looks over her shoulder, back the way she came.

"We have to bind Zymarc," I reply. "I have a feeling his Vitiosyns will be coming soon."

Gemma queries, "Do you have enchanted rope, Skylin?"

Her attention whips back to us. "Of course! Always keep some with me, during the events." She pulls out a glowing rope from her main pouch.

Gemma takes it. "Which hand do you think is his dominate one? Left or right?"

I reply, "He must be equally good with both."

Gemma states, "Then we have to figure out a way to keep his fists clenched. Cross his arms in an *X*, at the wrists. Tie them that way."

Skylin exclaims, "You can do that with paper. Wet it, form it to his closed fists, then freeze it."

"I don't have paper," states Gemma.

"Nor I," Skylin admits. "All of King Aygor's young wards insisted on taking what little I had, to doodle pictures on."

I state, "I have the journals, and *The Dark Prince*."

"Dark Prince," both girls say in unison.

I pull the storybook out, tear three random pages from it, then put it away. I don't need to worry over remembering what the narrative is. The King's Wards have it memorized.

Gemma wets the pages, I form them to Zymarc's fists, then Skylin freezes them in place.

Satisfied with that, Gemma further instructs, "Hold his wrists together."

Skylin and I do as we're told.

Gemma's quick in wrapping the rope round Zymarc's wrists. First vertical, then horizontal. She finishes with the knot facing away from Zymarc. The leftover tail of rope, she wraps around his neck like a halter. The loose end, she holds near the start of the wrist bindings. It glows, weaving itself to be connected seamlessly with the rest of the rope.

Gemma breathes out her relief. "I did the knots right. Now to mute him, bury him in the snow."

"What?" I ask. "Shouldn't we be taking him down with us? We've captured him. The end. Game over."

Gemma shakes her head. "Do you really think the others won't try to kill him? Even if Jasper and Mekka try to stop them, the Vonsai won't listen. Together, they're like Awngeleik on steroids. They may even get her to join in again. No. We have to wait for things to settle. If we're lucky, we'll talk everyone down, and Zymarc will still be buried here, waiting for us to take him away. But I'm not counting on that."

Skylin points out, "Also, won't killing him by usual methods mean instant death for Talok?"

"Good point," I reply, even through the frustration.

Gemma adds, "We need to free Talok of that device, *then* end Zymarc. Not before."

I want to pummel my anger out on something. Gemma's right. I wish she wasn't. And the look on her face says she wishes that too.

"Fine, Gem," I state. "But, even with burying him, the Vonsai will be able to sniff him out."

Gemma glances to Skylin. "I was hoping Skylin and Awngeleik could help with that. Awngeleik's scent is strong. You could spread it around, and shift the bloodstains to being somewhere else."

"Yes," Skylin replies, "that will work." She starts combing her fingers through Awngeleik's mane and feathers. Then she begins her work of spreading the scent all over, heading in a maze of paths. After that, she works on moving the bloodied scene elsewhere. But she's having a difficult time of it.

Meanwhile, Gemma and I dig in the snow, using our hands and my daggers.

"This is taking too long," I state. "A little help, Awngeleik? This *is* partially your fault, after all."

"Don't guilt-trip her," Gemma scolds.

"But it works," I reply. "Watch." I sit back to give the Equidyn enough room.

Awngeleik pounces, using her two front hooves on the ground where Gemma and I were digging. Then she digs like a dog about to bury a prized bone in a dirt pile.

I give Gemma a wicked grin. "See?" I shrug.

Gemma stares at Zymarc. "I can't believe we're just going to bury the King of Vitiosus in the snow." She looks at me and laughs.

"He'll hate us forever," I add, as Awngeleik finishes digging the hole.

"Good." Gemma nods once with finality.

We take hold of Zymarc by his arms, and drag him to the hole to shove him in it. He's almost there. Then he starts mumbling something. His eyes struggle to open. We let go of him.

"Skylin!" Gemma shouts. "We need him muted . . . Now!" Gemma jolts up straight in a panic.

Only the calm voice of a woman approaching us, keeps that panic from getting worse. "Allow me," says Rorka. She rests her right hand atop my shoulder. The stain on her skin—the marks unique to her—pulses with a steady rhythm.

Looking relieved, Gemma gives no indication that she sees the changes in Rorka. Not even when that elaborate stain weaves itself around on the Greyvon's face like a living tattoo, before settling to stillness. Her skin tone is replaced by literal black-and-white marks woven intricately together, as she moves closer to Zymarc. My suspicions about Rorka are confirmed. Only those with the gift of whatever magic this is can see it upon others like them, like us, like me.

I grin inside. Hope rises up. Oddly, the fear of the moment has left me. Somehow, someway, Rorka's presence gives me the same confidence only my dad's did when he was alive; again, when seeing him after each instance of outwitting time.

"I've much to tell you, Ravier," she says. "But first to mute this Vitiosyn." Rorka's right hand reaches for Zymarc.

He's fully awake now. When registering the face of the one reaching for him, he actually flinches, then he uses his feet to push himself farther away from Rorka. He ends up trenching himself in the snow.

"Wait, wait!" he says, in alarm.

Rorka snaps her fingers.

Zymarc chokes on his words.

The Matriarch Candidate commands him with, "I bid you speak only words necessary for bargaining. Words of cunning, for Greyvons are such souls the very best at it. Think hard, dear Zymarc, for you toil with a female Von now, not a male. Most certainly not a dyn. Rather, the future ruler of Vondurheil. Do you dare, dear Onyx, to offend me?"

With each breath, Zymarc's chest heaves. His gaze has hardened on the Greyvon. Regardless, he simply says, "No. I dare not offend you, daughter of Shena's cousin. Did Jasper ever tell you that's who you are?"

Rorka stops the progression toward the Vitiosyn King. "That's not possible," she whispers.

Even as Skylin creeps into view of the scene, Zymarc continues, "Oh, but it *is* possible. I also know why LanSoren wished to avoid you at all costs. Shall I tell you of it? Don't you wish to know, before you mute me? Perhaps I'll tell you, if you let me keep my voice. Let me summon my army from afar, to end this war here in Vondurheil. Isn't that what all of you want? The final battle? To get it over and done with?"

I stand up. "No. And that's not going to happen. You're not going to summon them. Mute him, Rorka. Do it now," I command her.

She doesn't listen. Zymarc's captured her curiosity. It's what he does. The tempter of all. *Is there no one immune to him?* I wonder. I finish the thought, thinking, *My father. My father could resist him. And I'm his son.*

Realizing this, I grab hold of Rorka's wrist. "I said to mute him already. Don't you see what he's doing? Distracting you, distracting us. The others are going to find us. Talok isn't safe, Rorka. We have to get him away from here. Away from Vitiosyns. Please!" I tighten my hold on her. "Don't let the war come to Vondurheil. I don't want my cousin to die."

Even while I'm bargaining, Zymarc's quick to tell Rorka, "Your mother was frozen in stasis, you see. She was already carrying you almost to term, when a rather hated Withrasyn Taint froze her to glass and stone. Hid her in a closed-up cavern for thousands of years. Then Dezarin found her, thawed her out. But it was Jasper who woke her up. Woke her for long enough, so she could give birth to you. Then she died. Died in the arms of the alpha. That's why he raised you, for you would have no other Von equal to you." Zymarc laughs, adding in, "Well, Droediin was your close equal. He belongs to me now. A willing victim. The very best kind."

Tears have welled up in Rorka's juniper-green eyes. Quietly, she asks, "Why did LanSoren of Trauvo evade me?"

Temporarily lacking magic, I sink to the ground. No matter what I do, Rorka won't let this matter go. As I have my obsessions, so does she. I can't stop her curiosity. And neither can Gemma by the looks of her drained expression.

Then there's Awngeleik. Forgetful of us, she digs the hole deeper. She's halfway concealed by it.

Skylin edges closer to our group, unnoticed by the others.

"LanSoren, himself, told me why," replies Zymarc, sitting up straighter. "Perhaps I'll let the winds of Vondurheil tell you of it. Rather, show you of it. Come," hums Zymarc, slowly blinking. "Come, Equidyn, awaken the cold, awaken the memories. Wings of the Stag. Is there nothing you can't do?"

Upon hearing Zymarc's name for her, Awngeleik ceases her digging. That silvery black appearance comes over her. Sparks form on her wings. Blue sparks. The colors of Vondurheil's wind collect on her wings.

I try to move to safety. But I'm too exhausted.

Skylin bolts forward, rushing for the three of us, not a bit concerned over the Equidyn or the Vitiosyn. The sparks are about to burst from Awngeleik. Skylin covers us with her wings, right as the sparks explode out.

Skylin's hit by them. She screams. But she holds tight to us. We keep hold of her. Gemma touches Skylin's cheek, and the girl from Clan Jhire seems relieved of some pain. Then Rorka leaves the safety of Skylin.

At the end of the horrific burst, I grab hold of Skylin's waist. I drag her away from the Equidyn, who's crumpled down in the snow, unconscious. Zymarc, however, is still awake. Barely. His black mask has been ripped off his face, leaving his skin marred. He's taken the brunt of the sparks. His clothing has holes burned through the fabric. Blood oozes from the singed wounds of his face and arms. The bindings on him, however, have held strong.

The colors of Vondurheil swirl around us, then form into people. The figures of my father and Zymarc.

Skylin weakly hugs me, shivering. Her wings are limp, battered, and burned. Bleeding too.

I hold her closer and cry silently. The tears freeze on my face. "Stay awake, Sky," I whisper. "Don't close your eyes." I stare down into those blue spheres. They are as an ocean. So many flecks of different shades of blue.

Her own tears well up. "It's okay, Ty. I've woken up from death, before. It's what Darklyres do." She reaches up, to stroke my cheek, to brush the frozen tears off my skin. Her hand falls. She goes limp in my arms. Her eyes flutter shut.

I choke on the lump in my throat. More tears brim. But they do not spill down. They remain, making everything blur before me.

A gentle hand takes hold of mine, the hand of mine not clinging to Sky. I know Gemma's touch by now. I'd know it in the dark.

My father's voice plays out from somewhere nearby, saying, "I don't know what to do, Zymarc. No matter how I try to avoid a certain someone, she always arrives when I least expect it. I've barely escaped several interactions with her."

Zymarc laughs. But his laugh is different than what I've heard. Happier in its tone. "Do you *fear* this certain someone, Lance?" he asks. "I thought nothing could frighten you. Not after—"

My father interrupts, replying, "No, no! It's not that. I'm not afraid of her. Rather, afraid of what could . . . I mean, what *will* happen if I meet her."

"You speak as if you know the future," says Zymarc, in the memory. "You haven't been speaking with Vardiyas, have you?"

"Of course I have!" exclaims my father. "Why do you think I visit you so often? Vosh-Perida is literally a short jaunt away."

"Lance, I warned you of that." Zymarc sounds stern. "It's dangerous talking to them."

"I can't believe what I'm hearing. From a Vitiosyn, no less. You're one to talk of danger."

"Yes. I am most certainly one to talk of it. And warn against it," says Zymarc. "I and my people are an abomination to all Sorsryn Clans still in existence. Yet we have lived on. And we are stronger and stronger, each passing year. Why do you think that is? Do you think it was because I loved toying with danger so much that I slipped up, and made a mistake, thereby crippling my chances of success? Crippling the chances of my people to remain, long past when I am gone? That was Deezalo's mistake. He got greedy too soon. He became obsessed with personal vendettas. His vanity and lust were his ultimate undoing."

"Are you going away?" queries my father.

"Everyone goes away eventually, Lance. I've found my replacement for when I'm gone, though. You're going to like her."

Sounding skeptical, my father asks, "A woman will replace you? How did you manage that? Finding one with enough power? You know what? It doesn't matter. But I do wish to know why you think you'll be going first."

"Because you are young, and I am not. Don't you want to know my replacement's name?"

"Only if you wish to tell me."

"Caleiso," Zymarc says.

My father laughs. "She was named after a Geldryn?"

"Not just any Geldryn," says Zymarc. "The very one responsible for the fall of Deezalo. Jasper set that trap, using her as bait. She wanted to be used as such. Not many know the story. They only know the tales of Caleiso, and her violence. This girl I found, she's only a year old now, and well . . . she'll be much the same as the one she's named after. But tell me of this one you're avoiding. What's the race? What name? Tell me anything you like."

"She's a Vonsai," says my father reluctantly.

Zymarc chuckles. "Let me guess? She's that young protégé of Jasper's? Rorka, I do believe is the name."

The tears have dried enough for me to see. My father comes into focus. He's slimmer than I recall. I assume this is because he's about ten years younger. His next words confirm that it is so.

"Yes," he says. "She's eleven now. But she should be much, much older; more advanced in years than even Jasper and Merlynite are now, for she was conceived before them. But not born before them."

The projected Zymarc strolls around in the foreground. Then he stops in his tracks. "I don't follow. What have the Vardiyas revealed to you?"

"It was one Vardiya," says my father. "You know! That Aysivak. Soren confessed what Monel made him do. It was an order. He couldn't refuse him. He had to do what he did to Rorka's mother. Shena's cousin. Can you believe it? She's a cousin once-removed to the Von Matriarch." My father grins.

The younger Zymarc has a black mask on, the same mask that has been ripped off his face in the present. "What does that have to do with your avoidance of her?"

My father rushes up to the younger Zymarc, and grabs hold of the Vitiosyn's shoulders. "It has to do with the reason Monel ordered Soren to put Shena's cousin in stasis, in the first place. To shorten the tale by quite a lot, I'll just say that this Rorka of Pariah is essential for this era. Not the one when she was conceived. Her life would've been cut short, if she had been born on the eve of the War of Ichors Von. Therefore, Soren saved her for this time. Rather, Monel made him. If I meet her, the whole purpose for her being saved for this era will be ruined. She'll die. At twenty-two years old, her life will be forfeit if I so much as *meet* her."

The younger Zymarc pulls away, appearing dumbfounded by what he has heard.

My father continues, "Muraine needs her, you understand? Rubidyns need her. Jasper needs her. But, more importantly, my child needs her."

Zymarc comes out of his stupor to look hard at my father. "You've a child? When? And with whom?" He crosses his arms.

"I've a son. Born the same year as this Rorka." My father grins proudly. "He'll be ready for you, when you meet him, Zymarc. But will you be ready for him, I wonder." My father glances to me, then down at the dead Darklyre in my arms. Curiosity enters those copper-colored orbs of his.

I follow his gaze down to her.

Skylin of Jhire isn't waking up. She's lost more blood. Gemma has slipped into a slumber, after attempting to help Skylin. She has her hand resting on one of Skylin's burned wings. Renewed sobs start rising up my throat. I choke them down, to keep quiet. But barely. I keep hoping that Darklyres truly are the conquerors of death.

"Please wake up, Sky!" I scream inside. I'm shaking in fear. So cold inside. Numb outside. Yet my heart pounds and pounds, sounding as gushing water running past my eardrums.

"I wonder," says my father, looking back to Zymarc in the past. "Will you *wake* up, Zymarc? Will you *open* your eyes to the truth before you, when you see him? Will you see the *sky* for what it truly is? Will you search for what is hidden there?" He looks past the Vitiosyn, to Skylin. He seems to ask her, not Zymarc, "Will you *feel* again? Will you *breathe* again? Rise the way you did when you were a young warrior? For you are, in many ways, just a young warrior." He looks to Zymarc.

The younger Zymarc suddenly notices himself in the present. He rushes to his injured self and kneels down. "What has happened? Where are we?" He scrambles up, then directs an angry gaze at my father. "LanSoren! What are you doing? Are you mad? Do you wish to fracture time?"

"No!" my father shouts. "I wish to fix it, if even a little. I wish to give you the chance to save yourself in the future. Also, to buy myself the chance to save another. For fate's sake, girl, wake up!" He claps hard.

Lightning crackles down to hit Awngeleik. The Equidyn leaps up, renewed.

Skylin comes to life in my arms, gasping. She screams in horror, until she realizes where she is. When she sees my face, she quiets down, yet her eyes are wide and frightened.

Gemma rises. "What do I need to do, Mr. Ravier?"

"Be a Galloway," he says. "Be the ninth Galloway. The very best of them."

"What number was my father?" she asks through tears.

"A better answer," he tells her. "Your cousin is the eighth."

Gemma shakes her head. "That doesn't add up."

"Because," he replies, "Kaida isn't a Galloway. Not by blood."

The younger Zymarc has finished healing the present one. And that one is coming to full awareness.

My father grows restless. He moves toward the Zymarc there with him. "We must leave, Zymarc. Your future self can't know what's just transpired during his incomprehension." He grabs the younger Vitiosyn. "I'll ensure he doesn't recall a bit of this interaction in the future, Rorka. Get ready to restrain that present one, with you."

Rorka nods at my father. "I will see that the task is done, LanSoren."

He looks over his shoulder, asking, "Do I look as good as I did in your dreams, Little Sunset?"

"Better," she says. "For you are not as a phantom I must chase."

Amused, he laughs. Then the colors of Vondurheil come over him and the younger Zymarc. The two fade away, as Rorka bends down to the Vitiosyn King, fully awake.

In hatred, he stares hard at her. "Do what you feel you must, Von," he says. "But know that something has put us in a time-distortion. You're sure you can get out of it on your own?" He lifts his bound hands, saying, "If not, you merely need to—"

Rorka licks the middle finger of her right hand. She sweeps that finger across Zymarc's blistered lips. "Sh, sh!" she hisses, even while he presses his back harder against the packed, trenched snow. "No talking," she finishes. Then she holds her index finger in front of her own mouth.

Zymarc struggles, looking as if he can't breathe. Eventually he licks his lips, letting out a pained groan. The skin of his lips sticks together. Though he keeps forcing them apart, quite quickly he's unable to stop them from sealing up. His mouth takes on the appearance of a beast's sewn shut with strips of skin. Zymarc screams muffled sounds, then thrashes about.

Awngeleik steps down on his chest, using her front hooves. A few of his ribs crack. He grimaces, and tries to scream more. It's just mumbling. Then he kicks.

Skylin slides off my lap, to go shoot his feet with freezing water; his gaze at her is pure venom.

Fanning out her restored wings, Skylin states, "I feel vastly better. But you, Vitiosyn. You need rest. You've been through quite a lot. All that plotting must have made you tired. And, though you can div spell words, good luck getting them to work here in Vondurheil, where you're its enemy."

I go stand beside Skylin, looking from her to Zymarc. He huffs out a hard breath through his nostrils. I halfway expect smoke to burst out, with how angry he looks.

"Go on, then," he divs to me, in spite. *"Bury me in the snow. It will only delay me by a little."*

I pat Awngeleik's shoulder, and she steps off Zymarc.

His muffled cry brings a smile to my lips. I go to where Zymarc landed in his fall from the tree. Where Winter's Vondaen now rests in the snow. I pick it up, and feel a hot chill. I stride back, to let Zymarc see the blade.

He struggles, and his breaths quicken. He tries to yell again. It's no use.

Feeling the blade's edge, I state, "I don't know what you think you're doing with all these mind games and named weapons, Zymarc, but even Soren feared this blade. It has to be one of the best. I gave it back to you in Grevagg, out of honor, before making my request. But you got greedy. Perhaps you are getting greedy like Deezalo. Perhaps all your plots will lead to one outcome. The end of you. The end of your people. The death of your replacement. Caleiso. Perhaps all you've done, and will do from this point forward, is for nothing. For now, this weapon is mine. Soon to be with Alpha Jasper again. Its rightful keeper."

Gemma states, "Good luck stealing it a second time. I say we bury him now."

The marks are beginning to fade from Rorka. Her skin's almost normal. "I'll start work on bringing the distortion down." She winks at me. "Help your friends bury that. I tire of his stench. I would gladly devour his flesh and feed his bones to the Vonsai, but you seem to think he needs to live for a little longer."

I nod. "We think his life is presently tied to Talok's."

Zymarc sways his head side to side. I can't tell if that's a ploy to throw us off. Or if we truly are wrong. It doesn't matter. We're burying him, and that's that.

"The device?" Rorka asks.

Sighing unhappily, I confirm, "The device."

Zymarc's second look of venom makes me want to laugh. Especially with that mouth of his, sealed shut.

Rorka walks out of sight. Something softly crackles in her direction. She works to bring the distortion down.

Gemma and I drag Zymarc to the rather large hole in the frozen ground and shove him in it. He doesn't fight it; merely accepts this fate, only wincing in pain.

Skylin smiles sweetly at him, as she claps twice. "Have a nice rest, Vitiosyn. You've earned it."

If Zymarc could snarl at her, he would. With his mouth sewn up, however, there's no chance of that.

The dug-up ground throws itself over our captive.

Awngeleik happily flaps her freed wings, and makes snow swirl to cover the ground until it looks undisturbed.

Rorka whispers, "The distortion's gone. They're looking for us. We need to hurry out of here."

Awngeleik in the lead, the three of us run back with her. Rorka mostly covers up our tracks along the way. The winds of Vondurheil do the rest. We find the others at the front of the lodge, some frantic, others arguing. Arsyn just sits, surrounded by SynKievas with Sonya and the wards. His battered wings are being bandaged by Dea.

Talok spots us first. "Tyler!" he shouts, coming to grab hold of me. "You're safe. Where is he? I'll kill him."

I glance around at all the angry faces, then Merlynite encased as a frozen statue. I think, *There's no talking them down from this. Too many to convince, in such a short time. They'll stop at nothing to kill Zymarc. And I'm not ready to give up on saving my cousin. Not after everything.*

Ryco's gaze is the only one in the group before us that's not filled with hate. Rather, he understands. "He's escaped, hasn't he?" Ryco asks. It's as if he's giving me a way out.

And I take it, saying, "We need to abandon Vondurheil. I know it's your home, Jasper, but it's not safe anymore. Please, listen. Call your Vons to leave."

"I no longer have the voice," says Jasper. "Mekka and Rorka, it's your decision. Today, I'm simply an old Von-dog."

Transitioned to being in Von form, Rorka asks me, "You're sure you feel we've no other choice?" But she divs, *"Got to make it convincing, haven't we?"*

"Call for Vondurheil's evacuation," replies Mekka, sounding winded. "Tyler is our equal. Droediin believed it. Let us believe it. He's thought this over. Gemma too, by the looks of her."

Rorka begins the climb up the lodge, and rather fast. At one of its high points, she howls forlornly. Like a wild thing clinging to a slanted surface, she's determined, hanging on. Her wail is akin to the scream of a siren, but sharper and chilling. She continues. When her voice ceases, the echo continues out across Vondurheil. She climbs down. Still twenty feet from the ground, she leaps to land in a pile of snow. She trots out, shaking herself off.

"They'll only take minutes," she says. "We've been shortening the drill time."

Sure enough, thousands of Greyvons soon come as a horde from every which way, the Paragonian refugees riding upon the backs of only a third of the thousands.

Eight small, sleek Vons get to Rorka first. They surround her like guardians. Two are striped, two spotted, three tan, and one brown.

Once the horde has quieted to listen, Mekka tells them, "We're leaving Vondurheil, ne'er to return, until the end of the war. Head for the way out. And fast. Take our allies as riders. Move!"

Many Vons sniff Merlynite's frozen figure, when they pass by him, as if paying homage to him. They whine and howl or bark, but keep moving forward. Once to the dry, stone path, they run faster. Rorka's eight bound for the front. They set a fast pace.

Warren slips a bridle on Awngeleik. Holding her reins, he glances at me.

Mekka trots over. "You ride your Equidyn, Ravier. Keep control of her.

Pick a partner, someone who'll help you keep your head, should things go awry."

I'm about to say 'Gemma,' but I spot her mounting a multi-colored, slender Von with Ben.

Mounting up onto Awngeleik's back, I blurt out, "Skylin."

Mekka says, "I don't remember which Darklyre girl that is."

"The blonde one," I state. "Especially friendly. Talks too much. Claims she can overcome the mid-levels of death, in the Minor's Gauntlet."

"Oh, that one," says Mekka, the confused look gone. "I'll get her for you." Finding her, Mekka leads her to me, then trots off.

She climbs on, grabbing round my waist. Chills race up my spine. Not the kind from cold air, but the kind that excites me. The dimness of thinking she wouldn't wake up starts to haunt me. Then I recall our first kiss, and I have to hide a smile. "How's your dad?" I ask, spotting him watching me intently from the steps of the main lodge.

"He's been through worse," she says, adjusting herself for the ride. "Dea promised to keep a lookout on him. SynKievas also promised. He'll be fine. Bet he'll be taking those wing bandages off in a short while too." Pausing, Skylin rests her chin atop my shoulder. She whispers, "Mekka said you wanted me as a partner in the journey. Is that true? I thought for sure you'd pick your friend, Galloway."

"Nah." I shrug. "She's already picked Ben."

Offended, Skylin scoffs. "Vards, I'm second choice again? I even died for you, you know."

"You're not second, Sky. Gem's made her choice; I've made mine . . . if you know what I mean."

Skylin gives me a quick kiss on my neck, then huddles closer. "Let's go, then."

Awngeleik trots forward.

Jasper's in front of Merlynite's ice-statue. As we pass him, I hear his whispers of, "Goodbye, old friend. May you rest well, knowing you did not destroy us. We shall live on, always remembering you. And this I promise: I shall find your heir, Droediin, and save him."

My heart aches. The sacrifices are becoming too great to bear. I toss Winter's Vondaen, and it lands at Jasper's feet. Not waiting for his reaction, I tap my heels against Awngeleik's sides, and she bolts forward. We leave Vondurheil.

4

Soup of Ashes

Once outside in the hot sun, Mekka, the Paragonians, and I wait for the city of Vondurheil to be cleared. Rorka's Theocktras keep the pace at the front. I've almost exhaled a sigh of relief when shadows cross over the landscape. Vitasadyns roar overhead. Their red-hot flames hail down a blistering storm.

"As if the desert heat wasn't enough," says Skylin, from behind me. "Think Zymarc was able to contact them?" she whispers.

Jasper and Rorka trot out with another group of Vons.

"That's the last of them," says Jasper. Then he sees the dragons with their Vitiosyn riders coming for us. "Rorka," he says, "head to the front. Have your Theocktras pick up the pace. Mekka and I will keep the back running at full speed." To us, he says, "The rest of you, reflect their spells as well as you're able."

"Leave that to us," says SynKievas. "Darklyres are good at it."

Arsyn adds, "Narrow your line to no more than ten meters wide. Can't guarantee we can protect anyone outside of that."

Sounding worried, Skylin asks, "Father, what of your wounds, just healed?"

Shaking off the bandages, Arsyn fans out his wings. He glances at them. "They seem fine. It takes more than a mere Von shredding my wings to hold me back. Dea's a good healer. She'll be right up there with us, healing us so we don't fall and break our necks. Isn't that right, SynKievas?"

"Yes," he agrees, adding, "but it would be nice to have that ancestral garb Ravier misplaced back in Grevagg."

"Vards, SynKievas," I say, quickly digging out the green cloak. I toss it to him. "You could've asked for it sooner."

Enthusiastically, SynKievas replaces his own cloak with the ancestral garb of King Aygor. He shivers in delight. "I've waited a long time for this. Shall we go, Arsyn?"

Arsyn, in answer, simply flies up, each flap of his wings propelling him farther than I've witnessed with other Darklyres, when first taking flight. SynKievas quickly follows. Then Dea, after them. The three fly thirty feet or so above us.

"Dyns will!" Skylin shouts after them.

The Vitasadyns start for the front of the line. Rorka's almost there.

Once the dragons start hurling their fire in rapid succession, Awngeleik gets restless, wanting to run wildly all over the place. I hold tight to the reins.

Skylin stretches her wings to provide shade for me, making it easier to see the way.

"Let go of her lead," Skylin instructs. "Let her push the Vons faster. I can feel her wanting to leap. So let her. Let the Equidyn do something for you. She wants to please you."

I release the reins and shout, "Go!"

Awngeleik runs faster. She weaves in and out of the cleared spaces between the Vons. Her stride lengthens. She snaps at the nearby Vonsai, making them mad. Then she passes them, and they tear off after us. The group gets faster. Awngeleik makes for the front of the line. The forest edge isn't terribly far in the distance.

We're halfway to safety from the open air of the desert.

My body courses with adrenaline.

Fire makes it past the Darklyres. It takes dozens of Vons out right next to us.

Awngeleik screeches, losing her pace. She stumbles, nearly losing her footing, but she flaps her wings and keeps herself upright.

Skylin shoots water on the burning Vons, saving some from bursting into flames. It's all she can do, before we're too far away.

As I spot incoming fire, I take out my light dagger. I speak, "Ventus-pru-eina." Cold wind blasts out and encases the fireball in ice.

It still falls, disrupting the line. But the Vons are able to weave around it.

Skylin whoops. "Nice shot!"

We're nearly to safety, when the King Vitasadyn lands hard at the edge of the forest. Scepter's careful not to land on the sand. He roars, and the Vons slow to a walk. They pace back and forth. They know they cannot stop moving completely.

"Where is my king?" Scepter growls, lowering his wings to rest atop the darker ground of the forest floor. "Where is Zymarc? You have him. Tell me where he is."

Rorka lunges at one of Scepter's wingtips; she gets a hold of it with her sharp teeth. She rips a chunk from him, and he bellows out fire. Her Theocktras begin to mimic her. All eight of them snarl and bark and lunge in attack. Scepter latches onto some of the smaller ones, the tan ones, and flings them away. Relentlessly, the three get up. They fight again and again and again. The other five remain as pesky, barking, nipping distractions. None of the nine will back down, until Mekka has reached the front of the line in battleform. He faces the King Vitasadyn. Jasper's beside him. Both are undaunted by the flames. It seems only Mekka, Jasper, and Rorka can come to a complete stop on the sand.

When Scepter swipes his spiked head along the desert ground, the three relentless ones of Theocktras are forced to back off.

Scepter lifts his head high, shaking the sand from it, before he bends his head down enough to look at the alpha and his two candidates. "Where is Zymarc?" he rumbles.

I urge Awngeleik forward, whispering to Skylin, "Find Talok. Tell him to play dead. Go!"

Skylin jumps down to go find my cousin.

Once at the front of the line, I shout, "He's dead, Scepter! Zymarc is dead. And so is my cousin! See for yourself." I point back to where Skylin has started sobbing in heartbreak. Gemma quickly plays along, adding sounds of soft sniffling. Ben pretends to comfort her, by holding her hand.

Scepter stretches his neck up, to get a better view over the lot of us. He scoffs. "It can't be as you say," he rumbles. "I still feel his heartbeat."

I ask, "Sure it's not Caleiso's you hear? Where is she? Ask her if it's so. Ask her if she is now queen over all of you. That is her place, isn't it? Zymarc's heir to the throne."

"She's not here," Scepter rumbles more quietly. "And I know not whether she is the heir."

"How convenient," I state. "Let the king die. Then take his throne in Vosh-Perida, the very moment it's happened. Bet you all are missing her coronation."

Scepter scowls at me. "Where is his body?"

I smile wickedly. "Buried in Vondurheil. In the frigid cold, where he belongs. Now, let us pass. We wish to bury my cousin where *he* belongs. In Paragon, with all the ones you slaughtered. I bet your brother, Reign, is ashamed of you. But I will revel in telling him how you failed to save your king, when he's the one who had everything in his favor. Everything working for you, yet you still failed."

Scepter roars one last time at the Greyvons and me, then takes flight.

The Vitasadyns and their riders fly away, heading for the entrance to Vondurheil.

I know it won't take them long to find Zymarc, once they've reached the main lodge.

When Skylin gets back on Awngeleik with me, I kick my heels into Awngeleik's sides, commanding, "Run as if our lives depend on it."

She sprints forward with renewed force.

I say over my shoulder, "Let's hope Gemma's bindings cause problems for them."

"Oh, they will," Skylin replies. "As will the depth of that pit Awngeleik dug. Rorka's magic that sealed his lips shut too. You could make a winning bet that they'll have a hard time restoring their king to his former, wicked glory."

We are some of the first to make it to the safety of the forest, and I laugh. I *actually* laugh. I whisper back to Skylin, "I love the way you talk."

"Does that mean we can start making bets against each other?" she queries.

"One thing at a time, Sky," I say, as I start cooling down amidst the forest shade.

"Sure, Ty. But you're going to have to make bets eventually. Especially if you want that cloak back from SynKievas."

Aiming my hand over my shoulder, I speak one word. The spell word of: "Oonda!"

Skylin's blasted with water, and she squeals.

This time, I keep the laughter from bursting out, simply laughing on the inside.

* * *

After two days of travel, and no Vitasadyns coming to attack us, our group relaxes somewhat.

I lie wide awake, staring up at the stars that second night. Someone sneaks onto my bedroll with me. I halfway expect it to be one of the Darklyre children, in search of a warm victim to suffocate with their wings.

Skylin whispers, "Want company?"

My heart beats faster. I lift the covers, and she crawls in.

Pointing up discreetly, so that her arm isn't as a waving flag for attention, she whispers the constellation names to me. So close is she to me, her cheek is pressed against mine. I fall asleep to the sound of her soft voice, as she recites their history. I don't really care about all that. I simply find comfort in her enthusiasm for telling me.

Half-awake in dawn's dim light, I pull her close to me and then rest one hand atop her hip. The morning air's cool—not cold enough for me to see my own breath, but it's right on that edge. It's nice to have someone near for warmth. Peering over the edge of the blanket, I brave a glance around. No one's awake nearby, except for Musgrae and Ryco conversing quietly at the border of one of the canvas canopies. I trace along Skylin's freckled cheek, then along her pink lips. I want to kiss her. *Really* kiss her.

She startles awake, not making too much noise. She meets my gaze, and I grin. Then I motion with a glance that we should sneak off.

We creep off my bedroll and go some distance from camp. As soon as I think it's safe, I stop.

She looks back at me, her breaths shallow, eyes wide with anticipation.

Going nearer, I grip around her waist and then feel her back, where her wings attach to her skin.

"Just kiss me already," she whispers, near breathless, eyes already shut.

I brush my lips against hers, cautious at first, but I quickly let myself get lost in the moment.

She digs her fingertips along the tops of my shoulders, then into my neck. She claws her way up to my scalp, running her hands through my messy hair.

I cup her face and explore that mouth of hers. So many words come out of it, in a single day. I want to leave her speechless for hours. Then I won't have to wonder how I did. I'll know.

Behind us, someone clears their throat.

Skylin recoils, stifling a scream. She ends up whacking me in the face with one of her wings. I'm flat on my back, and groaning.

"As proud as I am, Ravier, that you've started your own expeditions"—Musgrae stands over me, haloed by the morning light—"I don't know how the others will take it. Arsyn, in particular. I've had my fair share of run-ins with overly protective fathers. They perhaps are as unpleasant as that Gatro was, trying to eat Keturah." He helps me up, then brushes dirt off my coat.

"You're not going to tell on us?" queries Skylin, playing with the feathers of one of her wings.

"It's not in the job description," says Musgrae. "Did I out Gemma and Ben? No! They outed themselves. You've both been through a lot. You shared a moment to unwind. All night long, I might add. And now that moment's over. We've got lots to do before we head out today." Musgrae points at us. "And no more sharing bedrolls. Understood? Or Ryco's going to be the one talking to you 'bout all this. Believe me, you don't want that."

Skylin nods.

I shrug.

"Good enough for me," he says, starting to collect firewood. He hands Skylin some, then points at me specifically. "Get busy, Ravier. You should always make it look like you've been doing assigned tasks, especially when you've been busy doing other . . . unassigned things."

We get back to camp, and fake looking forlorn. But I can't keep my eyes off Skylin. Not as she brushes her blonde feathers out, grooming them for flight. Not as she helps Dea with the King's Wards. Or when she drops picked fruit and pine cones down from some trees, to Siege, Eli, and me.

Once back on Awngeleik with Skylin pressed against my back, I ache inside. *Why do I feel this way?* I wonder. I can barely breathe, yet nothing's crushing me. I'm jittery, yet nothing's off in the immediate distance threatening us.

Partway through the day's journey, Talok and his Greyvon ride—one of Rorka's striped Theocktras—come alongside me. "Are you all right, Tyler? You haven't seemed like yourself all day. Are you worried that I'm mad at you for lying again? If that's what is on your mind, worry no more. It was perfect. Bought us time. And it was a brave gamble, saying what you did to Scepter."

"Thanks, Talok. I'm just tired, I guess."

"Then let Skylin ride with me for a while. Take a nap on Awngeleik. She'll keep you from falling." He pauses, then adds, "I think."

I shake my head. "But then I won't sleep tonight."

Talok glances to Skylin behind me, before he nods. "Sure, Cousin. But we could always have Quall mix up a nice sleep blend of herbs."

I rub at my forehead. "Nah! I'll be fine."

Talok grins. "Well, then, I thought Skylin should know that Dea—"

"What about Dea?" Skylin interrupts.

Startled briefly, Talok replies, "She suggested you tell us about Darklyre history. Your unusual quietness is making your father suspicious of a certain something." Cringing, Talok clarifies, "A certain someone, actually."

"Oh," Skylin whispers, readjusting her position. "Right! Darklyre history. One thing I've always loved about our history has to do with our ancestor Ezareen. Have you heard the story?"

I smile wickedly, saying, "Nope. What do you *love* about it?"

Skylin squirms behind me. It's been precisely five hours that she's been unusually quiet. I'm quite proud of myself. But then I want to explore her mouth again, and I can't even see her. That ache starts all over.

"Ezareen had two sons: AshCrawft and Ayzareel," Skylin states. "AshCrawft, the older brother, had two sons with a Metimora. I don't remember their names, but they started the GreyLyre race. Which, unfortunately, led to Grawllik's existence."

I burst out laughing, leaning forward a bit. Then I get serious. "You shouldn't say stuff like that."

"Why not?" queries Skylin. "I think he's creepy. You agree. And that's the end of it."

"You should feel badly for him. I mean, he was one of the ones taken by Zymarc. Perhaps you resent him for ruining your plan."

"He didn't ruin my plan. He *altered* my plan. Big difference."

"Only in a Darklyre's eyes," I reply.

"Shut up, Tyler." Skylin pinches my back. "Who asked you?"

"I did, in Mensa-div with myself. I was merely answering my own question aloud, for you to hear. Wasn't that kind of me?"

"Would it be kind of me to drown you with water, as I did in Grevagg?"

I shrug. "Will it stop me from feeling so tired?"

"I doubt it," says Skylin.

"You *doubt* it?" I ask. "Why?"

"Because if you don't want to do something, you won't. If you don't want to feel, you won't. If you *want* to feel *tired*, you'll keep on feeling tired. *You* cannot be controlled."

"That sounds like flattery and an insult, spoken with the same breath."

"She's good at that," says Arsyn, now a few mounts over. "Continue your story, Skylin."

"As I was saying," Skylin says, "Ayzareel became the ancestor of the Darklyres, which you already knew. He had eight children with a Withrasyn, Gaula. The first was born the same year Deezalo became the Prime Vitiosyn."

"What do you love about that?" Gemma asks.

"Our name—Darklyres," replies Skylin. "It literally means *Dark Harmonies*. I've always thought that we got the name because Ayzareel was pure dragon and Gaula was a Withrasyn, capable of performing Dragon Taming Magic. For the time they lived in, they were an unlikely couple. A dark sort of harmony."

Arsyn says, "Even now, they'd be an unlikely couple."

The rest of the day's ride is filled with lots of talk of Paragon. The younger Darklyres want to know all they can. Arsyn, SynKievas, and Dea are also curious, though less enthusiastic.

We'll be there, the next morning . . .

I miss having Skylin with me that night. But, recalling Musgrae's warning, I stay put on my bedroll. Sky doesn't come over, either.

Morning unfolds.

I'm anxious to return home to Eyo'el. It's been too long.

I'm packing up the last of my bedding, when Siege approaches me.

"It's time, Tyler," he says, glancing at Talok, who's still fast asleep on his bedroll.

"I don't follow."

Kent joins us, to say, "He took a turn for the worse, last night. Didn't keep a single bit of supper down."

Eli adds, "Quall and Ben's tonics aren't helping no more. Talok spent most of the night away from camp, so he'd not keep us up. But I heard him. Kept him company, though he insisted I get some rest."

Warren gives his input of, "That Dea's helped quite a lot. But I believe her shield abilities have diminished."

I hang my head, before braving the question: "You want me to ask Sonya to make her Soup of Ashes, don't you?"

Grimacing, they nod in reluctance.

"Sure it won't kill him?" I ask.

They shrug.

I laugh. "You're no help at all."

Musgrae grabs me by the shoulders. "We know." Saying that, he shoves me in the direction of the Darklyre girls; Skylin's among them.

I'm so nervous. It's hard to breathe.

Skylin and Sonya groom the children's wings. It's like watching a war of wills. They want the children to hold still. The children don't want to hold still. Some of them simply don't want to fan their wings out for grooming. They stingily keep them wrapped round their bodies, in penguin pose, making the task of the older girls near impossible.

Skylin spots me approaching. "Look, Sonya, Tyler's come to help us." She hands me a wooden comb. "Start on that one." She motions to the boy a head shorter than me, hunched over in that special pose, as he scowls up like a little monster.

I admit, "Skylin, I don't know how to groom wings."

"It's easy," says Dea, coming to grab the edge of one of the boy's wings. "You take the wing firmly in your hand, like so, and yank it out. Then comb down, lift, comb down. Repeat. If they're especially dirty, you douse them with cold water, and continue combing."

"Cold water?" the boy shouts. "But we're already cold! Can't we go back to the warm desert, and sunbathe?"

"Yes, sunbathe," a girl echoes.

"I want to sunbathe," a little girl pipes in.

Their chatter turns into imperceptible words.

Dea fumes, "If you don't quit talking over each other, I'm going to have Tyler clip your flight feathers."

They go silent, terror in their pleading, little eyes.

A different boy says, "But we want to be able to fly, when we get to Paragon."

"Then mind your manners," says Dea. "Or those feathers *will* be clipped, and I'll only let Arsyn grow them back for you when you start behaving."

"Will the Paragonians like us?" the littlest girl asks.

Dea doesn't know how to answer. She seems worried over this same question.

Seeing the need, I state for her, "Of course they will. You'll be guests of their King Talok, won't you?"

The young wards smile and then quiet down, to let Skylin and Sonya groom them.

I start on the young boy's wings. The other boys line up near me to watch.

"This is going to take me a while," I tell them.

The boy at the front of the line says, "We don't mind a bit of waiting."

"Yeah," the oldest boy agrees. "It's better than having girls groom us."

Ryco divs, *"But we mind waiting."* He, Ben, and Gemma come join us right then, asking Dea for combs. Ryco takes mine. "Why don't you and Sonya go see about starting that soup? Take Skylin, to help collect ingredients. Go."

I forfeit the comb to Ryco, as Dea asks, "What soup?"

"My soup recipe," Sonya says shyly.

"You make soup?" Dea queries, confused. "I hadn't any idea you were working on your own recipe. Do I want to know what's in it?"

Sonya fervently shakes her head. "And please don't make me tell you. It's my survival soup. Ketty hates it. But we're hoping it'll help Talok. Can I go now?"

Dea waves her off, and Sonya bolts away.

Skylin and I jog after her.

I'm tempted to grab Skylin's hand. But I resist. It'd be a dead giveaway.

Sonya instructs us, saying, "We need black bark, gray moss, and beetles. Any flowers you think will help with the taste might be a good idea too."

"*Any* black bark will do?" I ask.

Sonya nods, volunteering to get beetles.

"Gray moss it is for me, then," says Skylin.

We collect as much as we think Sonya needs. With no Sonya in sight, Skylin glances around nervously. She steals a kiss. My face heats up. Then she dashes back for camp. I start to follow.

I pause, when I catch sight of Rorka's brightly colored, flowing hair through the thick of the trees. She saunters along by herself, observing the forest, seeming to consider a secret thought. She glances my way. I stand by to wait for her, and she comes over. Twigs snap and pine needles crunch under her boots.

She stops an arm's length away. "Hello, Ravier." She smiles. It isn't a bright smile. Rather, a knowing one.

I glance at her arms. Her enchanted bracers have been replaced by different ones—plain leather, instead of metal-studded. I meet that juniper-green stare. "Did you let the visions play out?"

Her smile diminishes. She swallows hard. "I took the bracers off, yes. Not that night of your departure. In fact, it was the night before all of you returned. As I told you, I fear many things."

I take a step closer, to whisper, "And what happened? What did you see?"

She touches my left hand; the stain appears only where her fingertips brush along my skin. "I fell into a deep sleep. I had visions of another place. One I never could imagine, while awake. And I . . ." Trailing off, she withdraws her right hand.

"Go on," I encourage her. Reaching out, I firmly take hold of her right hand.

Her skin attempts to light with the stain of this different magic we share—The Prismatic of Magic. It doesn't finish the stain. It fades instead. Rorka finally admits, "I met people in the vision whom I've never met during consciousness. LanSoren was one of them. And that one who calls himself Arsyn. He was in my visions, literally a day from our first meeting. He never spoke to me. Only LanSoren did. There were two women in the distance. One stood before a wall of mirrors. The other amongst a multitude of dragon statues. The statues were of a species I've not encountered. There was a winged, black horse there too. His eyes turned red as he approached me, and—" Rorka stops short and squeezes her eyes shut. Tears seep from the corners of her closed eyes.

I ask gently, "What did my father say to you before that, Rorka?"

"I . . . don't remember."

"Try to," I say. "Please. It must be important."

Rorka roams about in an anxious circle around me.

I tightly cling to the ingredients Sonya needs for the soup, waiting for the Greyvon to recall what she does not wish to. She resists it. I can feel the tension in the air that has grown heavy with mist.

Rorka stops in her tracks, as recognition lights in her gaze. "It was an apology. Yes, that was it. LanSoren apologized for needing to choose your life over restoring my memory. He explained that he could have restored me to a former glory. Or he could choose for you to live on and learn, and be what Muraine truly needs. The answer. The cure. Then the black horse approached me, drowned out the voice of your father. He recited that thought we shared. But it was different. More complete. Something like, *Happiness was vanquished. Then the days of zeal became rime. Love was lost. With it gone, our sadness arose out of failure. You have failed fate.* Something, or someone, lit the black horse on fire. He stormed toward me in a full gallop. Great pain overcame me. I started to leave the dream world, for fright. As I did, I saw you in the distance, as you are now or slightly younger, frozen in a pillar of ice. Your father had his hand pressed to the ice. He looked as if he was saying a silent goodbye to you, while you slept in the pillar."

Unwanted tears form in my eyes. I blink them away. "What do you think it means?"

"I was hoping you would have some ideas," says Rorka, sounding tormented. "The black horse was terribly frightening. He bit into my arm, before I left the dream world to awaken in my bed within the lodge. I recall having the sensation of singed flesh, though no fire was near my bed before slumber. The burn is still here on my arm. It wasn't there, before I fell asleep."

Rorka removes the bracer from her right arm and pulls her sleeve back. Sure enough, there's a large burn mark, even scratches where sharp teeth could have grazed across her bare skin. She adjusts the sleeve and bracer back in place, as my thoughts whirl.

"Rorka," I ask, "is it possible you went to an actual place, not just a dream world?"

"I don't see how." Rorka shakes her head. "I've never heard of such a thing happening. I even checked for a trail of lingering magic. There was nothing out of the ordinary, save for the burn mark on my skin."

I'm about to talk more, ask more. But I hear someone sniffling nearby.

Rorka flinches, before muttering, "We can discuss it later, Ravier. I do believe one of those King's Wards is in distress."

Rorka leaves for camp.

Meanwhile, I search nearby for one of the wards. When I spot Sonya curled up on a fallen tree, I stop. She's mashed beetles and collected them in a large leaf. She's trying not to cry.

"What's wrong?" I ask, approaching her.

She wipes her eyes. "I just miss Ketty, is all. I didn't think I would so much. Nor King Aygor. But I do. I even miss my trainer, Orteel. And I *never* thought that would happen."

I grin. "I know how you feel. It'll get easier. I should know. I've not been home for a while. Possibly, I may never make it back."

"But aren't we arriving in Paragon, tomorrow?" Sonya asks, getting up to head in the direction of camp.

"I'm not from there," I reply. "I'm from Earth. Where Adair Galloway is from."

Sonya hesitates, then says, "I do hope you make it home. It's sad, thinking about never going back to RawZend. If it was safe, I'd want to go back there today."

"I bet you will, someday."

"I'll take that bet." Sonya picks up her beetle-filled leaf.

We head back. Once at camp, she starts on the Soup of Ashes. Initially, she adds a gallon or so of water. It doesn't appear too terrible. Nor is the smell off-putting. As it cooks down to a charred paste, however, all who witness the soup cooking struggle not to vomit right there. The smell becomes as bad as something that's been dead for days.

When it's ready, though I have no idea how Sonya can tell that it is, indeed, ready, she fills a bowl and then hands it to Ryco. Even he has to rally up the courage not to gag.

Musgrae drags Talok out of bed, to sit him down near the fire growing cold.

Ryco proclaims, "Sonya's made you her special soup, Talok. Eat up."

Talok scoops the spoon in the dark-gray mush, lifts it, then lets the contents plop back into the bowl. He turns up his nose to it. "Not having any, not until someone else tastes it first."

Growling under his breath, Ryco looks at me. He crosses his arms, then motions with a jerk of his head that I be the victim.

I sit beside my cousin and take the bowl from him, filled with remorse that I know the ingredients it contains. I can't look at the contents. I just take a spoonful and shove it in my mouth before I can talk myself out of it. I gulp down the gray paste as fast as I can. Then I press my lips together, willing myself not to puke it back up. My stomach churns, unhappy with what I've done. Something seems to tingle and crawl in my mouth, in the worst sort of way. It tastes like cheap blue cheese, times ten, coating stale peanuts. Bitter nuttiness, joined with earthy mold.

Gemma hands me a canteen of Farivoo; I gulp the liquid down, swishing the last sip before swallowing. I smack my cousin on the back, and say, "You'll survive."

Talok takes a bite. He spits it out. Throws the bowl. The contents splat on a tree. "Disgusting! I'm not eating that."

He runs away.

Warren captures him. "Oh yes you are, Talok."

Ryco snaps his fingers. "Ben. A syringe." He takes Ben's offering, and hands the needle tip back. Then he plunges the glass syringe into the pot of gray paste. He fills it, as Warren and Musgrae hold Talok down on the ground.

Talok yells foreign obscenities at Eli, who's about to stop my cousin's legs from kicking. "Eli of Kirja, you dare join in this torture, and I'll be biting your neck first chance I get."

Flinching, Eli brushes his hand across where Talok bit his neck days ago. Siege takes the position of holding Talok's legs down, by lying atop them. Talok clamps his mouth shut, his eyes spewing hatred at Ryco.

"You won't win, Talok," Ryco states, whilst Quall and Ben survey the scene from the sidelines (Eli has disappeared, altogether).

Kent says, "Cooperate, and it ends in minutes."

Quall adds, "We're not heading for home until you've finished that whole pot of soup Sonya prepared."

Keeping his teeth clamped together, only Talok's lips move as he asks, "Why isn't anyone else eating it? Why's it just Tyler and me?"

Kent replies, "She made it especially for you."

"I respectfully decline it," says Talok, teeth still clamped together.

I clasp my hands behind my back, making the comment, "Galloway's gonna tickle you soon, if you don't start behaving."

Gemma proclaims, "Ooh! Good idea!" She rushes to do the deed.

Talok fights it. Then he gives in, and laughs out angry sounds.

Kent lunges to keep Talok's mouth open. Ryco empties the syringe contents into my cousin's mouth. Quall stoops way down to pinch Talok's nose shut. Talok coughs and gargles, and his eyes water from the effort of the struggle. Eventually, he has no choice but to swallow the soup.

Jasper and Mekka wander into the midst of our group to watch my cousin being forced to gulp down every bit of Sonya's soup. Rorka stands with them, her gaze far away, as her Theocktras pant happily nearby.

Once Talok's released, all King's Guard rush away to prepare for the journey. Some Vonsai come and sniff the contents of the soup pot; one of them hacks in disgust, then runs off. The others don't even so much as *sniff* the pot. They trot away instead. Talok just lies on the ground, out of breath and grimacing. He clutches the front of his coat.

Gemma tosses a canteen to Talok. It lands on his chest. "Farivoo as solace for your wounded soul," she says.

"That is a weak apology," says Talok, sitting up to drink the whole thing. "But it'll do."

Finally, we're off.

Talok broods for most of the way. But at least he has some color back in his face. It eases away some of our worries. It does nothing, however, for my newfound worry over Rorka. She is troubled. I don't believe she told me all of what her vision revealed. Also, she studies Arsyn every chance she gets. Yet she won't approach him. I don't know what to do, other than let her work out her own misgivings.

5

Alchemist vs. Architect

Riding atop one of the spotted, slender Vons of Theocktras is Dea, adjusting her laced-up, black corset. Once done with that, she toys with the fine chains of her webbed necklace. Finally, she asks Ryco, "How will they welcome us do you think?"

"Hard to say," he replies. "I know for a fact that Paydinn and his family—the Jokryns—have taken root in Eyo'el, and in neighboring cities. Whether that's made Talok's advisers more or less welcoming of others, well . . . we'll see."

Ryco opens the new gate with a single, sweeping motion of his hand.

Eli mutters under his breath, "Showoff," as Ryco dismounts his ride of a young Vonsai and then walks forward.

Warren states, "It isn't Ryke's fault ya can't open the gate by yourself."

We follow Ryco in, as Eli retorts, "Neither can you, Warren."

"Yet I'm not the one sore over it," replies Warren.

They stop their argument immediately upon entering the city.

The rubble has been cleared away. Trees soar up toward the atmosphere again, the finished homes spotting them as would silver stars on a glistening-green sky. The trees aren't as tall as before, but their breadth spreads out, covering a far greater distance. It has an unkempt, feral appearance.

I climb down from Awngeleik; so does Skylin. The others soon find their footing upon the ground as well.

"Khyra's been busy," Ben comments.

"Last chance to ask her," says Ryco. "Have you changed your mind?"

"No," Ben replies. "I would not steal your sword, at such a time as this. But will you tell her what's going to happen to you?"

Reluctantly, Ryco strolls forward. "I'd not make my last moments with Khyra filled with sorrow over that. I want to see her smile one last time, before we leave tomorrow."

We head farther along.

Several horses rush up to Ryco. Brash is one of them. In fact, he's the first to reach us. He looks Ryco in the eye, then whinnies a deep, happy sound.

Ryco says to him. "Tell Reign his boy's returned home, a king."

Brash and the other neins gallop off. They take flight. I hold tightly to Awngeleik's reins; I don't want her out of reach, especially since we don't know how she'll react to this rebuilt city of Eyo'el.

We wait around, as Ryco paces back and forth. He rubs at his forehead. I've never seen him this nervous.

Reign roars off in the distance. He's quickly appearing, flying above us, and casting a great shadow over the green grass of shamrock regrown over the mangled mounds. Many dyns—some large, most small—gather at the tops of the refortified wall of black trees protecting Eyo'el. Those dyns rumble and roar and shoot fire into the air. They sound as a flock of chattering birds at mealtime, large and thunderously loud birds.

Reign lands hard on the ground, then does a slithering run the rest of the way to us. The ground shakes. Talok dashes to greet his dragon, slamming up against the side of Reign's great, scaly face. "I've missed you, Talok," Reign rumbles. "And your people have too. Welcome home. Especially you, Sivos-Paradyn. I see you've brought more of your kind, with you." Reign studies the Darklyres.

Ryco pulls at the collar of his coat. "Where's Khyra?"

"On her way," replies Reign. "When I roar, she knows she's needed at the gate. It's all I've done—roar and nap—until yesterday, when I discovered that my wings could again lift me."

Talok says, "Wait until you hear how Tyler duped your brother, Scepter. I've so much to tell you."

We don't wait for too much longer, before Khyra comes stomping her way toward Reign.

"Reign!" she shouts. "I told you I'd be working on the top tree canopy today. I fell, nearly broke my arm too, startled by your roar. Just look at my cloak. Torn in several places. You're supposed to wait until you're at the gate, before you go roar—"

When Talok steps into her view, she stops mid-sentence.

"We're home, Khyra," he says, his face beaming in happiness.

She shrieks and runs, then throws herself against Talok. She hugs him tight. Seeing the rest of us, she quickly goes round hugging us all, even Eli. He cringes. Then she stops at the sight of the Darklyres.

Talok makes quick introductions. When Khyra shakes Dea's hand, she pauses, tilting her head in curiosity.

"You seem familiar, somehow, Deamond," Khyra comments.

"As do you," replies Dea, casting a downward glance. "Although I cannot place what it is. Regardless, may I congratulate you on rebuilding a beautiful city?"

Khyra blushes. She turns an even darker shade, as Sonya and the other wards add their compliments on how beautiful she has made Eyo'el. Even SynKievas and Arsyn congratulate her on her skills in Green Magic. In shyness, she thanks them all.

Quall states, "I'll take these ones to the castle, give them a tour. Eli, Warren, Nyrim—you're with me."

They take to the path, as Mekka and Rorka instruct the Vons (the ones allowed into the city) to spread out and keep as quiet as they can. Jasper's not with them. In fact, I don't see him anywhere nearby. Mekka and Rorka realize it as well. They trot off out of sight, presumably to go look for him. The Vons of Theocktras follow close behind.

Ryco suddenly hands Khyra the small black box he's taken out, saying, "Happy birthday, Khyra. Sorry we're a little late."

Khyra turns serious. "Oh, was my sixteenth a few days ago? I quite forgot. I've been so busy." She opens the box, and her hands tremble. She pulls two somethings out, and they grow to full size. Two small birds colored of black, white, and blue, rest in Khyra's palm.

Awngeleik tugs us over there, so that she can sniff the lifeless creatures.

Pushing Awngeleik's head out of the away, Ryco snaps his fingers over the birds, and they come alive. Chirping, they then fly away together singing a crisp, pleasant song.

Awngeleik snorts and squeals, stamping her front hooves on the ground.

I hold the reins so tight that my knuckles go white.

After the two birds are out of sight, Khyra's erupting smile fades. She closes the box, and slowly looks to Ryco. She holds her breath. Her neck tenses. She starts asking, "Are you—?"

Gripping her hand, Ryco pulls her closer. He brushes her black hair back away from her face. Quietly, he asks the question: "Will you be my wife, Khyra? My equal, before we have to leave again tomorrow."

"Where are you going?" she asks. "You just got back."

Talok says, "We've found a way to get this rather tedious bracelet off me." He holds up his wrist, sporting the Geldryn device.

Khyra breathes in relief. "That's wonderful news. Can't I go with?"

Ryco shakes his head. "I—Paragon needs you here. Safe. Will you promise not to leave, unless you have no choice?"

"Is that the Second of the Guard asking me," Khyra queries, "or my potential partner for life?"

"Both," replies Ryco, walking around Khyra to stand behind her. He sweeps his gloved hand along her bare neck.

Khyra states, "I've not said yes, yet."

Ryco smiles in that special way. "I'm not trying to romance you, Khyra. I was checking to see if your injuries left scars. But I see that it's something else, which has marked your skin."

Khyra's violet eyes widen. "It was Madeleine's idea. 'You're of Von aura,' she said. 'You must get a mark of one upon your back.'"

Ryco states, "I look forward to seeing it."

"What makes you think you'll be seeing it?"

"Is that a no, then?" queries Ryco, his expression unreadable.

"I didn't say that," replies Khyra, momentarily squeezing her eyes shut. "Can't I think it over, on the way to Sosha's Castle?"

"Of course." Ryco motions for Khyra to lead us. "Who's the mark's carver?"

"Madeleine," she replies, starting the trek forward. "She's been learning new things, while you've all been away."

"That's wonderful," I state.

Kent asks, "How is she?"

"You'll have to see for yourself," Khyra replies.

"Fair enough," says Ryco. "Tell us about the city."

Gemma, who's holding hands with Ben, asks, "How did the rebuilding go?"

Khyra glances behind, eyeing the two of them. She frowns, then focuses on what's ahead. "It's been hard work. Not a lot of sleep. Used an exorbitant amount of magic, and got help from Rozeth's friends from the Aeown. Zepharre's had his hands in near everything, every step of the way. But not *my* city plans. I didn't tell him how it was going to be, until it was already done."

Ryco remarks, "I'm sure he was thrilled over that."

Gemma and Talok relay what's happened to us; Khyra's gripped by their recount, not asking too many questions. Reign walks, sometimes slithers, along with us. Awngeleik is reasonably calm too, and I'm relieved. We journey under the new city-in-the-trees. Once under its shade, geometric patterns can be spotted from various positions. It's exquisite yet wild, with its order among chaos. Ryco's quiet through it all, merely observing the handiwork of Khyra and the Emeralds. Pride in those yellow eyes, he grips Khyra's hand and ambles alongside her.

We draw nearer the castle. It's the same as it was when Gemma and I first saw it. No more battle scars. Simply the perfect place to house the King of Dragon Tamers.

Talok stops. He smiles up at it in wonderment. "Home." He sighs.

The double doors groan open, and a frazzled Zepharre tramps out onto the landing. It looks as though his dark-brown hair hasn't been brushed for days. No longer clean-shaven either, I hardly recognize him. He hasn't seen us yet, since his head is downturned during his quick descent of the stairs.

Khyra hisses the adviser's name, "Zepharre! I've been avoiding him all morning." She turns to Ryco. "Here's how it is, Ryco of Paragon. I accept your offer."

Even as she's talking, Zepharre spots her, and starts his rant, "Khyra, there you are. I've been looking for you—"

Khyra grabs Ryco's coat lapels right then, and pulls him down for a kiss. It isn't quite as sloppy as the one she gave Ben, down in the tunnels. She still doesn't know what she's doing, though. Hiding a smile, I look away to Zepharre.

He has stopped in his tracks, still talking, "All morning and—what is happening?" He sees Ryco and Khyra, then turns back to the castle. He walks in a confused, little circle, then looks at them again. "You're *still* there. Kissing Khyra. Isn't she your ward? Something isn't right." He looks off to the distance, studying the many places someone could use as a hiding spot.

Waving at Zepharre, I say, "We've made it home. How'd the food stores hold up?"

"Gone!" His attention snaps to me, as he jerks his hand up. "All those Jokryns finished off what we had. They especially loved the flavors. We must now suffer through the bland fares they brought with them. That's what's wrong!" he exclaims. "Last night's actually had flavor. They slipped something in it, and now I'm hallucinating. Wretched Jokryn children, taking advantage of their grandsire Paydinn not being here to control them."

Blinking rapidly a few times while staring at the ground, Ryco one-handedly wipes his mouth.

Khyra states, "No, Zepharre. They truly are here. Also, I passed my sixteenth year a few days ago. Ryco's asked me to be his equal. And I accepted. Isn't it wonderful?"

"Lies!" Zepharre shouts, rushing to Khyra. "I don't know who I'm talking to in this moment." He looks away, in alarm. "Oh no! What if I'm still sleeping rather than hallucinating? How does one wake from an induced sleep curse?"

At the top of the castle steps is Sonya, saying, "Love's devout kiss. That's what our storytellers say."

"Ridiculous." Zepharre shakes his head. When he looks to Sonya, his voice turns shrill, asking, "What is that? This isn't real. I know! I'll go engage in something I detest. It'll make my blood pressure rise. Then I'll wake from the sleep curse. Paperwork! I detest doing paperwork. And if that doesn't work," he says, then pauses to glance at Khyra, "I'll try something that will bring me the *greatest* of joys. I'll burn the City Architect's blueprints that she has on the wall. It doesn't make any sense. So, who cares if it gets burned up?"

He tramps up the stairs; Quall unintentionally blocks the doorway.

"My word!" Zepharre yells. "Get out of the way, Quallendeis! Does anyone have any hope of seeing anything, with you in the way?"

Quall's about to deck Zepharre in the face. He stops when Ryco says, "Zepharre thinks he's hallucinating."

"What luck," Quall mumbles, lowering his fist, "that Ryco's quick to talk. I was about to break your jaw, Zepharre, and keep you from saying another word." He moves aside, and the head adviser bolts past him.

Khyra laughs. "Can't we let him think he's hallucinating for a little longer?"

Ryco fails at stopping his cringe. "Not a good idea."

Gemma adds, "But it would be entertaining."

Awngeleik tugs me over to a patch of grass outside the castle, to lie down.

Warren assists me in staking her lead rope down, proclaiming when we're done, "She must be tired."

The Darklyres wait at the top of the castle steps. In pairs, we trail inside.

Madeleine greets us—Ryco, in particular.

"I can't believe you're all home," she says, hugging Ryco. She steps back. "I've remembered a great many things. Especially of you, Sylvadyn. I recall that it was you. You, who taught me stitchery, by making clothes and such, after I arrived in Eyo'el. I was nineteen, and you were twenty-one. Freshly made Second of the Guard. Now look at you. Nyrim said you're leaving again. You must come back, to teach me."

Khyra beams. "Yes, teach Madeleine again, so she can stitch together my wedding dress."

"Wedding?" queries Madeleine, as she accepts the black box Khyra offers her.

"Ryco and I will sign a contract." She turns to him, to add, "If that's all right. I don't want a ceremony, until my parents are home. Or until we've found out what's happened to them."

"You and Ryco are engaged?" Madeleine studies Ryco's face. "What about—"

Interrupting, he replies, "It didn't work out."

Madeleine quickly glances at Ben, who's standing beside Gemma, then back to the black box. She opens it. A gasp of delight escapes her. "These are as beautiful as you, Khyra." Returning the box, she cups the younger girl's face. "You shall make a lovely bride."

Musgrae shyly steps forward to ask, "How many years have you remembered?"

"Bits throughout, Musgrae of Bethsaide."

A broad grin creeps onto Musgrae's face. While he tells her of the ordeals we've endured, we head upstairs. Never once does he mention the part about having to kill Merlynite. I imagine many of us are still in shock over it. It's tough to push away the images, once they've started.

I run my hand along the warm stair railing, and Metsa greets me. *"Tyler! You are home, at last. No longer are we wounded. Merely asleep. We wait for you to waken. I am one of the chosen, and so is the Midnight Anemone. Though her power is not at slumber, her heart sleeps. You must waken it as well.”*

I div to Metsa, *“You mean the Arkivara of Trauvo?”*

“Not her. The Anemone I speak of is your poison,” replies Metsa, in div. *“And you are hers. Yet, together, you can heal a great many things, in the future. Resist her friendship, and all will be lost.”*

“Is she Awngeleik?” I div. *“Metsa, answer me.”*

Metsa’s replying div chills me to my core. *“I am not a commoner that I must answer you, Dark Prince.”*

I’ve no response for him. I’m simply left wondering why he’d call me that, as if I’m the character in that children’s book. I muse, *Perhaps my father read him the story, and it’s one of his inspirations for conversation.*

Halfway down one of the halls on the second floor, Madeleine stops all of a sudden. She turns, saying, “I’ve remembered something else to do with you, Tyler Ravier. Do you still not know what you are? Or, rather, who you are?”

“I’m the Son of LanSoren.”

“No,” she says. “Apart from anyone else. Standing on your own, who do you think you are?”

Hesitating, I reply, “Tyler Ravier.”

“Yet you think that name is ordinary, don’t you?”

I don’t know how to reply. So I tell her the truth. “It’s always sounded ordinary to me. Not a family name, not an Iraqi name, not a catchy name. Just plain Tyler.” I grin in sadness.

“You are wrong,” replies Madeleine firmly. “You are Savakaidyn. It’s the name of your coat. Sleeping Dragon. It’s a Rubidyn word. I meant to tell you, before the festival. When I couldn’t find you, I put if off for tomorrow. Then tomorrow came, and my part in your story was stolen away by some phantom of fate. I was one meant to walk with you. Now I’ve forgotten near anything of use to you. And the greatest irony is: you were the one who made me forget.”

“Why tell me this now?” I ask. “What difference does it make? We’ve found a way to save Talok.”

“But what of Zymarc?” she asks, in return. “How will you stop him?”

"I don't know."

Circling about me, Madeleine continues, "I'll tell you how you can't stop him. You can't keep on believing that you're ordinary. Not a bit of ordinary. None of you." She sweeps a glance over everyone. "You can take everything out around Zymarc, but if you believe you're just plain nothing, you'll never defeat him. He feeds off emotion, like a dragon. I should know. I tame dragons. I know one when I see one. He holds the aura of several dragons. I recall LanSoren telling me that. But he has not the one you do, Tyler Ravier. Though your true power sleeps, it will awaken. It waits for you to be ready."

I recall some of the words when Gemma put Zymarc to sleep. I speak one now. "Ravieras-Savak. What's it mean?" I glance at Gemma.

She replies, "It was something that came to mind, after reading King Aygor's letter. Right after the closing, I think. I don't know what it means. But it certainly worked on Zymarc, didn't it?"

Madeleine states, "Perhaps it is for you to know, and then believe. Believe that there is power in a name, Ravier."

A man adds, "Sleeping Dragon is an aura of both." It's Lokasi, coming to greet us. He looks on at Kent with pride, then to me. "It's why LanSoren and Madeleine picked that design. They didn't know which you would be—a powerful dyn, or a cunning Von."

Talok claps me on the back. "By those definitions, he's definitely both."

"Like that Onyx Prince, which Gyronawv talked of?" queries Ben, hiding a grin. "Prince Setharyn."

Dea adds, "That explains why I think you're a legend made flesh. In possession of Siveyra's Mark, no less."

Someone strides into the hall just then, carrying a tall stack of books.

"EmiKal!" Talok calls out. "Want help with those?"

The books go flying, and a shrill scream escapes the secondary king's adviser.

"Talok!" he exclaims, already on his knees and collecting the books. "You're home? It seems to have been ages. I can hardly believe it."

We help collect the books for EmiKal, then follow him farther down the hall.

He says, "I was on my way to give these to Zepharre. But tell me of your travels. Have you been successful?"

"We're heading for Zepharre as well," says Talok. "To warn you, he thinks he's hallucinating or stuck in a sleep curse, and he doesn't believe it's really us."

EmiKal grins nervously. "We should get to the Advisers' Quarters quickly, then. Who's to say the havoc he'll enact, in that frame of mind."

We practically run to keep up. EmiKal bursts into one of the rooms adjacent to the council room.

"Zepharre, what are you doing?" queries EmiKal, setting his book stack down on a table near the door.

"Paperwork!" shouts Zepharre, spectacles on his face, whilst he peruses the paper stack upon his desk.

EmiKal falters at the doorway. "Are you feeling all right?"

Sitting, with quill in hand, Zepharre pores over some ledgers. Never looking up, he replies too calmly, "Of course I'm not. Our new ally's children—Paydinn's progeny, to be exact—thought it'd be a good laugh to play one of their pranks on us. We're hallucinating. Or you're one of the perpetrators. And I'd rather not speak to you right now. I'm quite distraught. So, unless you can undo the damage, go away."

Khyra argues, "Zepharre, you're being ridiculous. Talok's home, and—"

Zepharre bolts out of his chair and strides toward Khyra. He cuts her off by saying, "And?"

Unsure of herself now, Khyra adjusts her tattered cloak. "They've found a way to remove the device from Talok."

"What else?" queries Zepharre, leaning forward in anticipation; his face is inches from hers.

Hesitating, Khyra chews on her lower lip. "Ryco and I are engaged."

Zepharre points at her. "See, that's how I know none of this is real. That! You are his ward!" he shouts, stepping back. "Ryco's too honorable to ask you that sort of thing, when you're so young that you can't even be on your own. *Someone* has to claim you. Ryco would never shift you from *ward* to *wife*, without there being some lull in time. Some years from the moment you come into your own, to when you actually marry. You've hardly even lived. You've never been outside of Paragon. You've *scarcely* been outside of Eyo'el."

"That's not my fault!" Khyra shouts, as angry tears build up. She balls her fists at her sides.

"Khyra, I hadn't meant to upset you that way. I'm sorry." Zepharre remorsefully looks about. "I'm apologizing to hallucinations, now?" That wildness returns to his eyes, as he talks to himself. "No. I'm *not* sorry. You know what else I won't be sorry for?" He strides his way to the largest picture hanging on the wall. He takes it down, spitefully looking it over.

"Zepharre, don't," says Ryco, taking a few steps forward.

We get ready to restrain the head adviser.

But Khyra's screaming jars us to inaction. "You *dare* destroy that, Zepharre, and I will *end* you!"

"Lies," says Zepharre, with a small smile. "Little Khyra wouldn't ever have the nerve to threaten me." He lifts the picture over his head, as if about to swing a hammer, then crashes it down on his desk.

The frame shatters. The blueprint inside is torn in half.

Khyra's face turns beet-red.

Ryco motions for us to let them be. "He shouldn't have done that," says Ryco, rubbing at his face, quite satisfied for what's about to transpire.

"I feel better," says Zepharre, his smile widening.

That smile quickly disappears, however, as Khyra lunges for him. She claws at his face, rips his spectacles off in the process. He barely manages to fight her off, before she's grabbing a splintered piece of the wooden picture frame. She throws it at Zepharre, and it turns to metal just before it smacks his arm.

He hollers. "That hurt, you little witchy Jokryn. You think 'cause you look like that girl, Khyra, I won't fight back? Ha!" he shouts.

We watch them go at each other, making a mess of the room. Khyra slams Zepharre down upon his own desk, choking him, then grabbing his coat lapels and beating his back against the desk. Paperwork and books go flying. The desk surface is cleared in seconds.

Zepharre gets free. He unsheathes his long-blade while he's at it, and points it at Khyra's throat. He gets her to settle down. "Make a move and I'll run you through, Jokryn. I mean it."

Ryco takes his Parasogyn form, his breaths sounding as a riled-up beast.

Khyra glances down at her black-leather bracers. The look in her violet eyes darkens. She smacks the blade away, using one of her protected wrists. "Put your sword away, Zepharre. No one wants to see it."

Shock crosses Zepharre's face, and he drops the long-blade. "You didn't have to sink to *that* level, Jokryn." He turns to go straighten the ledgers and paperwork, before putting all of it back on his desk. "And look, there's Ryco in his rather splendid Parasogyn form. You know, I've always been quite jealous of it. I would never admit it to his face. Perhaps hallucinating *isn't* so bad."

Scoffing, Khyra turns to us. "I give up. Just let Zepharre rot in here, until the war's over."

Zepharre pulls his chair in, then slips the bent spectacles on his face. He adjusts his coat lapels, before taking a quill in hand and restarting work on the ledgers.

"Snap out of it, Zepharre!" EmiKal exclaims. "Talok and the others *are* home, and you're just going to . . . going to do paperwork?" EmiKal fidgets with his hands.

"I told you," Zepharre replies, scribbling numbers in the ledgers, "we're hallucinating. How many times have I got to say it? The sick nerve of you, Jokryn, making me *repeat* myself over and over again, here"—his eyes flare at the paperwork—"the same way you make me do when we're all mostly sane and sober. Look what you've made me do now." Zepharre lays down his quill. "I'm starting to rhyme like Eli. I actually miss that little bugger, Kirjan. Come to think of it, however"—his focus strays upward—"it's rather rare for victims to have the same hallucination. Whoever you are, you shouldn't be hallucinating that Talok and the others have come home. Therefore, I must be asleep!" He calmly picks up his quill and resumes his calculations of the ledgers.

Gemma says, "Let's go with Khyra's idea. Abandon him."

Zepharre snaps his attention up. "You can't abandon what's already been abandoned, dear demon of Paydinn's making. Oh, and EmiKal? Just for laughs, mind telling me what those winged creatures are, standing next to Talok? Or, rather, the one who looks like Talok." Zepharre taps the quill end on his desk.

Dea steps forward, to say, "We're Darklyres, Mister Zepharre."

Startling, Zepharre says, "My word. Now I'm imagining Khyra older, and with wings." He laughs nervously and rips the spectacles off his face, bending them further. "And calling me Mister Zepharre. I've never been called *that* in my life."

"I had a feeling that would be the case," states Dea, suddenly studying Khyra.

Skylin touches Dea on the arm, whispering to her, "You two look like each other. That's the familiarity. She resembles a younger you, without the wings."

Sonya and the other wards squeeze past to get a look. They agree. Deamond and Khyra are near identical. Same height, coloring—everything, except for age and the wings.

Zepharre rubs his forehead, blankly staring at a wall. "I've never before heard her voice. It's so smooth, and calm. Not at all like a Jokryn. How could I imagine, in my sleep, something I've never heard? That doesn't make any sense."

A reddish-colored bird flutters through the open window right then, to land atop Zepharre's desktop. He startles in his chair, then he grabs a nearby book and slams it down on the bird. "Another letter!" he shouts. "Don't I get enough of those, when I'm awake?"

When he lifts the book, a crumpled piece of paper is left behind. He sweeps it onto the floor, using the edge of the book, then seems to remember something. He says to Ryco, "Oh! Did Reign tell you the good news about your name?"

Ryco, back to his usual form, goes forward to pick the letter up.

Zepharre continues, ranting, "We put it to a vote, before I fell into this sleep curse. And it's been decided. You are now the Paradyn. It means: the Dragon of Paragon. And, since this isn't real, I don't have to worry over hearing Eli's rhyme of—"

Eli pokes his head out enough for Zepharre to notice him, saying, "The Paradyn of Paragon." He smiles wide.

Zepharre growls, before he eyes Eli curiously, motioning at his own neck. "What are those two puncture marks on your neck, Kirjan?"

"Bite marks," Eli grumbles, glancing away to Talok.

"What *bit* you?" Zepharre asks. "For it couldn't have been a Sorsryn. The mark's all wrong. Not spaced far enough apart. And, when they bite out of ill intent, their fangs curve in like hooks and tear the skin quite badly. Ask me how I know."

Talok says, "I bit him."

"You, Talok?" Zepharre's brow furrows together. "But you're part Vaegon. You can't have blood. I mean, you can taste it. But not consume it."

"It's the device," replies Talok, walking closer to Ryco. "It's changing my physiology. Giving me a blood craving. But, not to worry, one of the Darklyre girls—Sonya of RawZend, in fact—made me her Soup of Ashes. It was sufficient, in place of the blood."

Ryco smirks, as he gives the letter to Talok.

Zepharre says, "Ash bits in food never hurt anyone, especially if you're a Jokryn. Or better? A dragon."

Gripping Zepharre's shoulder, Ryco states, "Blood for a Vaegon. It's like wine, for those too young. You can taste it, but then you're supposed to spit it out."

Zepharre warily stands up, to add, "Problem was, I never spit it out. That was a fun night, wasn't it?"

Ryco replies, "It was the one night I actually didn't mind you."

"You only liked me drunk?" queries Zepharre with wit, before he gets serious. "Are you really home?"

"We're *really* home," replies Ryco.

Zepharre grips the front of Ryco's coat. "By the Vardiyas! I've missed you, Paradyn."

"Where are the Jokryn?" I ask.

Sounding spiteful, Quall adds, "We didn't see them, on our way in."

"Hunting," replies Zepharre, letting go of Ryco. He glances to Khyra's forlorn face. He gradually looks over the torn blueprint in her hands. "My apologies, Khyra. I didn't think any of it was real. Or I thought that you were a Jokryn, trying to torment me."

Khyra states, "Perhaps if you had been more welcoming, Zepharre, they wouldn't wish to torment you."

Zepharre raises his voice in defense, "I followed all Sorsryn etiquette. I was proper, during all introductions. More than proper, truthfully."

Khyra says, "They're half Metimoran, though, aren't they? Have you seen how the Jokryn brothers behave toward each other? They think you hate them."

"Perhaps I do. But, yes, fine," Zepharre agrees. "You're right about the Jokryn brothers. Complete disregard for etiquette. Yet how am I to know what's proper for Metimorans? They've been off in their own little spot of hidden land, for longer than any of us have been alive." Pausing, Zepharre adds, "Look, I don't want to argue with you, Khyra. You're an intelligent woman—"

Khyra spouts off, "So I've advanced to a woman's status. And intelligent too? How kind of you."

"Well," says Zepharre, blushing some, "I can't have it being told that a girl tossed me about in the Advisers' Quarters, now can I? I can handle a woman putting me in my place. Not a girl. Besides, you've not been a Minor-Pristine, for two whole days. Yes?"

"Wait!" Khyra exclaims, grabbing Zepharre by the coat sleeve. "You knew, yesterday, that I no longer held a girl's status, and you had the nerve to talk to me the way you did?"

"Come now, Khyra," says Zepharre. "You seemed to have forgotten that your day of birth had passed, so I took advantage. It's what I do. And, with the events of today, you will have a great story to tell those eight children you plan on having with your future partner, which is Ryco, apparently." The head adviser laughs nervously. "It's still hard to believe you're not his ward any longer. I mean, you've always been his ward."

Ryco's shoulders tense. "Eight?" he asks, in alarm. "Why eight?"

Zepharre shakes his head, before motioning that we head out with him. "It's the luck of the Vardiya, Ryco. My parents believed in it too. I'm seven of eight. Five older brothers. Two sisters. The older one's my twin. All live in Kirja, near the sea. And I hate the sea. So I stayed here, after Guard School."

We trail out, except for Talok, preoccupied with looking out the window.

"Are you coming, King Talok?" queries EmiKal.

Talok swallows hard, folding up the crumpled letter. He says, "The Amethyst Queens are at the gate, waiting to be let in. They wish to be welcomed. I'm unsure if I'm ready to welcome them. What do they want, do you think?"

Zepharre states, "Let's hope they've come to tell us that they've taken in those of our people we sent their way."

"It *has* been long enough," EmiKal adds. "Weeks, in fact."

Looking over my shoulder, I ask, "Shall we go down?"

Skylin crowds close to me, and Arsyn close to her.

Talok sighs. "Yes, but you must promise me, Cousin, to remain quiet. Let the Sovereignty do the talking. The Amethysts hold tight to etiquette."

"Relax, Talok," I reply. "I only plan on standing at your side, quiet as can be. Unless you wouldn't mind if I stay up here and watch from the window, since I'm not part of the Sovereignty. I am very tired."

Talok thinks on it, then says, "Perhaps you *should* get some rest. But in the council room. There's a better view."

Just like that, they're gone, leaving me behind with the Darklyres.

6

Three Queens Bring Gifts

In the council room, King Aygor's youngest wards are forced into naptime. One by one, the others take to sleeping.

Arsyn and SynKievas are last to succumb to fatigue. Before they do, Arsyn rocks the littlest girl in his arms. Tears have seeped from the corners of her light-colored eyes. She breathes in fitfully, until she's fast asleep and limp in Arsyn's hold. Then her breathing steadies out. Gently, he lays her down among the others.

In quietness, I ask, "Do they miss home badly?"

"Home is where their guardian is," replies Arsyn. "It's him they miss more than anything."

SynKievas adds, through a yawn, "During the Clan Gatherings, Aygor lets them stay with Dea or himself. But, truth be told, they prefer Aygor. They have difficulty falling asleep, without him nearby."

"I get that," I reply. "Think he and the other two were able to get Ketty back?"

Arsyn shakes his head. "We've not had word that he has. And I'm too leery of sending a letter of inquiry to him. If he's in stealth, it could give his presence away."

"What about the Shield of Shylen?" I ask. "Think Zymarc's figured out that it's a fake?"

"Depends on what he intended to use it for," says Arsyn. "If he's collecting named weapons, perhaps he won't find out until enacting some sort of ritual that requires the shield."

SynKievas is about to say something more, but he glances to the wards and decides against it. "Shall we?" he asks Arsyn.

"Rest, you mean?" queries Arsyn. "Most definitely. Wake us, Ravier, when those Amethyst Queens have left, and we are allowed to forage the castle for food."

"Sure thing."

I watch the two Darklyre men lie down on opposite perimeters of the sleeping children. They then fan out their giant wings, and blanket the children with them.

Though he's motionless, Arsyn's gaze follows me as I sit at the window. Looking to the approaching stream of Sorsryns riding horses, I prop my chin on my fist. The entourage has brought many carts and carriages with them. All are plain, except for a few near the front. Now discernible are three riders on neins, leading the line; women clothed in flowing, yet fitted black-and-purple robes. Save for the cutout strips for their eyes, their skin is completely covered. Crowns of intricately woven metal rest upon their hooded heads. One is white, the second is silver, then gold for the third crown.

Startling me, Dea whispers in my ear, "Arsyn's asleep. And Skylin and I are going down for a better look . . . If you catch my drift."

I glance past Dea to Skylin, who's tucking her wings close against her body. She shyly grins at me.

Carefully, I leave my place at the window, to sneak out with the two of them. Dea closes the door and heads for the stairs. Meanwhile, Skylin grabs hold of my arm; she pulls me into the Advisers' Quarters.

She shuts the door. Quickly does she run both hands along the entire wall, which separates the quarters from the council room. She whirls around, proclaiming, "They shouldn't be able to hear us so well, now."

I stroll closer to her. "I really should rest. Or watch what's happening outside."

Skylin starts undoing the front of my coat. "But is that what you wish to do?"

Grabbing her wrists abruptly, I force her hands to the back of my neck. She obliges me, then she claws into my skin, and up to my scalp. She kisses me, and hard. I can barely take in a full breath.

I pull away, to grab Zepharre's desk chair. I collapse on its seat, overcome with fatigue. I say, "I'm too tired to keep standing."

"I don't mind," says Skylin, as she straddles my lap. She sits down, and kisses me more slowly.

My heart pounds. It's harder to breathe. I don't know what's wrong. *Is she drawing magic from me, or something?* I wonder.

Suddenly alarmed, she stops. Her posture goes rigid. She gets up to rush for the window. "I hear unrest out there."

I join her in looking through the glass windowpane.

One of the three queens stands on a castle step, conversing with Talok.

Silently, the window opens of its own accord, and we hear the dialogue.

"Sisters," says the woman crowned with white, "do as the City Architect has suggested. A third of the wares we've brought shall be taken to the lower Arkivara. Two-thirds to the castle's storerooms."

The other two queens lead their people to the designated places.

There's hardly anyone left, waiting before Talok and the Sovereignty.

The white-crowned queen questions Talok, "That is settled. Now I must know of something more important. If there were a long-lost daughter of Paragon, wayward in her ways, would you, King Talok, welcome her home?"

Cautiously, he replies, "If that daughter is not of ill intent, or a traitor, of course we'd welcome her back, Queen Kovin."

"Daughter of Paragon," Queen Kovin calls out to someone in her entourage, "you may approach."

The side door of the one adorned, black carriage opens, and out walks a woman cloaked in white and blue. Advancing to the base of the castle steps, she removes her hood, and looks up to the Sovereignty with those piercing Vaegon-eyes.

When Kent sees her, he breaks the line on the stairs, calling out,

"Mother!"

Lokasi goes to stand at the top of the stairs. "Leira, what are you doing here now, of all times? You're a little late."

"I've come home," says Leira. "Am I welcome?"

"I've already said that you are," replies Talok.

Leira removes her cloak. She lets it slip from her grasp, to fall to the ground. Though her dress is dark in color, there's no hiding the fact that Kent will have a new sibling very soon.

Lokasi takes a few hurried steps down, narrowing the distance. "You are still legally my wife, yet I've not been with you for eleven years. And you return with an unborn child? Do you ever have any thought for persons other than yourself, Leira?"

Leira's voice trembles, as she says, "I've written you many times, asking you to release me of my obligation to you. Why haven't you ever replied?"

Lokasi spouts off, "I was waiting for you to come home to Dysarda. There's now no Dysarda to go back to. I was there, three days ago. I've only just gotten back this day. The Arkivara slumbers. Too distraught is she over her city's destruction, to witness more violence. And, after this, I'll not have the strength to heal her—waken her—for you break my heart even now." Lokasi's expression is drawn taut.

"Go inside, Arkivy," Talok commands, "before you say too much and have regrets."

Leira takes a step forward. "Wait. I need you to release me, Lokasi."

Lokasi practically spits out his reply, "Vaegon marriages are for life, Leira. Only the king may break such a bond."

"I wrote to King Sosha years ago," states Leira, "asking him if he would release us of our obligation to each other. He gave his word that he would, if you were of a mind to willingly let me go. Please, Husband!" Leira begs. "Release us from each other."

"I released you in my heart, years ago. I no longer wish to call you *wife*. Nor can I stomach the thought that you are the mother of my son, and my dead daughter. You've not loved me, from the day she died."

Talok walks forward. "Kent, escort your father inside. You are to remain there in the castle, until I say otherwise. Go!" he commands.

From the halfway point, Kent storms up the remaining steps.

Lokasi takes a paper out from a hidden pocket in the folds of his robes, and forces it into Talok's grasp.

Kent grabs his father by the arm, to lead him inside.

Unfolding the paper, Talok looks it over. After some moments, he states, "This is your marriage contract, Leira. Are you certain that you wish to break it? It cannot be undone, after that. Even if you find love for each other, you cannot be partnered to Lokasi ever again."

Tears streaming down her color-drained face, Leira lowers her head. "Break it, King Talok, for it must be you to do so. You are the king."

Talok rips the document in half, from top to bottom; then again, from side to side. He stacks the four pieces together as neatly as he can.

Leira weeps. She clutches at her chest, as she sinks to the ground.

Talok makes his way down the steps to say, "The document has been quartered. You are free. Welcome home, Leira of Dysarda." He helps her to stand, then hugs her in a tight embrace. "Come inside." He motions, stepping back. "And rest a while."

After Queen Kovin bows her head to Talok, she turns to leave. She accepts Zepharre's aid in being lifted up onto her giant winged-horse.

"Another question for you, young king," says Kovin, reaching for the reins.

There's movement in the adorned, black carriage. Through the small windowpane that faces the castle, someone can be seen turning their head around for a look up at me. I register his profile, then his eyes colored like my own, which stare back. I rest my hands upon the windowsill, and lean forward, wondering who this could be.

"Make it quick," says Talok. "I don't know how long Kent can keep his father from breaking etiquette further."

Kovin asks, "Is the father of Leira's unborn child welcome here, in Paragon, as well?"

Leira clings to one of Talok's arms, waiting for his shock to wear off.

Talok at last snaps himself out of his stupor, to reply, "I give him the same response. If he is not of ill intent, nor a would-be traitor to Paragon, we shall welcome Leira's lover into our midst."

The Amethyst entourage, previously away delivering wares, now trails back.

Kovin looks to the other queens. "Sisters, we shall leave them. They are welcome here, as are the refugees—which King Talok sent to us—welcome in our home. They are well, Your Highness; many Vaegon women among them, however, wait to be with child to save their race. Have you any Vaegon men to send with us for producing draft children, as is the custom in Vaegon wartime?"

Hesitating, Talok glances about at the other Sovereignty members. He hasn't a clue of what to say.

Zepharre comes to his rescue. "That list is in one of my ledgers. Completed it yesterday, after a long talk with Grover, Eishal, and Lokasi. Allow me to go get it."

Pushing Skylin out of the open window's view, I call down, "Where is it, Zepharre?"

He scowls up at me. "Tyler Ravier, what are you doing in the Advisers' Quarters?"

"Straightening up your workspace," I reply, grinning slyly. "It's the least I could do, after some woman made a mess of it."

Zepharre's shoulders tense up. "Just grab the whole stack that's on my desk, and bring it down."

"Sure thing," I say, as papers rustle behind me.

When I turn around, I expect to see Skylin grabbing the paper stack. She's right next to me, however, trying to peer out the window for another look.

Standing beside the desk is a man, cloaked in black and blue, riffling through the stack. Waiting for me to turn around, more like. He's staring right at me.

"Tyler Ravier," he says. "I've waited a long time to meet you."

Skylin startles, and I'm quick to close the window, before she lets out a startled squeal.

He takes hold of the ledger stack. "Shall we go down? Queen Kovin is anxious to return home. The sooner, the better. Someone stole the Amethyst Bow of Three Queens, the day before we set out on the journey here. They mean to track it down. But we both know who stole it, don't we, Tyler?"

I click my tongue. "Zymarc most likely has it. Now, Sorsryn, you talk as if you know me. But are you going to give me your name?"

"Yes," he says, "And you don't even have to threaten me for it. You merely have to promise me you won't turn my name into a spell. I've no wish for that. I am ReNovak's named Onyx Prince. Prince, twice over, Lemawr."

7

Goodbyes to Our Men

At last, standing in front of me is the one we've been searching and searching for. Prince Lemawr. He's here not a moment too soon. I don't know whether to be happy, or terrified.

I wonder, *Where do I even start?*

"So," says Skylin, looking Lemawr up and down, "you're the one they've all been looking for."

"You start," says Lemawr, focused on me, "with the important and pressing bits, first. Like this." He holds up the paper stack. "This is hardly interesting, though. Not nearly as interesting as the pages you've on your person."

"That means you know about the journals?" I confirm, while following him out into the hallway.

Arsyn's there, leaning against the wall, cleaning his main blade with a small rag. I tell Skylin in div; she stops in her tracks, and frantically looks about the Advisers' Quarters for a place to hide. Arsyn glances up to watch Lemawr and me exit the room. When I close the door on my way out, and give him a small smile, his intensity shifts to perplexity. He glances at the door, unconcerned with me. For now, at any rate.

Lemawr and I trek forward. Behind us, a door opens and then closes. I briefly remember what Musgrae said about protective fathers, and make a mental note to avoid Arsyn and his daughter if at all possible for the remainder of today.

During our trek to the castle entrance, I ask, "Are you one of them?"

"A Siveyra?" he queries, giving me the papers. "Most definitely. In fact, I'm two. It's what's delayed me for so long."

"I don't mean that," I reply. "I mean, are you one like Aysivak?"

Lemawr slows his pace, seeming to ponder on something. "I tell you I'm two Siveyras, yet you're concerned over whether I'm like a Vardiya. Odd one, you are, Ravier."

"Didn't you get instructions from my dad, LanSoren, before he died?"

"Aw! That," says Lemawr. "I'm not too savvy on those details. That was for Dezarin to know. We're not yet in sync as well as we'd like to be."

Shocked, I ask, "You're Dezarin?"

"Well." Lemawr starts pulling on my arm to get us moving forward again. "Technically, it's *my* body, *my* mind. I'm merely sharing it with him. He took a mortal blow, two years ago, around the time LanSoren perished. He's been slowly dying from a rather nasty bit of Death Magic."

"Did Zymarc have something to do with it?" I ask.

"That is very likely, yes. Dezarin needed a vessel to transfer his consciousness into. When he found me, ten months ago, he was at death's door. I couldn't say no. I mean, think of what knowledge would be lost, or put on hold for ReNovamen? First, you'd have the ritual of rebirth. Then you'd have to wait for the child to grow up into adulthood. There's always a chance, too, that some knowledge would be lost forever. As it is now, we just have to wait a little longer for us to stabilize. Get used to each other, and such."

As the castle opens its doors for us, I div to Lemawr, *"Is Leira's child?"* I let the question hang out there, while briefly considering how the child's citizenship will work. *Is it Onyx, Emerald,* and *Vaegon?* I wonder, as I jog down the stairs.

I move past the King's Guard on the right, the Arkiveis on the left, then past Talok, standing near Leira at the base. Finally, I stop in front of Zepharre. "Here are the ledgers, Zepharre." I hand them over.

Lemawr stands beside me, saying in a hushed voice, "It's mine. Not his.

Not ours. Mine."

"Are you going to make a ring for it?" I ask, in sarcasm.

"A ring for an unborn child?" queries Lemawr. "That's a Geldryn thing to do."

Zepharre glances up, eyeing us curiously, before flipping through the loose ledger stack. He takes out two papers, and hands them to Queen Kovin. "Keep those. I've copies of them in the grand ledger." Glancing to Khyra, Zepharre states, "If you would, City Architect, summon Faction Five for duty, asking that they report at the gate, ready for a long journey."

Khyra takes a leaf-like paper from her pouch. She rolls it rapidly between her palms, whispering something. Snapping her fingers, a bow appears in her grasp. Paper now made into an arrow, she takes aim at the city-made-of-trees. Once released, the arrow bursts into dozens of sparking streams headed for the tree canopies. Putting the bow away, she looks at Zepharre.

He puffs out a breath, before turning back to me. "Right! Now that we're done with that, tell me, Tyler, whom might this be?"

Lemawr extends his hand, in greeting. "Prince Lemawr, at your service. Or, at least, the Paragonian Sovereignty's service."

Zepharre shakes hands with him, his face clouded in confusion.

I lean forward, to whisper, "He's Gyron's nephew. Named Onyx Prince."

"Ah, yes!" Zepharre smiles curtly. "How do your loyalties work, exactly?"

"A good question," says Queen Kovin. "I shall leave you, Onyx Prince, to get acquainted to your new cohorts. But, first, this list has a Kent of Dysarda on it. Is he not one of the king's men?"

"King's Guard," Kent corrects her, from his current position at the top of the stairs. "My father and I have discussed it, just now. He'll be taking my place, in traveling to the Zotek with you. He has some tasks to do, before departing. Once they are complete, he'll take a dragon's flight to catch up with you. Shall you be taking the main path to the Zotek?"

Queen Kovin bows her head in reply, then she says, "May the light of Vardiyas be with you all." She tugs on the reins of her horse, and it turns to trot away, leading the entourage out of the city. The lot of them are as a massive wave of white, black, and violet, with splashes of silver reflecting off their weapons, buckles, and such.

Talok strides over to Awngeleik, who's happily munching on a patch of long grass. Unclipping her lead rope from the stake in the ground, he leads her over. "Get on, Cousin. We shall say goodbye to our men, at the gate." Glancing to Lemawr, Talok adds, "After that, there's a bit of business we are to discuss with Prince Lemawr."

"Yes, much business," says Lemawr, holding his head high in pride.

I climb on to Awngeleik's back, and Talok mounts behind me. My pat on her shoulder gets her moving. Pacing forward, she snorts a few times at the horses in the entourage, who are beginning a gallop. Tucking her wings against her body, which then partially shield Talok and me, she bolts. After speeding past the entourage, she slows her pace for the three queens. They take a long look at her, their gazes joyful at seeing her. Queen Kovin acknowledges Awngeleik with a single nod.

Galloping faster, Awngeleik screeches and then lets out a guttural sound. It's not quite a growl, but neither is it a roar. It's unique to her—the Equidyn's voice.

Dragons, gathered on the city's walls, launch into the air, roaring. They fly over the entourage, then circle back to the end of the group. Their shadows crisscross on the ground, appearing as many little rivers of flowing water.

Dozens of Vaegon men wait at the gate, all mounted on horses.

Awngeleik halts all on her own, to stand tall.

The dragons take to the walls again.

The Amethyst entourage slows to a stop, and waits for us.

"This day," Talok calls out to the forlorn young men, "I and your Sovereignty ask a great deal of you. To travel to the Zotek, and secure a future generation of Vaegons. I do not know when you shall return, if ever you do return. Do you accept this key task? A task which ensures the survival of a portion of our people."

The men bow their heads, but one at the front says for them all, "We accept this, King Talok. If we should ne'er be able to return, however, what will become of the Arkivaras?"

Talok replies, "The Arkiveis shall put them to sleep, and they will slumber until it is safe for them to awaken. As you all know, slumbering Arkivaras cannot be destroyed. The land itself protects them, massacring all who would do them harm. If they must sleep, it could very well be you and your children who wake them. And that would be the greatest honor and testament of you—that Vaegons shall always prevail. Keepers of Memories. Tamers of Dragons. That is who you are. Never forget your roots, even as you start anew elsewhere."

This puts hope in the young men.

"Then we are ready, Highness," says a different male Vaegon.

The King's Guard, Khyra, Zepharre, and a few others trail onto the scene in time to wave farewell—Lokasi and Nyrim are among them.

I add, "Arkivy Lokasi will soon go to the Zotek as well, to be with you. Have a safe journey."

"You as well, Son of LanSoren," replies the oldest among them.

"Guard yourself," says another.

The front Vaegon states, "We can never thank you enough, Ravier. Look after our people, with that cousin of yours."

Talok lifts his hand high, in goodbye to them. I have not the heart to wave goodbye, though. I simply bow my head and pray that the spirits keep them safe. That Sivondel is not fed by their souls anytime soon. *"Not yet,"* I div to him, if, indeed, Death might be listening. *"Please, not yet."*

8

A Conscience from Afar

The three queens are about to start forward, when Jasper comes out from a grove of nearby trees, tiredly walking toward them in two-legged form. Also in human form, Mekka and Rorka aren't far behind him, appearing just as defeated.

Kovin, noticing the alpha, gets down from her horse. She gracefully strides the rest of the way to him. "You have aged, Alpha Jasper. It is true, then," she queries, cupping his face, "that you gave life's vitality to LanSoren, trying to save him?"

"It is true, Queens Kovin, Arkawna, and KaaVus," he replies.

Kovin reaches up to lift her white crown off her hooded head. She benevolently offers it to Jasper, saying, "It is such a small gift of thanks, in comparison to what you have sacrificed. Yet it is all I have with me of any great value. Please accept it."

Though Jasper kindly takes it from her grasp, he does not place it upon his own head.

Mekka and Rorka have come nearer. They are reverent in their stance, patiently standing beside their old, worn-out alpha.

Queens Arkawna and KaaVus dismount their horse companions and approach the candidates.

Kovin instructs her sisters, "KaaVus, you shall bestow your gold to the Matriarch Candidate. And, Arkawna, your silver to the mighty Von. It was fashioned by a Silverian, an era ago. Though he tried to make it smaller, it never properly fit any Queen of the Amethysts. It shall fit you perfectly. Are you the last standing candidate? The Alpha Candidate?"

Mekka gives his reply of, "Droediin and I were the last two. My rival has fallen to Vitiosus. He is now Zymarc's. I am the last, and the burden is heavy."

Arkawna, tallest of the sisters, places the silver crown atop Mekka's head of messy, dark hair. "May this then lighten your burden." Her voice is strong, yet carries gentleness. It's the sort of sound one could listen to endlessly. Arkawna continues, saying, "The White Crown symbolizes balance, impartiality. In essence, it stands for justice. The Golden Diadem represents goodwill, prosperity, and resilience in times of famine. It is courage amidst adversity. At its core, it is perseverance. But the Silver Circlet signifies something more personal. It is as a mirror for self-reflection. It reveals you as you truly are. The truth of your nature. Things hidden so deep within, you're not even aware of them. Yet, they drive all actions you take. Its heart tells the truth."

Queen KaaVus asks, "With it upon your head, mighty Von, what do you feel?"

"Fear," replies Mekka quietly.

"But you are Mekka of the Vons," says Arkawna, "the last Alpha Candidate. What have you to fear?"

"The title. My future position. I'm a target, and a big one, because of what I am."

Arkawna places her hands over Mekka's clasped ones. "Now that you know fear drives you, what will you do?"

"I shall strike it dead," replies Mekka, with more confidence. He gestures to Rorka. "And if that doesn't work, I shall have the Matriarch Candidate beat it out of me. It's better than being confined to a bed. Or trapped in a small room, with only one way out."

Arkawna draws her hands back, as she tilts her head to one side in thought.

Leaning closer to Arkawna, Rorka says, "It's a long story."

"It's *not* a long story," states Mekka. "It's a humiliating one. We shan't talk of it. Can we agree?"

Enthusiastically, Rorka nods. "Agreed. We shan't speak of it. Certainly not in front of foreigners."

Kovin focuses on Jasper. "Won't you put my crown on, Greyvon?"

Ignoring her, Jasper strides for Talok and me, who are still atop Awngeleik's back. Crown in one hand, Jasper offers his other to help Talok down.

As soon as Talok has faced Jasper, the White Crown is placed upon my cousin's head by the alpha. "This is for you. Not for me," says Jasper. "Today, you are not a young king. Simply, a good king. Take flight to The Sodon. Get what you need. Save your own life. Defeat a wretched soul. Come home. That is all."

Talok says, "I will."

I correct him, stating, "*We* will."

Jasper looks off to the distance. "Arkivy Eishal, if you would tell me where my friend has been buried, I shall go rest there with him for a while. For, on this day, I am a tired, old dog."

Eishal and Grover have gathered with the other five Arkiveis and Prince Lemawr.

Trauvo's Arkivy hesitates to answer.

Jasper says, "Please do not make me beg."

Eishal toys with his staff, finally admitting, "I cannot tell you, Jasper, due to my lack of remembering what I did. LanSoren gave me implicit instructions on what to do, if he should perish, which I must've carried out. From the time I whisked his body away from Eyo'el, to the point at which I returned to my home in Trauvo, I recall none of what I did. I am sorry. I do not know where he is."

"I see," says Jasper, staring at the ground.

Lemawr approaches him. "Is it that you wish for the company of a friend who understands you?"

Jasper turns to study the Onyx Prince. "Lemawr," he says half-heartedly, "what do you want?"

"To comfort a friend, deep in grief."

"We were hardly ever friends, Onyx Prince."

"Perhaps not," replies Lemawr. "But you were close with Dezarin, were you not?"

Jasper's expression is unreadable. "Dezarin is gone," he says. "I felt his essence fade, before I went into hibernation. He is dead. I am near sure of it."

"I am not dead," says Lemawr, in a different voice. As he takes more steps forward, he ages. His face becomes rugged; his eyes less amused; his hair flecked with many grays. Dezarin motions to the form he's trapped in. "I am a son of a Sorshrynak, no more. But this Lemawr is quite strong, and rather gifted. His form is pleasing to look at as well. He will serve my purposes quite efficiently. If only he'd stop being selfish, and let me talk more. I'm aware of all he says. But his punishment shall be that he won't know a single word I say."

The news that Lemawr and Dezarin share the same form ripples varied reactions from those around—mixes of surprise, curiosity, and hope.

Dezarin turns his attention elsewhere, saying, "Now, Ryco, where is Rozeth?" Dezarin strides toward him. "I told you *and her* that during times of war—where either one is involved—you were never to be apart, for you are dual apprentices. And what's a dual apprentice without the other half?"

"She went to look for you," replies Ryco, unfazed.

Dezarin interrogates him further. "Why did you not go with her?"

Ryco motions around. "I had other matters to take care of. As you can see."

"Yes, I see," says Dezarin, "as I see much in you. Why do you wear sadness, as if your mother perished only yesterday? Does time not help to mend all wounds?"

Ryco remains silent.

"Will you not answer me?" queries Dezarin.

"It is not for you to know what worries me," Ryco replies. "It does relate to the reason Rozeth went to find you, however. Seeing you as you are now, it wouldn't have mattered if she *had* found you in time. You could not honor her request, even if you wished to."

Dezarin seems to understand something unspoken. Then he startles, saying, "Lemawr presses to have the stage back." Turning to Jasper, Dezarin adds, "Allow me to do something for you, Jasper, before I go. For who doth know when Lemawr will let me talk again."

Standing in front of the Greyvon Alpha, Dezarin runs his right hand over Jasper's face, utterly confusing the Greyvon. Dezarin's intentions are unclear, until he spreads two fingers of his other hand far apart, and claws form, which he then pricks his own neck with, readying it for Jasper's bite.

Jasper recoils in panic. "I cannot. I won't be able to stop myself."

Dezarin replies, "I can make you stop, Jasper. If not me, then your candidates."

Jasper's chest heaves. He eyes Dezarin's neck hungrily. He lunges. Latching on, he drinks the Siveyra's blood. Slowly, Dezarin's appearance is replaced by Lemawr's.

Mekka starts pulling at Jasper. "You must stop, Alpha. The Vonsai outside the gate can hear you. Soon, they'll smell blood."

Rorka shouts, "They haven't been fed a full meal in days! They will tear our allies apart."

Yapping and growling sound outside the new gate of Eyo'el. Then the banging starts.

Screeching impatiently, Awngeleik paws at the ground, but she lets Talok return to her back.

"Make her advance," Talok commands, and I obey.

Khyra shouts above the noise, "Ryco, you have to open the gate! They're going to destroy it, otherwise. I haven't finished fortifying it. Took me a week to get it to its current strength. We cannot let it be broken."

Desperate, Mekka yells, "I cannot stop them all!"

The Amethyst Queens mount up, to lead their entourage into forming a barrier of riders on horses.

"They're not attempting to get in," states Queen KaaVus. "The Vonsai are trying to stop a Siveyra from entering."

Glancing over my shoulder, I ask Talok, "Whom do you think it is?"

"Let's hope it's RayVora, Paydinn, or one of the brothers."

All take positions of defense.

When Queen Kovin says, "We are ready," Ryco opens the gate with green sparks shot from his hand.

No sooner has the gate opened to shoulder width, than a horde of angry Vonsai storm in, some on two legs like werewolves; others gallop in, unsure of whether they should run like a wolf or cat or ape. However awkward they appear, their sound is deafening. The closer they get, the more frightening they become.

Talok calls from behind me, "Awngeleik, you have my full permission to use whatever means necessary to settle the Vonsai. Calm them, even if it means harming them a little."

Awngeleik remains still, as chaos surrounds us.

"Those are King's Orders, Awngeleik," I state. "What are you waiting for?"

Talok laughs. "She waits for you, Cousin, to tell her what to do. She's yours, after all."

I command, "Do as he says. Stop the Vonsai."

Awngeleik pins her ears back and hisses like a reptile. When a werewolf Von bumps her, she lunges for his neck. She flaps her wings and takes off running, dragging the squealing victim along. She hits many others with her wings, and shocks them some. There's lots of yelping and growling and barking. When she's almost airborne, she tosses the Von to the ground, then proceeds to stomp at him. Her would-be victim scrambles away, tail tucked between his legs.

All Vonsai give her a wide berth. Regardless, she charges them, and roars with that Equidyn voice. The dragons decide to help. As soon as they've landed, Awngeleik begins a gusting wind by flapping her wings. That wind pushes against the Vonsai, who attempt to go forward.

With the presence of dragons, they quiet down and then withdraw. Left behind is a curled-up figure, cloaked in black, lying on the ground.

His hands shield his head. Slowly, he unfurls.

I jump down in alarm. This is not Paydinn or one of his brothers. This is an Onyx. *Why aren't the dragons upset?* I wonder.

Everyone around is ready to attack the intruder. Yet I'm the first one to say anything, asking, "Why are you here, Onyx?" Unsheathing NeiSator, I ready myself for anything.

"It's my week off," says the figure, as he cautiously stands up. "Got Zymarc to overrule ReNovak, and give it to me." When Gyron removes his hood, he exclaims, "Vards, Ravier! Look at the shadow of stubble on that face. You're looking older by the week. I can't tell you how worried I've been for all of you. And, yet, you're here. Alive. It is of the Vardiyas' making."

I resist the urge to feel my face, feel the stubble Gyron claims I have. I clip NeiSator to my belt, instead.

Zepharre asks, "You've not come to deliver a message, nor start a battle?"

"No," replies Gyron, striding toward the three queens. "I've come to return something, and I'm glad I made it here in time." He takes off his cloak, before he removes a wrapped item that's strapped to his back. After the leather cording is untied, the cloth wrap unfolds and reveals a black-and-silver bow of intricate design in Gyron's grasp.

The queens leap down excitedly, to rush toward him.

"The Bow of Three Queens!" Kovin shouts for joy. "I didn't think I'd ever see it again."

"I knew that we would," says Arkawna smoothly.

KaaVus states, "But not so soon as this, Sister."

"I *was* instructed to steal it," Gyron confesses. "I gave it to Zymarc, three nights ago, to prove I had done the deed. I didn't have to wait long for him to use it, and to make his intentions clear. He killed a dragon with one shot to its head."

KaaVus gasps in horror. "It should not be as powerful as that."

"I know," Gyron agrees. "Yet, in his hands, it is."

Arkawna asks, "He's killing his own dyns, now?"

"It was a BlacKaidyn. It had caught word of something, and refused to let Zymarc turn him by way of Vitiosus. Said that Zymarc is no longer worthy to rule dragons, and that he intended to return home to Paragon. Zymarc shot him on the spot."

Talok's face clouds over in anger. "We will make him regret that course of action. I assure you."

"Good." Gyron grins. "Give it back to him, in style of two-fold punishment. He deserves no less."

Queen Kovin takes the bow in her quivering hands. "We shall see that it is properly purified, before used again. How can we ever thank you, Master Gyronawv?"

Gyron frowns. "Though I don't deserve thanks, I would wish to see your faces, and count it as the best gift I've been given. For last I saw your faces, you were three little princesses. Barely young women. And you've come far from that time."

The queens remove the cloth hiding their faces. All three smile brightly at Gyron. He opens his arms, and they rush to the Siveyra. Embracing them, he says, "You've all grown into three fearsome, beautiful queens."

The Amethyst entourage follows their queens' lead, revealing their own features.

Kovin cranes her neck to look up at Gyron. "You'll always be our favorite Siveyra and mentor, Master Gyronawv."

"When we see you on that fated battlefield, days from now," adds KaaVus, "we shall restrain you, protecting you then from harm."

Arkawna adds, "Waiting for the moment of when Onyx Neutrality is restored. We have brought the Onyx Prince. He shall see it done."

Gyron steps away from the three, and repositions their hoods to shield their features once more. "You must hurry away from here. Zymarc will soon discover that the bow's missing, if he hasn't already. Do not go by the normal way. He knows it well. Pass south to Kirja, then take to the Sea of Gradoelin."

Queen Kovin and her sisters flee to their mounts.

"May the cunning of Vons be with you," says KaaVus.

Faction Five takes to riding amongst the entourage. They are gone.

All the Vonsai, now visible, pant in contentment or groom themselves. Quite proud they are of their work in stopping Siveyra Gyron.

Jasper—at least, the one I think is Jasper—wipes blood from his face. His hair is no longer peppered with gray, but is a dark-brown instead. Those eyes, however, are unmistakably his. Wise beyond words, and fierce. The fire's back in them, like green embers about to ignite.

Lemawr stands up in shock, feeling his own neck. "Would I be wrong, in guessing that you've just met Dezarin?" he asks Jasper.

Gyron whirls around. He stares at Lemawr, dumbfounded. "You look familiar, Sorsryn."

Lemawr replies, "Nice to see you, Uncle. It's been a while."

"Lemawr!" Gyron exclaims, laughing. "You're alive. Many of us weren't sure, in the Nyxane."

Going over to pat his uncle's chest, Lemawr poses the question, "Tell me, Uncle Gyron. Am I still the named Onyx Prince? We've not heard otherwise, while in the Zotek."

"That's where you've been?" Gyron asks. "The Zotek? Couldn't you at least have written to ReNovak, telling him you still live?"

"There was no need," states Lemawr, "while the clan was neutral. Then, when it wasn't, I was in no position to travel. This journey's been hard enough as it is."

Gyron says in angst, "I wish you had. You *are* still the Onyx Prince. Though not for long. ReNovak has suspected you to be dead, for a while now. You've not responded to any of his letters, nor his summons. At the very start of The Sodon, he means to make his special request of the former Onyx Queen."

"Ayna?" Lemawr queries.

Gyron nods. "She is of near equal rank to him. Therefore, she's able to grant him his request, if she so chooses. He desires to name a new prince. Since he hasn't procured proof of your death, he was unable to legally do so, before this year. Will you go to The Sodon, Lemawr? Will you once more ask to be the Onyx Prince?"

"I cannot," replies Lemawr. "Uncle Gyron, I was made Onyx Prince during a time of neutrality. Asking it now means to risk pledging myself to Zymarc."

Gyron hangs his head in defeat. "I hadn't thought of that."

I ask, "Is there an instance of when an Onyx Prince was named, during the time there was also a victor?"

Lemawr points at me. "A good question. I don't recall any such instance, and the other Siveyra isn't talking. Do you recall any, Uncle?"

He replies, "Blood heirs have been born, during times of Onyx Victors being named. But I'm unaware of any named Onyx Prince gaining the title, after an Onyx Victor was named. I shall head for home, to search in Oniva's libraries. Send someone from here to The Sodon. I will let them know of my findings, and if it is safe for you to make your request of ReNovak."

"And Lemawr will stay here," I add, "to have a look at the dragon-wolf journal."

Gyron stops his forward progression to look at me. "Have you learned how, yet?"

"Not yet. But I will do what I can," I reply. Then, in div, I add, *I will find a way to free you, Gyron. I hate seeing you as a pawn.*

Aloud, Gyron replies, "As do all Onyx, Ravier. It is what it is. I accepted it, long ago." He starts to amble his way for the city exit, when apprehension overcomes him.

An odd buzzing sounds out from him. He grabs at a small piece hanging from his neck.

"Gyronawv," a metallic voice echoes out.

Gyron states, "It's ReNovak, trying to make contact. He shouldn't be able to, when I've been given personal time. I must be away from this place. He cannot know where I am. That I've come here."

Lemawr holds out his hand. "If *I* make the connection, will he see my surroundings?"

"I don't believe so," replies Gyron, taking the chain with the pendant off his neck.

Lemawr takes hold of the pendant. Blue light glows from within his grasp. When he releases his hold, the pendant stays suspended in the air. More light flares from it. It whirs, and the ground rumbles. The dragons grow uneasy. Many of us look to the sky. Nothing's amiss, there.

When blue light bursts out, it forms into a figure. ReNovak's figure. His back to Lemawr, he strides forward. "Gyron, don't you *ever* again delay a summon." He whirls around. Upon spotting Lemawr, shock fills his eyes, and his voice cracks when saying his prince's name. "Lemawr? Where have you been? I've sent out armies, looking for you. Has Gyron known where you were, this entire time?"

"He did not," replies Lemawr. "We sort of stumbled upon each other. He tells me you mean to name another prince. Is that still the case, knowing I've not died?"

"Are you coming home to Oniva?" queries ReNovak, his shocked sorrow ceasing.

"Oniva is not my home," states Lemawr. "Not while Vitiosyns are allies of the Onyx. Setharyn would've felt the same as I do."

ReNovak gets in Lemawr's face. "Don't you mention my dead son, as if you knew him. You didn't know him. He's not here."

"If he were," Lemawr shouts, "he would be ashamed of you letting the Onyx fall into Vitiosyn control!"

ReNovak turns on his heel, to stride around impatiently. "I'm not the one who let his guard down. I tried to do everything I legally could, to raise suspicion that Zymarc was close in winning the title. The Onyx were a part of the Withrasyn-Vaegon Festival. They hadn't been, for near one thousand years. Didn't anyone think it odd? I asked the Matriarch Candidate to sit on a throne, in place of Jasper. Etiquette states that is blasphemy. King Talok rules Paragon. Not me. He should've been the one to ask her, or give permission. I gave the Warrior of the Nyxane the night off, as well, to bed that very Greyvon. Was that not also unusual?"

"I didn't know that these things transpired," states Lemawr.

"Because you weren't there," ReNovak rages on. "You could've stopped all this, Lemawr, before it even started."

"How do you figure that?" queries Lemawr.

"You know all the Onyx scripts, better than any still living," replies ReNovak. "Better than me, more than Gyron was ever allowed, and more than Ayna ever cared to know. You know the stories of how past Onyx Kings have hinted a victor is close to being named. Only Dezarin knew the tales better, because he lived through them. But he is dead. Onyx Warriors found his body days ago. We shall have his funeral, in the last hour of The Sodon."

"I've known his fate, for a while," states Lemawr, calmly pacing about. ReNovak scoffs.

Lemawr stops abruptly. "Even if I had been there, and recognized the signs, then alerting the Paragonians of it, would they have stood a chance in challenging for the title?"

"Possibly not," replies ReNovak. "You would have, however. You could've done a Prince's Gamble, calling out a victor potential, by name, to fight you to the death. You could have killed Zymarc, when he was somewhat weaker. Again, you could've challenged his status, right in Paragon, as Gyron was announcing him and his people as victor."

Lemawr's now an arm's distance from ReNovak. "Gyron gave the verdict? That's your place to do so. It's the law. Where were you?"

ReNovak's mouth twitches. "I had a pressing errand to run."

Lemawr gives a half-grin. "You *are* telling the truth. I know it on your face." He folds his arms across his chest, before asking, "What errand was it?"

ReNovak circles around Lemawr. "That is my business. What was I supposed to do? It was my last chance to enact a fail-safe. Do not pry into the matter, Lemawr. I'm warning you. What I've set in motion is hidden from Zymarc. Don't undo the hard work I saw to, in order to protect my conscience."

"Your conscience!" Lemawr shouts. "What good is a conscience, when you are at the absolute command of a wretched soul? You are slaves to Vitiosyns."

ReNovak cries out in anger, "You left me!"

"I had no choice," Lemawr states.

ReNovak calms a bit, to say, "Then I have no choice but to remove you of your title, Onyx Prince. Ayna will grant my request, for she will not be hearing that you live. Not until it's too late. Send all the letters you wish. Take whatever dragon you think is fast enough. Neither will stop this from happening. I shall name another prince, at the end of The Sodon. Once I've announced that the title is open, requests will come pouring in. Unless you get all citizens of Oniva to chant your name, Lemawr, it is not a title you'll ever hold again."

"Seeing what you have become, Brother," Lemawr says, "it is not a title I wish to have. You've cast your lot with Deathasyns."

"They're not as bad as you think," says ReNovak. "See for yourself." He spreads his arms out gracefully.

What surrounds ReNovak, wherever he is, slowly fades into focus.

He continues, saying, "Under Zymarc's rule, they've come a long way from being the land's nomads, moving their temporary homes at a moment's notice of an oncoming Geldryn attack."

ReNovak stands on a hilltop. In the distance behind him, countless buildings of dark metal and mirrors reach up past the clouds. Lightning crackles down on them, illuminating the city. The sounds fade up to ReNovak. The sounds of the forge—metal being struck; fire being stoked; steam hissing off a water's surface.

Someone approaches ReNovak, unaware that we and Lemawr watch.

ReNovak briefly presses a finger to his lips, a signal for Lemawr to be quiet. "Say anything, and she'll hear you."

It's Caleiso, climbing the last few steps to the hilltop. A letter is in her grasp. "Your orders, ReNovak, from King Zymarc." Handing it to him, she starts to leave.

Lemawr whispers, "Brother, who is that girl?"

ReNovak eyes the letter, then turns to call out, "Caleiso, I thought you were a Prime-Warrior. Why are you acting as some messenger girl?"

She pivots on her heel to stride back and snatch the letter out of ReNovak's grasp. "You're right," she says. "A Prime-Warrior is entitled to know what orders are being given." She opens the envelope. "Shall I read it for you?"

"By all means," states ReNovak.

She starts reading. "King ReNovak: You are to report to the Prisons of Pilark, here in Vosh-Perida. You shall help me decide the fates of an important few. RayVora, three of her sons, and that detestable Greyvon half-breed, Nebukahn. Afterward, we shall enter into a game. One I very much want to win."

Caleiso pauses, swallowing hard.

ReNovak asks, "Why'd you stop, girl? Keep going."

She continues, "As I have lost a dear possession of late, and was blind, believing another was authentic, we shall instead make a game of running one hundred arrows into a set of dyns. I don't mean to kill them. Merely, to test our abilities in piercing them just right that they can hold precisely one hundred arrows, without dying. The dragon who dies, loses, along with its owner. I've been practicing for two days now, and I've got it down quite well. Tested my techniques on the traitor dyns. They are dead. But not before I got a hundred arrows in. We need to toughen up the young ones. And you shall assist me."

ReNovak's eyes turn wild. He starts sweating.

Caleiso reads on, "Also, bring that Darklyrian girl with you. Keturah. I've decided what to do with her. It seems, I have been fooled. I have been a fool. Even recently getting myself buried—" She stops short, looking up at ReNovak.

"Go on," he says, in amused anger.

She starts again, sounding irritated. "Getting myself buried under the snows of Vondurheil, by children and a red-haired dog." She skims the letter, then folds it up, and abruptly hands it to ReNovak. "He rants on about that, for several lines. See for yourself."

She quickly hurries down the hillside, disappearing from our view.

Smiling, ReNovak unfolds the letter. He reads the rest of it silently. Then he laughs. "It's that Ravier. It couldn't be anyone else." ReNovak walks about, in happiness. "He hates him, and he loves him. This letter reveals it to be true." Quieting down, ReNovak looks to Lemawr, while tucking the letter away in his coat's inner pocket. "You shall bring him to me, during The Sodon. I do not care if it's the first part. Or the second, which is the day after. I wish to speak with him, alone. Do that for me, Lemawr, and I may grant you the title again."

Uneasiness rises up inside. *What could he possibly want?* I wonder.

The other Paragonians seem alarmed as well. Even the Greyvons.

Lemawr glances at me. He tries not to be obvious about it, but ReNovak sees the brief desperation, and pries, "He's there with you, isn't he?"

I query, "Can he hear me?"

Lemawr rubs at his neck, then sweeps two fingers along his cheek, before lowering his hands to rest at his sides.

Gyron says, "That means no. Tell him what you need to, Tyler."

"We're going to The Sodon, regardless of what he wants," I state. "Why not use it to our advantage?"

Talok adds, "Have ReNovak leave Keturah where she is safe."

"With the former queen, Ayna," says Gyron. "The girl won't be harmed while in her company."

"If he does that," I state, "tell him I'll meet with him in Oniva, during The Sodon."

Lemawr relays our instructions.

ReNovak asks, "Lemawr, do you give me your word that he'll be there?"

"Absolutely. Even if I have to drag him there, to uphold his end of the bargain. Consider it my last act of duty, as the Onyx Prince."

ReNovak grins. "Then I accept his terms. I shall have to make a good excuse, for *forgetting* the girl in Oniva. It shouldn't be too terribly difficult. I bid you farewell, until The Sodon."

In an instant, everything of ReNovak's surroundings fades. His form turns back into blue light. Then the pendant draws the light back in. Gyron takes it from its suspension, slipping its chain round his neck again.

Gyron grips Lemawr by the shoulder. "Go on the old Onyx Warrior paths. They're hardly used anymore. But be careful. Especially you, King

Talok, and your Ravier. I must go quickly."

After a brief but longing glance at Rorka, Gyron jogs out of the city, then he bursts into a full sprint.

Lemawr puffs out a breath. "I think it's high time I had a look at that journal, Ravier."

I dig around in my pouch for it. The dragon-wolf journal grows to full size in my hands. I sweep my fingers across its cover, anticipating what Lemawr will reveal of its pages.

Will I see him again? I wonder. *My father. Or will it merely be more words on paper?*

9

Quill Strokes Spoken

At the council room table, Lemawr sits, carefully turning each page of the dragon-wolf journal. All who will fit in the room, have gathered round to stare at either him or the journal—Talok and his King's Guard, many advisers, a few Arkiveis, and some Darklyres.

Leira sits near him. Breaking the silence, she says, "Lemawr, darling, your audience is hungry for you to say something. What is it that LanSoren has written in ancient Sorsrynian?"

Lemawr straightens in his seat. Closing his eyes, he rubs them. "Something very complicated. It's going to take me a while to understand what he means." He looks at the lot of us, then lets his hands drop lazily to the table. They thud against the surface. "Come back in a bit. I should have something, then."

I glance at Ryco and Talok, who are sitting to the left of me. "You go. I'll stay."

Gemma and Khyra enter the symposium room. Gemma has on a simple set of clean clothes. But the City Architect has donned a delicate dress made of black fabric, with a blue pattern accentuated by thin piping of white satin along the contours.

Khyra nervously smooths out the front of her dress. "Were we going to sign that contract soon, Ryco? I assume, immediately after Lemawr has made the translation, most of you will be off to The Sodon."

Taking a deep breath, Ryco stands up. "Your assumption is correct."

Adviser EmiKal rises from his spot at the council table, and takes a letter out of his satchel. "I've already drawn it up. Did so, while the lot of you were at the gate. It merely needs the signatures." Setting the letter on the table, he slides it over to Talok.

My cousin opens it, musing aloud, "This will be the first unity contract I've signed, giving my approval. I'm glad it's for you, Khyra, and Ryco too." He looks at them. "Once it's signed in all the right places, I say we have a great big meal served here in the council room. Also, Gemma Galloway shall teach me—a hopeless soul—how to cook."

The room fills with sounds of pleasantry. Many agree. But Deamond states, "While you're at it, Gem, instruct Sonya in the way of recipes. I caught word of what her Soup of Ashes consists of, and, well, her formula needs vast reworking."

Sonya defends, "It's my survival soup, Dea. It helped the King of Paragon, didn't it?"

Talok tries not to cringe. "It did, indeed. It exceeded the creativity of even *my* oddest of concoctions."

Suddenly hobbling into the room, Grover queries, "Odd concoctions? Have you been practicing your cooking while away, King Talok? I'm ever so proud. Nyrim and Kent have given a full report. And what a report it was!" he exclaims, tossing up his hands happily. "So many things you have accomplished, and near escaped. My favorite part, though, was Tyler's work in fooling that Scepter. Ghastly dragon, he has become."

After adding his signature to the contract, and passing it to Zepharre and EmiKal, Talok says, "It was one of my cousin's finer moments. We'll not soon be forgetting it."

Grover's shoulders lift, as he takes in a quick breath. "Yes, yes! I wish I had been there to see it. Which got me thinking . . . you could donate that memory to the Arkivara. She'd like to have that memory. Most definitely, she would."

Talok frowns. "You can't have my memories to give to Eyo'el, Grover. Not today."

Indignant, Grover huffs. "Well, I've lost quite a few lovely memories. She won't let me know which ones they were. Fair's fair, King Talok. You've not given a donation for a while."

Easing up, Talok frowns at Grover. "I just got home. There's also a good deal I can't risk forgetting. Do you not even care that this device is changing me?"

"Certainly!" Grover exclaims, sounding irked. "I'm merely thinking of Eyo'el and her people. They would not wish to forget their King Talok. The last memories you gave her were of LanSoren's funeral. She grieves for you, Talok. She thinks you are still broken. Please let me cheer her with some hopeful moments of yours."

Talok shakes his head. "I can't risk too much being taken, Grover. You will *not* ask me again."

I slide my chair back. "I'll go. She's not had any of my memories. Do I have your permission, Cousin?"

Gemma sends me a look, divving, *"You actually asked him for once."*

"You may," says Talok, retaking his seat. He sends me that smile as if we're the only ones in the room. Briefly, the same look is in his eyes that he had when Gemma and I were brought into this very room for the first time. Then the shadow clouds over his face.

"Death and goodbyes," he divs to me, yet glances to Ryco. *"Are they always this unfair?"*

I div back, *"Yes, Cousin Talok. But we shall see him again. All that the Arkivaras have to show us of Ryco'Eldeis, she shall show us."*

Talok swallows hard.

I stand up from my seat, and flick my cousin on the arm. "Thanks, Cuz!" I grin. I start the stride out of the room, but stop before passing Khyra. "Don't have too much fun after dinner, City Architect."

Her nervousness falls away. "We shall have a party, while you are gone. Might even get Zepharre to dabble in alchemy, multiplying our supply of Farivoo."

"Ack!" Zepharre groans, right as he's about to sign the contract. He looks to Khyra, and wrinkles his nose at her. "Farivoo! Must it be Farivoo?

Never did like it. Ryco, quick, think of a different wedding gift the Alchemist can give you. *Anything* else for me to multiply. Please."

Gemma says, "I don't think Tyler much likes Farivoo anymore, either. Do you, Ty?"

I just wink at Gemma. "Back in a bit," I say, before I follow Grover out.

* * *

We're almost there, when I ask Grover, "What will it be like? My memories being taken?"

Hobbling beside me with use of his staff, Grover replies, "Hurts a tad bit. Generally hinges on how valuable the memories are to you. If something taken will alter you too much, she won't accept the memory. Therefore, you needn't worry over being different afterward."

The path Grover takes us on leads to the base of the Arkivara. Her rattling rhythm of leaves has ceased. She is silent. Her Arkivy knocks thrice. The main trunk shifts to form stairs leading up to an entrance. Glancing to different sections of the main trunk, I realize that there are several doors.

I ask, "Has she always had this many entries, Grover, and I just didn't notice before?"

Grover goes up the steps one at a time, hardly making a sound, except for his chatty reply of, "It's something new Khyra did to assist me in keeping my rooms organized. At least, that is what I told her all her efforts would be purposed for. In reality, I wanted my things protected from all prying eyes. There is merely *one* room for citizens to visit whenever they wish. It's a new room, empty. No bookshelves, no chairs, and *no* counter for all to unload their things upon. Also, it is disconnected from the rest of the Arkivara. And that is key in containing the mess."

"How will they let you know they've come to visit?"

"A silver bell." Grover's wobbling footsteps quicken. "It has been fastened to the wall. And if anyone should try to thieve it, it'll set their hands on fire. A Jokryn cast that enchantment for me, before they went on their long hunt to resupply the city wares. I'm quite grateful for it. Not the wares part, but the hands-on-fire part."

Grover takes the last step. The door creaks open of its own accord.

We enter the room, which is softly illuminated by blue-fire. The door closes. Grover leads us farther in. Passing under a white, wooden archway, we're now in a circular room fashioned of Blackwood. At its center is an elliptical shape of what appears to be water. It swirls with the colors of Vaegon-eyes: blue, black, and white. It's as streams of paint swirling with each other, but never quite mixing fully.

Grover takes off his spectacles. He tucks them in a hidden pocket of his Arkiveis robes. "When you are ready to meet Eyo'el, step into her heart, Tyler. If she doesn't greet you, then you're not Vaegon enough, and we'll have to go to a different room for memory extraction."

I blurt out, "That sounds painful."

"I wouldn't know, personally," replies Grover, tearing his gaze off his staff to look at me. "LanSoren has given memories both ways. He said the extraction was far worse."

I hold up my hand. "Maybe you shouldn't tell me more. Or I might not go through with this."

Silencing himself with fingers pressed to his lips, Grover goes to stand near the archway. He bows his head, then folds his hands. His stature exudes reverence for his Arkivara.

Yet I, as if it's any ordinary day, take a step forward. I'm oddly at peace with myself. Closing my eyes, I reach out. When my fingers make contact with a liquid-like substance, I startle. After progressing two more steps, a weight presses in on me. Not like I'm being crushed, but rather as if I'm being wrapped up in a blanket. I open my eyes, and a face is in front of me. A pitch-black face. The whites of her eyes glow, and her eye color I liken to blue sky at dusk.

"Hello, Ravier," she says.

"It's nice to see you, Eyo'el." I grin back. "What would you like to know?"

"Everything," she says, her face moving away from me, as a darkened figure forms, showing the rest of her. "But your lifetime will do, as it is all my Arkivy Grover has offered for me to glimpse."

"You can view my life," I ask, "without taking the memories?"

"Yes. And when I sleep, I remember bits of the lives I have viewed throughout. But my dreams twist reality. The only time I truly know what is real, are the memories committed to me."

"Have there been instances," I ask her, "of entire lifetimes being given to you?"

"When they pass from the land of the living," she says, "to the shadows of Black Heaven, my Arkivy brings them. Many lifetimes have been given over to me, of late. All ending in violence, and deep sorrow. I weep for my children. Please. Give me a happy memory. A good memory. Your favored memory. Ease my burden, for it numbers in the thousands. Give me hope, for I've near lost it."

The weight around grows heavier. It starts to hurt, and I wonder: *Is this what she feels? Literally the weight of all the deaths that have occurred in her city?*

I tell her, "View my life. Then I will give what I can."

My life literally flashes before me. Like quick reels of film, so fast, I barely make out what's happening. It starts when I'm a small child, about three years old, ending with as I am now. I don't know if minutes have passed or hours. It's a timeless feeling—invigorating then balanced then peaceful.

Eyo'el says, "I *like* your life, Ravier. Filled with so many new things. And this world you call Earth. It's not too terrible, either. I see why LanSoren enjoyed going there. Couldn't rely on mere magic for everything. He had to adapt. Make friends. Form another identity, absent of Muraine. He and his sister, alike."

"His sister," I ask, "where is she?"

"She waits in England. You should write to her, if you should make it home to Earth. Ask her to visit you. Tell Grover to give you one of LanSoren's enchanted quills. Then she will know you've been to Muraine, and she may be open to telling you more. We have now come near this meeting's end. What shall you give to me?"

I sift through, searching for what memories to give Eyo'el that I don't necessarily need to remember. I pick the one of Gemma leading me from room to room in the Galloway mansion, making me study up to twenty paintings; but I choose to remember the dinner Molly served us.

Eyo'el gasps. "What fun! So many paintings. Metsa is jealous of their patterns."

Picking another, I know she'll like this one. The night of the festival. The part when Gyron grabbed Rorka and took her out for a dance with the Onyx Warriors. I skip forward to when Callie and I caught him kissing Rorka. I stop the memory right as they begin talking.

Prideful, Eyo'el says, "Siveyra Gyronawv: the good Sorsryn. Perhaps the best of them. Delivered to Paragon, our dearest Metsa. Centuries ago, Gyronawv gave the sapling as a gift to Queen Awleesia. Metsa was the last sapling of the last trees that grew in the Monel. This is a good memory I shall cherish always. A moment between lovers. Now give me hope. The turning point in *your* heart."

I search and search for the last memory to give the Arkivara. Nothing seems right. I either *need* to remember it, *want* to remember it too badly, or feel as though it falls short of what Eyo'el requires. Then the sequence stops. I find the one memory that will put fire back into the heart of Eyo'el. It's a section of conversation I had with Zymarc in Vondurheil.

His voice fades in, saying, "Can't you feel him here, Awngeleik? Can't you smell him? His body went through here, after his death. You know it to be true, Equidyn. Take the two, and the third might be revealed to you."

The surroundings of Vondurheil appear, as my distant voice cries out, "He's a killer. Don't listen to him. Listen to me. LanSoren would never wish for you to become some kind of slayer. He would want you to heal, not wound. To restore, not destroy. Don't be a demon of death, but a demon of light." I see myself sink to the ground of wet snow and beg with a whisper, "No more dark, no more night. Choose the light."

The memory stops there and then slips away, gone forever from my mind.

"Eyo'el?" I ask after a time. "Were the three enough?"

She speaks words of, "Krim-Karasa dim-drim. Harin nae-Varin. Din-drim Delaysarin. You are him: Ravieras-Savak-Kavas. Soon. To ruin. To doom. Laevarye, there is a time to die. Nice to be meeting you, Ravier. We shall talk again."

"Wait!" I shout. "I don't know what any of that means, Eyo'el."

"Talk to your riches," she says. "Give ashes to the witch, for she has the thought you need."

The weight lifts off, and I'm forced to take three steps back. I fight it, but I lose. The Blackwood room surrounds me. The liquid-looking heart of Eyo'el darkens to just black. I rush forward to enter her mind again. But I'm shocked by sparks. I collapse.

Grumbling in his sleep, Grover startles awake from his resting place of a chair set against a wall. He hobbles over to help me up. At least, as much help as the oldest Arkivy in the land *can* offer me with his trembling hands and weak, wobbling, chicken-skinny legs. "Ravier! Good! She's released your awareness. I started to worry. Tried to talk to her. She wouldn't listen. Neither would she let me out, to call Eishal and Lokasi for aid. Are you all right?" He blinks at me, waiting for an answer.

I shake my head, trying to process what's happened. "Do you have a quill that belonged to my father? I need it."

Grover straightens his posture as well as he's able to. "Right here, in my pocket," he replies. "Stays with me, always. If you have need of it, keep it. I can always swindle Eishal into giving me one of LanSoren's lesser ones."

Grateful, I tuck it away in one of my supply pouches, then rush for the exit.

"Wait, Ravier," he calls after me. "What happened between you and Eyo'el?"

"Ask Eyo'el. I don't have time. Have to go." I swing the door open.

Dawn's light creeps through the tree canopies, casting an orange glow across the land. In a panic, I step down. But there are no stairs. Only a twenty-foot drop. I yelp, scrambling to catch hold of something. I'm unsuccessful.

A dozen or so Vonsai napping nearby hear me. They leap over. Rorka's Theocktras join them. I haphazardly land on them, fighting off their curiosity for licking my face.

Once I have my feet under me, they settle. I pat one on the head, saying to them all, "Good Vons. Saved me from breaking my neck."

They pant happily. Then they start nibbling on each other's limbs. I roll my eyes, and start the trek back to the castle. The Vonsai follow me like curious pups, while Rorka's pack lies down for another nap. I've not gone far, when I spot Arsyn on the path that passes the Arkivara. I jog over to him, the Vonsai right at my heels.

"Are you headed out for the journey to The Sodon before the rest of us?" I ask, while eyeing the bulging travel pack that's slung over his shoulder.

Tugging on his cloak's hood, he shakes his head. "I have business farther north than that. I know my way to the Plateau of MarcKand, however. I will be there, in time for the ritual involving Ryco. I must leave now."

"Then may the speed of dyns be with you."

"It will," he says, pointing at a small dragon, who's restlessly clawing at the ground. "See that two-year-old grunt? He's itching to see the skies past Paragon. He hasn't been on a real flight, and a dragon's first flight is perhaps their fastest, until they are much older."

"What about Skylin?" I ask. "Do you want her to stay here, or go with us to Oniva?"

"To The Sodon," he replies. "Be sure to get those Blades of Neutrality, at all costs. And will you promise me something, Ravier?"

I purse my lips. Suspecting it has to do with Skylin, I simply nod.

He says, "Will you *try* to show a little restraint, when it comes to my daughter?"

"Tell that to her," I argue. "She's the one who let me drink spiked Farivoo, then used me afterward."

"You used each other," says Arsyn. "And I *have* had a talk with her. Now I'm having a talk with you. Watch yourself. You have an unusual amount of magic. It makes you a bit magnetic. To both sides of this war, it would seem. I hope this doesn't offend, but it's as if you are a toxin. Everyone wants you. But whose poison are you, I wonder."

"Let's hope I'm Zymarc's. A toxin that will be his undoing."

"Let us hope for that." Arsyn waves goodbye before he leaves on the back of the young dragon.

Huffing out a sigh, I peer at the Vonsai. "That was less painful than I thought it would be. Shall we make a run for the castle?" I take off toward the distant structure.

They trot beside me, still panting cheerfully; some yawn, though. I climb astride one. *Then* they run. Unlike horses, they hardly make a sound. We arrive at the castle steps, as the younger-looking Jasper opens the double doors. His features are ridden with worry, until his Vonsai yip at him from their positions at the base of the stairs.

The tension of his face subsides. "Ravier, I was about to go check on you and Grover, in the Arkivara. You were in there long enough; two-thirds of a day."

"I know. Is Lemawr finished with the journal?"

"He's still in the symposium room," replies Jasper. "Not sure if he's still hard at work, though. It's possible he fell asleep."

Nodding, I state, "Go check on Grover. I left him in a hurry. I'll see to Lemawr."

We go our separate ways, and the Vonsai follow their alpha.

As I head into the castle, and climb its interior stairs, I ponder on what Eyo'el said. *Talk to your riches. The witch has the thought you need.* The words dance in my head, and I wonder, *What did she mean?*

Something pinches the skin of my wrist. It's the watch. While repositioning it, I recall my father saying, *Words for riches . . . Kindling for thought.* It had to do with what despairion is. I take out Rozeth's letter that contains my father's poem. I walk down one of the hallways, seeking privacy, and read the letter over; it doesn't mention *despairion* at all, simply Despairing Marion. I put it away.

When I'm almost to the council room, Madeleine comes into view.

Wandering the hallways by herself, she looks at me in a daze. Her eyes shift to a glowing blue.

"Your riches are in there," she says, slowly pointing to the door that's three down from the council room. Her eyes return to normal, and she turns, continuing her stroll in the hallway. I'm about to enter where she indicated, but noise in the symposium room startles me. I rush to fling the door open.

Lemawr sits at the table, slouching in his seat. Furiously, he rubs at his eyes. No one else is there to keep him company—only a multitude of papers covering the wooden surface, and the dragon-wolf journal, now closed.

I ask, "What'd the journal say?"

He startles and falls out of his chair in fright. "Ravier!" he cries out, scrambling to get up. He takes hold of my shoulders. "You'll not believe what that whole section was about. A use for Enchantment Circles as I've never read about. Many thought the original art was lost. Shifting a name to a spell, containing the same strength as base spells, themselves. Nyxavond—a name turned to a spell—pales in comparison to what this can do. It involves mirroring upon water, or ice, depending on the character of your magic. The amount of magic needed is enormous too."

"Lemawr!" I shout. "Slow down. You lost me at 'shifting a name to a spell.' How?"

He trips over himself, picking up the thinnest, neatest stack of papers from the mess. "These diagrams will assist you. LanSoren was smart, in only writing down how to draft them out. He didn't actually name the different types of Enchantment Circles. Instead, I had to sift through a myriad of riddles and calculations, to get the final angles. Once I figured out that *ellipse* actually meant *circle*, it all started to come together. I believe he knew many—not well versed in ancient Sorsrynian—would recognize the terms Enchantment Circle, Cresynt Circle, and such." He shows me the diagrams. "LanSoren wasn't sure how your magic would develop, at the time he wrote that journal. So he provided four options to try."

"Why are there eight diagrams, then?"

"Two variants for each circle. Four for water. Four for ice," replies Lemawr. "There are a total of eight types of Enchantment Circles. Your father suggested only trying half of them. Cresynt, Tri-, Diamynd, and Hexyn Circles. Two-, three-, four-, and six-point enchantments. He said if you're feeling lucky, and especially ambitious, go for the Hexyn Circles. From what I've heard of your boldness, I'm near sure you'll go for one of them." He takes two papers from the bottom of the stack. "Hexyns require the ritual to be completed in six minutes. Placing six iconic weapons, and casting six non-elemental spells. There's no room for error. You must be perfect. The one on ice will be a little forgiving. But not the one in water, for it requires a levitation spell to hold everything in place. Rather than the circle being below you, on the frozen water's surface, you'll have to be underwater, doing all the motions in the space in front of you."

I leaf through the diagrams. "What about these other three?"

"Cresynt must be done in ten minutes, with two weapons, and two spells at its points. Tri-Circle in twelve minutes; three and three. Diamynd in eight, four different types of weapons and spells. None require iconic weapons, except Hexyn and Octyn. Merely any enchanted weapons will do. You can also use elementals. I've laid out further instructions in this letter." Lemawr gives me a sealed envelope. "Read it during your travel to Oniva for The Sodon. You must leave soon."

Lemawr and I exit the council room.

"Almost forgot," he says, handing me a small, black book. "Your first spell-book. Talok said you don't have one yet. Now you can copy these diagrams to it, and fiddle around with different things to try at all the points. Discuss it among your friends. They're quite gifted. Especially Ryco and Warren. Talok too. If it weren't for that device changing him, he'd be far stronger than he currently is."

"Thank you for everything, Lemawr." I now stand in front of the door three down from the council room. "I just hope I'm able to complete one of them in time."

I turn the knob and peer into the room. The bedroom's covered in feathers, ripped pillows, and tossed bedding. The lot of them—Talok, the King's Guard, some advisers, the Darklyres, *and* Gemma—are fast asleep. Of the guards, only Kent is missing. All the men in the room merely have their pants on. Gemma just has on her thin suit of diving armor. But Khyra is in a nightgown, resting in the same bed as Ryco. The newlywed couple has black, white, and blue paint on their faces. They're almost unrecognizable. They are content, however, sleeping in each other's arms.

Lemawr whispers in my ear, "They signed the contract. The lot of them had a lovely dinner, served in the symposium room. Then they came in here. Got quite rowdy. It was very distracting, while I was trying to concentrate. There was lots of dancing. Herb drinking. Pillow fights. Laughter and shouting. You'd have thought the war's won."

"It was," I tell him, "for a night."

After a quiet laugh, Lemawr says, "I must check on Leira, then get back to that journal. There's more to be discovered from it, I'm sure. Greet ReNovak for me, but tell him I've no wish to be the named Onyx Prince. I doubt my Uncle Gyron will find anything that proves the safety of being named prince again, anyway. I must let the notion go."

"With what you told him," I ask, "won't he be suspicious of your absence?"

"If it comes up, tell him I bound you to go."

"Will do." I enter the room, as Lemawr leaves.

After slipping Rozeth's letter out of my pouch, the younger Soren's advice creeps into the forefront of my mind: *When in doubt, burn it.*

I write the two important phrases on the envelope, using my father's quill: *words for riches* and *kindling for thought.* Then I make my way for Gemma, who's splatted between Ben, Siege, and a few of the young Darklyre wards.

"Gem," I rasp out in a whisper.

Her eyes flutter open, and she wipes at her sweaty face. Some of her hair strands have plastered themselves to one of her cheeks.

"We need to have a talk," I tell her, holding Rozeth's letter up for view.

She eases over Ben, and we leave the room quietly. I lead her to the second story's alchemy alcove that views the castle's center gardens.

She trudges along, yawning a few times. "What is it, Ty? Did you talk to Lemawr?"

"Never mind that now," I reply. "It's something the Arkivara said to me a bit ago. I think it has to do with you."

Gemma sits at the bench where Jasper napped weeks ago. "What did she say?"

"Something about giving you ashes, and that you have a thought I need." I begin searching the alcove for any metal container. At last, I spot a shallow bowl and snatch it up. After dropping the letter in, I hesitate.

"What's the matter?" queries Gemma sleepily.

I ask, "What was the word for fire, again?"

"Oostrina," she replies. "Snap your fingers, if you just want a spark of it."

Doing as she says, I go sit with her on the bench. The flame eats at the letter, turning it to blackened cinder in the silver bowl.

She asks, "What's supposed to happen, once you give me the ashes?"

"Don't know," I reply in truth, as the smoke gets thicker. Its scent stings my nostrils.

Gemma coughs, waving away the smoke that wafts in front of her face. In a short while, the smoke subsides.

"Do you plan on putting my face in that?" Gemma asks.

I laugh. "I was going to have you dip your hands in it, once it cools. Are you offering to paint your face with ashes?"

"If I must," she says, "I will, for you."

I lean over to press my lips tenderly against Gemma's cool cheek. Then I straighten my posture and gaze forward to the window, remarking, "I think after The Sodon, the real battle's going to come. Zymarc will catch wind of Talok being freed of the device, and that Ryco . . ." I trail off, unable to finish.

Yet I manage to think one thing: *Death and goodbyes . . .*

Gemma huddles closer and hugs my arm.

Tears sting my eyes. "I don't want to say goodbye to him, Gem. I have the means to create a really powerful spell. I don't know what it will be, yet. But it'd have enough power to save him. With so much to do, will I have time to complete it?"

"Only the Vardiyas know, Tyler," Gemma says. "Maybe a Rubidyn or Borrower of Time would know too. What does your heart tell you is currently the most pressing matter?"

"This." I slightly lift the bowl of cooling ashes. "Then making it to The Sodon."

"Then focus on those," says Gemma. "Have they cooled enough?"

I hold my hand over the top of the bowl. Oddly, I can't feel warmth emitting from it. I realize that the bowl never felt hot in my hands, as the letter burned.

That's when I whisper, "My senses have been numbed. Will you test it?"

She gently stirs the ashes with her index finger. "They're still warm," she says. "But not too hot." She dips four fingertips of each hand in, then smears ashes on both of her wrists. Dipping again, she sweeps some across her forehead, then down the bridge of her nose. Closing her eyes, she dusts a little on her eyelids and then inhales a deep breath, before waiting in stillness.

When she opens her eyes minutes later, she bolts upright. "It's a word. I can hear it. Yet I can't speak it. It sounds similar to despairion. Three syllables, maybe four or five."

Searching for some paper, I ask, "Think it's a spell word?"

Gemma shakes her head. "It could be. From what I've learned of spells, this one in particular might be an acronym."

I hand her a paper, then my father's quill.

Luckily, she's able to write it down. She gives it to me.

I read it off aloud, "De'eispar-Rione. Thirteen letters. It probably is an acronym. Think the others will know?" I look to Gem.

Someone with heavy, plodding footsteps approaches. "We should discuss it, on the way to The Sodon."

We turn to see Kent, who's sickly pale.

"What happened to you?" I ask.

"I had six tasks to complete," he replies, "before I would be allowed to leave the city with all of you. I've just completed the last one, and had wondered, Gem, is there any dinner left from last night? I'm frightfully hungry."

Gemma giggles. "You *must* be. You didn't even notice the ashes on my face."

Kent takes a second look. "I thought that might've been from last night's celebration. How was it?"

Leading us through the castle, Gemma tells the story, "After the contract was signed, Quall and Musgrae hauled Ryco into that bedroom. Siege and Eli shoved Khyra in there with him. Then Mekka and Rorka confined them to the bed, in a similar way that Jasper did to them. Talok pronounced them partners for life and then asked Warren to start a time-distortion, set for eight hours. We abandoned them, so I could teach Talok and a few others some of Molly's cooking tricks."

"At what point did all the men lose their shirts?" I ask.

Eyes twinkling, Gemma says, "Two words: Quall's herbs."

Chuckling, I ask Kent, "Were you and Ben there for that too?"

"Ben was with me, during most of the celebration," replies Kent, sounding exhausted. "He wanted to comfort me. The six tasks I had coming, were not something pleasant. Vaegon obligations rarely are."

In the kitchenette on the first floor, Gemma serves up last night's dinner. We eat in silence, savoring the blend of pleasant spices in a perfectly thickened soup.

Finishing a bowl of it, Kent tells Gemma, "I do believe you've worked a miracle, Miss Galloway. Talok can cook an edible, even pleasant, meal after all."

Musgrae, fully armed and ready, strides into the kitchen to be with us. "There you are. Ryco!" he shouts over his shoulder. "Found them in here. And Ravier's eating. Such a rare sight, you know."

I smirk at him.

He smirks back, as he playfully punches my arm. "It's all right. It must run in your family. Talok's the same way, and LanSoren was too. It's as if you feed off the very air you breathe."

"Knowing Tyler," says my cousin, ambling in, "I wouldn't put it past him. Are you ready to head out?"

"Yep! Lemawr has translated enough for now. We'll talk about it on the way there."

"Good!" Talok beams, sounding like his old self. "We got all the bags packed last night, before Quall brought out the herbs, and Eli the pots of hot water."

Gemma giggles. "Don't forget the Farivoo the Darklyres smuggled into the room. Once Zepharre caught a whiff of it he was gone, even though we made the Darklyres promise they didn't spike it."

I look to Talok. "Think we can invite Dea and Skylin to go? Arsyn said Skylin could. I'm sure Keturah will be glad to see familiar faces."

"Already thought of that," he replies. "They're ready now."

I ask, "We're really headed off?"

Talok rubs at his face, before replying, "Yes. To Oniva, the capital city of the Nyxane. I've never been there. It'll be the first for both of us. Let's make the memories worth something, before we must go to MarcKand."

Ryco comes to stand behind Talok, a bleak smile on his face now cleared of the paint. His yellow eyes are that straw color. He tries to appear strong. In reality, he's breaking under it all. And so am I.

How will I survive the loss of this new friend? I wonder. *Will I be changed forever? Will I be willing to sell my soul to Zymarc, King of Vitiosyns, to bring this one back? Or will I finish a spell that can save both Talok and Ryco?*

I'm left to wonder if that sleeping power everyone keeps telling me that I have, will awaken in time for me to accomplish my deepest desires. To have the power to save the ones I love. I simply have no idea if I can do it, and that makes me feel scared. More scared than anything.

II

Of the Other Half

*"When calls the darkness,
find it. Bind it to light.
Defeat it forever."*

10

Do What Feels Right

Before we go, we entrust Awngeleik's care to Jasper. I hate to leave her again. At least she's in Paragon with dyns, neins, and those familiar to her.

"She is safe with me, Ravier," Jasper tells me. He hesitates as if inclined to say something else. Whatever it is, he decides against voicing it. Instead, he gives my shoulder a squeeze, then retreats into the castle, pulling Awngeleik by her lead rope. Though reluctant, she goes with him. She looks back at me, as the double doors close.

My head throbs sharply. The worry over her well-being starts to consume me. I've no choice in this. This is how it must be, for she would not be safe in Oniva, nor on the way there, and most certainly not safe on the way to the Plateau of MarcKand.

Zepharre eyes the shut doors curiously, then snaps out of his thoughts to briskly shake my hand. "Ryco refused to tell how you all mean to free Talok of the device. I almost pulled rank to force him to confess the plan. Khyra, however, asked that I not pry. And how can I refuse her, after I so rudely tore her blueprints in half?"

"Is that another apology?" I ask.

Zepharre startles, hiding his hands in the folds of his long coat. "Apology? Did I apologize? I've not the recollection for certain of that. Though I'm not sorry now, for I thought it was a hallucination. Therefore,

I'm absolved of needing to apologize for my behavior. Yet I'll not be escaping the consequences of my actions. You could say that *wrong* deeds must be righted by *good* deeds. So that is what I shall do. Right the wrong with good."

A sickness creeps into my gut. But I tell Zepharre, "I'm sure you'll find a way to make up for it, while we're away."

Zepharre's gaze softens. His shoulders relax. "I do hope you are right, Ravier."

Khyra, having said her goodbyes to the others, hooks arms with Zepharre, who then rolls his eyes. She says, "Of course Tyler's right. I've already started a list of things for you to do, Alchemist. We're going to make Eyo'el quite a beautiful city again. Different, to be sure. Yet beautiful. And strong too."

Zepharre sneers. "So long as it doesn't entail me putting a Farivoo fountain anywhere, I'll do most of the things on your to-do list, Your High—I mean, City Architect." He keeps another sneer from emerging.

Khyra's violet eyes light up. "That's a grand idea, Zepharre. A Farivoo fountain in one of the taverns that's just being built. In fact, how about having one assembled in each of them?"

With the hand not held captive by Khyra, Zepharre claws at his neck. "Can't we have at least one tavern, absent of Farivoo? Honestly, I don't understand this love of Farivoo everyone has. Are you with me or not on this, Ravier?"

"I'm with ya!" I grin. "One tavern, absent of Farivoo."

Zepharre glances at Khyra, who's covering a smile. "There you have it," he says. "Ravier has spoken on the matter. And thanks are in order, on a different matter, before you go, Tyler. Namely, the bargaining of more days for our Talok. You are braver than I thought one of your age and race ever could be." In div, he adds, *"Only Ryco has done braver things than you, in the circle I've personally met."*

"Vards!" Khyra tightens her hold on Zepharre's arm. "Can't you just tell Tyler what you mean? Zepharre is vastly impressed by your gifts, Tyler, and he thanks you profusely for everything you've done for us."

Adamantly, Zepharre shakes his head. "I didn't say any of that. I don't claim that. Woman! Stop putting words into my mouth. You could ruin my reputation. And then my nieces and nephews, and great-nieces and great-nephews, could hear of it. I'd be at their mercy. Their greed exceeds my own, I fear. Especially my great-nephew Reptestro. My eldest brother's grandchildren are monsters. I hate them almost as much as I hate the Jokryn playing their pranks." He hisses that last *S* sound.

Zepharre's out of breath by the time Ryco comes over to say, "We need to be leaving, Zepharre."

"Tell that to your bride," says Zepharre. "She's the one who keeps lengthening the conversation. And it's not in my nature to ignore someone who's talking. I just keep responding until they stop talking. Unless I fear for my life. *Then* I stop talking. Only venturing a Mensa-div to say anything."

While Zepharre prattles on, Ryco cups Khyra's smiling face. Then he kisses her, and I smirk at Zepharre. He glances to the pair beside him, kissing, and stops his trail of words. He rolls his eyes, then looks to me. "Why do I even bother talking? No one listens these days. Ah! But I suppose that's my own fault." More loudly, Zepharre says, "Come back soon, Ryco, and start on those children with Khyra. I very much look forward to you being a father of eight. I shall spoil them, behind your back. And who knows? One might even become like me. Farewell," says Zepharre smugly, prying his arm free of Khyra's hold so that he may stride away with EmiKal and the other advisers.

Khyra pulls away from her new partner, about to shout something at Zepharre. But Ryco holds her back.

Attempting to stifle a laugh, he says in a hushed tone, "Try not to kill each other while I'm gone."

"Then tell him to behave properly," she retorts. "And by proper, I mean benign."

"He doesn't know how," says Kent from behind me. "If he becomes too unreasonable, have Madeleine accompany you to 'Zepharre' meetings. You'll find him much more agreeable."

Madeleine strolls up beside Khyra. "I will be there for her. Speed of dyns, Tamers. Bring both our king and our Paradyn home."

"They will," Talok replies. He hides the truth of the sacrifice that's soon to come, quite well.

I wonder if he feels as sick inside as I do over Ryco's impending death. Perhaps he's holding out for the same hope as me. That some spell or Enchantment Circle will save him.

Once we're all piled on a dragon's back, and have our horse companions settled down, one of which includes Brash, we wave goodbye to those still lingering near the castle.

The journey out is a daze. I study those eight diagrams, until my eyes can't focus anymore. I ask loads of questions to do with iconic weapons. I still can't decide which to use for the Hexyn Circles. My twin daggers can fill two spots. The Blades of Neutrality, two more. The Spear of Guyheiz, which Warren has with him, can be the fifth.

While resting the first night, I muse, *That leaves one more spot to fill, unless it's better to have a weapon set. There's also the spells to decide on. Non-elemental ones. I don't even know where to begin with those.*

Drifting into a fitful sleep, I startle awake sometime later. Someone has weaseled under the thin covers of the bedroll with me. I roll over, expecting it to be Skylin, after she's finished her task of tending the horses. But it's Deamond.

She whispers, "What circle is it you mean to do? Your questions haven't given it away. Many of us are wondering."

"Hexyn," I whisper back.

Dea scoffs. "You don't start with Hexyn. Even the most gifted don't start with Hexyn. My advice to you? Start with half of Hexyn. A Tri-Circle. We have loads of enchanted weapons with us. You also can use elemental spells. Get a feel for how a successfully completed circle is. Then, when it comes time for you to do Hexyn, you *might* be successful."

"Show me."

We sneak off out of earshot from the others.

Deamond draws a large circle in the dirt, about ten to thirteen steps in diameter. Then she explains that the triangle is imaginary. The points where weapons are placed is with the top triangle-point facing away from you. Then you imagine it being picked up, mirrored, then set down again. Those are the points for the spells to hit. We go through several tests. I place the weapons; Dea casts the spells.

Sometime later, Dea sets an ordinary blade in the circle's center, and says, "Whatever you are trying to enchant, always goes in the center."

"What if you're trying to enchant a word?"

Her eyes grow wide. "That is beyond my knowledge. You'd have to ask one of your friends."

"I don't want to worry them."

"Very well," she says. "Theoretically, you'd have to put something in the center, to stand in place of the word. A representation of it. To merely write it down on paper with an enchanted quill, then place it in the center, is not enough."

"What about a book?" I ask, studying the Tri-Circle, imagining all the possibilities.

"That could work," says Dea. "It'd have to be enchanted, and be a true representation of the one word or series of shortened words you're trying to enchant and string together. A book, though, may have too many words to serve your intentions properly."

Chewing nervously on my lip, I ask after a time, "What about me? What if I stood in the center?" I motion to it.

Even in the moonlight, I spot the look of horror on Dea's face; the tears she tries to hold back.

She subtly shakes her head. "That is dangerous," she rasps out. "It could kill you. Perhaps not standing in the center of a Tri-Circle. But a Hexyn? Standing in the center of a completed Hexyn Circle, enchanting something tied to you—a word—the ritual would be too much. It would kill you, Ravier."

"What choice do I have?"

Dea looks away. "Please, Ravier, try one of the others Lemawr gave you. Don't choose Hexyn. What good are you, to anyone, dead?"

My nostrils burn. I wipe at my stinging, watery eyes. "The ritual that saves Talok, kills Ryco. How can I just stand by and watch, doing nothing, Dea?" I sink to the ground and rest my forehead on my palms, elbows propped on my bent knees.

Dea comes to sit with me. She grips my shoulder nearest to her. In a trembling voice, she says, "Ryco is a King's Guard. It is his duty to save the king. Don't take his act of sacrifice from him. You don't take duty away from such a guard, nor do you take duty away from dyns. He is both. Don't make him grieve your death. He will blame himself. It's what loyal dragons do. They take responsibility, even if the blame does not lie with them."

"We're done for tonight," I say. "I can't do anymore. I'm too tired. Too scared."

"No, you're not," says Dea, standing up. "I'm going to reset the circle. You're going to cast three spells to enchant that weapon in the center. Then we'll go sleep, wake up, and make it to Oniva. Get up, Ravier."

I obey, yet my heart is numb while watching Dea do the motions.

She stands aside, instructing me, "Use fire, wind, and water. Oostrina, Ventu, and Oonda. But *feel* out their placement. Don't just cast them anywhere. This is the hardship of Enchantment Circles. They are unique to the caster. The effect is never identical, unless the same caster matches everything as they did before. Do what feels right to you, Tyler."

Closing my eyes, I reactively reach out with my right hand. Envisioning one of the three points, I cast Oostrina, merely thinking the word in my mind. I hear the flame lick over the ground, in the distance. With my left, I cast Oonda. The noise of water sprays goes forth in the cool night air. Cupping both hands together near my chest, I slowly open them. Moving them away from me, I cast Ventu. The warm wind blows toward me. Then it churns around. I open my eyes to see the three spells swirling with each other, in the circle's center.

The short-blade shakes. It steadily lifts off the ground. Vibrating, a whirring sound rings out. The three elements burst outward. The wind sweeps away the drawn circle, and moves the placed weapons a bit.

Dea rushes to the newly enchanted weapon. She carefully picks it up. As she takes hold of it, a wide grin spreads across her face. "Equal parts of all three spells, Ravier. That is hard to do."

Approaching, I reach for the blade, nervous to hold it.

Someone softly claps three times, nearby.

I whirl around.

Those citrine-yellow eyes are aglow, in the darkness. Ryco comes up to me. "Well done, Ravier. That was not an easy task."

Quall strides up behind him, to add, "Your father would be proud. You should be too."

I pass the blade to Ryco.

After inspecting it, he inquires, "May I keep this, until that day we save Talok in MarcKand?"

I reply, "You can keep it forever."

He sighs in sad longing. "This is one of the few times in my life that I actually wish I *could* keep something forever. Yet I cannot. I need you to remember this, however." He studies me hard.

"I will," I reply. "Tell me."

"I believe Zymarc intended to destroy Paragon," states Ryco, "on that second day of the festival. Then his apprentice must've sent word that the Son of LanSoren, or some soul of great power, was in Paragon. You saved us from being utterly destroyed, with your very presence. I can't help but wonder, if a soul can spare so many from death in that fashion, what can that soul do when actually working to save a nation? In other words, don't worry over saving me."

Dea adds, "Don't merely save a nation, either. Inspire them to rise up, to take action."

Quall voices his thought of, "Opportunities await in Oniva, Tyler. On the Day of Neutrality, Oniva's eyes, and all visiting her, will be on you. Use the attention to our advantage."

I make the statement, "Then, what other choice do I have than to ask ReNovak to name me as the Onyx Prince?"

The three of them give me their knowing looks, but it's Quall who says,

"I cannot wait to see you ask that of ReNovak."

11

You are Your Father's Son

Yesterday, we decided to cover ourselves with hooded, black cloaks. Also, we bid farewell to the dragon who brought us as far as a day's ride on horseback to the Onyx city. No need to announce to all of Oniva that the Paragonians have arrived. We currently wait at Oniva's gate. I don't know why I expected it to be an impenetrable, black wall. What waits to be opened is made of graceful, intertwined streams of metal—black, silver, and white.

Eli asks, "You sure they heard you, Ryke?"

"Oniva is vast, Eli," he replies. "And it's early. Barely dawn out. Be patient."

Along with Eli, our horse companions grow restless. Brash, however, remains calm. He reminds me of Ginger Snap, only much bigger, and colored differently.

Siege whispers, "Someone's approaching."

"'Bout time!" Musgrae grumbles.

Siege glances over his shoulder, and shakes his head. "Not beyond the gate. Behind us."

Quall firmly instructs, "Don't any of you draw your weapons. We're on neutral ground."

A hooded figure on foot slows to a stop a short distance away. He stares at us. We stare at him. No one says anything.

When Dea registers who it is, she jumps down from her horse companion. "King Aygor!" she shouts, rushing to embrace him.

He takes off her hood, to cup her face. "Is it merely you and Skylin, with the Paragonians? No SynKievas or Arsyn?"

At ease atop Brash's broad back, I tell the Darklyrian King, "Arsyn had business to the north."

Dea replies, "SynKievas was sentenced to stay in Paragon with Sonya and the others."

"They are safe, then?" he queries, coming closer to the rest of us.

"Better than safe," she says, getting back on her horse. "They are taken with the land. The dragons, the horses, the people. Don't let me get started on how they feel for the Greyvons. When the time comes, you're going to have difficulty convincing them to go home to Grevagg."

Aygor grins. "I consider myself warned. Thank you, King Talok, for ensuring their well-being. They are the world to me. Which is why I now find myself here."

Talok asks, "For Keturah? She's a reason we are here as well. I feel partially responsible for her being taken. I want to set it right, if I can."

Dea flicks Skylin's boot, as she looks up at her. "Let King Aygor have your nein. Ride double with Ravier."

Aygor asks, "Am I not allowed to enter Oniva on foot?"

"You are," Quall replies, "but their etiquette states only warriors and commoners enter on foot, for The Sodon. Neither of which holds the status to make a special request of Nyxane's nobles, with the exception of Onyx Warriors. But they have a separate sorting system."

"Once thousands begin arriving," Siege adds, "the Onyx divide nobles from commoners. There's a lot of logistics that go into keeping order on such a day as this."

Dea states, "In other words, King Aygor, get on the high horse."

"Fine," he says. "But I don't have to like it."

Skylin has dismounted her horse, to walk over to me. I help her up on Brash. She sits in front of me. I like her close. Especially, I like the warmth of her wings on my core, the softness of them as they brush against my hands that currently grip the reins. Not realizing it, I've fallen for this girl.

As Aygor gets situated on the one black horse among our group, the gate shifts, and the metal scrolls move to form a symbol resembling an abstract branch facing north. The two wide doors, taller than the surrounding trees, grind open.

The ground shakes; my heart pounds.

Gears squeal to a stop. The gate's fully open. Only two have come to greet us. Gyron, accompanied by a tall woman, who's dressed in a black, iridescent dress with long sleeves and a low neckline. The bottom hem reaches all the way to the ground, and hides her feet. Not a single weapon is on her person. Merely a necklace with a single pendant.

The good Siveyra beckons us to come forward. We do, but slowly.

When he motions that we should stop, we obey.

"From where do you hail?" queries Gyron, in seriousness.

Quall states, "Paragon."

"From what city have you just come?" Gyron asks.

"Eyo'el," replies Ryco.

"And who is head of your company?"

Talok shoves his hood back. "King Talok of Paragon. I have brought my cousin here, for an audience with King ReNovak. Are we permitted?"

The lady with Gyron replies, "You are. Let me introduce myself. I am former Queen to the Onyx, Ayna. You are most welcome here, this day. Please allow Gyronawv to show your tired horses to the stables, as they are not permitted to wander in our cities, as you let them in yours. A few of you may accompany him."

Dismounting, we collect what things we need from our supplies. I pet Brash on the neck, to reassure him I'll be fine. Then Kent, Ben, and Gemma volunteer to help Gyron lead the neins to some black stables in the distance on our left. I smile at the sight of the stable structures made of Blackwood with white trim. They must be where my dad got the inspiration for our smaller barn back home.

"Follow me," says Ayna, turning to head up a hill. She grips the skirt of her dress, lifting the hem off the ground. Her stride is long. Nearly three steps of mine could fit in the span of one of hers.

Almost to the hilltop, Eli bursts ahead. Then he stops, awestruck.

Ayna saunters up behind him. "The Oniva of Onyx. It isn't usually this still."

We join the two of them.

My cousin drinks in a deep breath. "It's better than the stories."

Glistening, black buildings, fashioned similar to old cathedrals, are scattered around. In addition to their two towers at the forefront, there's a third that rises at the back of each cathedral. I can't tell what the larger cathedrals farther away are like. These stand tall, as a testament of order, sharpness, and perfection.

I ask Ayna, "Let me guess, Onyx are fond of Tri-Circles?"

She faces me with enthusiasm. "Most definitely. We are. All those buildings with three towers have permanent Enchantment Circles etched into the center of their floors. They are our schools, libraries, and particular places to practice magic. The ones beyond them, with four towers, five, or six, those are for scholars and warriors to practice becoming Nekrosyns. That is, those equally a scholar and a warrior. Come, I've spotted ReNovak down the way. I'll tell you more, as we go."

We follow Ayna's sure steps, listening to her.

She continues, "For near fifty years, we train in the ways of war, or the studies of scholars. Then we are expected to become as proficient in the other class of thought or action. I started out as a scholar. A Saigryn. At least, that is what I got everyone to believe. I've always dabbled in the ways of war, however. Although the Diamynd and Heptyn Cathedrals are a sight to see, I don't recall my first time entering them as a Saigryn. But I shall never forget how the Hexyn Cathedral's majesty brought me to my knees. It was Nyxane's favorite cathedral. All things Onyx are in it. As such, only Onyx are permitted to enter. I desire to take you there, this instant. It is our pride and joy. Yet, we can never share its treasures with outsiders."

We get to the base of a wide, sloping hill.

Nearby buildings fashioned of gray-stone choke out our view of the city.

"Did ReNovak make his request of you already?" I ask.

"He did. How is it you'd know he'd be asking me?"

"There aren't too many nobles ReNovak *can* ask," says Talok. "Are there?"

"No," replies Ayna. "And many of the nobles are away, due back later."

Getting to the end of a moss-covered, stone path, the view opens up to a space of landscape. Rising and sloping softly, it's blanketed by spindly, flattened grass. Rich in its green color, it's not starved of water, but I've no desire to lay upon it for a nap.

Ayna continues, "I'd tell you what it was he asked, but he asked it in private. I gave it to him in private. Therefore, it is upon him to announce it."

Seeming unconcerned with anything except for the surrounding sights, Talok simply says, "We understand."

"More than you know," I add.

King Aygor interrupts, to ask, "When may we see a certain Darklyrian girl?"

"That has been recently complicated," replies Ayna, still journeying forward. "The girl's care was given over to me. However, on this day, a neutral day, she technically belongs to the one who took her. Zymarc. He can't come take her while she's on neutral ground. If he waits until tomorrow evening, though, he can. And ReNovak has been forbidden to give her care to anyone else."

Aygor asks, "Tomorrow, she is no longer safe?"

"Potentially," says Ayna, "that may be so." She stops to look at Talok and me, then points off to our right. "That is ReNovak, over there, conversing with someone. He's been with the visitor since shortly after I granted him his request. It's unusual for him to talk this long with the same individual. Something isn't right. My advice to you is this: tread lightly with him. I shall send Onyx Warriors to you soon, to show you to your sleeping quarters."

Once she's out of sight, Talok says, "We discussed it last night, Tyler, while you slept. You will go to ReNovak alone. We'll wait here, staying in your sights. But it is to you the Onyx King wishes to speak. And we desire to give him that."

Quall grumbles, "I had wished to hear how this conversation was going to turn out between you and the Onyx King."

Warren adds his input of, "Don't make us regret giving you this chance."

"I won't," I reply, before striding toward ReNovak and the figure. Panic rises, the closer I get. The figure's cloaked in midnight-blue—the same color Zymarc wore, while in Vondurheil. I try to stop and turn around, but ReNovak has seen me. I can't cease the progression of my steps toward him. I continue, only stopping an arm's length away. I bow on one knee and then rise to stand tall.

"King ReNovak," I state, "you wished to speak with me."

"Yes." He nods. "Before we get to that, however, it might interest you to know that I've been conversing with a Vitiosyn for a long while."

Hidden by the hood, the figure's face remains in shadow.

"Why would I care of that?" I ask. "This land is neutral, today. I need not fear any Vitiosyn. I should hardly fear anything at all."

"Did I not tell you?" he says to the figure. "Is he not more brazen than that day in Paragon? If he is of a mind to give it to you, then I shall give you your request. Ask him, Vitiosyn."

The figure yanks the hood off, revealing Belzara's gray-skinned, tearstained face. "You wish for me to ask a boy? To put her fate into his hands? I will not!" she shouts.

ReNovak coldly replies, "You will ask him, or I will not give you what you desire."

"Her fate?" I ask. "Whose fate do you mean?"

ReNovak replies, "Belzara's Beloved, slain down during the first day of the festival, if memory serves right."

Distressed, Belzara's chest heaves up and down. "They've kept her here, the decay in suspension, so that she may be brought back. The prospect recently taunted before me by Zymarc, himself, when he was drunk with dragon's blood."

"Why do you want her back?" I ask. "Is it to have her beside you, as you face us on the battlefield?"

Belzara's scarlet-red eyes narrow on me. "I'm tired of war. I do not wish to be a Vitiosyn any longer. I wish for family. It's what was promised to me by Deezalo after the wars ended. But his wars *never* ended. Then he was caught—executed shortly after that. Zymarc, as well, tried to give me a sort of family. Each time, it was wrecked, again and again. I was given one last chance at family, with Caleiso. But she never loved me, because Zymarc had stopped loving me well before he ever found her."

"Even if she's brought back, Belzara"—I shake my head—"how can you stop being a Vitiosyn?"

Belzara steps closer. "I was one of the first Deezalo turned with Vitiosus, before it was as strong as it is now. I had a choice. I chose to be a Vitiosyn. I can choose to stop being one. It's a choice that not even Zymarc has. Though I must always have a master, I can't be goaded into doing everything he wants. He hates me for it. But he loves how his goading of you gets you to show a strength rare few possess. He cannot control you, and he admires you for that. At least, he did." Belzara cackles out an ugly laugh.

ReNovak stuffs his hands in his pockets. "What is so amusing, Belzara?"

"Zymarc," she replies, "was buried beneath the snows of Vondurheil. He stopped loving Ravier so much, after that. You should have heard him screaming about it to Prince Azabahk. It was soon afterward that I learned of her presence here in Oniva."

Pausing in thought, Belzara comes to kneel in front of me; she and I are eye to eye. Her harsh demeanor falls away, and she begs, "Please, Ravier, agree to have my loved one brought back, and I will pledge myself to you for the rest of my days. I will choose to let you be my master." Tears stream down, adding to the streaks on her dirty face.

I bend forward to cup my hands over her filth-covered, clasped ones. "I have no desire to be anyone's master. Be free, Belzara." I grip her hands tighter. "Go watch your loved one brought back to life. Then run away with her, and be happy." I release her hands, before braving a glance at ReNovak's rigid expression. "Give Belzara as she desires. That is my decision. What is yours?"

Belzara cries out, sounding broken, "You are your father's son. Merciful and kind, Tyler Malik Ravier; I will remember you."

Not waiting for his answer, I turn to stride a few steps away, and cut off the flow of tears before they start.

ReNovak says, "It will be as Ravier has decided."

Overwhelmed, Belzara weeps. "I shall never forget this, Ravier. The day my heart was made glad again."

Too distraught to look back at her, I stride toward the Paragonians.

"Aren't you going to watch the product of your words?" queries ReNovak, walking beside me.

"I don't wish to hate her, ReNovak." I stop to face him. "How can I bear watching Belzara get a loved one back, while I cannot? I've come here to have a talk with you. So what are you waiting for?" I throw my arms open in frustration.

The ground trembles.

I startle, then realize it's Oniva's gate opening again.

Ayna and some warriors are approaching the Paragonians to assist with our things.

ReNovak strides the rest of the way to them, asking Talok, "Do I have the King of Paragon's permission to take Tyler Ravier behind closed doors? What I wish to talk of, cannot be spoken out in the open. Nor behind simple doors. I must take him to an enchanted room, where all magical bindings fall away."

Talok replies, "I leave it to Tyler to decide."

ReNovak adds in, "I'll have to blindfold him, before taking him there. I wish to be the only one who knows where the room is."

"I don't like that at all," states Quall, a frown on his face.

"It's all right," I reply. "If it's what ReNovak has to do, I'll agree to it."

ReNovak takes a black cloth out and covers my eyes, tying it tight at the back of my head.

Footsteps approach. I listen as Ayna says, "It's your older warriors, ReNovak. They've made it back from their two-year tour." Her voice catches. "They have the body of Dezarin with them."

A small hand grips my arm, startling me.

Skylin says, "Don't trip and fall, hurting yourself, Tyler. There will be lots of dancing tonight. Won't there, King ReNovak?"

"Certainly," he replies.

Skylin brushes at my neck, then kisses me lightly where she bled the intoxication out in Grevagg. Warmth seeps into my veins, then dissipates.

"I'll be fine," I reply, "so long as ReNovak isn't a klutz."

Skylin moves away.

A heavy hand takes hold of one of my arms.

"Come with me, Ravier," ReNovak commands. "And Ayna? See that my recent visitor is given as she desires. Ravier has agreed to it. Order Gyron to bring Belzara's Beloved back to life."

He pulls me away. Part of me wishes to know what the others are thinking. But perhaps it's best I leave them now, even if it's leaving them angry or confused. It'd be no different from how I feel: dazed, with a building fire in my heart the closer ReNovak brings me to the enchanted room.

There's lots of stairs, and echoing hallways.

We pass by others, who are conversing in hushed tones. They speak in a foreign tongue; therefore, I don't understand a word they say. One phrase, however, catches my attention: Ravieras sa-vel LanSoren.

Oniva knows who I am, I muse. *Perhaps that will give me an advantage tonight, when I make my request of King ReNovak.*

12

Secrets Kept

A door opens, then shuts.

My blindfold's removed.

I'm in a black room; torches on the walls are lit with soft-white flames.

ReNovak stuffs the blindfold in his pocket. He intently watches the one seated at a metal, octagonal table. A giant being, cloaked in black and scarlet-red. Blackened-gold gloves protect his relaxed hands that rest on the table's surface. All fingertips of the gloves come to a point, and tines forged into the metal would most certainly tear his enemies' flesh more on the way out, than the plunging into muscle.

As I sit in one of the smallest of the seven empty silver chairs, it takes everything in me to remain calm. I ask the stranger, "Who might you be?"

He doesn't answer. Nor does he move. He only breathes in and out steadily.

I glance at some of the exposed skin of his arms, and a lump forms in my throat. Faint stripes colored of blood-red, black, and copper glint in the torchlight. It reminds me of something. I cannot recall what.

If he's a Sorsryn, I muse, *he's no ordinary one.*

ReNovak takes the seat opposite of me. He looks to the stranger. "Meet Tyler Ravier. The one you've been hearing so much of."

"Has Jasper come?" asks the stranger, his voice unnaturally deep.

"It would've been too bold of a request," replies ReNovak, "as well as near impossible to get him down here, without setting off suspicion. Ravier was more easily obtained."

"Obtained?" I ask, thumping my heel nervously on the floor. "What do you want with Jasper?"

The stranger's cloak sets itself on fire, turning to reddened soot that falls to the floor. His clothes, made of shimmering scales, match his skin. But holding the intensity are his copper-colored eyes, glowing akin to flickering fire. This fearsome one replies, "He and I have unfinished business. But you and me, our business dealings are just beginning."

In coldness, I comment, "Not until you tell me who you are."

"I don't like introducing myself. Dyns rarely do. And when we are forced to, we get rather hungry, wanting to devour the one who dares to solicit us for our name."

"Dyns?" I ask. "You are Rentwar, King of Rubidyns, aren't you?"

He poses a question, in return, "How was my recruit? She wouldn't tell me how the journey went. Merely that Jasper has given up hope. Is that true?"

I ask again, "Why do you care so much about Jasper?"

"Boy!" He pounds his fist on the table, leaving a scarred dent in it. "Stop evading my questions. Where *is* the Greyvon Alpha?"

"He's with the Equidyn, guarding her."

ReNovak's expression is intent on me. "And where is that, Ravier?"

I laugh. "I'll be telling neither of you, because I don't trust either one of you."

Rentwar calms down somewhat. "I need to talk with Jasper, of a matter I cannot—"

I cut him off with, "Rubidyns cannot be bound *not to say*. Try a different lie. One I might actually believe."

"Very well," says Rentwar, his eyes darkening to dull-copper. "The Equidyn can only have one master. Are you that master?"

I'm about to claim it. Then I stop, and wonder if it's true. I panic, saying aloud to myself, "The third memory. I shouldn't have given it away." I meet the Rubidyn's gaze. "I don't know for certain if I am. I gave three memories to the Arkivara. One from Earth. One from Paragon. The third from Vondurheil. It was when Zymarc challenged Awngeleik to kill him. I had to convince her not to. I don't recall what was said. I just recall her about to rip into his throat. Then, suddenly, she was coming down. There's a gap. I don't know if I'm her master. Merely, I *think* I am."

Rentwar says, "If you do not know whether you are master to Awngeleik or not, then you are of no use to me."

I scoff under my breath. "Well, I'm certainly not your toxin, am I?"

"You might have been," says Rentwar with wit. "But I have encountered others like you, and dealt with them accordingly. There is also the fact that your power and influence are not yet to their level."

"You mean Soren? Others like Soren of the Monel, right?" I ask.

Rentwar drums the metal tips of one gloved hand on the table. "He had power, to be sure. Near his beginning, he had some influence as well. Yet he lost it. No. The true influence always rested with Shena and Fayel. The day after the Battle of Queens, in which both perished, was the striking of the first ShenawFayel."

"It means *Truce for a Day*," ReNovak clarifies, leaning back in his chair.

Rentwar continues, "It's stronger, and more binding than The Sodon, for it is two names forged to one; made into a spell, unbreakable. Not even Vitiosus can break it, for it was made after the Laws of Magic. Jasper and I forged it together, in the Cave of Ichors Von. The two queens were at the points of the Cresynt Circle. Their lingering power and influence forged forever into the symbol of strength and cunning. Even now—over six thousand years past their end—a spell forged from their very names, and bound by the flesh and bones of their bodies, is struck among all habitants of Muraine. Particularly in times of war."

I ponder on a string of thought: *It's no coincidence that he's talking of Enchantment Circles now. Does he know of the journals? And if he does, how much?*

"All of it," replies Rentwar aloud.

ReNovak looks about the room. "What? All of what?"

Rentwar's gaze on me is unwavering. "It's between me and the boy. I must tell you this, Ravier, for your not knowing would open you up to believing a lie that could control you."

The intensity of his expression frightens me into a cold sweat.

He states, "It was not Zymarc who killed your father."

My head wants to explode. I shove the table away, enough to stand upright without moving my chair. "You know who killed him?" I ask. "And you're not going to tell me? Merely, you'll tell who *didn't*? Why does it matter knowing he didn't? I'll end him for what he's done!"

"Yes," says Rentwar calmly. "Punish Zymarc for what he *has* done. Not for what he hasn't."

"I do not understand you, King Rentwar." Seething inside, I press my palms flat on the table surface to lean forward. "What is it you want?"

"To see the Equidyn," he replies. "Since you are not sure of your being her master, you cannot give permission for me to go see her, wherever she may be. If Jasper were here to talk with me, I could ask him to confirm something of her physiology that I need to know. Although you are useful to others, Ravier, I'll say it again. You are of no use to me."

"Then we're done here." I head for the door. "But I'll tell you this; I'm not completely useless in telling you what you wish to know. Jasper's hope has been restored. And Awngeleik possesses two hearts—one dyn's heart, one nein's heart."

Rubbing his forehead, ReNovak asks in disbelief, "She has a dragon's heart? How did no one know of this?"

"Perhaps it was dormant, until recently." I shrug. "Now, will you let me out of here? I've no wish to stay."

Moving to stand up, Rentwar suddenly has hold of a long, cloth-wrapped parcel. He sets it down on the table. "I, as well, am finished here, King ReNovak. I've brought the prize you mean to give to the next named Onyx Prince. May he aspire to deserve them: Enyxar and Aevimeis."

ReNovak replies, "You can't leave until nightfall. That's what we agreed on. Otherwise, I can't ensure that you won't be seen."

"Very well," he says. "I'll wait." He sits back down.

ReNovak blindfolds me again, before we head out.

Wanting to make it back to this room later, to see the Rubidyn again for further questioning, I start counting my steps—first five, then a left turn; up eight stairs, right turn; then eight more stairs. A door creaks open, and we pass through. It slams shut. I pretend to startle, losing my balance. Flailing my arms out, I catch myself. The floor is cold, smooth stone.

Helping me up, ReNovak says, "Should've warned you it'd slam like that, on our way out."

We walk a bit farther. Eleven steps. Then we stop.

I keep repeating it in my head: *eleven, eleven, eleven.*

ReNovak lets go of me.

I start to worry.

When his breaths cease, I call out, "ReNovak, why have we stopped?"

Something wallops me on the back of the head, and pain surges over my scalp. I land on my knees, then someone squeezes above my temples hard enough that my head goes numb. Though I fight to stay conscious, I soon pass out.

13

Let Loose

My awareness fades back in. It's dark outside. I'm standing in a long line of people. Many are ahead, and even more behind. Tall pillars of metal contain flickering flames at their tops, illuminating the space surrounding the line of people.

What happened? I wonder. *Did someone jump ReNovak and me?*

I feel the back of my head, the spot where I was struck. Oddly, it isn't sore.

My hand lowers to rest at my side. I peer past the others ahead of me. We're waiting at one of the cathedrals I couldn't make out before. This one has six towers of four different heights. The tower layout is odd, akin to a pentagon with an added point at its base. The structure's shorter in front than at the back. The back tower's parallel with the short, front one that doesn't even reach past the roof pitch. The following two sets of towers gradually rise higher. The very back wall and tower soar hundreds of feet high, reaching for the night sky.

Lining each roof pitch in view, warrior silhouettes stand still. I wonder if they're statues, until a cluster of them climb down, and more shadowed figures take their place.

After a deep sigh, I glance around for a familiar face—anything familiar, really.

A rugged warrior, meandering toward me, poses his question of, "You are Tyler Ravier, no?"

"Who's asking?"

"Hydvar of Oniva." He holds out his roughened hand, while two other warriors take up his side positions. His expression's pleasant enough.

Yet I cross my arms in nervousness. "No offense, but I'm not comfortable shaking hands with a complete stranger."

Hydvar doesn't appear upset, as he pulls his hand back to rest it on his blade hilt. "Is it that you fear me taking a spot of magic, or that you might take a splash of mine?"

"Both," I reply, reaching for my own blade hilt, NeiSator's, to be precise.

This amuses the other two warriors with Hydvar, whose faces give way to the fact that they are holding back a laugh or two. All their smile lines are showing, but no true grin has broken through. They eye me with interest, yet say nothing.

Hydvar suggests to me, "Perhaps an old type of greeting will suffice better? A tap of our blade hilts, or the neutrality of crossed blades?"

The scrawniest of the three finally lets out a bursting laugh. "So long as you don't start tapping hilts of swords, Hydvar. If that happens, Gyronawv will put you in your place. And you won't like that. But I shall enjoy watching."

Hydvar's pleasant expression turns lethal. "Sawrro!" he shouts. "Shut your vulgar mouth. Kaalon." He turns to the shortest of them. "Are you simply going to stand there, letting Sawrro think the wicked things he is?"

Kaalon frowns. "We're all tired, Hydvar. Let Sawrro be amused by his imaginings. Besides, you're the one who got the lady to accept you as night partner. I don't see the need for your complaint."

"Yes." Sawrro spits the word out. "You didn't even give us other warriors a chance to draw for the request. I had rather wished to bed her, you know?"

Hydvar puffs out a held breath. "Again, your vulgar mouth, Sawrro. This is the Son of LanSoren, standing before us. Could you find it in your heart to have even a minuscule amount of respect?"

"It's fine." I shrug, as I take my hand off my blade hilt. "A friend of mine back home says worse things. Probably needs his thoughts sanitized every hour."

Kaalon issues forth a wide grin. "Only every hour? Why, you, Sawrro, you would need it every minute. And Hydvar, here, every half-hour."

The four of us laugh together, before I ask, "And you, Kaalon? How often do wicked thoughts infect you?"

"More and more," he says. "Every day, since hearing Vitiosyns are the Onyx Victor. The notion is absurd. King ReNovak should not have let this happen."

Hydvar winces. "I hate that we were away on our two-year tour. Many of us pledged ourselves to Gyronawv, decades ago. And where were we to protect our one male Siveyra? Gone! That's where."

Sawrro's smile lines diminish. "Ayna truly meant to ask him for a partnership? I thought that was hearsay."

"There's only one Siveyra among the Onyx men?" I ask. "Isn't ReNovak a Siveyra?"

"He should be," replies Kaalon. "However, he never went through the journey. He is over a thousand years old, yet not a speck of Siveyra."

Sawrro leans closer, to whisper, "Many believe he is cursed."

Hydvar states, "For his entire rule as king, he's only had one wife; one blood heir too."

I quietly voice the name: "Prince Setharyn."

Somberly, the three of them nod.

"Given his age," Sawrro adds, "he should have many more than one. More than one wife, though not during the same space of time; but most definitely more than one heir, even if they are illegitimate."

Kaalon lets out a sigh. "Don't let us bore you with our Onyx woes. You're in line to ask ReNovak your Sodon request, aren't you? It must be your first time, seeing how young you are."

"It is," I reply, as a blonde girl strides past. Spotting her near-matching blonde wings, I exclaim, "Skylin! Wait!" I reach out for her but keep my place in line.

"Tyler!" She beams. "Look, you're much closer to the end of the line now. It won't be too much longer."

"How long have I been in line?" I ask.

"Hours." She approaches me. "Just before dusk, when it was still full light out. Don't you remember? What about that thing on your wrist? I thought it told time."

"It doesn't tell time, here," I reply, talking fast. "It tells time back home. Where are the others?"

She points to a patch of darkness, past where the pillars' light reaches. "Platform up there."

Unconvinced, I ask, "They're sitting in the dark?"

"We can see the happenings around better," she defends, as a scowl creeps into her features. "And don't get a *tone* with me."

"I'm not getting a tone," I argue. "At least, I wasn't." I glance at Hydvar. "Am I allowed to ask someone to keep my place in line, until it's my turn to make a request?"

The kindness reappears on his face. "You are. But you must return while at least eight are ahead of your fill-in."

"Your fill-in," says Sawrro, "must be someone from the company you arrived with as well."

Kaalon adds, "Or you forfeit your request of King ReNovak."

"I'm not standing in line for you!" Skylin exclaims, her wings fluffing out. They now appear big enough to belong to a male Lyre. "Really, Tyler, have you no patience at all?"

"Come on, Sky!" I beg. "Hours, I've been here. You said it yourself. Take pity on me. Let me walk around for a bit. I'll come back, well before there are only eight ahead of you."

"No!" she near yells at me, puffing her wings up further.

I huff out a loud breath. "Fine. Will you at least send Gemma over to me? Tell her to bring me some water. And food. I'm starving." I turn away, refusing to look at her a second longer.

"I'll contemplate doing so," she says. "I *was* going to bring you water. Seeing the way you're behaving, though, I'm not now."

She stomps away.

I glance at her half-hidden hips. I ask, "How old are you, Hydvar?" while refraining from another look at Skylin's retreating figure.

He stands tall and proud. "Not even thirty years away from my Siveyra Journey. I very much hope to complete it."

Kaalon shifts his weight to a different foot. "The three of us, in fact, are not thirty years away from it."

Sawrro's smile lines rush back. "We're quite excited for the prospect."

I quickly motion forward to Skylin, who's fading into darkness, then back to me. I ask Hydvar, "Does this type of interaction get any easier, as you get older?"

Sawrro peeks toward Skylin. He looks at me and shakes his head.

The other two try not to laugh, but Hydvar's the one to reply. "I'm afraid not, Ravier. Women only get more complicated as the decades, then centuries, pass on."

"More creative too," Kaalon adds, "in how they humiliate you. Reject you. Best you, with blades and magic."

Hydvar says, "Yet some become more loving."

"Perhaps," Sawrro mutters, "too loving."

"I suppose," says Kaalon, "you can be loved a little too much."

I reply, "Sure you haven't got that confused with 'wanted'?"

"Aren't they the same thing?" queries Kaalon. No emotion touches his voice. "Want and love?"

My hands are clammy, when gripping my wrist. A pang crawls across my chest. I don't want to voice what's coming to mind, but I do anyway. "Love doesn't seek its own gain, Kaalon. If you truly love someone or something, you seek to add to it. Not take away. Nor tear it down. But to build it up to be something stronger. Something good. It's what my parents used to do for each other. Then my dad died, and . . . well, I'm sure you can fill in the rest."

"You are a kind soul," says Hydvar after a minute, a sad grin on his face. "I'm honored to have met you. All of us are."

"We are, indeed," Kaalon agrees, his eyes looking dead. He seems not to appreciate my objections to his belief.

Sawrro adds, "You talk like your LanSoren. He was here for the last Sodon, you know. Gave a mighty speech. Inspired us all."

Kaalon shifts his weight again. "None more than ReNovak, though, I think."

Hesitant, Hydvar then asks, "If you find someone to stand in line for you, or after you've made your request to ReNovak, will you do a small favor for me, Tyler?"

"I'm not sure what I could do for you, but I'll give it a go."

"I hate seeing ladies sad"—Hydvar glances down—"on what is the most upheld, celebrated day for the Onyx. But Lady Rozeth despairs over a scene that happened earlier today."

Sawrro butts in, to say, "It's to do with that Siveyra Dezarin's body we brought back with us this morning. A transfer of inheritance. Dezarin never had children. Therefore, his apprentices were his heirs."

Kaalon clarifies, "More importantly, his last two apprentices."

"Ryco and Rozeth?" I ask, surprised.

Sawrro bobs his head up and down. "That's how it was *supposed* to be."

I interrupt, to say, "I don't get why his body matters. It's sad he's gone, but what are we to do?"

Kaalon further clarifies, "Siveyras hold residual power in their bodies, for up to one year past their end."

"Dezarin," Hydvar adds, "hasn't been dead for a year yet. Still had some power in his bones. That's how we were able to find him, regardless of the fact that he was buried."

"We were digging him up," says Sawrro, "when that Rozeth founds us. Attacked us, more like. Tried to kill us."

Hydvar says, "She thought we intended to desecrate his body, or deliver it to Zymarc. Can you blame her for attacking?"

"It was well known among the clans," Sawrro argues, "that our company was sent out to look for Prince Lemawr. And also to inquire after Dezarin, while we were at it. We were just doing our job. She didn't have to nearly kill five of us."

Kaalon says, "She gave them back their life force, didn't she? No harm truly done in the end."

Sawrro gets in Kaalon's face. "What would you know, Kaalon? Were you one of the five, digging up his body?"

"I was at the back, guarding the rear with several others. Is it my fault the front guards weren't doing their job of watching out for you?"

Hydvar pulls the scrawny one back. "Sawrro, if you were one Rozeth nearly drained of life, why is it you're sore over not being able to bed her? Wouldn't you rather not be in her company at all?"

Sawrro teems with anger, clawing into the fabric of his coat. "I wanted *revenge* on her, for almost wrenching the life right out of me. I wanted to win in the end, by being on top. Now I have to find someone else to get on top of, and compel into submission." He storms off.

Hydvar calls after him, "Good riddance to you, and your foul mouth."

"Why don't you go find a dragon's tail, Sawrro," Kaalon hollers. "Ride that."

"Shut up, Kaalon! You should be the one riding the tail. For I am not the one whose parents named him after King Kailon of the Vaegons, now am I?" Sawrro shouts his rhetorical question, before fading into the dark.

Hydvar laughs, nudging Kaalon's arm. "What a night that was, when we fell into a dragon's nest, eh?"

Kaalon's mouth curves slightly upward. "It was a night revealing many things to do with dragons, to be sure."

Suddenly curious, I ask, "Why were you named after King Kailon?"

Kaalon opens his mouth to answer, but Hydvar answers first. "Many Sorsryns were thankful for the Dragon Tamers taking in the Withrasyn women. It was never the people who refused them, who turned them away."

Kaalon adds, "No. It was the nobles, rulers, and other influential Sorsryns. They sent the Withrasyns on their way. My mother had a distant Withrasyn cousin, at the time the curse was laid forth. And that distant cousin of hers was one of the women let into Paragon, before it in fact had that name. My mother soon after vowed to name her firstborn son after the gracious king who helped to save the Withrasyn Clan from extinction."

Hydvar's eyes gleam, as he says, "Many Sorsryns, especially Onyx couples, named their children after notable Vaegons and their dragons. Once they got word from numerous Withrasyn sources of the hospitality of Vaegons and the tameness of their dragons, many Sorsryns vowed to name their offspring after them. Our Kaalon was named after King Kailon. The king's name was typically pronounced as *Kaalon*, but sometimes was said like *Kylon*, but never *Keelon*. For *Keelon* is the feminine version of that particular name."

I share a look with Kaalon, who coughs a bit. He afterward holds back a grin.

Hydvar keeps ranting, unaware of our lessening interest. It's as if I've hit the 'play' button on him. He must go until he's finished, and on he goes more. "Then there was the king's brother, Kristos, whose name many passed on to offspring. I was once with a *lady* named for him, Krystosa. *Y* rather than *I* in her name, for that is what most Onyx prefer for the spelling. And I distinctly recall there was a BlacKaidyn called Prelude." Narrowing his gaze on a far-off point, Hydvar seems to search his mind for the rest of the pre-recorded rant.

Kaalon takes the opportunity to add, "Yes, that was Prince Kristos's dragon. Female dragon, if the history books are correct. Didn't we train in the finer points of Gendras with a girl named Pralueday, back when we were young Onyx Warriors?"

"Yes!" Hydvar's eyes light back up. "Pralueday, the joy that comes before an important event. She was part Onyx and part Emerald, with a fraction of something else. She was one of the ones Siveyra Dezarin brought with him, for the lecture and demonstration he gave on Gendras Magic in the Hexyn Cathedral."

"With how this one talks of it," Kaalon says to me, "would you believe that happened over nine centuries ago?"

I remark, "He talks of it as if it happened just this past week."

Hydvar blushes, sheepishly looking to the ground. The 'stop' button has been pressed.

Getting serious, I ask, "Where did the lot of you find Dezarin's body?"

"In MarcKand," Kaalon replies, "near the base of the plateau."

"Not the Aeown?" I ask. "Wouldn't he wish to die near his homeland?"

"You would think that," replies Kaalon. "That's not how it was, though."

Hydvar grows restless, fidgeting with his hands. "He was missing his heart. We searched. Rozeth searched. No one found it."

"Then he was killed somewhere else," I state, "and buried in MarcKand."

"Possibly," says Kaalon. "If we weren't allied with Vitiosyns tomorrow, we could look into the matter further."

"As it is now," Hydvar says, "we'd have to petition Zymarc tomorrow, to go on another tour to find answers."

"He's not likely to allow that," I comment.

Hydvar says, "We also don't want Zymarc to know of Dezarin's death any sooner than can be helped."

I ask, "Once he knows?"

Contempt fills up Kaalon's eyes. "He'll know a great adversary of his is no more, and be bolder than ever before."

"We're none too happy for it," says Hydvar, sweat beading on his forehead. He wipes it away. "Come find us, Ravier, when you're headed over to your friends. See if you can't inspire cheer in Lady Rozeth for me. Though I asked her before her sorrowful moment, I still wish to be with her tonight."

"I'll do what I can."

Hydvar brushes his hand along my coat sleeve—the gratitude apparent in his posture, as he and Kaalon walk out of sight.

Gemma watches them leave, then approaches. "I didn't come right away, then I didn't want to interrupt your conversation. But I knew something was up with you, as soon as Skylin said you *actually* asked for food. You never ask for that; only nibble on some, if it's available. What's happened?"

Leaning closer, I whisper, "I lost several hours of time. No memory of it. I'm not sure if ReNovak was responsible, or if someone did something to the both of us. Were either one of us acting unlike ourselves?"

Gemma replies, "You said you needed to think about the conversation you and he had. So we honored that, and let you be. You got in line an hour later, and that's where you've stayed. You looked fine, though. ReNovak too. Nothing out of the ordinary."

She hands me bread, and I take it. I bite into it. Food rarely tastes this rich and pleasantly sweet.

After Gemma beckons to someone, Eli and Musgrae stride over. "I also convinced *them* to stand in line for you. You're welcome."

Musgrae pulls me out of the line, as he and Eli step into my place.

"Go on, Ravier," says Musgrae.

Eli adds, "Go stretch your muscles for a mighty bit."

Gemma lights a lantern, before indicating to a patch of darkness. "The rest of us are over this way."

* * *

Neither being Onyx nobles, nor Onyx Warriors, it takes a while for us to navigate through the packed crowds as they wait for various Onyx nobles to give them their requests. Many are denied ridiculous ones, simple ones, and on and on. Only half or less of those I overhear are given.

One request of a male Emerald to an Onyx noble is: "If I do indeed giveth over my family's named weapons, ten in number, passed down for many generations, may I be shown the inside of the Hexyn Cathedral, my lady-noble of the Onyx?"

"That is forbidden," says the female noble to the man. She hands him a small paper. "Inside the Hexyn Cathedral is only for Onyx view. You may, however, make another Sodon request of a lesser noble, tomorrow at first light, with the commoners."

Taking the paper in defeat, the man leaves the front of the line.

I take note of the cloak he wears. A trio of green colors—lime, sage, and forest green—embroidered with silver thread that forms a pattern of leaves on the fabric. If I run into him later, I mean to ask him about the ten named weapons he has to offer.

The lady-noble shouts for the next in line to approach.

Another request I overhear is from a tall, pale-skinned woman. "I have studied long and hard to earn favor, my liege-noble, and I request on this Sodon year to be given over as an understudy to one of your oldest of the old Onyx Warriors, to learn from him all he has to offer me in under a day."

The Onyx nobleman smiles. "I grant you your request, fair lady of the Silverians. Follow these directions, and wait for us to bring you your Onyx Warrior for the night." The nobleman gives her a folded-up paper, and calls for the next in line.

The last request I catch, before Gemma and I get to the others, is from a male cloaked in shimmering, blue-scaled fabric. "I have brought with me nine scaled armors and a Vardiya, in trade for a princess not belonging to anyone but the Ruler of the Deep. We know she is near. Will you make with us this trade, liege-lord Onyx of Oniva?"

Gemma stops traversing forward. So do I.

"Is that Brink?" she whispers in alarm. "Do they really have Krina?"

Because we've stopped, the crowd soon swallows us up. I only hear the noble's reply to Brinkorr: "We have not possession of her, yet we do know of her whereabouts. King Zymarc of Vitiosus obtained her. It is him you must ask. But tomorrow, in the dark hours after The Sodon, for he is not part of Clan Onyx." There's a pause, then the noble adds, "You may, however, make another Sodon request of King ReNovak, himself, before dawn's light, with those who have found favor by his nobles to do so."

The noble calls for the next in line.

Gemma and I finally arrive on the platform, overlooking all the ones standing in separate lines. I glance over the crowds, searching for Brink, even calling to him in Mensa-div. He doesn't answer.

Gemma divs, *"We'll look for him later."*

After a slight nod at Gemma, I can't help but wonder about the requests. *Is there a precise way to ensure you get what you ask for? Certain wording, for specific types of requests? And why did the noble give Brink a chance to make a request of the Onyx King, when that other man with ten weapons was thrown in with commoners by a different noble? That doesn't make sense.*

I begin to doubt that ReNovak will give me my own request, to make me the next Onyx Prince. Looking around at the others, I notice someone's missing. I ask, "Where's Ryco?"

Rozeth leaps out from the shadows in hysterics, coming into the lantern light. "Tyler! You must convince Ryco to let me give him his inheritance. Dezarin left it for us both. And, for the shortest of breaths, we shared the lingering power that remained in Dezarin's body. Then Ryco bit into my neck, forced me to take his share. I didn't want it. I *hate* him for forcing it into my veins. Please! Do something, Ravier. Talok will not command Ryco to let me—"

"Rozeth!" I shout, taking hold of her arms. "Calm down. Explain what—"

She cuts me off. "I can't calm down. I was to find Dezarin. Get him to assist us. But he's dead. I've failed the last good thing I set out to do before, well, you know what it is. Why do you let me stand here, shouting at you, Tyler?"

"Because I understand," I reply firmly. "Dezarin was like a father to you, wasn't he?"

Hydvar and Kaalon timidly climb the platform's steps, and come into our midst.

Wiping her angry tears away, Rozeth calms somewhat, managing an upward twitch of her lips meant to be a smile. It just looks as if she wishes to punch someone in the face. Probably Ryco; after that, it's a toss-up between Zymarc and whoever killed Dezarin.

I ask the two warriors: "Couldn't wait for me to come find you?"

Kaalon replies, "We saw the lantern light on the Paragonian's Platform."

Hydvar's chest heaves up and down. He's sweaty, looking much the nervous mess. "Lady Rozeth, is there anything I can do to—"

Rozeth bursts into tears, her hands cupping the front of her face to muffle her sobs.

I glance around at all the distressed expressions. Only Warren's is different. Annoyed. He pretends to read a book, divving, *"Please do something, Ravier. Ryke won't come back, until Rozeth has either left or calmed down. I don't care a jot which one you get her to do. But, if you fail, I'll be forced to drug her with some of Quall's herbs."*

"And I shall happily provide them," replies Quall, to our div.

Talok adds in div as well, *"She's driving us all mad. Even Musgrae wanted to escape her. I envy him and Eli down there, filling in for you."*

An idea comes to me, and I tell Rozeth, "You're going to write a letter to express yourself."

"A letter?" She balls her hands into fists. "That's not going to help a near whit."

"This one will." I clasp my hands behind my back.

"Fine!" she shouts. "Afterward, I shall go hunt Ryco down, tie him to a chair, and *bite* him. Show him how it feels, power being forced into his blood." She takes the paper that Ben gladly offers. "I'll have the added benefit over curiosity being satisfied, as well, to what dragon's blood tastes like. I've always wondered."

Kaalon whispers to Hydvar, "Sure you still want to be night partner to this one? . . . Partner?"

"Absolutely." Hydvar's gaze is keen on Rozeth.

I snap my fingers, imagining my father's quill appearing in my grasp. Instantly, it's there. I offer the instrument to Rozeth. "I'll tell you what the opening should be, then the first line, the last line, and the closing. The rest, I want you to imagine you're saying goodbye to Dezarin, while he's on his deathbed. Can you do that, Rozeth?"

Nodding, she takes the quill.

I start, "The opening should read: To future partner to Leira of Dysarda, father of her unborn child."

The quill scratching the paper pauses in Rozeth's hand. She looks up. "Lady Leira? Kent's mother? She is with another man, not Lokasi? I don't know who that is, Tyler."

"It doesn't matter," I tell her, but I hesitate to say what comes to me next. Regardless of how I feel, I say the words aloud. "First line: I know you, but I have never spoken to you. Familiar as my own face staring back at me. How can that be? The next part is yours, Rozeth. Tell me when you're finished." I turn and then bump into Rorka, who's cloaked in a torn, dirty, brown cloth.

"Tyler," she says, in a strained voice, "I know I'm not supposed to be here. It couldn't be helped. I felt obligated to tell you that something rather disconcerting has happened, while the newest ally of Paragon was looking at those pages. We got distracted, and the Vonsai, well . . ." She bites down on her lower lip.

"What happened?" I ask, though I don't really care to know.

"You should know," says Rorka, "that she has escaped. But, not to worry. Mekka and I found her. You're not going to like where, though."

My posture goes stiff. I force myself to ask, "Where?"

Rorka squirms in place, then she grips my neck, saying in div, *Awngeleik was let loose by the Vonsai. She and Jasper got in a horrific fight. He shredded her wings something awful, trying to restrain her, keep her from flying away. She still managed an escape. Jasper had to stay behind. But Awngeleik ran the whole way. Mekka and I could barely keep up. Then Ryco saw us. Helped to hide her. In spite of all efforts for the contrary, Awngeleik's in Oniva.*

Anger rising, my shoulders lift. My neck tenses so hard it makes my head vibrate. "You had one job, Rorka!" I shout, trying to gather my composure. I claw at my scalp. I shouldn't be so livid at Rorka, but I am.

"I know," Rorka says. "I'm sorry. But I wanted to tell you. You had a right to know what's happening back home. Didn't you? Also, that other thing you asked me to do a while back, I've not found out anything of use. Perhaps I can learn something here in Oniva."

Alarmed, Talok stands up. "What's happening at home?"

Talking faster than usual, I tell Rorka, "Yes! There's something you can do. And you must not forget anything I say. Go find the shortest line that leads up to a request from an Onyx noble. A man. Not a woman. For the lady Onyx nobles seem to be stingy to foreigners, who miss a step in the process of requesting." I stop to take a breath.

Talok's about to say something; I clamp my hand over his mouth. When he fights to pry my fingers off his face, I squeeze harder. Then I snap the fingers of my other hand.

"To sleep," I growl at him, my teeth clenched tight.

My cousin falls unconscious.

Wild-eyed, Gemma berates me, "Tyler Malik Ravier!"

I shout back, "I haven't the time, Gem!"

When she and Ben, Siege and Quall, even Hydvar and Kaalon start to make a move to do something (something about my behavior, most likely), Warren slams his book shut. "Yo!" his voice booms. "Give a brother the stage. Let him keep talking."

I go back to giving Rorka instructions. "Do you have weapons with you that Jasper has enchanted?"

"He gave me two, when I got my own Von pack."

"Good! When it's your turn to make a request, offer them to the nobleman. Call him by liege-lord. Say that you've trained long and hard to find favor, and that you request on this Sodon year, to be given over as an understudy to the former Queen of the Onyx, Ayna, to learn from her all she has to offer you in under a day." Out of breath, I just stand there, panting for air.

Talok starts coming to; Ben helps him up.

Rozeth proclaims, "Tyler, I've finished the letter."

My last speck of calm, I give to Rozeth, saying, "Last line: Ease my burdens, for they number in the thousands. Give me hope, for I've near lost it. Closing, write this: Forever in service to Paragon's new ally. Yours truly, Rozeth of the Aeown."

She writes it.

I whip my hand out toward her. "Give me the letter."

She does.

I'm so angry. So scared. So *many* things. I envision the letter reaching Lemawr this instant.

Rozeth interrupts my thoughts, to ask, "How is this new ally going to help me, in saying goodbye to Dezarin?"

I reply, "Because he was the last one to see Dezarin alive. The last to speak with him. The last to practice magic with him. For all intents and purposes, he might as well *be* Dezarin to you, in this moment."

I crunch the letter lengthwise, wringing it in my hands, imagining it turning into an arrow; then I want a bow in my grasp. They both appear, ready. I aim to the angle I think is right, and let it launch out into the night. I grip the bow so tight it bursts into embers. Then I softly play with the arrow's tail of rope-light, speaking to it, "I need this letter to him *now*." I release my hold. The arrow shoots out of sight.

"Tyler?" Skylin queries, while coming up the stairs. "Have you asked King ReNovak your request yet?"

"Not yet," I reply. "Musgrae and Eli were kind enough to hold my place in line. But there *is* something you can do for me."

She draws her wings closer to her body. "So long as it's reasonable."

I glance at her full, pink lips. She breathes faster, licking them nervously. No longer does she appear angry with me.

Before I can vent over Awngeleik's escape, or overthink the ramifications of my actions, I rush to grab hold of Skylin's waist. I pull her close. I kiss her on the mouth; she kisses back. Flashes play in my mind of King ReNovak leading me down to the enchanted room, then back out again. Then of King ReNovak, himself, hitting me over the head. He helped me up, told me to do exactly as he said, before he took me to the others. For hours, I was in a trance-like state of action.

I muse, *What didn't he want me to see, during that time? What's he hiding?*

Pulling away, breathless, Skylin divs, *"I put a tracking spell on you, in case that Onyx King didn't bring you back in a timely fashion. When you acted strange, waiting in line, I went to where he took you. Dea and I did some digging around with spells. Got in the room. All it contained was a table, chairs, and a painting of some striped dragon in flight. A title at the bottom read:* Rentwar, King of Rubidyns, by Adair Tomatsu Galloway. *Dea and I just uncovered the flash of ReNovak hitting you, while you were blindfolded. I don't think you should make a request of him, Tyler. Something's very wrong."*

I give her a quick peck on the cheek. "I feel better. Thank you, Sky.

And, vards, try not to worry so much. You'll get gray hairs." I begin the dash down the stairs.

Dea's in my way. "Sky-lin and Ty-ler. King Aygor will have your hides. He's in charge of her well-being, while Arsyn isn't here."

I state, "And neither will ever know, if you don't tell them, Dea. Take me there. After that, I have something to ask you. And, Rorka, you come too."

"What about waiting in line for a male noble?"

"That can wait."

Deamond scowls. "You're lucky I think highly of you, Ravier."

Kaalon makes his comment of, "Don't be too long."

"Your fill-ins," Hydvar adds, "are twenty out."

"Run fast," I tell Dea. "And, Warren, will you put that book down, to come do something useful?"

He slams his book shut, yet again. "Reading is useful, Ravier. Not that you would know. You're always busy, being pulled in copious directions. No wonder ya don't eat enough. Never enough time."

I state, "Just be happy I'm not Paydinn, with a Book of Time."

The four of us rush off, leaving the others utterly confused.

14

The Sodon Request

Crouched down, Dea whispers, "It's too heavily guarded, now." Several Onyx Warriors patrol by the building Dea claims has a vacant room, containing one of Adair's paintings of a dragon—King Rentwar, specifically.

I ask Warren, "What building is that?"

"Pentyn Cathedral," he mutters.

Rorka asks, "Is that five point for Pentagon, or Pentagram?"

"Either shape works," says Warren, "just matters on what the intentions are for your Enchantment Circle."

I turn away from the hedge bush we've gathered behind, trying to think of what to do.

Warren sinks down to sit on the ground. "You's going to tell me what this is about or what, Ravier?"

"Awngeleik's just outside Oniva's gate," Rorka whispers.

Warren tries to form words. None come. He's in as much shock as me. He barely blinks at all.

A commotion of shouting extends from the direction of the crowds in line; we glance there.

"That doesn't sound good," remarks Dea. "I do have an idea on how to solve your horse dilemma, though." Dea looks to us. "King Aygor has only come for Keturah. I can ask him to take Awngeleik back to Paragon, along with Ketty and Skylin. Will that suffice?"

"I like that idea." I nod.

"Mekka and I will also travel with them," Rorka adds. "They'll be as safe as is possible, given these circumstances."

When we hear the distant Equidyn's voice, chills stab into me.

Warren bolts up. "I better go help Ryke. Have Aygor come find us."

"Be careful, Warren," I plead.

"Stop your worryin', Ty." He flashes a crooked grin. "You'll get grays."

"Rorka?" I start to ask.

"On watch duty with Warren," she says. "We got this. Go on."

They jog away.

Dea and I stand up. I start to run back for the lines, but Dea catches hold of my arm.

"Hold up. We've still got a few minutes. And I wanted to tell you something earlier."

"What?" I ask, impatient on my feet.

"King Aygor brought the other piece containing the shield's power." She fans her wings out proudly, pushing her cloak aside. "He merged its magic with my wings. I've been made whole again. And your cousin can feel it. He started getting color back in his skin. But that's beside the point. I was wondering . . . do you want to use me as one of the weapons for Hexyn?"

I'm speechless, overjoyed by what she says. Yet also afraid. Fearful of performing the Hexyn Circle.

She plucks one of her longest flight feathers. Instantly, it takes on the look of metal. She offers it like blades being given to warriors, who are worthy of their country's honor. In the low light, the metal shimmers a deep violet that's akin to her eye color. I reach out to brush my fingertips along its textured, metallic surface. It's cold, though the air around us is not.

"Take it, Tyler. You may not have another chance, for we do not know if I'll be there, watching you perform the Hexyn Circle."

"You actually want me to do the Hexyn one?"

"No," she cries. "But I also think that you need to do that one. Whether it's to save him, or for something else entirely. Only the Vardiyas know. Enchantment Circles aside, will you allow me to do a quick favor for you, before you get back in that line to shove it to an Onyx?"

"What'd you have in mind?"

"Will you just trust me?" she queries.

I tell her, "With my life."

* * *

Now wearing the green ancestral cloak of King Aygor's that, come to find out, Dea won back from SynKievas in a bet before we left Paragon, I finish securing its hood in place over my head. Then I pull Musgrae and Eli out of my spot in line, trading places with them.

"Thanks for saving it." I give Musgrae's arm another squeeze, then let go of him.

"In the nick of time, Ty," Eli says.

Musgrae, in a teasing tone, adds, "Ten left ahead of us."

"I know," I grumble. "Yet I made it back, didn't I?"

Musgrae shakes his head, before saying, "We'll come down to hear your request, when it's your turn."

They leave.

My nerves are completely shot, as I think, *How will Oniva react to me? What will ReNovak say? Will I be able to keep calm, while not letting on that I know part of the truth of what he did? And what is the complete truth of what he did that I cannot recall?*

The last ahead of me approaches the cathedral's steps, a young Deathasyn by the looks of him—tall, lanky, and gray-skinned, hardly clothed at all. His eyes are burgundy-red, not scarlet.

Though he's close by, I don't catch what he asks. But ReNovak's heterochromian eyes darken over with spite, as the Deathasyn requests whatever it is.

The Onyx King replies for all nearby to hear, "I deny your request,

Deathasyn Viido's Hymn. Zymarc of Vosh-Perida is not present for any challenges, today. Come back tomorrow, to ask to be his next apprentice. However, if you wish to alter your words, you may challenge his *former* apprentice, Caleiso." ReNovak motions to a group sitting along a lighted exterior wall of the cathedral.

One, cloaked in white, stands up to remove her hood. There she is. The one I hate with every fiber of my flesh. The one I blame for all the bad that happened in Paragon. Caleiso of Vitiosus. I did not fear her presence until now. Awngeleik's not safe. She's close. Much too close to her, to me.

The Deathasyn youth subtly shakes his head, then turns away, and trails off into darkness, defeated.

I'm next. My heart beats wildly. The pressure's on. I must perform my most convincing lie. Ensuring my hood's still in place, I start the count of my steps, if only to calm myself. To focus. Twelve steps, then I'll be there at the base of the stairs. And only too soon I'm there, looking up at ReNovak.

His hands are in his pockets. Among Sorsryns, it's a mannerism I've only ever seen Zymarc do.

I am unnerved. I mentally put the metal mask on his face. Crimson-red eyes too, peering at me from above that mask. The clothes. The expressions he had, while impersonating Soren. I even imagine him without a full head of hair. It all matches, except for his height. I think, *But that could be because he hunches slightly, as him. Can he really be, though? The errand on that day, and so many other things? All a ruse? If it's true, he's mastered deception. He's cheated magic, and hurt death itself.*

ReNovak asks of me, "State your name."

"Tyler Malik Ravier."

"Where do you come from?"

"Paragon," I reply, as I try to think of what to do. *Do I still ask him such a bold thing, now? Or should I run away?*

"What is your home city?" he asks.

"Eyo'el," I state.

"Your age?"

"Fourteen."

"Race?"

"Withrasyn, Vaegon, and human."

"Occupation?"

"A student of magic," I reply, not knowing how long this is going to go on.

"Status?"

I hesitate, unsure of what he's asking. "Cousin to the King of Paragon," is what I reply.

ReNovak chuckles, at last asking the one question I wish he had started with: "And what is your request, on this year's Sodon?"

Slowly, I unclasp the Darklyrian cloak. I remove the hood. I let the green cloth fall to the ground. My coat of the Sleeping Dragon shows, for all in view of me to see.

Boldly, I begin, "I ask that, if I have found favor in sight of the Vardiyas—not simply an Aysivak of Vosh-Perida—that you name me the next Onyx Prince. That I might aspire to deserve the Blades of Neutrality: Enyxar and Aevimeis. That, with them, I might set trapped souls free." I bow my head, then bend down on one knee in reverence, unsure of how I look after Dea trimmed my hair.

When I look up, I know I must sound and appear different, for ReNovak has startled back a few steps from where he stood. His hands are tightly clenching the front of his coat. His breaths have become shallow.

"Come approach," he commands, "but stop on the landing just down the way from me."

I do as he bids, standing taller than I feel inside.

"Many have told me," states ReNovak, still breathless, "of that day, in Paragon. That Soren asked of you, what you saw. Zymarc, himself, has stated that you thought you were Soren. Or, at least, like him. Do you still believe that?"

I ask in return, "Who's requesting of whom, now?"

Having gathered composure again, ReNovak coldly says, "Do not test me. Not when I'm up here, a king, and you're down there, nothing but a brazenly bold child."

"I'm a lot more than that." I scowl at him.

"Prove it." He makes a quick, harsh gesture around us. "A command to tell the truth. Truth admitted, for all of Oniva to hear. Do you accept? For you must be tested, if you are to become an Onyx Prince."

"I don't want to be an Onyx Prince," I state. "Rather, the very one, as if I were a blood heir. Your rightful heir. If you agree to that term, then I accept the testing."

ReNovak points to the marble landing that he stands upon. "Come before me, and let us begin."

Eleven steps, then a twelfth. I'm there.

When he puts his hand on my forehead, I gasp. It hurts.

Voice reverberating, he states, "A command to tell the truth."

He lets go, and the air around forces me to kneel.

ReNovak calls out, "Sorsryns of Oniva, this one has asked to be our next Onyx Prince. A blood heir prince. My rightful heir. And he is able, as he is one-quarter the other half of us: Withrasyn. As well as nobility, cousin to a king. Three times, I shall ask him of his beliefs of himself. Three times, he *must* tell the truth. For he is bound by magic now."

Numerous, hurried movements rustle from behind. Then everything goes silent.

I manage to say, "I'm ready."

ReNovak starts by asking, "Citizen of Eyo'el, in your heart, who are you?"

"Tyler Malik Ravier, only child to LanSoren of Trauvo."

He asks, "Son of LanSoren, whom do you believe you are?"

"A legend made flesh, keeper to the Sleeping Dragon aura."

ReNovak puffs out a breath. There's hesitation. He then asks the third question, "Sleeping Dragon, whom do you wish to be?"

"I desire to become the next Prince to the Onyx, keeper to the Blades of Neutrality. To be an upholder to the Laws of Magic."

After a time, ReNovak says, "You may rise."

Standing, I look upon the Onyx King.

"You are found true," he states. "For the title, you are good enough."

Ayna is nearby, holding the blades still wrapped up like a package.

"All that is left," says ReNovak, "is for you to take hold of the blades, see if you can bend them to your will, to obey you, conform to you, assist you in your time of great need."

I smile, remembering Madeleine's last statement before her memories faded. *When the time is right, you will see Rentwar.* I think, *She knew, before, that this would happen. That he'd be bringing those blades to Oniva. I wonder how Rentwar even got hold of them, though.*

Ayna unwraps the package. Long, straight blades are revealed. They glisten, akin to something new. Perfectly symmetrical to each other, their etched metal is a dark silver, their sharpened edges bright. Their blade hilts are wrapped with black leather, and equal parts bronze, steel, and copper make up the pommel. The guard of each blade appears as an eye—the outer circle is of oiled bronze; the inner one must be of steel; and polished, golden bronze creates the pupil.

While observing the blades, I can't help but be reminded of Soren's words: *beginning, end, and everything in-between.* Enyxar and Aevimeis, symbolic of the end and the start; Eyo'el and Sivondel, entities of life and death; and my own daggers—RotaSyn and NeiSator—could be the in-between.

I wonder, *Am I the in-between? Not a place, but a person, wielding merely half the power I'm meant to have?*

Ayna's face seemingly contains a light that comes from within. She stands in front, offering me the blades. "Take hold of your inheritance, Onyx Prince."

Obeying, I grip the hilts. I lift the twin set. They are heavy. Forged for a man to lift, or a warrior to wield. I realize I'm neither one yet. When their hilts conform to a fraction of my grip, however, confidence replaces doubt.

Resolved, I think, *I must do this. I must accuse the Onyx King of being false.*

I ask of King ReNovak, "As your Onyx Prince, am I allowed to ask something of you, mighty ReNovak of Nyxane, Second Son of Aygawnax?"

"You are." He grins in pride.

Approaching to stand in perfect alignment at the front of him, sudden strength comes upon me, and I pound the blades into the marble landing, then step forward. "A command of truth!" I shout. "Are you Zymarc, cheater to the Laws of Magic?"

The crowds gasp. Some shout. Many rush forward. Warriors leap down from the roof pitches of the cathedral, to stop them. Gyronawv, himself, is on the landing, ensuring that Caleiso and the other nobles do not leave. Ayna stands by, as would an elegant lady undaunted by it all. She merely watches in anticipation.

Green flames wisp off me. Also do they wisp off the Blades of Neutrality, still embedded in the marble. The Onyx King falls to his knees. He mentally fights me, tries to resist. It's then that the Sleeping Dragon coat catches fire, burning away. It re-forms itself beside me, empty. The Prismatic of Magic ignites on both hands, racing up my arms like fine strokes of paint. I reach for my coat. But the coat floats around, and a form slowly fills it to its full size. He stands behind the trembling King ReNovak, who's been forced to kneel. I recognize his wicked grin. I'd know it anywhere. It's not Soren's, but mine.

It's me, only older, coming to take the Blades of Neutrality out of the landing. Their green fire goes out. He crosses them in an X and then aims them at ReNovak's throat. "A command of truth, Onyx. Are you?" He pauses to laugh. "Are you a cheater of magic, King ReNovak?"

The Onyx King can't help himself. He must reply, "Yes."

"Then I shall cheat too!" he proclaims, rushing closer to the cathedral. He cuts into its black brick, a circle, various curves and sharp angles contained within it. It's to one side of the front tower. He runs to the other side, cutting a different symbol there.

The people around sound utterly terrified and confused. I'm not far behind them. But I also admire the expertise with which this older-me performs all movements. He whispers words unclear, and seems to dance with the intensity of feeling that Vitiosyns did in the Dance of Death, yet pure light is held in his features rather than darkness.

"These are for setting the Onyx free," he calls out. "As it was not for Soren and Adair to kill Zymarc, some centuries ago, it is not for me to free all Onyx. That is for another." He strides to the edge of the landing, to face Oniva. "*But* it is for me to end Vitiosus forever." He lifts the blades above his head, crossing them in the Sign of Neutrality. They light with green fire, once again. He shouts, "It is for me to defeat Zymarc of Vitiosus!" He bangs one blade against the other. The sound echoes out.

The crowds in Oniva shout. I turn to face them. Hands are lifted. Weapons are pointed to the night sky. The people cheer. Not just Onyx. Sorsryns of the other clans join in too. Even Deathasyns not garbed in rags, but rather, clothed as nobility. Talok and the others stare up, mesmerized by who I will become. Only two do not look to him, but, rather, to me. Gemma and Ryco. Awngeleik's there with them.

She screeches her Equidyn call, and the crowd's reverie breaks. Those near her, back away in fright. She approaches the stairs, looking to the older-me, while letting her shredded wings droop on the ground and then the stairs as she starts to climb. Her hooves clack on the marble steps, sounding sluggish and heavy. I hear them as if they're in my head. So loud.

Lowering the blades, my older self speaks, "Krim Karasa dim drim. I am him. Ravieras Savak Kavas. Soon. To ruin. To doom. Laevarye, there is a time to die."

Awngeleik's wings heal, and she shifts into her silvery-black, demon form.

He continues, saying, "When calls the darkness, I will be there to find it. To bind it to light. To defeat it forever. For I am the Sleeping Dragon. May the patience of Vons be with me. Might the strength of a dragon's first flight lift me. Give me the will and wings, to rise above the many oceans of death." He reaches out to Awngeleik. "Come," he hums. "Equidyn, let me send you home, for the younger-me can only handle so much."

He grins wickedly at me.

My breath catches in my throat.

Awngeleik's on the lower landing.

He snaps his fingers, and the sound of glass cracking fills me with dread. I look down at my wrist. The crystal face of the diver's watch has fractured; Awngeleik has simply disappeared in a puff of smoke and embers.

He shrugs at me. "It was only going to be a distraction. In time." He snickers. "It will be fixed. Until then, oh well." He strides to be an arm's length away. "Now I shall ask what you are not strong enough to ask a second time. A command for a king to tell the truth."

My older self aims one blade toward ReNovak, who tries to catch his breath. "Are you, King ReNovak, in fact, Zymarc in disguise?"

ReNovak doesn't answer.

Older-me continues, "If you are not, rise up. Go confess before your people what you have done."

In agony, ReNovak grimaces. He stands up to approach the edge of the landing, His confession begins. "I am not Zymarc of Vitiosus. I'm not a servant to Vitiosus at all. But I'm guilty, nonetheless. For I cheated magic, to bring about a blood heir: Setharyn. I was young, and I could not wait for the Onyx to be free. I must confess, we are not free because of me. Because I could not wait a hundred years for the Vardiyas to send us the Onyx Prince, bearing their mark upon his head. More importantly, their power in his veins. And, now . . . we've waited hundreds of more years. It is my fault we are still slaves to the Laws of Neutrality." ReNovak collapses on the landing, bitterly weeping. "Please, forgive me."

Leaning down to me, my older self shakes the blades twice. "You, Ravieras-Savak, stand strong. Aspire to deserve these, for they are not yours yet. Free the girl, and free yourself. Take up the Shield of Shylen, for she is an all-consuming power. Not a commoner. Even if you strike her, she rises again and again. Redeem your Midnight Anemone, or all will be lost." He offers the hilts. "Goodbye, Ravier."

I take hold of the hilts, and he slowly turns to embers. The green ancestral cloak is folded up neatly where he stood. The coat re-forms, and creeps its way back onto me. Turning, I see the crowds kneeling, their heads bowed. I'm overwhelmed, as I look around. When I spot a sad, dark-haired girl standing with the nobles near Caleiso, my heart melts. Keturah's trying to be strong, but tears still trickle down her pale cheeks.

After picking up the garb, I aim a blade tip in Caleiso's direction. "I'll challenge any who stand in my way of placing Keturah of RawZend back in the care of her loving king and guardian, Aygorinaith."

Gyronawv states, "Such a duel must be a duo's duel of offense and defense."

Taking out her cruel, curved daggers, Caleiso grins. "I'll accept that duel of duos. Prince Azabahk will be my defense. Who is to be yours?"

"Deamond of RawZend." I lower the aimed blade, as I look to where Dea stands amidst the Paragonians. I toss the green cloak to her, and she flies up enough to catch it.

Gyronawv announces, "In the arena, you may begin this duel."

15

A Duo's Duel

The arena we're in is at least twice the grandeur of the vast one in RawZend's city of Grevagg. All of Oniva and its visitors are seated in I know not how many main levels. Peoples of numerous races and cultures stand, anticipating what's to come: a duel of duos for the possession of the King's Ward Keturah. She's up on the king's balcony with ReNovak, Ayna, Gyronawv, and the three warriors I met in line. Talok's also among them. But not King Aygor.

Caleiso has removed her cloak, and I, my coat. The extra layer of protection isn't allowed for the primary contenders of the two teams. Dea, however, is allowed to keep on the ancestral garb.

Gyronawv calls out to the four of us, "Discuss with your partner, a strategy. When ready, go to the center."

I turn to Dea. "Should I go with the Onyx blades, or my daggers?"

Dea, first stretching her wings, then her other limbs, replies, "Which feel better in your grasp?"

"The daggers."

"Then go with those. What I know of duo duels, there are three rounds, unless said otherwise. After each one, you may switch out weapons. But not during. The third round, they may alter rules, before you begin. It forces you to adapt fight styles."

"What spells should I try? I only know elementals. How about we

197

count this as practice for the Enchantment Circle?"

"Good idea. Let's start out slow. White spells should be easier for you, since you're part Withrasyn. I don't know Vaegon magic. So we'll leave that out. Compression is a good one. It can act like a third hand in combat. Speak *Spizatio* after your gaze has pinpointed where you want this Caleiso to be crushed. Add an *S* at the end, if you want it to squeeze harder. It'll use more magic, though. And, remember, you're not allowed to outright attack Azabahk. If you hit him while he's trying to shield her, you must pause for one second, before continuing."

I look ahead to my opponents, resolving in my heart to win. "Give me one more spell to try."

Dea replies, "Caleiso might try to chain you with an Onyx spell: Vinklayem. It burns like you wouldn't believe. In case I don't get to you in time to break it, speak the Withrasyn spell: Yodeshyn. It's meant to free of restraints. Works on elemental vines and other things too. Ready for round one?"

"No. But we'll begin anyway."

We approach the center; Dea and Azabahk don't go all the way, however.

Head held high, Caleiso declares, "This time, I will crush you. Humiliate you. You're not that older version of yourself yet, Ravier. You are still ignorant, weak, and inexperienced. Years, I've prepared for duels such as this. Training since I could walk to win wars. I gave you the chance to go home. Yet you refused. How were the poisoned stores?" She sneers at me.

I clench my teeth. I must not reply. Must not let on how confident I'm becoming in myself. I must appear calm. I must be as a Von, waiting for the perfect stroke to strike to win Keturah back for King Aygor.

We ready our stances.

Ayna calls out, "The Minor-Pristines may begin."

Unlike before, I'm the first one to strike and jab.

Caleiso's stronger than she was, less hesitant than before. She has a speed she didn't possess in Soren's Library. I also am not the same as I once was.

We cut into each other rather badly.

Our defense partners are there to restrict our bleeding with spells, even to heal the skin completely some of the time.

When Caleiso shouts, "Vinklayem!" red-hot chains form from the air near me.

They wrap around my upper body, and I scream from the searing pain.

In div, I speak, *"Yodeshyn!"*

The chains break.

Caleiso steps back, surprised.

I rush her.

We go and go, wearing the other down.

A loud snap rings out.

Caleiso stops, mid-swing at my head. But RotaSyn's tip already pricks at her neck ever so slightly.

"A stalemate," Gyronawv announces. "Talk with your partner. Prepare for the second round."

Dea and I jog out of earshot from the other two.

I try to catch my breath. The pain stings sharply. My arms tremble. I drop the daggers.

Dea grabs both my wrists tightly. "Try to relax," she instructs. "I need to replenish your Mazhrein a bit."

Blowing breaths in and out, I try to do as she says. Slowly, the pain dulls to an ache akin to the soreness after a long, hard run.

"Forget Spizatio," says Dea. "You need something stronger than that. She's toying with you, only using half her potential. You need to break her. Here's three Black spells to try: *Tasawn* for blind, *Dayellos* for weaken, *Jextowan* for confusion. Time that last one right, and you'll get her to hit her man, Azabahk. She'll be required to pause for a second. You can do this, Ravier. I believe in you. Let's go again."

I stride back to the center in confidence. I breathe hard, not because I'm tired, but because I'm ready for a real fight. Caleiso's crimson-red eyes tell me she's ready for that too. The first round was spent feeling each other out. Now we're each ready to destroy the other.

We're merely an arm's length apart.

"Begin!" Gyron shouts.

Flicking my daggers to point downward, I shout, "Tasawn!"

A blank look crosses Caleiso's features.

I cut deeply into the flesh of one of her arms. She cries out, dropping one dagger. I kick it away.

Caleiso bolts. She looks this way then that. Azabahk chases her down to heal the blindness. She gets her sight back, as I pace around nearby, waiting.

I think, *It's my turn to toy with her.*

Smiling, I glance at her neck, and speak another word: "Spizatio."

She chokes, clinging to her one dagger, while grabbing at her neck with her other hand.

Fighting that off, she rushes to set the ground on fire beneath me.

Dea pushes me to the ground, rolling me, then covering me with her wings. She chokes the fire out. The ancestral garb protects most of her.

I cough from inhaling smoke; also, from the smell of burnt feathers. My lungs burn. Dea shoves me back into the fray of the fight. I scarcely keep my balance.

When Caleiso casts something else, I lose that balance entirely. The world spins as if I've drunk some spiked Farivoo. I collapse on the ground. It takes intense focus simply to keep sitting upright. Mouth dry, and panting, I manage to speak another word, as Caleiso comes to cut me up. "Dayellos."

She trips, then falls flat on the dirt. She claws her way for me, her arms trembling in fatigue. Once close enough to strike me, she shakily raises her dagger, screaming in effort.

I pant out each breath, only focused on not passing out.

The snap sounds out.

Caleiso yells in anger, letting her body collapse.

I collapse back too.

Our partners come assist us up.

"Another stalemate," ReNovak calls out this time. "You are now permitted to use Death spells, simply not to their full strength. Also, your defense becomes secondary offense. Do not waste the opportunity."

Dea and I trudge away to discuss a strategy. She works on healing me, as we talk.

All huffy about it, she says, "That Caleiso paired *Hathaysa* with *Idawn*. Imbalance with lethargy. You did good in not instantly passing out, Ravier."

"Tell that to my body. It hurts all over."

"I know. There's just one more round. And now I can fight beside you. Pity we can't use Kyanistic or Geldryn spells. They'd have to expel more magic, in defense against them. It's frightfully fun using Volisos—levitate. At first, opponents think it's Hathaysa. Once they've realized they're wrong, it's often too late. There are rather vile Death spells we need to watch out for, though. That Azabahk must know a nasty lot. Best all-around defensive spell is *Deflamo*. Make it plural, if you get too worried."

"What Death spell should I try?" I ask, now able to stand without the world spinning round.

"Easiest to get right," she says, "is blood tears: Sareustranen. Victims bleed from their eyes, and their heads become ridden with searing pain, leaving them unable to think. Ready?"

"Not quite." I tell her, "I want to start this round with something that'll make them afraid. Or, at the very least, uneasy. When's the last time you were dispatched?" I grin like a devil.

She laughs. "Days *and* days ago."

"After Skylin taught me some dance steps," I state, "we saw Grawllik. He said you're something wild, after waking from being dispatched." I hold up RotaSyn and NeiSator. "Which one do you want plunged in?"

She glances at NeiSator. "That one. Have I permission to take up these other blades of yours, Onyx Prince?"

"Definitely. Let's start."

She takes up Enyxar and Aevimeis; their edges briefly flicker with green embers.

Side by side, Dea and I go to the center.

So do Caleiso and Azabahk.

"Begin!" ReNovak shouts.

Whirling to face Dea, I stab her in the chest with NeiSator. I yell out a war-like cry, as it happens.

The crowd screams in horror. Some join the war cry. All soon grow silent.

I quiet down too, only to let out a little chuckle. I pretend to be Soren. I slide the blade out, Dea's blood on its edge. After sweeping my fingers over its flat part, I pretend to lick Dea's blood off my fingertips, then wipe the blood on my face and neck. It heats up where I've streaked my flesh with her blood. I laugh maniacally, looking at my two opponents.

Caleiso and Azabahk *were* about to attack. But they're frozen. Horrified, they only gawk at me.

Power emanates within my chest, rushing in my veins. I walk forward, and Caleiso seems to grow smaller. I realize, however, that I'm the one growing taller. My steps sound as metal, drumming on the ground. Yet my movements are fluid, as if in water. I'm weightless, seeming suspended in the air, though my feet touch the ground. That green fire wisps off my skin, and the Prismatic of Magic ignites, painting across both hands then arms.

My voice deeper, I shout, "Come fight me, Caleiso!"

Dea revives right then, screeching and screaming. Her wings are that metallic-purple, not looking like soft feathers at all. She flies upward, then lands hard beside Azabahk. They begin their battle. The Prince-General has well met his match. Perhaps, even, his superior. It's a blood bath between the two.

Caleiso, in possession of both her daggers, slits her own wrists, and speaks a string of words, "Vitiosus-sev-dev-Gree-awleis." Hissing the end sound, she, too, grows to appear older, looking like a woman. A warrior. My equal in a fight.

We begin.

On and on, it goes. We cut and jab and kick, casting elemental spells to throw the other off. It's as a dance. We're trying to best the other, while also attempting to impress.

The crowds drum their feet in the stands. Some clap to the beat of our rhythm. Occasionally, deep horns sound out, shaking the surroundings still more. The ground quakes from them, from us. It's thunderous. Yet no thunderstorm I've heard is this boisterous. No event before compares to the sound, the feeling, the sight.

My only wish is that my father could be here to see it. Me, fighting with expertise to save an innocent soul from being a pawn.

In a flash, Caleiso's eyes turn pure-black.

I'm thrown off balance, my body turning ice-cold seemingly from within.

"Dea?" I div. *"I need an ice counteract."*

Dea gets away from Azabahk long enough to assess me. She divs, *"She's cast* Sareusprine, *that is: blood cool. She's freezing your blood, for hypothermia. Cast its opposite on yourself.* Sareustriavas—*blood heat."*

Azabahk restarts his attacks, and Dea's unable to help more.

Unsure how to cast a spell on myself, I wonder, *What if I'm like that young dyn in Paragon, clawing at the ground, so anxious for his first dragon's flight that I use too much magic and overheat my body?*

My arms have grown stiff with cold. It's hard to move. I figure, I must touch a hand to my wrist. My right hand—the weaker one—to the wrist of my dominant side, the left.

This older Caleiso circles me, reveling in her work.

My lungs burn, as if breathing in winter's freezing-cold air. I hold my breath. There's no one to help in this moment. I'm on my own. I close my eyes, unwilling to accept defeat. I imagine my heartbeat warming my insides back up. I think with all I have left, one word: *Sareustriavas.*

I have not enough magic to say that one again. Thinking of Aysivak, I plead, *Please work!*

Caleiso comes to prick my neck with her daggers. "I like you on your knees," she says, in a sharp voice. "I shall now do what my master, Zymarc, has bid. To mark you for death. For Sivondel." She slowly adds, "For you will keep Sivondel eternally satisfied. And, when you are dead, Zymarc will use your body—the Onyx Prince's body—to seal Vitiosus forever, so that it may never end. So that it may never be defeated. So that it may become the sixth particle, to join the five magics in the air. Vitiosyns will become a new clan, the ninth clan. They shall rise above the rest. Yet you won't be here to see that, for you'll be dead, feeding the Vitiosyn Circle forever."

I gasp. I try to cry out. This cannot happen. This should never be. I must fight. I must rise.

Although my breaths are ragged, I manage to say, "You will not do this."

My body warms up, and I speak the words I'm sure will work, "NeiSator, Vinklayem!"

NeiSator rises from the ground by itself, waving around in the air. It slashes in the direction of Caleiso, and a glowing, golden-orange whip wraps round her body and flings her around a bit, before releasing her. She spirals away, smashing against the arena's lower wall.

Rising, I run toward her. I pick her up from the ground by her neck. Choking her, I gaze into her dark, hateful eyes. "I am a legend made flesh. You will not use my body for such vile things."

Her black eyes fade to crimson-red, then slowly to the heterochromian colors of one blue and one green.

Struggling, she becomes smaller, returns to the thirteen-year-old Callie of Dysarda again. "Please, Ravier!" she begs.

I deem it as deception. I'll not be a fool again. I hiss the word: "Sareustranen!" Then I tell her, "For red belongs in your eyes."

She screams in torment. Blood tears run down her face. Her body convulses. She barely gets out her next words of: "Don't be a demon of death. But a demon of light."

Those words call to me, seemingly from afar. It's as if I've heard them before. Yet I know not where. Regardless of where I heard them, they soften my heart. I release her, and she falls limply to the ground, wheezing.

I turn away and spot Dea just finishing her bite of Azabahk's neck. He lies motionless, as if dead.

A snap sounds again.

ReNovak announces, "The Citizen of RawZend and the Onyx Prince have won."

Oniva and The Sodon visitors roar with cheers.

Dea comes to me, her grinning face covered in Azabahk's blood. "You did it, Tyler."

"*We* did," I correct her. "Go retrieve Keturah, soon. Travel with the other Lyres, and Greyvons, back to Eyo'el. Wait there. Be the shield to my home."

"I will, Ravier," she cries, overwhelmed. "You get that Hexyn to work. Bring them both back with you, from MarcKand."

Exhausted, I collapse. Dea lowers herself to prop my upper body up so that I'm not lying flat on the ground.

Feeling myself getting small again, I look up at her, to say, "I couldn't have done it without you. Thank you for believing in me."

16

To New Beginnings

The exit out of the arena is a task in and of itself. Many unfamiliar faces show expressions of pride and gratitude, even sheer awe of us. I lean on Dea, during our exit. She knows I'm very spent from it all. Gyron is some distance ahead, leading a team of Onyx Warriors along. They clear our way. One of those warriors holds a torch. He steadily pushes the crowds back, but he keeps pausing his task to look at me. Talok and the others are farther beyond him, standing there, waiting.

My cousin catches sight of Dea and me. He comes to grip me by the shoulders. "Tyler!" he shouts above the noise, laughter in his voice. "That was incredible. Come. We'll help you get cleaned up to dine with the Onyx. We want you looking stately, when you go before King ReNovak. He requests an audience with you."

The noise increases too much to catch anything else he says. He tries divving more conversation to me, but my head hurts too much for that. Dea shouts something. Talok nods at her. He leads the way out from the crowds who linger around the arena's exterior.

Once out of that loud throng, I still can't hear much of anything—only the static, ringing in my ears. Though I lean on Dea, I stumble. I fall to the ground. I try to push myself up, but my limbs shake too much. They've no strength left in them.

Not missing a beat, Ryco scoops me up off the ground as my dad used to do when I fell asleep on the couch in the living room while watching my favorite TV show. I'd wake for a brief moment, long enough that I saw his expression of love for me. I see that look in Ryco's face now, only displayed differently. His expression is stern yet stoic; his yellow-colored eyes brighten to look like the morning sun cresting over the horizon.

My body is near limp in Ryco's grasp. My legs are draped over one of his bent arms, and my feet dangle down past that. My arms, I have folded up close against my chest. I find comfort in resting. Even comfort in the scent of pinesap, which Ryco always seems to emit when he's either mad or scared or . . . something like that. My thoughts swirl, unable to determine the exact meaning of things.

During Ryco's long strides to wherever, he takes a moment to glance down at me. His mouth twitches. Then he looks straight ahead. "You did well, Ravier," he says. "Although you've work to do on your form, and the quickness with which you cast spells could be improved upon too, you're better than most I've witnessed in a duo's duel."

"I say brav-voh!" Eli whoops.

Many in the group chuckle. I haven't any energy left for that. I fall asleep in Ryco's hold, to the sound of them—the Paragonians and Rozeth, the Darklyres and Rorka—all chatting of their favorite part of The Sodon so far. I start to wish Awngeleik was here. I very much want her company. My dad's Equidyn. I wonder what she's doing right now in Paragon, after being sent back from Oniva.

* * *

Sometime later, I startle awake at sensing Awngeleik's loud screech in my head. It's exactly like that first time I was awoken by her, in the middle of the night. I halfway expect to be in my room, on my twin bed, under the cozy covers. I look to the side of me, where my nightstand would be. I even reach for it, for my alarm clock. It isn't there. Neither are there. Only Warren's there, reclining on a fabric-covered chaise.

207

"Yo, Ravier," he says, closing the book in his hands. "Did the two-hour nap help ya out?"

I stretch out on the long couch. Amazingly, my body doesn't ache. Just a little sore. "Yeah," I reply, as I cover a yawn that forces its way to the surface. I glance around the grand room we're in. Soft light lets me see the ones gathered in here. My fellow Paragonians. No one else. Eight King's Guard and Talok. But then I spot Brinkorr. He approaches.

"Are you now a prince, twice over, Tyler?" he asks, managing a smile though his eyes are full of defeat.

Sitting up, I make myself stand before this Laykonian. "I don't believe so, Brinkorr. Just one prince. How did Krina get kidnapped?"

As Brink tells me, I look over the clothes I wear. They've been cleaned and straightened. I glance at Warren. He opens his book back up, and covers the view of his face with it, pretending to read.

"We waited for a time," says Brink, "before braving a trip to the surface. Krina was supposed to stay down in Deivahl while we resupplied up top. But, being Krina, she didn't listen."

"Why didn't King Lemara come for The Sodon?" I ask. "Why'd he send you to ask after Krina?"

Brink explains, "I did my fair share of traveling around with Prince Lemawr, many centuries ago. Though the land has changed much since last I ventured out from Deivahl's shoreline, I still know it well enough to find my way around. Lemawr and I used to make the journey to Oniva so often, we could navigate it while blindfolded. King Lemara, however, has hardly ever left Deivahl. Never had a reason to."

As I listen to Brink carry on, I glance at my clothing again, then over to Ben. He looks away in guilt to Musgrae. Musgrae sharpens his weapons, seeming to ignore all else. I start a stroll about the room, smelling the various soaps and potions set within mirrored, golden trays, before feeling the many small, odd objects laid out for occupants to look at or touch. On glossy, wooden, sideboard tables, all these little things find respite, not a speck of dust upon anything. Partway through my stroll, Eli joins in. Quall quietly chortles at us, giving a slow shake of his head. He sits in a large rocker made of dark wood, whilst he sips from a steaming mug of brewed herbs. Kent is near him, also drinking from a mug. Ryco and Siege sit at a table, playing a game of cards. Capture the Wolf, Free the Dyn, most likely. Talok switches between watching their game, listening to Brink, and looking at me. Through it all, my cousin's expression remains blank.

When Brinkorr pauses, I set down a bottle of cologne, and ask, "Do you wish for me to get Krina back for Lemara?"

Brink lets out a held breath. "Onyx Princes, I tell you, you never can tell what they are thinking. Lemawr was much the same. And he told me that a certain Setharyn was as well."

I hold back a grin. "Is that your way of saying yes?"

"Yes, Prince Ravier. Bring back our Krina." Brink collapses on the same couch that I napped on minutes ago. "Even if that means taking her to Paragon, we will come to get her. Or, rather, *I* will. Broena's likely to murder the girl, upon retrieving her. She's livid with the princess, for disobeying instructions. Lemara's distraught enough too, he hasn't had time to delve into that journal you left behind."

I knock on one of the sideboard tables' surfaces. "Consider it done, Brink." I look to the others, Ryco and Talok, specifically. "Shall we go dine with King ReNovak? I assume the invitation still stands?"

"It does," says Talok, sounding worn-out.

Brink asks, "Mind if I remain in this room of yours? I've had quite the long journey on foot."

"Course ya can!" Warren bellows out, as he bolts up from the chaise. "Here! You's can even read my book. Borrowed it from one of the archives of Oniva. That was my Sodon request. To borrow a book for a day. Might as well share it." Warren looks at me. "That Skylin's already read half of it. Did so while waiting for us to clean you up, Ravier. I had to pry it from her greedy, little hands. And I thought *I* loved reading books." He pats his chest, looking around, as Brink pages through the book. "Has anyone seen my—"

Eli throws a quill at Warren. When it hits the Veldarian on the chest, ink splatters to make a mess of Warren's white coat.

Warren throws his head back in dramatics. "Ee-lie!" he yells. "Do you know how long ink stains take to remove?"

Ben raises his hand. "I know that answer," he says. "An hour."

"Yeah! An hour. *One* hour, little Kirjan," Warrens spits out.

"I don't get what your deal is, War." Eli lifts his shoulders up in innocence. "You just want to stay in here and read your book, don'tcha? I've given you a good excuse to stay behind. You should be grateful."

Musgrae has ceased sharpening weapons. He scratches at his throat. His mouth parts open. But then he decides against interrupting the altercation. He instead puts his things away carefully.

Warren makes a move to grab Eli. The skinny Kirjan darts out of reach.

Not holding the book anymore, Brink taps his fingertips together, curiously observing Warren and Eli. Then he snaps his fingers. Warren's thrown to the ground, his breaths hammering out. A frightened squeal escapes Eli as he cowers away from the Laykonian, who's suddenly standing near him.

"Ink stains are easy," says Brink, bending down to brush his scaly-skinned hand over the stain upon Warren's coat.

Brink stands back. The stain starts to glimmer as if wet. Drops form. The black liquid pulls away from the fabric. Suspended in the air, it then races its way back into the quill.

Ben's eyebrows lift. "After we're back from dinner, you must show me how that trick works."

Warren stands up, looking his coat over in skepticism.

"Certainly," says Brink, taking up Warren's book once again. "But you'll not have the same ease of it as I do. Water—in fact, any liquid—is more obedient to Laykonians than it is to other races. Lemawr never had as easy of a time of it as me. At least you may now make it to dinner, Warren of Veldar, and looking quite sharp, I might add, in that black-edged, white coat of yours."

Warren claps Brinkorr on the back. "Thanks to you, Brink. Want us to bring some food back for ya?"

"Whatever pleases you," says Brink, before lounging down on the couch.

Quall firmly sets his mug down on the coffee table in front of him. "Let us be off to dinner, then."

We follow Quall out the door and down a long, dimly lit hallway.

We are passing by many doors on both sides of the hall, when I ask Talok, "Where are we?"

"The inn that Ayna and some warriors led us to," he replies, walking beside me.

Quall adds, "They were going to have us stay in one of the cathedrals meant for Onyx royalty, but we didn't think you'd like that. Being treated like a prince and all."

"Were we wrong?" Siege asks from somewhere behind me.

I shake my head. "No. You got it right. Plus, Rorka would have a harder time avoiding a certain Onyx Warrior."

"True," says Talok.

Ryco, in stride with Quall, stops at one of the doors. He knocks. It flies open.

Skylin rushes out. "Is Tyler awake yet? Is he okay?"

"I'm fine, Sky," I call out. "And, before you start doing that thing you do, can you do me a favor?"

She's already at my side, eyeing me up and down to be sure that I didn't lie; that I truly am all right. Before she answers me, Gemma marches out through the doorway all tense.

"Don't you dare agree to his favors, Skylin." Gemma scolds me with her gaze. "Tyler has a bad habit of getting you to owe him favors. One favor becomes three. Then he *cheats*, and gets an extra favor without you realizing it. Don't you, Onyx Prince?" She purses her lips in mockery, even bobbling her head side to side.

I fake a pompous attitude. "Well, if you hadn't been such a Rich Witch with everything, I never would have gotten the opportunity for favors, now would I, Gem?"

I offer her my arm like a gentleman, though my smile feels more wicked than ever. Gemma's pursed lips crease further with rage. She stomps toward me. I fear she's going to slap my face, wipe the grin clean off it. So I soften my look in her direction, and it's her scowl that's wiped clear away.

Gemma rolls her eyes. She complains, "I despise you, and your stupid grin, Tyler. Or should I say, Ty-Ty?"

She smirks, as she hooks her arm with mine. Her fingernails dig in; I ignore the action, pretending to have won.

Dea pokes her head out of the room. "Are the two of you quite finished? Can I talk now?"

Ryco smirks. "Jump in at any time."

"Skylin is to go with you," Dea says. "King Aygor and I are staying with Ketty for a bit. We'll be along later. And, Ryco, will you send back a letter, giving us directions to the King's Hall?"

"Already thought of that." Ryco takes a few steps toward Dea to hand her an envelope. "The walk's about forty minutes, if the way is clear. Be there before midnight. None are allowed admittance to the hall after that."

Dea flutters her wings a little. "So it's fifteen minutes to fly there. Got it!" Her violet eyes tease him.

Looking embarrassed, Ryco quickly pinches the bridge of his nose. Regaining composure, he says, "I forget about them. The wings, I mean. Possibly because I'm envious of them, in the way that Zepharre is jealous of my abilities as a Sylvadyn Pairos. I've always had to walk everywhere I want to go, while in foreign cities. Therefore, I only know how long it takes to walk from place to place in Oniva, and also within much of the Aeown." He stops looking at Dea at this point. "And I've memorized all of Paragon's cities, and the journeys between each city are also committed to memory. Obviously, I have to relearn all of Eyo'el, though." Ryco pauses to scratch his neck. He looks blankly at the floor, seeming surprised that he just rattled off a whole lot of useless information.

Grinning in her naughty way, Dea wiggles her bare shoulders back and forth.

Ryco takes in a sharp breath. "See you at dinner." He bows his head, then turns to face forward in the hall. He quickly strides away.

Kent comes over to grab one of Dea's hands and kiss the back of it, saying to her as well, "See you at dinner." He winks at her, then follows after Ryco.

Quall, softening his furrowed brow, takes his turn to kiss Dea's hand too. But he says, "Make it before midnight." Then off he goes down the hallway, a nice little bounce in his step.

Once the three retreating guards have started the trek downstairs, loudly stomping down every step, Siege edges his way over to say to Dea, "It's the herbs. They were worried over causing a scene at dinner. We're all so tense, being in this city, with all that could transpire come morning. They drank some herbs to ease the edge off things."

Well," says Dea, delighted, "tell Ryco he should have herbs more often, for I like the way he talks when under their influence."

Siege squares up his shoulders, standing tall. "I'll tell him . . . tomorrow."

His expression confused, Eli opens his mouth to say something. Warren backhands him on the chest, knocking the wind out of Eli.

Eli wheezes.

Musgrae says under his breath, "Shut up, Kirjan," before he sends a charming look in Dea's direction. "Are Rozeth and the wolves in there with you, by chance?"

"No," Dea replies. "Should they be?"

Musgrae lifts his shoulders. "Nah! We just don't know where those three have gone off to, is all. Enjoy your flight to the hall."

Talok takes the lead down spiraling, wooden stairs. So faded and worn are they, the wood grain is barely distinguishable. Down a full flight of stairs (which ends up being twenty-two steps), there's a hallway to our right, identical to the one we left behind. We traipse down yet another flight. Same amount of stairs. Same kind of hallway to the right. But in front of the stairwell, there's a door. Talok opens it. Chattering noise blasts us in the face. Laughter, cheers, music, singing, silverware clinking, and dishes clattering.

Once in view of the room, I can't help being filled with joy. Many tables made of black glass—each surrounded by five chairs looking to be of etched, silver frames with white cushions—fill the enormous room. Many occupy this dining area. They converse and drink; a few drum one of their boot-clad feet on the wooden floor. They look across the way to the section cleared of furniture—to the people dancing there with a partner or two; or to those who duel with weapons; or others competing in magic, drawing symbols and colors in the space in front of themselves. The ceiling isn't set very high. And I cannot see the opposite wall from where we are.

Talok points to our left. "That way's to the exit!" he shouts over the racket.

Gemma's arm is still hooked with my own. When Skylin comes to hook hers with my previously unoccupied one, I feel much like a rag doll, being pushed and pulled along by these two girls of a different rhythm. Skylin's excited, and quick on her feet. But Gemma is steady, seeming suspicious of the room. And I see why. All the walls are made of mirrors, containing no seams. Merely covered are they by a thin veil of sheer curtains—curtains that fade from white up top, to gray two-thirds down, and then to black at the bottom. It's reminiscent to the dress Khyra wore that day in Zima's Kitchen, minus the flame pattern.

I start to wonder how much the Paragonians have designed things in the way of the Onyx, to show honor to them. Now, look what's happened. Never were the Paragonians named the victor. Never were they saved by the Onyx that they so seemed to love. Nothing the Onyx have done has shown any return of admiration. Only Gyron has done such a thing. Saving my cousin, by asking that he be given twenty-two days to surrender the dragon-horse to Zymarc. But we will not surrender her. We won't back down. We will stop Zymarc's plan from coming to fruition, whatever that true desire of his may be.

Many in the room spot me. They call out my name, 'Ravier,' in cheers, raising their drinks to me.

I simply smile at them, or incline my head in their direction, as both my arms are occupied by Gemma and Skylin. There's no chance of waving, or offering to shake the hands of many reaching for me. Gemma bats the grabby hands away, and the Sorsryns recoil in shock. Soon, they laugh at her. And she smirks. Skylin only has to fan her wings out, and most of the Sorsryns in here (wasted at this point) are mesmerized by her perfectly aligned, groomed feathers. They stare in a daze, not saying anything.

One, however, says in a slur, "What creature be you, girl?"

"A Dark Harmony," says Skylin in pride, barely slowing her stride.

The asking Sorsryn blinks in confusion. He goes back to drinking.

Others, also looking much filled by drink and the festivities, whistle or holler in teasing. Mostly at me, I think, as I have a girl on each arm. And I don't like that image. My insides heat up.

I begin to get uncomfortable, until an especially well-dressed male Sorsryn (though I know not of which clan) calls to me, "Prince Ravier to the Onyx, shall you be taking Sodon requests soon? For I wish to be first in line, if ya are."

"Am I allowed to do that?" I ask.

"Certainly, ye are," says a woman at a counter, serving up food and drink.

I'm poised to ask her more, when Skylin makes a sudden forward movement. A short little *ah* sound escapes my mouth, as I'm pulled along, Gemma right with me, pushing against my back.

The woman dressed in a colorful, bright coat laughs. Her darkened skin glimmers with perspiration. She starts wiping down her serving counter, saying to the male Sorsryn, "Looks like those two mean to ask 'im before ye, kind sir. Best to try in the mornin'."

"Ah, well. That's always my luck."

They fade out of eyesight.

We're finally to the door that leads outside.

As we exit this Sorsryn's pub, and into the darkness of nighttime, I look over my shoulder to the four-story, black-brick inn we are leaving behind. It's enormous. Part of me wishes to go back in there, to join the celebration. To ask all the ones inside as many questions as possible. But there's no time for that.

Quall, Ryco, and Kent linger outside, standing around a high lamppost made of scuffed, engraved silver. Oniva is lit by many of these same lampposts. Soberly, the three guards come join us in the walk to the King's Hall. We traverse along a winding road of stone, lighted by many lampposts. The group strolls along in silence. It seems I'm not the only one who's spent.

Gemma releases my arm to go walk beside Ben. They hold hands. Then Gemma leans her head against his shoulder.

Skylin eases up on her pace so that she's parallel to me. Finally, she is content to slow down.

"You know what I wish?" says Gemma, after a time.

"What?" Ben asks her.

"That I wasn't so homesick," Gemma admits. "Or that my home was hidden among all these buildings. More importantly, that I could see the people I'm really starting to miss."

My chest stings. I sigh, feeling sad inside.

Gemma peeks over her shoulder to me. "Who are you missing most, Ty?"

I think on it for a few moments, not too sure who it is I miss most. Then I reply, "My mom, telling me what to do, believe it or not. Decisions have never felt harder than here or now."

Talok taps my shoulder. "What? It's not that Molly Smith, with her epic cooking skills? Or Tadashi, and his weapon collection?"

Eli asks, "Or those two friends of yours, very Vonsai in nature?"

"Don't forget that Ginger Snap, neither," Warren adds. "First unscathed night watcher for Awngeleik. That's quite the accomplishment. One none of us can brag of."

"All right, all right," I give in. "So I miss home."

"So do I," says Kent, staring straight ahead to some far-off thing. "My Dysarda. It shan't ever be the same again. Those were my father's words to me, before I left."

Ryco leads us off the well-lit way, to tread atop a footpath made of lumpy, beaten-down grass. Down, we beat the grass further, adding to its wear and tear. There are no high lampposts along this trail. "It's a shortcut," he says to those looking back longingly to the even roadway.

We don't get very far before encountering an Onyx Warrior, who stands along this trail. A torch is in his hand.

Skylin unhooks her arm from mine.

Small, cottage-like buildings dot the area to either side of the path. This Onyx is most likely their guardian. He steps forward in confidence, lifting his torch a bit higher. His gaze I liken to spitting fire. "These are barracks to the Onyx Warriors. Only those of the royal—"

I come into the light, and he stops short. He averts his gaze.

"Forgiveness, Onyx Prince." He starts to bow. "I didn't expect you to be out at this hour, for it is very late. You must be worn right through." He's bent down on one knee now. I swear he's about to kneel all the way. And I don't want that at all.

"Please," I ask, "don't bow to me. I don't deserve that." I make a move to help him to his feet. He refuses to stand. Even when I take hold of his arm and pull, he holds to bowing.

"Aye," says the warrior, peering up at me. "But you do deserve it. I am honored to bow. There's not been an Onyx Prince to bow to, for more than a thousand years. And it is my generation whom the spirits have given an Onyx Prince. A blood heir." His voice quivers. "A blood heir prince, whom we have heard whisperings of, who can do remarkable things. And, tonight, I can proudly confirm that all the whisperings of him are true. For this Onyx Prince, I would vow to serve if even unto my death. For this Onyx Prince, I would gladly accept a curse to save him. I ask of you, if you are giving out Sodon requests, Prince Ravier, that you let me pledge myself to you, for I would rather serve you than the other." He deepens his bow to me. His face is not even twelve inches up from the ground. The torch in his hand is barely lifted higher than that.

The flames of it are near enough to my person that I feel their heat. My own heat within increases too. I don't know what to say to him. I'm speechless, taken aback as if I've just been punched in the gut. Out from my confusion, a thought rises to the surface. I give it a voice, confirming, "Even being an Onyx Warrior, you are able to pledge yourself to me? To serve me, over your King ReNovak?"

The warrior nods. "Yes, for you are Prince of the Onyx."

I let go of his arm, easing to an upright position. "And it would extend past today?"

"Of course," he says. "For today is the day of The Sodon. And Sodon requests cannot be revoked. They must be honored. Come what may."

"Tyler!" Quall rasps out, sounding sober. "Do you know what that means?"

"Not quite. Only that I can give out requests to Onyx Warriors."

"Exactly!" Quall's face lights up even more. "If Gyron hasn't asked his request yet, he can ask you. He can pledge himself to you."

"May I stand, my prince?" asks the warrior.

"You don't have to ask!" I nearly shout. "I never asked you to bow in the first place."

Ryco states, "He was following etiquette."

I swallow hard. I'm about to apologize. But, somehow, I don't think the Onyx Prince is supposed to apologize for such misunderstandings as these. So I apologize with a look, softening my face, even relaxing my stance.

A small smile plays across the warrior's lips, as he stands. "Do you accept my Sodon request, my prince-Sorsivyte, Ravier?"

I'm about to answer 'yes' without a thought. But I catch myself. I search for the proper response. It comes to me. "I grant you your request, brave Onyx Warrior of Oniva."

With utterance of that last syllable of my first given request, power leaves me. I must breathe all the way out. I've no choice. Lightheadedness overcomes me. I sway a bit. Reaching out, the warrior steadies me.

Tears wash over his eyes. Tears of joy. He pulls his hand back. "Have you a mark, Prince Ravier? An emblem that is yours with which you may brand me?"

A minute passes as I work to regain my senses. I'm able to take in a full breath. I shake my head. "I don't." I glance around at the others. All but Gemma, Ryco, and Skylin shrug at me. Then Ryco adds his shrug a couple seconds later, that know-it-all smirk upon his face.

Memories flash in my head of that first night in the woods. Seeing Ryco at Mirror Lake, healing Awngeleik with sparking magic. Ryco's expression that scared me into sprinting in the opposite direction. Talok, when he caught me by the wrist. I was so scared. But why? Look at all I've endured, with hardly an ounce of fear stopping me. I look now to Talok. He's deep in thought, thinking of what could be my brand most likely. He keeps feeling his face absentmindedly. The buttons of his coat cuffs glimmer in the firelight. They're a solid, glossy black metal. I try to recall the symbol he had on the buttons of his other coats. I never asked him about it. What that symbol was for. And now I can't quite finish imagining how it looked. I glance down at the fasteners on the sides of my boots, knowing the mark was on them. The symbol has been ground off all six buttons of each boot. I've no idea when that could have happened. It must've been in the arena some hours ago; Caleiso, in her malice, trying to strip me of all things Paragonian.

"Talok," I blurt out.

He startles. "What, Tyler?"

"The buttons on your other two coats, they had a symbol carved into them. And that same symbol's been ground off the ones of my boots. What is that symbol, and what importance does it have in Paragon?"

"It's the Withrasyn symbol of Wyeisa," says Talok.

Ryco hides a smirk. "Oh, Ravier." A hushed laugh comes out. "That's a perfect mark for you to make your own."

"If it's a Withrasyn symbol," I argue, my hopes getting dashed, "wouldn't that mark belong to Paragon? I mean, it was on two of Talok's coats after all."

Quall comes closer. He bends down to get a better look at my face. "As all of us and this Onyx Warrior will tell you, Tyler, that symbol merely stands for remembrance of an extinct clan. The Withrasyns.

Only Matron Avilon may still be alive. We suspect that as truth, less and less with each passing year. There are none still living to claim that symbol as their own. So take it as yours, Ravier. Bring it to life again, renewed for a new purpose. To mark those who would pledge themselves to your service. For serving you is as if serving Paragon and all that lives there." Quall gestures to the warrior, who waits expectantly.

Warren flicks a coin to me, and I catch it in my right hand. He says, "That's a Wyeisa coin. He was one of the Withrasyn Kings. The last to call for the use of such currency as that. I've kept it with me for good fortune on my fate, ever since I was a boy, training with the Kyanites."

"Heat the metal, Tyler," Ryco says. "Brand your warrior, so that he may be free of a cheating, cowardly king to serve a good and bold prince."

My throat constricts, like I'm being choked. The coin rests directly over that *M* etched into the very lines of my right palm. The face of a man looking forward is stamped into the metal. I turn the coin over to see the Wyeisa symbol. Its mark I liken to a *W* turned on its side, with an elegant *Z* sharing the slanted line. Looking up to those around, I ask, "Do you think I can give it another name? Rename the symbol to something meaningful for me?" I close my hand around the cold metal. It quickly starts to get warmer.

"Yes," the warrior affirms. "Be sure of the name you give it, however. For if it is of false meaning to you, those branded by you could be stolen away as pawns."

Looking down at my right hand, as I open it to observe the heated coin resting there, the lines of my palm glow white. My hand is stained to that familiar black. At least, familiar to me now. The warrior gives no indication that he sees the change of my skin. No one does, save for Skylin. Her eyes are wide in fear. She comes to survey me, while I weigh the coin in my darkened hand. I'm grateful for her silence on the matter. I can tell she wishes to say something. But even she knows better.

No colors race over my palm. It makes me worry that something isn't right. Then again, I have used much magic today, and given out my first Sodon request. I look to the warrior once more. "Where should I put the mark?"

He lets go of the torch, and it stays afloat where he placed it. He opens his hands to me, palms facing up. "You must pick one. Place one mark upon the palm only, just below the thumb. For that is the location that shows a master has good intentions toward those he marks. You must also choose the mark's orientation. How do you wish for me to view it, when I have nothing with me to mirror its reflection?"

"First, which is your dominant hand?" I ask him. "I'll place it there."

"Both, my prince. My right best wields weapons; my left loves magic. Though that isn't normal. Typically, one hand is better overall than the other, be it left or right. I am proficient with both."

"You're sort of"—I pause—"in-between, then?"

"You shouldn't say such things as that, Prince Ravier." The warrior grows nervous, sweat beading on his forehead. "The in-between is something a former Warrior of the Nyxane talked of, long ago. It is a very dangerous place. Only Vardiyas dare tread there, untroubled by any of the happenings that occur in the in-between. That is what we are taught, at least."

I'm about to tell the warrior to offer only his left hand, but I've two things left to ask him. I study his face a moment, before I speak. He's beyond nervous, unwilling even to look at me. I give my questions a voice. "Do you prefer magic or weapons, dear Onyx Warrior, whose name I do not know?" Waiting for his response, I reposition the coin in my palm to be upside down to me but right-facing to him.

He sees this action. A genuine happiness brightens his face. His eyes are happier, the crease lines of joy showing through. "To new beginnings," he whispers in conviction, his voice getting stronger with each spoken line. "To the people and world I never knew existed. To a love for magic. To the death of Vitiosus. Though I was not one there that night in Paragon to hear you, nor see you speak that, I heard much of you from my brothers-at-arms. And I must tell you, my prince, it is magic I love. Same as you. Magic." He lets his right hand rest against his side. He only offers his left for branding.

I pick the coin off my right hand, and turn it over. It feels hot to neither of my hands, but I know that is a false perception, for steam comes from it, swirling in the cool breeze of night. "Can I name the brand, afterward?" I glance from the warrior's palm to his face.

"You may," he says. "But be quick of it."

He's a step away. So I take that step and press the turned-over coin to his left palm. He shows no sign of pain. He waits patiently, keeping still, as I hold the hot metal to that perfectly sized spot for this mark. My mark. The Mark of Malik. What better name to give it than my own? My middle name. For a middle name only seems to have the use of distinguishing me from other *Tylers*. What are the odds other parents named their sons Tyler Malik? Also, what are the odds this world has another Malik going around, naming symbols after himself? Highly unlikely, I decide.

As I pull the coin from the warrior's freshly blistered skin, the metal has become cold. I flick the coin back to Warren, and he catches it. Then I make my request of the warrior: "I've thought of a name for it, but tell me more about renaming things. And what your name is. You never said."

Ben comes to rub salve on the warrior's wound, even as I'm talking.

The warrior thanks him with a single nod of his head. He takes up the torch in his right hand, before standing as a guardian to the barracks once more. He says to me, "Those who bring something once dead to life again may rename the entity. It is their right to do so, for it is written in the Laws of Magic. Upheld by Tree Stag and The Black Flame. And life and death are held to the counterbalance of time. For with time, comes life and growth; with time, there are greetings; with time, *is* there folly or *is* there wisdom; with time, *are* there dreams or *are* there wars; with time, *are* there losses or victories; with time, goodbyes are said; with time, decay must obey; with time, death must come. And in time all things become balanced and complete."

Warren has his head bowed in reverence. When the warrior has ceased speaking, Warren's voice drops an octave. He's quiet to say, "Thank you, kind warrior. I've never before heard the Warrior's Song spoken by a true Onyx Warrior. Only heard the Kyanite Konverts recite it as history."

"And do you know its history?" the warrior quizzes, staring forward. He stands as a statue, watching the darkness. Only his eyes move. Only his chest too, as he breathes in and out.

"Oh, I *wish* I did," says Skylin, her face forlorn.

"We do," says a strong voice, approaching from amid the dark.

Three warriors advance toward us, coming up behind the barracks' guardian. First Hydvar, then Kaalon and Sawrro, their faces weary and garb wrinkled from the hustle of the day.

"You're supposed to be sleeping. Or, at least, pretending to sleep," says the guardian warrior, still unmoved.

Hydvar comes to pat the guardian warrior on the back. "Sawrro has been summoned for duty for a day, to be a scholar to some Silverian woman."

"He's much excited." Kaalon rolls his eyes. Then he looks Sawrro from head to toe. "Look at him. He can barely keep from dancing for joy. Be happy it wasn't you, Smythe. It's why Gyron put you on barrack duty. It was going to be Sawrro, until Gyron went through the granted requests of dusk, and saw the Silverian woman's request. He was sure Sawrro, here, would be only too overjoyed at the prospect."

"Ack!" Sawrro sneers. He takes hold of the front of Kaalon's coat. "You shut your mouth, Kaalon. Or I'll be stitching it shut."

Kaalon makes not a move to push Sawrro away. "You are the one in need of a stitched-shut mouth, not me."

Hydvar adds, "For it is you, Sawrro, guilty of all the vulgar talk. Even more of ghastly musings, which are never given a voice. Thank the Vardiyas."

My first marked warrior, Smythe, side-glances to the other three warriors. He keeps silent, looking forward again.

I study these older Onyx Warriors before me. I start to imagine if one of them *could* be Zymarc. And, if so, which one? Then I recall that they were away for a two-year tour. I think, *How could he be one of these? It seems impossible, even in a world reliant on magic.*

Sawrro suddenly loses interest in Kaalon. He looks to our group. It's as if he hasn't noticed us till now. "Onyx Prince, Ravier," he says in a smoother tone. He bows, barely bending his stature forward (Kaalon and Hydvar join in bowing, synchronized). "Why did you not speak up, to let us know it was you, visiting us in the dark? Visiting Shmighty, here." He waits for my answer.

Smythe turns to face Sawrro. "For the umpteenth time, Sawrro, my name is pronounced as a combination of *smite* and *smith*. Not as a combining of *shy* and *mighty*."

Eli proclaims proudly, "The Smiting Smith! Seems easy enough to remember."

"It is a title Yigoshi would be fond of, "Siege adds. "Rarely did he have time to wield the many weapons which he forged. Only time for testing them."

"Don't encourage him, Siege." Musgrae points at Eli. "They're going to string you up, Kirjan. Don't you continue with your rhymes."

"I shan't string him up," says Smythe, sounding serious and looking it too. "For it is very likely he'll remember my proper name, whilst my brothers-at-arms are sure to forget how to say it."

Eli lets his vampire grin show. But then the three older Onyx Warriors return a similar grin. They've got his beat, for their canines are more pointed than any Paragonians' set, except for maybe my cousin's. Eli looks as if he wishes to run away, wide open are his eyes set into his face that has drained of color.

Talok starts chuckling. "Eli, they aren't going to bite you as I did."

"You . . . you don't know that!" Eli shouts. He runs away.

Warren has to go after him—grab him, bear hug him, bring him back to our fold.

Eli sounds like a squalling bird, trying to escape its death. Finally, he screams words of, "Let me go, Warren! Let go, or I'll use that spell to bleach your skin, make you look spotted beige-and-brown."

Ryco purses his lips. It suggests a scowl. He crosses his arms. His citrine-colored eyes begin to glow bright. Yet the corners of his eyes turn upward. He's doing his best not to laugh.

I'm in no mood to laugh.

"You'll do no such thing," says Warren, as he sets Eli down. He pushes him to be closer to Musgrae. "Watch that one, will ya, Grae?"

Musgrae rests his large hands upon Eli's tense shoulders. Eli side-glances to Sawrro, who now has a ghastly look of pleasure set into his features. No longer does he smile.

Eli's breath quickens. He tries to bolt forward again. Musgrae yanks him back. Kent takes to one side of Eli, Siege the other. Ben's there in front, clearing the Kirjan's coat of the creases it's collected throughout the day.

Sweat running down his face, Eli manages to say, "I feel as if I'm some poor creature, being fattened up for a meal. A Sorsryn's meal!" He spits out that last phrase.

Ben's hands go still, resting on Eli's coat lapels. He stares into Eli's face. Then he playfully snaps his teeth at Eli. Eli punches him right on the jaw. The two start wrestling.

Musgrae steps back and lets it happen.

My cousin is bent over with laughter, laughing so hard that the sound soon vanishes.

Quall goes to break up the fight, but Ryco stops him. "Calm down, Quallendeis. They are at that age. Let them get it out."

Though Quall looks not a bit happy about it, crossing his arms, he lets the two youngest guards go at each other.

Talok composes himself, to merely watch them. He divs to me without looking my way, *"I wish we could join in. But Ryco would turn furious. A lecture would soon follow, about etiquette and all that."*

I add in div, *"True. And I've just won his approval. Possibly respect. Not going to risk losing it now."*

"Cousin," he divs, *"you actually care if Ryco respects you? Well, isn't this day a day of improbabilities being dashed to pieces."*

I shrug, playing it off as a readjustment of my cloak.

Throughout the wrestling spree, Eli can scarcely land a hit on Ben.

Pretty soon, Eli is flipped onto his back.

Ben's on top of him, holding a dagger to his throat. "You are stealth and a thief, Kirjan. But I am not. I am of the strength and stamina of Yharss-Rawshuen. Next time you complain that your load's too heavy, during our journey, I'll be telling Ryco the truth. Understand?"

"Yeah!" Eli flashes an angry look.

"No more running away?" Ben asks.

Eli grumbles, "No more running away."

Ben gets off him, but it's Gemma to help Eli up.

"A kiss, as solace for your wounded ego?" Gem asks him.

"Vards!" Eli grumbles. "Why not?"

Gemma pecks him on the cheek, then she retreats over to Ben to giggle in safety.

Eli scoffs. "Ya never cared at all, Galloway."

Talok holds up his index finger, as he looks to the Onyx. "I've a question," he says. "What happens on The Sodon . . . ?" He trails off, waiting in anticipation.

"Is not reported, until the next," says Hydvar.

Sawrro adds, "For it is considered bad manners, so long as the matters that happened are trivial in nature."

Kaalon shakes his head, letting his focus linger on the ground.

Smythe, in seriousness, asks Gemma, "Has a king ever kissed you, girl?"

Gemma stops giggling. She glances to Talok. She swallows hard.

I don't like the way he looks at her. I feel as if a shadow looms overhead, darkening my mind with worry. When my cousin goes toward her, I command him, saying, "Talok, don't."

Talok pivots to face me. He's gone pale again. Deathasyn pale. His eyes are wild like a monster's.

Less commanding, I tell him, "I don't think it's a good idea, Cousin."

"Do you ever stop to ask me what I think is a good idea, Tyler?" He wets his lips. His expression is one of hunger.

"You are the King of Paragon," I point out. "You can tell anyone *anything* you like, anytime you want. But you don't. And that's not my fault. So don't go getting that look with me, King Talok. I am no threat to you." I say that last line, truly meaning it.

"You are every threat to me!" he yells.

Gemma takes in a sharp, fearful breath.

I step toward Talok.

The four Onyx are restless on their feet. Sawrro has the added look of amusement. I see it out of the corner of my vision. How the others react, I don't know. I don't look. My focus narrows on Talok. In seconds, he is all I see. Malice has started to sink into his features, and I hate it. I hate it more than I'd ever care to admit. In this moment, I hate him yet I love him; I pity yet fear him.

I admit, "You only say that, Cousin, because, for some reason, you must think it's your throne I want. But I've no wish for that. Keep your throne. And ReNovak can keep his. There is but one I never wish to have a throne. Zymarc. Can we agree? Agree that a Vitiosyn should never have a throne?"

Talok stands there, seething with every breath.

Regardless of how intense he appears, I start to calm down. The others come back into my focus.

Gemma softly grips Talok's arm. "I would wish to be kissed by a king. It'll give me something to brag about to Tyler, when we get home."

I can tell she's lying. Tears threaten to spill down her face.

Talok doesn't notice. He is merely distracted by her attention directed at him. This Geldryn device is ravaging all the kindness right out of my cousin. And there's nothing left I can do to ease his symptoms. I am powerless to help Gemma.

When she pulls Talok down for a kiss, I fight back a gag. It wants to erupt from my throat. I turn away. Watching that, makes me sick.

One of the four warriors asks me, "Onyx Prince, do you wish for us to do something?"

I just shake my head. The world seems to spin. I sink to the ground, exhausted. I sense power being drained from me. My vision blurs too much for me to tell who or what could be doing it.

Somewhere behind me, Gemma whispers words of, "To sleep deep in the keep; dim-drim-nae-Varin. Ha-Shyn."

Someone snaps their fingers.

Something thuds to the ground.

Many rush around, whispering too many things for me to comprehend any of it.

Soon, I can breathe again. My senses return to normal. I glance over my shoulder. Talok is passed out on the ground, surrounded by many of his guards and Smythe, who's holding up the torch for them to see better. Gemma, however, stands by, watching it all. She turns a glance of apology to me. She mouths the words: *I'm sorry.* Gem was siphoning magic from me. In past times, I would've been livid with her. Now I'm only grateful she thought of some way to disarm Talok, and make him sleep.

Someone offers me their hand. It's Skylin, giving me a look of reassurance. I accept her help, even lean against her once I have my feet underneath me. She wraps a protective wing around me, and I relax in that warm, feathery-soft embrace.

The others quiet down enough to hear me say, "We can't go to dinner at the King's Hall. Not with Talok about to snap like this. He isn't well. I don't want anyone else to see him this way. Will some of you go to King ReNovak? Explain only this to him: that the Onyx Prince wishes for peace and quiet tonight. Bring food back with you, and whatever else the king is inclined to give you."

Hydvar steps forward, frowning in sadness. "Kaalon and I can go, in place of you, Prince Ravier. For we are Onyx Warriors at your disposal."

Kaalon nods his agreement. "It is as Hydvar says. But you, Sawrro, won't you leave us already? You're only delaying the inevitable. And speak to no one of what you've witnessed."

Sawrro narrows his gaze on Kaalon, yet leaves without a word, nor so much as a nod of acknowledgment directed at me.

Smythe stares on down the path that the others and I haven't crossed yet. Someone's approaching, fading out of the darkness. "There'd be my replacement for the night into dawn." Smythe looks to me. "I shall help the lot of you back to the inn. You are still where Mistress Ayna set you up for the night, no?"

Quall speaks up, "Yes, that is still where we intend to sleep."

Smythe's replacement is now within clear view. Tall and gangly, he looks familiar to me. I can't place him.

"Vards," Kaalon says under his breath. "Your replacement, Smythe, is that gangly Zenzar? He's too scrawny to be a Barrack Guard. This encampment will be in shambles by morning, with that one at the helm of order and control."

Hydvar puts his hand on his hip, just above where his blade is clasped to his belt. "That Zenzar is better than you give him credit for, Kaalon. He is the same young warrior whom ReNovak named as Warrior of the Nyxane, should our dear Siveyra Gyronawv succumb to the battlefield."

Kaalon looks furious. "Tell me he's joking, Smythe. That little scrawny thing, the future Warrior of the Nyxane? No."

Smythe hides a grin, as he looks my cousin over. "How should this one like to be carried, do you think, Prince Ravier? Dignified, like an innocent, sleepy child; or degraded, over the shoulder like a sack of meat?" He whips his attention to me.

I raise an eyebrow. "Was he acting dignified, before being put to sleep?"

Smythe clicks his tongue. "Right! Over the shoulder it is." He picks up Talok's limp body, throws him over his shoulder, then proceeds to head back the way we came.

Talok's body flops and flails and sways with each of Smythe's footfalls. I want to keep watching the sight of my cousin for quite some time. But I must look away, for I mean to commit the memory to the Arkivara, and I don't want a gaping hole in memory left behind because I stared for much too long.

Warren leans down to tell Gemma, "That's a mighty fine sleep spell, Galloway. He's completely out." Warren straightens his stance. "Ryco, I believe that deserves high marks."

"I'll be sure to write it down," says Ryco, as he watches Hydvar and

Kaalon go converse with Zenzar.

Too far away are they, for us to hear the words they speak.

Ryco whispers to Musgrae, "Go with those two. Take Warren and Ben with you. Make sure there aren't any backhanded schemes being planned. Come straight back to the inn without stopping."

"Will do," says Musgrae. He tags the two who are to go with him. The three take off toward Hydvar and Kaalon, jogging to catch up to them.

I wrap my arm around Skylin for support, as we turn to head for the inn.

Skylin opens her other wing in invitation. "Are you chilled, Miss Galloway? I've got two of these, you know." She flutters her wings a bit.

Gemma takes to Skylin's other side, crowding close for warmth. Quall leads the group with Siege and Smythe, and my unconscious cousin. Ryco, Kent, and Eli take up the back, conversing in hushed tones.

Meanwhile, Musgrae, Warren, and Ben fade into darkness with Hydvar and Kaalon, headed off to the King's Hall. I wish safety for them *and* us.

Though we're not far from the four-story inn, it feels like the longest trek I've made in a while. So many thoughts run through my head. Before one has finished, another is taking its place. All that keeps me grounded to the present it seems is Skylin's wing tightly hugging me, and Gemma's icy-cold hand reaching behind Skylin to touch me on the arm.

Gemma says to me, in Mensa-div, *"Hold on, Tyler. It's not too much longer, before Talok will get better. Not too long before we stop Zymarc. Just keep being that brave, bold version of yourself."*

Her words revive me. Each step becomes easier. I'm grateful for the company of others but especially grateful of Gemma and Skylin.

17

Dragon's Flight

The roadway, leading back to the inn, got more and more congested with foot traffic, the farther we went. Yet the crowds were quiet, whispering to each other, any laughter sounding like low wheezes, any yelling sounding as hushed tirades. It must be one of the rules of the city: after The Sodon requests, comes peace and quiet. So, unless you must speak at full volume, you'd best hush.

At last, the inn comes into our view. All torches on the building have been lit. The lampposts' light grows dim.

Talok is still draped over Smythe's shoulder. It was difficult not to stare at him, while we were headed back, especially when his mouth dropped open and drool drizzled out.

At one point, Quall peered at Talok's face, and whispered, barely audible, "Serves you right."

I had to suppress a laugh. No one else heard him, for they gave no response. Before we went onto the crowded roadway, Kent took out a cloak to cover Talok. That cloak still conceals my cousin, carried like a sack by Smythe. Only my cousin's hands and feet poke out from beneath the fabric, limp and dangly.

The dangling subsides, when Smythe comes to a stop. "Your cousin is waking, Ravier. Shall I set him down, let him wake while lying still upon the ground?"

"Yeah."

I gently pull away from Skylin, immediately missing the warmth she puts out. I remove the cloak. As soon as I have, Quall starts to slide Talok off of Smythe's shoulder. I assume he's going to ease my cousin down all nice-like. That isn't what he does. He simply grabs hold of Talok's wrist. He pulls.

My cousin splats on the grass that's just to the edge of the roadway.

Smythe startles away, looking from Talok to Quall. "Isn't that one a king?" He hyperventilates. His gaze darts about to see if anyone on the road witnessed Quall's act of disrespect. None look our way.

"He'll never know"—Quall glares at us all—"unless someone tells him." Quall stuffs his large hands into the pockets of his white coat. Challenging any rebels, he cocks his eyebrows up.

"I shan't ever tell," says Smythe, following Quall's example of putting his hands in his pockets. "For I fear I would lose my head for letting you do that. To your own king, no less."

Quall only lowers his head, letting his mouth curve upward.

Talok groans in grogginess. He rolls out of the splat pose, onto his hands and knees. "What happened?"

Kent stands beside Talok. "You weren't feeling well, so we headed back for the night."

Talok grumbles something inaudible.

"Want a hand?" queries Quall, mockery edging his voice.

"No," Talok manages to say. He stands up all the way. "Sorry we had to miss meeting with King ReNovak. There's always tomorrow, at breakfast."

"Don't apologize to me, King Talok." I hand Kent the wadded-up cloak. "I wasn't really feeling a dinner with King ReNovak, in the King's Hall, anyway. I'd rather be here at the inn."

Siege asks, "What's the last thing you remember, Talok?"

My cousin rubs his forehead. "Not a whole lot, after leaving the vicinity of a certain person. Why? And how was I not feeling well? I feel fine now, aside from a lapse in memory."

"More like a lapse in judgment," Gemma says under her breath.

"Gemma cast a spell on you," Skylin blurts out. "It didn't go in your favor. You soon passed out. We had to ask Smythe to carry you like a sack of meat." Skylin smiles sweetly. "Which he did."

Smythe stares at the ground.

"Don't you worry, Cousin." I add in, "When you started drooling, we covered you up with a cloak."

"That way you could keep your dignity and all," says Kent.

Grimacing, Talok shuts his eyes. His jaw clenches tight. The pain seems to pass, as he reopens his eyes. "Thank you for covering me."

Kent merely nods.

It's Ryco to say, "You're welcome." He has that snarky tone and know-it-all smirk.

Talok huffs as he turns on his heel to stride for the roadway. He joins with the lingering crowds traversing it. We jog to catch up. Smythe stays close to me, still holding his torch. At the sight of the torch, those in the crowd give us wide berth. Before long, Talok's opening the front door of the inn. We follow him inside.

There's a pause in all the chatter. Many notice that I've returned.

The woman at the counter calls out, "The Onyx Prince has returned. Have ye come back to give out Sodon requests?"

I open my mouth to say something else, but "yes" rolls off my tongue. I grin wickedly at the woman; more so at the Sorsryn man, who asked to be the first in line earlier.

Smythe calls above the constant noise, "Would there be Onyx in here? Gather round, for Prince Ravier has a mark with which he may brand us, to steal us from a king. It is blasphemy, I know. Yet it is blasphemy I have committed." He holds his left hand high, for all to see should they look. "And it is blasphemy I ask all of you brothers and sisters of mine to commit. To be branded by the mark of Ravier. And what *is* that mark's name, Ravier? For you never said." He lowers his hand and looks at me.

"A part of my name. The name: Tyler Malik Ravier." Loudly, I declare, "The Mark of Malik! It means much to me. For it is the name my mother wished to be the first part. But it is the second part. The part only those close to me know by heart. The unsaid part of my name, when first introduced. I should like to give you that part of my name: Malik."

Smythe's face is bright with a genuine look of joy. His eyes have life back in them. Fire. A fire of the soul, I imagine. "Come!" he shouts. "Ask for the Mark of Malik, as I did. Make your Sodon request, even if you've been turned down once already this very night."

The chatter in the inn grows louder. Many Onyx Warriors come first, then the other Onyx men and women, young warriors too.

I search around for Warren, as he is the one with the Wyeisa coin, now the Mark of Malik. I don't know if he and the others will be back soon.

Nervousness starts to rise up and choke me.

Something glimmers in the air, spinning. It hits me on the chest. A small, metal object. I catch it before it falls to the floor. It's the Wyeisa coin I hold now in my left hand. My attention jerks up. Warren's grinning face towers over the crowd. He points to the dining section of the room.

I give him a nod, showing I understand.

Hydvar and Kaalon approach Smythe, asking what's going on. I don't listen to what he tells them. I simply try to decide how I want to orient the mark on all the ones beginning to form a long, winding line in the pub of this inn.

Only too soon, that male Sorsryn of earlier stands before me, making his request of: "If you should indeed find me worthy, fair prince-Sorsivyte Ravier, brand me and make me yours. Steal me from the clan of my fathers, and their fathers before them, all the way to the beginning. When Sorsryns replaced Sorshrynaks." He kneels, then offers his right palm for branding.

In that moment, I realize each request is going to be worded differently. Therefore, I decide the mark should be oriented differently on each palm. It should look unique to the one wearing it, for they, themselves, are unique. Each one important. Each one needed. Each one wanted. Wanted by me.

I tell this warrior, "I accept your request. This day, consider yourself stolen away from the clan of your ancestors."

The metal is ready. Power leaves me, as I press the heated coin to the warrior's hand. He solemnly speaks words I do not understand, as it's happening. When I pull the coin away, the warrior stands renewed, even overjoyed.

"Forever at your service, my prince!" he declares. He moves aside for me to begin the process all over with the next, then another. I start to run out of ways to orient the coin to be placed down uniquely.

"Smythe," I ask after a while, "is there some other way I can make the mark? I want it a little different for each one."

Smythe searches for an answer.

Having heard me as well, Hydvar and Kaalon start feeling around in their pockets.

Hydvar pulls a thin object out from his pocket. A quill. He offers it to me. "Heat the tip," he says. "Then draw the mark. It is an enchanted quill. Therefore, the strokes will remain."

I lift my splayed-out hand, refusing his writing instrument. "If a quill works, then I'll use my own." I take out my father's enchanted quill—the one Grover gave me. Part of me wishes I had the engraved one my father bestowed to me as a gift years ago, though. It must be enchanted as well, for the words I wrote at Mirror Lake remained in the depths, even though the paper had succumbed to the water—to the grasp of Aysivak.

The next asking Onyx is a woman. The woman from the counter, who was serving up all the tenants of the inn. She is the first I will give a written mark to. I wait until she's made her request.

"All me life," she says, while kneeling before me, "I've been servant to that Crown of King ReNovak, enough Onyx in me veins to be an Onyx Warrior, yet ne'er enough male in my blood to make it happen—the Kyanite half of me scorned that my clan is lost, hidden away, or destroyed. Still, I wish to be a warrior. So make it happen, my fair Prince-Sorsivyte Ravier, will ye? Steals me away from the Crown. From the House of Dovak. Make me an Onyx Warrior, for it is what I truly hope for. To take a stand with my fearsome and bold brothers—warriors all. Will ye?" she pleads, looking up at me.

Without hesitation, I tell her, "I will give you your Sodon request."

She laughs and sobs and holds both palms out for me to choose.

I ask, "Which one loves weapons?"

"My left, fair prince." She pulls her right hand back, still offering her left.

I begin the mark on her offered palm, careful to transpose it as if it's reflected in a mirror. I finish. She jolts up, triumphant.

"Ghebina!" an already marked warrior shouts, grinning. "How's it feel to be now one of us? Which of us do you want for the night? You need not have permission from ReNovak now, you know."

"'Twas great, till ye opened your fat gob and said that," Ghebina shouts back. "Not a one of you do I wish to bed, but ye all do I wish to duel and defeat."

A great cheer rattles my head, making my hearing ring.

Ghebina rushes for her serving counter and dives over it. She soon returns, wielding a long-blade. She starts dueling the warriors I've already marked.

I briefly stand near the Paragonians and watch Ghebina defeat five Onyx Warriors, in five minutes flat. I can tell she's been waiting her whole life for this very opportunity.

Smythe waves me back over, and I go to restart the process of requests again, even amidst Ghebina's duels with the other warriors.

Much later, when the noise has lessened a little, I spot Rozeth coming through the inn's entrance. Rorka and Mekka are right behind her. They navigate through the crowd to Skylin, Gemma, and the Paragonians, gathered in the dining section. At some point, Aygor, Dea, Keturah, even Brinkorr joined them there. They're all looking my way, save for the few scanning the room, making sure I'm safe, that they're safe too.

Relaxing further, I fall back into the rhythm of listening to and giving out requests. I orient the mark as if it's mirrored, for a while, then I switch back. I start to embellish the brand. More and more, it becomes intricate or sharp or soft in appearance. I base it all on how I feel inside, when I see the asking person in front of me.

More hours have passed, when a certain feeling wrenches my stomach (it's not hunger). I look up. A woman watches me, from beyond the line. She must be tall, for I can see her head above the gathered crowd. I meet her bright gaze. Former Queen of the Onyx, Ayna. A slow smile plays across her lips. She holds a book up for me to see. She wiggles it back and forth.

Quall goes to take it from her. He strides back to the others, while Ayna lingers in place. She looks around at the scene, seeming to take it in with a fresh outlook.

I go back to drawing the mark on a man's palm. I've almost finished, when Ayna Mensa-divs, *"I shall keep King ReNovak occupied for you. You needn't worry over being caught tonight. But you must leave very early in the morning. For when he catches word of what has transpired here, he will hunt you to challenge you for ownership of the warriors. He might even try to kill you."*

My hand trembles. The mark has a little squiggle line in it at the finish. Panicked, I look up at the man.

He merely laughs. "More unique is mine than all of yars, brothers and sisters. Look!" He holds his hand up in pride, showing my mishap for all to see.

I briefly hide my face in my hands, taking a moment to rub my dry, scratchy eyes.

While the room chatter grows loud again, Ayna continues the div, saying, *"On The Sodon, he is beyond your strength, Ravier, for each asked request gives power to the Onyx King. You are but the prince. My advice is to wait to challenge ReNovak. Wait for The Sodon to pass. For his power to lessen, if even a little."*

"What about these warriors, Ayna?" I ask. *"I'm worried about what will happen to them, if they stay here."*

"Do not worry, Ravier," she says soothingly. *"For, as a queen to a former Onyx King, I am a free Onyx. I intend to take your branded warriors, every single one, and head for Paragon. We shall guard it for you while you are*

away."

My chest is about to burst from the great relief I feel in my heart. Quickly, it starts to not seem right, however, to let Ayna take the warriors to Paragon. The Jokryns are there, to protect it. So I div to her an alternate course of action, *"No. Don't go to Paragon. Go talk with King Aygor of the Darklyres. He's with Talok and the others. His people are without a home, because of Vitiosyns. Ally yourself with him, for he is good. Please, do whatever it takes to help him."*

"I shall see it done, my prince," she divs. *"But in the morning, for I must be away to ReNovak, or he'll soon hear of this commotion."*

Before she leaves, I ask one last thing in div, *"Will you please send Siveyra Gyron? I want to free him too."*

Ayna's demeanor grows sad. *"His fate is sealed, Ravier. You cannot free him, as you have freed all of these. He is Warrior of the Nyxane. Only ReNovak's death will now free him."*

Holding her head high once more, Ayna turns and strides out of the inn.

The door closes behind her.

As quickly as my joy came, it leaves. Yet I continue penning the marks on many palms of many warriors—all genders, near all ages and sizes and abilities too. I pen the mark on that patch of skin that means a master only has good intentions for those he brands. That little spot, touched by the power of the wielder. The power of the branded. It is my hope that their power within leaches out through the mark, to their choice of attack or defense, be it magic, weapons, or otherwise. That, in their moment of need, my mark will give them just a little more strength. A fraction more to hold on. To stay alive. To win.

At the end of it all, I can barely keep hold of the quill, and my eyes fight to stay open. Hydvar and Kaalon have left for the night. Smythe stayed behind, though. He's still to my left side, holding that ever-lit torch. The crowd has died down to a few stragglers, and Ghebina at her counter, who returned to serving up food and drink a bit ago. When I've finished writing that last brand for the night, Ghebina comes over to me.

She hands me a bag. "This, here, be for ye journey. I shall have breakfast ready, before first light. I reckon your lot means to run tomorrow. I dinna ken where it is ye mean to run to. But I can feel it. You's will run. And I must ask ya take a dragon's flight there. Be swift and quiet and watchful, will ye?"

I hold out my hand, in thanks. "I will. Thank you. It was nice to meet you, Ghebina."

"Ack!" She scoffs. "You shouldna be thanking me." She shakes my hand anyway. Before going back to her counter, she takes another look at me. "I still canna believe what I see in ya, Ravier."

Skylin comes to pull me away. I wave goodnight to Ghebina, as she starts clearing the pub of the great mess left behind, beginning with the dishes.

Our group leaves the dining section.

I give Ghebina's satchel of food and supplies over to Siege, since he's the nearest guard. We all trudge up the stairs, single file.

Once back in the room, Warren sets a small box on the coffee table. "That'd be food for you, Ravier. Sit, eat, rest, then—for fate's sake—get some sleep. We've a long day tomorrow."

I quickly relay in Mensa-div to Warren, what Ayna told me. I didn't think it was possible, but Warren grows a shade lighter.

He whispers, "I'll tell Ryke. Now eat, Ravier."

I heed his words. Also, I take note of the look on Ryco's face, as he enters the room. Weary doesn't begin to describe it. Brink and all Paragonians, and Greyvons and Darklyres, who've made the journey to Oniva are now in this room.

Smythe pokes his head in. "I shall be stationed outside this door, Prince Ravier. Hydvar and Kaalon are set at the inn's entrance. Have yourself a good night. You've done well. Don't you let anyone tell you differently."

I thank him, while in the middle of opening the food box. I sit down on the floor, right as a glorious, savory smell wafts up, making my mouth water. Smythe smiles. Then he closes the door. I start eating the food that was meant to be served at the King's Hall. It's delightfully spicy and satisfying. Somehow, Warren's kept it hot and fresh this entire time.

Timidly, Keturah joins me at the coffee table. She never says *thank you*, and I never hint that I want her to. I simply offer the box of food, and she picks out what she wants. She crowds closer to me on the floor.

After a time, she whispers, "I never got to ask a Sodon request. What's it feel like, asking one?"

"Terrifying," I tell her. "Even worse giving them out, for I fear the consequences that could come of it all. But if you want to ask one, you can ask me." I continue munching away on some meat bits.

Keturah says, "All I ask is that you crush those Vitiosyns, and soon. For I hate them, and how they stole me, and used me for bait. They wanted you to duel that Caleiso. I'm just glad you had Dea to partner with you. It is the one time I was truly glad she's wickedly wild in duels. I don't like dueling against her."

"I don't think I'd like that either," I reply.

Sooner than I wish, Ketty and I finish the rest of the food.

All of us settle down in the prepared beds, only having to share our own with one other. That's how large this room is. Surprisingly, I end up being partnered with Ryco. He must be worried that Talok will have another outburst in the night and come attack me—a perceived threat.

I try divving to Ryco. He doesn't respond initially. Then he divs, *"We are tired, Ravier. We wish to sleep, so let us."*

I lie there, wanting a cuddle partner. Knowing Skylin won't be with us after tonight, I start to slide off the bed to go to her. Even in the dark, a hand grabs me, pulls me back onto the bed.

Ryco whispers tiredly, "Absolutely not."

Though I grumble, I listen. Soon, I'm fast asleep.

* * *

The next morning comes. I stand by the window of our room that's on the third floor of the inn. There's no light outside yet. The lampposts have been put out. But light is approaching. Soon, it will be cresting over the horizon. I unlatch the lock and swing the window open. Hardly do I believe that this moment has come. Today is the day we take flight from Oniva, to make for the Plateau of MarcKand.

Siege and Kent are down below, barely visible in the dimness. They've summoned three Mystadyns—those soft, white-and-gray dragons who fly in the thunderstorms, while clouds flash lightning and pour down rain. The two guards lead the dragons closer to the inn's entrance. I don't see Hydvar or Kaalon standing around anywhere out there.

Kent calls to me, "Tyler, is Talok up yet?"

Slowly, I shake my head.

As he saddles the dyns, Ryco instructs, "Better get him up, Onyx Prince. Before I do."

Siege says, "Aw! Let him sleep, right until we must go. We were up into the wee hours. All of us celebrating, except Ravier, stuck taking those requests."

"And me, nursing all the bruises Ben gave me!" Eli exclaims, before biting into a biscuit. He continues talking around his mouthful of food. "All that excitement made me straight-up tired. Then helping that Ghebina with cleaning the inn afterward. I'm rightly exhausted."

Musgrae reaches for the biscuit, trying to take it from the Kirjan.

Eli stuffs what remains of the biscuit into his mouth. His cheeks bulge like a chipmunk's.

In disapproval, Musgrae smacks Eli on the back.

Swallowing unexpectedly, Eli chokes.

"Yo, Eli!" Warren scorns, approaching him. "That biscuit was for Tyler or Talok. You haven't eaten all that food we gave you, did ya?"

Eli, red in the face, is dazed. Gripping at his throat, he says, "I thought you's were being nice, giving me another breakfast. I did only get an hour of sleep. One hour." He holds up his index finger.

Warren snarls. His attention whips up to view me. "You's want me to beat him, Onyx Prince? I'll be happy to do so."

Quall purses his lips, divving to me, *"Doesn't seem to matter where we go. This lot's always misbehaving some."*

"Would you have them any other way?" I div back, then say to Warren, "Nah! I'm not hungry. The food last night was enough. If I need something later, I'll just have a bite out of Eli's neck."

Eli squeals, drawing his shoulders up protectively. "Is this going to become a family tradition, between you and your cousin? Feeding on me?"

Ignoring them, Ben assists Gemma onto a dragon, then climbs up to join her.

Musgrae helps Ryco finish saddling the last dyn. Then he nods at me once, before lowering his gaze.

My heart sinks. This flight won't be a happy one. Not unless I can forge a spell to save Ryco, prior to when Talok's freed of the device. I shut the window, then amble to my cousin's bedside. Gently, I shake him awake.

He rolls over to face me. "Sit a moment, Tyler."

I do, and he grips my left arm. The device bumps against my skin. It's hot as a pan just beginning to heat over a fire.

Eyes glistening, he tenderly says, "I didn't know I could ever be so proud of a person. That I'd ever admire anyone more than my own father, or Uncle LanSoren. Watching you last night was surreal. It was as the legends of Sorsryns I've grown up reading about. Last night, for the first time, I watched it play out before my eyes. Memories held in the Arkivara do not compare. Perhaps that's to do with me not being pure Vaegon. I cannot feel as she feels. But, yesterday, we all felt something we never had before. All of Oniva did."

"And what was that?" I ask in humility.

"It's hard to explain." His grip tightens. "It was like watching magic become a person. You, Tyler. It's as if you're a sixth particle in our air. We cannot look away from you, and we do not want to. Do you realize that you have near the highest status in Muraine? You're even above the Onyx King, when it comes to freedom. If ReNovak and Zymarc are not present, you hold command of the Onyx."

"Even Gyron?" I ask, hopeful.

"Yes. However, that pendant round his neck makes it easy for ReNovak to overrule your commands." He lets go of me, then gets out of bed. The covers are tugged away.

I stifle a gasp, seeing how much weight he's lost. I can count each of his ribs. Tears well up in my eyes. He doesn't notice.

He starts dressing, instead. "We know you mean to use your circle, to save him. But Ryco told me something last night, after he apologized to Rozeth."

"Please, Talok. I can't listen to this." I bolt off the bed.

"You have to," Talok says firmly. "Your life matters more than his. That's what Ryco believes. So, you may attempt to complete the circle, and save him. I won't dare command you not to try. But don't you *dare* sacrifice yourself, in his place. Ryco can't tell you, so I'll tell you for him. He's come to love you as his little brother. He's lost so much, over the years. Let him give something. Let him die with honor, if it comes to that."

I shake my head. "It won't come to that. It can't."

"I hope you're right," says Talok, now fully dressed. "But if it has to be you or Ryco, who must die to break this device off"—he taps it—"let the Paradyn save me."

I refuse to acknowledge the request. Rather, I storm out of the room. I race down the stairs, so full of rage. A few people are already being served up breakfast, in the pub. One warrior sits alone at a table. I can't help but stop to further observe him. He has his chin propped up on his clenched fists, elbows on the table. His green cloak is draped on the back of his chair, the fabric pooled on the floor.

"Everything all right, fair warrior?" I ask him.

He breaks from his thoughts, his attention jerking to my direction. "Don't mind me, nor my woes, Onyx Prince," he says, moving to take hold of his water glass. He sips from it.

His voice is familiar. I dig through all the memories I can recall of yesterday. They are great in number. I can't place him. He's not a warrior I branded last night, though.

I take a seat across from him. "Was your request denied yesterday?"

He sets his glass down. "It was. I was given another opportunity to ask today. However." He meets my gaze then. "The ten weapons I brought with me from the Aeown, to offer in trade of a given request, were stolen from my room sometime in the night. While I was down here, most likely, watching all the commotion of the Onyx Prince giving out Sodon requests."

Confusion filling me, I muse, *Ten weapons. Why's that sound familiar?* Then it comes to me.

I ask the man, "You were in line, prior to my Sodon request and then accusation of ReNovak, weren't you?"

"Aye, that I was."

"You had ten *named* weapons, didn't you?"

He only nods. Then he stares down at his untouched breakfast.

I'm starting to panic. Zymarc is collecting named weapons for whatever goal he has. If they've been stolen, there's a good chance it was him, or one of his men. I highly doubt Caleiso would show her face, after yesterday. Also, she and Azabahk were looking very poorly after the duel. I'm not even sure if Azabahk made it out alive. I never thought to ask.

The warrior interrupts my panic only to add to it, by saying, "Also, there have been reports from a few Onyx Warriors that a Silverian woman was murdered last night. That Smythe, who was with you. I overhead him telling a few in here. That's when Ghebina snuck off to wake some of your men, get them started for the journey." The man shakes his head. "This Sodon isn't going at all how I expected."

I bolt out of the chair, not sure what to do first.

Talok is just opening the stairwell door. I rush to him, grab him, practically drag him toward the inn's exit. In quiet hysterics, I tell him, "We've got to leave right now. Please don't ask me to explain."

Ghebina stops us at the door.

"Please, Ghebina," I beg. "You must let us leave."

"Aye, I intend to." She holds out a brown satchel. "More food to replace what that skinny guard ate. Good luck to ye." She cups my face and plants a kiss on my cheek.

I blush.

Talok takes the satchel.

She opens the door for us.

Talok and I stride out. We pace forward, side by side. Each dragon is saddled, and carries one large supply box behind the back of the saddle's hardened-leather rims.

Light crests over the horizon.

Kaalon approaches on the roadway all calm-like.

"Kaalon," I call to him. "Have you seen Sawrro this morning?"

"No," he says, now closer. "Why? Is something the matter?"

Hydvar comes around a corner of the inn. "You're not leaving, are you, Tyler?"

I'm starting to not know whom to trust. I'm suspicious of everything, everyone. I push Talok to the saddled dragon in the middle. "Get on!" I shout at him.

Ryco and Rozeth, already on that dragon, pull my cousin up.

Quall and Siege are with Ben and Gemma. The other four quickly climb onto the third dyn.

Smythe is jogging down the road. Once he sees us, he breaks into a run, running past Kaalon. He draws out his long-blade. He whirls around to aim it at Kaalon, whose features crease in shock. Kaalon holds up hands of surrender. The flickering fire in Smythe's other hand, he aims at Hydvar.

"Sawrro is missing!" Smythe shouts. "And the Silverian woman he was with last night has been killed. Murdered in her bed. All the Onyx of Malik are nowhere to be found, save for me. Many others have perished in the night. All who brought weapons or artifacts for trade. They are dead. Former queen, Ayna, has disappeared without a trace. King ReNovak was the last to see her. He's on his way here now, to look into the matter."

Hydvar has gradually closed the distance between himself and Smythe.

Smythe sees it. Frantically, he begs, "Stop, Hydvar! Don't come any closer. There is a traitor among us. I pray it is Sawrro. I want it to be him. Not you, nor Kaalon. Don't delay these Paragonians another minute.

Don't make me fight you, for I will. I will, even unto the death."

"We know," Kaalon says, while lowering his hands of surrender.

Hydvar adds, "We've not seen King ReNovak this morning. Nor Gyronawv."

Kaalon grins. "Therefore, we've not gotten our orders for the day."

"We could," suggests Hydvar, coming closer still, "conjure up small talk with the king, distract him, make him think nothing is at all the matter."

"We could do more than small talk, though," Kaalon adds, "if commanded to do so." He flicks his gaze from Smythe to me.

I let out a held breath, to give the command, "I command you, Onyx Warriors, do whatever it takes to distract, even detain, King ReNovak. Do all you can, without committing wrongs against your king. Be on your way. Buy us time."

"It shall be done," says Hydvar, bolting away. His boots pound on the roadway. He fades out of sight.

Kaalon stares at me. "Where is it you mean to go, Prince Ravier? Home to Paragon?"

"I can't tell you that."

He cringes. "Yes. Stupid of me to ask."

I climb onto the same dragon as Talok.

Kaalon lifts a hand in goodbye. "Speed of dyns."

"Hang on tight," says Ryco. "Don't want you falling and breaking your royal neck."

I do as he says.

Kaalon paces on the road.

Smythe stays planted near our dragons.

"Go on, Smythe," I tell him.

He shakes his head. "I mean to stay right here, block any spells fired at you."

"Right!" says Siege. "Has anyone anything to retrieve, before we get going for our destination on this lovely, quiet morning?"

Ben states, "We've checked, even tripled-checked, supplies."

"So long as Eli"—Warren scowls at the Kirjan sitting beside him—"isn't on the dyn with all the food, we'll be fine."

I ask, "Which dragon carries the food?"

"Which do you think?" Musgrae smirks. "It's behind you and Talok. With the lack of appetite you two share, we figured it'd be safe there."

"Let's be off," Talok commands. "I hear Hydvar talking with ReNovak now. Kaalon's just joined them. They are close."

Siege addresses the dragon Talok and I are on. "Claudys, you lead. And be quick about it."

He eases forward, making a wide turn away from the inn. The other two dragons, smaller in girth and length, follow his lead.

ReNovak's voice is getting closer.

"Yes, Sawrro is missing, Hydvar. He's been missing for hours."

There's a pause.

"Well, Kaalon, why do you think I didn't notice sooner? I was busy in bed, *not* sleeping!" ReNovak shouts. "And why haven't Tyler and his cousin come to breakfast? Nor replied to the note I sent back last night, asking them to dine in the morning."

I wish this Claudys would be faster about his preparations for flight. All three dragons line up to an open path ahead—a clearing of seventy feet or so. After the seventy feet, a grand cathedral stands unrepentantly in the way.

Midsentence, ReNovak stops talking.

I look to my left. Fear crawls all over me.

He's standing not even thirty feet away, a lethal glint in his gaze. "Where do you think you're going, Ravier?" ReNovak shouts, enraged. "Oh, I heard about what you did last night. So, where are they! Where are the warriors you branded, and stole from me?" ReNovak bolts toward us.

Hydvar and Kaalon tackle him, pin him down.

"What are you doing?" ReNovak shrieks. "Get off me! Stop them from leaving!"

Smythe leans down to ask, "Is that a command, King ReNovak?"

"Yes, you fools! It's a command! Orders for the morning: don't let them leave!"

As the warriors are busy, detaining their king, Claudys breathes in deeply, sounding as a gust of wind. He exhales, and his body rushes forward. The movement's smooth. His wings create perfect dynamics. Only a gentle breeze stirs about, as surroundings blur to streaks of colors.

Blasts of fire smash into smaller, nearby buildings. Debris crosses our path, but Kent and Warren clear it with wind magic.

Already to the grand cathedral now, Claudys bounds upward with force. Even as he climbs the cathedral's wall, and pushes off from the roof, the motion's fluid, akin to bounding from a wall while underwater. There's power behind it, yet not the roughness.

A horn blares in the distance, and ringing that sounds akin to large bells clanging. A great, resonating call races over the city of Oniva. All warriors on the ground, now far below us, line up.

The dragon, Claudys, rumbles the command, "Hold on tighter! They mean to pull us down with magic. But we are stronger than what they can send, for we are Mystadyns, made of a wind stronger than any Sorsryn could ever hope to cast."

And he's right.

I hear the great gusting beneath us. We hang on with a death grip. The pull the wind has on my feet or anything else that hangs over the sides of the dragon is fierce. But the dyn does not notice. He continues making the ascent, unbothered. As do the other two.

Seconds later, Claudys becomes agitated. He rumbles, "Enough of them, I say. Guard your ears."

Ryco casts a spell over us, as lightning flares from Claudys's wings. It crackles and thunders down to the ground. The other two follow in his example. Even with Ryco's guarding spell, I still hear a great crashing below. A roar of horrified shouting. Then silence.

My hearing comes back into full volume.

The dragons level out in the air.

I look over my shoulder, to the city we're leaving behind. No one is coming after us, in the air.

We've escaped Oniva, only to head for MarcKand, some days' journey away.

***

That first stop for the dragons to rest is pleasant enough. Silently, we agree not to mention the narrow escape.

Ryco and Warren prepare supper.

Gemma asks, "Where'd the saddles come from?"

"Me," replies Warren, as he spices up the stew with herbs. "Finished what our head blacksmith, Yigoshi, started but never got to complete. Found them in Eyo'el, when we stopped to resupply. Reduced their weight and size. They've been holed up in my pouch, from that time forward. Teeny, adorable, little saddles. Looked like they could fit those squeaky tree lizards I've seen around, from time to time."

"Is that a Sylvadyn joke?" Ryco smirks, pausing to add vegetables to the pot.

"What?" queries Warren, confused. Then he catches the special glint in Ryco's glance. "No, Ryke. I didn't mean the Sylvadyns. Vards! They're not teeny at all."

"Certainly. They are not," Ryco agrees.

Claudys and the other two Mystadyns curl up round our camp in a circle, like lean, long cats, hugging the warmth in. Yet a slight breeze always swirls around, when they're near. The scales not covered by tiny, velvety feathers are slick and tightly knit together. It's as if thick, smooth skins have been etched with the pattern of dragon scales.

Gemma asks Claudys, "Now that The Sodon is soon to end this evening, will we still be able to fly all through the day, without fear of being attacked by Vitiosyns?"

The voice of Claudys is a soft, metallic timbre as he answers Gemma. "Mystadyns are often left alone. We side with no one. And that's by choice. The Dyns' War was long and hard, and Mystadyns came out at the bottom of the rung. My grandest dame and sire told me of it. We are not strong enough to make much difference in a war against

BlacKaidyns or Sylvadyns. Certainly not against Rubidyns. We are the weak ones, simply enjoying the storms in the sky, rather than the storms down below."

"I love the sky, and lots of clouds," says the skinniest dyn.

The other hisses, "Thunderstorms! Those, I love. We can defeat the lightning, absorbing it. But we can't cast it too well. If we could, we'd be a storm. Back there was a mere fluke, I think. Us, absorbing the magic of Onyx Warriors."

The skinny one fervently nods. "Yes, that's how it was."

"In other words, Galloway," says Claudys, elegantly crossing his furry, scaled paws that rest on the ground. "We're allowed to fly anywhere, mostly free."

"And much we see," says the skinny one.

The other adds, "But do not tell, for none do we side with, but ourselves."

"We're merely practice dyns," Claudys states, "for tamers to attain high enough levels to tame BlacKaidyns." He pauses, and what appear to be swept, elongated feathers above his eyes draw together. They might as well be sleek, angry eyebrows. At least, when Claudys is scowling. For when he is at peace, his face has a softness to it that near no other creature possesses. He adds in sorrow, "When they no longer need us, they forget us."

Siege argues, "I do not forget you."

Claudys laughs, and a burst of wind almost puts the fire out. Warren shields it, standing with outstretched arms and coat spread far like an ostrich fluffing its body out.

The fire's saved.

He sits down.

"That's due to your kindness," replies Claudys to Siege. "Got to be mean, taming those stubborn BlacKaidyns. And though you can, you don't prefer it, Dragon's Voice."

Reminded of something my father said, I speak it as a question to the dragons: "Reflection gazes into the ages. Confirming it and seldom more? For their fear is near, when that reflection doth, indeed, confirm it."

"Yes, exactly," says Claudys. "We fear recompense for ratting out the happenings of the surface."

"Reflection?" the skinniest perks his head up. "Mirrors. That reminds me of mirrors. I love mirrors."

"Mirrors, I hate," the other grumbles.

"You hate everything but storms," the skinniest says.

"By the Dyn's Spike!" Claudys grumbles. "Having you two around, why, it's like being round an echo."

Gemma smiles. "You should call them Delta and Echo."

The grumbly one lifts his head higher. "I like that. Delta. I claim it."

"Oo!" the skinny one squeaks. "I am Echo. That is mine."

"But those aren't Mystadyn names." Claudys scowls.

"Doesn't matter," Echo says. "They're our new names. Named by Galloway. Ha!"

I ease up, wanting a moment away from the noise. In div, I ask Warren, *"Do you have the Spear of Guyheiz, and may I have it for the circle?"*

Not even looking away from the arguing dragons, Warren slips it, in miniature form, off his belt and gives it to me. No one notices.

I quietly trail away, eager to start practicing for the Hexyn Circle, as the spear grows to full size. I wish Dea or Skylin were here with me. Or, better, that Gyron was here, as a free Onyx of Malik. Instead, it's the six weapons that are with me: my daggers, the Onyx set, the spear, and the shield's power disguised as a long, metal feather that Dea bestowed to me. I know the real Hexyn will either be on ice or underwater. For now, I just draw lines in the dirt. I rearrange the weapons' placement, completely lost on where they should go. It goes well into the night, until Ben wanders to where I am.

"Have you picked your spells yet?"

I shake my head, gathering the weapons to restart. "They can't be elementals. That's all I know."

Ben points to the weapons I've gathered back up in my arms. "They need to resemble the weapons, to a degree. Relate to them, somehow. Want suggestions?"

Tiredly, I nod. We sit down together, and I take out my spell-book. Jotting down the ones I recall Dea telling me, I show the list to Ben.

"Deflamo is good," he states. "Pairs well with the Blades of Neutrality. *Zeekstoneis* is another you should do. That one is cast, in preparation for being attacked. Deflamo is for mid-attack. But both nullify spells, good or bad."

"Makes sense." I write it down. "What about my daggers? Night and day?"

Ben smiles. "The perfect ones, if that's what you feel they are in nature, would be: Zotekavond and Nyxavond."

"Whiteout, blackout?" I ask.

Ben nods.

I write those down too. "That leaves the spear and shield. The spear's Kyanistic, right?"

"Yes. And it deals with time. Time is Metimoran. *Temporiavas.* Slowing or speeding it up is Blue Magic. It matters what you intend to do with the enchantment, as to which you should choose. *Rempori*, to slow down time. *Velotemp*, to speed it up. As for the shield, *you* must choose that. Have it relate to the heart of your intentions. Are you protecting something? Do you mean to destroy? You must answer that, for yourself."

I lift my shoulders, feeling defeated already. "I don't know enough words, Ben. There's not enough time for me to learn it all."

After he licks his lips, Ben takes something out of one of his supply pouches. With a trembling grasp, he offers me a worn, teal-leather book. "That is why I want you to take this. My spell-book. After becoming Eighth of the Guard, I wrote all meanings and instructions down in English, to get better at the language. How to pronounce it all, using its rules, rather than rules of the language of Vaegons or Sorsryns. It's indexed in the back."

I hesitate to accept it. "Won't you need it later?"

"Ryco has given me his. And it's in a language I prefer. Now, will you come to bed? Gemma won't go to sleep, and she's refused to so much as look at me, for as long as you're out here, alone."

"Here I was, thinking you wanted to chat." I tease, "But you's just wanted Gemma cuddles."

He blushes. "Yes. That, and a girl's goodnight kiss. Will you help me out, Tyler?"

Clutching Ben's spell-book, I get up. "Come on then. I suppose one of us should get the girl tonight."

We head for camp.

At one point, Ben nudges against my shoulder. "That Skylin, we approve of. None more than Talok, though. She's been good for you. And you for her, it seems."

"Tell that to Arsyn. I don't think he cares much for me. Called me everyone's toxin."

Ben clasps his hands behind himself. "No. That's a good sign. It means Skylin cares for you deeply enough that her father sees it, and worries. Khyra's parents didn't even know who I was, until I made Eighth of the Guard, and found favor in Ryco's eyes."

"Did you happen to see the Darklyres off?" I ask. "I haven't had the heart to ask about it, till now."

Ben slows his stride, coming to a complete stop.

I turn to face him. "Did something happen?"

Ben swallows.

I'm starting to sweat.

Finally, he ends my misery by saying, "It did. Dea and King Aygor got into a bit of an argument. She had wanted to come with us, especially after that Ayna and your marked Onyx Sorsryns joined with Aygor, promised to escort the Darklyres to wherever they wished to go. King Aygor eventually had to dispatch Dea, tie her up, take her away. Skylin was quite upset over it all."

My head lowers. A lump forms in my throat. "Why wouldn't he let her come?"

"Fear, Ravier," Ben replies, that look of wisdom about his eyes. "Where we are headed is very dangerous. And King Aygor cares for all his wards greatly. Imagine how hard it was for him to let his wards go with us to

Paragon? I imagine he only asked that of us, because Arsyn and SynKievas also accompanied us. Neither are with us now." Ben restarts the walk for camp.

In quiet misery, I follow. My feet drag along the grassy dirt for that last bit of the walk. Before we're to camp again, I end the silence by saying, "Thanks for keeping Gemma happy, Ben. I haven't been the greatest friend during our time here."

"She understands, Tyler. As Warren said, you're pulled in all directions."

I stop to look at him. Anger swells within my chest, as I voice the thought, "But there's only one direction I truly want to go."

Ben's features take on pride. He stands taller, as if at attention. Victory dances in those wise, brown eyes. "And what direction is that?"

I tell him, "To face Zymarc and Caleiso, and utterly destroy them."

18

Circle of Enedei

Hours of flight, with only enough time to rest on the ground, are what fill the next days. I practice the Hexyn Circle as much as I'm able to, but I haven't chosen the shield's spell word yet. Nor what the intent should be. Night after night, I study Ben's spell-book until my vision goes blurry.

The answer evades me.

I sink to the ground in defeat, as desperation takes over one night. The last night that I have to figure out the Hexyn Circle to save Ryco as he saves Talok. My eyes sting. My throat burns. I want to scream. Instead, I take hold of NeiSator. I throw him as hard as I can in the direction opposite of camp. Out in darkness, he thwacks into some tree I can't see. I hug my knees to my chest and silently cry. I lower my head, until my forehead rests on my knees.

A warm hand presses on my back. I didn't even hear anyone approach. I startle to my feet, quickly wiping the tears away, to stand tall. Taller than I feel inside.

Those familiar yellow eyes glow in contrast to the blackness of night. They are dimmer, however. Straw-colored. Ryco comes a little closer. I'm able to make out the rest of his features in the moonlight. "It is all right, Tyler," he says. "It will be all right."

My chin quivers. My shoulders hunch. I can't keep hold of the façade

255

any longer. My voice trembles in saying, "If you help me, I bet I can get it. I feel like I'm close to having it right. Please, Ryco, help me. Help me save you. I don't just want Talok to be saved. I want you to go home to Paragon too. I want you to hear all the people, returning after the war is won, call you the Paradyn. To welcome you back as a good family would. I want them to care for you, as I have come to care . . . for you." I trail off, sniffing back the sobs building in my chest.

Ryco has taken the position directly in front of me. The glow of his eyes is all but a dim light. He reaches slowly, to rest his hands upon my coat lapels. No warmth radiates from them anymore; only coldness. I shiver.

"I would like that," he says. "That which you've described. It sounds nice. Happy. What I've learned of happiness, however, is that it always fades. I am a Sylvadyn, and true happiness isn't meant for them. For us. My kind. Though I'm a quarter Sylvadyn, it doesn't matter. My mind is as a full-blooded one. My father was of the Sivos line, not the Sylvas. The Sivos are only good for two, perhaps three, things. War. Producing many offspring. And being the kind of monster that preys on children, scares them, breaks them, enslaves them. Sivos Sylvadyns are not good, Ravier. My advice to you"—Ryco grips my coat lapels tight in his fists—"if you ever come across a Sivos, kill it. Cleave its body in half. Bury the halves far apart from each other. For Sylvadyns can otherwise use spells of Nekrosis. Reanimate each other. They become worse than how Merlynite was, for they can control the forest. Haunt it, devour it, make it rise up against any who dare step foot in it."

"Why are you telling me this?" I ask. "Are we in danger of being surrounded by Sivos dragons?"

"Not now." He lets go of me. "But on the way back to Paragon, you might encounter them. I'm telling you what to do, should that happen. I've not told any of the others this." He looks away. "I've had to take care of keeping the Sivos dyns out of Paragon, by myself. Ben caught me one night, though." Ryco seems to cherish the memory. The brightness of his eyes slightly returns. "He offered to help. So I let him. I killed the Sivos.

Ben dug the graves. We buried the halves together."

Suddenly, it makes sense to me why Ryco gave Ben his spell-book.

Continuing, Ryco says, "The first time I saw him, he was six years old. Fancied himself a victim of 'love at first sight' with little Khyra." Ryco steps past me. He's gone only seconds. He returns with NeiSator in hand.

I take the dark dagger and clip him back on my belt.

When I look back to Ryco, tears have wet his face. He says, "I wish I could watch Ben become a fearsome warrior. I know that's what he'll become. Will you watch that, for me? Be the witness?"

I don't trust my voice to work, so I only nod.

"And don't tell them what I've told you, unless you need to. I fear too many questions would arise in their minds, to do with my past sorrows. I've no wish for that subject to be the lingering thoughts they have of me. Rather, I want them to think of what my last act of service will be for Paragon, its king, and my friend."

I state, "I think Talok's more than a friend to you, Ryco."

He looks surprised. "Ravier, I wasn't talking of Talok. And if you consider yourself my friend, will you do something for me?"

"Anything."

"Good," he says, then pauses, searching for words. After a time, he says this: "Save the Hexyn for something else."

I start to argue. But the desperation, the torment on Ryco's face stops me. I find that my words of argument slip away.

He continues, "Save it for something better. Something that will save many others, not just one. If you must pick one, have it be a good one. One capable of stopping Zymarc. I can't. I've tried. And I have failed. Don't you fail, Ravier." Fire returns to Ryco's voice. His eyes are like bright fire too, burning the sorrow right out of me. Or perhaps *scaring* it right out of me.

He offers his hand. "In case we don't get another chance, I have one last thing to say to you, Tyler. I'm glad to have met you, my friend. Take care of Paragon, and all that it entails."

Gripping his offered hand, I reply, "I'll try my best."

Ryco smiles. He leans closer. He whispers, "I've got news for you, Ravier. I believe your best is good enough." He releases my hand.

We walk back to where the others are, side by side, as friends.

* * *

The next day is the final day, that last leg of the journey, spent with the Mystadyns. As they have taken us farther from the cities—any civilization—they flew lower and lower. We're now able to make out more of Muraine than we could before. Exquisite and colorful don't begin to describe it. It's not until we approach the Monel that the colors fade away to bleak. It's barren. All trees are leafless and twisted, covered in thick, brown moss in the stages of decay. The grass is pale-yellow. When Claudys and the two land softly upon it, it crunches loudly.

Echo complains, "This place, I do not like."

Even while climbing down from Claudys, Ryco states, "This isn't the plateau."

"We know," says Delta, glancing yonder to the tall, crumbling, dust-colored buildings.

Claudys clarifies, "It's believed to be haunted by Soren, himself. None but the bravest go there. And you are brave, Sylvadyn. All tamers hold a bravery we simply do not possess. We shall wait for your friends, down here."

Delta adds, "And we shall be honored to carry you home for eternal rest."

"Yes, rest eternal, Sylvadyn," Echo adds with sorrow.

"Speed of dyns," says Ryco, patting Claudys on the shoulder. He turns to lead the way.

The three Mystadyns have bowed their heads. Further they bow their heads, as we turn away to finish the hardest journey I do believe any of us have ever made.

We trudge through the dead land that's spotted with crumbling structures and muddy water puddles. The worst, however, are the remains of the Withrasyns. Thousands of skeletons, picked clean. Cloth decayed, clings to bones—the bones, which are as smooth as prepared ivory, except for where they have been fractured. Broken by visiting creatures, most likely. A hot, dry breeze ripples the dirt further, rattles the bones where they lay, and stirs the frayed cloth.

There are no other sounds than us, the bones, the wind, and the Mystadyns gently moving about. Then they are too far away for us to hear.

The cold hits us like a wave. We draw our clothes tighter about our bodies. We huddle closer together too. On the path Ryco takes us up and up farther still, snow grows deeper and deeper. Gemma keeps stumbling. Musgrae eventually has to carry her on his back, as if she's a small child spent from an entire day of running about. In her case—in fact, for all of us—it's been an entire month of running about, fearing for our lives.

Warren jogs to the front of the line, where Quall and Ryco lead. He motions that we stop. He and Eli resize some supplies—more cloaks and coverings for our boots. We layer on what they give us. No one says a word to each other. We can't bring ourselves to. The sorrow is too sharp. And the fear too great that speaking will awaken ghosts of the fallen Withrasyns.

By nightfall, we're at the top, depleted and shivering. The plateau is absent of everything. Everything except snow. More of it starts flaking down from the shadowed sky.

Gemma huddles near Ben, and I beside Talok.

Ryco hands Warren the pamphlet Arsyn gave him weeks ago. "Please, Warren, prepare this Circle of Enedei for me."

Alarmed, Warren stiffens his neck. "A circle of nine points?" He flips through the small pages, going faster and faster. He's panicking. "Ryco, why didn't you tell me this uses nine spells, so strong, so vile, that no weapons are even needed? You're not going where Deathasyns go!" he shouts, furious. "Your soul will be sent to the worst of places. The place where souls killed upon Blackwood Spikes go." Warren throws the pamphlet aside, and it lands in the snow.

Gemma starts to sob. A scream escapes her, echoing out. Musgrae clamps his hand over her mouth. He shushes her. Ben stares at the ground in silence.

"Gem, please," Musgrae begs. He glances about, afraid.

Talok comes forward, enraged. "Is this true?" He glares at Ryco.

Ryco admits, "I knew you would rather die, yourself, than let this happen, Talok. I deceived you, fully meaning to confess when we were already here."

Talok's eyes blaze. He turns pale, and his teeth grow sharper, looking more Deathasyn by the minute. "I forbid this—"

I know what I must do, yet I despise myself for it. Stepping in front of Talok, I interrupt him. "Let Ryco go, Talok. Let this Paradyn save you. We've come all this way. Don't force him to watch you die. This is how it must be. I hate it. You hate it. We all do. But it is what it is. I *will* show honor to the Sylvadyn. So should you. Must I pull rank, and give the Onyx Prince's command? Please! This hurts more than I thought possible."

Talok's color returns. His teeth shift back to normal. To Warren, he whispers, "See that the circle is prepared with the utmost care."

Warren picks up the pamphlet. Hatred rules each movement of his thereafter. Sooner than any of us are ready, Warren has finished the preparations. I couldn't bear to listen nor watch him do it. I now watch, as he gives Ryco the pamphlet. "This vile spell dies with you."

Ryco nods, his breaths sounding choked out.

Warren walks away with a stiffness, but then he rushes back to embrace Ryco. He smacks the Sylvadyn on the back, hard. Then, in agony, he lets go.

Rozeth's next. "For luck," she says, "that you may go to a better place than where we believe you are going." She kisses him firmly on the mouth, then pulls away.

She lets him bite into her neck, to draw magic from her veins.

Ben holds a cloth out. "For your face." He forces a grin.

Ryco takes the cloth. He wipes the blood off, before gripping one of

Ben's shoulders. "Take care . . ." His words trail off.

Ben finishes, "Of the lot of them. I know. And I will. Light of Vardiyas be with you, Ryco of Paragon."

They all say their own goodbyes.

I'm last. Approaching, I hold my left hand out. "The way Deamond believed in me, that night of first learning Enchantment Circles, I believe in you, Ryco. May true happiness be at the end, for you."

He gives back my enchanted blade. "You're the best of us, Ravier—of Paragon, of Oniva, and, now, of Monel." He heads for the circle's center.

I put the enchanted weapon away.

Warren poses Talok, with his device-entrapped wrist, along the circle's outer rim to specific positions to each other. He then comes to join the rest of us, and raise a sound-dampening barrier.

Ryco takes one of the five pouches off his belt, setting it down beside his feet. He stands tall, as he begins to read the pamphlet aloud. We hardly hear the words, and Ryco covers his mouth as he speaks them. Spells ignite at the nine points, one by one.

Warren whispers, "Ryco doesn't want us hearing it." He turns to Rozeth. "Also, he wanted me to tell you that Lemawr gave him the heart of Dezarin, when learning of what we intended to do. Dezarin ain't dead, Rozeth. His body's gone. It's true. But Dezarin lives on, in Lemawr. Two Siveyras in one. Ryco wanted you to know, and to have some hope to hold to for this moment. Especially since he means to use Dezarin's heart for solidifying this spell. Ensure it's an absolute success and all."

Rozeth balls up her fists. "That wicked Sylvadyn. Deceitful for the good of others. I hate him and I love him."

When the ninth spell ignites, whispering chants emit from the circle; chants that do not come from Ryco nor anyone seen. But from the unseen.

Warren erases the barrier. The chants get loud, and louder still. Blood comes up from the ground that the circle's drawn on. Then that blood flows, forming into three things at the circle's perimeter. The beings are of equal distance to each other. Figures take on characteristics. Deathasyns, who are cloaked in grungy, torn rags of metallic-teal cloth, stand as eight-foot-tall monsters. Sharp, jagged teeth show, as they finish their chant. Their maroon-red eyes pierce through the night and cold, melting the snow wherever they gaze. Arms spread out, they touch fingertips to the wrists of the other two. The three easily complete the circle, in this way.

The broadest of them speaks first, in a deep, chilling undertone reminiscent of metal scraping at bone. "I am Vosh-Vendei, ninth born child, fifth and last son to Father of Geldreis and Gendran. Twins of Geldryn, they were. High, did they become. Cursed, did they maketh me and my half brothers." He steps toward Ryco, and motions to the left.

The left one strides forward the same amount as his brother, speaking the words, "I am Vit'Athos. The youngest of these is Perida's Kree."

The third saunters all the way to Ryco, while making the statement: "You hath summoned the three. Dei-Athos-Kree. Your life you forfeit for another. That is the deal of this Circle of Enedei. Have you all pieces? Have you two hearts to satisfy my hungry, older brothers?"

Never looking away from Talok, Ryco replies, "Heart of a Son of a Sorshrynak, Dezarin's, and my own—Sylvadyn, Withrasyn, and Vaegon. The one I wish to free is he, in the blank sliver of the circle. Will you free him of the cursed Geldryn device of old?"

Vosh-Vendei pivots his attention to Talok. Then to the device. He screeches, sounding far worse than Awngeleik when she's terrified. The sound brings sensations of a knife gently scraping along my skin, threatening to cut me open at any second.

Vosh-Vendei's maroon eyes begin to bleed. He claws at his own face. His voice hisses, "Give me that Dezarin's heart. For I must wash away the horrors of this binding. Wrist Bind of Blood Thirst."

Ryco stands, resolute. "Not until your brothers begin the freeing of him, Talok of Paragon."

"Do as this Sylvadyn mutt dost say," Vosh-Vendei commands. "Destroy that wretched binding forever. What my own Geldryn brothers did curse me with, it was. This day forward, it shall be no more. Great thanks I must give you, Sylvadyn. I shall show you the making of this spell, as your reward. It shan't save your soul from the striking. But you shall see what none have, save for those who made the spell. My preferred spell of the Dei-Athos-Kree spells."

The brothers fade to embers, then shift into looking more alive. Not in rags. Vosh-Vendei has the Geldryn device on his wrist. He's drenched in blood. His two brothers have him chained. He screams and screeches, sounding as a wild animal.

"I must feed!" he pleads. "I must have more blood. Soren, save me of this fate. Please, I beg you. I beg for my life. Again and again. I am wretched!" The Deathasyn weeps.

A fourth figure approaches the circle, seeming from long ago. It's the younger Soren.

"I must cheat, to do it," he says. "I have searched the world over. Even in time, I have sought something to save you, Vosh-Vendei. There are only two I've found who can do it. An older-me, and his apprentice, Adair Tomatsu Galloway."

Soren opens a book of time. Most likely one of the greater Books of Time. One of the six. The pages turn. The older Soren, in all his horrific glory, steps out from the pages. A small man—clothed as an Amethyst Sorsryn, but absent of a hood—comes from behind the older Soren.

Gemma gasps. She clamps her hands over her mouth and leans closer for a better look.

Cold as ice, Soren of the Monel commands, "Do as this young Sorshrynak bids us, Adair. It shall be our undoing, meddling with time, in such ways. He does not yet know how broken he makes the timeline. While he strives to save but one soul, he, indeed, condemns many." Soren laughs.

The younger one watches in horror.

The older Soren shuts him out of the circle. "You're done here, stupid soul. It's my turn now. You had your show, in Eyo'el. But my work starts here. The Circle of Enedei. Nine. The Geldryn think it—nine—as an abomination. They think many things are an abomination. Dragon-horses, for example. They think those are the worst conceptual sort of creature. But they are perfection. Two hearts, beating in one body. Perfect for a Circle of Enedei. Yes! It shall free me. Nine! Let this be done by you, dear Adair. Start what another will finish."

Swallowing hard, the small Adair steps into the circle's center with Ryco. He doesn't know the Sylvadyn's there. Or doesn't show that he knows. His eyes glow, swirling with copper and red, akin to Rentwar's fiery, flickering ones. He reaches out toward the nine points, one at a time. Strands of light then connect him to those points.

Others appear, for a flash. The Galloways.

Adair speaks, "Heirs to Neftelliim. A portion of their power, I shall, in fact, take. Bind to the Enedei. Soren's Enedei of Dei-Athos-Kree. None do I care that it saves, but one. A true innocent, far into the future. Nine watches. She weeps for him. The other. For them. She cannot stop that fateful trade of souls. One must perish, that the other may live. Laevarye, there is a time to die. And it is time. I shall begin."

My chest aches. I want this to be over. Yet, I cannot look away. I cannot abandon Ryco, in his time of sacrifice.

Adair takes matching blades out. I realize, in dismay, they're my daggers. Only longer. They begin to glow, while in Adair's grip. Then they wisp with fire to match their dusk and dawn colors. In succession, Adair cuts three light strands. Two flashes of Adair's descendants go by. Moments in which one danced exquisitely, or another ran faster than the other kids. Adair draws magic from himself, and these two. Memories fade. Six strands remain.

Soren speaks, "One, two, three. They are for you."

Vosh-Vendei is released by his brothers. In a trance, he takes up the position where the three strands have faded from.

Adair cuts three more.

Flashes of a younger Tadashi start. He practices with a Katana blade, by himself. Slashing this way and that, he cuts a symbol in the air. Yet he's unaware. Adair reaches for that symbol, and pulls it into the circle. Tadashi fades. Two others are shown. One a painter. The other, a musician. In the thick of their artful moments, they, too, draw symbols, not knowing what they truly do. Adair takes those symbols. Those two Galloways fade.

Soren counts more, "Four, five, six. They are for him."

Vit'Athos enters that now-vacant space.

With more force, Adair cuts the last three strands, then falls to his knees, breathing hard.

A young woman duels with Tadashi, besting him at near every turn with her Katana. In the end, Tadashi's at her mercy. Seven symbols has she secretly drawn in the air. She laughs. "Won again, big brother," she says.

She fades to another scene with Tadashi, who holds a newborn child in his arms. He shows the child to the woman—his sister—as she lies on a hospital bed.

Tearful, he says, "Kathryn, you have a daughter. Isn't she beautiful? Please, will you hold on to life for her?"

"Name her Katie Galloway," says Kathryn, "after me, for she is beautiful. But yours will be better, big brother."

Tadashi holds his little sister's hand, trying to find a response. He can't. He clings to the baby girl in his arms.

"Take care of her, Tadashi," says Kathryn weakly. "Life will be hard without a mother. We should know."

They fade, and it shifts to a different girl. Older than Gemma, perhaps the same age as Deamond. Her eyes are bright-green, but her smile shines brighter than the light in her gaze. It flashes through her talents. Music. Singing. Fighting with weapons, even dueling against Tadashi. There seems nothing she cannot do. It goes through her ages, and nine symbols she makes, throughout her years, in secret. Adair reaches, to take them. As the girl dances on a stage an artful ballet in front of a massive crowd, she draws the ninth symbol with her footsteps. When Adair takes that symbol, the girl loses her balance and falls. Landing wrong, she screams. She grips at her ankle.

Looking up, she meets my gaze. Her tears cease. She's seen me, or someone, as the scene fades out. Her terrified expression is the last to disappear, before it shifts to my father. He's sitting at his desk in the study, writing letters. He reaches for his coffee mug to take a sip, as one of the daggers floats up from somewhere in the room. Soren appears, aiming it at my father.

"Stupid, Ravier," he coos in a singsong voice, "leaving these around for me to take hold of. They were mine, once. And they remember. Recall the days I put them to good use."

My father replies, "Killing thousands is hardly good use, Soren. Put the dagger down. And let's have a talk, shall we?"

"Tired of talking," says Soren. "More doing is what I want. Teaching a little Galloway a spot of magic. She saw me, the other day. A Galloway *actually* saw me. In this world. I asked if she wanted to learn magic. And she agreed. I've been teaching the ninth one, at the lake." He laughs. "She's there, now. Swimming. Swimming on down. Down . . . to drown." He laughs maniacally, pointing the dagger away from my father's neck. He amuses himself.

My dad panics. He runs out of the house. He dashes toward the lake, sprinting at full speed, through the forest. He gets to the lake's rocky shore, then yells out one word. One name: "Gemma!" He sees something in the water and dives in. He takes hold of her limp, little body, then swims for shore. Once on shore, he yells, "No! Why has this happened? It can't happen! Wake up, Gemma. Come back! Tyler needs you. He just doesn't know it yet. Don't die, Galloway." He sweeps his hand tenderly over her lifeless, child's face. Then he silently weeps.

A high-pitched voice calls to him, asking, "What's the matter, Mr. Ravier? Are you all right?"

He looks up. It's the young Gemma, sitting beside him, looking at him with concern.

"What were you thinking?" he shouts. "Why were you swimming alone? You could have drowned. You could have died."

"I was napping, Mr. Lance," she says. "I couldn't have been swimming. My clothes are dry. See?"

He touches the hem of her sleeve, then a dry strand of her hair. "Yes, you're perfectly dry. I don't know what's happening. What's wrong with me?" He looks about in fear.

The young Gemma keeps silent.

Then my father gales in a breath. "I need you to do something, for me. For Tyler too. Will you?"

She nods.

In sadness, he instructs, "When it's time to blow out the candles of the cake for your eighth birthday, I want you to think three things. Focus on them *so* hard, as if you're about to speak them. But don't speak them aloud. Merely, think. Can you do it?"

"Yes," she replies.

"Here's the first," says my father. "I *wish* a thousand wishes, to see the good in Soren one last time."

"Got it." She nods.

"The second: I hope for *one* soul in one hundred million souls to save."

"One hundred million," says the child-Gemma, with wonder. "That's a lot. But I'll hope to save the one."

"Good." My father grins. "The last, and third: I will be the one to set the Sorshrynak free. For it is me, the binding Ninth of Enedei. Heir to Neftelliim."

The present Gemma is next to me, as she takes hold of my left wrist. She digs her nails in. She starts speaking through her younger-self, to my father, saying, "It's all right, Mr. Ravier. We're here at the Circle of Enedei, on the Plateau of MarcKand. I see the one in one hundred million souls to save. Your nephew, Talok. Ryco, Lemawr, Dezarin, and I are the main parts. See it through, LanSoren. For, here, in front of me, you already have. Your son's been named the Onyx Prince. He has branded Onyx Warriors. Called them the Onyx of Malik. You did it. You saved your son."

"Galloway?" My father's voice cracks in relieved sorrow. He cups the child-Gemma's face. Then he glances around, searching. He can't see us. "I cannot believe it. I defeated Soren? I defeated that demon?"

Gemma speaks again, "We don't know for sure, but we believe so. Rest well, Ravier. You won. Soon, we shall defeat Zymarc."

My father's smile fades, as he says, "When the time is right, tell him everything. Remember that phrase, Tyler. It's important, in this timeline. Despairing Marion, and despairion," he speaks to the young Gemma. "These two words for riches are safe kindling for thought. When the Witch of Galloway is given the ashes, she shall remember more. Thirteen things, as well as ghost memories of Soren and me, magic and Muraine. When Vardiyas light her path, she'll know the third set."

Soren, within the circle, looks on at us with murderous intent. He speaks the phrase: "Thirteen things, to be done."

My father's figure dissipates like smoke.

The child-Gemma begins aging. The clips of her secretly drawing symbols flash by so quickly we don't see what she does. Then she stops, and fades away. It's over. Adair draws the thirteen symbols of Gemma's to himself.

Soren says, "Seven, eight, but nine completes it for them."

Perida's Kree steps into the last section.

The Deathasyn brothers grip each other's wrists. They complete the circle, a second time.

The spell pamphlet in Ryco's hands burns up. His breaths quicken. He's gasping, then shouting. His hands are drawn out as if pulled on by rope. He cannot shield himself with his hands. He cries out.

Adair softly touches Ryco on the chest. His face crumples in fear of what's to happen—the taking of one life, to save another. But Adair still initiates it, then he steps back. And when he steps back, a bright-red, horizontal beam of fire sears from the hands of Perida's Kree to slam against Ryco's chest.

Ben comes to shield Gemma's view. He hugs her close, as she screams in horror.

Eli faints, falling to the ground.

Kent collapses to his knees.

The rest of us stand by, helpless. We can't do anything except watch, and lean on each other.

Rozeth runs away, throwing herself down into the snow to weep.

I look back to those citrine-yellow eyes, refusing to look away until it's over.

The fire beam stops.

Ryco still stands. But a hole's been bored through his chest.

Talok has shifted to look as a Deathasyn. He lies lifeless on the ground, within the circle. I fear we've lost them both, in the same instant.

Ryco divs weakly, *"It's not over yet. When my eyes close. Count to thirteen. The device should break off him. I'll start falling. Thirteen more. I'll be gone. I'll miss you."*

I div back, *"I'll carry you in memory, forever."*

A small smile plays across his lips. His eyes deaden, then close. He falls to the ground with a sickening thud.

The Deathasyn brothers chant and laugh as it happens. Vosh-Vendei takes the pouch resting by Ryco's feet, then he and his brothers disappear to feast.

Soren of the Monel and Adair go back through their Book of Time.

The younger Soren is let into the circle again. He looks around in horror, whispering, "Vardiyas forgive me for this atrocity of magic. I do not know what I have done. I fear, I shall never be the same."

He, as well, fades from our view.

Something cracks, sounding as glass. We rush to the circle, but Warren makes us wait.

Checking that it's safe, he nods.

We go forward.

Talok's color is coming back. The device has not only broken off him but has shattered into dust. My cousin is starting to sit up. He crawls over to Ryco. Hugging his Second Guard to his chest, he whispers, "Well done, Ryke. You saved me. Be at peace, dear Paradyn."

Footsteps crunch in the snow. Someone's approaching. He asks, "How long, since he fell?" It's Arsyn, looking on sternly at the horrific sight.

"Just over thirteen seconds ago," I reply.

"Then I don't have long to start preserving him, do I?" He sets down a simple casket made of Blackwood.

He rushes forward, to take Ryco's maimed body from Talok's grasp. He carefully sets Ryco in the casket, then quickly places the lid over the opening. A barrier flashes and clicks over the wood.

Eli starts coming to, looking on at the happenings.

"There," Arsyn says, sweeping his hands over the top. "I've preserved his body, within a minute of his death."

"What can you do, Arsyn?" I ask. "How can you hope to bring him back? Look what that ritual did to his body. Did you see it? We had to watch it!" I shout.

"I know, Tyler," he says quietly. "But I'm a Darklyre. And we like challenges."

I shout louder, "Don't taunt us with that! Don't give us hope you cannot fulfill. It took everything in us, to say goodbye. Don't make us do that again."

Arsyn places a finger on the closed casket. "I have to try to save him, especially after hearing what you did at The Sodon. I went to find a way to assist in easing the place of death Ryco would go to. Then I caught rumors of how you inspired Oniva. So I've decided to take a greater risk, one that could bring him back. If only I can muster enough strength from within, to do it. But it must be in Paragon. Eyo'el. His home city. We must take flight for there, and now."

Talok asks, "How long will that casket keep him from decay?"

"For as long as I can hold out," Arsyn replies.

Rozeth rushes back, in hysteria. "We must leave this instant. But our Mystadyn friends have flown off. Something's frightened them away."

Kent looks off to the distance, to the flickering fire in the night sky. "It's Vitiosyns, with their Vitasadyns. Something's drawn them here."

"That might be my fault," Arsyn confesses. "A Rubidyn brought me. There was no faster dyn to do it. Save for Rentwar, himself. She calls herself Rentwar's Recruit. Claims to know the lot of you. Do you trust her to take us back to Paragon?"

Talok's the first to find his voice, saying, "Yes."

Warren fixes straps to Ryco's casket, then Musgrae carries it behind him like a backpack. Quickly, Arsyn leads us down the path we took up to the Plateau of MarcKand.

19

In Times

It's a race, slipping and sliding down the path of trampled snow. Gemma clings to Ben for support. I'm running beside Siege, as he conjures a bow and arrow in his hands. He releases the arrow, never stopping his forward journey down the hill. Quall aims one of his hands at that moving arrow. The arrow bursts into blue-fire. It transforms into a mighty-sized Mystadyn. So real does it look to be that the approaching Vitasadyns, and their crazed Vitiosyn riders, are distracted by it. Kent joins in firing off arrows. Dozens of times, he and Siege alternate turns. Quall is the one to make the fired-off arrows burst into conjured dragons.

"Warren!" Quall shouts over the roars of dyns and riders and us, as we crash through the snow. "Give them a voice. Make it more convincing than you ever have!"

"Can't!" Warren calls out. "Circle took too much. Not enough magic left in me to do it. Veins burning as it is. Can't keep us hidden from their notice much longer."

Rozeth goes to run alongside Warren, matching his stride. "Able am I to boost your levels," she says. "Yet it will take more than a minute." She grips Warren's wrist. Warren has to slow down for her. They keep running in unison.

Ben sprints to catch up to Eli at the front. He grabs a fistful of Eli's coat, and the two youngest guards stumble, tumbling into the snow. They roll down the rest of the path, only stopping at the bottom of the plateau. Gemma cries out, reaching a little too late for Ben. She doesn't dare to rush forward too fast, for risk of losing her own footing. Arsyn takes flight, flying low. He gets to Eli and Ben first. Talok is there, seconds later. Then the rest of us.

Arsyn steps aside.

Ben has already stood up. He extends his hand, demanding, "Give it to me, Eli. I know you have it. An Arkiveis staff. Hand it over, unless you wish for all of us to perish here."

Even in his sudden anger, Eli quickly digs through one of his supply pouches. He throws something small at Ben. He shouts, "Hushilios!" That object grows to its original size—an Arkiveis staff.

Ben grabs hold of it, before it falls to the ground. He aims it up. Blue-lightning flashes from the stone at the top of it. Something whirs, vibrates the ground Ben stands upon. We sense it from where we stand too.

The conjured Mystadyn flock is given a voice. And that voice sounds as a storm of constant, rolling thunder. The first conjured one, however, has a booming roar. Loud like a cannon going off beside you, while you haven't any ear protection. Loud, loud, loud! My eardrums throb. Yet I still hear all the happenings. Wind rushes for the surface. Snow blasts downward. We run for cover, but it reaches us, slams us down. We claw our way along, crawling.

Quall yells, "Ben! You made it too convincing. Force it let up a little!"

"The spell is cast," Ben shouts over howling wind. "It'll last however long the Arkizadan Staff wishes."

Quall is so furious, we clearly hear him over everything. "Eli. Of. Kirja! You stole Arkivy Aruus's staff? And you've had that artifact this entire time?"

Eli keeps clawing his way forward through the snow. He's headed for shelter, any shelter that will come into view. "Guilty," he confesses.

I get to Arsyn. He's actually stopped to take a moment to look skyward to the sight of conjured Mystadyns. Some sort of understanding sinks into his features.

"Silver magic," he says in brief delight. "That's how it's different. That's how they do it. Tamers use Silver Magic."

"Why's that matter?" I ask, while glancing to the others ahead of us. They're getting farther away.

Arsyn snaps himself out of his trance-like condition. "I guess it doesn't. I've always wondered, though: how does one tame dragons? By reflecting it, it seems. Mirroring magic. And in mirroring it, they make it something different. In reflecting a heat source, they can pinpoint it at something and intensify the effect. Just look at that storm of Mystadyns."

I follow his upward gaze.

The snow flurry pelts against my face. I must squint my eyes, to even see through the blizzard. Snowflakes collect on my lashes. My eyes sting from the cold. But I spot the conjured dyns, weaving round the Vitasadyns. They summon lightning to themselves. The snow flying about dampens the crackling sound only by a little. It's as that fading sound of a rifle that's just gone off. Over and over again, that sound ripples out. Vitasadyns cry in alarm, in agony, in anger. Some conjured dyns fall to the ground. They appear life-like, until smacking the surface. They turn into a wave of snow, and that snow blends with what was already there, swirling about.

Vitasadyns start falling too. One is encased by a dozen conjured dyns. Lightning crackles in the air and strikes those Mystadyns—consequently, the Vitasadyns they have hold of are struck too. Those struck Vitasadyns land hard in the snow. Smoke churns around their forms. Their bodies remain motionless, after hitting the ground. They are dead. Or nearly so.

Arsyn grips my shoulder. *"Come!"* he divs. *"We must leave. Their riders might still be alive."*

I sprint after Arsyn to the largest, nearest weathered structure. Though it has most likely stood for quite a long time, its stones look as if a fearsome gust could topple what remains of the building. The others are there, however, already taking cover within its meager protection. They've stripped off enough layers to regain some mobility. And there she is. The Recruit in human form.

She calmly turns to face Arsyn. Her red cloak softly aglow, it sways with her movements. Luminous in the dark are her Rubidyn-red eyes. "Are the lot of you and Arsyn ready to go home?" she queries. "For home to Eyo'el is where I've been instructed by King Rentwar to take you. He shall join us, soon. King of Rubidyns. He is coming in search of the Onyx Prince."

I *must* speak now. I can't stop myself. "Is this what he's been waiting for, Recruit? For me to be named the blood heir of ReNovak?" I start stripping off the extra layers.

"I do not know," she says. "I wish I did. Who am I, but a servant to the king of the mightiest of dyns? Nothing, I have come to learn." She strides out of the crumbling building's doorway. Sounds of cracking and hissing sound out. Even with all the thunderous noise around, we can hear her transformation. We step out, only to see the end of it, her long tail growing and growing. By the time she's transformed, that tail appears as a whip, with a flattened, triangular spike at the end of it. It's big enough for a person to stand upon.

We leave our extra clothes behind, in the building.

"Climb on," she commands. "Strap that Sylvadyn's box down. Nail it to my flesh if you must. My task is to get you home. Every single one."

Kent has taken out his personal Arkiveis staff. Ben still has hold of the stolen one. The stones of the two staffs emit enough light for us to find our way around, for the moonlight has been choked out by clouds. We're all on The Recruit, finding the best place to grab hold. Musgrae lets Ryco's casket slide off his back for Quall and Warren to move around.

Warren searches for somewhere, anywhere, to secure Ryco's casket. Desperately, he says, "Your scales are too loosened, my lady dyn! I can't use hooks. I must nail down the ropes."

The Recruit twists her neck round to look at us. Only one of her eyes is visible. She tilts her head enough to assess Ryco, hidden by the casket that's centered between where her wings attach to her back. "Nail it down," she says.

Quall hesitates to help Warren. "The nails have to be long, lady dyn. If it is a rough journey, and it will be, you risk bleeding out much blood and magic."

The Recruit moves her head to face forward. She gazes upward to the darkened sky. After a deep breath, her voice is strong, in saying, "I am of the mightiest of dyns. A Rubidyn. I fear nothing except failing my given task, to see all of you safely home. I will tear through any who get in my way. What are little nails but a mere speck of pain? And what is a mere speck of pain, but less than a breath within a lifetime lasting thousands of years?"

Quall turns back to the casket. He takes a hammer out. Musgrae comes to grab it from him.

"Let me, Quallendeis," Musgrae says. "I've got to do something for Ryke."

Quall offers the hammer, but unhappily so. Musgrae has to tug it from his grasp. Resigned, Quall comes to huddle down with Ben, Gemma, and me.

Talok shouts, "Start us for the sky! Grae and Warren will have him ready, before you take off."

The Recruit has been lining up this entire time. She now starts a fast walk, then a slither. She gets faster and faster. Her movements are smoother. Last time, she just bolted off the ground and headed up. It was rough. This is not.

Warren has taken out nails from his supply pouch. They fit in his palm. Then they grow large enough to be spikes, which are near two feet in length. He tucks four under his arm, and holds one ready. Eli adds to the necessary items, throwing coiled rope to Musgrae. Musgrae shakes it out. Siege assists in drawing it taut over the casket. Warren, using his great strength and weight, pushes each spike in enough that they are started for Musgrae to hammer in the rest of the way.

The Recruit holds true, not flinching a bit. She keeps up her smooth run atop the ground, kicking up minor amounts of snow.

Musgrae hammers the first spike in.

The Recruit rumbles and groans, though muffled. I can tell she is screaming in pain, her teeth tightly closed. Fire flares in front of her. Most likely from her nostrils, for the pain must be too great to suppress all signs of suffering.

Musgrae skips a spike and pounds a second one in all the way. Five great strikes on the nail head, and it's in. Again, he skips a spike, but pounds a third in completely.

The Recruit lets out an earsplitting wail. She can't help it.

My skin crawls. My body is struck with fleeting pain.

Fire blazes out of her mouth. The snow in front of her melts. The water turns to steam. It crackles and sizzles, as water does in hot oil. Her back begins to feel hot.

Sweating, I wipe at my forehead when that sweat threatens to drip down. It's like standing in front of an open oven, set to broil.

The Recruit's fire goes out. Her wings start flapping. She warns us, "They have spotted me. I must make the jump. Have you got him secured?"

Musgrae's about to go back to the two spikes he skipped. He shouts, "Only a triangle secures it. Two more to go for a Pentagon."

"Three are enough." The Recruit flaps harder, runs faster, breathes deeper.

She lifts off the ground, as Vitasadyns descend. We're soon in the thick of them. They fire at us, missing only by some meters. Arrows come whizzing by overhead, then some from below.

One from above hits Arsyn. It sears straight into his wing. He cries out, but he quickly dislodges it without snapping it. Forming a bow in hand, Arsyn stands steady. Aiming back at our attackers, he releases the arrow. A great bang explodes behind us, and not very far behind either.

Siege crawls on his hands and knees. He yanks out one of the skipped spikes. He cauterizes the small wound with a bit of fire. Then he tosses the spike back.

Eli doesn't miss a beat. He casts a spell of sparks. It connects with the spike. Soon, there's a great flash. The spell is as snapping static electricity, exponentially multiplied to wound dragons.

They roar in pain, then in awakened anger.

Talok stands up.

Quall, from his place of huddling with three of us, shouts, "Talok, get down, and hold onto something. She's going to have to ascend higher than this. I don't want you falling off."

"Let me be the King of Paragon for once, Quallendeis." Talok glances at him. "With that device off, I'm feeling better already. And I mean to tame a dragon. It's been far too long."

With his knee bent, Talok lifts his foot back enough that he's able to tap his fingers on his boot's heel. He does the same with the other. His boots form shallow spikes on the soles. And those spikes sink into The Recruit's scales enough to assist Talok in staying upright during the rougher ride, but not enough that it seems to bother The Recruit. Talok steps forward with little difficulty.

Quall shouts, "No one's ever tamed a Vitasadyn, Talok. Once the BlacKaidyns have been turned, they are lost. Please! I'm begging you! Get down! Protect yourself. Will you nullify Ryco's sacrifice? Make it for nothing?"

"It's not for nothing." Talok holds his hand out. "Ben of Yharss, give me the Staff of Arkizadan. Let us see if a corrupted dragon can be made to see things in a new light."

Ben looks on in pride. He gives his renewed king the staff.

My cousin wraps those long, thin fingers of his round the staff. "If you would, Quall, please attend to Arsyn's wound."

Arsyn has collapsed from blood loss, possibly some nasty magic added to the arrow that pierced his wing. Somehow, he remains conscious. Gemma and Ben do what they can to help. Kent throws over some ingredients that Quall needs to revive Arsyn's strength, as Rozeth further attends to Warren, still depleted of magic.

Meanwhile, Siege removes the other unused spike, repeating what he did before. Eli sends out another spell. This time one of ice. Sounds of shattering glass ring out, jarring my senses.

The dragons wail. They are farther back than during the spark attack.

We've not gone far, by the time Talok has readied himself. He stands tall, looking over the vast Vitasadyn army. They are banded near each other in the sky. Dozens and dozens of them. They spread out, as we ascend higher. One is bigger than the rest, faster in flight too. He gets closer and closer.

I'm all alone in my little spot by The Recruit's left wing. She levels out, and I must watch this horrific sight. Even as I crawl closer to my cousin, I can't tear my gaze from all these dragons chasing us in the air.

"Stay there and watch, Cousin." Talok glances down. "Learn what you can. For you are a Dragon Tamer too. I was going to show you, on the second day of the festival. The chance was taken from me. It was meant for show, then. This is for necessity."

He refocuses in our enemies' direction. So do I. He reaches out. His voice resonates over the noise, as he says to the approaching dragon: "Come, Vitasadyn, come. You are old and mighty. You refuse riders. Not a single one is upon you—steering you, controlling you. Yet you fly with them; the dyns with riders. Is it that Vitiosyns control you from afar? Is it that they steer you with invisible chains?"

The dragon speeds up more. So does The Recruit. He gets no closer to her than before. All the while, his other Vitasadyn friends and their riders fire assaults at us. The Recruit flies expertly, dodging most of it. Only some attacks graze her scales. They deflect, leaving her and us unharmed. Behind me, some of the guards—though I can't tell which ones over the racket—shout to the others the side they mean to protect of The Recruit's.

Talok continues conversing with the dragon. "I must tell you, old and mighty dyns do not take orders. You were meant for freedom. And freedom you have earned, through time. Through time and wisdom and knowledge. All things you've added to your days, give you claim to a truth. Old dragons bow to no one. Take orders from no one. No one, that is, but kings or the alphas of dragons. Even then, challenges may be made for status. Has Zymarc of Vitiosus proven himself as either, to you? A king or an alpha? Has he?"

The Vitasadyn hasn't answered Talok yet. But, during that last line, he manages to outfly The Recruit. He's just out of Talok's reach now, staring him down. He breathes an especially hot breath out, adding to what The Recruit already puts off. His inhales, however, cool the nearby air, bringing some relief to the exposed skin of my face and hands. Then it's stifling hot all over again. The sensations are on repeat.

Talok waits for his answer. He still reaches for the dragon. Then he says, "I am King of Dragon Tamers, Talok of Paragon. Son of Miriam of Trauvo, a tamer. Son of Sosha of Eyo'el, an architect. Like my parents, I mean to restore things, starting with you, mighty dragon. What is your answer? Are you for me, or against me? Will you turn on your winged brothers and sisters—now Vitasadyns, once BlacKaidyns. Will you become a Black Dragon again? Will you let me help you?"

The dragon's breath grows hotter still. His eyes open wider. A billowing sound rumbles in his throat.

As Talok presents his wrist, now free of the device, his voice gets louder. "Look! Zymarc of Vitiosus has failed to kill me with that Geldryn trinket. I'm sure you've heard of it. Heard the stories. And now that piece is gone forever, never to return to the land of the living. It is destroyed. Yet I live. I fought to hold on, waiting for an answer. And that answer came. So tell me *your* answer? Will you help me in battle? Will you help the King of Tamers, the one Zymarc couldn't kill?" Talok whispers that last part. Then he closes his eyes. Blue-and-silver light swirls about my cousin. It never comes to rest upon me, the one who is *not* the King of Paragon.

The dragon has turned his face to better see my cousin's wrist. The slit of his one visible eye grows thin. I wonder if the dyn is going to open his jaws, and snatch my cousin up whole for a meal of flesh and bones.

I hold my breath, waiting.

The Recruit's tail sways in the air. I try not to let my gaze follow it, as she lines up that triangular spike to strike the dragon, should he make the wrong choice.

Attacks continue. Arrows find the loose spots of The Recruit's scales.

They sink into the flesh of her wings. She cries out great moans of pain, now too distracted to attack.

The dragon breathes out deeply. The rumbling in his throat subsides. On his exhale, he stretches his long neck forward enough to touch his snout to my cousin's outstretched hand.

Talok's eyes open. They are aglow with a bright-blue color. His sandy-blond hair turns platinum-white. Other than that, he appears no older. He pulls his hand away.

The dragon slows down some, moving away.

Talok looks into the dragon's eyes. He lifts the Staff of Arkizadan, then strikes it upon The Recruit's back. She shudders, but holds to her task of flying while injured further from all the arrows in her wings.

Blue-light races around, fading out into the open air.

Images of The Sodon flash, looking hazy like dreams. Images of my request, the duo's duel, my branding of the warriors, but they are seen from Talok's perspective. Never once did he look away for those moments, not even as others tried to converse with him. He only broke line of sight if needing to move to get to me.

Talok's voice resonates, as he says, "That is my cousin, the Onyx Prince. He, the blood heir of ReNovak, means to make it to Paragon. His warriors wait for him, though we know not where. Will you help me get him there? Get him home? Fair Black Dragon, take us there."

I stand up. I hold tight to my cousin's side, to his coat; Sosha's Waking Dragon; my father's coat, resized for the much smaller frame of my cousin. Boldness returns to me. I add to Talok's dialogue, words of: "You are welcome to come home, BlacKaidyn. Come home to Reign. He's alive and strong, despite what you may have heard from Vitiosyns. He is there."

The Vitasadyn opens his mouth. Fire forms at the back of his throat. It sparks and crackles. It grows blistering hot. I'm so afraid, I can't even tremble. I'm paralyzed in fear.

The dragon's voice is deep as he speaks, and fire swirls around with his words. "Reign of Paragon lives? That cannot be. I saw him fall, many spikes sunk deep into his flesh. Fresh dragon spikes. No BlacKaidyn, nay, no dragon could survive that."

"But he did!" I shout, though my insides shudder. "And he flies again, over all of Eyo'el."

"You lie!" the dragon growls, venom in his voice.

"Why would I?" I ask him. "I care for Reign. So does my cousin, Talok."

"You are coozins?" the dragon asks. "I have coozins too. That Reign is my coozin. So is Scepter. Never did like the older coozin. But the younger one. That one I do like." The dragon blinks, and he doesn't blink often. Only once every few minutes I realize. He seems to be thinking. He looks to Talok. "Truly, you can make me a BlacKaidyn again?"

"With this staff." Talok lifts it slightly. "I believe so."

The dragon replies, "With what you have shown me, with what you have made me feel, and with what your coozin has said, I am yours, King Talok of Paragon. You may turn me. Or attempt. If you should fail, I cannot keep my Vitiosyn lords from taking back control of me. May you be as strong as dyns are swift on their first flight."

Talok tightens his hold on the staff. He aims it at the dragon. Silverlight, looking as a piercing beam, flares from the stone. It hits the dragon's forehead. He roars, and the force almost knocks me off my feet. My grip on Talok keeps me steady. Talok has hold of the staff, in one hand. The other is lifted, fingers splayed out. He blocks the erupting fire the dragon has aimed at us. His arms don't shake in effort at all, during his dual task of defending and attacking.

The dragon's fire cuts out. His dragon-eyes become like two, domed mirrors. They reflect the lot of us, on The Recruit. In that reflection, I spot the dark blood that's pooled on the bright-red scales of The Recruit's back, where Ryco's casket is tied down by ropes nailed into her. Much blood has streamed its way around too, like many little, red rivers trapped in between her scales. Also, I see the numerous arrows lodged into her flesh. Her breathing has become labored.

My chest tightens. It's hard for me to breathe too, I'm so afraid.

The light of the Staff of Arkizadan ceases.

Talok's blocking hand lowers. He leaves himself open to the dragon.

Eyes still akin to mirrors, the dragon sheds his Vitasadyn scales like unwanted dirt. The raven-black color of BlacKaidyns replaces the dinginess. The mirrors become dragon-eyes of violet—no red of Vitasadyns. He turns in the air and heads for our attackers.

It's frightening, at first. He lunges for smaller Vitasadyns. Grabbing them in his hand-like front paws, he tears those ones apart.

Their silhouetted pieces fall from the night sky.

His spiked tail pierces the sides of the larger dragons in the flock, or simply sweeps all the riders from their backs. They attempt to save themselves with magic. But he roars, and shoots fire at them. The Vitiosyn riders have no chance of surviving that.

Still clinging to my cousin, I can finally take in a full breath.

Twenty have fallen in minutes, and who knows how many riders along with them.

This restored dragon anticipates their every move, their every attack. The element of surprise pays off, and pays off beautifully.

Just to the side of The Recruit, a small dragon rises up to the same level as her. He flaps hard enough to be parallel with her. He has a rider. A giant, cloaked rider in black and scarlet-red. That rider's blackened-gold gloves glint in the moonlight, as he holds to straps tied on his smaller dragon.

"Arsyn of the Jhiresons," the figure calls out, sounding familiar. "You promised me he would be here. And I have looked. But, here, he is not. Where is Zymarc?"

Arsyn, somewhat healed of his wound, carefully steps away from Quall. He makes his way for a better look, keeping his wings tucked close to his body. "He should have been. I don't know why he would delay coming." Arsyn lowers his head in shame. "I rarely misjudge an enemy's choice of retaliation."

I glance at my comrades. They aim weapons and magic at this visitor in the sky; even Gemma has fire held in the grasp of her right hand. They guard Ryco's casket from him. Arsyn does nothing but stand silent.

The Recruit struggles to catch her breath. Unable to say a word, she can only wheeze and cough and hiss out many sounds. No fire leaves her mouth.

"King Talok of Paragon." The figure laughs darkly, sounding like Soren.

He's about to say something more, when a slew of magic and arrows are launched at this stranger. He blocks it all with a wave of his hand. Only Warren's one attack of Blue Magic hits the stranger, and Gemma's ball of flames whizzes past the stranger's head.

My heart pounds. I want to shield my cousin. I find that I cannot move. Panic hits like a stranglehold.

The stranger tilts his head, seeming to want to look at us from an upside down view. He shakes his head, straightening himself to be an upright, stoic rider. He turns his attention to me. "Ravier," he whispers. "Did I not tell you before? We are at the beginning of our business dealings. You and I. Did you think you'd not be seeing me again? That I'd be so impolite as to never meet your Paragonian friends?"

Business dealings? I wonder. *What's he talking about? Soren wouldn't say* business dealings, *would he?*

The figure looks to The Recruit's face. "And how fare's my recruit?"

The small dragon replies, "I believe she's been better."

"That she has," the figure agrees, as his cloak sets fire. It's turned to reddened soot that swirls in the air. It forms into many little dragons. Red dragons. Rubidyns.

"King Rentwar?" I ask. "What are you doing?"

"Frightening little children." He grins. "Did it work?" Those faint stripes on his skin are aglow, his matching garb too, as if light within him seeps out. It makes sense why he would always have a cloak around. There'd be no sneaking up on anyone, otherwise. And with those flickering copper-colored eyes, well, I certainly don't like being under his scrutiny.

"We are thoroughly frightened," Eli replies. "Truly, you's are the Rubidyn King?"

"Who's asking?" Rentwar turns his scrutiny to Eli.

Eli looks away. "Just . . . just a King's Guard . . . of Paragon."

Rentwar grunts. "There are other races that have their own King's Guard? Since when? For I've only heard of the Withrasyn King's Guard, and the Geldryn Guards. Both clans, gone. Only a remnant of one lingers on. Lingers in most of the ones now before me."

Quall queries, "You had expected to find Zymarc here? How would he know where to find us? Not even our countrymen were told where we were going after The Sodon. Only that we intended to save Talok."

Remembering something, I add, "I bet it was Grawllik. I was asking him about the plateau, how long it took to get there and all. Do you think he was tortured into giving Zymarc that information?" I focus on Arsyn.

Breathing heavily, he replies, "Grawllik would willingly give it. Even happily so. He is a soul for hire. Only loyal until a greater reward for him looms in the near future."

Behind us, the Vitasadyns are getting closer.

Talok turns back to face the dwindled army of them and their riders. There are still many. Just not an innumerable many. Talok's restored dragon isn't faring too well. My cousin quickly aims the staff's stone at the dragon. A beam of light bursts out. Once hitting the tamed dyn, his scales shift into mirrors. All attacks are reflected back at his enemies. He's able to get away, but he flies sluggishly.

The light beam cuts out. Talok collapses. I catch hold of his arm, keeping him on his feet.

Rozeth grips his wrists and gives him a boost of magic. "Better, King Talok?" She lets go.

"Yes, but what are we to do? Is there a lingering fleet down on the surface, waiting for us to come to them, do you think? Is there another flock already in the air, coming? And what if they are cloaked by magic? What if we don't see them, till it's too late? What plan of action is best for us to take? Master Quall, any suggestions?"

Quall is tying down all the loose straps and weapons about his body. "It depends on who is coming for us. Zymarc, his Prince-Generals, or Prime-Warriors. The warriors prefer dyns." Quall motions back to the ones attempting to catch up to the mirrored dragon and us. "The generals prefer travel by horseback. And Zymarc uses all methods. You never know what means of travel he'll take, nor what form of attack or defense he intends to use. There is no pattern. Believe me, LanSoren and I tried to find a pattern. We never did. Only that he goes after what he wants most, in the moment. And that changes by the day. Perhaps by the hour, of late. It's why he still lives. All bounties put out on him over the centuries have failed."

While Quall is in the middle of talking, Rentwar looks over his shoulder. His copper-colored eyes narrow on something off in the distance. I follow his gaze. A great silhouette of a dragon rises from the deadened forest yonder, back in the direction of MarcKand. Green sparks crackle up from the forest. Lightning crashes down from rain clouds that are forming. Those clouds start concealing the moon again. Everything gets darker. I spot Gemma's frightened expression, before the moonlight is gone completely. I carefully find my way to her. I want her near.

"Tyler," she divs, as soon as I've bumped into her amid this darkness. *"That's an Imperial Sylvadyn. Ryco told me about them. That they can fly above a forest, as long as its trees remain tightly packed together. And only old Sylvadyns can rise to fly in the air as that one's starting to. It will be faster than those other dragons, for it means to draw magic from the forest, a near unending supply."*

Disquieted, I hold tight to her. "Gemma says it's a Sylvadyn."

I search the darkness, trying to spot those around. I only make out Rentwar, his skin still aglow.

Gemma calls out, "We need to land! Start thinning out the trees."

"Yes," Warren agrees. "Was just about to suggest it."

"Can't we thin them out from here?" queries Eli. "Stay in the air? Don't like the idea of what could be hiding down there. We're so far away from home, far from all things familiar."

"He's got a point," Talok admits. "But we are much exposed, and low on magic. Air's been depleted of what we're able to absorb. Perhaps the forest can restore our reserves, and offer shelter."

"Can you manage to land, Recruit?" Rentwar asks. "Or do you wish for Rah'Zyock to take them down to the surface, before hunting the Vitiosyns there? I can already smell them from up here."

The Recruit rumbles. She suddenly finds her voice, and she is livid. The heat of her back restarts. So does my profuse sweating.

She roars her question of: "You have named that scrawny dyn, before giving me my name? Do tell when that one, barely with a voice, earned his name. Earned the name: Outcome, born of disobedience! Rah'Zyock!" She roars louder.

Rentwar adjusts those gloves meant for tearing things apart. "Why, it was that day you were in Deivahl, playing keepaway with the EquiVon. Rah'Zyock was instructed to wait for the signal to attack one of Zymarc's cities. Instead, he disobeyed. He went in of his own accord. Couldn't help but have a quick feast of Vitiosyns too, before opening up the dragon stables, and freeing many dragons held captive inside. He found one of the old Rubidyns, who has been missing for some centuries."

"What of him?" The Recruit asks.

"Found dead," Rentwar replies. "Body full of arrows. One hundred arrows, I do believe it was. Shot from the Bow of Three Queens. He didn't stand a chance."

Rah'Zyock falters in flight, dipping down a bit.

Rentwar grabs hold of the straps. "Rah'Zyock! Warn me next time your strength wavers."

"Yes, King Rentwar. Apologies. It's been a long several days of much flying, little resting."

Rentwar growls under his breath. He stands up. "That Sylvadyn is taking too long to reach us. If I can't have Zymarc for a duel in the air, I shall play with that Sylvadyn crow." He turns around. Fire ignites around him. Red-hot fire. It resembles energy rather than flames. It is an unnatural red.

Rentwar shouts, and all that lies in the direction of his shout is illuminated. It becomes like daylight shining around us, when he speaks: "Eekawsynd! Have you come to see your descendant, brood of a Parasogyn? The Parasogyn, Son of Crenza? He has fallen!" Rentwar side-glances at us, more quietly saying, "This should make him mad." He looks forward again, proudly proclaiming the last part. "Ryco of Paragon *is* dead! And I have killed him! Come fight me. Restore the honor of your Vaegon-dyn line. Come for the Rubidyn, who sleeps no more."

The great Sylvadyn's sound is thunderous—likened to a building toppling down, the noise carried on a howling wind.

I cover my ears. We all do. Except for Arsyn. He still looks off, seemingly at nothing.

The mirrored dragon of Talok's now appears as a battered, bleeding BlacKaidyn. He is near to us. Just another minute or so, and he'll be right by us.

The Vitiosyn riders keep testing the distance that their magic and arrows will go. Their attacks are getting nearer. Their remaining Vitasadyns, however, hold their fire. Surely, they know how far their flames will reach.

Off to The Recruit's side that faces an open meadow below us, something is illuminated by the light of King Rentwar's voice. It is dark and menacing, amidst the bright meadow. Its eyes are red, eyes that are looking right up at us. He forms a bow in his hand. He aims upward.

"Get down!" I shout, pulling Gemma down with me.

The arrow sounds as quiet, whistling wind, whizzing past.

Gemma holds tight to me, assessing our surroundings.

Talok spots the arrow when it reaches its pinnacle. It's starting its haphazard descent. He rushes to whack it with the staff.

A rope-light attached to the arrow's tail forms. Someone's coming. That someone lets go of the rope he used to quickly ascend. He lands atop The Recruit's back right as Talok is swinging the staff. My cousin hits the intruder square on the chest. Blue-light explodes from the stone. The figure is thrown off. Though he falls off, he doesn't cry out.

The King's Guard gather round, each one looking in a different direction.

I crowd against Gemma. We're still lying low, unsure of what to do.

"Stay down," Talok instructs.

Rentwar says, "Keep flying, Recruit. Hold true to your given task."

"I will," she says. She flaps harder, taking us higher. Her breathing becomes more strained.

Both heat and the cool night air swirl around. Each breath is sporadic. My nostrils burn from the constant change of temperature. I can't help but cough. Yet Gemma seems fine, alert, ready for anything; her responses are quick, but not so quick as to make her appear frantic. Then she smacks me on the back, and hard. She beats the coughing fit right out of me.

The intruder has shot off more arrows. Not for attacking, really, but to save himself from falling and hitting the ground.

The King's Guard keep burning up those arrows.

The intruder must be close to hitting the ground below, by now.

Rentwar looks down. The glint in his gaze says he recognizes the one harassing us. He's about to do something, when a hailstorm of arrows heads for him. Many of those arrows form that glowing rope. It's not just one intruder to ascend onto Rah'Zyock's back. Rentwar stands. He strikes all down with his flesh-tearing gloves, save for one. That smallish one dodges well enough, until Rentwar is able to grab hold of him by the neck. "King Zymarc of Vitiosus." Rentwar grins darkly. "How rewarding this is. I was plotting to hunt you, put you down myself. What luck. You came right for me."

"Should've stayed asleep in your cavern, old dragon." Zymarc smacks his head against Rentwar's face, then claws any exposed skin of Rentwar's.

Rentwar tightens his hold on Zymarc's neck, even as blood runs down his forehead and gets into his eyes. Somehow, Rentwar's gloves have no effect on the King Vitiosyn.

When Rentwar tears Zymarc's mask off, the King Vitiosyn instantly takes on Soren's appearance. He laughs at the Rubidyn.

The others try to aid Rentwar, but Zymarc's shielding wall absorbs each and every attack.

Breathless, Warren yells, "Yo, stop!"

"It's an absorption spell," Rozeth says for Warren. "Have to find its weak point, as well as the spell it's vulnerable to."

Zymarc reaches behind his back for something under all the fabric of his garments.

"Rentwar!" I call out a warning, as many send attacks at us from the ground.

The Vitasadyns have caught up to The Recruit too. Only the restored BlacKaidyn keeps their attacks on us restricted. Even still, their attacks hail forth. Rozeth faces the hailstorm and holds up her hands. She stops the spells that were coming straight for us.

Arsyn is with her, giving her a boost of magic when she needs it. He says, "I've not enough to expel magic for spells. Only enough to give for another to do so."

Zymarc has uncovered a small, metallic something.

The Recruit shrieks, "Let me abandon my task to assist you, Rentwar."

"No!" he shouts. "I've almost found the weak point of his neck. I shall break him. Let him fall like filth to the ground. I shall let the Sylvadyns feast on you, Zymarc. And Sivondel shall take up what they leave behind. The bones."

"That's not going to happen," says Zymarc, revealing the war axe. Deezalo's Hammer.

It's not at its full size, but quickly it grows. He swings. That sharp edge, glowing red, strikes Rentwar's side. It gets lodged there.

Crying out, Rentwar releases his grip on Zymarc.

Zymarc yanks the axe out, as The Recruit screeches in fear. She flies faster, going higher. Somehow, she's found renewed strength. Strength born out of fear. Zymarc has landed on his feet. He runs atop Rah'Zyock's back. He expertly leaps at the right moment when The Recruit's wings are facing downward. He lands on the tip of her right wing. As she lifts her wings, Zymarc slides down, being propelled toward us.

We band together, to surround Ryco's casket. Arsyn, Quall, and Talok are at the forefront, and that terrifies me. I would rather it be no one or all, not a few in the greatest line of danger.

The daylight of King Rentwar is fading. Rah'Zyock can't keep up with

The Recruit. She's grown too fast.

Spitting steam hisses nearby. Rentwar has taken his dragon form. And *what* a form. The daylight is restored. But only where Rentwar has cast his gaze. That gaze is on Zymarc. The darkness of night closes in elsewhere.

Zymarc squints. He counteracts with a darkening spell. It absorbs Rentwar's light, even the moonlight at first. He's then able to fully open his eyes.

Rentwar, still in dragon form, keeps growing in size. He is as a striped dragon of copper-and-gold, like that one sitting atop a mound of gold, in Adair Galloway's painting: Vision of the Dragon.

Zymarc swings Deezalo's Hammer. He goes to plunge the axe-head into The Recruit's neck.

I reach out, willing it to stop. And it does. Zymarc struggles against my strength. At least, I think it's mine, until I realize nothing is leaving my body. I'm too spent. I glance around.

Quall has his hand extended, as if wanting to claw the Vitiosyn. "I wouldn't be doing that."

Zymarc twists out of Quall's invisible hold. He throws the war hammer. It glows brighter. It plunges into Rentwar's scaly neck, before he has finished growing to full size.

He roars. His gaze grows brighter. Zymarc's darkening spell wavers. The Paragonians launch attacks.

Quall lunges forward, his energy pushing Zymarc back a few steps.

The Recruit cries out, yet she holds to her task of flying. Her wails do not cease. Only grow quiet, sounding heartbroken.

Rah'Zyock flaps erratically. He keeps changing direction. He doesn't know what to do.

Rentwar shifts back into his two-legged form, the axe edge still embedded in his vastly smaller neck. He lands on Rah'Zyock's back.

Zymarc races off The Recruit. He leaps toward Rentwar. In seconds, he's on Rah'Zyock, and has hold of his mighty weapon.

Rentwar rasps out the words: "Keep to your task, Recruit."

"Please, Rentwar!" she begs. "Let me help."

"No!" He raises his voice, holding the hammer's head. He's preventing Zymarc from pushing it further into his flesh.

Zymarc is trying his hardest to, but his arms shake in effort.

"I'll buy time," says Rentwar. "I—War Bringer, Truce Maker—and Rah'Zyock will keep Zymarc and his Vitiosyns at bay. Get the ones with you to safety. And quickly."

Talok lifts his hand in goodbye.

The Recruit bursts forward, flying faster than I thought possible. She is incredible. I decide, yes, 'the mightiest of dyns' description is right.

The distance grows wider.

I ask my cousin. "Won't you Mensa-div to him about the device, Cousin? Let him know he's lost that chance to kill you?"

Talok lets a small smile play across his lips. He whispers, looking across the way, "You've not defeated me, Zymarc. Even if you were to wish me dead from that device, were to try, you'd suddenly find it ineffective. So go on, Vitiosyn. I dare you to kill me with it now."

We stare back at the two kings, as they try to kill each other. Zymarc has yanked the hammer out of Rentwar's neck, and has started hacking into Rah'Zyock's back. Rah'Zyock lets him, though I know not why he does. It breaks my heart. My throat hurts.

Zymarc takes a pause in his violence against the small Rubidyn. Somehow, I feel his gaze upon us. A sudden chill swirls about. Then heat. The heat of hatred.

Zymarc's enraged shout carries on the air. "Kaesh ah suundah!" he yells after us, whatever that means. It sounds like a great curse of frustration.

Fire flares from the small Rubidyn's wings; Rentwar draws that fire to himself. He restarts the process of taking his dragon form. His form of War Bringer, Truce Maker. Only Sivondel can compare to the dragon of daylight before us. Rentwar.

He snaps at Zymarc. The Vitiosyn dodges as well as he's able to. But Rentwar is fast like a young dragon. Rah'Zyock assists his king in not letting Zymarc escape with one leap to the ground. Although it's a long way down, I imagine Zymarc could survive it with a spell or two. The small Rubidyn, though wounded, keeps Zymarc corralled, as Rentwar snaps again and again at his foe, trying to catch him between his sharp dragon teeth.

A cry rings out in the night. A man's cry of anguish.

Rah'Zyock stops flying. He goes limp and falls to the ground, crash-landing in the forest.

The Recruit keeps up her speed. The rushing air has grown colder.

Rentwar starts up the fire in his throat, and we spot a struggling silhouette amongst that fire. Zymarc's silhouette, caught between Rentwar's teeth.

Eekawsynd, the Sylvadyn, has been delayed by much. Mostly by the restored BlacKaidyn warring with Vitasadyns. He's now caught up to Rentwar. He looks as a gale-storm made of an entire patch of forest. He flies past the King Rubidyn. Those glowing yellow eyes of his are fixed on us above, in the near distance.

Gemma exclaims, "We've got to start on thinning the forest now. Stop the Sylvadyn from advancing."

Talok agrees, "Yes! Except thin it out at random. Create a place of safety for us to land. Recruit, I know you were tasked with taking us all the way to Paragon. You are now too weak for that. And I feel a Vitasadyn army of reinforcements getting nearer. They are almost upon us. We can't stay with you. Would you, instead, draw them away from where we land? Warren can cast a spell to make it appear as if we are still with you. It won't last long, but long enough is what we need."

"Yes, King Talok." Her voice trembles. "For you have proven to be the King of Tamers. You may override orders as you see fit; especially when no decision provides absolute safety."

Ben looks at Talok. Almost smirking, he says, "There's no avoiding the Belly of the Snake. It'll be the best way to get down there quickly and, hopefully, unnoticed by the coming ones."

"Right!" Talok ties straps over anything loose on his person. "We'll do it for Ryke. It'll be the gentlest descent we can give him."

Warren works on the false images of us, using Blue Magic I presume. Lots of images appear, blurry as if far off during the heat of summer.

Ben says to Arsyn, "Can you fly, go to the surface, catch the arrow I fire off at you?"

"That is about all I have left in me to do." Arsyn readies his stance. He gets a running start before leaping for the surface. His trajectory isn't as smooth and calculated as usual, but he holds up during his descent.

Ben forms a bow and arrow. He keeps his focus in the direction of Arsyn.

Gemma has begun setting a tree here and there on fire. It's a rapid fire that only burns one or two trees, before going out. Though smoke rises, we're going too fast to catch even a whiff of it.

Eli assists Gemma with her tree burning.

Musgrae and Siege assess the nails and ropes that secure Ryco's casket.

Quall and Rozeth keep a lookout over our surroundings. Then Rozeth joins Gemma and Eli, but she doesn't use fire on the trees. Her shot off spells end up encasing small clusters of trees in metal. They die off, reflecting like marred metal; the Imperial Sylvadyn has to reroute his path around those clusters.

Her voice sounding old, The Recruit says, "Only cut the ropes. Leave the nails in. I can survive it longer. Bleed less. Make it far enough away that the coming army may not find you."

Gently, Siege replies, "As you wish, lady dyn." He cuts the rope.

Musgrae holds the casket in place—at least, tries to. "Quall!" he yells, right as the casket lurches. "Help!" Musgrae practically kneels, as he grips tight to the casket.

I rush to help Grae. Quall does too.

"Ben!" Quall yells. "You're out of time. Fire it off."

Ben takes quick aim. The arrow is released. I close my eyes, willing Arsyn to be ready to catch it.

Ryco's casket lurches again. It violently bumps against one of the long nails.

More blood of The Recruit's oozes out. She screams in pain. She falters.

We slide around. I clench my teeth. My head feels as if it's about to burst. The loudness subsides. I hear only my heart drumming in my ears. Then the sound of branches creaking, reaching for us. The Sylvadyn's here. His roar is akin to a thousand daggers flying through the air, especially as my hearing comes back to full volume.

A great burst of light comes from behind me. From the direction of Rentwar. I hope with everything it's the result of Zymarc being crushed to death and eaten. Can it truly be so simple as that? No grand duel with the King of Vitiosus? No face-off of two or three, even four armies? Simply, the King Dragon above all king dragons, making a meal of the King Sorsryn above all king Sorsryns.

Madeleine's words come to me then. *In times of great need, you will see Rentwar.*

I look back; I can't help it. I must see him, in this moment of need.

Eekawsynd has come to our level. In fact, has risen above The Recruit. He's hot on her tail, sounding as branches of dozens of trees smacking against each other during a gust of wind. His great big jaw, filled with teeth made of metal thorns, opens wide. He's about to plunge down, to sink those teeth into The Recruit.

The army of Vitasadyns is gone. Their ashes are falling to the surface. Talok's tamed dragon drinks up those ashes nearest to him with each inhale.

The silhouette that was in Rentwar's mouth is gone too.

The King of king dragons takes in a giant breath.

Eekawsynd is yanked back.

That's when The Recruit flies in a wide circle.

Warren pulls the casket out of Grae's grasp and mine. "We gots to go!"

Quall scoops me up; Gemma too. He throws us down the long roller coaster-looking slide, made of black-and-white wood. Smooth as polished glass, it's cold too.

Gemma screams. I hyperventilate.

Quall calls after us, "Tell Arsyn to catch the casket!"

Darkness blankets our surroundings. We're tossed about. Not too badly, though. It's simply fast; frightening too, for we don't know what waits at the end of it. I hope nothing's descended upon Arsyn to attack him.

At last, we exit the ride. We roll a ways on the ground.

Arsyn's there to help me.

Breathless, I manage to say, "The casket," before I run out of breath and cough.

Gemma finishes, "Got to catch it." She rushes back to the slide's exit.

Arsyn bolts that way. The casket rattles during its descent. I watch in horror as it thwacks Gemma on the abs.

The wind's knocked out of her. She wheezes.

Arsyn dashes over to keep the casket from hitting the ground hard.

I claw my way for Gemma, finding my footing along the way. Got to make sure that *hit* didn't break her ribs.

"Gem?" I ask.

She starts wailing. "Oh Tyler! What if that damaged Ryco's casket too much? Arsyn." She looks at him. "Is it?" She can't finish her question, before another sob escapes her.

I grab hold of her shoulders. I've no words to comfort her. I wonder, *What if she's right?*

The others quickly join us. Ben severs the connection to The Recruit. She flies off, heading north. Her blood drips down like rain, as she leaves our sight.

I bow my head. It has grown too heavy to hold up. Even if for just this moment.

A soft rumbling of a dragon approaches, nearby.

I snap my attention in its direction. It's not from above, but from within the surrounding forest. The guards ready themselves, though their strength is at least half of what they are normally capable of.

Gemma grows quiet, crowding closer to me.

"Quiet, little Paragonians. Must be quiet," the dragon rumbles. Rah'Zy-ock limps forward into view.

Arsyn brushes his hands along Ryco's casket, as Rozeth kneels beside it. Tears roll down her face. She pats the casket lovingly. "Ye did good, Paradyn. Cousin Evie would be proud."

The guards lower their weapons.

Rozeth looks to Talok. "Let's get this one home, King Talok."

Talok steps forward. "If we work on healing you, Rah'Zyock, can you fly away to go assist the lady dyn? She's not doing too well."

"I could do that, after enough healing. But the lady dyn asked that I stay with all of you."

I straighten to full height. "How are you even still alive? I saw what Zymarc did. How he hacked into you."

"I am a Rubidyn." Rah'Zyock lifts his head proudly. "It's what we do. With each full breath, we heal, if only by a little."

Siege queries, "Can you still fly?"

Rah'Zyock's head lowers. "What strength I had left in my wings, I used to catch up to you."

"No matter," says Talok, closing the distance to Rah'Zyock. "Walk with us a while. I'll do my best as the King of Tamers to heal you."

Musgrae and Warren carry the casket, resting a corner of it on their opposite shoulder of the other; Arsyn supports the middle with one of his wings—the uninjured one. As he passes by Gemma, he gives her a reassuring look.

She takes in a relieved breath, and so do I. I dare not ask if the spell on the casket was weakened, however. I'm not that brave.

20

Of Great Need

The forest is still dark. Rah'Zyock has stopped in his tracks. He must have Mensa-divved something to someone, for he is looking around. Talok, glancing behind at the dragon, also comes to a stop.

The small Rubidyn, small in the world of dragons in fact, lifts his head high. He declares, "I am able to fly. And I mean to, with or without the lot of you. You've time to climb on, or watch me fly off yonder. If you do not fly with me, I will not go to Paragon. Rather, I must be away to the lady dyn, or my king."

Talok studies the gathered group of us, who are looking to him for an answer.

Quall asks, after a time, "Where will the dragon go, King Talok?"

"To Paragon. Get Ryco secured, but no nailing him down with ropes. We'll not do that again."

Musgrae lets out a held breath. Warren's tense shoulders relax somewhat.

Once we're on Rah'Zyock, he takes off. He leaps up, bolting from the ground. The use of his wings and tail keep his back horizontal, which I'm thankful for. So do Arsyn, Musgrae, and Warren appear grateful, as they're the ones still watching over the casket. Rozeth is with them, this time. With Ryco.

Hours pass into the night. We have escaped the Vitasadyns and their riders. Who knows what became of Zymarc, though. The lot of us discuss it. *Can Zymarc really be dead?*

Crowding near Gemma and Ben, Eli poses that question, adding to it: "If he truly has been killed, what comes next?"

Talok focuses north. "We take the war to them, in Vosh-Perida."

Quall counters with, "It's not as simple as that. Caleiso's not dead. Nor is Azabahk. And we know not what became of Belzara. At any rate, what we saw of Caleiso in Oniva may only be the beginning for her. Do none of you recall how she aged herself to be older, the same way Tyler did? She was mighty strong, considering it was only a duel. What if that was the beginning of some power awakening in her too? What if Zymarc dying gives her an inherited power? She has learned much of us. What if this is why? So she could utterly destroy us. What if Zymarc's deepest desire all along was to *actually* die? What if he was tired of being the King Vitiosyn? What if he is in the beginnings of replacing Sivon—" Quall stops, to finish with a whisper, "You know, The Black Flame. What if Zymarc means to become The Black Flame? What if The Black Flame, indeed, becomes The *Red* Flame of Vitiosus? We don't know how the Spirits came to be, do we? It could be that Zymarc knows how, has learned how, and is tired of this world the way it is. That he intends to change it to his liking."

"Stop!" Warren yells. "This cannot be, Quallendeis!" Warren shakes in anger. He has stood up, to loom over Quall, who's sitting down. "You're scaring us with this sort of talk!"

Easing up, Talok goes to grip Warren's forearm. "Settle yourself."

Warren drops down to sit in silence, his dark-brown face darkening over with emotion.

Calmly, Talok says, "If what Quall suggests is true, where do we fit in it all? As a people? A nation? Why would he come after us? Why would he see us as a threat, do you think?"

I point in the direction of MarcKand. "You can tame Vitasadyns. Make them good again." I lower my hand. "Perhaps that's something no other Dragon Tamer has been able to do. To revert the process of Vitiosus, whatever that process may be. You undid it once. You can undo it again. Maybe Zymarc suspected this. Maybe he tried to take you out, because you'd be a threat to Caleiso at the start of her rule."

"More and more," says Kent, "it's looking like Zymarc really did kill LanSoren."

I can't keep sitting. I go to Talok's side, to get a better look at everyone. I shake my head. "No. It wasn't him. Zymarc is nearly as upset as we are, over how my dad died. And King Rentwar admitted that Zymarc didn't kill him."

"When was that?" Gemma suddenly asks.

"Shortly after I left with ReNovak that morning in Oniva. He took me to see King Rentwar, in a room below one of the cathedrals."

Rah'Zyock loses his rhythm of flying for a few seconds. Then he's back to flying strong.

Siege queries, "What troubles you, young dragon?"

"My King Rentwar would only say who didn't kill Master LanSoren, if, indeed, he could identify the guilty party."

I admit, "Yes, that's how I felt about it too."

"Any ideas on whom it could've been?" Ben asks, as he keeps an ever-watchful glance about the surroundings.

Rah'Zyock continues, as if no one said a thing, "And if he knew who did, why would he hide it from Rubidyns? For I know that they do not know. We do not!" The small dragon gets louder. "To and fro, for two years, he has had us searching for any signs of Zymarc, while Zymarc was at home in Vosh-Perida. To and fro, searching for the Equidyn for two years. To and fro, the lady dyn searching for Jasper of the Greyvons for nigh a year. Why, why, why? And why did King Rentwar lie about that old Rubidyn? We did not find him shot up, full of arrows. No! That one attacked Rentwar, and King Rentwar had to kill him. 'Twas a fight to the death, it was. A duel for status."

We grow silent. Whisperings come into volume around us. They get louder, as if speaking inside my head. It's a woman. So quickly does she shift from subject to subject, I've not enough time to catch a single word.

I glance at Rozeth. Moonlight gleams on her raven-black hair, as it swirls about in the wind. Her mouth is moving like she's whispering without sound. I know better. She's not whispering. Her thoughts have become as a Mensa-div.

I ask, "Hey, Grae, how does Mensenglos work?"

"What?" He gawks at me. Then he catches a glimpse of Rozeth, and grins. "Don't think so, Ravier. You've got to suffer the noise right along with the rest of us."

Arsyn's confused expression lights with understanding, once he spots Rozeth. "Lady Rozeth?"

"Quiet!" she yells. "I'm practicing!"

"Practicing what?" Musgrae ventures to ask.

"Bird's-eye view, paired with *through the looking glass.*"

Musgrae frowns. "Through the looking glass? Is . . . is that a spell? Warren, what spell is that?"

Grumbling something inaudible, Warren then replies, "Lets ya see through small creatures' eyes. Ya use bird's eye, to find the small creatures around ya, then looking glass to see what they see. If you're *really* good, you can hear what they hear too."

"What do they hear, Rozeth?" Kent queries.

"Shh!" She fumes, reaching to smack the arm of the nearest guard (it's Eli, greatly offended by her abuse). "Over the lot of you, I can't hear them."

Soon, we only hear Rozeth's Mensa-div, spilling out, and Rah'Zyock's rhythmic flapping.

As our Emerald Sorsryn gains potential intel from the nearby creatures below us, the rest of us aren't much for talking—too afraid to incite Rozeth's wrath.

Rah'Zyock isn't one for asking any more questions either. He's still deep in thought. When he does interrupt Rozeth in her task, it's to tell us: "We're approaching Sylvadyn forests. They might sense that a dead one of them is passing over. Thought I should warn you, they might cry out in grief."

No sooner has he finished saying that, than they let out mournful wails from below us. The treetops glow with yellow dots. Sylvadyn eyes look up at us, as we fly in the night.

"Look out!" Ben shouts.

Rah'Zyock dodges something.

We scramble to hold on tighter.

Musgrae grips tight to the casket, and Warren to him. Arsyn fans his wings out, shielding them.

Rozeth leaps to her feet. "Vitiosyns wander down there."

Rah'Zyock states, "I need to land, hunt them—"

Bright-red fire cuts his words short, explodes in his face. Arrows, imbued with magic, pelt Rah'Zyock's wings. We hear them thrust into his underbelly too.

Screeching in pain, he calls, "Prepare for a hard landing. I can't keep myself up. Soon, they'll start with the spikes, now that they know I'm a lone dragon."

The spikes launch up, buzzing with energy. Rah'Zyock dodges most, but one grazes his wingtip. Sparks make that wing go limp. His clawed feet grab for the tops of the trees that we're plummeting toward.

Kent uses wind magic to keep the limp wing elevated. It's a rough descent. If it weren't for Warren with his Blue Magic, we'd have a much more jarring ride.

Branches, even trunks of Muraine's smaller trees, snap, and give way to the Rubidyn's body tumbling down. When he slides to a stop on the mangled forest floor, he's too worn-out even to whimper. His chest just heaves infrequently. I fear he won't last long.

"Leave me," he sputters. "Others will come to my aid. It'll take Vitiosyns some time to kill me, for I've been healed by the King of Dragon Tamers. And his healing is sure and true. Perhaps Vitiosyns will deem me valuable enough to keep alive. But they won't, with the lot of you around. Go. Run. Don't take the normal way. They know your scent. They will find you. Kill you. And the war will soon be over, if that happens. Paragon will be utterly defeated. Vons too."

Arsyn takes Ryco's casket from Musgrae and Warren, secures ropes round it to assist him in carrying it like a backpack. All of us are beyond exhausted, except for Arsyn it seems. He sets the pace. Quall takes up the back, like a guardian.

We run. Then run some more. It turns to jogging, then walking, then dragging our feet. When too tired to go on, we stop to sleep for two hours. In pairs, we take turns watching while the others slumber.

On one of those stops, Siege and I are paired together.

Sitting with my back against a tree, I whisper, "We've been going like this for two days. How long is the journey home? Is there no way to summon dragons, to fly us there?"

Talok trudges over to join us. He plops down.

Siege asks, "Can't sleep?"

Talok sighs. "That metal cuff has been draining me for so long. Now that I've had a few rounds of rest, I find that I'm not tired at all. Simply broken. But I do believe we'll make it home."

"We must," states Siege. "To answer you, Tyler. Flight isn't safe. I consider us far from home, if we keep going on foot."

"An entire month, at least," says Talok. "And that's if our stamina doesn't waver."

I ask, "What if Arsyn can't hold Ryco in suspension for that long?"

"Then we'll all give him some magic," replies Talok, "to keep him revived."

So that's what we do. When it's my turn to give Arsyn some of mine, somehow it feels as if he barely takes any at all. It makes me mad. He's holding on to Ryco's last bit of life—the one chance he has to come back to us. I wonder, *So why's he taking a gamble, now? Why's he not taking more magic from me?*

I brush the thought aside, too worried over getting caught by Vitiosyns. They're at the forefront of our thoughts, night and day. We listen for them, as we march along in the dark. In daytime, we look for them. But we do not stop the march, unless it's to eat, sleep, or resupply our stores.

Ryco's casket is traded off between the strongest and tallest among us:

Arsyn, Warren, and Musgrae.

One night, Quall volunteers to bear the load of Ryco.

Ben scowls at him. "I'm a healer. You're a healer. You need your hands free, unoccupied, Quallendeis. I forbid you to carry Ryco. Your hands are better put to other use. For healing. For shielding."

"Very well, Rueisvben'el," says Quall. "You make a good point. For healing and shielding."

"For herb picking and brewing too," states Eli. "The ones for stamina."

"Best idea that Kirjan's ever had," says Warren, his voice weary.

The idea puts a glimmer of joy back in our thoughts. We get to taste some of Quall's herbs. He brews a pot, stirring in many bits of partially dried plants and seeds, spices and flower petals. Once the bits are strained out, he ladles the brew into our cups, and we gulp down the smooth, sweet, steaming liquid, afterward feeling revived some.

Rozeth finishes first. She sets her cup upside down on top of Ryco's casket. "Soon," she says. "Soon, we'll have you home, Sylvadyn."

We copy Rozeth's example. Twelve cups are upside down on the casket. We stare at it. Stare at the cups. Can't help it. Ryco's sacrifice may be permanent. He may never be coming back. That thought defeats us. I see it. The disbelief in each one of us. Some eyes are dim. Others have features drawn taut. Near all heads are lowered, looking too heavy to hold up all the way.

Musgrae takes out a silver cup from the supplies. Raising it a bit, he whispers, "It's one of the silver pieces he always packs for me . . . packed for me. It's only fitting that it never be used again." He sets it upside down on the casket's center, then turns and walks away.

Rozeth's composure cracks. She covers her mouth to quiet her sobs.

Warren sits on the casket, where Ryco's feet would be if we could see him. He pats the casket lovingly. "Ya did good, Ryke. Outdid even Ravier."

I start to wonder if I can see past the wood of the casket, to see Ryco as he is now: held in suspension, moments after his death. I think, *Does he look any better than after that moment?*

Arsyn grips my shoulder. He divs, *"I wouldn't be doing that, Ravier.*

Remember him, while he still lived. For that is how I wish to make him again. Living, not sleeping. Most definitely, not dead."

My chest tightens. I look elsewhere. Anywhere except at that casket.

Ben finds a small piece of wood. He starts whittling it into a shape. Gemma watches him, if only to keep herself from sobbing as Rozeth still does.

The Emerald woman's weeping doesn't last long. She gathers her senses, dries her face with a cloth that Musgrae offers her. He rests one of his big hands on her shoulder as a means to further comfort her.

Kent gathers the cups and puts them away. He gives the silver one to Musgrae.

Siege takes up the casket for the first time. He won't let anyone talk him out of it. Truthfully, we don't try hard.

Once Siege has the casket secured like an enormous sack on his back, we start again. The farther we have gone from the Plateau of MarcKand, the more the creatures of the forest sing and chirp and rattle about in the branches.

One morning, they suddenly stop; we look about in renewed terror.

Rozeth holds her breath, before whispering, "It's a Gatro. It's been through here recently. See, there are its footprints." She points.

A low growl rumbles nearby. We're too late to dodge our attacker.

The Gatro leaps from the underbrush of fallen trees, swiping at us. It goes for the one who carries Ryco's casket at this point in time—Arsyn.

Caught off guard, Arsyn can do nothing as the casket is wrenched off his back.

The Gatro's already running off with it. We chase him down, spreading out in pairs.

An arrow whizzes past my ear, nicking my face. It stings, before burning harshly. Onward, that arrow continues till it plunges into the Gatro's backside.

The six-limbed creature hollers. He seems frozen to the spot. Ryco's casket falls to the ground beside that beast, and I shudder in dismay.

Warren and Musgrae go hack into the Gatro, using their short daggers.

By the end, the two are covered in Gatro blood. Kent and Siege search for the archer. I, too, look for who it was.

A small Deathasyn woman approaches, her words having the sound of an irritated snake. "Don't you dare be off with my dinner. Look how you've mangled it. And they call Deathasyns beastly? You've gone on and ruined the flavor it should have had. Not that you weaselly, meat-hating Paragonians would know what Gatro meat's supposed to taste like."

"Do we know you, Deathasyn?" queries Talok, aiming ice magic at her. One twist of his wrist, and he'd have her at his mercy.

"Perhaps not you," she says, as she indicates to me. "But he should. In fact, half of 'em should. Don'tcha recognize me? It was you, Onyx Prince, who did convince a king to give me my life back."

When Belzara approaches behind the smaller Deathasyn, we understand.

Relieved, I confirm, "You're Belzara's Beloved."

Belzara bends down, to wrap her arms about the waist of the smaller Deathasyn. "I listened to you, Ravier. After seeing you on the landing of the Hexyn Cathedral, giving that speech, then taking my chances by staying to watch the duo's duel, I couldn't help but be inspired. Immediately after the duel ended, I ran away with my Ethelvrise."

"Still getting used to that name," says Ethelvrise sheepishly.

Belzara leans down further, to kiss the neck of Ethelvrise. She adds, "We heard rumors of another faction of Onyx Warriors, shortly after leaving. A faction who call themselves The Onyx of Malik." Belzara studies me. "Would ya happen to know who they'd be belonging to, Ravier?"

In sarcasm, I admit, "Not a clue."

No one around contradicts me.

I cement it with the go-to, lifting my shoulders in that way. The others join in.

Belzara laughs. Ethelvrise grins tensely.

Quall asks, "Neither of you are Vitiosyns any longer?"

Belzara releases Ethelvrise, to step closer. "It's as you say, Quall of

Trauvo. I am free. No master may ever claim me. Nor her." She looks to me. "Are you in want of more company? I assume you're headed home?"

Talok confirms it. "We're still weeks out, though."

"We shall make for you a supper," says Ethelvrise, as she cuts chunks of meat off the Gatro with her crimped dagger. It reminds me of the daggers Caleiso carries. "Have you had Gatro before? I don't truly know if y'all are meat-haters in Paragon. Simply, it's what I was always told." Ethelvrise pauses in her task, to glance at us.

"We will, as of today," states Warren. "Just cook it well-done."

Ethelvrise smiles, but it is a dark, menacing sort of look with all those sharp teeth of hers filling her mouth.

Arsyn, inspecting the casket, ignores everyone.

That's when Belzara glances around at the different faces. She takes to sitting on a smooth, flat rock. "I see you've added two new persons to your company. But one's missing. Where's your Sylvadyn, King Talok?"

Talok motions to the casket in front of Arsyn. "Gone," he whispers, grabbing at his freed wrist. "But so's the device."

Belzara's gray skin pales to a murky white. "Your Sylvadyn is dead?"

Siege queries, "Why does that disturb you?"

"You need to be home, soon," she says. "Eyo'el is without her Sylvadyn."

Irritated, Musgrae motions around. "We know. You don't have to tell us. We're bitterly aware of it."

Ethelvrise pauses in slicing up the meat that's laid on a fallen tree. "You misunderstand my Belzara. The Black Flame was the first Sylvadyn, long ago, before made into a spirit of death. The one and only Spirit of Death. No legend gives way to how he became that. But all Sylvadyns hold a certain power, when near Arkivaras. If Zymarc learns your Ryco is dead, he'll know there's near nothing to stop him from giving Paragonians over to The Flame for a feast."

Gemma blurts out, "Zymarc's dead. He was eaten by King Rentwar. We as good as watched it happen."

Belzara stands up. "When was that?"

"Over three days—" Siege starts to say.

"I saw him less than two ago," Belzara interrupts. "Or, rather, I sensed him."

Talok asks, "You're sure—"

Belzara scowls. "You're questioning me? *Me*, Belzara, formally known as Ethelvrise? I've lived for thousands of years; gone through ReNovamen multiple times, because the Geldryn never let Deathasyns have any Siveyras. I served under Deezalo for three of those lifetimes. I know the presence of the Prime Vitiosyn like I know my own heartbeat."

"Could it have been Caleiso you felt?" I ask. "Not Zymarc. We're fairly sure she would inherit his power."

Ethelvrise has started a fire, and is now preparing to roast the meat on spears made of pointed sticks. "A Prime Vitiosyn must be male. It cannot be Caleiso. Or else Belzara would have tried some years ago to overthrow Zymarc."

"I did try," Belzara mutters, as she paces about. "Didn't work. Couldn't kill him and take his power." She stops. "It could have been my brother whom I sensed . . . former brother, that is—Azabahk."

Quall snaps his attention to Belzara. "Prince-General Azabahk is your brother?"

"*Was* my brother. We were twins in our first life, and in some of our other lifetimes. Given to Deezalo, as children, during one of those lives as twins. We were brought up in his courts. And nasty courts they were. Violent and cruel. Azabahk and I always stayed close, except for the lifetime when Deezalo was captured, and executed soon after." Belzara looks to Warren, whose face darkens over. She asks, "What became of Deezalo's Hammer?"

"We don't know," says Talok, in place of Warren.

Belzara states, "For that weapon, alone, Azabahk would kill, in order to get it back." She glances to Ethelvrise. "Cook that meat to rare. We've no time to waste. They must be on their way, and quickly. Us, as well, to hunt whomever it was I sensed lurking nearby."

Cringing, Eli looks at Ryco's casket. "The things we'll do for you, Ryco. He *is* all right in that casket, yeah? No real harm done to its seal?"

Arsyn slumps back against a tree trunk. "I had to refortify it. It's left me drained. The seal won't hold the way I intended. I'll have to refortify it every night."

"We will travel with you," says Belzara, "for as long as we are able. Let us hope that I not sense his presence again."

Ethelvrise says, "Let's eat, then be off."

* * *

For weeks, we travel with the two Deathasyn women, as they lead us on new paths. Shortcuts. They assist in carrying the burden of Ryco's casket. In refortifying it as well.

Warren's silent hatred lets up by only a mere fraction, each night. The others seem numb to the fact that Deathasyns, former Vitiosyns, are assisting us. It truly lives up to the saying, an enemy of my enemy is my friend. I still don't know how I should feel over the ordeal, though. Relief is the closest description.

Many times, we must alter course, because Belzara senses that Vitiosyns are near. She can smell them out, and Ethelvrise can hear them from miles off. Yet they do not sense that *one* Vitiosyn. The one we all fear, though we don't want to admit to it aloud.

One morning, before dawn, Belzara announces over breakfast, "By nightfall, you'll all be half a day out from Eyo'el. We shall leave you from here."

Ethelvrise adds, "We shall run away again, and be happy. For we have helped the little Paragonians. Also, we mean to hunt that one, ruling Vitiosyn, whomever he may be now."

Belzara states, "When we catch word of your victory—wherever our journey takes us—we shall come back to Paragon and celebrate with you, King Talok of Dragon Tamers. For you are Vision of the Dragon, destined to take your people to heights they've not known before."

Talok swallows a mouthful of food. He focuses his gaze down at his bowl of stew. "You're sure you don't want to come with us?"

Belzara chuckles. "Deathasyns shan't ever be accepted by your people, Talok. Take that as a warning. Tamers are proud folk. Always have been. Death magic is not for them. Hardly is it a magic for me, anymore. I've seen what it does to innocent people."

We can't help but look to Ryco's casket. I recall the sight of the beam searing through Ryco's chest, before he died. The image makes me almost lose my breakfast over the campfire. Not another word is spoken until after breakfast.

We finish.

The Deathasyn women bow to Talok.

Once Ethelvrise straightens her stature, she says, "Will of Vardiyas, and Onyx Prince be with you."

They depart; we go forward.

Nightfall comes.

We lie down to rest. The others sleep. I just can't will myself to slumber.

Frightened beyond words, I torture myself over wondering if I shall ever see Ryco again, alive, well, and happy. Those images of his chest being seared through haunt me. I want to beat my fists on Mirror Lake's rocky shores till I feel nothing.

I get up from my bedroll. Cricket-like sounds chirp around. Intermittent clicking and birds warbling add to the chorus of night.

"Pst!" someone whispers. "Tyler?"

It's Gemma, calling to me. I sit on the bedroll with her.

"Want company?" she asks, turning down her blanket.

I crawl in; she covers me. That's when the burning tears start.

She hugs me close to her chest, digging her fingers through my shorter hair. It's a little longer than it was, when Dea gave it a good trim. I miss the Darklyres. I miss the ones in Paragon. I miss all the ones back home, on Earth. So many do I miss.

My few escaping sobs are silent, shaking my shoulders, as I hug her back. Eventually, I drift to sleep in her arms.

Later, though I know not how much later, I'm jarred awake. Gemma's not on the bedroll with me.

Scuffling footsteps sound from somewhere nearby.

Dread seems to pierce into me from the very air.

I ease up, trying to judge where the sound is coming from. The two on watch are Kent and Eli. They're passed out, positioned as if they've been struck. I rush to them. They're coming to.

I shake Eli to awareness. "Where's Gemma?"

Kent stands, a bit wobbly. "Something made the trees strike us."

Eli rubs the back of his head. "Didn't even hear it until, *Bam!*"

Muffled screams come from somewhere far away from camp.

Terror-stricken, I hear too much sound. All the sounds of every moving thing. It's so loud. Like buzzing in my head.

Kent calls out to everyone, "Wake up! Gem's missing."

The group startles awake. We begin the search.

Musgrae finds the drag marks. "This way."

Arsyn and Warren stay behind with Ryco.

The rest of us run to find Gemma.

"Tyler!" Gemma suddenly screams from somewhere close.

We rush into a small clearing. It's the portal clearing, where the streams of water flow. A figure looks back at us, his eyes glowing crimson-red. He has hold of Gemma, his gloved hand clamped over her mouth.

I wonder, *Is it Azabahk? Could it be?* My heart sinks. Sounds grow quieter. His voice is smooth. It is the only thing I hear, as if whispered in my ear.

"Return to me the Equidyn, Onyx Prince," says Zymarc. "And you'll get the girl back."

I rush forward. We all do.

The two of them disappear together in a flash of bright energy, the captor with his victim.

Rozeth gets to the space first, where they were standing only seconds ago. "I know not what spell that was," she cries. "We cannot track her. She's lost to us."

My heart pounds painfully in my chest. "I was right next to her! Why didn't I sense him? Why isn't he dead? Why didn't he take me? Why her?

Why Gemma?" I break down in sobs.

Quall carries me back to camp, my strength drained from me.

We are defeated.

21

Battle for Status

After a fitful rest, we rise a few hours later. We make for Eyo'el. All the while, I keep one thought at the forefront. A thought of, *I will not lose Gemma.* I've determined in my heart to give the Equidyn over to Zymarc. I dare not tell the others.

Now we stand at the edge of the forest, speechless.

Eli lets out a soft, choked gasp.

The great trees surrounding Eyo'el have been stripped away for miles. Cut down and splintered, not even stumps remain. Merely ashes. Tiny bits of wood. Beyond the sum of debris, the Blackwood walls of Eyo'el stand as fortification. The journey to the gate looks to be a death wish. That flat, barren land offers no protection. Only danger.

"This happened weeks ago," says Siege, recovering enough to speak.

Quall states, "I wonder why we didn't see the signs of it, prior to now."

"They would've made it rain," Warren says, "to keep the smoke down. Wouldn't have seen it, unless two kilometers out."

"Siege, can you summon dragons for cover?" queries Talok.

Siege looks down. "We're too far away from the city. They won't hear me."

Rozeth poses her question of, "What of that tamed dyn, Talok? Do you think he is near enough to hear you?"

"I do believe he went back to Vosh-Perida," says Talok. "That he intends to stir up the dragons there. Nowhere near here."

Arsyn adjusts Ryco's casket, strapped to his back, while he stays in the shadows.

Dawn's light illumines the landscape more.

Anger rising, I stride out into the open.

"Tyler, what are you doing?" Arsyn calls after me.

I yell, "We didn't travel all that time, doing all that we did, to be defeated while our home's in sight!"

I run forward, taking out the Shield of Shylen feather as I do. I brush my left hand across the flat part of it. Then I stab the shield piece of Dea's into the barren land. "Dea," I call, "we're home. We've brought Talok and Ryco back. Come to us. Help us . . . We're here." Whispering that last part, I fall to my knees, exhausted.

Dawn breaks out its full light. We wait in agony. The others still stand at the forest edge; Arsyn within the shadows of it, as he draws his cloak tighter about himself. I'm alone, out in the open, sitting and waiting and hoping. Tears refuse to give way. My eyes are as dry as the very land before me, beneath me, as I just sit there, thinking, *Beautiful Eyo'el, do you still live beyond that gate? Or have you died? Have we failed you? After all we've done to save your king, have we only come back to find you dead?*

Footsteps approach. Their owner continues on past me. Arsyn. I recognize his boots, made of the thickest leather, symbols etched all down the outer sides. The others of the company go bravely out into the open too. Most of them pass by me. Some stop, not going any farther than I have.

The city shows no signs of waking up.

Vitasadyns roar in the distance. They come from the north. The others quicken their stride. I remain sitting, defeated.

Someone returns to stretch their hand down to me. Then another on my other side. Arsyn and Talok. My cousin says to me, "Come, we'll ease each other's burdens."

"We shall give you hope," says Arsyn, "for you've near lost it."

Gripping my arms, they haul me up to stand on my own two feet.

Ben clips the shield's metal feather piece to my belt, then moves in front of me to lead.

Scepter and other dragons land on the ground some distance away, letting Onyx Warriors and Vitiosyns pour off their backs in hordes. They take flight again.

We walk quickly, trying to find our stride. When we do, we run. Us, toward the closed gate of Paragon. Our would-be attackers, toward us. Both Onyx and Vitiosyns alike. The thunderous multitude storms toward our measly group of eleven. Twelve, if counting Ryco in his casket.

The closer they get, the more the ground trembles.

The gate remains shut, not budging. We continue forward. I can only hope that, soon, it will open. That soon, Paragonians and Greyvons, the Jokryn and Darklyres, even my Onyx of Malik will come to our aid.

Magic and arrows pelt the ground near us. Talok, Rozeth, and the seven King's Guard take action, blocking and then firing back. Arsyn blocks enemy fire too. I'm standing on my own, swaying unsteadily. The ground shakes more. I fall to my hands and knees. I'm too weak, too scared, when a thought occurs to me. *What if there's a barrier around the city, shielding against attacks and, also, against sound?*

"Eli!" I shout over the noise, while kneeling on the ground. "Do you have the Staff of Arkizadan? Give it to me." I hold up a hand to catch it.

In a moment, he has it out. He tosses it. A fiery arrow hits him, goes right through his shoulder. It stays lodged there. Stumbling, he screams. Kent's there to block other attacks directed at Eli.

I grip the staff tight in my right hand, as it feels more natural in that one's grasp. I focus on a single sensation—the image of light after storms—thinking: *Wake them up, Eyo'el. I'm here. Krim-Karasa-dim-drim. I am him. Ravieras-Savak-Kavas. Soon, to ruin. To doom. Help me bring our enemies to their doom.*

I aim the staff stone at the gate and think the word for sparks: Ignicuel. Silver-colored fire akin to liquid bursts from the stone. One shot like lightning. It crackles, then cuts out. The staff starts vibrating. I can't keep hold of it. I toss it away. It bursts into dust.

I collapse in shock. My heart pounds. I think, *What have I done?*
Rumbling comes from ahead. From the gate.

My body shakes. I'm unable to breathe. The thought repeats, *What have I done? What have I done?* Unwanted tears seep from the corners of my eyes. I stare ahead. I've no care for the chaos around me. Only care for Eyo'el. A hope that all is safe inside. But, also, that they are now wide awake.

The silver-fire ignites on the walls of Blackwood. It continues up, to encompass the air above the city.

A breath of horror is wrenched right out of me. I gasp and choke and cough.

A black cloud rises up from Eyo'el. It's as a deafening cloud rising up from the surface to rest amid the sky. I know not whether it's good or bad. It comes to fly over us. It has not the sound of great dragon wings. Rather, like a tumult of birds. Large birds.

Arsyn shouts over it all, "It's King Aygor and his Lyres of RawZend!"

Many cloaked Darklyres land near us. Other armor-clad ones remain up high, their hammered breastplates glinting in the light. Both groups battle against our enemies on the ground, and the ones in the air. We bump past our allies, our hearts renewed.

Scepter and scores of Vitasadyns take to the ground. They slaughter numerous Lyres around us—crushing them underfoot; sweeping spiked tails at them, piercing some; others are snatched up, mid-flight, and swallowed whole. We can't go forward, nor back. We're slowly surrounded, any chance of escape choked out.

ReNovak comes into our midst. "Stand down, Paragonians. You've lost. Let this bloodshed end. Be taken prisoners, instead."

The gate of Eyo'el begins to open. A Black Dragon has crawled up enough to be seen from over a section of the wall. He leaps from his place there, to glide down. A quaking roar rumbles out from him—Reign—coming down to attack his brother, Scepter. It's all any of us can do to scramble out of their way.

More Darklyres are cut down. But so, too, are the enemies' forces cut down. Dyns fly upward, leaving the city. The young, the old, and the ones somewhere in between. The Greyvons burst open the city gate the rest of the way, barking, snarling, and howling. Thousands of them, they run for ReNovak and his forces. Onyx move back to let the Vitiosyns be torn apart and eaten first.

My heart wants to rupture. I need it to stop. The Onyx are mine, and I am theirs. But so are the Dragon Tamers. I cry out.

Jasper strides out in wolf form, weaving in and out around his forces, looking much improved from all the other times I've seen him. He roars that Greyvon Alpha howl, and his enemies cower. Only one Onyx in his direct path does not succumb to fear.

Siveyra Gyronawv stands in the way of Jasper—that alpha threatening his people, our people, the slaves to the Laws of Neutrality. I focus on Gyron. He's close enough to cut ReNovak down. I reach out with my mind and grab hold of the Siveyra. I find that it's easier this time, for this time I am the Onyx Prince, and I am awake. I grip Jasper's mind too. I stop him from killing a great soul.

Forcefully, I will Gyron's hands, the hands grasping hold of two blades, to move their aim toward the Onyx King. The good Siveyra resists me. Perhaps he must put up his best fight. Though I am of the dragon aura, I wonder if I can be of the Von aura too. Both power and cunning. Logic and improv. It's worth a try.

I div to him, *"I am Ravieras-Savak. Your Onyx Prince. Listen to me, Siveyra. Let me free you. Strike your king's side. He deserves no less, for being a cheater of magic. Come, join with my Onyx of Malik, wherever they may be."*

Something gives way, like a great sigh of rest after a long night of torment. Gyron gives in. His blades move swiftly to pierce ReNovak's side. The king cries out, falling before the Warrior of the Nyxane.

Gyron calls out, "Justice has been served for your treachery toward magic, King ReNovak. You are made whole, in the eyes of Vardiyas now."

Blade pulled out of him, ReNovak falls.

As Talok helps me stand up all the way, he exclaims, "Now, Tyler! Give a command."

"Onyx Warriors!" I shout, making the motions. "King's Command! Cut down Vitiosyns who would dare to strike your Onyx Prince."

Thousands upon thousands are cut down.

Their great cries ring out, chilling me, haunting me, stabbing my mind with pain.

The land is covered with more blood. And that blood finds every gap and slant, trickling like red streams not very far from where I stand.

The ground shudders, as remaining Darklyres take off to fly upward. They land upon the walls that protect the city. Familiar faces are aimed downward, watching us from those walls. My Onyx Warriors. Smythe is up there with them, smiling down at me. He's been fitted with a white coat of the King's Guard, similar in design to what Quall, Warren, Siege, and Eli wear. He lifts a hand to greet us. Beside him is Ghebina, ever watchful of our surroundings. She lingers her gaze on the patch of forest the others and I exited a short while ago.

Only Reign and Scepter continue the fight. They get in the way of us making it through the gate.

Smythe calls down, "I've been told by one of these Arkiveis—Grover, I think it was—that this is a battle for status among dragons, and not to interfere, Prince Ravier."

"Yes," Ghebina adds, snapping to attention. "And don't ye be interfering neither, Ravier. Stay put, looking pretty. Or else we must disobey an Arkivy to save our prince."

Smythe mutters to her, as if I can't hear him, "Looking pretty filthy, ya mean, Ghebina? Look at the lot of them. Half-dead in appearance. It's a good thing King Aygor made the move to have us and his forces return three days ago. City would've been razed to the ground just yesterday, otherwise."

"Sh! Smythe," Ghebina warns, flicking him on the arm. "He might hear ye. Knowing the close call that it was might be the last pebble in his shoe, before he be breaking down. He is still young, ain't he?"

"Have care of your words, Ghebina," says Smythe, glancing away. "Look, our Siveyra has been freed because of that young one. Even if it doesn't last, Gyron is free in this moment. Bask in it, for moments are all we are promised."

The Onyx on ground-level near us, stand at attention beside Gyron. All are in awe, watching the two dragon brothers brawl.

Kent, Musgrae, and Siege start preparing an ammo I've not seen them use before. Curved arrows, cork-screw stakes, grappling hooks, and other things.

Talok tells me, "Reign is my dragon. Keep your Onyx out of the way. We're going to help Reign kill Scepter. The Darklyres and other dragons won't assist with this. It's a fight for chief dragon status."

Nodding, I say, "I'll stand between. Go. Make sure he wins, Talok."

Talok pats my arm, before he runs off toward the fray.

Scepter, being bigger, can't dodge his brother's quicker jabs, nor the strikes from spiked wingtips.

Talok, short-staff appearing in hand, draws a symbol in the air. He sends it to Reign. Scepter roars in anger, his blood spurting out of his fresh wounds. Right as the symbol lands on Reign, fire flares from the open jaws of Scepter. Reign leaps from the ground, spinning upwards. Spikes are let loose from his wing's edges. They pierce Scepter deeply in the neck.

Talok and the three rush closer to the King Vitasadyn. Their ammo's launched with wind Siege sends forth.

Turning his head, Scepter rears up surprisingly high for his size. He grabs Reign by the haunches. He pulls Reign down, then proceeds to beat him with the dozens of spiked-horns upon his neck, and with the lodged ones given to him by his smaller brother.

The launched ammo reaches Scepter, while he digs his claws deep into Reign's back legs.

Reign rumbles like a thunderstorm that's building, growing, then he opens his mouth wider, and an exploding sound deafens us all. I'm thrown down, disoriented. My hearing rings. Onyx Warriors are brought briefly to their knees. Then clacking sounds come from the forest. Clicking, tapping, slithering.

I force myself to get up. But it hurts. My ribs hurt. My throat burns. My exposed skin stings. And my eyes? Well . . . they've felt better.

"Sylvadyns!" Gyron points. "Light the ground with fire, there and there!"

The remaining Onyx army heads up the back of our company. They continuously fire at the edge of the forest where the barrenness begins.

Ghebina lets out a war cry. Arrows are shot by the warriors from atop the entrance wall. The attack sprays out as it hits the ground near the forest edge.

Jasper, with Mekka and Rorka's assistance, herds his Vons as close to the city wall as possible. They wait for an opening, to attack or defend. Whichever is needed. After some time, the candidates nip at the Greyvons' heels. The mass starts climbing the wall made of trees, getting faster as they ascend higher. They're over the entire wall, before the dragon brawl has ceased.

Jasper remains on the wasteland side with us, watching as would a guardian. At some point, my control of his mind must've broken.

Scepter's weighed down. Even more so from the ammo shot into him that has ropes attached to the ends.

Onyx continue their fire at the forest edge; Darklyres too.

A loud sound of creaking, crackling wood catches on the wind. Branches race toward us like rushing water down a hill. Large citrine thorns throw themselves over the mound of fire. Many Onyx are shot through the chest by them. The branches follow the thorns like a comet's tail and burst over the flames. When nearing the city, the thorns, branches, and leaves slow somewhat. Deep-brown dragons take shape, their scales appearing as different kinds of tree bark merged together. They roar and click, reminiscent to wind rippling over water or fire torching all in its path. If elements had voices akin to creatures, that's how these dragons sound—the elements, come to life. Sylvadyns. Four of them. They're as fast as dolphins, diving in and out of the sands of Paragon's barren strip of land.

Musgrae and Siege work hard to stake the ropes into the ground that are swirling about Scepter's body, but Talok and Kent are the ones to initiate shocks through those rope fibers.

Scepter screams.

My head vibrates.

Reign, Kent, and the four Sylvadyns are unaffected, as well as Warren, who's coming over to me.

He yells above the noise, "Those are Ryco's tamed Sylvadyns! Tell the Onyx to cease their attack on them. Or more will die. They're strong, sure dyns. Ryke would have only picked the very best. The most stubborn. They'll fight to the death."

I give the command in Mensa-div to Gyron, Smythe, and the other Onyx; they cease their attacks on the four beasts.

More Vitasadyns come into view from the west, the direction of MarcKand.

Arsyn sets Ryco's casket down. "The seal's about to break. I must attempt to save him now."

Quall shouts, "We must get inside the city!"

"There isn't time," Arsyn says, "to wait for those dragons to claim status."

"Really, Ryke?" Eli grumbles. "You couldn't hold out for two more minutes?"

Scepter's voice fades out. Though he tries to catch his breath, he can't. He's tied down. The Sylvadyns shift their bodies back into branches so that they can latch onto Scepter's wings and legs, further pinning him to the ground.

Landing, Reign gazes at his brother. It's only a moment. Then he lunges for Scepter's neck, and rips him open. Blood sprays from that torn neck. Scepter's dying cry echoes out, then gurgles, and fades to quietness.

Arsyn shifts to take his Parasogyn form, speaking demonically, "Sasak-Concalos-Sadyn-el."

The enemy dragons from the direction of MarcKand have reached us. Reign has killed his brother. He's now tearing off his brother's wings. The Sylvadyns release the dead dragon. They retake the form of dragons, to fly up to land on the city's wall of trees. The Darklyres and my Onyx give them much space. The four dyns sit like statues of hounds guarding their home, narrow-eyed and alert. Ghebina goes over to pet one of them. He actually lets her, leaning his wooded head down a bit.

The Onyx Warriors not under my direct command begin to flee. Gyron stays.

Arsyn speaks the last part, one word of: "Sivondel."

The ground rumbles as if it wishes to tear itself apart.

With a great gust, the bodies of the fallen draw together, including Scepter's. His wings stay behind with Reign. The gust only touches the dead. Ashes and dirt of the land join with them. Black-fire burns it all together, to form into one creature. Sivondel, thrice what he was at the shores of Deivahl.

Citrine thorns of the trees behind us come whirling through the air and form his eyes. He roars, and it booms out. We're thrown back from the force of it. My eardrums burst. Searing pain almost makes me faint. It takes everything in me to focus on something else. Like not dying or fainting or screaming.

Ryco's Sylvadyns bellow from their place on the wall.

More pain surges in my ears, rattling me.

Enemy dragons turn away, fleeing to the north. They are too scared to land. But the Sylvadyns are not scared. They leap into the air, to begin a chase. I wonder how they are able to fly over a barren land. No trees below them.

Suddenly, a deep chill overcomes me. The pain in my eardrums leaves, as I hear Ryco's last words to me: *It's not over yet. When my eyes close. Count to thirteen. The device should break off him. I'll start falling. Thirteen more. I'll be gone. I'll miss you.*

I whisper the phrase forcing its way up, "I'll carry you in memory, forever."

The casket seal breaks.

Rising to his feet, Arsyn directs his shout upwards, "I have summoned you, Sivondel. I, Arsyn of the Jhiresons, heir of Taazar, direct descendant of Jhire, himself. Friend of Sylvadyns. I am a Parasogyn of the line of Ayzareel and Gaula. Feast on this death, but save one for us. I petition you to bring him back to the land of the living. Ryco'Eldeis de Pawv'Ragaen. The one of the Power of Two Dragons."

Sivondel beats his wings harder. The wind gales as a tropic storm. Though there isn't any body of water nearby, many ice-cold droplets are flung down from those wings.

At the mercy of his terrifying majesty, we cling to the ground. Yet I brave a look into his eyes, and any tears I had burn away. My eyes are made dry. Not because hope rises. Rather, a hot terror comes from staring death in the eye, and finding that death looks back.

"One, every thousand years," I whisper, my gaze steadfast, "you can bring back. Bring us our Paradyn. I, the blood heir Onyx Prince, request of you. I ask you, Spirit of Death, go against your nature, and bring back one life. That is all. One."

Sivondel dips his long neck down, and tenderly bites into Ryco's cracked, battered casket. He does not crush it. Instead, he flies over Eyo'el with purpose in his movements, headed for a very specific place within the city. The Castle of Sosha, most likely. That, or the Arkivara.

The gusting wind fades with him. The torrential downpour that's begun too.

We get up and hurry inside the city.

22

What Spirits are Made Of

Just inside that open gate of Paragon, two wait right there for us. Deamond and Khyra. Relief, perhaps pride, is on their faces for the sight of us coming home. Quickly, terror replaces the relief in their matching set of violet eyes. They take in our appearance.

Dea frowns.

Khyra's chin quivers from sadness. "Where's Ryco?" she whispers.

Talok approaches her, reaches for her.

She backs away. Tears trickle down her face. "Where's Ryco!" she shouts, before sobs begin.

The remaining seven of the King's Guard gather round, heads bowed in respect. Ben has the hardest time remaining calm. He can't decide what to do with his hands. He searches his pockets. He finds that cloth, the one always ready for those who need it. He hesitates, then stuffs the cloth in his pocket. Both hands he buries deep in his pockets, in fact. Pain washes over his face.

Talok has started telling Khyra the news.

Her loud sobs turn to screams. It chills me, makes me shiver. I hate the feeling. Hate that we couldn't tell Khyra sooner. Warn her, or something. Surely, she must've known there was a chance one of us could die? It being Ryco, though? Ryco, and no one else? Now that will shock all of Paragon.

I recall the woman in blue, the day we left for Vondurheil, those months ago. How she shouted at him, *"That's not fair! No one can beat you, unless they're actually intending on killing you. Even then, it's doubtful."*

I look up at Sivondel, carrying Ryco's casket. I struggle to keep composure, as I walk forward. Heading for where I think Sivondel is going to lay Ryco down, I leave the others to stay with Khyra. I've not given up hope. Sivondel is still the Spirit of Death. I have faith that this one of death will hear us out, will listen. But will he make Ryco one of those counted among as 'saved every one thousand years'? I simply do not know . . .

Dea follows me. She's a few paces behind when, even through her fear, she declares, "I knew you hadn't perished, Ravier. No one wanted to believe Khyra and me. I must ask, though . . . what dyn is that, flying over us? Friendly like Khyra's new Sylvadyns, I hope." She has a look about her. A look of knowing in those reptilian eyes. She knows there's a good chance Ryco may not be coming back to us. Knows that I wasn't able to save him. She knows that fact is weighing heavy on my shoulders. She walks faster, coming to grab me by the arm. "Ravier," she says sternly.

"He's neither friend nor enemy," I reply. "He's The Black Flame. The Spirit of Death."

Dea's mouth drops open. She gazes up at Sivondel, wonderment on her face.

I grin. "How's it feel, looking at Death?"

She manages to say one word: "Incredible."

Khyra runs past us in hysterics. "No, no, no." She says it again and again, louder each time.

I pick up my pace, telling Dea, "We've asked him to bring Ryco back to life."

Ahead of us, Khyra stares up at Sivondel. She screams at him, "Ryco! I want to see him! It cannot be true. Please, fair dyn, let me see my friend, my mentor, my partner. Ryco'Eldeis!" She collapses to the ground, choking on her sobs.

Talok and the seven with Rozeth plod their way closer. There's no hope in their expressions. Only defeat.

I wonder, *Why won't they believe that Death* does *hold the keys? That he can use them how he will?*

Arsyn flies upward. He assists Sivondel in lowering Ryco's casket carefully to the ground. It comes to rest on a patch of dirt near the base of the Arkivara.

The Darklyre of Jhire opens the casket.

Sivondel growls, grinds his teeth together. I liken the sound to dozens of dry bones grating against each other.

"He is not in The Kievas," rumbles Sivondel, hovering over the entirety of Eyo'el. "I cannot bring back what is not there, waiting for me."

"He has not fully died yet," says Arsyn. "His spirit lingers. Soon, he will be delivered to you. And when he is delivered to you, will you bring him back to us, fair dyn?"

"What has happened to his heart?" Sivondel's growl grows deeper. "This ought not to be done to a body. Spell of Dei-Athos-Kree. Abomination of abominations. I shall try to overcome. But it is the other spirits I must now battle. Can death win, I wonder?"

Bolder than ever, I speak to Sivondel. I tell Death, "When calls the darkness, find it. Bind it to light. Defeat it forever. Krim Karasa dim drim. I am him. Ravieras Savak Kavas. Find Ryco for me. Win against the spirits. Bring him back to us. That is all." I take out the Blades of Neutrality. I clang them together, their flat parts, speaking those words of: "Thirteen—Done, when you find him."

Sivondel roars violently, lifting his enormous head. He focuses on Khyra, and quiets down to say, "Can I indeed deliver to thee, most favored Sylvadyn of all? One-quarter fearless, one-quarter arrogant, the other half afraid."

He bends his head down, to study Khyra as she weeps quietly beside the casket. She holds one of Ryco's hands, kissing the palm of it lovingly.

"Widow of Paradyn," Sivondel rumbles at her. "Petition Tree Stag to guide me. To unite me with power of Vardiyas, for I feel your Ryco's spirit fading now to darkness. A darkness not even I dare tread amidst, alone. Abomination of abominations. Where Deezalo doth, indeed, lie in wait to torment all who are given to him. A never-ending war he wages. Where blood rains from black clouds. Where fire boils the seas to steam. No metal can withstand. No spell overcome. No soul escape. For Ryco of Paragon, I would but try to search for him. Pull him from among these oceans. If Life, the other half of me, goes with, I shall have heart. The Heart of Arkivara, to call me back with memories."

Deamond has hidden herself away. She leaves that hiding place now, wearing the green ancestral garb of Aygor. She runs toward Sivondel. She stops near Khyra. "Take me with you, Sivondel, Spirit of Death. For I have the complete strength of the Shield of Shylen."

King Aygor has come to view the commotion just now. He shouts, "Dea, don't! You will die!"

He rushes toward her. Arsyn gets in his way. The two begin a brawl with weapons.

Arsyn shouts, "Let her, King Aygor! She is stronger than you'll ever know."

Dea leaps off the ground. She takes flight.

"Do not fail, Dea of RawZend," I div to her, though she doesn't acknowledge that I do.

Death's face comes to greet her. Gently, she touches him on his scaly cheek. She begins the transition into fiery, black energy. Fading to join with Sivondel, she looks back to her guardian. "I've died loads of times, King Aygor. Is this not what Darklyres train for? To conquer death. This is the greatest test of all. If I cannot overcome it, as the Shield of Shylen, with the power Khyra shall give us, no one can overcome the Death of deaths."

Dea finishes her fade, to join with Death.

As she does, it's as if a part of my heart is chipped away, thrown out to die. Barely can I breathe. Only Skylin, standing across the way directly in front of my vision, gives me a speck of joy. She's all right. I had wondered

. . .

I lift my hand pathetically. What else is there to do?

King Aygor transitions into that Parasogyn form. He yells like a beast gone mad. Arsyn manages to hold him back, barely. It's when SynKievas and Seqwhyett come to help restrain Aygor that the Darklyrian King can be tamed a little.

Sivondel laughs, and the sound thunders all around us. He roars upward at the sky. His wings grow feathers; violet metal like Dea's own plucked feather given to me.

Getting to her feet, Khyra releases Ryco's limp hand. She speaks to the Arkivara, "Go with them, Eyo'el. Go with your Death. Come back with my Sylvadyn."

Eyo'el is unmoved.

Kent glances around. "Where's Grover to wake her up?"

Zepharre peers from amidst the cowering Vonsai. "Castle. Deep in grief. Now, I'd wager a bet, afraid beyond words. As are the rest of us."

Kent makes a black staff appear in his grasp, the same one used to assist Nyrim with his memory overwhelm. He aims its stone at the Arkivara, pausing for words, searching for what will wake her. Then his features take on severity. No more do we see Kent of Dysarda, but, rather, an Arkivy. His eyes glow blue, and he shoots silver-colored fire from the stone of his staff to strike the Arkivara. It ignites the black-and-white wood bark of her, without burning in destruction.

"Wake up, Eyo'el," he speaks out. "Be free of the land. Join your other half, Death, for a time. Your Sivondel. Aeowneis-teras-metsas-sadora-vyn-kryn-dei-Sivondel. Share in your burdens. Come back into the light, when it is done. I release you, to go do this."

Kent's eyes cease their glow.

The fire on the tree bark goes out.

A thin smoke dissipates from the area.

Rhythmically, the Arkivara begins her rattling of leaves. Some leaves are shook free, hurrying toward Sivondel. He absorbs her turquoise leaf-spikes. Crystals of blue, black, and white—the colors of Vaegon eyes—form on his mighty outstretched wings, adding to the violet already there.

All creatures have long fled to cowering in the shadows within the city of Eyo'el. The Vonsai tremble, tails tucked between legs. One of the littlest of them, Zepharre pets on the head. The Greyvons whimper when their alpha in Von form, Jasper, comes out to be before The Black Flame. He howls low. The wind colors of Vondurheil emit from his Greyvon fur, turning to fire that pushes Sivondel up faster, sending him higher for flight.

Sivondel soars, flying toward the light rays of the star Rentwaramein. Suddenly, he plunges downward toward the ground. We run back for the gate, to watch as he joins with the barren land. When the tip of his tail fades to energy and then all energy catches on the wind, floating away, a blast sounds out. Black waves of sand roll over the colorless wasteland. Then it's gone. All of Sivondel. Dea too. And a portion of Eyo'el.

Stuck in an oppressive stupor, we trail back. No one says anything to the other. It's all too much. I sink down beside the casket. I lay my enchanted blade down on the Paradyn's chest, the one he gave back to me. Both of Ryco's wrists I grab. I place them over where his heart should be. All he has to do to grip the hilt is tighten his hands into fists. They remain still. His face is lifeless. The lines of it tell that he didn't die in peace. Instead, torment. Hot tears sting my eyes. My hands are filthy from the journey, so I wipe the tears away with the back of my right wrist.

Heavy footsteps approach.

I'm about to shout at whoever it is, tell them to leave me be. Let me grieve.

The owner of the footsteps talks softly, asking, "Onyx Prince, where would you like the body of King ReNovak?"

I look over my shoulder. Siveyra Gyron is carrying the body of his fallen king. Smythe and Ghebina quietly stand with him, glancing at the Paragonian citizens, as they start to emerge from their homes or hiding places. Some among them have reptilian eyes. Those ones are dressed in garments of earthen colors. Their hair has that pattern of snakeskin.

Jokryns, I realize. *They are Jokryns.* I return my attention to Gyron and the limp body he holds in his arms. "He is dead?" I ask, a glimmer of excitement in my voice.

"Not exactly, Prince Ravier," replies Gyron. "But, for all intents and purposes, he might as well be. For a few days, at least."

Smythe sighs, sounding delighted.

Ghebina smirks.

But I'm confused. "What do you mean?" I ask.

"True justice has been served to ReNovak, for cheating. What your older self did in Oniva was only half the punishment," says Gyron. "The Vardiyas immediately took him away, for his Siveyra Journey. If he completes it, he will wake up. Three days is the longest journey in history. If they do not succeed by that time, the Sorsryns never awaken. Death claims them."

Gyron's arms begin to tremble. "As I asked before, where do you wish for his body to rest, while he journeys?"

I grin wickedly. "Siveyra Gyronawv. I command you to, within reason, do to his body whatever makes you feel better."

Smythe joins in with his own dark grin.

Ghebina gazes up at Gyron, before eyeing an empty spot of ground.

Gyron's eyebrows lift. His eyes are playful as a cat's. He glances to where Ghebina is staring. He surveys that empty section of the regrown grass of the Shamrock-green. He chucks ReNovak's lifeless body that way. ReNovak lands hard, rolling to an unnatural position. Gemma's sleeping pose is peaceful, in comparison.

Paragonians clang their weapons against those of their comrades, shouting, "May the Onyx King stay dead!"

They cheer some, but stop when the pendant around Gyron's neck begins to glow.

A voice talks from it, saying, "Gyronawv. Where is ReNovak?" It's Zymarc's voice.

Gyron takes off the chain with the pendant. Energy bursts out, and a projection of Zymarc appears.

From wherever he is, he faces Gyron. "I have word that the city besiegement of Eyo'el has ceased. Why?" Getting angrier, his crimson-red eyes darken to near black. "I told ReNovak to attack Eyo'el, until all are dead, save for the wretched Equidyn. So why has he stopped?"

Going to stand beside Gyron, I shout, "He's been struck down, Zymarc!"

Zymarc commands the Siveyra, "Then go, Warrior of the Nyxane. Head up the Warriors of Onyx. Make them restart the attack. Go now!"

Gyron grows in stature. "Warrior to the Nyxane, I am no more. Instead, I am Guardian to the Onyx Prince, for he has completed the justice ReNovak deserved for cheating, by the forcing of my hand."

Zymarc's eyes at last flicker in fear. It's brief. But I see it. And it emboldens me.

Furious, I point at him. "You can have the Equidyn. I'll give her to you. But you'll be giving the Galloway back. After that, we fight the deciding battle of this war to end it. We're tired. We want it over. Come death or victory, I challenge you to this, Zymarc of Vitiosus. Combat to end one of us, forever. And good luck getting the Onyx to attack the city, while their Onyx Prince is here. Even more luck is needed, for the Onyx of Malik are here to protect me too."

Contempt in his eyes, Zymarc grips something behind him. He drags it to be in front of him—a chair, which Gemma is tied to. Her ankles are secured to the chair legs, and her wrists are strapped down to the armrests.

She struggles.

Zymarc inhales a victorious breath. He runs his gloved hand through her frazzled hair.

Her body trembles. She whimpers.

Zymarc says, "What shall I do to her, I wonder? I believe . . . blood tears is fitting. You did that to Caleiso. I shall do it to her. Fair's fair. Or would you rather I strangle her to the edge of death three times?" He laughs. "Two for repayment of your actions toward Caleiso, plus another for good measure."

He looks down at the top of her head, and starts speaking, "Sareus—"

"Stop!" I shout, falling to my knees. "You can have Awngeleik. Just, don't hurt Gemma. Please!"

Zymarc inhales, sounding disappointed. He strokes Gemma's cheek softly.

Tears roll down her face, trailing across some scabbed-over nicks. Her eyes are tightly closed. Her lips quiver in fright, as Zymarc feels along her jawline.

He forces her to look up at him.

She screams sharply, yet she cannot look away.

I shout, "I'll kill you for that!"

"Yes, try to kill me for this!" he yells, releasing Gemma. His projection steps closer to me. "I want a fight with the Sleeping Dragon. I need not fear, for you're no Waking Dragon. Nor are you Dezarin. If your father were here, I couldn't have accomplished all that I have. He would've been there to anticipate me. To stop me. But he wasn't. He was dead. He *is* dead. And there is nothing that can bring him back."

"It doesn't matter," I reply, in a quiet rage. "I'm here. I'm alive. And I will stop you. I'll even risk dying, if it means stopping you."

Zymarc cracks his knuckles, before intertwining the fingers of his gloved hands together. "That older version of yourself could put up a good fight. Might even have succeeded in killing me. But you? I think not. How to, for this? For I'm not completely unreasonable. I give you something to make you feel better, before I wipe Paragonians out of existence. Give me Awngeleik. I give Gemma back. Then we fight." He lets out a deep laugh. "It's a win-win. You'll not be defeating me, Onyx Prince. Even without the Onyx forces, I can still claim victory. And quite easily."

Talok comes nearer. "We'll stand behind my cousin, in this decision."

"Good," says Zymarc. "I want to see that Equidyn now. I want proof of your possession of her."

I stand up to look at all the ones gathered round. Awngeleik isn't among them. "Bring her," I command.

Khyra grips my arm. "We thought she was with you, Tyler. She's not here."

Wide-eyed, Siege exclaims, "What do you mean, she isn't here?"

Zymarc snaps his attention from Gemma to us. Slowly, his laugh grows in volume. "Has that older version of yourself played a joke on you, Ravier? Oh, the irony." His laughs now sound as mockery.

I shout for Awngeleik to come. Her silence is all that is given to me.

Those in Eyo'el search, though they've been here for weeks, unlike Talok and us. It's no use. She doesn't come. She isn't found. She's not here.

Turning murderous, Zymarc takes a dagger out from its sheath and heads for Gemma.

I don't even have time to scramble toward him and shout obscenities, before he's aiming it at her. He grabs hold of her long hair, and slices.

She screams a tortured cry.

All of Paragon cries out in livid fear.

Zymarc says, "Relax, girl. It was just a bit of hair. Didn't hurt you at all." He winds Gemma's black strands round his right hand. Then he flicks the mass of hair away. He talks to Gemma more, saying, "You're starting to hurt my feelings, Galloway. I've protected you from true harm. I didn't let Vitiosyns drink your blood. Not a single taste of it. Nor did I let them tear your garb from you. I didn't even let them scratch one little mark on your sad face. These marks are from tree branches last night, as you tried to get away. A lot of good that did you."

Gently, he runs his ring finger along her forehead, tracing her profile along her nose, her quivering lips, stopping at her chin. He grips there and makes her bloodshot eyes look up at him.

Quietly, Zymarc says, "I don't like doing this to a Galloway. Believe me. I never thought I'd be forced into this, that day Adair spared my life. He and Soren set a trap. Adair had me at his mercy. Then he changed his mind, saying, 'It is not for me, to end you. Nor is it for Soren to kill you. That is for another. It is for another.' He lowered his weapon, then disappeared. Took Soren with him. I do not believe that Tyler Ravier is this *other* mentioned. He's not this year. Nor will he be next year. Possibly, not ever."

I ask, "Then why wish for me to be your apprentice, if you think I'll never be good enough?"

Zymarc leaves Gemma, to come stand before me. "You'd better worry over other things, Ravier. Such as finding that Equidyn." He stuffs his hands deep into his coat's pockets. "I realize that you're too far away to bring her to me by half a day's time. I'll accept nothing less than seeing her *within* half a day, however. Have Gyron give me a call, using that pendant. I'll complete the connection. Upon my witness that you have the Equidyn, we'll plan where to do a trade."

"Can't wait," I reply, irate.

Zymarc waves one hand at us in an arrogant way. "Until then," he says. "I bid you farewell."

The connection's severed.

23

Restless Seeking

Hours, we search. Awngeleik is as a ghost unseen, no trace of her.

Rozeth and Gyron have been sending dozens of arrow-letters to Ayna in Oniva. Lemawr, throughout those hours—grouchy and untalkative—simply snapped his fingers over the communications, to add protection of obscurity. Then he focused on the dragon-wolf journal once more. He won't let anyone have it, nor touch it, nor look upon all his notes strewn on the council room table.

I'm headed back to see him again, ask him what we are to do. Before I can race inside the castle for the umpteenth time, Smythe stops me.

He comes closer. "What do you wish for us to do, Ravier?"

One of my feet is already planted on the first of those thirteen steps of the castle. My hand has hold of the rail. I pause to go forward, thinking of what to have my Onyx of Malik do. I'm about to tell Smythe I don't know, when an idea comes to me. "Do you know how to forge weapons? Good, powerful weapons? Zymarc's kept the best of our blacksmiths. Our warriors, also. If you haven't already, begin helping Paragonians with these things. Weapons and warfare."

Ghebina comes up behind Smythe. "We've already been teaching them Onyx logic and tactics. I've also taught them a Kyanistic spell here and there. Couldn't leave the city for weapon-making supplies, though. And your people have already made what they could, long before we arrived."

"We *are* good in the forge. Good at gathering raw materials as well. Now that it is safe to leave the city, it is an excellent idea." Smythe glances behind to Ghebina, then refocuses on me. "Who is best for us to be speaking to of weapon-making?"

"Musgrae, Warren, and the Arkivy of Bethsaide. I think his name is Yevolta. May also want to talk with Zepharre. He knows locations of materials the best, I imagine. Or Khyra."

"Ack!" Ghebina wrinkles her nose. "Zepharre! Don't like 'im. Yet he be good at alchemy. You's want us to make him help us, saying it was a special request of our Ravier?"

"Yeah, tell him that." I nod. "Keep him busy. So busy that he hasn't time to interfere with the plan to hand over Awngeleik."

Smythe and Ghebina give a slight bow in unison, then they're on their way to find Zepharre and the others I mentioned.

Meanwhile, I race up the stairs, and into the castle.

I'm in a daze, worrying over Gemma. What might be happening to her this very minute. Not even remembering the trip up to the symposium room, this time I stand just inside the room.

Lemawr is still unbothered by the chaos, only concerned over the journal and his notes.

I shout, "Lemawr, for Vards sake!" I ball one of my hands into a fist that's aimed downward at my side.

He snaps back, looking like the older Dezarin, "Don't you take their name lightly! This isn't their fault. If you can't be patient, Ravier, get out! And don't slam the door. It makes the papers—"

I spin around, walk out, then slam the door.

Dezarin yells, "Now it's going to take me even longer!" Then he mumbles to himself, "Paragonians, impatient creatures. Vaegons? Slightly better. I'm glad it was a Vaegon you chose, Lemawr. I wholly appreciate waking up, looking into such mysterious eyes as what Leira possesses."

There's a pause. A voice change.

"Thank you, Siveyra Lord Dezarin," says Lemawr, in boredom, "for your approval of my most recent lover. Wait! What do you mean—"

Dezarin interrupts, "Oh, yes. She *is* a fine lover. She'll make an excellent mother too. When's your little tyke due to begin its cries of life?"

Lemawr queries, "How'd you be knowing she's fine? Dezarin, what have you been doing while I'm in the dark?"

Dezarin cackles. "Well, what do think I've been doing? I'm enjoying being in a younger body. It's been quite a long while. I can read without my spectacles again. And I can stay fit, without getting winded. I'm keeping your form nice and strong for you, while you have a little rest from consciousness. You should be grateful. You'll need to be strong, once you have a little tyke running about. Unless we die tomorrow. Then it won't matter. Now, shut up, Lemawr. Stop interrupting. You've made this take three times longer than it should have."

I sense someone behind me.

Whoever it is leans down, and whispers over my shoulder, "Eavesdropping, are we, Ravier?"

It's Gyron.

I turn to face him. "You have another letter?"

Standing at attention, he nods, offering it to me.

With a shake of my head, I say, "I think we should stop with the letters. Ayna doesn't know where Awngeleik is. No signs of the Walking Terror in Oniva, or anywhere close by. Also, Dezarin needs to be left alone."

"Left alone?" Gyron's shoulders go stiff. "What does he hope to get out of that journal?"

I shrug. "Who knows? As it is now, he and Lemawr are at war over sharing the same mind. Would you do me a favor?"

"Of course."

"I want a sign put on the door. Have it read, in all languages you know: *Do not disturb Dezarin and Lemawr, under any circumstances, unless we're about to die. Come back tomorrow, for that is when the dying is scheduled for.*" Tittering, I sense I'm breaking under the pressure. Barely can I determine what to do next.

Gyron lowers his gaze. He sweeps a hand over the closed door. Symbols and words burn into the wood. "Done," he says quietly. "I wonder, if that's what you feel is going to happen, might I have permission for something?"

Apologetic, I reply, "I don't know what I feel, but afraid. Truly afraid, Gyron. I don't know what to do. I've given a task to the Onyx of Malik. But what do *I* do? It's torture, being useless. Especially today."

He leads us away from the council room. "Go be with someone you love. Comfort them. Talk with them. For you may not get to, come tomorrow. It's what I wish for. To share a night with a lover, before the battle. May I be with Rorka tonight, Onyx Prince? I've never been with anyone quite like her. I confess, I crave her company."

I rub my face, hating what my answer must be. "I can't give that to you. It requires Jasper's permission."

He slows his long stride. "But you're open to letting me?"

"Yes."

"Then let us find Jasper." He restarts his stride, going faster.

I jog to keep up. "Is someone in a hurry?"

"You would be too, if you had found your superior, after centuries of searching."

"All right. You win. I can't begin to understand what that would be like. I do have an idea where Jasper might be."

We head for the alchemist alcove. Along the way, Gyron sweats in nervousness. Yet he acts giddy. Happy. A weight has been made lighter for him. It's evident in the proud way he carries himself, holding his head high. A slight bounce has been added to his step.

The alcove comes into view. Jasper, his complexion younger and darker, sits on the scuffed-silver bench. His back to us, he stares out the window. Approaching him, we find that actually *isn't* what he's doing. Using his mind, he toys with the Star of Shena. It floats about, spiraling every few seconds. It then bursts with the colors of Winter's Vondaen, without being destroyed.

Hearing us, he snatches it out of the air. The colors disperse. He gets up to face us. "Any word of Awngeleik's whereabouts?"

"Unfortunately, no," says Gyron, wiping the sweat off his forehead.

Jasper starts a walkabout of the alcove. "Then why have you come?"

I cringe, when Gyron silently prods me to take action.

"I came to ask you something," I reply. "In the grand scheme of things, it's not too important. But, in case we die tomorrow, I had wanted to give a loyal friend a chance *tonight*, to be with one he loves."

Jasper runs his tongue over his top teeth, before biting his jaw together tightly. He looks a little hungry. "Gyron wishes to be with one of my Vons?" he asks, all confident-like. "I could give that answer straightaway, unless it's to be Rorka he wants. She must be given by Mekka. As he would have to be given by her. They are each other's now. Have been, since we first arrived in Vondurheil weeks and weeks ago."

Gyron's face crumples in despair.

Emotionless, Jasper queries, "Do you still wish to bed her, knowing she's been to bed with the last standing Alpha Candidate?"

Gyron wrings his hands in front of himself. "I still wish to be with her. Even if it's merely for company. Companionship before we conquer, or are overcome."

Jasper speaks to the empty space in front of him. "Mekka, you are needed in the Alchemist's Cove."

We wait in silence.

As we do, I think of all the things I wish to discuss with Jasper, now that we'll be alone. The ShenawFayel's at the forefront. *How does it work?* I wonder. *Can I use it to advantage now? We're running out of time.*

Mekka stomps along almost past the alcove. Glimpsing us, he stops. "What is it, Alpha?"

Jasper studies some bottles on shelves. "Gyron has a question for you. His Onyx Prince has already given consent to it."

Gyron's about to ask, when Rorka comes up behind Mekka. The two Vons have shared stature; in size and magic, that is.

Rorka's breath catches in her throat. She's about to run off. "I will go."

Mekka grabs her by the arm. "Where do you think you're going?" he practically snarls. "I heard what you thought, just now. You *still* love him.

Even after all he's done as Warrior of the Nyxane, you still want to bed him?"

Quickly, I div, *"Mekka, let them have one day. One hour, even. We've all fought hard."*

"He's not that, anymore, Mekka," she cries, trying to pull away. "Tyler has freed him of the title, of slavery to the Onyx King. He is a free Sorsryn. A Siveyra."

Mekka yells at her, "I gave myself to you! Even when you had reeked of Onyx, days prior. I didn't force you into anything." Then he divs, *"Stay out of this, Ravier. Your loyalties are with Tamers, first, then Onyx. Greyvons are at the bottom of your priorities."*

I div back, *"My loyalties are with those possessing good hearts. Compassion. Ferocity. Willingness to do what it takes, to see justice done. Gyron can't help that he was born Onyx. Would you convict him for it?"*

Lowering his voice, Mekka says to Rorka, "I chose to love you, despite the fact that you didn't save yourself for me."

"I know," she says. "That's why I will go now. Get away. Control—"

Mekka interrupts. "No. You're not going to leave." Gradually grinning, Mekka glances to Gyron, who's still a frazzled mess. "At least . . . you're not leaving without him."

She blushes red. "Mekka? Don't tease me like this. It hurts!" Tears brim in her juniper-green eyes.

Mekka cups Rorka's face. "You misunderstand. Look at him! Poor Onyx fool has fallen for a Von. Go bed him. Wipe that sad sorrow away. Bed that Onyx so good, he howls."

I look down, trying not to laugh.

Vonsai come into view, panting happily within the castle hallway.

"And, there," says Mekka, letting go of Rorka. "Right on cue. They hear us arguing, and they think it might turn into a different sort of activity. Isn't that right, Vonsai?" Mekka playfully barks a few times at them, like a man mocking them.

They erupt in yaps.

"Just keep it down, will ya?" Mekka says to the two. "If not, *those* will be waiting outside your door. And, whatever you do, don't let any of them walk in on you. That's when the bad habits start. They'll become like Musgrae. But, rather than on two legs, they're on four." Mekka's amused, heading to look down the hall. "Where *is* that Grae? I miss the way we used to beat on each other, in our youth. Jasper, want to come play with your former Vonsai, all grown up now?"

"Be there in a moment," says Jasper.

Mekka and the Vonsai rush out of view, the yaps fading with them.

Jasper says, "Not that either of them are truly grown."

Rorka tilts her head, nodding.

Going over to her, Jasper caresses her face. "Enjoy yourself, darling, while you can."

Turning redder, Rorka covers her face. "I shall never live this down."

Gyron approaches. "And I shall never forget it." He pulls her hands away, and kisses her lips tenderly.

She digs her fingers into the cloth of his coat. "I want you now," she moans.

"Vards," I say. "Wait for Jasper and me to leave, at least. Or better? Find somewhere else." I motion. "There's no door, here, for privacy."

Gyron states, "You can build one." He starts kissing Rorka on the neck.

"True." I cross my arms. "But Jasper was here first. You leave."

"Tyler?" Rorka calls, peering past Gyron. "Can he and I?" She bites down on her lower lip, hesitant to finish. Then she does. "In the Advisers' Quarters? It'll make me feel rather naughty."

I snicker. "Promise me! On Zepharre's desk. Leave it as if it never happened."

"Deal." She smiles. "He'll never know."

The two flee in happiness.

Though I watch them head off for a moment of reprieve, my own joy fades.

Jasper toys more with the Star of Shena, now fastened round his neck.

I remark, "I thought The Recruit took that back with her?"

"She would not let me leave without it."

"What's it for?" I ask, paging through books left out on the alcove's tables.

"A symbol of promise." He offers it to me. "Hold it. Tell me what it makes you feel."

I take hold of the silver chain and gaze at the wavy, eight-point star encasing a turquoise-stone. It gently sways, as I hold it up. When no feelings of consequence overcome me, I offer it back to Jasper. "It doesn't make me feel anything, really."

"Odd," he says, starting to reach for it. Then he points. "Look again."

I begin to, when lots of pattering footsteps rush down the hallway and distract me. The herd of Darklyre children flap about, squealing. Mekka, in Von form, barks at them. Vonsai join in and paw at the children. Sonya and Keturah are there too, heading up counterstrikes of wind magic.

Musgrae comes to snatch a small boy up, but the wind throws him off-balance. He falls, laughing. "Ya got me! Keturah of RawZend, I pronounce you the winner of this year's Minor Gauntlet!"

Mekka, submissive as a dog on his back, adds in a growly voice, "For you have bravely fought, and defeated the mighty Vons with your army."

I can't help but smile, as the children cheer. The Vonsai try to howl. Yet their lungs can't sustain it. Their howls cut out, sounding as half-howls.

Jasper carefully takes Shena's Star from me, and slips it round his neck again. "Did I not say they never quite grew up? Yet I could gaze upon the sight forever." Watching them, he absentmindedly tucks the pendant behind his shirt.

I ask, "What's it mean, not to feel anything from that?"

"You have to be focused, for it to work. We'll try again, another time."

Grabbing Jasper's arm, I whisper, "Wait. I wanted to tell you that I saw Rentwar at The Sodon. Again, on our way back from MarcKand. He mentioned more about a ShenawFayel, the first time I saw him."

"Not here," Jasper divs. *"Meet me in the bunkers below. The castle's awareness can't reach one of the rooms down there. We shouldn't go there together. It will learn of your intent and try to stop you, you understand?"*

Ever so slightly, I nod.

Jasper leaves, calling back to Mekka and Grae, "I'm off to hunt Gatro. Alone. I'll be a bit, as the forest has grown thinner of late."

Busily restarting a game of chase with the Darklyres, they hardly acknowledge the statement.

It's easy to slip away, unnoticed. Jasper's gone for a few minutes ahead of me. I wonder how much time to waste, before going to meet him. Suddenly, I sense a bitter chill, as if I'm in shock. I hug my arms to myself, trying to warm back up. When heat ignites, I'm sweating. It's akin to when the beast got closer to me, back in the forest surrounding Mirror Lake. Only, more pointed.

Cold fear overcomes me. I rush forward. Something's not right. I think, *Merlynite should be dead. What if Zymarc resurrected him out from the casing of ice, in Vondurheil? What if Droediin's been sent here? Or what if Zymarc, himself, has actually snuck into the city?*

In record time, I find my way to the bunkers. Jasper isn't lingering at the entrance. Sprinting, I begin to check all rooms. "Jasper," I rasp out repeatedly.

He doesn't answer.

After entering another empty room, I start to turn back and leave. But there's something rectangular, glimmering on the wall. A painting. Tentatively, I approach. It's of a wolf. A Greyvon. With those emerald-green eyes, it must be Jasper. They flash green, then an envelope slips out of the painting. The glimmering ceases. I pick the letter up.

For Tyler, it reads.

Left to see Rentwar. I should've realized sooner, why he went to all the trouble of contacting me, via his Recruit. What other reason he would have, aside from restoring our former Von-dyn alliance. With the renewal of mind, it has become clear.

I know not when I shall return. I was going to ask you to go with me. But you have more important things to do. The ShenawFayel, for example. Strike one with Zymarc, if Awngeleik continues to evade discovery. It is, perhaps, the only way to get your friend back. You must tempt Zymarc with something he cannot refuse, or he'll not be striking one with you. I leave you, to determine what will be his temptation. Do not tell any what you intend to do. They'll stop you. Yet you must find one who can contact Zymarc, or has a way of learning where he is. Also, you must have someone to take Gemma back to Paragon. Again, this is for you to decide. Ryco would have done this for you, in a heartbeat. Perhaps there's another among the guard, equally as bold?

Before you set your mind to a ShenawFayel, I should warn you. It is an agreement, most binding, intended to force opposing parties to set aside differences for a day. Once struck, for precisely twenty-two hours, you cannot harm the other. Even more? Magic binds you to protect them, in case they should be attacked. Deathasyns grow restless, in Vosh-Perida. Attempts on Zymarc's life may occur, while you are in ShenawFayel. You could die, protecting him. And that would be a bitter end for you. To die, protecting your enemy of yesterday and tomorrow. But you had a right to know the truth. Now, I've told you. Light of Vardiyas be with you, Ravier.

Your friend and ally,

Jasper of Vondurheil

P.S.

Take this painting with you. If I am able, I'll come through.

Though Droediin's already confessed to being the one on Earth, near my home, I can't help but mentally compare the phantom's notes with this letter of Jasper's. Since Droediin destroyed the notes a while ago, I'm left unsure if the penmanship's the same. I don't believe it is. Still, why would I sense a chill similar to that day, here? It's more acute, now. Perhaps it's because magic's now more concentrated in my Mazhrein.

I tuck the letter away; then—while thinking the word: *Resilios*—I take the painting off the wall. It shrinks down to fit in the palm of my hand. I add it to one of my pouches, as I leave the room, pondering. I can't think of whom to ask for help in getting me to Zymarc for a ShenawFayel.

Once I'm out of the bunkers, and in the castle's grand entrance, the answer still hasn't come.

Talok spots me. "Tyler? Has something else happened? You appear as though you've just had the Soup of Ashes."

Thinking, *I need them distracted*, I formulate a perfect plan.

"Something's in the bunker," I remark, sounding worried. "I couldn't find anything out of the ordinary, but still." I shrug.

Talok slowly nods. "Yes, we shall have a thorough look. Make sure a Gatro hasn't taken up home there, or something."

"Yeah," I reply, forcing my eyes to open wider. "With the Darklyre children here, it might wander up. Try and eat them, while we're all distracted by something. It'd be awful." I muster up a tear, to sell the lie.

Talok runs off without another word. Eli's close behind. Soon, guards and many others come forth, rushing out from various places in the castle, to head down below with the two.

Skylin's ready to follow the commotion, when I go grab her, haul her to a tucked-away spot within the castle's architecture of the stairs.

"Tyler? What's wrong?" Her bloodshot eyes are wide in fright.

Relaxing my grip, I whisper, "It's a ruse, Sky. Try to keep them distracted here for a while, will you?"

"Where are you going?" She grabs at my sides.

That electric feeling fills me.

"I can't tell you. Will you be all right, with Dea . . . you know?"

She blinks, and tears catch on her blonde lashes. Her blue eyes captivate me, even during our shared grief. I can't look away. I want to stay. To comfort her. To hold her. In wrapping my arms round her waist, and drawing her close, it's all I've got to give, before leaving again. For the briefest of moments, I'm jealous of Gyron and Rorka. They get hours. I get seconds.

"Three days," says Skylin. "If she's not back in three days, then I'll be a mess. Not before." Tears roll down her freckled cheeks. Yet she forces a sad, upward twitch of her lips.

I stroke one of those wet cheeks, with the back of my curled fingers. I quietly ask her to kiss me.

She does, and more. She hugs me with her strong wings, pulling me so close I can't take in a full breath. Her lips have never felt smoother, nor tasted sweeter. Her tongue never so good, demanding that I take notice of it. I'm filled with warmth from within, and from her wings. But that wonderful mouth of hers fills my thoughts with a passion I fear could consume me.

Before I'm swept away, I pull back. "I've got to go, Sky."

"I know," she says. "I'll keep them going in circles for as long as I can. Be safe, but bold. Come back."

She bounds out of our hiding spot and is quickly gone.

My lips tingle. Happy for a moment, I exit through the double doors.

Siege sits on the top step, a little Darklyre boy on his lap. "See," he says, glancing back at me. "Tyler Ravier's still here. We're all very sad over Ryco. It's true. When we are able, we'll have a grand funeral for him, if he shouldn't come home. He'll always be home, in our hearts. And that's what matters. Be fearless, for Ryco."

The boy gives a sad smile, hugging Siege round the neck.

Siege squeezes him back, then smooths out some of the boy's unkempt feathers. "Now, I do believe Ketty's calling from the kitchen that it's lunchtime."

"Is it Gatro?" asks the boy.

"Let us hope so," says Siege. "It's what they hunt, in the bunkers. It's why I'm here. Waiting, in case it should outsmart them. Slip past to escape, or come capture you. I shall single-handedly cut it down, and give you the first portion. Or you can give Ravier, here, your portion."

"That one!" the boy exclaims, running off. "Bye, Masters Siege and Tyler."

I wave goodbye, then slowly take the stairs down.

Siege follows. "I know that look in your eyes. Ryco told me, warned me, of it. Said to look after you, make sure you don't do anything too stupid, after he's gone. So, what is it this time?"

At the last step, I stop. "If I tell you, you have to help me. It's all there is left to do."

"Then tell me," says Siege bravely.

"Why are you called Dragon's Voice?" I ask. "You couldn't summon BlacKaidyns to us, at the forest edge. With a name like that, shouldn't you be able to?" As I walk forward, Siege keeps pace beside me.

"I could have, on other days," Siege admits. "My voice to summon dragons carries on the wind. If it's not too loud, I can summon Mystadyns from many kilometers away. But BlacKaidyns don't listen to the wind. So, I must use other, less effective, methods to call them. After this, if I should survive, I'll train harder than I ever have, to see that this sort of thing never happens again, Ravier."

We pass below the city's many canopies, welcoming the shade.

"Your abilities are more than adequate, Siege."

"No, they are not," he corrects me sternly. "I shall improve myself. And that's for me. Not you, Talok, or anyone else."

"Yes, sir, Dragon's Voice. Could you call for me a Mystadyn, now, by chance?"

"Can have it here, within half an hour." He gives a triumphant look. "Have you thought of where Awngeleik might be?"

I'm about to tell the truth of the ShenawFayel. But I stop, knowing that perhaps only Ryco could know the whole truth upfront and still follow through with my wishes. It's how he was. Bold beyond words.

"She might be hiding in water," I reply. "I want to check some pond areas, farther out. Lakes, too, if there are any. And can we go out to meet the Mystadyn? Save some time?"

"It'll only spare ten minutes," he says.

I reply, "Let's be off. Not tell the others, in case I'm wrong."

We leave the city and soon reach the forest edge.

Sounds akin to horns and chimes ring out from the city limits.

Siege replies, "That'd be them, looking for us."

"Keep going," I tell him. "We need to hurry."

24

Through the Storm

elta's cousin is the one who shows up, to take Siege and me. Not very talkative, but fast, the Mystadyn gets us away from Eyo'el very quickly. Using the Bird's-Eye View spell, which I quickly read about in Ben's spell-book, I latch my focus onto bodies of water and lead us farther north. I div to Delta's cousin, asking that he make his movements subtle.

Night comes.

Delta's cousin gives off ambient, blue light from his scales.

After a mere thirty minutes, Siege is suspicious. "Tyler," he says, as if asking a question, "we're getting awfully far from the city."

"I know. I couldn't tell you, while we were still—"

Eyes wide, he scowls up at the dark clouds. "Vards of Deivahl! Now you've lied to me." He starts telling the dragon, "Turn back—"

"No!" I shout, standing up. "Dragon, keep going. Keep flying toward Vosh-Perida. Siege, I'm sorry. But I have to get Gemma back. I have to strike a ShenawFayel with Zymarc."

Siege leaps to action. "No, no, no!" he shouts. "Absolutely not, Tyler! By the spells! I didn't believe Ryco. I didn't believe you could do this. I will not be taking you to your death."

"What about Gemma?" I ask. "We don't have Awngeleik to offer. This is it. If I don't do this, she will die."

"Pardon me, Tyler. But Gemma values your life too. How do you think she will feel, if *you* die or are overcome by Vitiosus?"

"You don't get it," I reply. "That night at The Sodon, Caleiso gave away one of the things Zymarc means to do. A Vitiosyn Circle, Siege. He meant to use my body for it. To make Vitiosus unending. A sixth particle of magic. Imagine if he learns that Gemma is the Binding Ninth of Enedei. What if he probes her mind and finds out?"

Siege mutters, "We may already be too late. He may already be using her body for that circle. Her being part of the Enedei would power it possibly more than even you or Awngeleik."

"I know. Yet I don't believe he has started the circle. I *have* to believe he hasn't started on it. Soon, he may. A ShenawFayel—"

Siege finishes, "Buys time for us to get Gemma away, and plan an attack." Looking to the clouds surrounding us, Siege says, "Mystadyn, fly higher. Call your family to you. Seek out Zymarc, wherever he is, in Vosh-Perida. We need to be at his door, within the hour. Do what you must, to get us there."

"Speed of dyns," our Mystadyn ride hisses. "I shall fly my best. Once my family has come, we shall fly our fastest. To warn you, there's a storm approaching. You'll be soaked through."

Not much later, Siege and I are huddled together. Exposed to the torrential downpour, we cling to the furry feathers on the dragon's back. The wind is fierce, cold, and biting. We're driven to numbness, both inside and out, until thunderous sounds ignite a boiling anxiety in both of us. Only the Mystadyn and his family flock, coming to join us, are undaunted. Delta's among them. Soon, Claudys and Echo are seen bursting up from the ground below. The flight, less than an hour long, feels longer than the entirety of my time on Muraine. Colder, darker, louder than any of it. Fear is at my door in a way it never has been. Soon, I'll be before Zymarc, striking a deal with him that could end with me being the one dead. Or worse. Part of a circle—one solely meant to break the Laws of Magic. I'd be cursed forever.

* * *

Still twenty minutes out from where all the Mystadyns have assured us Zymarc is—the city of Vaydell—Siege sent a letter to him. We've now waited at the city's gates until dawn. Only the one Mystadyn (Delta's cousin) waits with us. The others have gone off somewhere.

"This isn't looking good, Tyler," Siege says. He has sat down, leaning his back against a tree. "I don't know why he'd be making us wait this long."

I pace around like an utter disaster of nerves. Scratching nervously along my hairline, I feel the shorter hair I'm unaccustomed to. It's not as short as it was on The Sodon. But still, it's not yet medium length. Then there's my face, surprisingly in need of a shave. It's scratchy like sandpaper.

Siege continues, "He hasn't even sent out a Prime-Warrior, or Prince-General, to greet us." After a glance in my direction, he huffs.

It's silent for a bit, until he says, "Dea made you look good."

"What?" I stop in my tracks.

Siege smiles. "Dea made you look older with that haircut. And you've filled out quite a lot. Sleeping Dragon's looking tight on ya."

Glancing down to the coat's open front, I begin buttoning it. I can't fasten the top two buttons. "So it is."

I start undoing the buttons, but Siege flicks his hand. "Nah! Leave it. It's better that way." Pausing, he asks, "So what's the plan? What are you going to offer, as Zymarc's temptation?"

"If you get back to the others, you won't tell?"

"Dragon's Voice can never be made to tell." Siege lounges on the ground with his legs straight out but crossed at the ankles. "For he has tamed too many Mystadyns. He lets the truth carry on the wind. And only Mystadyns hear some of it, but not enough to tell."

Taking out Jasper's miniaturized painting, I give it to Siege. "If Zymarc finds this, he'll destroy it, or absorb the magic in it. Jasper said if he's able, he'll come through. I leave it with you."

I'm about to tell him what I'll offer, when Claudys comes to relieve the dragon who brought us. "This way," he murmurs. "Zymarc's not accepting any through the main gate. There's been rioting, within the cities of Vosh-Perida. I suspect he's been injured but has just now recovered enough for visitors. After today, not even Mystadyns may freely fly over this land. We've had the most unkind greeting imaginable. One of our young ones was stolen, this past week. Unable were we to claim her as we had hoped for, today, since Zymarc put all attending Mystadyns to sleep but me, so that I could come fetch you."

Though troubled by this news, we follow Claudys to the back of the city. Delta's cousin stays behind. I hear him slither off on foot. He does not take to the air.

Azabahk, still worse for wear from The Sodon duel, waits there at the side gate. One of his legs is in a brace, and he leans some of his weight on a white staff in hand.

"Where's the Equidyn?" he queries coldly.

"I've come for a deal, Azabahk," I state. "We need to see Zymarc. Have a talk with him."

Siege adds, "And, at some point before we leave, we want to see Galloway."

Azabahk grits his sharp teeth together. "Zymarc anticipated that. It's why you've been kept waiting for so long. She was in a different city, farther north. Now, she's here. Follow me. And, you, Mystadyn. Leave. We'll call when our guests are ready to depart."

Claudys is reluctant, pattering his paws nervously on the ground.

Siege assures him, "We'll be fine. Go on."

Azabahk giggles in a creepy way. "Fine? Fine, says Dragon's Voice. Ryco of Paragon is dead, yet you are fine?"

Biting back words, I go in ahead of Siege.

Azabahk continues his rant: "Soon, your land will be void of food. Yet, 'tis fine? Vons will grow hungry. Dyns will fly away, in search of food. The land will become diseased, unable to grow anything quickly enough. Yet, it is *all* fine in Paragon. Eyo'el, specifically, yes?"

Siege and I stop, when Azabahk halts ahead of us. We look down at our boots. I don't know how Siege feels, but fear is making it hard for me to breathe, hard to think. Yet I think, *I cannot fail. But what if I do?*

Crowing, he says, "Wait here, or go have a talk with those Onyx we managed to wrangle to our side. The choice is yours."

The Prince-General hobbles off, meandering along the drab, flat stones of the city's streets. All buildings look to be weathered marble. Old. Nothing special about them. It's exactly opposite of Oniva, as well as very different from that city we saw behind ReNovak's projection on a hill.

"Dragon's rodent," says Siege. "I always thought he sounded like one. Now he looks the part."

"Sh!" I scold. "We don't want anyone here, hearing that."

"Why ever not?" inquires a deep voice.

I whirl around. "Hydvar?" I ask, in disbelief. "How is it you're here?"

Kaalon comes up behind him, saying, "This is where we got stationed, while our king and his warrior led an attack somewhere south. Was it in Paragon?"

"Eyo'el," Siege replies. "No need to worry. We're all right."

"For now," I correct him. "I thought you both were pledged to Gyron?"

Kaalon says, "I'm pledged to Hydvar."

The older, rugged warrior looks down in shame.

Kaalon continues, "And Hydvar was pledged to Gyron. Now Zymarc has made him the Warrior of the Nyxane, as Gyron is no longer."

"What about that Zenzar?" I ask, dreading the answer.

Furious, Kaalon says, "Put in a sleep, eternal. He might as well be dead, for only Zymarc can break that spell."

Hydvar squeezes his eyes shut. "Gyronawv and ReNovak are cut off from the Onyx. Zymarc won't tell us what's happened. We feel the power he's been given, though. Once King of Vitiosus. Now King of the Onyx. We shall be serving, for the first time in our victor history, a mad king."

Kaalon brushes sweat off his forehead. "I don't know how the Vardiyas have allowed this. He breaks order. He cheats laws. I even heard a rumor

. . . he hurts death."

Glancing toward the back gate, Hydvar grows uneasy. "You should leave, Tyler. It's dangerous here."

"I can't."

Azabahk shrieks from some distance away, "Hey! Hydvar, you are needed at the dragon stables. And, Kaalon, come help me search for Zymarc. He's not in his room, where he said he would be. Resting! Stubborn, hardheaded, coldhearted, dragontail-eating beast. What I wouldn't give, to be able to rest in bed, unbothered." The Prince-General hobbles off again, out of sight.

Hydvar bows from the waist, quickly excusing himself.

When Kaalon's about to leave as well, I grab hold of his forearm. "Where's Sawrro?"

"Still missing," replies Kaalon, glancing to where I have hold of him.

I think to myself, *Zymarc had to have been parading around as Sawrro, this whole time. It all fits, doesn't it?* Aloud, I voice, "If you find Zymarc first, tell him I've come for a deal."

Kaalon pulls away from my grasp. "We know that. All of us overheard it."

"It's not just any deal, Kaalon," Siege says.

I state, "ShenawFayel. I've come to strike one."

Kaalon grabs his blade hilt. He puffs out a breath of shock. "No, Ravier. Don't be doing that. At the end of it, he'll kill you."

"Then so be it," I reply, in firmness. "I'm not letting Siege leave without Galloway."

Kaalon clenches his teeth together a moment. "Then I shall try to find Zymarc quickly for you. I saw that friend of yours, last night. The girl's tormented by the sounds outside her window. Sounds of screaming deaths. She's not looking too well. She needs to go home."

"I agree. That's why I'm here."

Kaalon turns to head off again. Then he whirls back around, holding one finger to his lips. "Am I permitted to know the deal you mean to offer? Zymarc is unlikely to tell us what bound the ShenawFayel. And I fear for you, Ravier. You're the Onyx Prince. Why not, instead, command me to rescue the girl. I would gladly die, trying to help you."

"I don't see how that can work," I reply.

Kaalon sighs as if agitated. He says, "So long as I'm careful, not being seen by Zymarc or the Prince-Generals, I might be able to sneak her out here to you. I know which Vitiosyn has the prison keys. You'll need to give me the command of King's Orders. It'll work, in absence of either of the kings."

Gnawing on the inside of my cheek, I then reply, "How about this, instead?" I lay a hand on his forearm again, speaking the words: "Even in risk of death, bring me the Witch of Galloway: Gemma."

Kaalon holds his breath. He slowly lets it out. "You really are quite extraordinary, Ravier. Able to do things only talked of in legends. Stay in the open, but linger where you can easily hide in shadow. I'll either be back with your Galloway, or dead. Come what may, see you soon."

Siege and I head for clusters of small buildings. There's lots of spaces to hide in, or paths to make a run for the side gate.

On the way there, Siege comments, "That last part Kaalon said, what do you suppose he meant, Tyler?"

I shrug. "Don't know, Siege. Maybe once you die, it doesn't feel like much time has passed, before others join you. I've no idea what The Kievas is like. Do you?"

Siege shakes his head. "Warren was always jabbering on about it, until lately. When he did, however, Eli ended up asking stupid questions. Warren would get angry. Turned into arguments. Quall took out the herbs. Then I found myself the only one among Quall's Triad with his head on straight . . . ish."

The wait for Kaalon isn't too long, surprisingly. When Onyx Warriors come to shield him from the view of Vitiosyns lingering about, I can't help but smile at them and the evident loyalty they have for each other. Then I spot Gemma. She's blindfolded. Her short hair is more butchered than I imagined. She's slightly thinner too. It's everything I can do to remain with Siege among the clustered buildings.

Spotting us, Kaalon grins. His pace quickens, while he's in the open. He has hold of Gemma's arm, as he leads her along.

When Gemma's closer, I hear her scratchy voice, asking, "Where am I being taken now? I just got here."

Kaalon replies, "It's a surprise, girl. One you'll not believe, unless you see."

They're almost to us, as we make for a building's overhang. Close enough now, I tear the blindfold off Gemma and hug her close.

Siege tugs on my sleeve. "Ravier, we've got to go. Azabahk's headed this way."

"Is Sawrro with him?" I ask. "Or, rather, Zymarc?"

Siege looks, but then shakes his head. "Don't see Zymarc yet. And no Sawrro. Why would Sawrro be here? You don't think he's—?"

Interrupting, Gemma cries, "Tyler, you stupid fool! Why are you here?"

I brush tears off her pale cheeks. "To do a trade for you."

"Caleiso's with Azabahk," says Siege. "Come on, Ty."

After thanking Kaalon, I ask, "How'd you get her out so fast?"

Gemma blinks rapidly, looking to me, then Siege and then Kaalon.

"Tyler." Siege's voice fills with horror. "They're all looking in our direction. They're coming our way."

Kaalon takes in a deep breath, but he's not alarmed. He sniffs a bit, yet not in the way of sadness.

My heart starts to sink.

Kaalon inquires, "A ShenawFayel with Zymarc, to save your friend for another day? It's bold. It's brazen. It's what the Son of LanSoren would do. But what does it remind me of?" He thinks a moment, then his eyes shift to crimson-red. "Oh yes! The boldness you had in Vondurheil, as the both of you buried me in the snow. So what's this deal you'd be wanting to make with me, Tyler Ravier? It had better be good."

When he puts his hands in his pockets, my fear's confirmed. I'm looking right at the real Zymarc. A venomous grin creeps onto his face. He's overjoyed.

III

At the Precise Moment

"The strength that many and your father lacked,
lives in you. That is why they are gone,
and you are here."

25

Risk It All

My gut twists as if I've been punched there. *Kaalon is Zymarc. What do I say to that? I was so sure he was Sawrro.*

No further can I think on it, because Siege draws out his Katana blade. He points its tip to the ground. He holds his head high, as he steps between Zymarc and me. Given our situation, his confidence makes me cringe inside.

Zymarc eyes him with curiosity. "Dragon's Voice, indeed," he states, not even removing his hands from his pockets. "I've heard rumors of you. Until he died, I had thought LanSoren was Dragon's Voice. Imagine my surprise, those many weeks ago at the negotiating table, when I learnt that it was you: Siege of Gayza'Ragaen."

I'm about to speak, when Siege snaps his fingers. My voice is taken away. I merely cling to Gemma and attempt to comfort her. She holds tight to me, leaning against me. Strength has left her. It's almost left me.

Zymarc shifts his weight to his other foot. "I was starting to think that Ryco was the voice. That whispering sound, riding the wind, causing dissent among my dragons. Disobedience to me. Riots in my cities."

Siege is unmoved. "You give me much credit. Credit that belongs not to me. It matters not. Before Tyler makes an offer, and strikes a ShenawFayel with you, I must know what rules you play by. Deathasyn? Or your own?"

359

Zymarc glances at Gemma, and she trembles violently. "A mix of both," he replies.

"Whatever suits your needs, I imagine," says Siege, subtly grinding his blade tip into the ground.

Flinching, Zymarc slips his hands out of his pockets. "I know what you're doing, Gayzawan, and it won't work. The Mystadyns are fast asleep. You cannot wake them. They cannot aid you with sight and knowledge. Merely Claudys is permitted to be awake, for he'll be taking the lot of you back to Paragon, whether you are alive or not so much. Either way, you need transportation."

Gemma starts weeping. Then she shouts at me, "Tyler! Why couldn't you just leave me here to rot? You're not supposed to be a hero of one, but an entire nation. An entire race!" Her voice gives out suddenly. Exhausted, she lets go of me and falls to the ground. She cries out a haunting scream of grief.

I shake in fear. A cold sweat makes it seem as though I'm out in a blizzard, dressed in clothes meant for when it's hot outside. The tears stinging my eyes add to that sensation that I'm in the midst of a storm. I can't see anything, save for the blurred-out surroundings. Nor can I move. I'm paralyzed.

Someone touches me on the arm. I'm given my voice back, as well as the ability to move. The tears subside, while I reach down for Gemma and pull her up. I stare into her scared, brown eyes. "I'm repaying you, Gem, for all the *sorrys* you spoke that year. I heard them. Every single one. One hundred forty-four spoken. Three hundred sixty-five silent, but shown nonetheless. You don't owe me a damn thing. But I owe you my life, for it was you who saved me. I was numb. You made me feel again, when I didn't want to. You made me shout, when I wanted to sink into the lake and drown in silence. You snapped me back to reality, so I could move on."

Gemma cries out, "Don't, Tyler! Don't send me away. You're not going to send me away. I know it's what you're about to do. To take my place! I'll hate you forever. I'll never forgive you for not giving me a choice."

Siege rushes up behind Gemma and wraps his arms around her. He restrains her, keeps her from running away. Or from stepping forward to strike me. Gemma fights him, and screams and cries some more, sounding beyond angry this time.

In quiet heartbreak, I reply, "I did give you a choice. On that day we came here. Again, the day after the attack. You stayed both times. And now it's my duty to save my friend. The most loyal one I'll ever have. Gemma Galloway. Let me do this *one* thing for you."

"Settle your fear, Miss Galloway. He shall not be struck down yet. Nor you," says Caleiso, coming to stand beside Zymarc. She's grown taller, and she has packed on more lean muscle since I last saw her. Scars are on her face too, from when we dueled. She clamps her mouth shut, as she studies me. A hateful glint enters her features.

Gemma quiets her sobs. Her eyes are puffy and red, as endless tears stream down slowly. Once a glistening tear or two have dropped off her chin, others flow down in their place.

Siege releases her. She goes silent. Her lips still quiver, though.

She looks to me. "What's the deal you mean to make, Tyler? Or will you not even let me know that, before we say goodbye?"

I want to answer Gemma, but I know I've only the courage to say it once. So I look to Zymarc and tell him: "I've come to offer myself. Or, rather, the chance to turn me. The chance for you to make me your Apprentice to Vitiosus. I beg that you give in to the temptation of me. Let the next words from your mouth, Zymarc of Vitiosus, be your utterance of acceptance. Strike this deal with me, without hesitation. Even if it doesn't serve all of your purposes the way you may have intended, you know that it is me you want. The Onyx Prince. Blood heir to King ReNovak."

Slowly, Zymarc steps forward. He offers his hand to me, before speaking the words: "Shena of the Vons."

Siege pushes enough on my back that I must take a step toward Zymarc, before saying, "Tyler isn't privy to the wording. May I have him repeat the words I utter?"

"No," says a confident voice from nearby. Jasper ambles into view, divving to me, *"It appears I've regained my speed. I shall set this ShenawFayel. You must repeat what I say, exactly. Understand, Ravier?"*

"Alpha Jasper." Azabahk's voice strains a little. "Nice of you to join us."

Caleiso's stance goes rigid. "Who let you in?"

"Greyvons go where they please," Jasper replies. "Especially when talk of ShenawFayels ride on the whispers of wind."

Zymarc clenches his jaw tight. He appears to want to speak, yet he stays quiet.

Jasper, toying with the Star of Shena round his neck, looks to me again. He instructs, "Extend your hand to Zymarc of Vitiosus, then speak these words: The Dyns' Fayel."

I do as Jasper commands.

Zymarc grips my outstretched hand and is next to speak more words. "Cunning of wolves be far from me, in this day of truce against my foe: Ravier."

Jasper continues, "Strength of dragons be in me this day, in defending my enemy of yesterday and of tomorrow, should any attack this Zymarc of Vitiosus."

I repeat Jasper's words.

"By the enduring power of the Greyvons and Rubidyns," says Zymarc, squeezing my hand tighter. His gaze is fixed on only me.

Jasper finishes the vow with, "And by the witness of Alpha Jasper of these said Vons, this ShenawFayel is bound for a day. A day of truce between I, Tyler of Vondurheil, and you, Zymarc of Vosh-Perida."

My body courses with energy; something stronger than adrenaline, for it feels as if my very insides are trembling, aching for me to finish speaking the vow. When Jasper's words finish rolling off my tongue, and the sound of my voice ceases, and my mouth presses shut, all the anger I felt for Zymarc slips away. I close my eyes. Tears seep from the corners of them. When I open them again to look upon Zymarc in front of me, I feel nothing but a brotherly love for him. That should disturb me. Yet, somehow, it doesn't.

Zymarc's expression of malice drops off. He swallows hard. He looks away to Jasper, who's hiding that storm inside. His wise, green eyes narrow on Zymarc.

"You lose, Vitiosyn," Jasper whispers the words. His face brightens with delight. "You gave up your one chance to complete an enduring Hex of Vitiosus. You had all the keys. Now, there is no guarantee you will be getting them back in time."

Releasing my hand, Zymarc takes a step back. Jasper's words have unsettled him. "In time for what?" he asks.

Jasper glances to Siege. "Get on the dragon with Galloway."

Before Siege can capture her, Gemma rushes to me, and throws her arms about my neck. She hugs me tight, and I hug her back, desperate to think of a way to help ease her pain for the journey home to Paragon without me.

As I pull away, it comes to me. "Do you want a needle or an apple turnover?" I ask, doing my best to sound playful.

"What?" Gemma cocks her head, her grief taking a pause.

Clearing my throat, I say, "Sleeping Beauty or Snow White? Technically, a spindle or poisoned apple." I shrug. Then I clasp my hands behind my back and confidently stare Gemma down.

Her lips slowly press together, before she says, "Mushy, mutilated apple pieces swimming in my mouth? No thanks. I'd rather have a cinnamon roll." She manages a sad grin. "But I'll take the spindle. Or dagger. Whichever you want to give me."

"Hey, Gem," I ask, "guess what?"

Her brow furrows in confusion. It's adorable. I smile slightly.

"What?" she says, her tears all dried up now.

"Bear-Wolves," I state, matter-of-factly, "they're real. Wouldn't it make a great headline for an article?"

She laughs bitterly. It shifts to quiet sobs. She's about to bury her face in her hands.

I reach to cup her face but find that I can't bear to. Not like this. Instead, I brush my fingertips along the hair strand, now butchered. I pluck a single hair of hers with my right hand. I twist it between my thumb and forefinger, willing it to change its form, its properties. It goes stiff. It turns into metal, shining like silver. I will it to become sharp like a needle, thick like a spike, and it does. It grows to be the same length as my palm. Then it shifts to being as clear as a spike formed of ice.

"Make it home safe," I tell her. "To your dad, my mom, Molly, my friends. Kane and Haru. Even Snap. If I don't make it back, take care of them all, will you? And write that article. Get pictures of Mek before you leave."

With no tears left it seems, Gemma simply nods. "I will, Ty." Her voice is thick with emotion.

I start Jasper's sleep spell, saying, "Sleep, slumbering deep in the dark. To summoning a slumbering Rubidyn's keep to sleep." Hesitating, I say goodbye to my best friend. The ninth of the Galloways. Truly, she is the best of them. At least, she is to me.

I hold up the thinnish spike for Gemma to prick her finger on. And she does. She goes limp. Her gorgeous chocolate-brown eyes close. Siege catches her up in his arms, as I tuck the spike away in an inner coat pocket of mine.

"Dyns' will, Tyler," he says brokenly, before he makes his way to secure Gemma on the back of Claudys.

Jasper holds Winter's Vondaen out to me.

I, sounding as Gyron that day, say to him, "I do not know your meaning, Alpha Jasper. What am I to do with that?" I look from the blade to the alpha's face.

Jasper hides a grin. "After that day in Grevagg, when I nearly perished, the blade stopped answering to me. It is reluctant to serve me the way it did before. It's been leading me to its new master for some time. Today, it led me here. Gave me the legs of my youth to carry me quickly. It's just a thought. I do believe that you, Tyler, are its new master. If not you, perhaps Zymarc. Since you are in ShenawFayel, there's no harm in letting the two of you test its loyalties. I'll come back for it, tomorrow. And, however it ends, fate and your father have decided the outcome. Of that, I am sure."

Jasper turns on his heel and strides away. He joins Siege and the slumbering Gemma on Claudys.

"This isn't over, Vitiosyn," Claudys rumbles softly to Zymarc. "I shall be back for my friends and family."

"We will see," Zymarc whispers.

I lift a hand in farewell to my friends. There's nothing else to be said. Not until a different day.

Zymarc simply waves off his entourage, and they disperse. The last to leave us is Azabahk. He hobbles away, using his white staff for balance.

Caleiso, however, remains beside Zymarc.

The Mystadyn leaps off the ground with force. Wind rushes from him.

Standing still, I lower my hand. I look to the sky. I keep watch, until the four of them are out of sight.

Once I've lashed Winter's Vondaen to my belt, Zymarc looks to me. He says, "I was going to ask Jasper why he calls you Tyler of Vondurheil"—Zymarc makes a point to glance at the Greyvon's blade—"but I see now, they must think you are one of them at heart."

I look around for Caleiso.

Zymarc says, "She's gone to prepare your room for the night."

"Is that where you're taking me now? My temporary quarters?"

"Temporary?" His eyes briefly narrow on me. "No. Though you think you are leaving tomorrow, Ravier, you are not." Zymarc starts a stroll toward the larger buildings of the city a ways away.

As there's nothing else to do, I follow.

"What makes you think that?" I ask, while keeping pace with him. "Do you mean to make me a prisoner, after the ShenawFayel has ended, and you've failed to make me your apprentice?"

Zymarc declares, "You won't want to leave. Not after I show you what the land of Vosh-Perida has to offer."

"And what does it have to offer?"

He stops to look hard at me.

I stop too, and hold his gaze.

"Wholesome food, for starters," he says. "Mostly protein. And not the kind they serve in Paragon or Deivahl. But perhaps in Grevagg. Yes, Darklyres have a wholesome diet and exercise regimen. Their magic is exquisite as well. Especially that Deamond's." Zymarc starts forward again. "Grawllik has told me all he knows of her."

"Why do you care to know more of Dea?"

Zymarc pivots his attention to me, as we walk along. "Are you really so daft? Of course I would need to know more of her after witnessing the Duo's Duel at The Sodon, when you stabbed her in the chest and she rose again, enraged like a rutting bull-dragon during the season. Except for, she wasn't rutting; simply channeling a power. A magic I've not seen in any, except for you and your father. Yet, hers is different. She's left my top Prince-General crippled. Not an easy task. He heals fast, usually. This has left permanent damage to him. He'll not be seeing a battlefield again."

I remark, "Poor Azabahk, destined to be a teacher and scholar now, is he?"

Zymarc lets out a few laughs, sounding pleasant and bright. His Vitiosyn appearance wavers. His eyes become green like mine. Like Soren's. His skin darkens to an olive tone. He doesn't quite look like the Kaalon he's been pretending to be. Nor like Soren or me. Yet, there is something familiar about his features. It reminds me of someone. I saw so many Onyx at The Sodon. Perhaps I caught a glimpse of him as he truly is, and didn't know it.

A sudden pang of hunger hits me, while keeping pace with Zymarc. I ask, "Are we having dinner in the city or elsewhere?"

"At the Prince-Generals' banquet table. It's outside, in the courtyard. We like to eat outdoors. No one can trap us that way. That's the first mistake of the Paragonians. They keep too much closed up in that castle. And, unless you're gifted in Gendras, able to convince the castle to alert you to intruders, well, it's quite easy to hide in there."

I ask, "How long?"

"How long, what?" he asks, in return.

"How long were you in Eyo'el, that day of the festival?"

Zymarc gives a lengthy sigh, confessing at last, "I was one of the bystanders that night. Didn't dress as a Sorsryn at all. Rather, I came in with the survivors from Yharss, dressed like one of them."

"Why didn't you just take Awngeleik, then?"

"I told you. To be named as Onyx Victor, I had to play by their rules. Revealing myself like that, and killing more of the Paragonians, was against etiquette. I had already had a show of force. Next, I had to be patient and cunning."

"That's not your only reason," I remark.

"True. You were the other part. That night, I saw you for the first time. Then I desired you. I wasn't sure what I wanted you for, then. The next day, I knew."

"You pretended not to know I was LanSoren's son?"

"Not entirely," Zymarc replies. "I expected you to be older. In your twenties. I thought maybe Lance had another child, or something. When I glimpsed into your mind and saw that you are an only child, well, I was a little surprised."

"According to Grover, I should be twenty-three."

Zymarc nods. "Yes, that is closer to what I thought. You were born before your cousin, yet he is the older one."

"Here's what has me a little confused." I glance at Zymarc. His attention is directed straight ahead. I continue, "My father died two years ago, Murainian time. Where I'm from, it's barely been a year. Shouldn't I be eleven or twelve, not fourteen, based on that time difference?"

That's when Zymarc focuses on me. In fact, he comes to a complete stop.

I study him, his expression.

He looks away, seeming to contemplate on something. Most likely to calculate his interactions with my father over the years, and the many key events mentioned. After a time, he states, "I haven't an explanation for why you are fourteen, not eleven. Vardiyas could be blamed for it, I suppose. I am certain that you were born twenty-three years ago. I remember the day your father told me. Warned me, actually. He said you would come one day, and that you would change things. That things would never be the same after nine. He didn't say what these nine things were, however."

My heartbeat gets faster. I think to myself, *Never the same after nine? Vards! He was right!*

Zymarc restarts our stroll forward. "Right of what? You know what the nine things are?"

"Maybe." I shrug.

He laughs. "That was a favorite response of your father's to me. Always irked me. Coming from you, the one-word reply is slightly more bearable."

I ask, "Any chance you'll tell me why you gave my father the Equidyn in the first place, thereby starting the whole premise for this war?"

Zymarc slows his pace. His grin turns smug. "Not a chance."

"Ah!" I nod. "Going to play hard to get, I see. Should've asked Quall for some herbs, before I left. Could've loosened you up that way."

Zymarc laughs again, but the sound is deeper, quieter, frustrated-like. "ShenawFayels. Aggravating, aren't they, how they strip you of your true feelings? Where is that temper of yours, Ravier? You should be shouting at me, by now. Or brooding in that dark way of yours. Or better? Trying to bend me to your will."

"Yeah? Well, where's your gloating? It's nowhere near the level it should be. You're slacking off. It's rather disappointing." I stuff my hands in my pockets, mimicking the way of Zymarc when he's smug.

"You're right," he agrees. "I blame it on being Onyx, for they don't like to gloat to foreigners too much."

"But you're a Vitiosyn," I point out. "Not an Onyx. Not anymore."

Stopping again, Zymarc makes sure no one is around, watching, as he grips one of my shoulders. "Vitiosyns are made, Ravier. Onyx are born. I was born as an Onyx. In the history of Vitiosus, there has never been a child, born of a Vitiosyn. Believe me when I say, it was an obsession of Deezalo's. Not really an obsession of mine, though. I tried. It didn't work out. I gave up, and moved on to other things."

"Like stealing dragons," I remark. "Then making a gift out of them and their offspring?"

He slides his hand off my shoulder. I find that I'm indifferent to his touch and the absence of it. I don't care either way what he chooses—to keep his distance or to act in the way of a concerned friend.

We start forward again, much closer to the old buildings now.

Zymarc stands an arm's length away from me, while we continue on. He must not feel the same indifference that I do. As he leads us down a narrow pathway in the shadows between darker brick buildings, he says, "I had to give them something to do. My Vitiosyns, I mean. Almost all were Deathasyns, before I turned them. Under Deezalo, indeed, all of his were Deathasyns. They were vile, grotesque creatures. By Siveyra Dezarin's written accounts, barely Sorsryn at all. I made them into something better. Something with structure and restraint. I gave order. Deezalo let them run rampant. He stripped them of dignity. But I gave it back . . . to an extent. They do still, on occasion, revert to the old ways of Deathasyns."

I comment, "How kind of you, Zymarc, doing that for them. How they must love you for it."

Zymarc's chest shakes with restrained laughter. "Mockery in place of anger? I'll take it. Though I do prefer seeing you angry." His subsequent footsteps bring him closer to me.

We emerge into the light of the midday, and approach a large, stately courtyard surrounded by greenery, and guarded by a great many statues and small dragons posing as statues. Horses, as well, stand as statues. Only their scarlet-red eyes move, watching those who enter. All are saddled, horse and dragon alike, ready for a journey to be made in haste. The stone statues are of weathered, white marble. But the motionless, living creatures are a mix of colors, ranging from smoky-gray to shiny-black.

Zymarc lowers his voice, so that the many men and women wandering around, dressed in that scanty, worn-out Deathasyn garb, cannot hear.

"No need to introduce yourself. They know who you are."

Grinning, I ask, "But do they know what I am?"

Looking about, Zymarc starts to answer but then stops himself a few times. At last, he says, "What do you *think* you are?"

"The Savakaidyn," I say, with pride. "The Sleeping Dragon."

Zymarc sweeps his hand over his mouth, before saying in a quiet voice, "Best not to tell them that." He motions with a nod at the dragons. "They get jealous, if I give any single dragon too much attention."

Slowly, I start to say, "Then I shouldn't mention Awnge—"

Zymarc quickly clamps a hand over my mouth, whispering into my ear, "Do not say her name, in their presence. My courtyard dragons hate her, abomination that she is." He releases me and steps back.

I wish my heartbeat would calm somewhat. There's no chance of that, when I realize that the dragons around us are eyeing me with hunger.

"Have they been fed today?" I ask.

"Of course! I don't starve my dragons, unless they deserve it. And never do I have a mass starvation. The majority must be strong, at all times. That's just good practice."

"What about your prisoners. Do you starve those?"

"Again, only if they deserve it."

"What prisoners do you have now? You know, besides the one-quarter of the hostages you never gave back."

Zymarc's neck tightens. "Let go of the matter, Ravier. I've decided to keep them here indefinitely. I've kept enough genetic variety among them. The Paragonians and Vaegons shall not go extinct. Not for a while, at least."

"Am I to understand that you're treating them like animals, in need of saving from extinction?" Exasperated, I raise my voice. "They wouldn't be in danger of dying out, if it weren't for you killing them."

Zymarc walks slowly away from me. "The more you see of Vosh-Perida, and those who live here, Tyler, you will start to understand why I didn't have a choice."

"I will never understand that, Zymarc. Never. But I'm here for a

ShenawFayel with you. So I must listen to what you have to say. Also, for what you feel you should teach me. For now, take me to where the dragons are fed. We'll give them a double feeding. I've never fed a dragon, and I'd like to learn how."

Zymarc adjusts his coat. "Nothing to it, really. You just put something moderately edible in front of them, and they eat it up."

"So," I ask, "no hand feeding them?"

He chuckles. "Not unless it's your hand you're intending on feeding them. Most likely they'd get greedy, however, and rip off the entire arm. Depending on their size, they might just swallow you whole. Never a fun thing to watch a promising warrior being swallowed whole by a dragon."

"You speak from experience?" I ask. "Or did someone relay the news to you?"

"Both," he says.

Zymarc's about to say something else, when he notices that many of the Deathasyns around have their attention directed at us. They eye me curiously, some spitefully.

Lifting a hand, Zymarc calls out, "Grawllik, have Tyler and I time to visit the dragon stables, before supper?"

From among the fray of gathered Prince-Generals, readying the courtyard for a banquet, Grawllik emerges. His wings are hidden beneath much fabric. It's not really a cloak he wears, nor robes. Just fabric positioned to hide what he physically is—a GreyLyre. It does nothing to hide what he truly is deep down, however: a traitor to King Aygor of RawZend.

26

To Know a Heart

Grawllik strides toward Zymarc and me. He stops at the center of the courtyard. He must fear getting too close to me. His gaze of confidence belies that assumption, however.

Merlynite is dead, because of him; Droediin was turned; the Darklyres of RawZend were displaced from their home; and Zymarc has been one step ahead of us all. All . . . because . . . of . . . Grawllik. I hate him. I hate this GreyLyre, pretending to serve one side, while he truly served the other.

The hairs on the back of my neck stand on end. A hot chill sears through me. "So, Grawllik," I ask in coldness, "you were a traitor, all along?"

"Not a traitor," he corrects. "Simply a hunter or mercenary for hire. King Aygor hired me for a job. Procure a book to awaken the Statue of Soren. And that one standing beside you hired me for a different job. A job that held no conflict with the first, until the lot of you Paragonians showed up and ruined it."

Zymarc *was* glancing off to his Prince-Generals, in the middle of assembling a vast, long banquet table, but he is now focused on Grawllik. "What was ruined? The plan went perfectly, if you ask me."

"Dea," Grawllik grumbles, stepping closer. "I had intended on stealing Deamond, and selling her to you for a high price."

I clench my fists.

372

Zymarc folds his arms tight against his chest. "And why do you think I would've paid a high price for her? I had not yet witnessed what she can do."

"I would've accepted a delayed payment," Grawllik admits, before covering a yawn with his hand.

Zymarc breaks out an amused smile. "Well then, you are foolish, Grawllik of, hmm . . . nowhere." Zymarc chuckles. "You have no home. No fellow countrymen. Do you know why that is?" He turns serious.

Grawllik's expression clouds over as well. He's in no danger of yawning now. His lips draw into a thin, tight line.

"I'll tell you why." Zymarc practically snarls out the words, moving forward to get in Grawllik's face. "Because you are lower than even Parasogyns. Lower than abominations, for you are servant *to* abominations. You, your father, that uncle of yours. All his children. GreyLyres. Where are they?" Zymarc asks in mockery. "Where is your family?"

"You know where they are," Grawllik growls.

Zymarc smirks in that way of his. Arrogant. "That I do," he says. "Most of them are dead. One of your distant GreyLyre cousins grew weary of the lot of you being servants to the Darklyres, first, then mercenaries for hire, second—and whatever else the laws and land allowed for GreyLyres to partake in—that he went mad. He killed all GreyLyres, save for a few dozen, in a single week of utter terror and heartbreak. Needless death. Death, born out of spite. Not a single death have I caused, with no purpose behind it. All death in my wake is used to my advantage. For I am an Onyx, at heart. I can't help it. Nor can you help being what you are—the worst kind of creature imaginable. The kind that simply will not pick a side." Zymarc glances back at me. "Have you anything to add to that, Ravier? Anything to contradict?"

I search my thoughts. The two simply stare at me. I break into a sweat. I wish I had control over it, for it is aggravating, always showing signs of my angst. After a deep breath, all I say is, "Death is death, none can escape, for no one can live forever. But murder, betrayal, they have intent behind them. Emotion. Death is indifferent. At least, I used to think so."

Looking away, I begin the walk toward the center of the courtyard. I stare up at the sky—to the washed-out teal, streaked with pale-gray clouds. They appear as smooth as white frosting, swept over a layer of light-teal clay by a clean knife. My hands are tucked loosely in my pockets as I breathe in the crisp, cold air of Vaydell. Part of me wonders if my father has stood in this very spot where I am. How I miss him.

Behind me, Zymarc says in a hushed tone, "When you die, Grawllik, no one will shed a single tear for you, unless it is a tear of joy."

I glance over my shoulder in time to see Grawllik's eyes flicker in anger. He's starting to shake, he's so angry. Even as tears of pained hatred well up, Grawllik says in a low voice, "If any could bear you a Vitiosyn child, Zymarc, it would've been Deamond of RawZend. I would've waited until she bore you that child, before coming to collect my reward."

Zymarc slaps Grawllik's face so hard, the GreyLyre is thrown to the ground. He scrambles on all fours. His wings struggle to rid themselves of the concealing fabric. When Zymarc walks toward Grawllik, Grawllik's breaths become shallow.

"It's true," Grawllik says as if begging. "Dea could be the first mother to a Vitiosyn child. Isn't that what you want? A child? A real family? A Vitiosyn family?"

Zymarc slips Deezalo's Hammer, miniaturized to the size of a normal builder's hammer, out from the holster strapped to his coat's belt. Though smaller, the hammer quickly grows to its massive proportions while in the Vitiosyn King's grasp.

Grawllik cries out in terror, "Please, please, my lord! Zymarc, tell me what to do? What have I said to upset you?"

"All of it," says Zymarc, raising the massive weapon. It glows a hot-red. And I feel the hot air drift out from it. It vibrates. It whirs akin to a machine longing to do the task for which it was made. To destroy things. Kill things. End Grawllik in this moment, so it would seem. I cannot move, only watch. Only breathe.

Grawllik scrambles to get up. To get away.

But Zymarc's wind magic is too much for the GreyLyre. I spot signs of

Blue Magic being used too, when Grawllik looks around in bewilderment.

"Please!" he screams, utterly terrified. "Tell me what to do!" His hands search the ground in desperation. He's starting to weep in fear. I'm reminded of Nyrim that day, when memories overwhelmed him, burst out of him. How I eased his burden, and saved the Arkivy of Yharss-Rawshuen. I have no such urge to reach out to Grawllik now. No desire to help him. No want for him to live. He is wicked.

Zymarc Mensa-divs to me, *"One word from you, Ravier, and I'll let this one go. No further harm done."*

Images of Dea flash in my mind's eye. Anger wells up at knowing what Grawllik had planned to do with her. I hate him for it. Though I am terrified, though my body starts to tremble, though I am sick to my stomach . . . I don't want Zymarc to stop what he intends to do.

I lower my voice, to say, "He's a traitor. And traitors deserve no pity, whatsoever. The decision is yours, Zymarc."

Grawllik flaps his wings and flails his arms. He scurries away as if he's blind. He probably is.

Zymarc simply waits, resting the axe head of Deezalo's Hammer on his shoulder, as Grawllik crawls around the courtyard in blind, frantic confusion.

The gathered Vitiosyns and Prince-Generals and Deathasyns laugh at him. More so, when Grawllik bumps his head against one of the stone planters beside a stone statue.

Zymarc strides forward in perfect calmness. He eases the hammer head off his shoulder.

Those gathered stop laughing. Only water gurgling in a nearby fountain fills the courtyard with quiet noise; that, and sounds of Grawllik's desperation.

The GreyLyre weeps, and his hands move off the planter, to feel the statue within his reach. He tries to determine what it is, where he is.

Zymarc's to him, and Grawllik knows it, can hear the metallic hum of the hammer approach. He cries louder. Scrambles away from Zymarc. But Zymarc steps on the long cloth that partially conceals the wings. The traitor can't get away.

The courtyard dragons hiss or rumble; the horses paw their hooves at the ground. Deathasyns hold their breath. Vitiosyns bow their heads. The Prince-Generals stand at attention, looking straight ahead. Only Azabahk moves around, hobbling. Then he stops. He enviously eyes his former weapon.

The Vitiosyn King raises the war axe high, overhead. Taking aim, he swings its sharp edge downward at Grawllik, who's lying on his belly, attempting to claw his way forward. In the end, he rests there, prostrate, afraid, and shouting. The hammer lands perfectly on the neck, cutting through it with ease.

Grawllik's shout of horror abruptly ends.

Blood sprays out from his body.

I look away, as a scream is wrenched from my lungs. I collapse to my knees. I hear Zymarc kick something. It rolls. I'm sick.

Soon, the feelings that I had when receiving the news of my dad overwhelm me. Such sadness. Hopelessness. Anger.

I look over to Grawllik's lifeless, headless body. His blood stains a good portion of the courtyard. Taking NeiSator out, I grip the sleeping-dagger in my trembling grasp. I rush for Grawllik, and scream in rage when I'm a mere arm's length away from him.

Zymarc drops the hammer to stop me, catch me by the waist. "Ravier!" he shouts. "It is blasphemy to desecrate a body twice. He's been removed of his head, and that is enough for what he was. What he did. What he had intended on doing. There is only one body truly worthy of being desecrated twice."

I fight against Zymarc's hold, not to hurt him, but to get free. I want to cut Grawllik's wings off. He doesn't deserve such a magnificent thing, in fact two things, to be attached to his filthy form.

But, as Zymarc continues to restrain me, my pulse grows steady. Tranquil, even. Zymarc lets go.

I stare down at Grawllik. I want so badly to kick his side in. It takes everything in me to turn and walk away. I don't know where I'll go, but *away* is best. I spot Caleiso as she's coming around the corner of a building. She exits the shadows, right as I reach her. I grab her by the collar of her coat, and whirl to slam her backside against the building.

Gasping, she struggles, until I will her to stop. I stare into her crimson-red eyes. I convince them to change to the heterochromian colors of Callie of Dysarda—one blue, one green—for if I do not see a glimpse of Callie now, I would kill Caleiso this instant. Her eyes are full of fear.

Inches from her face, I say to her, "Stay out of my way, Caleiso of Vitiosus. Or suffer the consequences. Your choice." I release her, and it's a good thing too, because Zymarc is there, scowling at me.

He waits for Caleiso to regain her composure. Regain the color of Vitiosyn eyes. Then he asks her, "Is Tyler's room ready? He's in need of rest, before dinner."

"And a bath," she mutters, wrinkling her nose.

The anger starts again. "What'd you say?" I make a move for her.

She pushes away from the brick wall of the building.

Zymarc positions himself protectively in front of her, remarking, "I'm in need of one, more than he is, if we're being honest. Look at this mess." He grabs at his coat. He's drenched in blood.

I realize that I'm covered in blood too. Grawllik's blood. I puke right there, barely aiming the vomit away from Zymarc and Caleiso. I'm on my hands and knees. Weak, lightheaded too, I get up. I start removing my coat, the Sleeping Dragon. It's going to need a good cleaning. And I've no idea where to start except to first remove it from myself.

"His room is ready," Caleiso mumbles. "So is yours. So are all the sleeping quarters of the Prince-Generals, Lord-King Zymarc."

"Very good," he says. "Feed that head to the best-behaved dragon currently in the stables. Ravier and I will be down for the third course, and we will stay to the end. Or until he has had his fill of our food wares. Whichever comes first."

Zymarc takes me by the arm and leads the way around the building where I saw Caleiso emerge. There's a door, which he opens. Then a steep, seemingly endless flight of stairs. He pushes me forward, and I start the climb in silence.

* * *

In a daze, I follow Zymarc's verbal instructions of where to go, each line of his sounding softer. Possibly grieved. At last, he takes the lead, striding past me. We're on the second level of whatever building this is. He opens an unadorned door. In fact, the entire inside of the structure is simple, not vying for any sort of attention.

Zymarc stands just inside the room, holding the door open for me. He sighs as he stares down at the dull, worn floorboards. He won't look at me.

Even as tears, hot tears that I hate, roll down my cheeks, this Vitiosyn will *not* look at me.

"Please, Ravier," he says. "Come inside. Clean yourself up. Have dinner with me and my men."

"Why?" I ask in stubbornness. "Give me one good reason why I should?"

He looks at me, then. He briefly lifts his shoulders in frustration. "Because we are in ShenawFayel together. This is how it works. Two enemies or would-be foes try their best to come to an understanding. An agreement to stop an impending war, or end one that's already begun. If no agreement can be made, then at least both sides can rest in the knowledge that they did everything they could to save their people from the pain of war and violent ends."

Wiping my tears of anger away, I storm into the room. I throw my bloodied coat to the floor.

Zymarc shuts the door softly, then strolls farther in. He, as well, takes off his coat, but slowly. A trail of blood has dripped along the floor behind him. Not that much. Most was at the start of our journey through the building.

The room is quite plain, even with all the furniture that's stained a walnut-brown or warm chestnut. A few small secretary desks are gathered together just off to the room's center, looking like an area for studying or doing paperwork. A mess of papers and books and odd instruments I do not recognize are on their surfaces. Bookshelves are near that. Also, a little seating area and small, round table are near those shelves. All of *that* is to my right. There are framed diagrams of devices dispersed on the walls. Diagrams of Geldryn devices, most likely. To my left, there's a recessed area. One must take three steps down, to get to it: the place for bathing in a large, black square tub made of marble. Nothing conceals it. No curtains, privacy walls, or anything.

Zymarc walks past me, past the study section, continuing on toward the back section where the four-poster bed with dark-red sheets rests. A few simple wardrobes are back there too, lined up against the wall opposite of the bed. He drops his soaked coat along the way. Then he removes his clothes from the waist up. He tosses the wet wad of them atop the discarded coat.

"What are you doing?" I ask, alarmed.

He pauses in undoing his belt. He turns to face me dead-on. Thankfully, his pants are still on. His boots too. Exasperated, he says, "They're soaked all the way through." He indicates to his pants. "What else am I do to, but remove the bloodied clothing?" He momentarily squeezes his eyes shut. "Right. I forget that you Paragonians are overly modest. Deathasyns certainly are not so. Nor are Onyx Warriors, when gathered together on a long, exhausting tour. My tiredness has made me lose my manners. I'll change behind a curtain." He strides toward one of the wardrobes.

Suddenly, I look down at my own clothes. The ones Madeleine finished stitching for me on that first day of the festival. Blood has soaked through my coat as well. I hadn't realized it till now. It stains that fabric of my pants and vest, though not as badly as Zymarc's clothes.

My heart pounds. I hear its beat throbbing in my eardrums. I can't stand having the stained clothes on. Without thinking, I undo all the laces of my boots. After I've wrenched those boots off my feet, the rest is easily stripped off my body. Very quickly, I'm naked in the room with Zymarc.

He's opened the wardrobe, taken something out, and is now unfolding a thin, black cloth. He startles, when he spots me just standing there, naked and hyperventilating, my hands balled into fists at my sides.

I start to take in his expression. But then images of Grawllik meeting his end by way of the sharp axe flash in my mind and more unwanted tears roll down my face. I go sit on the floor, lean my back against a sofa chair near a table, and draw my knees closer to my body. I hug my bare legs to my chest, attempting to calm down. Cold tears drip off my chin and land on my knees.

Zymarc studies me a moment. "You've not ever witnessed a head being removed from its body, have you?"

My voice croaks, when I reply, "No . . . yes." After a pause, I admit, "I've never witnessed that, before."

Zymarc drops the black cloth. He comes to sit beside me, slightly mimicking my pose that seeks modesty.

I swallow in nervousness.

He takes a deep breath, not looking at me. "It is a bit shocking, isn't it? Never did like beheadings. So messy. Sadly, Deezalo's Hammer prefers that method of killing. And I must indulge that weapon, if I intend on keeping him loyal to me." He glances at me, then to the pile of my discarded things. "And just think, one of us has done something to gain the loyalty of the Greyvon's blade. One of us is more worthy to wield Winter's Vondaen than even the Alpha of the Vons."

My racing heart slows down. So does my breathing.

Zymarc continues talking, "I confess, I very much wish to test that weapon's loyalties. But we can't do that with you being broken the way you are, at present. So, what's it going to take to cheer you, Ravier? Or, at the very least, convince you to put some clothing back on? I can't be dueling you or teaching you, or anything, with you as you currently are. Naked. Filthy too. Both of us are."

"I wouldn't be filthy, Zymarc, if I had ever had the time to stop, rest, and bathe. And you wouldn't be, if you weren't so nefarious, always plotting and stealing and killing."

"Nefarious!" His eyes brighten. "I'll take *nefarious* over, what was it?

Oh yes! Vacant, Vitiosyn shell. Isn't that right?"

I shake my head. "Do you want an apology?"

"Far from it. I was so disturbed at being perceived as *vacant*, I've done all I can from that moment forward, to be *more* than that. To rise *above* that title—your name for me. Even if it meant increasing my level of violence. I never want to be seen as empty. Deezalo was empty. Depraved. Demented. He had no grand purpose, except to destroy *eventually* everything he touched. Everything he laid eyes on, he wanted marred, marked, or broken. Be happy I'm not him. The things he would've done to your cousin, the Paragonians, to you. It'd make my actions look as child's play. He was that much of a menace."

Zymarc's attention snaps toward the direction of the door.

A knock sounds out.

Zymarc relaxes his neck, then taps my arm, whispering, "Put your pants back on. That's Caleiso at the door."

He stands up, and so do I, but with the added scrambling to get my pants back on.

Zymarc waits until I'm ready, before calling out, "You may come in." He strolls toward the recessed bathing area.

The door silently swings open. Caleiso strides in. She has donned a fresh set of clothes—a dark-teal tunic that resembles a short dress, and brown leather boots that reach all the way up to mid-thigh. Her blonde hair is done up quite elegantly too. Many small weapons and bottles hang from the three belts of varied width that rest about her waist and hips. She takes in the sight of us, absent of our shirts. "Apologies, Master Zymarc. I thought Tyler would be in his room, bathing. Not in yours. I'll come back, after dinner."

Zymarc pauses from his assessment of the marble tub to consider her. "For what reason, Caleiso? We've not any updates to discuss."

"It is of a matter I've wished to tell you for some time. But it can wait." She drops into a curtsey, before turning to leave.

"Wait, Caleiso," Zymarc calls out. "Since you are here, do a favor for me. Measure Ravier for a new set of clothes. An Onyx set. Those pieces of his will take more time to clean—then starch and press—than a new set will take to alter to fit him.”

“Very well.” She approaches me resentfully. “Have you a tailor’s tape, Lord Zymarc? I’ve not one with me for measur—”

“Use your hands,” says Zymarc, interrupting. “You *can* take the measurements by now, using your hands, I should hope.”

“Yes,” she says guardedly.

“Then get to it.” Zymarc snaps his fingers. Water starts gurgling up from the base of the tub, filling it steadily. Steam rises from it.

I turn my back to her. Surely, she can take my measurements that way. I glance to the window that’s perfectly centered on the wall perpendicular with where the wardrobes are and the wall behind the head of the bed. Birds flutter about, out there, beyond the glass. Dragons fly in the far distance. Evening hours are approaching.

Has it been as long as that, I wonder, *that it’s close to nighttime already?*

Caleiso places her hands on the small of my back right then, running her hands up the length of my spine. I shiver. I don’t want to. Yet I can’t stop it. She feels about my natural waist, going as far to the front of me as she can without getting too close. I must reek. I can’t smell a thing, though. The air is neutral to me. Must have deadened that sense, with all the things I’ve endured of late.

She sweeps her hands down my sides, roughly pushing my arms out of the way.

My shoulders tense. I’m halfway tempted to take a step back, try to land my heel on her foot to crush her toes. How I hate her.

Next, she’s grasping my arms and grating her nails from the tops of my shoulders all the way to my wrists. I let out a yelp. I step forward, turning to scowl at her. The backs of my arms still sting. I check to ensure they aren’t bleeding.

Taking some forced steps toward us, Zymarc laughs low. “Caleiso,” he scolds her, trying to quiet himself. He succeeds.

“What?” She smirks. “He deserved it. All those times he’s choked me, then slammed me against the wall outside, just now. In front of all the Prince-Generals, I might add. He has humiliated me on multiple occasions. So what if I claw his skin a bit? It's kinder than what he's done to me."

"Fine," Zymarc concedes. "But no more of that. Or I'll be repaying you twice over. Whether I wish to or no. ShenawFayel, remember?"

Huffing, Caleiso nods.

The gurgling water ceases. The tub is full. More steam swirls above the water's surface. The room grows incredibly quiet.

"Finish up," says Zymarc. "Then leave us. Don't come back without those clothes for Tyler."

Caleiso approaches again, seeming apprehensive this time.

I think, *What's with the sudden shyness?*

When she places her palms on my abs and feels her way along, I know why. I have the sudden urge to bite into her neck, much in the way Skylin bit into me that night in Grevagg. What an oddity it is. Why would I want to do that, here? And now? And with Caleiso? No!

I fight the urge. And the more I do, the more my senses heighten, almost to euphoria. I hear more, see more, feel more. I hear her heartbeat. It's beating fast. I catch a long line of her thoughts.

Thoughts of: *"Why does he have to look so good? Why so good with magic? Why couldn't he be a Deathasyn? Why do we have to be on opposite sides? Will Zymarc give me, little me, just* one *thing I want? Will he listen? Will Ravier listen?"*

I blink rapidly a few times, trying to grasp what I've just heard. I glance at Zymarc. He's filing his nails, while sitting on one of the steps that lead down to the marble tub. He pauses the filing, to blow nail dust away. He gives no sign that he heard her too.

I force myself to barely take notice of Caleiso, as she feels all along the curves of my neck, arms, and torso. It's when she hesitates at my beltline that I stifle a gasp. The urge to bite into her neck increases. More so, when she slowly starts moving her hands along where my belt should be.

I gnaw on the side of my tongue. The pain is enough of a distraction from whatever this is that's happening to me. *Why is it happening, anyway?*

I wonder. *I can't stand her.*

Taking a peek down at her face, I find that she is studying me. Intent on my expression, her eyes are the heterochromian. I'm about to call her *Callie of Dysarda*. Then her eyes change back to red. I don't call her by that name. My chest hurts, instead, and I'm forced to look away to make the pain subside.

"You've taken enough measurements, Caleiso," Zymarc states. "Now get out."

"Yes, Master Zymarc," she says quietly. "I'll be back as soon as I am able to, with those clothes."

Once Caleiso has exited the room, and shut the door firmly behind her, Zymarc strips his remaining clothes off and enters the bath first. I only catch a glimpse of his bare backside. It's scarred with old whip marks. Even with what and who he is, I cringe at the sight.

I slip out of my pants again and make for the hot, steaming bath. I should be mortified. I don't even let Jed and Jaxson see me naked in the locker rooms, if I can help it. But, here, with my enemy of yesterday and tomorrow, I am at complete ease.

I glance to Zymarc, as he enjoys the heat of the bath, and shake my head. I simply say, "ShenawFayels."

Zymarc somewhat chuckles. "ShenawFayels, indeed. I don't know whether to love or hate this one."

"Same," I agree.

He tosses me a small, dry cloth that was resting on the edge of the bathtub. He already has one for himself. He dunks it in the water, then begins scrubbing his arms free of the grime, of the blood. Somehow the water keeps this odd mirror finish. I can't see anything below the surface. Only the reflections atop.

Zymarc pauses his task of scrubbing. "It's *Argentus* that's been adapted for water, to give you the privacy you hold so dear."

We wash in silence, for a time. I know not how long. When Zymarc has deemed that he's clean enough, though, he tosses the washcloth aside. He leans back with a sigh. "Can I ask you something, without you fighting me in that way you do so fiercely, Ravier?"

"I didn't realize I fought answering you."

"Well, ya do." He smirks. "You've done well in learning how to guard your thoughts. So well, in fact, I cannot see the truth of something. Have you never tasted lust? Truly? I find it hard to believe."

"I don't know what that means. Tasted lust?" I shrug, while still gripping the washcloth in my left hand. "Do you mean, have I bitten into a girl's neck? No, I've not done that." I go on scrubbing my neck and arms.

"Hmm," he mumbles something. I don't understand it.

Then I admit to him, "I've never bedded anyone either, if that's what you mean."

He leans forward. "But you *have* been in bed with someone, haven't you?"

My mouth goes dry. I pause my scrubbing.

He continues, "I never imagined it would be the girl comforting you, holding you to her chest. I thought you'd be the one comforting her, holding her head close to your heart. But I guessed wrong, on that especially dark, clouded night."

I let go of the washcloth. It sinks into the water. "You meant to grab me?"

"Of course I meant to grab you. What would I want with that Galloway, except to use her as bait? She is not Adair Galloway." Zymarc shakes his head. "Yet it worked. You're here with me. You gave me what I wanted."

"And what *do* you want? Surely, it's more than just me."

He opens his mouth to respond, but I interrupt to say, "Answer this, instead, since it's unlikely you'll tell me that, outright."

"Ask away," he says.

"How are you able to practice Metimoran Magic?"

Zymarc's neck stiffens. "Why would you think that, Ravier?"

"I don't think it. I *know* it. You gave it away with those twin, black snakes, used to control Belzara from a distance."

Zymarc makes no attempt to hide the pleased grin emerging on his face. "So I did. Not that the knowledge does you any good, now."

I ask, "Who taught you that magic?"

"A dragon." He eyes me calmly.

"What dragon?" I return his calm stare. "The Black Flame?"

His eyes flicker like fire. It's brief. I break eye contact for a few seconds.

He voices the statement, "You wish to know how I managed to hurt Death. Simple. I starved him of his fodder, so he'd give me one desire. And what feeds Death, save for more death?"

The image of Sivondel in Paragon, drawing the bodies of the fallen to himself, flashes in my mind. I answer, "Blood. Bones. Decay."

Zymarc nods, finally unlocking his stare from my face.

I take in a full breath. "If that's true, who was given the bodies of the dead for a time?"

"No one. I and my people used Vitiosus to bring the dead back to life enough that Death could not claim them. The collective strength needed was immense. But we did it. Most of my people were unaware, however." Zymarc begins to massage his neck.

I search for more to probe about. There must be something. I ask, "Why do you need to learn the various classes of magic, Zymarc?"

He ceases massaging his neck, and flicks his attention my way. "I already know all the classes of magic, Ravier."

"No you don't," I contradict. "You don't know Red Magic, nor Crae-Shand. If you did, well, I believe the war would've been long over by now."

Leaning forward slightly, Zymarc reaches down to the water with one hand. He flicks his fingers across the mirrored, liquid surface. Water splashes me.

I flick water back. "Tell me why you wanted Talok and me to fight Caleiso in Grevagg."

Zymarc sweeps a hand through the water. "To make her stronger than before, for she's never dueled against one of the Paragonian Sovereignty. It could've been a great lesson."

Water laps against my chest, as I comment, "And if we *had* managed to kill her, you simply would've staved off her death with your collective strength of Vitiosus?"

"Something like that," replies Zymarc, as he leans back to rest his arms on a step leading into the tub. "Aren't you forgetting to ask me what I thought of the Shield of Shylen?"

I swallow hard. *So he did figure that out,* I muse, before asking, "You wanna talk about it? I'm up for listening."

Zymarc's green eyes turn wild. He bursts out of his sitting position to splash a tumult of water at me. The water resembles a shattered mirror made of liquid. I lift my hands to block my face. As I gradually expose my face, Zymarc is standing in the center of the bath, the water chest-deep.

Scowling at me, he mutters, "If we weren't in ShenawFayel, Ravier, you'd receive quite a blow to the face for your insolence."

"So this wouldn't be a good time to ask you what you did with Monel's spell-book, or why you needed the Bow of Three Queens?"

I cringe when Zymarc splashes another tumult of water my way.

He retreats to his former position. "Has anyone ever told you what an annoying little prick you are, Tyler?"

"Only you," I reply. "Next time I see her, want me to have Rorka practice her mute spell on me, the way she did on you in Vondurheil? You seem to have made a full recovery from that. It's astonishing."

Zymarc straightens his back, looking more imposing in the process. "You will regret such talk, come tomorrow, when the *Truce for a Day* no longer protects you."

I force myself to settle down, to quiet down.

After many moments of silence, I tell him, "I know about the Hex of Vitiosus. Caleiso told me at The Sodon. And that you mean to make a sixth particle of magic."

"I'm not going to use you for that," Zymarc assures, relaxing somewhat.

"Then whom?" I ask. "It won't be Awngeleik."

"You already agreed to give her to me, though. And, yet, you came empty-handed. Why?"

"We don't know where she is."

Zymarc looks away, muttering, "Well, that must be the truth, for the

ShenawFayel would keep you from outright lying to me."

A great scowl creeps into his features. Then he swipes his pinky finger across one of his eyebrows. It's the same type of mannerism my mother practices. Exactly the same. My heart drops. The room spins. I think in horror, *Could it be that Zymarc is? No! It can't be true.* Yet as I go over my mother's features and Zymarc's, there's enough physical resemblance to make me worry. What if my mother, Amira Hajjar Ravier, is somehow, someway, the daughter of Zymarc? That would make me his grandson. But wouldn't he know? Then a different line of thought occurs to me … Not if my father made him forget. And what if, in making the King Vitiosyn forget, my father sealed his fate of death? What if he broke Laws of Magic to make Zymarc forget, in order for my mother and me to be safe? Safe from being hunted by him? Or hunted by someone else.

Zymarc starts talking again, oblivious to the battle going on inside my head. He says, "There is much Caleiso doesn't know. One fact she is unaware of—what no one knows except for me, and now you—is that it is already done. The sixth particle is already there, among the original five. Has been, for some time. I'll show you, later. The proof is not here, in this room. It's in the *one* cathedral Deezalo managed to build, before he was caught and executed. There's a certain statue there now, with a certain spell-book at its feet. I already had the book. But I had Grawllik go back to Grevagg, after the city was abandoned, and steal the statue for me. He only just brought it here this morning. I was going to give him his payment, while we were out in the courtyard. Then he opened his mouth. Oh well! He got what was coming to him. I blame it on the curse of Soren's Statue. Always does he, even from the grave, seem to bring ill will to his statue's tenders or, rather, the thieves who keep moving him about. It's why I didn't dare be the one to steal him, nor transport him."

In horror, I ask, "You have the Statue of Soren here? In Vaydell?"

His green eyes flash to the crimson-red. Zymarc nods. "It seems fate is after you, Ravier. Fate and Soren. Sometimes, there isn't much difference, him being the Sorshrynak that he was. Soren of the Monel: forever the ghost, there to haunt me. And now? Us."

27

See Things Differently

Since we're finished with getting cleaned up, and Caleiso hasn't returned, Zymarc decides to find the smallest set of his own garb that he keeps in one of the three wardrobes. It doesn't drown me in fabric too terribly. We're headed for the door now, physically refreshed. But I am unnerved, barely able to hide it from this Vitiosyn King. He hands me my daggers, after looking them over for a moment. Accepting them, I fasten them to my belt, then glance to him again. He's taken on the pale-faced, red-eyed appearance. He's a little taller now too. And more unsettling to me. The ease with which he controls himself is something I do not understand. *Cannot* understand. Not even a day ago, he decapitated a being. Yet he seems fine, as we ready ourselves to leave. He has not the storm always about to burst the way Jasper does. Part of me thinks I have the beginnings of that Greyvon storm. Inner rage that builds and builds, until *Bam!* I act out.

I make some final adjustments to the worn, black coat I have on—mostly, I pull the right sleeve down so that it covers the diver's watch and its cracked crystal—then I ask, "How far did she have to go, to find a set of clothes that'll *kind of* fit me?"

Zymarc shuts the door behind us and locks it. He tucks the key away in a hidden pocket that's layered between the seams of one of his coat sleeves. "A city to the north. Pil'Drouka. The dragon's flight isn't far to get there. Even less so, to the outpost where some essential supplies are kept. She'll look there first. Should be back very soon, if they had what she needed."

We navigate back the way we came earlier. Once at the foot of the stairs, Zymarc hesitates to leave through that same door where we entered. Instead, he turns the corner, and goes down a long hallway. I follow in silence, taking note that there isn't a single door down this way. It eventually leads to a round room with three doors. One directly in front of us, and one to each side.

Zymarc comes to a standstill. With a heavy sigh, he tells me, "I'm about to do something I have never done, Ravier; intentionally use a living soul as a shield. I mean to use you to secure my own safety from rioters and assassins. Will you hate me for it, do you think?"

"Will your security measures ensure that I get to see the Statue of Soren?"

He nods.

"Then take us there." I indicate that he pick one of the three doors.

As he takes a moment to weigh his options, I take a moment to study him. Study his mannerisms and features, once more comparing them to my mother's. I just can't decide either way if he's my mother's father.

Striding forward, Zymarc chooses the door directly in front. He holds the door open for me. I exit first. He pulls the door shut behind him.

Some Vitiosyn men (a dozen or so) linger there in the colorful, fading light of dusk, cleaning or sharpening their many weapons. They startle at the sight of their king. Quickly, they stand at attention. One dressed in the finer garb of Vitiosyns, which still isn't too refined, must be near the rank of a Prince-General.

That one approaches us, saying, "Lord-King Zymarc, what are you doing, leaving the General's House via this way? It isn't safe. Go back through the courtyard. We've cleared that area for your safety."

Zymarc pats the concerned Vitiosyn on the arm. "A few minutes won't kill me. I came to ask that your best team clear the cathedral, its grounds, and the pathway leading there, for my safety." He pauses to glance at some Deathasyns strolling about in the distance. One of those figures startles, and runs off out of sight. Some of the men at attention spot the figure. They look to Zymarc. He subtly shakes his head at them.

"Is that all?" The more refined Vitiosyn man breathes a sigh of relief, for he had his back turned. He didn't see the fleeing Deathasyn. But then he spots me. His glowing red eyes grow wide.

Zymarc adds, "And that you take special care to be thorough in your patrol, as the Onyx Prince means to accompany me there to the cathedral."

The Vitiosyn bows his head. He stutters, "Of . . . of course! We would not want to create the need for reparation to the Onyx, should he suffer any injuries. We shall take care of you and the Onyx Prince. However, my top squadron men here wish to know, King Zymarc, are we permitted?"

"You are." Zymarc smiles in authenticity.

The colors of dusk have faded into the beginnings of a dark, cloudy night within these past few minutes. Tall torch poles light themselves with fire, or someone puts the fire in them. Either way, a warm light blankets the group of us gathered near the base of one of these poles.

The head Vitiosyn of the squadron takes to one knee, bowing to me. His men follow his example. Though they hold the position for seconds, it is as an eternity of confusion. I find that I love these men, would die for them, would *kill* for them. I glance at Zymarc, and know it is his attachment to them that I feel. His eyes have changed back to green. He looks upon them with his Onyx eyes, the eyes given to him at birth, rather than the set given to him by a magic, most violent—Vitiosus.

What is happening to me? I wonder. *No one warned me of how the ShenawFayel would really be. That I would feel as my enemy feels. That I would love what he loves. What if I truly am his grandson, and that is why no one warned me? Perhaps what I'm experiencing is entirely new.*

I'm starting to regret my decision to strike a ShenawFayel with Zymarc. All these pieces fit. Neither friend nor foe to my father. Many have said *that* of Zymarc, regarding his relationship to LanSoren. He could've been the father-in-law, unbeknownst to that in-law, if my father used all magic within himself to hide that fact from Zymarc.

Is it a fact, though? I wonder, still. I'm not convinced. Simply alarmed.

Interrupting my thoughts, Zymarc tells his man, "Let me know by letter, when you are done. Tyler and I will wait inside."

I turn on my heel and head back for the door. I thrust it open. I startle at the sight inside. It isn't the same room we left moments ago. It is an open room with windows on both sides, thick curtains covering them. On the far side, I can see the turn by the staircase that we took. I slowly glance back to Zymarc. He's right there at my side, scowling. Gentle, but persistent, he pushes me out of the way, and grabs hold of the doorknob.

He pulls the door shut, saying to me, "It is customary to say parting words to any warrior, before you simply leave their presence. Especially when those warriors are older than yourself."

"Oh," I say in nervousness. "Sorry, I didn't know." I turn to face the Vitiosyn men. "I meant no offense. It's just that I've not had much to eat today. Not much to eat for while, actually." I stare at the ground. I take that posture of reprimand I get when my mother is lecturing me. Also do I search for what else to say.

I look up, when the head of the squadron addresses me. "Ye be fine, Onyx Prince. Go to the courtyard. Get yourself a spot of food. They've already started serving up the wares."

The remaining men have broken their posture of standing at attention. They've spread out a little too. The quiet ones again take to the task of preparing their weaponry for battle. Also do they keep watch of their surroundings.

One of the men, a deep-voiced one, adds, "Yeah? And I heard they're serving Dragon's Tail tonight."

"You don't say?" a tall, scrawny one asks, all excited.

Zymarc quietly huffs.

Oblivious of him, they continue.

"Ooh! Ye must be trying Dragon's Tail, Onyx Prince," says Tall and Scrawny.

"He can't be having that!" the shortest exclaims. "He hails of the Tamers. Have respect for his origins."

"Why can't he taste the tail? He only be half Tamer. No! Less than half. For he is Paragonian and, well . . ." That deep-voiced, broad-shouldered one hesitates. The scar running down his face, marring across one of his eyes, a blind eye, glows a soft red. His dead eye always looks forward. But the other, the glowing red one, studies me fiercely. He asks, "Why, we know not what race your mother hails from. What is she of? LanSoren never said. And we never caught rumors of her, neither."

My skin is starting to crawl. I think, *For good or ill, here it goes.*

I reply, "I used to think she was just *human*. Now, with all I've learned, I couldn't really say for sure."

In interest, the shortest one—barely taller than me—asks, "What is she called by? Her name, I mean."

"Amira Hajjar Ravier," I answer. The sound of it comforts me. Even so far from the home I've always known, my mother's name, alone, brings solace. Then despair for whose daughter she could be. Confusion, after that, for thinking: *Could she have been the one, not Droediin, writing those notes? Droediin seemed to be hiding something, even after his confession. What if he was hiding my mother's real identity? Has she secretly been a Sorsryn all along? Or is she something else?*

Tall and Scrawny grins in that Deathasyn way, all crooked-like. "A name that sounds as a spell," he says. "Enchanting. You must look like her, for you look like not a speck of LanSoren, save for his aura."

"Do you mean he was an aura of both?" I ask. "Wolf and dragon? No one's ever said that."

"No, no," the leader states. "He was of the wolf aura."

"You're sure of that?" I quiz.

"Quite sure, yes. Wolf auras, many generations back on his mother's side." The squad leader is starting to get restless on his feet. He keeps glancing to Zymarc.

"And his father?" I ask. "You ever hear rumors about him? My grandfather?"

The squad leader hesitates, even stutters, "I . . . I know—"

Zymarc clears his throat. "LanSoren never knew his father, never found out his identity. Though he searched for answers for many years. Even asked me to help him, one time." Zymarc points at his men. "But you didn't hear that from me."

"Hear . . . hear what?" the shortest stutters.

The one with a blind eye adds, "We heard nothin' but of a head falling to the ground in the courtyard."

"Yes, Grawllik's head!" says the squad leader. "Gruesome, glorious end for a GreyLyre such as that, wasn't it, King Zymarc? Should've buried him alive. Nothing glorious or epic about that."

"I'll take that into consideration, for the next time," says Zymarc.

I can feel that we're about to turn and leave them. I want something answered first, and I don't want to ask Zymarc of it, outright. "Before I go have my first taste of *Dragon's Tail*," I say with zeal, "I wonder . . . if no dragon aura is on my father's side, how could I have an aura of both Von and dyn?"

"Ya couldn't," says Scarred-face, his scar's glow flickering. "It would have to come from your mother's side."

Zymarc taps his foot impatiently. "But, quite likely, whomever your paternal grandfather was, had a dragon aura."

"You're probably right." I nod, faking consideration of the matter.

Zymarc settles down, even starts to massage his neck a bit.

Then, all innocent-like, I ask, "What aura are you, Zymarc?"

"Wolf aura," he replies.

"Yes, that makes sense. All the sneaking around, plotting, and such. You'd have to be of the wolf aura." Inwardly, I breathe a sigh of relief. *That's that,* I muse. *He can't be my grandfather. What a relief! I wonder why Madeleine was so sure he's of the dragon aura.*

Zymarc stops massaging his neck. He lowers that hand. He eyes his men in curiosity. "But, prior to Vitiosus—I mean, before I became a Vitiosyn—when I was simply an Onyx Warrior, I was of the dragon aura. All the subsets of dragon auras, save for one. The Sleeping Dragon. That aura of both Von and dyn, with a propensity toward dragon." Facing me, Zymarc adds, "If my former self could be merged with me, as I am now, one could come to the conclusion that I'd be an aura of both, much like you are, Ravier." He hides a grin. Then he directs all attention to his men, even points at them again. "But you didn't hear that from me."

The shortest answers, "What? Hear what? I only heard one thing."

Scarred-face says, "Yes, all we's be hearing was that Ravier means to taste Dragon's Tail."

"What a delight!" Tall and Scrawny grins especially wide.

Squad Leader adds, "We're sorry to be missing out as witnesses to it too. Make sure to give us a detailed recount, Lord Zymarc, perfectly describing his reaction to the tasting."

"Certainly," says Zymarc, "I shall." With that, he heads for the door, turns the knob only using his fingertips, then opens the door enough for us to enter. He repeats that gesture of preferring me, by holding it ajar. He eyes me with a less-than-friendly look, though, as I walk past him.

Quietly, obediently, I go inside. It's that room with the three doors and a long hallway.

The door shuts firmly behind me.

I whirl around to face Zymarc.

He glares at me.

I go with the shrug, the go-to. There's really nothing to be said. I caught Zymarc, doing one of his tricks, and he knows that I know.

After a time of awkward silence, I point both index fingers downward, then ask, "Are we actually in the General's House?"

"No," he says. "Too many rioters and assassins know I prefer the General's House. That room with all the covered windows is to ensnare would-be assassins into making an attempt. We've caught many that way. Play a false image of me, traversing through the lower room. I leave the house through a different way, or wander about inside in no particular pattern, whenever I can. We are currently in the building opposite of the house. The Observer's Villa."

"So, when we turned the corner, at the bottom of the stairs . . . ?" I trail off, waiting for Zymarc to finish.

"We passed through a distortion. Not a time-distortion, mind you.

Merely a transporting one."

I stroll about the room. "That's how you've gotten everywhere so quickly, isn't it?"

"Yes," he admits after a time. "I learned information more quickly, however, through Kaalon's eyes."

"Wait! Kaalon?" I stop in my tracks. "I thought you were pretending to be Kaalon? Do you mean to say there actually is an Onyx Warrior by the name of Kaalon?"

"Come now, Ravier," he says in a low voice. "You don't truly believe I could pose as both Zymarc and Kaalon at the same time, do you? Someone would've caught on to the ruse, long ago. No, Kaalon is . . . well . . ." Zymarc looks off in shame, then refocuses on me. "Why don't I show you after dinner and the visit to the cathedral?"

"Fine. But I won't let you get out of explaining yourself."

"I would expect nothing less from the Son of LanSoren. Inquisitive little prick he was, at the beginning. You're just like how he was, around the same age."

Zymarc strides off down the hall, and I jog to catch up.

"How old was he, when you first met him?"

"Fifteen," replies Zymarc, as we pass through the distortion.

Something booms close by. Windows shatter. I take a peek back. Vitiosyns are running into the room with all the covered windows.

After some moments, someone shouts, "Lord Zymarc!" It's Squad Leader. Alarmed, he looks at us.

"I'm fine," Zymarc calls back. "Catch whoever set that trap, though, will you? We're headed out to the courtyard now."

"Sure thing!" The leader and his team leave to go hunt for the would-be assassin.

Passing the bottom of the staircase, Zymarc goes to the door that leads out into the courtyard. He rests his hand on the doorknob. He peers over his shoulder to make eye contact. "Just before I met your father in person," he says, "your grandmother, Marion of Trauvo, came to visit me. Said a great many things to me. Asked that I lie to her son, LanSoren, *when* he came to see me, asking after his father. How she was certain he would come, I don't know. You Raviers, you're such an unnerving lot. And Lance! He was the worst! I swear, he even made up words to annoy me."

Zymarc yanks the door open. This time, he doesn't hold it open for me. He just walks out.

"What kind of words?" I ask, barely keeping pace with his quick jaunt.

We make for the courtyard's center that's illuminated by lit, floating candlesticks.

Zymarc growls. "I asked them not to use the candlesticks. Drips wax everywhere. Leaves such a mess to clean up." Calming somewhat, he asks, "What was your question again?"

"Words—"

"Right! Words," he interrupts. "There were many unfamiliar words he spoke to me, or wrote in a place where he knew I'd eventually see them. You should *first* know this, however, Ravier. I apprenticed LanSoren, from the time he turned sixteen, all the way until his eighteenth year."

My heart wants to explode. I've no words of my own for that revelation. I just keep going forward with this one beside me.

Zymarc continues, "Shocking, isn't it? The great LanSoren of Trauvo was apprenticed to the King Vitiosyn. Indeed, he was my first apprentice. One I did not want. Rather, was coerced—threatened by your grandmother—into accepting. Marion, terrifying that one. She could"—Zymarc pauses to clear his throat, and sweat glistens on his forehead—"in fact, *did* steal thousands of my memories to prove her power to me. That she was not one to be trifled with. And I didn't trifle with her. I merely did all that she asked of me."

Zymarc comes to a complete stop. The music of wind instruments being played near the banquet table where dozens of Vitiosyns are gathered, eating and chatting or singing and dancing, drifts out to where we have come to a standstill.

"How can all that *possibly* be true, Zymarc? How can you expect me to believe it?"

He shakes his head. "That's just it, Ravier. Even after all these years, it still sounds ridiculous to my own ears."

"Why would she do what she did?"

Zymarc sighs. "I was hoping there was some explanation in those journals of your father's to do with Marion, and what she had planned. She even, at one point, let LanSoren and me believe that he could be my son. It was absurd." Zymarc lets out a soft laugh. "Due to the stolen memories, I couldn't refute the claim. And I never got a blood sample of LanSoren's to test, either, and put that matter to rest."

"What?" I ask. My pulse hammers. Dizziness grows thick in my head too.

Zymarc's about to answer, when Azabahk comes hobbling over to us. "King Zymarc, come to join us for a meal?"

Zymarc grins wide. "I have, indeed. And to give the Onyx Prince his first taste of Dragon's Tail."

Using a cane for balance, Azabahk lets out his Deathasyn smirk, contorted features and all. "Dear Deathasyn brothers!" he shouts over the noise. "The Onyx Prince means to taste the tail."

The chatter stops. The music subsides. The dancing and singing cease.

Feigning confidence that I simply do not feel, I stride forward. One of the Prince-Generals hands me a plate, once I'm closer to the table. His expression is one of being dumbstruck. He steps away, to watch me intently. All those sitting down seem to be on the edge of their seat, as I look over the contents of the plate. The meat resembles a rack of ribs . . . sort of. I try not to study it too much. I dig my fingers into the cooked, seared flesh. A chunk is easily torn off. I eyeball that piece. Part of it shimmers somewhat in the candlelight.

The serving Prince-General leans toward my direction to whisper, "The shiny parts are the scales. Not good for eating, if ye be a two-legged thing. Could break a tooth, otherwise."

"Thanks for the warning," I tell him. Then, before I can think too much on what Dragon's Tail actually is, I stuff a piece of it in my mouth. I peel the scale off, and drop it on the plate. It clinks, sounding like metal landing on porcelain. After a few chews, the meat has an excellent smoky flavor that builds and builds. It reminds me of seasoned meat that's been stuck on a spit and cooked over a fire near all day. My mother insisted I learn this particular skill. It was at some event she made me go to. I dragged Jed and Jaxson along. Their complaints nearly ended our friendship right there, that hot summer day when I was twelve years old. After swallowing, I admit, "It's pretty good, actually."

A Prince-General at the head of the table bursts to his feet. "The Onyx Prince likes my cookin'! Suck on that, ya bags of bones!"

I can't help but laugh. Then I look for a spot to sit down. There's a chair near the middle of the banquet table that's empty. I head for it, filling my plate along the way with fruits and seeds and, well, more Dragon's Tail.

The General-cook keeps talking as I move along, saying, "For bags of bones is what we all shall be, come the morrow. Couldn't be standing a chance against the prince and his Onyx of Malik." He pauses as I take my seat.

Oddly enough, I've picked the thirteenth chair from either heads of the table. Zymarc pulls the chair out that's across from me, but another is coming to sit in it. Caleiso. I glare at her, and her fancy, done-up hair.

The General-cook restarts his talk. "Unless that one there means to be joining our side. And do ye, Onyx Prince, mean to join us?"

Caleiso licks her lips. She glances away to Zymarc. He's already at the other head of the table. He ignores her, ignores the exchange, instead starts up a chat with Azabahk. They're too far away for me to hear what they're saying.

Truthfully, I remark, "I don't believe so. Then again, I don't know. Come tomorrow, when Zymarc attempts to turn me, I believe we all will have our answer."

Those able to hear what I've said, grow solemn. They eat in silence. The music stops completely.

The General-cook at the table's head sits down again. "Aye, that could be. Perhaps I shouldn't have said anything. Should leave that bit to Zymarc, for asking ya."

When that General turns his attention elsewhere, I Mensa-div to Caleiso, *"When did you get back?"*

"A short while ago," she answers. *"I put your new clothes in your room. I first looked for you in Zymarc's quarters, though. Neither of you were there. Where'd he take you?"*

"Around." I shrug subtly, then continue to stuff my face. Food has never tasted this good.

"Fine," she divs, while also stuffing her face. She takes a huge bite of tail meat and chews hard (I can hear her teeth striking together). *"Don't tell me, if you don't want to. Will you at least come back for the night, in time for me to ensure the pieces fit you right? I'll be reprimanded, if the clothes are ill-fitting."*

"How long do you need, for the adjustments?"

"Only some minutes."

"I'll be back in time."

In sarcasm, she divs, *"Beautiful."*

I counter with, *"Terrifying. I bet your work will look hideous on me."* I smirk at her, before gripping a glass filled with water. At least I assume it's water, since it's clear in color and not bubbly. I start by taking a sip. It's all right. So I gulp it down.

Caleiso snaps her fingers.

The liquid going into my mouth thickens. I ease up, alarmed. I stop swallowing, even pull the glass away to see the contents. It's filled with a dark-red liquid. The sour, metallic taste is recognizably blood in my mouth. I spew it out. All. Over. Caleiso.

Gasping, she pushes away from the table to examine the mess of blood on her teal tunic, yet she remains seated.

I take hold of a napkin that's laid next to my plate to spit into it, then cover a few coughs. I'm fine after some seconds. I toss the napkin to the table and sit back down. I try to catch my breath, try to swallow away the foul taste.

Zymarc has stood up from his place at the table, to shout, "Caleiso! What are you thinking? He's half Paragonian. He can't have blood. I've not taught him how to guard against it either." His red, Vitiosyn eyes blaze at her.

She goes from irritated to apologetic. She stands up and straightens her ruined tunic. She stammers, "I ... d-didn't ... know you hadn't taught him that yet. Apologies, King Zymarc. I forgot myself. Merely behaved as I would toward a fellow citizen. Or, even, a fellow Deathasyn." She swallows hard. Then she bows her head, aims her stance of respect in Zymarc's direction.

Zymarc places his palms flat on the table. He leans forward, to say in an icy tone, "Let me make this clear to you, girl. You are not a Deathasyn. If I stripped you of Vitiosus, you would merely be a Sorsryn of origin which we do not know. As far as we know, you are a true orphan, who has been under my care your entire life. And this is how you behave? This is how you show gratitude? By treating an honored guest of mine in this fashion? You could have killed him, for his guard was down."

Throughout the exchange, Zymarc does not yell. Only has he shouted her name.

Caleiso shyly glances at Zymarc. "Well, what do you want me to do for amends toward you?"

"For starters, apologize to Ravier."

Her expression of meekness evaporates, as she focuses on me. "Sorry ... for making you taste blood? I thought you might've liked to know how it tasted, when the blood from my eyes slipped into my mouth, that night at The Sodon."

"Oh!" I exclaim, easing out of my chair again. "Is *that* what you were doing? Giving me a taste of your blood. Does it taste like that, when taken from the neck?" I tap a forefinger on my own neck. "If so, then it tastes delicious. Doubtful anyone else's would taste so much like the cheap metal coins my classmates used to secretly slip into my food while in the cafeteria, much to my annoyance and their amusement. Do you eat metal like a dragon to get your blood to taste that way? Rather than being served your supper here, amongst the king and generals of an army, should you instead be taken to the Dragon Stables and given your supper there?" I find that I've clawed my fingernails into the wood of the table. I'm practically shaking in anger. But that last part fills me with remorse. It was low. Really low.

Tears have welled up in her eyes, those eyes that have turned heterochromian again.

I say, "Look, Callie, I didn't mean to put it like that." The old name for her slips out, before I can stop it. More coldly, I add, "What I should've started with is . . . you never should've been with me that day of the festival."

The tears slip down her pale cheeks, as she argues, "I never could've infiltrated the castle the way I did, if I hadn't deceived you, Tyler."

I hold up a hand to silence her. "Don't call me by that name. I am not your friend. As I said, you never should've been with me that day. Never should've lied, letting me think you were scared for your parents in Dysarda. Never *ever* should have let me come to care for you by the end of that night. For, now, I hate you more than I've ever hated anything in my life. Fourteen years. It's a short life to some. But it's all I've got. One life. Same as you. For I imagine, even in ReNovamen, nothing could ever be quite the same as it was before the change. Before the rebirth."

"I'm sorry," she cries, finally sounding genuine. Broken. In silent misery, she sits back down.

My heartbeat settles. And, though I hate myself for it, I pity her. My father's voice seems to call from afar, telling me that violence and deceit is all she's ever known.

I reach out with my left hand. If I can't wrench the wickedness out of her, perhaps I'll scare her a bit. I focus on all the bloodstains of what I spit out. I will it to become liquid again, the way I witnessed Brinkorr do with the ink and quill. Many implied that removing ink stains is a difficult or lengthy task, unless you're a Laykonian. Or, rather, someone who's able to practice their magic. Bloodstains are most likely the same as ink; time-consuming to remove. Steadily, then quickly, the blood lifts away from the table, from the fabric of Caleiso's tunic, and wherever else the droplets have landed. It happens in seconds. Not minutes. Not hours. Within a minute, they've drawn together to resemble a red snake, absent of eyes. I gradually point to my glass, then touch the side of it. The blood is drawn back into the glass. I dip my left ring finger in the blood, then drag it softly along the edge of the drinking glass. The glass vibrates in that musical way. The stain of blood leaves the liquid. It's soon crystal-clear.

Gripping it in my left hand, I raise my glass to Caleiso's shocked face. I say, "To a love for magic. Cheers!" I toast the generals, who then raise their cups to me in silence. I down all the liquid, before firmly setting my glass down. "Still tastes like metal." I exaggerate a grimace.

The generals snicker. But one says, "Wash the taste down with more tail."

A different general plops more meat on a plate, and leans over to hand it to me. "Snap your fingers," he says, "and that plate'll levitate, following you around and such, till you've practically licked it clean. Makes eating on the run easier."

"Yeah? *Easier* he says," one interrupts. "It ain't easier when those plates get packed away, still enchanted to levitate. Then those packs get ripped open during a scuffle, inevitably, and the plates start following you around, smacking your hands, demanding ya taste their invisible contents. Levitating plates. It seems very much like a Kyanite habit or, at the very least, a Jokryn thing to do."

"Jokryns!" another general exclaims. "How be those Jokryn brothers, down in our prisons? Haven't heard much about them, of late."

"Alive," says Azabahk in resentment. "You may go, Lord Zymarc. I'll stay, make sure they don't get too rowdy."

"I thank you," says Zymarc, folding up a letter and tucking it away in one of his pockets. "Shall we, Ravier?"

After I bid a good night to the Prince-Generals, I give my two-fingered wave to Caleiso. She still hasn't resumed eating. I turn to leave anyway, lowering my hand. I follow Zymarc away from the center of the courtyard.

* * *

We've been walking a ways outside of the protection of the innermost courtyard. The two of us pass by many other courtyards that are only partially shielded. I've also finished the last bit of Dragon's Tail that was on my plate. Now that plate's just following me around like the generals said it would.

Zymarc finally snaps his fingers over it, twice. The plate falls to the ground. It breaks into several pieces. I go to pick them up, but Zymarc says, "The dragons will come by later and crunch that into bits. Leave it."

We walk along in the darkness of night. We're not too near any of the tall, torch poles. Just close enough to see our way. Or, rather, for me to see my way, for I need light. Most likely, Zymarc doesn't. Either way, all the nearby shadows seem ominous like spindly fingers stretching across the ground, reaching for victims. It makes me uneasy.

After a time, Zymarc restarts our conversation from earlier, saying, "I never got a sample of LanSoren's blood, to find out if he and I were related. It's why I was in Yharss-Rawshuen that day. I heard, via Kaalon, that LanSoren finally gave over a blood sample well before his day of death. *Kaalon* overheard King ReNovak telling Ayna of it; and ReNovak heard it from Gyron, who heard it from King Sosha, who, apparently, ordered LanSoren to give the sample over as if a blood sample is something that can be owned or forcibly relinquished." Zymarc chuckles.

I ask, "Why do I get the feeling you want a sample of my blood?"

Turning serious, he buries his hands deep into his coat pockets. "Because I do. Many times, I've considered biting into your neck to get it too. Almost asked Caleiso to do it at The Sodon. But . . . I was fairly certain that would put you over the edge. Make you tear her apart. Seems I wasn't too far off."

"Could you do more with a blood sample of mine, than merely check it for a blood relation between us?"

"Such as?"

"Can you test me for Siveyra's Mark?"

"I could," Zymarc replies. "It would require a trip back to the Observer's Villa. Rather, a trip down to the dungeons below. Pay a visit to Matron RayVora and her sons. Not all four sons. But three out of the four. Not too bad, for all my efforts to trap the first members of the Jokryn family. We've time to visit them in the morning, however, get that sample as well as test that blade of the Vons. Today has been a long day. For both of us."

I scoff. "How's it weighed you down?"

"*You*," he says. "You've made my magic leech out, save for what's there for Vitiosus. Either that, or it's the ShenawFayel putting us on an even playing field. I'm sure I'll feel like myself again, come tomorrow when the spell breaks."

"How many ShenawFayels have you been in?"

"Enough. This, however, is the last ShenawFayel I intend to ever strike with someone." Zymarc starts walking faster.

Keeping up, I ask, "Why's that?"

He lets out a slow breath. "Because this one's different. Feels different."

We approach a tall gate, which looks to be fashioned in the way of wrought-iron. Rather than made of dark metal, however, it is a golden color. Still has the creepy vibe about it, though. Both it, and its fence to match. They tower like fences belonging to old estates. Only, they are much, much higher. Probably older too than any estate I've read about or seen pictures of, back home.

Zymarc undoes the heavy latch, then pushes the single gate wide open. He goes forward along the black-stone path. I follow. Our footsteps are silent.

Even so, floating glass orbs burst with flames—colors of blue, yellow, and red. It's as if they alert the cathedral's grounds to intruders. The sound of shattering glass startles me. But not Zymarc.

He continues forward. "This ShenawFayel is harder, because of who you are. His son. LanSoren never called me a friend. Yet I considered him to be mine."

The white-stone cathedral trimmed with gold comes into focus. Deezalo's Cathedral. Rather than having gargoyles, or angels and demons, or important figures for its statues of adornment, it is the golden statue of a bird. Images of the same kind of bird—an incalculable amount in this dim, colored light—are purposefully dispersed on the cathedral's exterior to make the building look as a living, elegant thing. I know I've seen that bird somewhere, before. *But where?* I wonder.

A breeze drifts about the area, coming from the sides of the path. It howls as a strong wind, yet it has not the strength behind it.

Even so, the gate slams shut behind us.

I whirl around. Zymarc doesn't. No one's there. It's just us. The two in ShenawFayel together. Turning to face the cathedral again, I glance to either side of the path. The courtyard has numerous black-stone walkways, and its grounds are filled with dead-looking trees of many sizes and shapes. They are encased in metal. Many colors of metals; gold, silver, bronze, iron, copper, brass, even some are as clear-crystal. They are beautiful and terrifying all at once, for, what if—like many of the things of this world—life can be breathed into them, and they can then decide to attack? Their branches are mighty thick, and those branch-tips are as pointed as freshly sharpened knives.

Zymarc interrupts my growing fear, to quietly say, "I miss that Ravier. Long for him, actually."

My face gets hot. "Then why are you doing all this? If you ever cared about him, why are you tormenting his people? You even tried to kill his nephew, my cousin."

Zymarc sighs. "I didn't have a choice. *Don't* have a choice."

"There's always a choice."

"Not for me," he says. "Not if I want to get what I desire most of all."

"And what is it you want most? Please, Zymarc, just tell me. Be out with it. You can't keep it to yourself forever."

"I dare not speak it, dare not even finish the conscious thought of it, or I'll never get it."

Arriving at our destination, a staircase of twenty-two steps which lead to the cathedral's grand, empty landing, Zymarc races up them.

He slows his movements to draw symbols of magic on the door, and that door opens of its own accord. Clouds draw away, laying the moon bare and bright. Moonlight shines down on the landing. No light goes beyond the door's threshold, however. Its doorway is wide enough that we're able to enter together, side by side.

I quickly fall a few paces behind Zymarc, for the sight before me. Like a switch being flicked up, the room is abruptly lit. White pillars, flecked with burgundy-red and midnight-blue are the center supports of the second floor, high above. I don't finish looking up all the way, because the murals on the walls of many scenes catch my attention. A cloaked figure, dressed in black and gold, is in all of them. Various Deathasyns, whose names I do not know, are with him. Not the same ones in each scene. But many men and women of various statures and ages. All scenes are of war, intimidation, or the practicing of magic. A fearsome-looking magic, which warps and contorts the things within those scenes to be frightening. It is not as the distortion of Blue Magic, per se, which always feels temporary. No. This magic, I fear, warps the very soul of the one casting it.

The door clicks closed. Something cold brushes against my arm. So cold is it, it instantly pierces through the fabric of the worn, black coat I have on. Suddenly, I very much wish I had my coat of the Sleeping Dragon. I think, *Why didn't I at least miniaturize it, tuck it away with my other things?*

Quickly, whatever it was is gone. It couldn't have been Zymarc, for he is walking ahead of me, and has been, since we entered. Also, he's given no indication of using magic. I glance around. No one has stepped foot inside the cathedral with us. No one lingers by the door either. No one is waiting around for us, directly ahead.

Even so, a masculine voice laughs from somewhere deep within the cathedral. Somewhere we cannot see. It echoes around us, then fades. I'd know that voice anywhere. Even in the depths of water, or the quiet of a snowy-white winter, I'd know it. I'd know him. Soren of the Monel.

I hear his voice say in Mensa-div, *"'Tis fate, you see. Given what he is. He cannot hide from me."*

I say aloud, "Zymarc?"

He stops. He turns around. His eyes are green. And he's become shorter. The same height he was as Kaalon. "What, Ravier?"

"Was that Soren's Statue, laughing up ahead?"

Zymarc hesitates to answer. Then he confirms my fear with one word. "Yes."

My eyes burn from the lack of blinking. My breath catches in my throat. And that also burns. In a frenzied whisper, I tell him, "I'm afraid."

"Don't be." Zymarc comes back to me. "I'm right here with you, in a ShenawFayel. I am bound to protect you, Ravier. Protect your life. Keep you from The Kievas, or any other similar fate of death. I sense no danger ahead. Only an old statue, forged by a mighty hand. A mighty dragon, in fact. But that is all. If continuing forward would put either of us in jeopardy, we would simply come to a stop. The magic of ShenawFayel is stronger than the normal senses, for it knows the future. Can feel it."

"You're sure?"

He lets out an irritated sigh. "No one, in the history of ShenawFayels, has died while still in one. We are safe. Unless you know something of ShenawFayels that I don't?" He studies me a moment. Then he does that same mannerism my mother does, when irritated.

I can't stand it anymore. I ask him, "Where did you pick that up? That habit of swiping a finger across your brow?" I copy it, so he stops looking all confused.

Now expressionless, he stands up straighter. "I ... don't know. I suppose I've always done that. Quite forget that it even happens. Why do you ask? That's a very odd thing to ask, in a place like this."

Gripping my arm where the coldness touched me, I state, "It's something I do. Change the subject when I don't feel right, inside."

"Why don't you feel right, inside?"

"Look around us, Zymarc!" I shout, even gesture toward all the murals on the walls. "We're in the cathedral Deezalo built. It might as well be called The Vitiosus Cathedral. And now Soren's Statue is laughing from somewhere up ahead. All of it is horrifying! Yet, you tell me not to worry?

How can I *not* worry? Can ShenawFayels guard against every danger? Can they outwit the Books of Time?" I stop talking. I've run out of breath.

Zymarc rubs his neck. He glances up at the ceiling. "Well then, Ravier, if you're that alarmed by this place, I should tell you . . . don't look up all the way. You won't be liking what you see."

Exhaling a heavy, frustrated breath, I reply, "Thanks for that. Now, I must look."

Zymarc smirks. "Thought you might say something like that." He goes to lean against one of the pillars. He waits for me to look. And I do, but slowly.

Dozens of snippets of scenes stare down. Rather than the cloaked figure in black and gold in all of them, it is a Sorsryn in a white coat, trimmed with black. I recognize it from the painting in my father's study. It's Soren's coat. Soren is in all the scenes up there on the ceiling. His younger self, bright and happy, looks upon a vast landscape. Eight Arkivaras are off in the distance, towering above a much younger landscape than what I've seen of Paragon. There's one more of him as the younger Soren. He's with a sunset-red Von and ruby-colored dragon. The three appear to be conversing, completely at ease with one other.

I glance to Zymarc. He's pulled out a small book from one of his pockets and is reading.

"Shena, Fayel, and Soren?" I ask. "They all knew each other?"

Not glancing away from the pages, he says, "Yes, but keep looking."

So I do.

The scenes get darker in subject. Soren never started to look gradually different. Those two scenes of his younger self, he looked very much like me. Then he suddenly had the lighter skin, and appeared older, with an evil glint sunk into his gaze. Many series of scenes portray him being given bounties by various Withrasyn kings. None are Monel, however. One such bounty is worse than all the rest, for they paint a picture of him creating dissent amongst Greyvons and Rubidyns. He had help too. From the Geldryn. I recognize their armor as those brass-colored, jewel-studded devices of old. To me, those things are an abomination to magic.

Then comes the Battle of Queens. It shows Soren watching from a great distance away, as Shena and Fayel rip into each other. Fayel kept her beast form. But Shena did not. She wore garb of red, as red as her sunset-colored hair. She is mighty in the scene, wielding Winter's Vondaen. She cut into Fayel's neck, but not all the way. In the next scene, Shena had turned her back to the fallen Fayel, but Fayel had not yet died. Suddenly, the scene comes alive. It's as if I'm there. I hear the sounds of war. Clashing metal, roars of dragons, cries of wolves. I even sense the ground underneath my feet tremble. I go lean against a cathedral pillar to remain standing. I look up again, for I must. I must see the horrible end of the War of Ichors Von. And I do when Fayel thrusts a spike of one of her wings straight through Shena's midsection. I hear the flesh tearing; the short gasp of Shena dying; of Fayel exhaling her last breath. I even hear Soren weep. I feel what he feels. His heart ripping in two. It's as if watching Gemma and Skylin kill each other, or my friends Jed and Jaxson ending the other one's life. I cry out, and fall to the ground. It isn't the marble of the cathedral that I sense beneath my hands. Rather wet dirt. The scent of blood drifts up to make me sick.

"Tyler?" a male voice calls from afar.

A hand touches the back of my shoulder.

I'm drawn back to the cathedral. I gasp for breath, as all the horrible noise and odors vanish.

Someone's helping me stand up.

I blink away the few tears that have gathered in my eyes. Zymarc stands in front of me, gripping my shoulder. I wish it were Tadashi there, right now. Tadashi Galloway, with his wise, kind gaze, rather than Zymarc's unreadable one studying me.

I ask, after a time, "Does that happen to everyone who looks upon those scenes?"

Zymarc lets go of me. "No," he replies, taking a step back. "They react in a worse way. Most run out of here, in terror. For, you see, no one ever witnesses the same thing, there at the end. What did you see?"

"The end of the War of Ichors Von. The Battle of Queens."

"Aw, yes." Zymarc grins in a knowing way. "My point is proven. I've never witnessed that, here. Only ever read about it, in textbooks. One of the things I've witnessed has to do with your coat and someone wearing it. The scene never showed his face, never let me hear his voice either. But the figure had on that coat with its hood up, and had hold of those daggers you always carry with you. Well, always *did* carry with you. I replaced them with replicas before we left the General's House."

Zymarc turns on his heel and continues forward again.

Hurriedly, I take hold of the daggers on my belt. He's right. Though they look the same, I feel not their power available to me.

"You had no right!" I shout.

"Yes I did," he says, not pausing his stride at all. "You wished to see the Statue of Soren. I knew that's what you would want. There was no chance of being able to bring you here safely, while you had the coat and daggers with you. They are tucked away in the General's House, where only I can find them. They'll be returned to you, as soon as we get back for the night."

I catch up to Zymarc to tell him, "Those daggers can be summoned by me, at any time."

That's when Zymarc stops to look at me. "Well then, it seems I cannot take another step forward, until you've decided on what to do. What'll it be, Ravier? Will you trust the ShenawFayel, in her wisdom and intent to protect, or will you go with your young folly and apprehension, by summoning your daggers while in this place?"

Calming only slightly, I ask, "What did you see, that you'd be inclined to take those things from me?"

"An interaction between Soren and that figure who was wearing your coat, or a coat very much like it. Also, that figure had hold of your daggers. They were different, however. As great in size and might as the Blades of Neutrality: Enyxar and Aevimeis. Soren feared the mightier versions of your daggers. But he hated the one wielding them. His hate in that moment was only matched by Deezalo and, well"—he hesitates—"you, Ravier. Believe me, when I say, Fate and Soren are after us. I wasn't making a jest, earlier."

"I didn't think that you were. But why must we keep going? Can't we come back in the morning? Please. I can't take so much revelation. So much truth. It hurts! What if it was me you saw? Could it have been? Did you catch even one glimpse of his face?"

"I did not."

I start shivering. I don't like his answer. A hunger comes over me. One that nothing could ever fill. I can't put a name to the sort of ache it is within.

Zymarc contemplates for a moment. Then he says, "We'll come back in the morning."

I'm overcome with relief. More so, as Zymarc starts for the way back. When he pauses his confident stride forward, the door opens. He continues onward. I follow close behind. Also do I want to grab hold of his arm, just to keep from feeling so alone. I've never been this frightened of anything in my life. And I don't even know exactly what it is that has made me scared.

Even so, I find that I'm able to stand on my own, walk forward on my own. Once stepping off the last stair, and onto the black-stone pathway, I can finally take in a normal breath. We head back, not saying a single word to each other the rest of the way.

28

By a Vile Touch

Once back inside his room within the General's House, Zymarc takes off his coat. As he hangs it on a standing coat rack that's off to the right side of the room by the seating area, he says, "I'll give you back your things, soon. The coat and daggers, to be clear."

I wander in, still shaken by the recent visit to the cathedral. I ask the first thing that comes to mind. "Why do you need Awngeleik?"

Zymarc has barely left the seating area. He stops to consider me, consider my question.

"Is it for her heart? Do you need her heart for some kind of ritual? Did you plan on killing her? Do you plan that, even now?"

Rather than answer me, he asks his own question. "Did you know that Awngeleik had an older twin? Xiedyn." Zymarc unbuttons his shirt cuffs, to start rolling up his sleeves.

Shaking my head, I give my silent reply of *no*.

Zymarc's about to say something more when a few guards and Prince-Generals pass by the doorway, talking amongst each other. He motions that I close the door.

As soon as it's shut, he says, "Xiedyn was opposite in color to Awngeleik. All black, but with yellow eyes. Sylvadyn eyes. That Eekawsynd you met some weeks ago? He was a foundation sire, the Sylvadyn Patriarch, to the twin Equidyns. He was much closer in relation to Ryco of Paragon

413

than the twins were. I do believe he was Ryco's grandfather, possibly his great-grandfather."

"How did you survive a face-off with Rentwar?" I inquire, as I wander about the room, discreetly glancing around for where Zymarc could have hidden my things. There's a few cupboards by the desks where they could be. Also could be in one of the three wardrobes.

"You don't care that Awngeleik and your Ryco'Eldeis are distant cousins?"

"Were," I correct him. "Ryco's gone, remember? Or did you forget? I could never forget."

Sighing, Zymarc ambles toward one of the desks. He sits down. He begins paging through a thick stack of wrinkled papers. After some silence passes, he asks, "How did he die?"

I stop my wander about the room. "You have no right to ask me that."

Zymarc doesn't look up. Simply does he . . . nod? I wonder, *Why a nod? Does he agree with me?*

I try again, stating, "You have no right to know how he died."

Another nod!

I stride toward the congregated desks, to stand opposite of where Zymarc sits, still calmly leafing through the stack. I shove some book piles out of the way, and a few volumes fall to the floor. My palms press against the oiled-wood surface, as I lean forward for a closer view of Zymarc to study him, to compare him to my mother; I can't decide. The anger builds. My palms get sweaty. I shout at Zymarc, "How are you still alive, King Zymarc? Are you going to tell me that you killed King Rentwar? The idea seems impossible."

He finds what he was looking for. He slips three horribly stained, creased pages out from the stack, setting the rest aside. He looks to me at last, though, not with a look I understand. "I am a Vitiosyn, Tyler. No," he corrects himself. "Rather, I am king over *all* Vitiosyns. I serve them as much as they serve me. It is a symbiotic relationship. Neither of us have a choice about it, really. Not any longer. We are slaves to each other. I give them protection, most complete; they, in turn, do my bidding. Whatever it is at the time. They also supply me with enough magic that, even from afar, I can never die by a normal means. Not by the blade. Not by typical magic. Not by near everything."

I remark, "My daggers could, couldn't they?"

Zymarc does that swipe across his brow again, using his pinky finger.

My mouth twitches. I can't help but be unnerved by how much he and my mother are starting to look alike, the longer I'm around this Vitiosyn.

At last, he answers with: "I don't know for certain. LanSoren, years ago, wielded them against me during a duel. He was seventeen or eighteen, I do believe. The wounds they inflict are hard to heal. That much I know. But no one's ever wielded them against me with the intent to kill. Until you, that day in the library. Soren preferred using magic and the Bow of Three Queens against me. Hooks, chains, axes, vines also, but never those daggers. Or, rather, the daggers when they were still great in size. In regards to the King Rubidyn, well . . . Rentwar underestimated me. He let me fall to the forest floor, while thinking, 'Surely, he must be dead.'"

There's a knock at the door.

Zymarc lets out a sound of impatience. "Come in," he says, "state your business, then *go* away."

I glance over my shoulder, as Caleiso timidly enters the room.

She closes the door behind her. "It is late, my Lord-King Zymarc," she says quietly, bowing her head. "May I show Tyler to his room, fit the clothes to him as well, before turning in for the night?" She braves a glimpse in his direction.

"Not before you do something else for me." Zymarc stands up. As he goes to approach Caleiso, he sets the three wrinkled papers on the spot of desk I've cleared of books. Then he continues on, talking to her.

As I look down at the papers, I overheat—getting all worked up. They're pages from *The Dark Prince* storybook. The same three used in Vondurheil, to restrain Zymarc's hands by first conforming the wet papers to his fists and then freezing those papers over.

They read: *But he didn't have any wings. He didn't have anyone with him who had wings, either. He was all alone, searching for the way home; You see, he had lost his way. Chased out of the circle of six pillars. Though he knew not by what. He couldn't remember. All he remembered was that the circle was of color. Of hope. The last time he had been happy, together with those he loved. And now? He couldn't even remember their faces. The faces of the ones he loved.*

Behind me, Caleiso and Zymarc still converse. I've not taken in any of what they've said. I just keep staring down at the pages, the words, the illustrations, wondering, *Does Zymarc know what to do with these? In fact, with that whole book?*

"You want me to what!" Caleiso shouts.

I whirl around.

Caleiso's face has gone pink with rage. Her crimson-red eyes literally flash like a slow strobe light.

"It will only be for a few hours," says Zymarc. "I have the document right here." He pulls a folded, wax-sealed paper out from an inner coat pocket. He hands it to her.

She grudgingly takes it, tears the seal away. Practically stomping over to me, she reads whatever the document says.

As she's stewing over that, Zymarc rummages around in his desk drawers. He takes out a black, spindly mask—the same kind of mask that has covered the lower portion of his face on other occasions. Not even putting it on all the way, he speaks into it: "Azabahk, you are needed in my chambers to sign a document regarding Caleiso, Ravier, and myself. Hobble up here straightaway." He pulls the mask away, then drops it back in the drawer. It clatters against other metal things contained there. The drawer slides shut. He knocks on the desktop a few times, much in the way I do after closing the drawers of my dresser, yet he doesn't say anything. No *thirteen done*. He just eyes me curiously. I look away. Even walk around Caleiso to peer over her shoulder, spy whatever the document says. I don't expect it to be written in English, yet it is.

Before I catch the exact wording, Caleiso yanks it to the side, out of my view.

"You don't need to read this." She focuses on Zymarc. "Because I won't be signing it. Won't agree to it."

"Come, come, Caleiso." Zymarc's voice drops an octave. "I have errands to run, and I can't be taking Ravier with me, where I mean to go. It would put him in undue danger."

"And what of you?" Caleiso shrieks. "Would you be putting yourself in undue danger?" She furiously folds the document back up.

"Consider it tit-for-tat." Zymarc's eyes darken over to near black. "You disobeyed me, when you set yourself up in Dysarda, three years ago. Months had passed, by the time I knew where you had gone off to. In fact, LanSoren was the one to mention it to me in passing. It was far too late to retrieve you, without being noticed. So Belzara convinced me to let you stay, until we could safely extract you from there without starting a war with the Tamers. I, thinking that she loved you as a mother would her own child, allowed myself to be persuaded. Convinced myself that it would be a good learning experience for you. Little did I know then, war with the Tamers was inevitable."

Caleiso looks down in shame. The strobe effect of her eyes subsides. Slowly, she offers me the document, and I accept it.

Zymarc inquires, "So, was it a good learning experience? You never told me, and I've not thought to ask till now."

"It depends on your definition of a 'good learning experience,'" she replies, still staring at the floor.

I unfold the document. The title at the top reads: Contract of Transference — provisional agreement.

"If," says Zymarc, "the Tamers were the enemies at our gates, come tomorrow, would you know how to defeat them?"

Does he mean to transfer something to me or her? I wonder, as I glance at Caleiso.

She lifts her head, before answering, "By that definition, yes, it was a good time of learning. A time I'll not ever be forgetting."

I go back to reading the document. Essentially, it's transferring the ShenawFayel agreement between Zymarc and me, to me and Caleiso for a time of no more than three hours. There must be one witness. And that witness, Azabahk, can be heard, hobbling up some stairs, then making his way for the door to the room we're in. He doesn't even knock. He just comes in, looking frazzled, a wild sort of tiredness about him. Rumpled clothes too.

Once the door is shut, Azabahk has eyes only for Zymarc. "Whatcha mean by *document* between the three of you? Don't tell me you're going to try that musing of mine I had earlier, at the dinner table, to do with ShenawFayels." Azabahk slightly leans on his cane for support.

"That's exactly what I intend to do," replies Zymarc. "I've already written up the magically binding contract. Look it over. Make amendments to it, if you want. Then bear witness to the three of us signing it."

I take a few steps forward. "What will I be signing, exactly? Are you handing over your position in the ShenawFayel to Caleiso? I don't see how that could work." I refold the document and hold it out for Azabahk to take, which he does.

Zymarc clarifies, "You'd not be in a direct ShenawFayel with Caleiso. Rather, she would be bound to protect you, as if she is me. You wouldn't need to protect her, per se. Nor could you do any true harm to her, however. And, once I'm far enough away, you won't feel the need to come to my aid, should I put myself in danger."

I ask Zymarc, "How can you be sure of that?"

"Because there has been an instance of two in ShenawFayel being taken captive by a common enemy. Through an unfortunate turn of events, they were separated. One got battered around a bit, while the other had no inclination of it happening. I believe if they hadn't been in ShenawFayel, the battered one would have perished."

Clicking my tongue, I then pose the question: "I don't suppose you're going to tell me what this important errand is?"

Zymarc adjusts his rolled-up sleeves. "You suppose correct, Ravier. Won't you sign the document? Afterward, you are free to go sleep for the whole three hours, if you wish. More hours, if you need them."

Azabahk glances up from reading the document. "This be fine wording, King Zymarc. No loopholes that the ShenawFayel should be able to find.

Therefore, nothing she can do to stop this contract from working. At least, that is my speculation, given all that I have come to learn during my lifetimes."

Caleiso smirks. "You mean, what you recall of them, don't you?"

Azabahk smirks back, and he is far more intimidating with that look of Deathasyn-turned-Vitiosyn about him.

Zymarc gestures at Caleiso, then to a cleared-off desk. "Sign it, so I can be on my way."

She goes to take the document from Azabahk.

But he withholds it. "You don't have to agree to this, if you don't want to, Callie. Remember that."

"You're wrong, Awza," she says. "I've no wish to become like Belzara, in our king's eyes."

The wildness leaves Azabahk's appearance. He lets go of the paper.

Caleiso lays the paper down on the cleared-off desk, and is first to pen her signature.

Zymarc quickly signs his too. He offers me his quill. I hesitate to accept it.

I ask, "Can't you take me with, on this errand?"

"It's far too dangerous. I can't keep an eye on you the entire time. It's better that you stay here, under Caleiso's watch. Perhaps you can even work on that matter I pointed out to you, earlier."

In div, he clarifies, *You know what I mean. That hatred thing. It controls you, at least half of the time. So learn to control it. You've been fortunate, in how things have worked in your favor. But fate always grows impatient with sloppiness.*

I clench my jaw. I don't Mensa-div back. Instead, I rummage around in my own things for my father's quill. I pull that quill from one of my three supply pouches. I stride forward, to sign the document, using my full name—Tyler Malik Ravier: The Onyx Prince.

Zymarc taps his foot impatiently.

As I tuck the quill away, I tell Zymarc, "Don't be forgetting who I am, Vitiosyn. If this is some underhanded scheme, you *will* regret it."

He stops tapping his foot. "No scheme this time. Just need to leave the city for a short while. Three hours is plenty of time."

Azabahk adds his signature.

Zymarc sighs in happiness. "Keep that with you, Awza. I can feel it working already. No longer do I worry every second for the well-being of the Onyx Prince. Rest well, Ravier." Zymarc strides for the door. He pauses, to ask me, "How's it working for you, Ravier?"

"I feel no different," I reply, sounding bored.

"Even toward Caleiso?" he pries. "No difference, there?"

I glance at her. My mouth twitches. I suddenly don't hate the sight of her face so much.

I Mensa-div to Zymarc, right as he's yanking the door open, *"You just said you weren't scheming!"*

"Aye! That's still true. I wasn't scheming to dampen your hatred of her. I simply hypothesized that it could be a side effect. Sweet dreams, Tyler." He ends his div, as he strides out.

I rush for the door, but he shuts it in my face. I yank it back open. The hatred for him returns, disguised as annoyance. I shout after him, "I'm not going to sleep, Zymarc, while you're off on some errand!"

"If you say so, Ravier," he calls back, not turning to face me. He goes forward, and fades out of sight. Presumably, he has used another distortion spell to exit the General's House. Those ripples of Blue Magic in the air, which resemble heat waves hovering over the ground, are now visible. They gradually fade.

I retreat inside the room and slam the door.

Azabahk lets out a quick, giggling cackle. "Apologies for the laugh," he says. "Can't help it. You remind me of him."

"My father, you mean?"

"Not LanSoren, no." Azabahk shifts his weight. He begins to hobble toward the door, his cane thumping along with each step of his. "Zymarc, in his younger days. Back at the beginning. Before my most recent ReNovamen was scheduled. I remember some things from that time. How Zymarc was very . . . spontaneous. Nowhere near as calculated as he is these days. Good luck resisting his Call of Vitiosus, come morning. He's been wearing you down this entire time. And *this*." He looks from Caleiso back to me. "Is one more way for him to erode your defenses. He knows with near certainty that you can survive the call. He's simply ensuring you can't resist it. Can't say no to Vitiosus."

"I will not succumb to it, Prince-General. You live in a fantasy, if you think I will say *yes* to Vitiosus. It's never going to happen."

"We shall see." Azabahk's grin grates on my nerves more than usual.

I envision clawing his face a bit, leaving a scar or two behind. Not that he needs more. He already has lots of tiny scars on his face. Maybe one large, diagonal scar across his forehead would look nice.

Azabahk cackles again. As he makes his exit, he says, "Sleep tight, Ravier. Don't let the little mice bite."

With that, the door shuts.

"Mice?" I cringe, even brave a glance at Caleiso.

She rolls her eyes. "There are only some on the first floor. Occasionally, they make their way up here. But, on the third—where you'll be sleeping for the night—there's not a chance of them being up there. Shall we go? Fit your clothes to you and such?"

Reluctantly, I nod. Then I recall that Zymarc never gave me back my coat and daggers. I go grab the three pages of the storybook, and stuff them into my pouches.

"What are you doing?" Caleiso queries sharply.

"He was giving these to me, right as you came in."

"A likely story." She puts a hand on her hip. "I shall ask him, when he gets back."

"You do that," I reply, deciding that I shall later sneak back here. Sometime after I've ditched her somewhere, and made my escape.

We exit the room.

Caleiso turns back to face the door, as she removes a key from a hidden pocket of her coat. I don't see exactly where the hidden pocket seam is. At any rate, she locks the door; and I think, *A lock isn't going to stop me. Didn't before, at the Galloway mansion. Not going to now.*

I grin inside, recalling that night of dodging Tadashi, as he slaughtered ballistic dummies with a new Katana blade. Also did I evade his security guys: Kane and Haru. Then the cat, Minksy, who snagged hold of that cloak I used to stay hidden. The same one used for concealing Awngeleik, when Talok and Ryco visited on the night of my fourteenth birthday.

Already, I'm scheming ways to find that key on Caleiso's person. As she leads the way to the third floor, and my temporary quarters, that scheme deepens to something quite underhanded. I recollect Azabahk's comment of how I'm like Zymarc, when he was younger. That brings a pause in my scheming, but only briefly, for I wonder, *What things hidden in that room could I find, when no one else is in there? I'll stop looking right away, if I find what belongs to me right away. But . . . if I don't find them right away, well, I might as well learn all I can of the King Vitiosyn. Perhaps I'll learn what all the fuss over Awngeleik is about too.*

* * *

Sometime later, Caleiso and I have been in my room for at least twenty minutes. I'm growing tired. The dark, warm colors of the room, with that added yellow-colored light emitting from glass sconces on the walls, don't help a bit either. It's a plain room. In it are only six pieces of furniture: bed, dresser, couch, table near that couch, and a small desk with a chair.

I stand on a small, wooden platform that's only inches in height. Caleiso started the adjustments to my new clothes as soon as we entered the room, and I had changed into them behind a privacy wall, which I could barely see over the top of.

After a time, I end the silence. "I thought this would only take minutes."

"It would have," she says, while fastening some pins in the sleeves, "if you didn't squirm so much, standing in place."

Some more minutes pass. I glance down at the pins fastened in the fabric. It looks like a mess of confusion to me.

"There!" she announces. "Last one." She straightens to her full height.

Stretches her back too, before massaging the lower portion of it.

The underhanded scheme begins. I see the opportunity. *But will she be suspicious?* I wonder.

I carefully shrug off my coat and hand it to her. "Where do you want the rest?"

"Go change into those robes I placed for you on the bed," she says. "They're vastly more comfortable for sleeping in. What you have on, put atop the privacy wall. These adjustments shouldn't take me more than an hour. They're very slight adjustments. Then we'll have passed half the time Zymarc will be gone."

As I stride for the privacy section, I ask, "Any idea where he's gone off to for his *errand?*"

She takes to sitting on the couch. She lays the coat on the table, and begins her work with a needle and thread. "I've a few ideas, yes. And he's right. Better that you stayed here."

I've stripped off everything. Folding it nicely, I set it atop the wall. Then I realize I forgot to grab the robes off the bed. There's no hope of sneaking over there, without being fully exposed to Caleiso.

So I add it into my scheme. "Callie," I call to her, using the calmest tone I can manage. I stand on tiptoe to place my arms on top of the wall. Even do I rest my chin atop the cold marble. I do my best to become her temptation.

"What, Ravier?"

I grin wickedly, when she looks over at me and blushes. She goes back to stitching.

"I forgot to grab the robes. Would you . . . ?" I trail off, looking as innocent as possible. I give her my look of pleading. And I know exactly how that look appears, for I've practiced that one to perfection in front of the mirror.

When she looks at me again, her breaths quicken. She jolts off the couch. Hurriedly gets the robes for me, whilst her movements are stiff and irritable. She throws the large garment at my grinning face.

I say, "Thank you," to patronize her.

She says, "Wel-come!" mimicking Soren's singsong voice. She goes back to her task.

After I've secured the long, black robes in place, keeping it closed with the buttons and leather ties, I exit the privacy section. I saunter over to join Caleiso on the couch.

She marks the fabric with a triangle of white chalk, then removes pins. She stitches along those marked seams. She repeats this with each pinned section.

After some silence, when I see that she's almost finished with the coat, I comment, "I heard your thoughts earlier."

Her frantic task of stitching slows way down.

I continue, saying, "And, I wondered . . . why do you wish that I was a Deathasyn?"

Suddenly distracted, she stabs the needle into one of her fingers. The side of her index finger. She gasps in pain, pries the needle out. Sucks the side of her finger. It's healed when she pulls it away from her mouth and rubs her thumb across the tiny wound. She shoves the coat away, pushing it to the opposite side of the table.

I add in, "Any particular reason you'd rather not be on opposing sides?"

"Vards!" she shouts, before gawking at me. "How much did you hear?"

I reposition myself on the couch, to better face her. All innocent-like, I ask, "Do you really think I'm good with magic?" Pausing, I feel a tinge of guilt for the next part. I go through with it anyway. "And that I . . . look good? I never thought I looked all that attractive."

She quickly glances to my lips. She licks her own. Then she stares at me wide-eyed. She's obviously fighting some kind of urge. I just make it all the harder for her, really sticking the knife in. By the end, I'll twist that figurative knife, and steal that key from Caleiso. Go explore Zymarc's quarters, unhindered. I think, *I'll even bite into her neck, if I must.*

I lean in closer. I make sure she spots my glance at her mouth. Then I ask her, in the most sensual voice I can muster, "What did you want to ask me, Callie?"

She doesn't answer. Her breaths get quicker, still. I hear her heart beating. It's faster than her breathing.

I fake the anticipation, softening my gaze on her face. Forcing myself to match the appearance of nervousness—squirming in place, sporadic breaths, that sort of thing.

"Ravier," she starts, but she can't finish. She instead leans in to kiss me. Immediately, she explores my mouth with her tongue. Slowly, at first.

Remarkably, it's not as horrible as I thought it would feel, kissing her, using her, running my hands along her body's curves. I start with where I think the key might be hidden. The sides of her coat, the front portion by her abdomen—it's in neither of those places. I realize it might be easier if her coat were off, and I later searched it when she isn't looking. So I return her kisses, and pretend to enjoy them. I do all I can with a decent conscience to get her worked up. Overheated to the point that she'll be taking the coat off of her own accord. I unbutton the front of it, to speed the process along. Then I run my hands to her back. I massage the lower part. She grows wild, clawing her fingertips into my shoulders, then my neck, yet she doesn't draw blood. I imagine that's because of the document she signed. Oh the irony that she can't hurt me.

A slight grin touches my lips, as I pull away to catch my breath. Though I don't truly enjoy kissing her, I still lose my breath as if I *do* enjoy it.

Caleiso studies my expression, while she catches her breath as well. Before I know it, she has climbed onto my lap. She straddles my hips, pushes me back against the couch. I find that this position is a little harder not to enjoy. I try to think of a way to distract my body, the instinct, from how it wants to react. Her neck is looking all the more tempting. I wonder what it would feel like to bite into her, taste her blood for real. I pull her closer, and start kissing her neck, nibbling a little. Then biting.

She lets out a quick moan. Then she says, "Wait, wait! I don't want blood on this." She pulls back to take her coat off at once. She throws it aside.

I grin in success.

She leans closer once more. Openly, she offers her bare neck to me. I restart, biting that skin harder and harder. I grip around her small waist.

She whispers, "You have to want to taste blood, Ravier. Or your teeth won't be working the way you want them to. Your Withrasyn genes are buried deep. Therefore, they will need a little coaxing from you, to—"

Suddenly, as she's talking to me, I focus on my teeth, willing them to grow sharp. Pain starts throbbing in my mouth. My front teeth hurt as if I've just bitten into an ice cube right after downing some hot cocoa. It's a quick, sharp pain that brings forth a grimace. But I can feel that my canine teeth have, indeed, grown longer, sharper. I gently bite into her neck, and she gasps in pleasure. Then she holds her breath. Her legs tighten. She's crushing me. I'm grateful that it's just my hips she's squeezing with her legs rather than her hands around my neck to choke me. She buries her hands in my hair. Claws her way along my scalp. It tingles. But, again, she doesn't draw blood.

Meanwhile, her blood has halfway filled my mouth. No longer metallic in taste, it has a rich tartness to it. Almost like some kind of rich berry dessert. A lot of it runs down, and soaks into her shirt. I'm sure that my robes are getting soaked with blood too. At least it won't show on the dark fabric. I start to pull away.

"Careful," Caleiso whispers, grabbing a fistful of my hair to keep my head from moving easily. "Or you'll tear the skin too much, and it will leave a scar. And don't you dare swallow that blood."

Gently, I open my mouth wider. My teeth release their hold. The blood runs out of my mouth, makes a mess of me and her. Her neck still bleeds too. She seems all right, though. Better than all right. In fact, quite happy. So am I, as I laugh a little. She smiles. Then she kisses me, not caring how messy it is. That's when my body betrays how I want to feel, which is to feel nothing. Instead, tingles race through me.

I think to myself, *I need a distraction. But what?* I reposition to shove Caleiso down on her back. She lies down, lets me lay on top of her. She pulls me down for a kiss. But I lift myself up. On cue, my stomach growls. It is my rescuer. For once.

Caleiso raises an eyebrow. "Want me to get us some food?"

Desperately, I nod. "Yes. I'm starving."

"Wait here, then. I shouldn't be long."

I finish sitting up all the way. I'm back to being upright on the couch.

She slides off the cushion of it, and gathers her footing. As she strides for the door, she asks, "What are you in the mood for?"

"Is there more Dragon's Tail?"

"Not unless I harvest one. Which I could, if you want."

"Just bring me whatever's available. Whatever you think I'll like."

"Sure thing," she says, with a spark in her gaze.

She leaves.

The pleasantries I've been faking fall away to be replaced by guilt over what I've done. Regardless, I scramble to pick up her coat. I search and search its pockets, its seams. I even shake it, listening for a clinking key. Nothing!

I groan out the words: "All that? For *nothing!*" I lay her coat on the table next to my unfinished one.

Using a spell of water, I clean myself up, while in the privacy quarter. Even do I clear the robes of the blood that got on them, before putting them on again.

My front teeth slowly stop hurting. They return to the way they were. Caleiso isn't back by then, so I go rest on the bed, and wonder how I will get into Zymarc's room, before he makes it back.

Not wanting to, and most certainly not intending to, I start nodding off. Before I know it, I'm fast asleep.

* * *

A draft swirls about the room. It's pitch-black, until my eyes adjust. The sconces have gone out. Someone thrusts the door open, but closes it quietly. Soft footsteps pad toward my bed. I nearly shout, as someone climbs onto the bed with me and shakes me to full awareness. I can't spot who it is in this darkness.

"Shh!" Caleiso shushes me. "Quick, get under the covers." She frantically tries to help me with the task.

But I lie there, clenching the front of my robes, saying, "Absolutely not! Look, that thing that happened earlier, well, you shouldn't let it go to your head. I don't want you that way."

"I don't care about that, Ravier!" she says in an angry, hissing voice. "Deathasyns have slipped past the Prince-Generals and various patrol squadrons. They heard about the Onyx Prince being here in Vaydell. They've found out why you are here. They only just learned which building you've been put up in. I don't know if they mean to hurt you or me or Zymarc. But you must do as I say. You must pretend I've bedded you. Claimed you. Please! They're coming. They're on the stairs now. We just need to buy time, topics of conversation, until my letter reaches Azabahk or one of the others."

"Surely you can take on a few Deathasyns?" I remark.

"A few? Sure." She finishes getting the bed covers over the both of us. "But these are riotous Deathasyns, driven mad with hatred for Zymarc. Dozens of them. Dozens outside. About a dozen on the stairs. If they think I've claimed you, it may give them pause in whatever thing they were planning. To be sure, though, they mean to commit violent acts."

She crowds closer. Even undoes the front of my robe, and touches her hand to my bare chest. I'm overwhelmed, suddenly very scared. I break into a cold sweat. I hear them now, talking and laughing in hushed tones within the hallway. The door creeps open, letting in a sliver of light.

"Where be this Onyx Prince we hear of, Caleiso?" queries a deep, masculine voice.

I lie on my side, inching my left hand to where Caleiso has her hand pressed against my chest. I interlace my fingers with hers. She starts kissing the back of my neck. In between kisses, she says, "He's right here. Leave us. We are occupied with things . . . things you've no business witnessing, Voldrake. Leave." She growls that last word.

This Voldrake laughs low. The sconces light up, but not all the way. Rather, they light with a cold, bluish light. "Perhaps," he says, "we've no business watching. But I cannot, will not, believe that Zymarc would allow it. You are as a daughter to him. And you are young. So go on,

Caleiso. Show us the things we've no business witnessing."

Half a dozen or so enter the room, along with this broad-shouldered Deathasyn rioter. Glimpsing them over my shoulder, I see all are armed with many weapons that sport the stains of war—much tarnish and dried blood. Some of the blood is fresh, however. They take to sitting on the couch, the floor. Two climb the privacy wall, and sit there to stare at us hungrily. Those two shove my folded clothes to the floor.

Voldrake takes a seat at the foot of the bed. He reaches for where Caleiso's feet are beneath the covers. She pulls them out of his reach, recoiling at his touch.

He says, "I call your bluff, little girl. Get out of that bed. Leave this room. We want some alone time with the Onyx Prince." He studies me intently. "There's much we are to discuss. And if we like not his answers, well . . . We'll make this a night he'll never forget."

I roll over to face Caleiso. If, for no other reason than for a distraction or self-preservation, I start to tenderly kiss her face. I let her feel along my chest. Then I get an idea of summoning my daggers. Rather, merely one; the sleeping-dagger. It prefers night, and it's quite dark outside.

"Ack!" says one of the accompanying Deathasyns. "They are little fakers. They've not been together. Nor do they intend for it. We are not interrupting any sort of sacred moment; most certainly no sacred union is underway either. Clearly do they wish to delay us, let us be caught by a patrol. They are distracting us, letting us think that Zymarc has actually procured a match for the fair Princess of Vitiosyns."

I stop kissing Caleiso.

Voldrake stands up. He comes around to my side of the bed. He bends down to rest a hand on my arm, and I feel defiled. His intentions bleed out with that touch of his. The blue light reveals cruelty in his expression. He means to violate me. So when he sits at my bedside, and starts inching his way to touch my face and then digs his fingers painfully into my skin, I panic.

I hold my left hand out, and shout for my dagger, "NeiSator!" to come.

A wind bursts into the room. The sconces shatter. That sleeping-dagger slips into my grasp. I jolt upright. Without thinking, I plunge its tip into Voldrake's chest. He lets out a sharp breath, as if being punched unexpectedly. Only ragged breaths come from him. The others screech and growl and burst into action. Caleiso leaps off of the bed. I can't see her anymore.

I yank the dagger out. Voldrake's body collapses on my legs, crushing me. A hot liquid soaks through the bedding. His blood. Struggling, I at last free myself to crawl off the bed, barefoot. I rush for the door, groping around in the dark. I scream, when stepping on pieces of the broken sconces. Yet I manage to quiet myself enough not to be easily heard after that. I keep going, limping along.

There are shouts, fighting, and blasts of magic. The spells illuminate the path. I make it to the door, and rush out, thinking that Caleiso can handle herself. I run for the stairs, galloping down them, yet with great agony. The shards of sconces embedded in my feet make each step forward excruciating. Along the way, I fasten my robes as tightly closed as they will allow for. I go to Zymarc's room, hoping that there are guards standing there. There are. As I get closer, I realize that those guards are dead. Their hands and shoulders have been pierced by long nails, fastening them to the walls so they appear to be standing watch, at first glance. But their throats are slit open, and their eyes are blank. I gag at the sight. Yet my fear of what's behind quickly overcomes the sick feeling from what's presented directly before me.

The Deathasyn rioters Caleiso said were outside are rushing up the stairs. They're on the second floor, as one comes down from the third level. I go cower by one of the dead Vitiosyn guards. I make myself look as small as possible, pulling the fabric of the Vitiosyn's cloak around me. I draw my black robes tight to my form, to be as hidden as possible. I hold my breath, my grip tight on NeiSator.

Quickly do I realize, I've left bloody footprints that lead straight to where I'm hiding. Through my panic, I focus on the footprints nearest to the rioters. I will the liquid to draw together. Gradually, it does. I envision it being pushed to where the walls meet with the floor. The line of blood is hardly noticeable, stuck there in those crevices opposite of each other. As the Deathasyns converse, I work on hiding the rest of my tracks that way. I suddenly have the thought that this is perhaps what was done at Mirror Lake, when something was hunting Awngeleik. Maybe the evidence is still there, hidden away under rocks; or in the cracks of tree bark; or feathers, disguised as leaves high up in a tree, out of normal view. If I ever make it home, I must have a second look around.

"Where did that Onyx Prince go?" asks one of the rioters, who's come in from outside.

Caleiso is dragged down the flight of stairs, to the second floor, kicking and screaming. A total of three that were in my room have made it out alive.

"Where are the others?"

"Gone. This one got a few. That little prince took Voldrake, though. Took him with the special dagger."

"Soren's dagger? That must mean the other is close by. They are here in Vaydell? What luck."

A different rioter with a scratchy voice says, "It shall be me, who gives the statue the daggers. And that coat. Got to find that coat."

Another says, "Zymarc would keep it close to himself."

"Well," says Scratchy Voice, "where else would he keep it, besides on his person or on the Onyx Prince?"

"His quarters, my liege," says a deep voice. "This way."

Trying to settle the trembling that's come over me, I crowd closer to the dead Vitiosyn's body. I'm thankful for their large size, or there'd be no hope of hiding beside him. No hope of escaping notice, as the Deathasyns approach where I am. So, too, does a scraggly, dirty rat approach. It makes its way for the dead guards. Rather than picking one of them to torment, that rat picks me. Crawls over the top of my feet. Its pointed claws bring pain to that sensitive skin. I want to scream, as it starts climbing my bare legs. I clench my fists, press my lips tight together.

Caleiso spews, "You shall regret this."

"Shut up, girl. Not a one asked you." The Deathasyn who has her by the arm, shakes her.

She glimpses me, as I peer out from behind the dead Vitiosyn's cloak. She grows silent. Yet she keeps resisting her captor. Keeps their focus off me.

The rat has made it up to my knee. It's so hard to hold still, hard to keep quiet. Sweat runs down my back. I hope these Deathasyns won't smell me. That their senses aren't as good as I think they are.

A Deathasyn starts working on the lock to Zymarc's quarters.

One of them finally demands, "You stop this, girl, or else I'll be giving you something to fight and scream about."

Sounds come from inside Zymarc's quarters. I hope, for a brief second, that Zymarc's in there. That he's returned. Then again? I'm terrified that they may have isolated the General's House to have a better chance of killing Zymarc, which in turn would mean the end of me, for I'm in ShenawFayel with him. Bound to protect him, even if unto death. Yes, I very much regret this deal I've struck with a king, who's gone off on some errand. Must be an Onyx thing. To always stay busy with secret errands.

I wonder, *How are Caleiso and I going to escape this?*

The rat climbs up my thigh. I inch my left hand into position so that the varmint must crawl onto my hand. He starts to, and it hurts when he slips a bit, and claws me. He keeps climbing.

A fleeting thought—*I hope I don't catch a disease from this thing*—sweeps over me.

Then a familiar sound wanders closer. Not the footsteps of Deathasyns. Indeed, it is not a Sorsryn descendant at all. Rather, a four-legged thing that's a quiet walker. A wolf sort of thing. I feel his aura getting closer. Droediin, Eighth son of Merlynite. He growls low.

The pain in my cut-up feet returns, throbs, in fact. My left hand throbs also, where the rat has clawed me.

The Deathasyns grow nervous. One pivots his attention to look upon the approaching beast.

I glance at Caleiso. She gives me a look of understanding. We need to run. She knows it; I know it. She quickly looks to her right. I recall there being a window at the end of the hall.

"Don't mind us," says Scratchy Voice to Droediin. "We are merely searching for artifacts that don't belong to the King of Vitiosus. We'll find them, and be on our way, little dog."

In a flash, I grab hold of the rat, and its squeal is shrill. I toss the varmint to Droediin, as he's passing by where I'm standing, hidden. He snatches that squealing varmint out of the air, and crunches down. He swallows it, as he takes on the appearance of that metal beast. His eyes become like red-hot coal. I can't run yet. Too many congregated Deathasyns could grab hold of me, use me for Von bait.

I wait for Droediin to ambush the one who dared to call him *little dog*, for I know he will. When he does, that one squeals in terror, far louder than the squealing rat. Droediin drags him around like a plaything, and he is especially vicious about it. The Deathasyns begin attacking the Von.

That'll be their last mistake, I muse.

Droediin turns his attention to them, and roars that earsplitting, alpha-Von sound. Caleiso rushes to grab me, pulls me toward the window. We run full speed toward the shut window. She's the one to leap, and break through it. I follow, fully knowing that if I don't jump, death waits for me in the General's House.

Even so, I cry out as I fall. But then I land on something soft. A black, winged EquiNein. He glides down. Landing, he trots about the area. Many Vitiosyns are swarming the courtyard. They attack any remaining rioters Droediin let live. Many have been slaughtered by the turned Greyvon. It's a rather horrific sight. Yet welcomed, for Caleiso and I would be dead if Droediin had not been here. I glance back at the window where Caleiso and I made our escape; Droediin, in human form, stares out into the night. He's covered in blood, yet he seems calm—too calm—as if he's already dead inside. Sickness crawls into the pit of my stomach.

"Callie," I ask, as I rest my forehead against her shoulder, "please take us away from the city for a while. I beg you. I cannot bear being here."

"Zebulon," she says, "you heard the Onyx Prince. Make for a peaceful place. Take us to the Pools of Vosh-Perida. I am certain the Vardiyas will value meeting the Onyx Prince."

Zebulon starts galloping, finding his stride.

Something comes whizzing from behind.

Caleiso is quick to snatch an arrow out of the air. Her speed startles me, until I recognize those distortion ripples of Blue Magic lingering in the air. She slowed time enough to catch the arrow.

"A gift from Droediin to you, Ravier," she says, as Zebulon takes off, flying upward.

I grab hold of the arrow. Something attached to it glimmers in the faint light that surrounds us. I unwind the leather cording, which secures the item in place, then let that fall away to the ground that's quickly fading as we ascend higher up into the night sky. Left behind is a small, mirror-like disk.

Why does this look familiar? I wonder, turning the disk over in my hand repeatedly.

It dawns on me. It's the mirror disk Jasper stuck in my coat pocket, back when I met him and Paydinn. Droediin stole it, when I was in Vondurheil the first time.

Why is he giving this back? I can't help but think, *What purpose does this item have, which it didn't before, that Droediin would be returning it now?*

I contemplate what it could be, but I'm much too tired. Much too worried over all the things that have transpired this day. Caleiso gives me a tonic for my feet, and they're able to heal during the ride atop Zebulon. I just let my mind rest for the remaining trip to the Pools of Vosh-Perida. I very much hope that the present-and-living Aysivak will be there. That he will have some words of guidance for me the way the future one did, for I am in much need of knowing what to do, and how to resist the Call of Vitiosus. The outcome worries me more, the less time I have before the ShenawFayel is over.

29

The Telling of Fate

As soon as Zebulon has landed and come to a complete stop among a maze of beautiful trees—trees that are no more than thirty feet tall—I leap down from his back. Striding away, I wander among the Pools of Vosh-Perida. They are like reflecting mirrors, perfectly still. I think they are frozen over with a thin sheet of ice, until a white, glittery leaf falls from one of the dark-metal trees to land in a nearby pool, and create ripples. Quickly, the water goes still.

I continue on, in quietness. Plants and shrubs glow with cool, calming colors likened to winter. The forest sounds as if it's wintertime too, any sound dampened by snow. Yet there isn't any snow. Only fallen leaves and a squashy, black material blanket the ground. No grass.

Caleiso calls out, "Tyler, wait!" She rushes to catch up.

Zebulon trots along with her. His hooves striking the ground hardly make a sound, and the red glow of his eyes chills me, makes me shiver.

Caleiso's about to say something, but Zebulon beats her to it, asking me, "Is it true that your cousin, King of Paragon, is free of the Geldryn device? That the freeing of him occurred on the Plateau of MarcKand?"

"What of it?" I ask. I still have hold of NeiSator. The metal disk is safe in my other hand.

Zebulon bites his teeth together in viciousness. Unlike horses of Earth, he has sharp canine teeth that could rip me apart.

He steps closer. "Do not believe that the EquiNeins of this world are as the little horses of where you hail from, boy. And do not question me as my son, Nebukahn, does. I have not the tolerance. Time is short. But a breath and a heartbeat, and you could miss your moment, your purpose."

Caleiso startles. She turns her focus on the great horse before us. "That Von, half-breed mutt is sired by you? Why didn't you ever—?"

Zebulon cranes his neck to view Caleiso. He inhales a giant breath, as she's talking. Then he slowly exhales, focusing on the finger she has directed at him.

Caleiso stops talking, when her hand starts to freeze over. A look of horror creeps over her face. The ice crawls up her arm. Before she can cry out, she's completely frozen in place like a statue.

I shiver more, only in utter fear this time.

Zebulon returns to gazing at me intently. "Now that we are alone, no little Vitiosyn ears to hear us, there are things you must know. First, cast your weapons into one of the pools, for it is sacrilege to enter onto this sacred ground wielding weapons."

I toss NeiSator into a pool. I fear this EquiNein too much, not to do as he bids. I don't want him to freeze me over as he did so easily with Caleiso.

When NeiSator's tip touches the water, the water freezes immediately. NeiSator appears suspended in the air, his tip barely pricking the ice.

I wait for Zebulon to make the next move. He tries to grin; it looks as a snarl. Only his tittering, laugh-like sounds tell of his amusement. He turns serious. "Your other weapons, also; that mirror-crystal and the broken timepiece it can fix."

My pulse races. I hold the mirror disk over the cracked sapphire crystal of my diver's watch. They are the same size. I feel much the idiot for not realizing it sooner. And now this giant horse wants me to toss both of them in the water? No way!

Boldly, I tell him, "That's not going to happen. I'm keeping them with me."

When Zebulon steps closer, I step back. I snap my fingers and call for

NeiSator. He doesn't come. So I call for RotaSyn. Neither does he come to my aid.

Zebulon keeps coming forward. I keep backing up. Caleiso stays frozen in place. Then the great horse charges at me.

I panic, turn, then run for it. I almost trip, in my haste. I dodge in and out of the trees. Several times do I barely miss falling into the round pools scattered around. The trees suddenly shift to look like mirrors. It's as a house of mirrors. Quickly, I'm disoriented. I can't tell which direction Zebulon is coming from. So I close my eyes to block the disorientation. I listen for a second, then rush in the opposite way of him. This goes on for many minutes. My heart pounds so hard, my chest aches. I come to a stop. I sink to the ground, and press my back up against a tree. I catch my breath.

Everything is eerily quiet, until something splashes and swims around in the many pools of water. Many somethings, in fact. Vardiyas have risen to the surface of each pool. Dozens, no, hundreds of them. Their little waterfox faces greet me. But when a cloaked figure comes onto the scene, and I spot him on the mirrored trees, the Vardiyas startle. They dive back underwater.

I remain still, holding my breath, as that figure passes by. He fades away. When I think it's safe, I stand up, to head back for Caleiso. I know not what else to do. I've not gone far, when a horse screeches beside me. I startle, then trip and fall; the watchband snaps on impact; the mirror-crystal slips from my grasp; I scramble to catch them, but they land in a pool; that pool freezes over. The two items sink below the ice, fading into the darkness of the water's depth. I glance back to the one who startled me. Zebulon. I scowl darkly at him.

Standing up, I shout, "How I am supposed to get those back?"

"Vardiyas only keep what is theirs. Come, he is this way." Zebulon turns and walks away.

Still livid, I follow him. "I don't know who you mean. *Who* is this way?"

"One who has waited for many eras to meet you. Now that you are armed with merely your name, he will accept you into his midst. You, the Last of the Ashenawks, are also the first. The in-between. There is none like you, Savakaidyn of Ravier. The strength that many and your father lacked, lives in you. That is why they are gone, and you are here. I know not *how* LanSoren died. Merely, why. It was to make way for you. The path he couldn't bear to go down, he left for you. For you are better. The Sleeping Dragon. The Onyx Prince. These are but two titles many will come to know you by, as you get older. Are you ready to meet him? The Phantom of Time?"

Sickness of heart overwhelms me. How do I answer that? I don't know. So I nod. One nod given to a winged-horse, and everything could be revealed to me just like that.

Will the truth break me? I wonder. *Will I ever be the same?*

Zebulon remains still. He seems to muse over my apparent distress. Then he starts speaking, reminding me of things my father told me. He adds quite a bit more to it. "Happiness was vanquished with mortality and the days of zeal became rime. That love, our love, was lost in the sea of time. With it gone, our sadness arose out of failure. We had failed fate. Yet he means to set it right. But, first, her hatred's pain would turn to nirvana, numbness of mind, and she may never again remember who she was, what she was. Our anguish stayed after her memory had gone. They feared the obscured. In fact, still do. But I, Zebulon of the Rime, did not, will not. Though it is near and last of the end, never will I fear what is to come. For my core is a core of ice, and only my other half could ever hope to thaw it out. Then there's reflection, gazing into the ages; she confirms it, yet seldom more. Merely reason and resolve can mend it all. You are one of us, made different. Your other half has forgotten who she is. So you must find another, to make up for the loss of her. And she must be mighty in all she doth do. Or you will perish. And if you perish, all is lost."

Someone calls from afar, a male voice I don't recognize, saying, "Zebulon, bring him to me."

We go toward that voice. We must pass by Caleiso, still frozen as a statue of ice, as we approach the Phantom of Time. Onward, Zebulon and I continue, side by side. The Vardiyas resurface to watch us from their pools.

After going farther along, as I spot a cloaked figure—who's still a ways away, standing near the one bubbling fountain in all this bit of forest I've seen among the Pools of Vosh-Perida—the Vardiyas are withdrawn. They dare not break the surface of the water. They only stare out, from just below that motionless surface.

Sooner than I'm ready for, we enter into his midst. It is the most beautiful part of the forest, where he is. Blues, greens, and purples glow about the area, emitting from the trees. The foreground is blanketed in sparkling snow. And that bubbling fountain swirls with metallic colors of magic: white, black, blue, brass, and copper-red.

The cloaked figure has his back to me. He stands in front of the fountain, unimpressive. He isn't tall at all, nor broad-shouldered. His presence is nothing awe-inspiring. "Light the fountain with fire," he says. His ageless voice is gentle, perhaps weary. He strolls away, as Zebulon nudges me forward.

Going forward, I snap my fingers, and speak the word: "Oostrina." A flame forms like a drop, and drips off one of my fingers. Once that drop lands in the fountain's liquid, that liquid lights on fire. Gentle flames lick the surface of the flowing water. I step back, suddenly feeling the awe. My whole life, lived up to this point in time, is revealed in the fire. Tears, endless tears run down my cheeks. They burn like flames on my skin. Tears of joy, tears of heartbreak, angry tears of not getting my way. So many feelings come over me, watching my life play out.

The fire goes out.

I gasp for breath, and I fall to my knees, for it is all overwhelming.

The phantom has his back to me, as he asks the greatest question any on this world have ever asked me: "What do you desire, above all else, Ravier?"

I swallow hard. I have to think about it. Then I answer with this: "To know the truth, come what may."

"Then I shall tell you the truth, come what may," says the phantom. He turns around. He slowly removes his hood. The young Soren is there, before me. He transitions into the older, wild one. Then to me, as I am now, and then the older me—the one I saw at The Sodon, correcting the Onyx King's deceit. This phantom keeps that form, as he says, "These are the faces I prefer to take as my own, for my own face no one would believe is real. You would hunt for me, night and day, in all the legends of Muraine, but you would never find me, for I've not yet been born in your timeline. But once I was born in one timeline, like a flash of lightning, I infected them all. Interacted with them all. Time is mine to manipulate. There are but few to stop me. Only the Ashenawks can stop me. For the Spirits of Muraine are only for there. Not for me. Not for where I am from. Where your power hails from is of another world as well. At heart, we are of another world. And so is Zebulon, here. You may leave." He flicks his attention to the great horse.

Zebulon perks his head up. "How will he get back?"

The phantom laughs. "Why, Zeb, I will escort him. Him and that girl. Did you truly freeze her over? I had wished to have a talk with her too. Meet her for the first time, and all, you know?"

Zebulon grunts. "Key words. *Had* wished. See, I knew you would not want to make her mind rupture with compulsive inquisition. Though there would have been a different cause, she would've been driven mad the way Soren was. So pick another time to meet her. A better time." As soon as he's done talking, Zebulon leaves our midst.

The phantom strolls near the fountain. "Zebulon of the Rime. Always giving bits of epiphany. There is also nothing that fazes him, truly. But what of you, Ravier? I know you must confront the Call of Vitiosus, come morning. And *that* morning is not too far off. Are you worried?"

I go sit on the edge of the fountain, and bury my face in my hands. I'm exhausted. I don't know how to take all this in. At last, I uncover my face, to reply, "*Worried* is too small of a word. I dread that I'm destined to become the next Apprentice to Vitiosus." I look up at the phantom. "Do I become that? Do I join Zymarc?"

"I can't tell you. What I can tell you is, in half the timelines, you succumb to the call or the death. Other times, you are left shattered, broken. And it takes you much time to rebuild your strength, both of body and mind. There are, however, a few ways to defeat Zymarc of Vitiosus. A few ways that you can end his reign of Vitiosus forever. To bring about the death of it. It will not be easy."

"Nothing is easy," I confess, "when it comes to Zymarc."

The phantom sits down on the fountain's edge beside me. "You worry over who he is, don't you?"

As I nod, my throat burns. I wonder, *Why have spoken answers suddenly become so difficult?*

The phantom says, "I understand. Truly. My father is . . . was . . . something to be feared. It took more than I could ever tell, to overcome him. Believe me when I tell you, we can face our demons. And we can overcome them, even when the cost is great."

"How great will the cost be?"

Pondering a moment, he replies, "It will be survivable. Though others may not have, *you* can survive this path. I approached your father one day, well before you were born, telling him much of what I'm telling you now. He had the strength, then. But when he saw you, held your newborn self in his arms, he couldn't bear to part with you. His love for you was all he could see. He had to save you. And the only way to do that, was to forfeit his life."

I bolt away. "Did you kill him?" I shout in horror.

The phantom eases up, to stroll about the foreground again. "No. Fate claimed him. His day of death was determined, the day you were born. He would die, on your thirteenth birthday. There was no escaping it. The only thing that could be altered was how. The way he was to perish."

I rush away from that spot in the forest, then run faster. In seconds, though, I run right into someone. I cry out in fury.

The phantom grabs me by the shoulders. "Please, Ravier. Listen! *Thirteen-done* was for you. For many eras, Murainians have been speaking that phrase, to leave the place of in-between, to escape it. I made that phrase what it is, as a way to commemorate one of your greatest losses.

The loss of your father, when you were just thirteen. LanSoren never knew the truth of that; I never told him. I had not the heart to tell him his fate, either. He learned it, nonetheless. And he accepted it with dignity."

Too overwhelmed, I beg him, "Take me back to Vaydell. Please!"

I'm trembling uncontrollably.

The phantom releases me, before asking, "When the ShenawFayel is over, do you promise to come back to the Pools of Vosh-Perida to meet Aysivak?"

Again, I only nod.

"I will hold you to it, Onyx Prince. You can be sure of that."

He leads the way back to Caleiso. She's no longer frozen. Instead, she's on her knees, reaching for NeiSator, who's still suspended in the frozen water of the pool.

"Come on," she mutters, as she places one hand on the ice for balance, "Tyler will kill me, literally, if I leave you here by yourself. Can't have some Deathasyn coming along to collect you."

The phantom, who still appears as my older, eighteen-year-old self, snaps his fingers. The ice quickly melts, and Caleiso falls into the pool of water, as does my dagger.

The phantom offers my diver's watch back, but no mirror-crystal.

I open my mouth to complain, but the phantom says, "Look again. It has been turned into something different. Possibly better."

Once more, I study the watch. That cracked crystal has been replaced by the mirrored one.

The phantom grins at me in a wicked way. "Oh, and fish that one out of the water, will ya? Give her a warm welcome for me too."

"I thought you were taking us back to Vaydell?"

He shakes his head. "Now that I've seen her, I know that Zebulon is right. I must pick a different time to meet Callie. Farewell, Tyler Ravier. See you in a few years."

Living up to his name, the phantom simply disappears in a swirl of smoke.

I rush to Callie as she breaks the water's surface, and tosses the sleeping-dagger to the ground. She coughs and sputters. I pull her out of the water. Her clothes are no longer stained. Though she gets my robes soaked, I don't care. I just want to hold tight to someone, even if that *someone* is someone I hardly know. Someone I hated just yesterday. That was yesterday, however; this is now. Seconds after my world has come toppling down over my head. I'm drowning in the sorrow, the confusion, the fear. I wonder, *How can I ever hope to be better than all those who have come before me?* The notion seems impossible.

"Ravier," she says, "what happened? Where'd you go, and why'd you leave your dagger behind?" Callie looks up at my face. "Vards, Tyler, are you all right? You look as if you've just encountered Soren, or something."

Managing a weak grin, I reply, "Or something." Then I wince at the sudden pain in my feet. "Do you mind giving me another tonic for my wounds? They reopened."

She gets up to rummage around in her supplies. She gives me a tiny blue bottle, and I take it, drink its contents. Several minutes pass, before my feet feel better.

As I wait for the wounds to heal, Callie takes out a little box from a pouch of hers. She resizes it to its large, original size. She finds boots in that resized box. "Here we are," she says. "I'll alter these to fit you. Should keep your wounds from reopening. Zymarc will have your wounds healed permanently, in minutes, if you'll allow it."

She miniaturizes the box, then puts it away. She begins reworking the large, somewhat tattered black boots to fit me.

I remark, "Those don't look like your size."

"They're not. They're Zymarc's. It's customary for an apprentice to carry two full sets of clothes and armor as well as five weapons of their master's. Though I'm not his apprentice any longer, I never took the time to clear out his belongings. I've been carrying his things since I was nine. Wasn't officially his apprentice, though, until I was eleven."

"So," I remark, "the same year my father died, you became Zymarc's apprentice."

Callie pauses in reshaping the leather. She presses her lips together.

Guilt washes over her features.

I ask, "Why?"

"It began with Zymarc trying to figure out what had happened to LanSoren. He called me home for a time. Not long enough that I'd be missed in Dysarda. Only long enough to further my training."

"To be a spy, you mean?" I try to remain calm.

She lets out a heavy breath. "Tyler, I don't want to fight."

"I didn't want to fight you either, when I first met you in Paragon."

"What did you want, when you first met me?" She looks up from her task.

"I had wanted to get to know you better."

Callie goes back to resizing the boots. She's nearly done. "And now?"

"I wish you hadn't done what you did." Before I see her reaction, I stand up. The pain in my feet has subsided. I reach down for the boots. "All done?"

She hands me the boots, then lets me help her up. I pull her close. I let go of her hand. But I can't resist brushing the fingers of my left hand along her cheek. I cup one side of her face.

Contentedly, she sighs, even closes her eyes. Yet I do not. I merely wish that she and I had had a different beginning, a different story. That she had not been cruel, while trying to impress a king of a violent, warp-minded people.

My hand lights with the Prismatic of Magic—black hand, glowing white nails, colorful streams racing over my palm lines. The colors bleed out onto her cheek. She doesn't respond as if anything unusual is happening. When I pull my hand away, her eyes are the way they were when she was Callie of Dysarda, pretending to be a Paragonian girl. I have the realization that, though it doesn't last long, I can make Vitiosus diminish. Her eyes are the crimson-red color again.

Hiding a grin, I ask, "Shall we head back?"

"Yes, but where did Zebulon go off to?" She wanders about, searching for him.

I tell her, "He got tired of us. Went back on his own."

Callie scoffs. "That's just like an EquiNein. KaaNeins, specifically, all high and mighty." She sighs in frustration. "Well then, we'd best get going. There's an outpost, not far from here. We can get fresh mounts there, pick ones that can't yet talk. They're more compliant. Meaning, they don't just go wandering off when they feel like it."

I ask, "Then Awngeleik behaves more in the way of a young dragon?"

"No. She gets her difficult traits from both lines. Perhaps she's a tad bit more like a dragon, though. If nothing else, she has the confidence like one. Much the way you do, Ravier."

Ignoring the comment, I ask, "Which way is the outpost?"

"This way," she says, starting the trek back to Vaydell.

* * *

We've been walking for a time, when I ask Callie, "Won't Zymarc come looking for us? Surely, the three hours have passed."

Glancing up, Callie focuses on the night sky. She searches for the moon, then she spots it. "Vards, you're right." She starts walking faster. "We're almost to the outpost. Just keep quiet. Don't tell them who you are. If you must say something, tell them you're a prisoner of war."

"Wouldn't I have on restraints, if I were such a prisoner?"

She stops midstride. "Are you offering to let me bind your wrists with rope?"

"That's not what I meant. Only, that it should be something else we tell anyone who asks about me."

"Like what?" Callie faces me. She folds her arms across her chest.

I go with the fail-safe shrug.

Callie lifts an eyebrow. "Well, I've thought of something else that will make many Deathasyns ask no further questions about you, or your identity."

She saunters off, and I reluctantly follow. Not knowing what she'll tell them makes me nervous.

Three smallish, stone buildings come into view. Torch poles, half the height of the ones in Vaydell, light the area. About a dozen or so warriors wander around. Only a few stand alert, watching for any who approach. They spot us, and lift their long-range weapons of bows. They are ready to fire arrows at us.

In confidence, Callie calls out, "Lower those weapons, for Prime-Warrior Caleiso and her guest."

"Who be that guest?" queries one of the three warriors at the ready.

"A potential," replies Callie, going forward. She pulls me along with her.

The warriors lower their bows, and put away their arrows.

One of those three warriors approaches, meets us halfway. "A potential?" he queries. "And before your fourteenth year has come and passed. That is mighty good luck, when considering the old traditions. Think King Zymarc will approve this one?"

She says, "I do, yes."

"Then, dear Princess Caleiso, I wish you more luck than Soren, when he was trying to escape his fate." The Deathasyn holds his head high.

"You would." Callie smiles. "But you should be wishing yourself that luck. I hear you've not had much of it."

"Aye, I didn't"—he pauses to scratch his face—"until this night, however. I've been freed of Vitiosus."

Callie's stance goes stiff. "What do you mean?"

"Exactly what I said. I am freed of Vitiosus. By Zymarc, himself. He came nigh three hours ago. Told me the last of my family had perished in the battle at Yharss-Rawshuen. That there is no one left to oppress me, should I wish to live as a simple Deathasyn rather than a Vitiosyn. My family threatened to sacrifice me to The Black Flame, or worse, if Zymarc had not taken me on as one of the young ones he would train up in the ways of Vitiosus. When I was thirteen, he turned me. He had to. My family was growing restless, agitated. So, against his will and mine, he turned me. Neither of us wanted it. My family would have murdered me, had I not carried on the family custom of serving the King of Vitiosus. Some of them, back in the day, served King Deezalo. At any rate, it was centuries ago when I lost my freedom. And now that I will have freedom very soon, for this is my last shift of duty, I don't know what I will do."

Callie has a dumbfounded expression. "Why would he free you like that, when we're at war with the Dragon Tamers?"

"You will have to ask Lord-King Zymarc that, my lady. For I do not know." The Deathasyn shifts his attention elsewhere a moment, before saying, "But you can ask him yourself. For he is coming this way, by way of the Pools of Vosh-Perida, from the looks of it. You must've barely missed each other."

I turn to glance at the bit of forest Callie and I just exited.

Zymarc meanders closer to the outpost, with a giant, winged horse strolling beside him. A black horse, his eyes aglow with red. Zebulon. The EquiNein stares at me, and his gaze pierces through the darkness. Wherever his gaze is set, lights with a soft red. And it gradually gets hotter, the longer he stares at the same spot of me—my left hand.

When Zebulon meets my gaze, he Mensa-divs, *"Zymarc of Vitiosus still yet has a part to play. Do not get in the way of that, Last of the Ashenawks. You have much to learn of fate. Do not become like Soren, thinking you can become a master of fate, and the telling of it. It was his downfall. Will it be yours as well? You must make a choice. So what will you choose?"*

"Truth," I div to Zebulon. I saunter toward the two.

Zymarc startles when he realizes that it's me, approaching. "Ravier," he whispers, "what are you doing here? You should be in Vaydell."

"There was an attack in Vaydell. Caleiso and I escaped some rioters, who had entered the General's House. Zebulon, here, took us out of the city for a while. We figured it was best to let things settle down, before returning."

Callie comes up behind me, to add, "We were heading back now."

"Zebulon!" Zymarc scorns him. "Why did you say nothing of that?" Zymarc doesn't wait for a reply, before he's striding closer to the outpost buildings. He commands the warriors on standby. "We need two of your most rested mounts. Bring them out."

Zebulon talks, even while Zymarc commands the warriors and they flee to go do as they were told. The dark horse says, "Why bother the King Vitiosyn with reports of near-tragedies? Best to tell him of tragedies that have actually happened."

Zymarc whirls around to glower at the great horse. "Zebulon, why is it that you talk as if you're a dragon? EquiNeins are not supposed to be this, well, I don't know. Dark hearted? You've spoken rather cold-minded things over the entirety of our knowing each other. Is there something you want to tell me, Zeb? For I am trusting you less and less, each day."

I interrupt them, to say, "There's something I want to tell *you*, Lord-King Zymarc. Rather, something I wish to ask."

"What, Ravier?" He huffs. I can tell by Zymarc's slumped demeanor that he is growing weary.

"Once we're back in Vaydell, will you take me to the cathedral again?"

"Why?" Zymarc queries.

"Because I mean to learn the truth, come what may."

He circles about the group of us. He stares out into the forest. As two mounts are being brought out, Zymarc climbs up onto Zebulon's back. "No," he says flatly. "I'm not taking you back to Deezalo's Cathedral while you are still the Onyx Prince. Rather, I will take you after the ShenawFayel is over, and you are my Apprentice to Vitiosus. That's the end of it. Get on one of those horses, Tyler. And do not test me."

It's a feeble attempt, but I ask anyway, "There's nothing I can do to change your mind?"

Not looking at me, Zymarc says, "Nothing whatsoever."

Giving up for now, I mount a horse that's much smaller than Zebulon. Callie gets on the other one.

Zymarc glances to the Deathasyn we spoke to only moments ago. He says to him, "You'd best be leaving before morning, dear Deathasyn. You're not welcome here, anymore. Come first light, I only want the most loyal of Vitiosyns at my side. Though you have served me well, that servitude is at its end."

The freed Deathasyn lowers his gaze, but not his head. "Farewell then, lord-king. You'll always be better than Deezalo, in my eyes."

Zymarc's mouth twitches. He looks as if he wants to shout. Yet he doesn't. He merely unclips a weapon from his belt. He tosses it to the freed Deathasyn. "Zymarc of Oniva enchanted that as a boy. I've kept it with me all these centuries. I'm not him anymore. I'm not an Onyx Warrior. Hardly Onyx at all. Therefore, I don't need that anymore. Leave before your fate becomes what Grawllik's was this morning."

The freed Deathasyn slowly looks up at Zymarc. "Goodbye, King Zymarc. Light of Vardiyas be with you."

Zymarc digs his heels into Zebulon's sides, and Zeb bolts forward. Our young mounts gallop forward too. The outpost is quickly behind us. We head for Vaydell, getting closer to some altercation. I'm sure of it. But what will it be? I venture that only Vardiyas and the Phantom of Time truly know what is coming. Also, what is happening in Zymarc's heart. I do not know whether he has gained strength this night, or lost it. And that uncertainty is frightening.

30

Beyond the Veil

The mood of Zymarc is volatile. So volatile, in fact, Callie and I didn't dare question him further. About anything. Not when we arrived back in Vaydell. Not as he got updates from Azabahk, regarding what occurred during his absence. Not even as Callie finished making alterations to my new clothes. And I dare not ask for my coat of the Sleeping Dragon, nor RotaSyn and my other things. I hide NeiSator, however, behind my vest of black fabric. He's not too noticeable, there.

Now we're on a mighty fast dragon. A type I've not seen before. I'm told she's one of the ancestor dames of Awngeleik and Xiedyn. Primarily an Aysadyn, she has the same blue snake-eyes as Awngeleik—dragon eyes that stare into your soul, and disarm you if you look for too long. Her scales are mixed shades of shiny black and dull gold. Bright-ivory fur is upon her long, narrow tail; along her back too. The fur stops around her neck and head, resembling a lion's mane. Yet her face is one of a kindly dragon: soft and relaxed.

Zymarc tells the two of us to sleep. That he'll wake us when we're closer to the destination only he and the dragon know. I don't argue. I *am* tired. And the ShenawFayel doesn't prevent me from sleeping, because of some impending danger. So I sleep. That is, until Callie shakes me awake. "Tyler, we're almost there."

"Almost where?" Sitting up, I rub my scratchy eyes. It's still very dark out. Clouds have covered the moon.

She's about to answer, when Zymarc replies, "The Graveyard of Blackwood Spikes. The place where many thousands of souls were taken from this world, but not given over to Sivondel. Once, every eight years—always the same year as The Sodon—they awaken. We can see them. Sometimes, they can see us. That is not usually the case, though."

Callie queries, "You're actually taking me there this time?"

"You weren't old enough the last time," says Zymarc.

Clouds shift to uncover the moon—a crescent moon. I think, *No, it should be a full moon.* I realize then, a lunar eclipse is unfolding. My pulse quickens. Yet the magic of the ShenawFayel doesn't insist that I do any particular thing. Regardless, I'm ready for something to happen. *What will it be?* I wonder.

The Aysadyn descends for the landing. It's what I imagine she's doing, until she slows to a hover over the shoreline of some dried-up lakebed that's filled with countless tall spikes. A far-off light illuminates the graveyard of stripped trees. Trees that go on for many miles. I cannot see the end of them. It is as a sea rather than a lake. Glistening, black spikes, which appear as a semi-translucent glass, must be fifty feet in height. One, near the center of what I can view, is triple that stature. It still has possession of its branches. Yet it is as a dead tree, while all the others bear resemblance to spikes. Statues of golden birds, the same ones on the cathedral in Vaydell, are resting on the dead branches; they must be enormous, up close. And, no matter the slight variations in shape and contours of the myriad of grave markers, all these tree spires have been sharpened to a fine, piercing point at the top, including the one with bird statues among its branches.

Zymarc interrupts my fixation, to say, "Climb down the rope, Ravier."

I look at him. He has hold of a thick rope.

"And don't worry," he says, "this rope has handholds woven in. Should help you climb down faster. Get going."

First, I go. Then Callie. Once our feet are firmly planted on the ground, Zymarc tosses the rope down. He immediately leaps off the dragon's back like a swimmer jumping off a diving board. The fall is at least seventy feet.

I find myself scrambling forward and shouting, "Zymarc! Are you insane?" I cast wind to slow his fall.

He blocks it, pushes it back at me; I'm thrown to the ground, as he casts his own spell of water. His body cuts through that floating bit of liquid, and he slows down. When he exits the hovering stream, he lands, rolls forward onto his feet. Water hits the ground. The dragon flies off.

Zymarc walks toward us, as if nothing spectacular happened. He's sopping wet, though. And it's proof that I *did* witness him make that horrifying leap like it was nothing.

Grabbing the rope off the ground, Zymarc begins to coil it. He strolls forward, heading for the large group of gathered Deathasyns, dragons, and Vitiosyns. "The answer is *yes*, Ravier. I am most insane. I'd have to be, to do what I've done. To carry out what I envision. Also, to be here in this place, during a ShenawFayel with you."

Following alongside him, I ask, "Why are we here? Do you mean to frighten me into not ever going back into Deezalo's Cathedral?"

"On the contrary. I mean to give you an informed decision. You will see the first summoner of Vitiosus. For Deezalo, once every eighth Sodon, awakens. This is the eighth Sodon, before the count resets. I, myself, have seen Deezalo here, multiple times. This will be my sixteenth time."

Zymarc begins to navigate through the crowd. Some Vitiosyn guards attempt to clear the path for us. Zymarc hands one of them the coiled rope.

While walking amongst the many people, Callie queries, "How many Sodon years have you been here at the graveyard, lord-king?"

"One hundred twenty-two times. For my other Sodons, I was still an Onyx. And a young one, at that. During one of those, I was under an apprenticeship." Zymarc pauses going forward. He glances over his shoulder. "Bet you'll not guess who I was apprenticed to, when I was sixteen, Ravier." He continues forward. "I was a twin apprentice with a woman. A Deathasyn woman. She and I got along well. Until, one day, we didn't."

Before I can ask Zymarc of that, he exits the crowd. Callie bravely goes with him. I linger behind with the people, however, as they quietly converse with one another.

A storm rumbles overhead. Lightning crashes down upon the grave markers made of trees. The lightning is not the usual kind in that the bolts are red, which slow their descent the closer they get to each pointed tip of the tree spikes. The Blackwood Spikes. Once each bolt has made contact with the intended mark, they then turn bright-white. Those bright bolts retreat to the clouds in a thunderous flash.

Zymarc calls over his shoulder, "How much longer?"

Beside me, a Vitiosyn guard replies, "Minutes, my liege. You arrived right on time. As usual."

This gets a sly grin out of Zymarc.

I stride away from the protection of the crowd, for I feel called to do so. Whether pushed or pulled toward Zymarc, I do not know. I only know that something is brewing to the surface. The ShenawFayel has summoned me to be near this enemy of yesterday and tomorrow. Soon, whatever is coming will happen.

Once I'm next to him, I ask, "Please, Zymarc, can't we watch from farther back?"

Zymarc lifts a hand to silence me. "Quiet," he says. "This is where I always stand, for this gathering of my Vit—"

Something erupts with red light. I can't hear the rest of what Zymarc says. Frantically, I crowd closer to the King Vitiosyn. I shield him from the red light, or try to, as thousands of red bolts electrify the tree that has branches and birds. A wind rushes through the graveyard; sounds of the imminent gust can be heard. It's coming for us.

Zymarc startles, grabs me by the arm, and pulls me back toward the crowd. We don't make it there, before the wind has caught up to us. It bites at our heels. We slip. We almost fall. Callie shoves the both of us just a little farther forward. We're saved from whatever the gust had intended for us. Callie, however, is not. Zymarc whirls around to reach for her, but she's slammed down, dragged away from us, away toward the graveyard, screaming.

"Zymarc!" she shrieks. Over and over again, she screams for him, *reaches* for him.

He and I cannot take one step in Callie's direction. Cannot cast a single spell, though we lift our hands to try. It's as if we press against an impenetrable wall.

I lower my hands. Zymarc does the same. I try to think of what to do. There are so many things about Callie that have come to light. Yet much remains a mystery. I cannot absently watch, as she dies here. I must do something. But what?

Zymarc yells in anger. Then he points to the graveyard. He shouts the command, "Go get her!"

The Vitiosyn who was given the coiled rope rushes forward. He leads hundreds of Vitiosyns onto the graveyard. They're almost to Callie. They slow her momentum with elemental spells.

The great tree in the distance is coming to life. The birds are waking up. They fly for the edge of the graveyard. All of it is a blur, as they attack the Vitiosyns. Those hundreds of Vitiosyns are slaughtered. Pierced by the wakened metal birds; carried up and ripped apart in the air; so many violent ends.

Zymarc lifts a hand to protect his people, to attack the living statues. Yet he cannot. So he turns to the remaining Vitiosyns. "Prepare for a battle without me. It seems I cannot help, for the ShenawFayel will not let me."

They do as he bids. Some rush forward, weapons raised. Others make preparations with arrows and magic. Many spread out, encompassing the shore of the dry lakebed.

Defeated, the Vitiosyn King lowers himself to sit upon the ground. He draws one knee close to himself to rest both hands atop it.

Callie can still be heard over the chaos, wailing in torment.

Zymarc watches it all play out, his face expressionless.

"What are we going to do?" I ask. My chest spasms. I cannot sit down as Zymarc has chosen to do. I pace about, testing where the boundary is. Where the ShenawFayel commands me to stop.

Zymarc replies, "Wait."

"Wait until what?" I shout at him.

"Until I think of what to do."

"Can't you summon The Black Flame?" I ask, desperate to get to Callie.

"No." He looks to the ground, and sighs. "I've already summoned him twice, in the span of a year. Once, to study him, learn what I could of the Spirit of Death. The second was to bend him to my will. I got what I wanted from him, that time. The law still holds: summon death a third time in a year, and your life is forfeit. Not even Vitiosus can break that law."

I sweep my gaze over the vast expanse. More Vitiosyns are falling by the second. "Zymarc, they're all going to perish, if you don't do something."

"Why do you care, Ravier? They're not your people. Not a faction of your army—the Onyx of Malik."

"I'm greatly disturbed at how you let them fall, while just sitting on the ground, doing nothing but thinking."

Jolting off the ground, he gets in my face. "I'm not just thinking. I'm waiting. More Vitiosyns are coming, as is our tradition for this day. My stronger ones. They always arrive later, after me. Also, a handful of captives are being brought here for a sacrifice to Deezalo. It won't be much longer."

I grow hot inside. "They had better not be from Paragon. And they had better not be any of my Onyx Warriors."

"They are not. Rather, they are Vitiosyn traitors. The ones I caught many weeks ago, when Belzara helped me overpower Alpha Jasper. Here they are now. And some other prisoners too."

Many dragons approach the scene of slaughter. They land in our midst. Countless people pile off the backs of the dyns. The traitors are bound, and led out toward the graveyard. Some others I recognize. Two in capacious robes, one in a white coat, and a dark-haired woman in a tattered dress. Also, Nebukahn is there, so many chains restraining him that it's a wonder he can even stand, let alone move. He's muzzled too.

They spot me. Or, rather, the woman spots me. "Ravier," she cries. "What are you doing here?"

RayVora, even in the dim light, is clearly worn-out and frazzled. Slumped shoulders; smudged, dirty face; but eyes now widened with terror.

Craesha stands near Nebukahn. He lowers his head in sorrow. Zeekryn is also much saddened by the sight of me in this place. The third man, however . . . his face I do not recognize. He's not Paydinn; that much is certain now that he's closer. He's rake thin. His cheeks are sunken in and pallid too. His glowing, magenta-colored eyes look on in boredom and then fury.

That one shouts, "I will not ever forgive you, Zeekryn, for that stupid, *stupid* spell of sleep you cast on my favorite chair. Look at this mess you've made for your older brothers to clean up. I and Paydinn have much to do. Craesha's been Mensa-divving to me all that has occurred, as Mother would not tell me. Most likely to protect you."

Zeekryn replies, "YaeVorkk, I do not need our mother's protection. I came in search of her and you. Also went looking for Craesha and his pet horse. I left the Paragonians at a very inopportune time. But I did so, for my family."

Looking up all puzzled-like, Craesha queries, "You don't need her protection? Look around, Brother. Is there anyone here who doesn't need protection?"

The Jokryn brothers start that angry, ridiculous reunion banter. RayVora is none too pleased, her neck rigid enough that the main tendons protrude.

Nebukahn starts walking forward, though slowly. He seems done with the company of the Queen Mother and her Jokryn sons. I go to him. I find that I am free to go past the border the ShenawFayel set earlier.

Watching me, Zymarc realizes it as well. He commands the newly arrived Vitiosyns to watch the Jokryns. Then he rushes to catch up to Neb and me. He breaks the chains off Nebukahn. "As a sign of good faith, I release you, Nebukahn of the Rime. You shall not be sacrificed to Deezalo."

Once the muzzle is removed from Nebukahn's long, wolfish snout, he asks, "Where did you hear that title . . . ? Of the Rime?"

"Your sire. Zebulon," Zymarc says. "He is watching. Waiting for you. He asked to join me, for a time. Turn him, for a time. He knew you would be captured, in time. In fact, ensured that you would be. I don't know how he knew, nor why he'd want it. Regardless, he asked that I free you this night. He means to take you from here." Zymarc pauses to survey the area. Spotting his target, he calls out, "He's all yours, Zebulon. Bring Caleiso to me, then be on your way. Do not return, after tonight."

Zebulon comes from the north, charging with great strength. He can be heard over everything, getting nearer. He covers the distance quite quickly. His eyes are still aglow with red. The closer he gets, the brighter that red becomes. The red light of his gaze is focused on his son.

Nebukahn cowers on the ground, screeching that odd Von-horse sound.

I bolt out of the way. Barely in time too, for Zebulon doesn't slow down. He speeds up. The ground in his wake ices over. He becomes a galloping figure of ice. He tries to trample Nebukahn, but Neb scrambles out of the way. He shifts into a black bear—only much larger. Quickly, he swipes at Zebulon, hits him, sends him sprawling.

Zebulon doesn't quite fall down. His wings help him stay upright. He repeatedly charges at his son; Neb alters into a different creature each time. He evades his father's tirade. But once Neb has transformed into a sort of werewolf—tall stature, longish neck, black fur that absorbs light like a living shadow—Zebulon grows docile. His ice form fades away. He's back to that of a KaaNein. He circles Nebukahn. Speaks to him too, saying, "It is you, to go fetch Caleiso. Deezalo awakens. Even now, he means to entrap—"

Nebukahn cackles, raises himself up on two legs. His thick, hairy arms are tensed up at his sides—his clawed, beast hands ready for attack. "I am not some dog to play fetch for you, Father. You are a traitor."

Zebulon charges so fast, Neb couldn't hope to move a single, clawed foot before he's struck in the chest. He's briefly turned to ice, but he breaks free of it.

The two stare at one another.

Taking the opportunity, I shout, "Please, Nebukahn, help Caleiso! Zymarc and I are in ShenawFayel together. Or we would go ourselves."

Neb glances to me. "Why's you want me to save that one, Ravier? Isn't she an enemy of Paragon? Your enemy?"

Approaching Neb, I admit, "Yes, but she's not my enemy, in this moment. Not while I'm in ShenawFayel. I don't wish for her to die yet, and certainly not here. Not like this. I'd rather it be any other way, any *other* place, than at this graveyard of Blackwood Spikes."

Nebukahn glances to the sea of grave markers resting amid the dry lakebed. To Caleiso, getting closer to that tree with branches. Her comrades did what they could. It wasn't enough. Only a third of all Vitiosyns gathered around are left alive. And that third have given up. They turn and head back toward us. Among them are the Vitiosyns I met earlier, the squadron leader with his team.

Scarred-face watches me with his one good eye. He carries a dead Vitiosyn in his arms—the one Zymarc gave the coiled rope to. That rope has strangled him, wrapped around his body like a large snake crushing a victim. Scarred-face throws his fallen comrade down at Zymarc's feet. "You." He points to Zymarc. "You bring this one back." The Vitiosyn's scar glows bright-red.

Zymarc replies, "I do not take orders from—"

Scarred-face bellows out an angry sound. His teeth get sharper. He grows in stature. Red spikes even pierce through the skin of his shoulders and upper back. No longer does he resemble a Sorsryn at all. He is as a creature that could survive any level of death. "He is my brother," Scarred-face growls. "He means as much to me as Princess Caleiso does to you."

Zymarc states, "I've not named her as my direct heir, Belgorr of the Moors. She is of—"

Belgorr interrupts, comes closer. "She might as well be a daughter to you. Do not tell me, Lord Zymarc, after all you've done, that *now* you will not save her. You have moved mountains, destroyed kingdoms, committed genocide. All for her."

"You misunderstand," Zymarc tries to say. He trails off, looking to the distance.

Belgorr has more to say. "We know she is cursed, my lord. We understand why you've done all that you have. *I*, Belgorr of the Moors, understand more than most, for I've glimpsed the future, in the Cathedral of Deezalo. I know why you need *her*."

Squad Leader adds, "Stop being afraid of the creature you become, when provoked. Rather, become it. Accept it. You have the power to break the protection the ShenawFayel forces upon both of you. But you both must fight it, together. And once you temporarily break it, my lord, I ask that you offer me as a sacrifice to Deezalo."

Zymarc takes in a sharp, startled breath. "I could never—"

Squad Leader holds up a hand. "You must. For it will confuse Deezalo, being offered one of his own kind—a Vitiosyn. You will get your one chance to snatch Caleiso from this place of death."

Zebulon adds, "We will remain to help you, Zymarc. Also, have I called for my own aid. Someone is coming. A soul of great power. One whom few can withstand. He will require the blade, Veldakryn. Do you have it with you?"

"Of course," says Zymarc, "but—"

"But nothing!" Zebulon shouts, coming to stomp at Zymarc's feet.

Getting in Zebulon's way, I draw out my dagger, NeiSator, for I must. I've no choice. However, I start to resist that force of the ShenawFayel. It hurts like an ache in my bones. A bruise radiating out to the surface. My showing skin starts blistering. I refuse to cry out.

Squad Leader digs his fingertips into his neck, until his skin splits open, and blood runs down.

Tears well up in Zymarc's eyes. He fights the temptation to bite into his faithful Vitiosyn man.

The scent of that Vitiosyn's blood is intoxicating to me. I suspect if Zymarc doesn't soon bleed the Vitiosyn, I will. I even move in his direction. Zymarc lunges for him instead, bites hard into the Vitiosyn's neck.

Squad Leader looks to his team members. He reaches out for his comrades. Then that arm goes limp. His eyes go blank. He is dead.

Zymarc catches him up in his arms. He confidently makes his way toward the graveyard. I follow.

Others do as well.

Many Vitiosyns start chanting sorrowful sounds.

A winged-creature flies toward us, from behind. I whirl around, thinking it's a wakened statue come to kill us.

The creature lands, his blond wings aglow. He tucks them out of his way, better showing his face. Hardly do I believe that Arsyn of Jhire has come to this horrible place. Then again, he's starting to feel like a guardian, there to save me from the worst. There to give hope during hard times, and a possibility that Ryco may yet be brought back to life.

He looks to me only for a moment, before rushing toward Zymarc.

Vitiosyns block his path, yet he does not attack. Merely shouts, while trying to push past them, "King Zymarc of Vitiosus! I'll be needing that blade, Veldakryn. For I mean to tear the veil separating the planes of existence. Deezalo intends to awaken, and he can with that girl's body as a host."

Glancing back, Zymarc yells, "I shall not be handing that weapon over to you, for I do not trust—"

Arsyn shouts over him, "Trust that I am a keeper to the Laws of Time, of Magic. Trust that I would never break it, bend it for my musings as Soren did. Never have I run from my fate. Merely accepted it with grace and dignity. Surely that Onyx part of you can respect that, understand that. I pose no present threat to you."

"Please, Zymarc," I beg. "Let Arsyn help us!"

Zymarc lays the dead leader on the ground, then rummages in his own things. He takes the miniaturized Veldakryn out. Tosses him high and far. The blade regains its size while in the air.

Vitiosyns move out of Arsyn's way, to let him one-handedly draw the great blade to himself. He catches it, looks over its sheath of black-metal. He runs past many, but pauses to glance at Zebulon and the son in werewolf form. "You," he says to Neb, "you will go through the veil, once it's torn. For you are as a creature of aura, in this form. The Shadow Wolf. Deezalo cannot inhabit you."

"Nor can he inhabit me," says one of the Jokryn brothers, stepping closer. YaeVorkk goes on to say, "Allow me to offer further hindrance to Deezalo's plan for the girl. A spell of Sleep Eternal should interrupt the process of Deezalo taking possession of the girl. And, since I'm much acquainted with Sleep Eternal spells, thanks to my wretched brothers, I'll have no trouble breaking it this night. No need to worry over me being taken up as a Vitiosyn to serve Deezalo, either, for I am protected via a gift given to me at birth by a Geldryn woman. Vitiosus holds no power over me, nor can it kill me."

"Your help incurs what price?" Zymarc asks, as he picks the squadron leader back up.

"Freedom for me and my family," replies YaeVorkk. "Let us work out the details, afterward. We must hurry."

"Fine!" Zymarc shouts over his shoulder. "Belgorr, release the second-born Jokryn son, and him only, to assist us. Guard the rest. Kill them, if they become unwieldy."

Arsyn strides to the edge of the graveyard. He speaks to the blade, saying, "I know I am not Veldar, nor my ancestor, Jhire of the Rime, but lend me strength to cut the veil, for it must be you, Veldakryn, to do it. Your master, Veldar, taught you how. Please remember now, mighty blade, who you are, and whom you've served. Greatest wielders of the shadow auras. Your cousins, RotaSyn and NeiSator are near, dear Veldakryn. You are not alone to bear this burden. They shall save your blade's soul from cracking. Have faith in me, for I am Arsyn of the Ravas." Arsyn draws Veldakryn out from his sheath, and the black-metal blade lights with green fire. Arsyn's wings light with green fire too. He does not hesitate in cutting the veil.

Wind bursts out from the cut in the thin, luminescent shield that keeps The Kievas and land of the living apart from each other. Also did that shield hold back the place of in-between.

Tormented souls awaken from the Blackwood Spikes. The ghosts are of either green- or blue-colored light. Their screams emit to be like a wild fire. Their wake is a trail of blood and tears. It all becomes as a river of red. That river lights on fire and burns the souls. They scream more. The fire grows to the same height as the forest behind us. Yet one can see through the flames, can see the sorrowful souls trapped in torment.

Arsyn widens the tear to a gate. He accepts the fire, absorbs it into his wings. His eyes are bright, glowing white. Zebulon saunters over to the gate. He rears up, flaps his wings. The bursting flames emitting from the tear subside to something the Vitiosyn Warriors can hold at bay.

Through it all, the ShenawFayel summons me to run the other way. I fight it. My bones feel as if something heavy is crushing them. But they don't break. Not yet.

I make it to Zymarc, and the pain subsides only somewhat.

A form is taking shape near Deezalo's grave marker. A laughing beast on two legs.

As soon as the fire has subsided, Nebukahn barrels through the gate, running awkwardly on all fours. YaeVorkk is right behind him, confidence in his posture.

Though sickened to say it, I tell Zymarc, "It's time to offer that one to Deezalo."

Zymarc looks down at the leader's face one last time, and says, "Good and faithful Ahmoset. I can never repay you for this sacrifice. Forgive me. Buy us the distraction we need." Zymarc approaches the gate. Using levitation magic on the body, he sends his fallen man off to the in-between.

Ahmoset becomes like the other ghosts, but made of red light.

The form off in the distance is here now. In an instant, he comes for the soul of Ahmoset. Ahmoset trembles, but he stands his ground when a large, fanged creature clothed in black and golden-colored rags grabs hold of him. That creature is adorned with tarnished silver chains and brass plate armor. Chipped jewels are set into his gauntlets, armor, and devices of old. King Deezalo of Vitiosus. Hardly can I bear the sight of him and his twisted expression. Warped like the one I saw in the cathedral. I realize that the wall murals were of him.

Ahmoset's ghost says, "I offer myself as a sacrifice to you, King Deezalo. Take my soul. Satisfy your craving for the blood of magic."

Deezalo's eyes are as an abyss of darkness, but his pupils are red. He considers Ahmoset a moment. His showing skin is blistered, cut, and peeling. He seems to be in partial decay, for there is a stench of rotting flesh about him during his slow walkabout. His voice is gravelly and biting, likened to water rolling stones before hitting hot coals and turning into steam. He says, "You are a son of Vitiosus, are you not? Why am I being offered such a one like you? I have never been given one of your souls to devour, before."

The sound of his voice chills me to my core; I turn to run, but Zymarc grabs me, keeps me in place. "Fight it," he says. "Take out that Greyvon blade. Let us test who its rightful master is. Let us conquer this ShenawFayel, even if it's brief. How could the former King of Vitiosus hope to stand against us, if we, indeed, conquer magic born of two matriarchs' souls?"

I tell him, "I'll start with my daggers. Trade Winter's Vondaen for RotaSyn. Then we shall begin in there." I look to the gate, then Zymarc.

"Tyler," he says in sadness, "if I die in there, will you—?"

I've already taken Winter's Vondaen out, to offer it to him. I say, "I'll take care of Caleiso, and wipe her memory; do whatever else it'll take to give her a good life. I promise."

Zymarc blinks away any sign of his feelings. He grasps the hilt of Winter's Vondaen, and quickly gives me RotaSyn. He rushes into the fray. In Mensa-div, he tells me, *You must cut down the ghosts. Do not pity them, or they will consume you. Do not stop moving. Do not hold still. Stay close to me, Son of LanSoren. We shall be cut down together, or not at all.*

I go into the deafening fray with Zymarc. My enemy of yesterday and tomorrow, possibly even the father of my mother. I hold to memories of her. Amira Hajjar Ravier. The lady's name that sounds like a spell. I start to imagine that Caleiso is a loved one like my mother. I find that such imaginings make the pain in my body—my bones especially—subside enough that I'm faster than Zymarc, faster than the ghosts, faster than Nebukahn with the other. I pass them by, cutting tormented ghosts down along the way. To keep sane, I must imagine that I am freeing them to go live out in peace. To be freed of the place of in-between. Free to go to The Kievas. I picture giving them the respite they deserve, for none but the most twisted deserve endless torture.

"Stay close to me!" I call back to Zymarc. I turn to glance at him. Only darkness greets me. It grows quiet. My comrades are hidden from my sight. I walk about, wondering where the ghosts have gone. It all goes black. I come to a stop. I slash my daggers around in the full darkness, hoping they'll emit light or something, anything.

Tree spires become as white pillars of fire. People are tied to them, two-thirds of the way up the sheared, fiery trees. I expect to hear the people's screams. And, though their mouths are agape with screaming, those screams are silent. Pain etches into their many faces. As far as my eyes can see, there are tree spires of white fire, all having people tied to them. Too many souls to count have died here, in this horrid place. But the center tree—Deezalo's tree—teems with life. Vibrant greens and yellows are its leaves, with blooms of blues and reds. Its tree bark is of black, silver, and white, glistening like etched metal. A tree of many colors, home to the enormous birds. The ones that were statues only a short while ago. One approaches overhead, and I ready myself to attack it. Then it grows smaller, to the size of a large eagle, with pale-yellow eyes watching me. Its face is red with a black stripe running down the center. A slight crook is in its beak, and on the bottom of that beak is a tuft of feathers that resembles a goatee. As it lands on the ground in front of me, I spot feathers of black and gray upon its wings. Reddish-orange tints its underbelly. Red feathers encase the legs. It eyes me curiously.

I now know where I've seen this type of bird. Just outside of Grevagg, when Gemma and I were separated from the others. It was the bird that watched us, while we were in the Fleishyn Forest.

I think, *How did it end up there, near Grevagg? Was Zymarc controlling one, using it to spy out unfamiliar territory? Or was it there for some other reason?*

The bird starts cackling out eerie squawks, reminiscent to crows, yet not annoying. Only unsettling. It's like the laughter of the original Deathasyn brothers, after they had burned a hole through Ryco's chest. I know the sound is in my head, imagined, for the bird hasn't opened its beak to make such a sound. No others are close enough to be the owners of the creepy bird laughter, either.

I take a step forward.

The bird grows angry, squawking louder in my head. It flaps furiously. Then it bursts up, flies at me. I lift my daggers to shield myself. It impales itself on RotaSyn. Its blood splatters on my face. I fling its body off my waking-dagger, or try to as smoke swirls around me. Large hands grab me by the wrists.

The smoke fades.

A warped expression greets me, as I look up at this immense and tall Geldryn. Deezalo. No longer has he the look of decay. Only strength in his form, and magnificence in his aura, to match that of Gyronawv. But he smiles with ill intent. His voice, strong and deep, says, "At last, Zymarc has given me one of my desires. The soul of a faithful Vitiosyn. More and more, Zymarc is becoming what Vitiosyns were always meant to be. Capable of anything. All powerful. There is nothing a Vitiosyn cannot do, if he sets his mind to it."

I don't know what to say to this depraved one. Surely, I must say something. So I start babbling whatever comes to mind. "One could say a love of power is a weakness. Is that yours?"

Deezalo lets go of me. "My weakness was *not* practicing Vitiosus more, sooner than I did. I heeded my master's words, and only dabbled in it here and there, at first. Then I learned how he feared me. Feared that I would become stronger than he, greater than he. He held me back. The white wretch."

Horrified, I take a few steps back. "You don't mean Soren of the Monel, do you?"

"Aye." Deezalo's head lifts proudly. "You know Master Soren? How is he? Has he come to see me? It was many Sodons ago, when I spoke to him last. He told me of a daughter I had, prior to becoming what I am now. He wouldn't tell me what became of her, though. Do you know? Know the fate of my daughter, Caleiso? Or of her mother, Gaula of MarcKand?"

I'm reminded of something Skylin said. How unkind it was that Caleiso had been named after a nasty Geldryn. I muse, *There must be legends of her. The original Caleiso.*

Before I can stop myself, my mouth opens to tell him of Ayzareel, Gaula, and the Darklyres.

Someone calls out, "Do not answer that."

Zymarc comes to be by my side. As he offers Winter's Vondaen, he says, "Give me those daggers, young Sorsivyte. Let us end this."

We trade weapons, as Nebukahn and YaeVorkk come into our midst, battered, bloodied yet alive.

"Where is the girl?" queries YaeVorkk.

"My, my, little son of RayVora?" Deezalo smiles in the depraved way. "Look at you, YaeVorkk. Where are your brothers? You are nothing without them."

"Ha!" YaeVorkk scoffs. "I am a Siveyra now, you filth. You'll find, my brothers are nothing without me. No other Sorsryn has trained up as many apprentices as I have. And none of my best apprentices have ever perished. Many have gained titles of Onyx Warriors, Amethyst Archers, Grim Reapers, nobles, leaders, many, many titles of honor." YaeVorkk boldly approaches Deezalo, to add, "You've been gone a long while, Deezalo. Therefore, I shall tell you, *all* you built, *all* you worked for, the only things that remain are these: Vitiosus Magic and that insult to cathedrals. Nothing else remains. Not even your daughter, your heir. Caleiso. 'Twas Soren, who was ordered to kill her by a Withrasyn King, all while you were off, flaunting your new spells of magic. How ironic."

Deezalo shows no emotion. He simply studies us; Neb and me, especially.

"Who is this boy?" he asks, once YaeVorkk has finished talking. "His face is familiar. It's as if I've seen him every day of my life, without actually conversing with him."

"His name is unimportant," says Zymarc. "You've had your amusement of bloodshed. Tell us where the girl is."

Deezalo stands up straighter. "Not until you give me a feast of faithful souls."

"Faithful souls?" Zymarc's brow draws together.

I clarify it for him and the others. "He means faithful Vitiosyns. It's what he has desired to feed on, for some time. He thinks you are becoming what Vitiosyns were always meant to be. Capable of anything. All powerful. Nothing you cannot do, if you set your mind to it. That sort of thing."

I know this will enrage Zymarc, for he hates being compared to Deezalo.

He starts to turn into something quite unlike a Sorsryn. Rather, he becomes a spike-backed beast similar to what Belgorr transformed into briefly. Red scales form along his skin. Then those scales peel off. They form into snakes. The slithering creatures race around the area. The darkness is chased away. The ghosts come back into the scene, as do the other sounds.

Deezalo covers his ears. He roars in agony. His body becomes clothed in rags again. The decay reappears on his skin, and his skin lights on fire, yet he doesn't burn up.

Glancing about, Nebukahn stops to focus on some far-off thing. "There!" he shouts. "She is at his tree's base. Already does she have her hand upon it. He's been transferring himself into her, this whole time." Neb, still looking like a werewolf, runs on all fours to get to her.

YaeVorkk rushes away too.

Zymarc lingers behind with me. His gaze is only concerned with staring Deezalo down.

The former king regains resistance to the sounds, and starts for the tree. He means to get to Caleiso first. Gathering courage, I run after him. Zymarc and I keep pace with each other. We slash at Deezalo's heels. He roars in anger, sounding like the monster he is inside. Ironically, Zymarc looks more the monster on the outside.

I imagine Caleiso as a loved one again, and my stride lengthens. I'm faster than Zymarc. I catch up to Deezalo enough to slash into his thigh deeply. He cries out, and falls. He tumbles to the ground. Quickly getting up to face us, he charges us. We're halfway to Caleiso. Neb and YaeVorkk are fighting their way through all the ghosts to get to her. They're almost there. Just a little farther, a little longer.

Zymarc and I fight the former King of Vitiosus, trading off our weapons when Winter's Vondaen starts to feel too heavy, too great to wield a second longer. My daggers are as nothing compared to the weight of the Vondaen.

Deezalo only fights us long enough to get an opening to run toward his tree. It's worse than trying to corral a wild horse. Far worse, for he is fast. And this beast bites hard. At one point, he clamps his sharp, vampiric teeth into my arm and lugs me around.

Zymarc stabs him in the back with NeiSator; Deezalo must let go of me.

I yell in agony, as my arm burns from within.

Zymarc douses me with freezing water, mostly my arm. It's frozen stiff.

"Use Sareustriavas to thaw the ice!" Zymarc shouts, as he defends us.

I cast the spell, and sensation returns. Too much sensation. I fear my arm is going to explode from the pain. But I get up, and help Zymarc.

Neb and YaeVorkk have made it to Caleiso. We can hear them arguing, as we fight Deezalo.

"She's in a trance," YaeVorkk states. "I can't cast Sleep Eternal while she's like this. It will kill her."

"What are we to do?" queries Neb. "We can't let him finish inhabiting her. I know many of them want us to save her. But I don't think we can.

Cast the spell, YaeVorkk. You must. Deezalo must never return to the land of the living."

Zymarc starts fighting harder. The Vondaen becomes too heavy for me to hold. I toss it to Zymarc, then summon my daggers. I'm about to rejoin the fight, when an idea comes to me. Zymarc and I need another distraction, so that we can assist with breaking Caleiso's trance. And I know such a one or two who are mightier than I could ever be in this moment.

I speak the words, summoning them from the past: "Invitios-RotaSyn-el-NeiSator!" I cross the daggers in an *X*, then I throw them toward Deezalo. The twin daggers plunge into the ground between Zymarc and Deezalo. Something explodes out from the daggers, and creates fog, making it hard to see.

From that fog, a figure emerges. Then another. One is tall and tan and thin. His skin shimmers like aged metal. Slicked back, white feathers cover his head, and his eyes glow akin to fire. Light emits from him. A soft light. The kind that could be sustained forever, for it never falters by flickering. RotaSyn. He smiles at me.

The fog disappears.

His twin, NeiSator, is a bluish, shadowed figure with copper-red eyes. His other features are too obscured to take note of.

"Ravier hath summoned us," says RotaSyn, with that strong voice. "We hath answered from across the distance, even passed through the veil Cousin Veldakryn opened. We have come at the call of Last Master."

I give the command, "Detain that one, Deezalo. Keep him from reaching the living tree."

"We shall see it done," says NeiSator, as he brandishes his blade. It is mightier. So is the one RotaSyn carries.

The twins begin.

Zymarc and I rush away.

Deezalo's cries of agony fade off in the distance. Part of me wishes I could bear witness to his pain.

We get to the tree. It's starting to die, from the topmost section down.

Giant birds fall lifeless to the ground. Flowers wilt and burn up. Fruit drops, instantly starting to rot. The leaves blow away in the wind, and turn into ashes that ride the wind.

YaeVorkk lifts his hand to start the spell.

"Wait!" I cry out, breathless. "Wait, YaeVorkk. Let us try to sever her connection to the tree safely, first."

Nebukahn informs me, "You only have minutes, Tyler."

I approach Caleiso. Zymarc gets in my way.

"I'm sorry, Ravier," he says. "The ShenawFayel is forcing me to stop you. I fear this will kill you."

"I don't care!" I shout. "Caleiso isn't going to die like this. She just can't. And I can't let Deezalo come back. This world wouldn't survive another King of Vitiosus. Especially not that one, who doesn't even care for his own people. Only wishes to devour them, his most faithful."

"Quite right," says a male voice from nearby. Azabahk hovers as a corporeal form. He continues on, saying, "Deezalo was vile. Still is, it seems. Do not let him have our Caleiso. I have risked death to help you, Zymarc. To tell you this: cut down his Blackwood Spike. Make it a stump, a reminder that you, and you alone, Zymarc, are the true King of Vitiosus. Fearsome and terrifying you are, but not vile."

"Our people would never forgive me," Zymarc argues. "They wouldn't understand why I had to cut it down."

"Yes, they will," says Azabahk, "for I bear witness, as do these, that you did it to save the Heir of Vitiosus. Lord Zymarc, she is your daughter."

Zymarc looks away in fear, returning to his Onyx form.

Azabahk says, "Do you mean to tell me after everything you've done for her, this is the one thing you will not do?"

Zymarc takes out Deezalo's Hammer. Determined, he strides up to the trunk, and lines up for the swing with the great war axe.

I ask Zymarc, "What of the ShenawFayel?"

"We'll continue to fight its hold together. Are you ready?"

In answer, I quickly go to Caleiso. I touch her on the shoulder, then the neck. She's ice-cold and barely breathing.

Zymarc starts the work with the axe.

Azabahk leaves our midst, fading out of sight.

YaeVorkk and Neb are there to revive Zymarc's magic, when he needs a recharge.

I talk to Caleiso. Call for her to turn around. I project all the images of our first meeting, into her mind.

Though her face is blank, tears trickle down her pale cheeks. She simply stands there, her right hand on the tree trunk, as red energy enters her body.

I go through our dealings together. Our duels, arguments, all of it. But then I show her my interaction with Zebulon and the Phantom of Time.

She blinks a few times.

I start reciting something I believe to be stronger than the ShenawFayel. If nothing else, it is older than that spell of *Truce for a Day*.

"I will tell you a story," I say to her. "Happiness was vanquished with mortality and the days of zeal became rime. That love, our love, was lost in the sea of time. With it gone, our sadness arose out of failure. We had failed fate. Yet he means to set it right. But, first, her hatred's pain would turn to nirvana, numbness of mind, and she may never again remember who she was, what she was."

Dark laughter travels down the way to Deezalo's tree. That depraved, renewed Vitiosyn comes closer, laughing louder. The twins race after him.

He calls, "Zymarc! Truly, you are the Vitiosyn among Vitiosyns, for you hath brought me the very best soul to consume. That of a child Vitiosyn. Though not born a Vitiosyn, she is perfect. More perfect than all child souls I devoured, while living."

Pausing with the glowing axe in hand, Zymarc shouts in anger. Wind goes forth to knock Deezalo down.

Turning to me, Zymarc states, "Keep working on breaking her connection to the Blackwood. And I'll keep up with the destruction of it."

Neb gives me a burst of renewing magic, and YaeVorkk to Zymarc. We continue on.

I recite more to Caleiso. "Our anguish stayed after her memory had gone. They feared the obscured. In fact, still do. But I, Tyler of Ravier, will not. Though it is near and last of the end, never will I fear what is to come. For I am resolved to finish what others have started. Please, Callie," I beg her, "wake up. Wake up! Come back to us. You don't deserve to die this way."

I wipe the tears off her cheeks. She is unmoved. No new tears stream down. It's unbearable to watch her being taken like this.

Drawing closer to Caleiso, I whisper, for I've not strength enough left to talk any louder. "Come back to Zymarc, back to me, back to Tyler Malik Ravier. He would never forgive himself, if you were to die this way." That last line, though spoken by me, didn't sound at all like me, as I am now. Rather, the way I do when I'm older. The mirror-crystal is glowing. The image of my older self looks out from it, then he fades away, looking troubled by something. The glow of the watch-face diminishes.

My heartbeat pounds in my eardrums. All else is drowned out. My vision blurs.

Chanting voices swirl around. Then ones in argument. Metal clashes too. The twin souls of my daggers chant above it all, saying, "Krim-Karasa-dim-drim. Delaysarin. Our master is he: Ravieras-Savak-Kavas. Soon, he shall ruin. Send some to their doom. Laevarye. There is a time to die. And your time is now, dear Deezalo of the Gressind."

The axe keeps chopping at the tree trunk. It becomes deafening. Wood starts creaking and cracking overhead. Zymarc has done it. Surely, this Blackwood Spike cannot survive now. Hope grows in my heart.

Someone grips my arm gently. "Tyler, are you all right?" It's Callie. I can't see her. But her voice is untouched by depravity. Deezalo didn't inhabit her. I'm relieved, until my vision comes back. The tree is starting to sway. It's about to fall.

YaeVorkk casts the sleep spell on Callie; she passes out.

"Run!" Zymarc yells, as he whisks Callie up in his arms. He leads the way to the tear in the veil.

"Get on!" Neb calls to me.

I climb onto his back. It's a bumpy ride on the back of a werewolf, who's running on all fours. All I can focus on is not falling off.

YaeVorkk is fast on foot, bursting ahead as energy, only taking a split-second to regain his sense of direction before bursting away again. The great tree groans in the wind. Then it snaps. It starts to tumble down behind us. It's going to crush us. If not crush us, its aftershock could kill us.

Arsyn stands at the gate, using Veldakryn to keep the tear from sealing back up. He's struggling.

"Hurry!" he yells. "I can't hold it much longer!"

The souls of my daggers quickly get there. They assist Arsyn and their cousin in holding the gate open.

Azabahk waits with the land of the living. Zymarc passes Callie to him, then turns around. He lifts his hands to brace for impact.

YaeVorkk makes it through.

But Neb trips.

I'm sent sprawling. The sight in our wake is horrifying. Deezalo has summoned an army of tormented ghosts. They are headed for us. I quickly stand up, and help Zymarc hold back the magic they cast at us.

"Zymarc, Tyler," Azabahk calls to us. "Quickly, you must come through. The Darklyre grows weak."

Sweat beads on Zymarc's forehead, as he shouts, "We must wait for a pause in the attack. Tyler can't hold it back, if he takes one step at all."

"Where is Winter's Vondaen?" I shout. "Can it absorb the magic for me, so I can move?"

Neb comes forward, then stands on his hind legs. "I shall hold it with Crae-Shand, for it is a magic that surpasses all others, no matter the location. Alpha Jasper taught me well." Nebukahn gets in front of me.

I stumble back as if letting go of a rope held by half a dozen people my own size. Zymarc and Neb get closer to the gate. I try going through. I can't. The ShenawFayel insists that I go stand behind Zymarc and press my left hand against his back.

A wind bursts forth from him. It gives us the pause in the attack we need. The three of us quickly retreat through the tear in the veil. RotaSyn and NeiSator turn back into blades that land at my feet. They shrink to dagger size.

Arsyn's grip on Veldakryn slips. He lets go, to leap back. The Darklyrian blade is swallowed up by the gate. The tear in the veil starts to seal, right as we watch the ghosts get hold of Veldakryn. They take turns attacking Deezalo with it. He screams in horror. It's like seeing a bear get ripped apart by a pack of wolves, only amplified.

The veil finishes making its seal.

A great snap of a whip sounds in my head. Pain erupts in my midsection. I glance down. A shard of something has pierced my belly. A bit of one of the bird statues. I'm bleeding profusely. Staggering around, I fall.

Zymarc was surveying Callie's well-being, as she sleeps. Now he's at my side, shaking me. "Tyler! Stay awake. Don't close your eyes."

My eyelids flicker, as I ask, "Did we break the ShenawFayel for a moment, Zymarc?"

"I don't know," he says, sounding desperate. He tries to bind my wounds.

I admit, "Zymarc, I can't feel my legs."

Touching my face, he studies me. His hands are drenched with my blood.

It's harder and harder to stay conscious.

Zymarc sees it, shakes me harder. "Tyler, don't you dare close your eyes."

But I do, for I can't help it. Young souls can only handle so much.

31

To Forge a Name

I sense my body moving amidst darkness. I have naught control over what happens to me. I'm at the mercy of obliviousness. It's cold too. I should be shivering. My body only keeps moving. Going forward to somewhere. I know not where. I should care. Yet I don't. In fact, something about it is hilarious to me.

I think, *I've died, while in ShenawFayel with Zymarc. If it's true, he's dead too. Oh the irony.*

Screams of torment echo around in my head. I see not the ones being tormented. Nor the owners of groans, moaning, and then screaming. It's hard to tell if their screams are of pain, or something else. Regardless, a laugh wants to rise up my throat. The kind of laugh I've heard only from Soren; recently from Deezalo too.

My own dark laughter fills my head. The darkness lightens to gray. A burst of bright light comes from somewhere behind me. A great snap of a whip cracks overhead. It jars me. Things start to come into focus.

I'm sitting at a simple, wooden table, much irritated by some sudden presence.

Voices fade into hearing, conversing in pleasant tones.

Zymarc sits opposite of me, at the other head of the table, talking with someone. He ignores me.

I hope I'm dreaming. Even do I think, *Please, no. Wherever I've gone to in death, do not let it be with him. Please, not Zymarc!*

Aloud, I beg, "Please, no!"

A spoon's in my left hand, poised to feed me some thickened soup. I drop it, and it clatters against the porcelain bowl. Soup splatters up, lands on my chin.

Biscuit in hand, Zymarc pauses from conversing with a woman, who's at the table with us. "Good morning," he says, before stuffing a bit of biscuit into his mouth. Morning light shines through the window behind him, illuminating the room.

The Deathasyn woman, hardly gray-skinned for a Deathasyn, startles when she looks at me and then Zymarc. She readjusts the wide straps of her elegant, midnight-blue dress. "Oh my. Zymarc, darling, did I forget to bid a 'good morning' to him?" She smiles at me, and it's a rather pretty smile, even with those sharp, Deathasyn teeth showing. "Good morning, Onyx Prince," she says, before curiously eyeing the space around my bowl of soup. "Darling, your barbarians have forgotten to give the Onyx Prince a napkin. Here"—she offers her own unused napkin—"you can use this one."

When I just sit there, trying to recollect anything after that moment of getting stabbed in the gut by a metal shard of a broken bird statue, the woman wipes the soup off my chin.

Flinching, I reluctantly take the napkin, and finish the job. I'm much confused by the lack of memory. Especially by the absence of pain. Nothing hurts anywhere. I feel fine. I'd feel better if I knew what was going on, though. What *went* on.

The woman turns her head to scowl at Zymarc. She's much smaller than most Deathasyn women I've seen. Her eyes are not that of a Vitiosyn. Rather, they are that beautiful burgundy-red. Her eyes seem much too big for her face. It must be due to the dark eye makeup she wears.

Zymarc admits, "He *was* given a napkin by my barbarians, as you call them. Then he complained of being cold. Set that napkin afire. Started laughing at it too. Laid it, still ablaze, upon his lap. I was forced to do something, you understand, Neeka. I had to take the napkin away from him. That's why he and I were wrestling, when you arrived for breakfast. Sadly, the napkin was rendered to ashes by Ravier's amused fury." Zymarc finishes his biscuit.

"A likely story," says Neeka. "Where are the ashes?"

Zymarc leans sideways to view the floor beside my chair. "Still there," he proclaims, straightening in his seat. Zymarc ladles out more soup from a cast iron pot, and refills his bowl. He grinds nuts and spices in a small mortar and pestle, then sprinkles that seasoning atop his meal. He's about to take a bite.

Neeka clears her throat. "Zymarc, darling, you should wait for them to bring up the rest of the meal, before you have seconds. You might find a liking to the other things."

With a sigh, Zymarc sets his spoon aside. He dumps his bowl's contents back into the pot. He gets up from his chair, to go open a window. He tosses his bowl out, then shuts the window. We hear the bowl shatter below.

He retakes his seat.

Neeka inquires, "Feel better?"

"No! I'm still hungry." Zymarc's indignant, now looking at me. "Eat, Ravier, before I pour that soup down your throat. Your hunger is driving me mad. Also did your short, curt answers drive me mad. Once you tired of words, you did that *thing* you do. The shrugging. You should work on ridding yourself of that habit."

I admit, as I clean off my spoon handle with the napkin, "I . . . don't recall anything, after passing out from the wound."

The one door leading into this room opens. Vitiosyn men enter, bringing more food to the table.

Zymarc slowly nods. "I know. All morning, you've been in a trancelike state of mind. I've done many things in your presence, hoping to jar you to awareness." He coyly gestures to the woman. "I even bedded Neeka here, behind a black curtain, while you were in the room with us."

My head swims with anger. "You did what?"

Disregarding my tone, Zymarc adds, "You blankly stared at a wall, as we went behind the curtain. And you were still staring at that wall when we emerged, fully dressed. There was some violence you bore witness to as well. You didn't react a bit. Honestly, I can't guess what in here has made you come to your senses."

I scowl darkly at him. "Couldn't find it in your heart to leave me outside of the room at least?"

"The ShenawFayel wouldn't let me." Zymarc gives a crooked grin.

"Lies!" I shout, throwing my spoon at Zymarc.

He catches it. Grins wider. Says, "Stop being a child, Ravier. It is a natural thing to bed another, especially when it is more than consensual."

I argue, "Consent is consent. How can something be *more than* consensual?" I squeeze my eyes shut. "You know what? I don't want to know."

"Well," says Zymarc, starting to contemplate.

"Please, no!" I whine. I lift the bowl of soup up to my mouth. I drink the hot liquid like it's the leftover milk from a bowl of cereal. Once finished, I firmly set the bowl down.

"Hello, Tyler Ravier," says a perky, yet smug voice. A girl's voice. Not Caleiso. Not Keturah.

I think in horror, *Oh no! It's her.*

Krina, *Princess Krina.* From the seat across from Neeka, she eyes me all gleeful-like. "Fancy seeing you here, Ravier."

I burst out with, "What are you doing here?"

"Having breakfast with—"

"No!" I shout, motioning around. "What are you doing in Vaydell? Brink was supposed to come get you, after I fought to free you and Ketty by dueling Caleiso." I whip my attention to Zymarc. "Why is she still a captive?"

"I'm not a captive," Krina argues. "And I'm not ready to go home yet."

"You can't stay here," I fume.

"Brinkorr of Deivahl came to collect her a while ago," Zymarc states. "She refused to go with him. Made threats on her own life, if I recall right, should we force her to leave."

She lifts her head arrogantly. "I'm not done seeing all there is to see, up on the surface. Surely, I've only seen half of it. *Less* than half."

My grip on the napkin tightens. I want it to be her throat.

As she ladles soup into a bowl, Krina continues, saying, "And, not to be rude, but *who* are you, Tyler? Cousin to a king? I'm a princess. I outrank you." After another smirk at me, she slurps some soup off her spoon.

I slam my napkin down on the table, bursting to my feet. "Like *hell* you do, Krina!"

She startles in her seat.

Composing myself, I lean down to ask, "Are you familiar with what Sodon requests are, *Princess* Krina?"

"Of course." She resumes the consumption of her soup. "Also did I hear rumors you made a rather grand request of the Onyx King."

I narrow my eyes on her. "That's right. Perhaps the grandest request to be asked in a long time, in fact. Before I tell you what it was, I must know. Do you not even care what I had to go through in that duel to free you and Keturah?"

"Oh, stop whining, Tyler." Krina sneers. "You freed one of the ladies in distress. Bravo! You should be proud of yourself. But I didn't need saving, dear boy. I was placed exactly where I wanted to be. On the surface, with someone who knows of the fate my mother suffered."

I cup Krina's face one-handedly, instead of slapping sense into her.

Her expression creases in confusion. She's only concerned with looking up at me.

I tell her, "I understand now why all the princesses in fairy tales get locked away, kidnapped, or otherwise. They had to be out of their mind, the way you are."

Krina glances down at her food.

I squeeze her face some, then yank my hand away. I resume my place at the table, calmly filling an empty plate with savory-smelling meat pastries.

Krina queries, "What was the request you made?"

Not looking at her, I reply, "To be made the blood-heir Onyx Prince.

King ReNovak's heir to the throne." I start eating bits of meat pastries.

"And did he give you your request?"

"Yes," is all I respond with.

After a while of silence, I say, "What I've come to learn of this world, there are few kings, few leaders, who outrank the Onyx Prince. It is a special role I play now, more than ever. As I said before, you're not staying, Krina."

"That's not for you to decide," she says. "For, I wager, there is one, here, who outranks you. Lord-King Zymarc. Surely, he—"

"Enough," says Zymarc. "Eat your food in silence, little girl. Tyler and I have suffered quite the ordeal, this past day. And the ShenawFayel weighs heavy on us." He cuts into a mini meat pie.

Krina eats more soup, no longer slurping it.

I glance at the Vitiosyns, as they retreat from the room with empty food trays.

Zymarc pauses his food consumption, to gulp down some sparkling liquid from a clear chalice. Neeka slides her chair out. She saunters to him, rests a hand on his shoulder, waits for him to set his chalice aside, then she bends down to kiss him tenderly on the mouth. He tilts his head back, to let her. She grips his face.

I look away. I start thinking of Callie. My pulse quickens. I don't know what's become of her. When Neeka starts for the door, I ask Zymarc, "Where's Caleiso? Is she—?"

"Sleeping," replies Zymarc, resuming his meal.

I swallow hard. "Then the Jokryns couldn't wake her?"

Zymarc quickly focuses on me. "She's resting, I mean. The second-born Jokryn spent two hours waking her. Then another hour negotiating the reward for his actions. RayVora had the nerve to request they be given a dragon for the ride home, wherever that home might be."

Neeka's about to leave. Before closing the door, she says, "See you tonight, Zymarc."

"Yes, of course," Zymarc replies. "Be sure to go see that little brother of yours. Viido's Hymn, wasn't it?"

Neeka lets out a quiet laugh. "You are hysterical, darling, pretending that you could forget his name."

Zymarc empties the remainder of his chalice, ignoring her.

Neeka closes the door. The swishing sound of her dress fabric fades. A distant door opens and closes.

Krina queries, "Viido's Hymn? That's her younger brother? Isn't he barely the age of a Sorsivyte? I thought she was well past a Sorsryn's Fifty. Nearly one hundred? It's quite the gap. Have they the same parents?"

Zymarc only nods in answer. He then pulls a small book out, and reads while finishing breakfast.

I remark, "It's not nearly the gap between you and Lemawr. Isn't it about, oh . . . a thousand years or so?"

"Something like that. However, he and I only share the same mother. And there wouldn't have been the great gap, if my mother hadn't been such a sickly creature. It seems, she needed the company of several Sorsryns in Deivahl. Also needed the waters of the Pools of Vosh-Perida with her always. My father captured some, put it in a pendant for her. Called it the Lumen of Vardiyas. She carried it with her always. At least, she did until giving it to my brother after I was born. Did King Talok and the others ever find him?"

About to speak the truth, I decide against it, saying, instead, "No. We never found him." I finish with the thought, *And that's the truth, for he was the one to find us. Therefore, I'm not lying to the princess.*

Zymarc slowly glances up from his reading. He considers me.

I cringe, now remembering that Zymarc didn't know Lemawr still lives. ReNovak must not have told him.

I ask, "When may I go see Caleiso?"

"In a bit," remarks Zymarc coldly. "She's not been sleeping long enough. Had a brew of herbs, to give her pleasant, healing dreams. It's best to let her wake on her own." Zymarc glances to Krina, telling her, "You may go."

Krina nods, then picks at the remains of meat pastries on her plate. She makes no motion to get up.

Zymarc's neck tenses. "I said, you may go."

In that Krina way, she retorts, "I heard you the first time, my liege. You said: 'I *may* go,' meaning I have a choice. And I choose to stay. To stay in this room. To stay in this city."

"Girl!" Zymarc pounds his fist on the table, making dishes rattle a bit. "Get up from that chair!"

Krina bursts to her feet. Her expression becomes taut with fear.

Zymarc gives more commands of: "Stop talking, and walk for that door; open that door; step through; *slam* it behind you. Now!"

Krina stiffly strides for the door. She seems forced to turn its knob, open it, step out. Her breaths quicken, then she slams the door.

Zymarc breathes in relief. He opens his mouth, about to say something to me. But then his gaze flicks to the recently slammed door. He firmly says, "And do *not* linger where you can still hear us."

Krina's voice is muffled by the door, asking, "But what am I supposed to go do, my liege?"

"I do not care," says Zymarc. "Go feed the dragons, in the stables."

"I hate dragons, unless they hail from Deivahl."

Zymarc suggests, "Go groom horses, then."

"I don't know how."

"Then learn!" Zymarc bursts out. He's turning red in the face. Then frightfully pale. His black hair starts falling out. His eyes become that crimson color.

There's a quiet huff from Krina, beyond the door. Her soft footsteps fade. A distant door opens then shuts.

Zymarc brushes his hands through his hair. It all falls out. Then it regrows. He's quickly back to looking like the Onyx version of himself. He says, "Lemawr lives, then? Did ReNovak know?"

I try to lie, but the ShenawFayel won't let me. I remain silent.

"Of course he knew." Zymarc asks, "When did you learn of it?"

I try to resist answering, but I know Zymarc is using magic on me. The tingle along my forehead gives it away. I say, "Just before The Sodon. ReNovak had already put preparations in place to name a new heir."

Zymarc says, "I'm surprised ReNovak did not summon him again, to rename him as heir."

I admit, though I don't wish to, "There was an argument between them."

"Over what?"

"I don't have to tell you."

"Fine. Then tell me how you fit in, Ravier. Did ReNovak want you for something?"

"He wished to introduce me to someone."

"And what is the identity of this *someone*?"

I stay quiet.

Zymarc pries, "Was it Matron Avilon? The last living Withrasyn?"

"No."

"What about one of the Amethysts?"

I shake my head.

"An Onyx? A Silverian?"

"No!" I shout, distraught that he'll guess it.

"Was it a Sorsryn at all?" Zymarc's gaze is wild.

Again, I shake my head. I try getting out of my chair, to leave this room. I can't. I'm confined.

Zymarc's gaze settles. He leans his elbows on the table. "Ah," he says, "it was King Rentwar. I should've guessed that, second. So, the Rubidyn King was there in Oniva for The Sodon? Met you for the first time, while there on other business." Zymarc's talking to himself now.

I'm free to move about. I head for the window, open it to get some fresh air.

Dragons have gathered below, in the courtyard. They are feasting on picked-over carcasses. The stench of raw, warm meat hits my nostrils. I close the window and stifle a gag.

Opening the door, I exit the small dining room. I find myself in Zymarc's quarters. A black curtain hides the bed and wardrobe area. Rage rises to the surface. I want to pummel Zymarc for his most recent offenses. I glance back into the dining room. Even hear his monologue.

He mutters, "He must've been in the crowd, as all were making requests.

Could've disguised himself as a Silverian, for they are about the same height as him, when he's in human form. But why would he wish to be at The Sodon, when he previously has never cared to be there?"

Thinking in silence a moment, Zymarc suddenly jolts out of his seat and strides for the exit out of his quarters.

I follow him. "Where are you going?"

"Deezalo's Cathedral." He points to one of the cleared-off desks. "Get your things, there."

I collect them, glad to have them back.

Zymarc asks, "Are you coming?"

We leave the General's House.

We walk in the morning light, headed to the edge of the city. The side opposite of where Siege and I were allowed to enter.

After a while, I ask, "Why do you think Rentwar went to Oniva? I thought it was to meet me, talk with me, for the first time."

Zymarc's quick pace hasn't let up. "King Rentwar would've picked a different place, if that's all he wanted. No. I believe there was something more. And it is this. He suspected what request you'd make of ReNovak. Somehow felt that Awngeleik would show up in Oniva that night. I couldn't follow her trail of transportation that your older self set in motion. As I was busy with other things, and had few Vitiosyns to command there, I couldn't follow her. But Rentwar could have followed her trail. Must've caught up with her. It's why he's involved in this war, now. He has the Equidyn. No other explanation fits so perfectly. He's had her for weeks. I must read up on Rubidyns, refresh my memory of their nesting locations."

I ask, "Does that mean there's a library in the cathedral?"

"Yes. It's much older than Soren's Library too."

"What about the Onyx Archives?"

Zymarc stops, to reply, "No library is older than the ones the Onyx possess. Unless you count the Arkivaras as libraries. The Geldryn Records were very old, however. Those are gone now."

I ask, "Because of you?"

"Because of me." Zymarc resumes the walk.

The cathedral comes into view. It's far less intimidating, in daylight. Nevertheless, Zymarc slows his stride toward the steps. I mimic his example.

Once we're at the landing, he says, "Put your coat on. And fasten the daggers to your belt. I wish to know if the time of day matters, in regards to the level of danger."

I happily don my coat of the Sleeping Dragon, and flaunt the daggers.

Zymarc tosses the other coat aside. Then he pushes the door wide open.

We go in, together.

Those eerie sensations do not come over me. I dare not look up at the ceiling, though. I even refuse to view the murals. I put on figurative blinders and go forward with Zymarc.

We traverse our way to a grand hallway. Then through many corridors.

"Almost there," says Zymarc.

I ask, "Mind if I spend time with the statue, instead of going to the library?"

Zymarc veers to go in a different direction.

My head starts throbbing. I wonder why I asked that question at all.

Zymarc's confident stride slackens. We're both sweating, our faces wet with it.

At last, Zymarc admits, "It's through that door, ahead. It seems we cannot go there together. I must wait here. If the ShenawFayel permits me, I'll head for the library. Go on."

And that's how I ended up going into the room with Soren's Statue alone.

I fear it was a mistake, for as soon as that door shut behind me, a golden light filled the circular room that contained six pillars. They lit with color. The three primary colors—gold, red, and blue. Then the secondary ones—copper, purple, then green. The statue set itself aflame. Soren's laughter echoed all around me.

I screamed for Zymarc to help. Pounded on the door that had locked itself.

It didn't matter.

The daggers were drawn into Soren's statue hands. Their former master woke up. He chased me about the room, slashing at me. I tried every spell I could think of.

Try as I did, I succumbed to exhaustion, and the older Soren stabbed me in the heart. His laugh was the last sound I clearly heard for quite a long time. He traded places with me. I know not how long I was trapped in the statue, before a young boy came along and put my divers' watch, mirror crystal in it, upon my right wrist.

The boy retreated to someone's side. He couldn't have been more than eight or nine years old, when my statue eyes perceived him beside an older Caleiso. She was dressed like a warrior queen, silver plate armor molded to the contours of her royal-blue dress. A delicate crown rested upon her head. One of black, gold, and blue metal.

Sounding wise, she tells the boy, "It must be you, to set things right, my son. Wake Tyler up. Return him to the past. Let him play his part. For no other can play it as well as he."

The boy approaches more confidently. His appearance changes. He grows up in seconds. He takes on the face of me, at age eighteen. "I have been born now, Tyler of Ravier," he says. "The Phantom of Time has come to set things right. I urge you to defeat Zymarc. You've already defeated Deezalo. But it was not enough. The land has succumbed to Vitiosus, most treacherous. Do not go into the cathedral with Zymarc. Choose another path. The ShenawFayel was outsmarted by a powerful being; one who wishes to use Soren for his will. The statue is a dangerous thing, when in the cathedral. It must not stay there, gaining power. Promise you will have it removed, thrown into the waters near Deivahl."

I manage a desperate whisper of: "I will."

The phantom activates the watch.

Everything turns blindingly bright.

I'm sent back to the past. Back to that moment of Zymarc telling me to get my things. That he intends to go to the cathedral.

Zymarc's asks, "Are you coming?"

Changing into my coat of the Sleeping Dragon, I ask, "Can't we talk a bit?"

"What about?" Zymarc turns to look at me.

After I get my things situated on my person, I shrug.

He scowls. "So it's back to the shrugging, is it?"

I shrug again.

He shouts, "Stop doing that, Ravier!"

"Or what? You'll hit me? Go ahead. Try."

He reaches up, as if to slap me. Instead, he pats my face. "You're such an annoying little prick." He walks away. "I've thought of something we can do this morning, as we wait for Caleiso to wake up."

We leave the General's House.

I'm a nervous wreck, as we walk in the morning light.

Zymarc says, "I apologize that my feelings toward that insufferable, little princess have affected you."

I say, "Nah! I didn't like her before the ShenawFayel. Now? Even less."

"Likewise," Zymarc agrees, before adding, "You know, I had considered making her a sacrifice to Deezalo, last night? Unfortunately, she's not a Sorsivyte, nor is she sixteen. Can't be used as a sacrifice, by Onyx Law. And that's the law that matters, as long as Vitiosyns are the named victor."

I ask, "So the Onyx Prince can't overrule the named victor?"

"Only if the prince wins a Prince's Gamble. The king would have to be available for a duel, however. And something's happened to ReNovak. Been detained, somehow. I can't make contact with him."

We're now to a plain, silo-like building made of metal. It's about sixty feet high. Nothing impressive about it.

Vitiosyn men exit from a door we approach.

"King Zymarc," says Belgorr, coming over to us. "We're near ready to set this afire. Had you wished to take one last look of your handiwork?"

Zymarc inquires, "They've been cleared away?"

Belgorr replies, "All but that one piece you asked us to save for you."

Belgorr's brother approaches, to say, " I left it in the case on the table."

"I'll take care of it from here," says Zymarc. "Clear out. And, Belgorr, tell your brother to get some rest, for Vard's sake. He just woke from death this morning."

This brightens the mood of the two Vitiosyn men. They head off with many others, going toward the center of the city.

Zymarc opens the door. It squeals on its hinges. He motions that I go first. First into the wide-open, circular room. First to see the horrific sight. Blood spatter everywhere. That dark Deathasyn blood. The concrete-type floor is smeared with it, pooled in places. Yet there are no bodies. No parts. Only torn clothing, and the stench of much spilled blood. Metal tables with straps and harnesses are dispersed around, for torturing victims. There are devices placed on wall hooks too.

I turn on my heel to exit this house of torture.

Zymarc gets in my way. "No, Ravier. You must take this in. You must see that *this* is what happens to those who dare to touch, to hurt, to violate those in my care. Voldrake laid a hand of ill intent on you. Tried to lay a hand on Caleiso as well. I know it's true. So I brought him back to life, to give him a proper ending. It wasn't hard, for your dagger hadn't completely snuffed the life out of him. Only paralyzed him. Held him suspended on the edge of death. I ended what you started with him."

I'm sick to my stomach. "I wouldn't torture a soul, Zymarc!" I shout. "Never would I do this!"

"Oh, but you will, Ravier." Zymarc goes to one of the metal tables along the wall. On the way, he says, "There will come a day that a soul as dark and defiled as Deezalo will rise up. That soul will commit atrocities that will make me look as a kindly king plagued by cowardice. I believe there is nothing you wouldn't do to stop him from hurting those you love." Zymarc opens a small box that's on the table. As he looks at what's inside, he says more, "Only last night, I was visited by a being, most mysterious. Shrouded from me. He claimed to know my fate. Convinced me rather well that he does not jest. Warned that my reign of Vitiosus is at its end. Only possessing the Son of LanSoren with Vitiosus, and gaining him as an ally, will keep my regime from falling. Ownership of the Equidyn could also spare me of the foretold fate, as well as aid me with my most wanted desire of all."

"I know you will not tell me what that desire is, Zymarc. But are you admitting to your own weakness? Love of power?"

He admits, "I don't love power. But I want it for my own reasons."

I haven't a thing to say, while Zymarc casts a spell on the box's contents. The sparking spell ceases.

Zymarc takes out the object: a hand encased by dark, reflective metal. "I believe this belongs to you." He offers it to me. "It belonged to Voldrake. The very hand that touched you."

I look it over. Feeling very devious inside, I remark, "You know, Zymarc, if I were Neeka, I'd think you were trying to romance me."

Zymarc laughs boisterously, and it echoes around, the sound absent of cruelty. He quiets down, wiping at tears that have seeped from the corners of his eyes. "Ravier, you really shouldn't have said that. For now I cannot let you keep it. It must go to a lady, fairest of them all."

I say, "Pity there's no Snow White around here."

"Oh, but there is a princess nearby." Zymarc stuffs his hands in his pockets. "A rather smug one, who can never be drowned. At least, that is her claim."

I comment, "Krina would only use it as a resting place for rings and jewels."

Zymarc chuckles. "What would Voldrake think of his hand being reduced to nothing but a princess's jewelry display?"

"He'd think it's a very Geldryn sort of thing."

"Right you are, Ravier." Zymarc glances around. "It'd be a fitting end. Deathasyns have detested the Geldryn throughout the ages."

"That may be. But I'm not giving this to Krina. It should go to the other princess."

Zymarc's about to ask me who I mean.

I state, "Princess Caleiso," before he can.

He argues, "Ravier, she's not a prin—"

I lift up the dark-silver hand, to interrupt. "Now, Zymarc. Stop being in denial. Enough have called her that, in my presence. There must be truth to it. If nothing else, she is your heir. Do you deny that?"

"No," he says, looking away. Then he starts speaking a spell, to cut me off, words of: "Sas-Sadora-vyn-kryn-dei-Oostrinas." Fire flares from his gaze. The bits of torn clothing, and anything that can burn, lights on fire. "Best we get out of here. Let the fire sanitize the place, ready it for those still waiting their turn."

I open the door, and we exit the repurposed silo building. Smoke soon pours out through all its crevices.

Zymarc digs a metal mask out from one of his inner coat pockets. He speaks into it, "Awza, is Caleiso awake yet?"

Azabahk's voice speaks out from the mask, "Yes, yes! Only just."

"Where is she?" Zymarc queries.

"Waterfalls. She wished to bathe outdoors. By herself. Had her take Droediin, out of precaution. Follow the paw prints. You'll find her."

Zymarc says, "Thank you, Awza."

Azabahk growls. "This politeness you've found a liking to, King Zymarc, is revolting. Stop thanking me, and tell Neeka to stop calling us *darlings*. We're not her pets!" He hisses the last word.

Trying to not to laugh, Zymarc puts the mask away.

He leads us in the direction of the forest.

I ask, "What had Voldrake wished to ask me? Did you find out?"

"He wanted your allegiance, as well as your coat and daggers. Toward the end, he said something about resurrecting Soren. No idea why he'd want to resurrect Soren. But to each their own."

"How'd they plan to do it?"

Zymarc huffs. "Only spirits know. All I interrogated from the group, withheld the means of their ritual. They had to have come across bones believed to be Soren's, though."

"What about the statue?"

Zymarc shakes his head. "I don't see how. Soren's Statue was forged to hold papers, books, and the like. Those Deathasyns were set on procuring weapons, not books. Therefore, how could the statue be involved?"

I nod, to hide what I'm thinking. Thoughts of, *That's why he let me enter that room. He was blinded by how much he knows of rituals. Yet, what could've fooled the ShenawFayel?* To further keep Zymarc from knowing my thoughts, I say with wit, "Well, well, dear Voldrake. Never got what he wanted most. May he rest in peace."

Zymarc adds, "I think you mean in pieces." He deliberates for a moment. "In fact, I do believe it was—"

Quickly, I interrupt, "Don't tell me how many pieces. I don't need to know."

Zymarc clears his throat. "Well, I can say this. Grawllik rests in two pieces. The devil. Should have made it six. Oh well. He's buried now. At least, the main part."

We're now well into the forest.

"Buried where?" I ask.

"In the dirt. To feed death."

I say, "Tsk, tsk, Zymarc. You should've let him join his head in the dragon's belly. What would Neeka say? Oh, and what if I remember certain things that happened during my trance? It could give me nightmares. Like what happened in the silo. Also, hearing you and Neeka, well . . ." I trail off.

"Why," says Zymarc, "we can make a trip to Trauvo, donate unwanted memories to her, for she's not far."

"I understand why you were in Yharss-Rawshuen that day," I state, slowing my pace. "But if Trauvo is closer to Vosh-Perida, why did Caleiso go to Dysarda?"

Zymarc catches sight of Droediin's paw prints. He starts following them. "Dysarda-Reine is the oldest Vaegon city. Has more history. Also, it's tended by a rather gifted Arkivy. The Warrior Arkivy. Only King Kailon was more gifted, for he had tended all Arkivaras. Even the one presently dormant in Gayza'Ragaen."

"Warrior Arkivy, meaning Lokasi?"

Zymarc nods. "Caleiso mentioned how he puts on a show of magic every month. I've even gone toe-to-toe with him, dueling as the Onyx

Warrior Kaalon. Lokasi is not one to be underestimated. I kept thinking he would challenge me, after the initial attacks. He never did. I'm unsure as to why."

Water gushes from somewhere up ahead. We get closer to it, nearly trip over a furry, napping Droediin. He startles awake and growls.

"Sh!" Zymarc scolds. "It's only us. Go on, Ravier." He shoves me forward. "I'll wait here with Droediin. I've a scene of slaughter to convey to him."

Droediin watches me intently, as I walk away, while Zymarc just flops down in a patch of long grass, and crosses his legs at the ankles. He starts by saying, "So you know those Deathasyns you didn't eat last night, Droediin? Let me tell you of their ends. 'Twas glorious."

They fade out of earshot.

The waterfall comes into view. It's thunderously loud.

I search along the shore for signs of Caleiso, only to find her outer clothes. *Well,* I think, *at least she has something on.* I wait on the shoreline, closer to the water's edge, and study the silver hand.

Someone approaches from behind. "What is that?" queries Caleiso, adjusting her shirt. She's already fully dressed.

"Something for you," I admit, holding it out to her.

She takes it. "A hand?" she queries, as her brows draw together.

"Voldrake's hand," I clarify.

Caleiso flings it away in disgust. "Ew!" She makes a face.

I cackle with laughter. "I guess that means you don't want it?"

"Definitely don't want it. Don't want a single reminder of that Voldrake."

"Well then," I say, "it shall go to fair Princess Krina." I fetch it off the sandy shore.

"What would Krina want with that?"

"Jewelry display," I proclaim.

"Good one!" says Caleiso.

We head for where Zymarc and Droediin are.

Droediin has transformed into human form, staring off into nothing.

Zymarc asks Caleiso, "Didn't want the hand, then?"

She scoffs. "Not funny, King Zymarc! What will be amusing is to give it to Krina for her jewels. I even have rings I can add to it, before Tyler gives it to her. What a joke it will be."

Zymarc turns serious, asking, "But do you have the one ring that rules them all?"

"What?" Caleiso queries, confused.

"Right!" Zymarc scratches his face. "You wouldn't understand that reference. Shall we go back? Give Krina the hand and rings, send her on her way to Paragon with Droediin? As you said, Ravier, she can't stay here. And I think Droediin's mind is broken beyond repair. Best to give Alpha Jasper the distraction of trying to *fix* him."

I ask, in suspicion, "What are you planning?"

"Exactly what I said."

"How much longer do I have until . . . you know?" I study Zymarc.

"A few more hours," he says.

"Then do you mind if I do my mental preparations, out here? I'd rather not see Krina and Droediin off."

Zymarc contemplates a moment. "It seems the ShenawFayel will permit me to leave you for a time. I have a few preparations of my own to make. Meet me at the Interrogation Silo we've only just left, when you're ready."

* * *

A short while later, I find myself practicing for the enchantment circle. The Hexyn Circle.

I take thirteen steps, counting them in my head, to get a visual of what the circle diameter should be. Looking forward rather than down, I try not to think about the steps as I take them. I must have overthought it, for, when I look back at the five attempts, they're all of different lengths.

Standing on the sandy shoreline, I groan as the waterfall gushes in the background, endlessly, unconcerned with my weighty task. I start again.

Rather than counting in my head, I count with my fingers, thinking about how I'll lay out the weapons: Enyxar and Aevimeis; RotaSyn and NeiSator; then I choose the Spear of Guyheiz and Winter's Vondaen, over the Shield of Shylen piece Dea gave me. The Vondaen isn't with me, however. Zymarc must know where it is. I'll have to get it from him, before I can finish the Hexyn.

How should I place them all? I wonder, visualizing the many combinations I could try for the six points. None yet feel right.

Once I've counted thirteen steps, I pivot, and start another line of footsteps parallel to the previous ones. I repeat a pivot and walk of thirteen steps again and again for an hour. When I check once more, the lines are still disastrous.

I sweep them away with a wave of Ventus, then sit down. I try to think of anything to relax me. Gemma's face, the first time she saw Awngeleik. Complete bliss. It ends with seeing Siege and Jasper take her away on Claudys. I switch to Skylin, kissing her. It ends in Arsyn telling me to show a little restraint, right before he compared me to being everyone's toxin. I rock back and forth, hugging knees to my chest. I search for the one memory that doesn't end in misery. They all turn sad, somehow. Bleak. Dark. But one calls for me to contemplate further. One I don't quite understand.

Even so, I rise to start the walk again, thinking on this memory that brings curiosity. Jasper's words of: *Sleep, slumbering deep in the dark. Light of the night, bright on the right of the Kyanite asleep. To sleep so deep you'll reap of the keep fast asleep. To summoning a slumbering Rubidyn to sleep.*

I wonder, *What does it* really *mean?*

Further, I remember more words. Gemma's, as she made Zymarc, himself, fade to unconsciousness: *Sleep, slumbering deep in the heart of the dark. Krim-Karasa-dim-drim. Light of night. Bright on the right of Kyanite asleep. Harin-nae-Varin. To sleep, so deep you'll reap of the dragon's keep fast asleep. Din-drim-Delaysarin. To summoning a slumbering Rubidyn to the sleeping dyns'hyn el Ravieras-Savak.*

It's near identical to Jasper's, but it has Ravieras-Savak at the end. My name. Sleeping Dragon.

What does it mean to be an aura of both? Why does it matter? I decide I have no idea. So I think about the weapons again—how the Blades of Neutrality likely represent a beginning and end. My daggers? The time in between that. But what of the spear or Jasper's blade? I think, *Where do they fit?*

Jasper's blade is most likely the older of the two, but which one might represent life and death? The spear saves time. Winter's Vondaen pierces the ethereal world, unable to be fooled. Some might claim that it cuts through time. Therefore, I decide they are equal.

Partly afraid, I peer back at my trails of thirteen footsteps. I puff out a laugh of relief. They're of the same length. In the sand, the parallel lines resemble the barbs of feathers, making up the vane. I pull out Dea's feather turned-to-metal, imbued with the power of the Shield of Shylen, itself.

I whisper, "Two races, made one. Not there at the beginning, but there at the end. Withrasyn and dragon. Darklyres."

It reminds me of Sivondel and the Arkivaras. He's the image of a dragon. And that dragon is death. Life, he claimed, is found in the Arkivaras: Tree Stag.

Is she represented as a stag, though? I wonder. *I never saw proof of that, when I was in her heart. Might she represent* all *life?*

I push the thought aside, for it leads nowhere. I wander around the area. My time is close, unless I can revert time, using my watch and the spear. I dig through my things, searching for Ben's spell-book. I take it out, quickly going through the index. I look up the sections on reverting time, making a mental note that I must soon lookup all I can on life spells, death ones, all things relevant to what I'm trying to accomplish, which is to resist the Call of Vitiosus and not die. So long as I live through the ordeal, there is hope of defeating Zymarc.

For now, I must buy myself time. Revert it, to the moment before Zymarc left. *Surely, a couple of hours can't be too difficult,* I muse. *Especially if I link with Droediin's power.*

"There's a thought," I say, already feeling a partial victory. I flip through

Ben's book again. I find the spell for time—Temporiavas—reading up what I can of it. There can be a pause before the syllable of 'avas.' In fact, a whole spell word can be said before the last syllable. There are other things Ben wrote of it. They don't help me right now.

Tucking away words I can use later, I search for what to pair with time. And I find it. A spell of undo—*Oonsilios*. The last *S* can be left off, if I'm short on magic. But I'm not. Just time. *S's* can also be added to the end or beginning of words, to aid with flow of strings of words. Again, there's much else I could glean from this spell-book. I move on to other subjects, though, like the notes Ben made of connecting words to aid in magic being released from the body in the right rhythm for the caster. It's different for everyone, apparently. We all have our own rhythm for magic.

Taking one last look over the connecting-word list, I put the book away and begin. I clear my mind of everything but three things: Temporiavas, Oonsilios, and linking my magic with Droediin; stealing his strength, if I must. This is the moment of practice. Overpowering my equal, so that I may resist my superior. Zymarc is held back by the ShenawFayel. Once it's broken, his power will be immense. His focus resolute on one thing: gaining me as an ally.

Closing my eyes, I search across the distance, mentally retracing the steps Droediin took to the forest. I speak the words: "Tempori-seves-Soonsilios-savas." I picture Droediin in Vaydell, last night, looking out the window into nothing. But he's not looking at nothing, as he comes into better mental focus. He watches the forest I'm currently in. He meets my gaze. His mouth twitches with a slight grin. He lifts his hand, holding a bow. He readies himself to fire off an arrow.

32

Within the Circle

From my place in the forest near Vaydell, I Mensa-div to him, *"Droediin, I need more time to make a spell out of a name. Help me, please. I don't know what I'm doing. But I'm close, cunning Von."*

While holding tight to the bow and arrow, he replies in div, *"Let us outsmart the Vitiosyn. You are one of us, Tyler of Vondurheil. Vons never leave each other behind. I've been waiting for you, here in Vaydell. I knew you would come to free me. So free me, Tyler of Ravier. Break the spell I cast on you."*

He releases the arrow. I mentally watch as Caleiso catches it. It was from last night, when she and I fled on the back of Zebulon, to make for the Pools of Vosh-Perida.

In the now, eyes still shut, I speak aloud: "To spells, binding and whole, not to tell, nor to say, and *absolutely* not to think the name . . ." I trail off. I can't say it in whole. Sure, I can think *The Phantom* and *of Muraine*. But not together. Whole strings of jumbled words fill the space, so that one could never put the two parts together. So I continue on, saying, "Is Droediin he? What do you think?" I struggle to say the one word I need to. Yes or no. It matters not. I must say one right after the two questions.

I end up on my hands and knees, pounding on the sandy ground, then clawing at my throat. Choking myself. Stopping, I scream in anger. I impulsively rush into the water, and dive down. I hold my breath. I think the two questions. My left hand lights with the Prismatic of Magic. It illumines my surroundings. I move that hand to write the word *yes* in the water. It's invisible, for it's not written with quill and paper. There's nothing to erase. But I did it. I swim to the surface. I ask the questions aloud, hesitating only a moment to say, "Yes. I believe he is."

Victorious, I exit the water. A fierce wind dries my clothes all the way through. Something grips me, throws me to the ground. Things fast-forward from Droediin's point of view, too quick for me to linger on any single part. Then it slows down to when Caleiso and I approached Zymarc and Droediin.

I gradually move back into my viewpoint.

Droediin's in human form. And he's not staring off into nothing. He's watching where I now am, and those mysterious Von-eyes of his are back. Recognition briefly flickers in them, as I meet up with my past self. My bodies sync. I'm made whole.

Zymarc asks Caleiso, "Didn't want the hand, then?"

The following dialogue is the same, only Droediin speaks this time, after I've said: "I'd rather not see Krina and Droediin off."

"Are you afraid, Ravier?" he inquires in seriousness. "Afraid that I'll eat the fairest princess of them all? If so, do not worry. I had my fill of flesh last night. Also will I have my fill in a short while, for Lord-King Zymarc means to give me pieces of the expired Deathasyns he spoke of."

"You didn't have to tell Ravier that," says Zymarc. Considering me a moment, he adds, "It seems the ShenawFayel will permit me to leave you for a time. I have a few preparations of my own to make. Meet me at the Interrogation Silo we've only just left, when you're ready."

He turns to leave. But I stop him by asking, "Would you happen to have Winter's Vondaen with you, Zymarc? Did it pick one of us as its new master? You haven't said."

"It neither resists nor rejects me." Zymarc takes out the Vondaen, to offer it. "Why don't you see what it decides of you, as you make your preparations?"

After I accept it, Zymarc and Caleiso start off.

Droediin gives me a quick wink, paired with a half-grin. Then he goes back to that numbed-mind appearance. The three leave my sight.

I quickly get to work, reviewing all I need to do, even thinking aloud, "If I'm the Sleeping Dragon, that should be somewhere in the spell. Somewhere in the middle. Ravieras-Savak. Maybe even add *Kavas* the way Eyo'el and my older self did. Also, if I'm an aura of both, there should be something of Vons and dragons mentioned."

Words of the ShenawFayel bleed into hearing like an eerie whisper. Someone's voice, saying, "Cunning of Vons, and strength of dyns." It is the voice of my eighteen-year-old self.

I search around. I don't see him. Then something casts a bluish light. The mirror-crystal of my watch is glowing. The glow fades. My older self appears on the crystal. He watches me. "Cheat death. Mirror the two. Hold tight to the shield, when—" Something stops him from saying more.

The crystal gradually goes black. It returns to being a mirror.

I recall the exact words of the ShenawFayel. *Cunning of wolves be far from me, in this day of truce against my foe: Ravier . . . Strength of dragons be in me this day, in defending my enemy of yesterday and of tomorrow, should any attack this Zymarc of Vitiosus.*

More, I read Ben's spell-book. I find what I need. Information about ShenawFayels. It seems, many spells have been rendered from the two Matriarchs' names, none greater than *Truce for a Day*, however. All of Shena's have to do with cunning or clarity; Fayel's spells to do with strength. *Shenawsafa* fits well in that it clarifies for the caster, but it fools the recipient of the spell. *Fayelondel* strengthens the caster's intentions. Never is this spell meant to be used alone. It always needs a partner spell.

I talk to myself, saying, "Guess I could've called out Ben as my partner in the Duo's Duel. He certainly knows enough."

I close the book, and mull over what to have the spell made-of-my-name do. My older self said to mirror cunning and strength. Cheat death. Hold tight to the shield, in a certain circumstance. The shield must be the piece Deamond gave of herself. The Shield of Shylen. Perhaps I can hold onto it, as the other weapons fill the six Hexyn points. Also, I should have on the clothes Madeleine made for me. It's only fitting.

Clean clothes in place, as soon as I've tied that last bit of boot lacing, I know what the spell should do. I must make death fall to sleep. And I can do it, for it's already a part of my name. If I make Death—Sivondel—sleep at the moment of my death, he's not awake to claim me. And once the moment of death has passed, I'm free of it. I'll be sent back. In the end, I will have actually died. Yet no one will have known it, except for me. None will be able to see it. It'll appear as if I never died. I'll rest in a place of in-between, as death's brought to sleep. Time passes over, and I'm free to go back to the land of the living. My daggers' cousin is even in there to aid with the immense power it will take.

A disconcerting thought dawns on me. That Dea was right. Performing this Hexyn Circle could kill me. Also, making Sivondel fall to sleep, when he's trying to find Ryco in The Kievas with Dea's assistance, could be disastrous. But I've no choice. Ryco accepted that he was going to die, with no hope of coming back. I *had* hope. And now that hope is gone. Possibly Dea will never make it back either.

I take a moment to sit on the ground and weep for my friends. I can't help it. Death and goodbyes are hard. My tears trickle down my cheeks. Dripping off, some tears land on the ground. Then I push myself up, determined to finish this. I wipe the tears away. Sloshing my way through the water, I find where it's deep enough, calm enough, to perform my enchantment circle.

Swimming around below the surface, I draw the circle with the quill of my father's, which Grover gave to me. Next, I use levitation magic—Volisos—in the water. My arms burn like deep bruises being hit. But I won't release those weapons from their place on the points. I've put the Blades of Neutrality at the top of the Hexyn. My daggers on east and west, ensuring that the sleeping-dagger will be on my left, when I center myself in the circle to complete the spell. The spear is at five o'clock; Vondaen at seven. The Vondaen will not stay in place, however. He's trying to tell me something. Perhaps that something is wrong. So I switch the Onyx Blades to be at the bottom, and the spear and Vondaen on top. Vondaen still refuses cooperation.

Frustrated, I go up for a deep breath of air. I dive back down to take Vondaen in my left hand. He conforms to my grip. In fact, he refuses to let go of me. I laugh inside.

"Fine," I div to him. *"I won't leave you behind, if you don't leave me. Deal?"*

The blade transitions its form to how it was when Gyronawv split apart the two Sorens stuck in the same body. The Vondaen then lets me trade which hand wields him. I tighten my right hand's grip on him, before taking out Dea's piece of Shylen. I place it at the top, the one o'clock spot—thirteen hundred hours, military time. The waking-dagger, I put at three. My sleeping-dagger at nine. The spear on eleven. Blades of Neutrality are crossed in an *X*, their sharp tips on five and seven o'clock.

I have a last monologue to clear my head, before I attempt to complete the Hexyn. *Laevarye, there is a time to die. And my time is soon. To ruin. To doom. But it is not at its end, for death will be made to sleep, to pass over me. I shall summon his strength, to enter the place of in-between. I shall outwit him at the time of my death, then free myself to rise up to the land of the living. This is my name's purpose. To make death sleep, so that a soul may survive and be returned, whole. No dismay of Nekrosis. No Law of Magic broken, for the shield shall hide me, guide me, protect me. Death will sleep at the beginning, but wake at the end. Time will pass, to complete the spell. May my name, tied and resting upon the points of Hexyn, save me. I shall begin.*

I Mensa-div the words of magic: *"Krim-dim-Karasa-Shenawsafa-drim, I summon him: Ravieras-Savak-Kavas-sev; Vayel-Ladel—Sivon of the del; Kryn-dei-Aevimeis-el-Enyxar-varin-nae. Temporiavas-safa—Fayel-londel; Merge to my name: Ravieras-Savak-Kavas. The Sleeping Dragon, able to make Sivon of the del sleep; Lomiiriavas, to awaken him after the tempori-el-Concalos-Sadyn-el-Sivondel."*

I've spoken five parts in Mensa-div. There's just one more point to take care of. I'll save it, until I'm at the Hexyn's center. I swim for that center, and turn around. I think on the words my older self said in Oniva: *"When calls the darkness, I will be there to find it. To bind it to light. To defeat it forever. For I am the Sleeping Dragon. May the patience of Vons be with me.*

Might the strength of a dragon's first flight lift me. Give me the will and wings, to rise above the many oceans of death."

I realize he was warning me of this moment. Foretelling of it. That gives me courage, as the circle lights with a fire the water cannot put out. Air rushes into my lungs, when I've lost all breath. I breathe in, I breathe out. The water is pushed away from the circle. I speak the spell words again, lifting my watch this time to collect the fire heading for the center, for me. Black, green, and white are sent forth from the Blades of Neutrality. The flames hit my feet. I cry out. Red and blue flames come from my daggers. Their fire hits my hands. I feel as though I'm being torn apart from within. I've no voice left to cry out. But it isn't over, for the spear bleeds out liquid of copper and gold. That liquid forges into a being in front of me. A spirit of both wolf and dragon. Head and tail of a wolf, wings and chest of a dragon. Body and legs equally of both. Eyes like two glowing emerald stones stare out. Metallic purple etches in the space between his copper and gold scales. His claws are matte black, and his breath like a white fog.

"Ravieras-Savak-Kavas," he speaks to me with a deep voice, sounding how I would if I were as ancient as Vardiyas and as strong as dragons. "You hath made me, Tyler Malik, the Savakaidyn. Sleeping Dragon. All whom summon me at the precise moment of their death, I shall save in time. I shall hide them in the gray mists of Kavas, above the oceans. Then bind them to the light of the land, Aevimeis, sister soul to Eyo'el. Laevarye, there is a time to die. But, also, is there a time to live. Aevimeis-teras-metsas-sadora-vyn-kryn-din-Savakaidyn. For now, it does not end with death. I release you, to summon me. Pierce my heart with the Vondaen. Be done."

As soon as I move that hand gripping the Greyvon blade, water rushes back to the circle. I swim forward through the strong current. I manage to pierce Savakaidyn's chest, while Mensa-divving to the spirits listening, *"Thirteen. It is done."*

The water becomes stronger, sweeps me downriver. It spews me out on a rocky bank, with the Vondaen. The other weapons soon land around me. For a while, I'm too weak to get up. Eventually, I do. I collect my things. I'm about to head for the Interrogation Silo, to meet up with Zymarc. I take a moment to appreciate what's around me. A beautiful place of tranquility. A forest teeming with life, because of decay. It's just how an ecosystem works, even on a world filled with magic. Some things here, however, are spared from decay. Trees encased in metal, their leaves too. They stand as timeless memorials, proclaiming that they are perfect and unchanging, yet dwarfed by the other trees. Perhaps the smallest things can be the strongest and most enduring, even as everything changes around them.

* * *

The door to the Interrogation Silo opens of its own accord, when I approach it. Hesitating, I gather my courage. I enter the place where I will either win or lose. This is where the last battle of the War for the Equidyn begins. Here, in a repurposed silo. No army—just two at odds with each other.

The entire interior has been cleared of the evidence of bloodshed.

Zymarc sits in a simple metal chair, looking over one of the metal tables with many straps, new straps I realize. He has one leg crossed over his knee. His posture is relaxed, but his expression is full of regret.

Interrupting his thoughts, I ask, "Droediin make it off all right with the princess?"

"Yes," replies Zymarc, still staring at the torture table. He lets out a weary sigh. "We must wait for the ShenawFayel to end, before we can begin this last bit of business."

He sits in silence. I remain standing.

After a time, he asks, "What was the verdict, regarding Winter's Vondaen?"

"See for yourself." I take it out, hand it to Zymarc. It has kept that inverted coloring as when Gyronawv wielded it.

Looking the blade over, Zymarc's eyes flicker with something. I can't

503

tell what he might be thinking.

He asks, "How'd you get it to do this?"

"Had a conversation with it, while practicing spells. Seems he rather likes being spoken to."

Zymarc's mouth twitches. A soft chuckle escapes him. "You know, until Arsyn spoke to Veldakryn last night, I'd only ever witnessed Soren speak to his weapons. Soren was rather insane, however. I figured that's why the habit never caught on." He sets the Vondaen on the clean torture table.

I pull out *The Dark Prince* storybook, as well as the pages Zymarc returned. I set them beside the blade. "What can you tell me of this book? Or the simple story it tells. Are there legends that reflect it?"

Leaning forward, Zymarc grabs the book and wrinkled pages. He reads it over. Even reads the note Soren left for Gemma. He straightens his posture, closes the book, looks ahead—says nothing, as he gives the items back.

"Well?" I ask, after a time.

He swipes his pinky finger across his brow, then lowers his hand. He gently shakes his head. "It could mean many things. But, coming from Soren, it could be telling a parable of Deezalo and Gaula. They were Soren's apprentices, long before Deezalo created Vitiosus. This might be telling of that. Deezalo may have used a Hexyn Circle, to create the first version of Vitiosus. Which has now become a class of magic, whether other Sorsryns wish to accept that fact or not."

"Why would Deezalo be called *Dark Prince*, though?"

"Magic might have been obscured from Deezalo; found it hard to perform, when he was younger. Perhaps Gaula opened his eyes to magic. It's interesting that this talks of purple."

I ask, "Why?"

"Because Withrasyn women predominantly had violet eyes. The trait dwindled out, however, the more mixed the Paragonians became. Awleesia had violet eyes. A brighter violet than I've ever seen. She used to dance beautifully too. Practiced magic with a grace and rhythm matched by few."

I walk to the side of the table, opposite of Zymarc. I study him. "You knew her?"

"Before I was a Vitiosyn and after, yes. Why do you care?"

"What if the story's of you? Did Awleesia ever try to open your eyes to some truth?"

Zymarc's breath quickens. He crosses his arms over his chest. "She might have, long ago. But I'm not a prince, Ravier, like you."

"You sure about that?" I ask. I think over the information my father showed me of ReNovak and Awleesia, while I was in Grevagg. *What if Zymarc is their son? Half Onyx, half Withrasyn?*

Standing up, Zymarc rests his hands on the table. He leans closer. "What are you trying to tell me, Tyler?"

Desperate, yet guarding my thoughts, I think, *I must get in this Vitiosyn's head, the way he has with me. There will be no chance of resisting the call, otherwise. Zymarc's too strong. Too cunning. I must be more cunning.*

"I believe that you are a prince, Lord-King Zymarc. That you were a prince, before you were a Vitiosyn. Not the Onyx Prince, nor a Prince of Withrasyns. But of both. That you are ReNovak and Awleesia's unclaimed child. Why else would ReNovak favor you, above others? Was it because of your gifts in magic, or was it that he knew who you were? An illegitimate son."

Zymarc's right hand grips the edge of the table. His knuckles go white. "That isn't possible. Queen Awleesia never would have treated me the way she did, if she knew I was her son."

I stroll about the room, watching Zymarc all the while. "What if she didn't know? What if a certain Withrasyn we both know took her to see the Kyanites? What if they had intended to unmake the child, but at the last second, Soren couldn't do it? Couldn't have you unmade? Instead, he never told Awleesia; never told ReNovak either. Rather, he took upon himself the consequences of you existing before ReNovak should've been able to father a child. He placed you with someone in Oniva, didn't he?"

Quietly, Zymarc says, "My mother was called by Ashar of the Nyxane, for she wasn't born in one of the main cities, but was still a daughter of the Onyx Clan."

I go on, "Though another raised you, ReNovak and Awleesia must've sensed who you were. Subconsciously knew you were their son, and loved you more than others, though they hadn't a clue as to why."

The Vondaen rattles a bit, while on the metal table.

Zymarc takes out Deezalo's Hammer, and puts it on top of the Vondaen, makes an *X* with the two weapons. The Greyvon blade fades to its normal form. It quiets down.

"The ShenawFayel is nearing its end," Zymarc says, as he starts a stroll about the room. We're separated by a distance of a few yards.

Putting away *The Dark Prince* and its wrinkled pages, I ask, "Then what?"

"Then we begin this last bit of business. I shall turn you, make you my apprentice. Or you shall die. Either way, you should not have said this thing to me."

The two weapons rattle violently, before they burst off the table, repelling each other. They spread out to east and west of how Zymarc and I are oriented.

The loathing for Zymarc comes over me, once more. The hatred in his eyes resumes. Only it is far worse. His Vitiosyn appearance returns, and I shiver inside. This enemy is beyond my power today. I've lost much magic this morning already. I cannot overcome the call *and* the death as I had hoped. At least I've created an escape from both. *But will I be able to time it right?* I wonder.

"At last," says Zymarc, "we are released. And after we're finished here, I shall look into the matter you've brought to light. If what you're saying is true, then I have a claim to the Onyx and Withrasyn thrones, one of which is now the Paragonian throne. By the Laws of Magic, and power of spirits, I must be given the thrones. Even if I should lose them later, I must be given them for a time. For your cousin's sake, you had better hope you're wrong."

"In time," I say, "we'll see." I congratulate myself. Mission accomplished!

I have thoroughly gotten inside this Vitiosyn's head. Now he is distracted. Now his power is less than it was. I have a greater chance.

Zymarc stops walking about. He presses his palms together, as if praying to a deity. Then he moves his hands out. All objects filling the floor space are pushed to the walls. Lowering his hands, he commands me, "Go to the center."

I do, then wait.

He says, "I was going to do a simple spell of possession with Vitiosus. But not now. You must have the lengthy process." He starts preparing a pentagram with the handle of the hammer, which he's snatched out of the air. First, the upside down star of five points is drawn. He trades the hammer with the Vondaen, to draw a circle around me. Then five small circles between the five points of the star. Again, he takes up the hammer, but uses its axe blade to cut lines that connect the five outer circles. In the end, there's the pentagram, five triangles, a pentagon within a pentagon, and me in the center, enclosing circle.

I comment, "Know much about enchantment circles, do you?"

"This is not an enchantment circle," Zymarc says firmly, as he lets go of the weapons. They return to east and west. "Though there is such a thing as Pentyn Circles, this is the Pentyn of Particles. It honors that five particles of magic exist. I've changed it somewhat, to proclaim that a sixth particle exists as well. As I said yesterday, it has for some time."

"What proof is there in Deezalo's Cathedral?" I ask.

"After this, I'll show you."

"Very well." I shrug. "I want this over with."

Zymarc adds, "We both do." He finishes making preparations on the Pentyn of Magic, saying all the while, "Many compare me to Deezalo, even though he and I are near opposites. Part of his downfall was his inability to change tactics, wants, needs, and the like. Whereas, that is my strength. To be as adaptable as a Von. While he wanted to make Vitiosyns like a natural occurring clan—in fact, was obsessed with the matter, unwilling to be patient, and plan it out to perfection—I simply wanted to give Deathasyns an equal say amongst Sorsryns. I wished to give them order, rules, law, culture. I never tried to make my Vitiosyns more than what they could be. Rather, tried to give them the tools necessary to be made better than they were. I united them more efficiently than Regal Deathasyns, that is, the Royal Family of Deathasyns, ever did."

"Is that why you slaughtered King Vit'Dod and his entire family?"

"I asked for their allegiance. If they couldn't give that, then I asked that they stay out of my way. They would do neither. They hunted me, instead. Sent out a contract, would reward the one who brought them my head. So, yes, in a way, they died because they were less determined than I was. Less cunning than I was. Shall we begin?"

I give my last feeble attempt to delay this, by asking, "Don't you want to put to rest if LanSoren was your son? Test my blood, and see if—"

"That's already done," replies Zymarc. "Got RayVora to help with the matter, last night. Gave her the dragon, in return. I saw the results of your blood panel, right before coming here."

"And?" I ask.

"And you'll not know the results, until after. If you die here, then never." Zymarc aligns himself outside of the pentagon's top point, directly in front of my view. "Now," he says, "I must warn you, this is the same type of possession I used on LanSoren. As you know, he resisted the call and the death. He later told me of the immense pain he felt. Worse than anything he'd ever experienced. Even *I* wanted to stop halfway through. He said I must keep going, or risk fracturing his soul into five parts, each part being tied to the particles, but not really a part of them. More like a parasite. He'd live out the rest of his days in pain. Never living, never dead. Just there, in torment, as the particles around him are used for magic."

I ask, "Don't I have a choice of the simpler Call of Vitiosus?"

"You do," Zymarc remarks. "But I wager you'd not want to be outdone by your father. You must know that you are his son in every way, even in the practicing and resistance to magic. Am I wrong?"

"You are not. Begin."

He does by speaking the incantation: "The fire of the soul is the life of the forest, forever. I shall not argue. Simply awaken them in the water. Breathe them into the air. Spill blood for the land to have, for death to drink. In return, I ask for freedom from the grave of the spirits. Of Vardiyas. I ask that a new breath be given first to me, then to him. The Breath of Vitiosus. I invite you to come. Come, Inviteis-Vitiosus." Zymarc kneels on one knee. He holds out one hand as if wanting an offering. He speaks more, this time, words of magic: "Oostrinas-delik-kaw; Viti'Aevus-sown-metsa-eek; Karas-Siveyras-Soonda-vay; Vosh-Fendi-Ventu-el-Kusi-Sareus; Soolana-sev-Vardiyas-Speridas-sar-Rentwar'Vamen. Inviteis-Vitiosus."

Zymarc's offering hand is filled with red fire that emits from the five points of the pentagram. Zymarc rotates his hand, aims it at me, pushes his palm forward, a devil's look in his gaze, before his eyes turn pitch-black. For a brief moment, I see the perversion in him.

A horizontal pillar of red fire shoots out from Zymarc's hand. I don't lift my own to stop it, nor to shield myself, as it heads for me, and hits my chest.

My screams of pain are heard at a distance. I'm pushed out of my body. I hover around the room, watching it all as if I'm a stranger. The pain becomes heavy. My fourteen-year-old self crumples to the ground. I hear his bones crack. Feel it somewhat too. Yet only he can cry out in agony. His eyes bleed. His skin splits open. His body convulses.

The pillar of fire continues on its own, as would Geldryn spells, while Zymarc strolls about the room. He watches, but as his Onyx self. He is patient and calculated.

With a snap of his fingers, the flames go out.

My broken body is made whole. I return to it, taking in gulps of air. I tremble in weakness. I can't stand up.

Zymarc says, "Get up. We'll start again."

"What?" I rasp, hurting and confused.

"This is a Pentyn. There are five stages. That was stage one."

"Please, Zymarc, I can't do that again."

"Too late. You must. And it will get worse, halfway through. I shall begin, whether you stand or not. But standing will lessen the initial pain, so I've been told. I don't recall my turning. Now get up, Ravier, and face me."

I do, but it takes several minutes.

The fire pillar starts again. I don't instantly leave my body. I experience the pain of breaking bones more sharply. I vomit right there, except it isn't vomit. It's fire. It burns my insides, coming up. Then I leave my body, and watch it happen. That boy's face becomes charred and bleeding. His screams are like an animal in torment, not a boy. Blood sprays out from his mouth.

Zymarc snaps his fingers again. "Stand up," he says.

I move back into my restored body and shout, "I can't!"

"LanSoren did! On all five. It was I who couldn't bear to see him in pain, for I loved him. But I don't love you, Ravier. I don't know you. You will not show me the truth of who you are. *What* you are."

"Because I don't know, Zymarc," I cry. "I don't know who I really am." I start weeping.

Zymarc waits with that irksome patience.

I hate him! And that hate gives me the strength to get up.

He starts again.

I stay in my body for longer, on the third occasion. I can't believe how much it hurts. I didn't know pain could be so great and powerful. I want to beg Zymarc to stop. My voice fails me. I leave my body again. I circle the room like an invisible ghost, desperate to stop this pain. I rattle the devices on the wall pegs, pull the tables and other objects closer to the silo's center. I feel a deep-seated hatred for everything rise up.

For the third time, Zymarc snaps his fingers.

I'm made whole, again. At least, I hope that I'm whole. The hate still lingers. I start to imagine torturing Zymarc. I manage to shake it off, and stand up without being asked.

"Is that all you've got?" I spit on the pentagram.

Zymarc laughs in a chilling way. "Oh no, Ravier. Just warming up."

He initiates the fourth attempt.

I stand for as long as my legs will let me, which is for minutes that feel as hours. I clench my teeth tight together. Hot tears burn my face. Liquid runs from my nose, also burning me. My eyes squeeze shut. I start seeing flashes of memories. They aren't my memories. RotaSyn's voice calls for NeiSator to come, to help save their Master Nerosh from death. Many weapons clash in the foreground. A great cry sounds out on the battlefield. The souls of my daggers wail. One of them later says, "We shall be given a new master, dear brother. Our story doesn't end here, on Jextoran."

More memories flash, bits of the other masters' lives, I imagine. Then I recognize Soren's point of view, watching that last battle of the War of Ichors Von. The two matriarchs kill each other. It switches to my father. He strolls about a place with trees like mirrors. Zymarc is with him. I only hear some of their discussion.

"When the time is right," says my father, in the memory, "tell him everything."

"You want me to tell that little prince," Zymarc asks, "that his father, King Sosha, was indeed a full-blooded Withrasyn? To what end?"

"Soren answered to Withrasyn kings, in the past. One must be slightly more than half Withrasyn to be a Withrasyn King, thereby able to control him."

"You do realize that Soren is dead, don't you?" queries Zymarc.

"He will return," my father warns. "And in a way none shall expect. There must be one here, able to stop him."

"That little prince doesn't have the strength."

"Then I shall teach him," says my father. "And if I fail, will you promise me one thing, Zymarc?"

"Anything."

"If something should happen to me, before he is ready, finish making my nephew strong. Do whatever it takes to ensure that he becomes immovable."

Zymarc asks, "Even if it means going to war? Or involving him with the war I already have with the Sorsryn Clans?"

"I urge you to do whatever you see fit, to make Talok strong. But I will warn you, Zymarc, should you go to war with the Dragon Tamers, there will be one to rise up and get in your way. Again and again, he will be there at the right moment to stop you from going too far. From getting carried away by the violence Vitiosus puts in your heart. My son shall tempt you; and you, him. I fear, the two of you shall be the other's undoing. Try it. See if I'm wrong. But of the matter to do with Talok . . . Will you tell him?"

Zymarc says, "I won't have to, Lance, because you'll be here, to tell him yourself. He should hear it from you. Now, no misusing this Vardiya. Took me quite a long time to find one who could serve your key intentions."

They fade.

The silo scene reemerges.

My screams come to the forefront.

Zymarc snaps his fingers.

I collapse, struggling to breathe. I somehow manage to shakily stand up.

Zymarc's mouth twitches with an emotion I can't determine. "Enjoying the pain yet?"

I stare some more, before answering him. "You are nothing to me, Vitiosyn. As I am nothing to you. So go on. Last attempt. Then it's my move."

I put my hands behind my back. I stand defiant, head held high.

Zymarc lights fire on the five points of the pentagram. Then he casts a color-changing fire within the five circles at the points of the outer pentagon. Faces form from those color-shifting flames. Twisted, demonic expressions. The ten flames begin swirling together to make a circle of fire. Whispering chants are like needles pricking at my eardrums.

Zymarc speaks the spell words again: "Oostrinas-delik-kaw; Viti'Aevus-sown-metsa-eek; Karas-Siveyras-Soonda-vay; Vosh-Fendi-Ventu-el-Kusi-Sareus; Soolana-sev-Vardiyas-Speridas-sar-Rentwar'Vamen. Inviteis-Vitiosus."

The entire Pentyn is filled by fire.

Louder, demonic chants echo around me.

The heat is too great. I see my life play out in the flames, similar to the fountain at the Pools of Vosh-Perida, only these memories are of violence I wished to do. To hurt my classmates, smash their faces in when they bullied me. My ill intentions over the years are revealed to me, and it's horrifying at first. Then it starts to feel good. A fire within burns. It's wickedness. I'm starting to like it. Starting to crave it. I realize that Zymarc's Call of Vitiosus is working. I'm turning. As my own laughter echoes around, I know he's winning.

So I push back, bringing to mind the words of the spell made-from-my-name. *"When calls the darkness, I will be there to find it. To bind it to light. To defeat it forever. For I am the Sleeping Dragon. May the patience of Vons be with me. Might the strength of a dragon's first flight lift me. Give me the will and wings, to rise above the many oceans of death."*

I manage a whisper, as I start to feel nothing but sadness inside: "Laevarye, there is a time to die."

My body slowly falls. I feel as though I'm falling through the floor, on down into a cold, gray void. I'm slipping farther into utter darkness. There's nothing to grab onto, nothing to slow my momentum.

Though terrified, I speak the words, "Ravieras-Savak-Kavas," and hope it is the precise moment of my death.

IV

To Become a Legend

*"When life grows dim, catch a fire.
Chase it, till it is yours. Bottle it up.
Store it for when all hope is lost. Then set it free
that it may go out into the world and save it."*

33

Surmounting Strength

The words of my name-turned-to-a-spell have been spoken. I know not if they'll work, nor when. I just keep falling through the pitch-black void.

Particles of light then illuminate the void as far as my eyes can see. Four colors. The colors of magic: blue, brass, red, and white. I imagine particles of black are here too. But the void is darker than any night. So it hides the fifth particle. Yet I know it is here. And it comforts me. The particles being here, akin to stars on a cloudless night, is a welcomed view while I wait for the end of this journey. Wait for Savakaidyn to show up.

I enter a deeper part of the void. Snowflakes float about, here. I catch a few in my hand. They don't melt. They instead glisten like tiny, clear crystals. The sixth particle Zymarc spoke of. It's why no one can see it. It's clear, invisible, but real. My left hand lights with the Prismatic of Magic, and one of those particles I hold grows to fit nicely in my palm. Its shape is a dodecagon—twelve-sided polygon. It morphs into a star with twelve points. Each point becomes a different color. Blue, brass, and red are near each other. Then black, silver, and white. Green, copper, violet, and clear. The north end is icy-turquoise; the south point a dark-teal. Deep, metallic magenta liquid fills the core.

Letting go of all particles but this transformed one in my grasp, I impale my palms with the north and south ends of the star. It shatters in my grasp. The liquid splatters on me. It's like glowing blood colored of dark-magenta.

The Prismatic of Magic fades from my skin, emitting into the void instead. The crystallized particles transform to be colored. They then become as all creation in Muraine. All flora, small creatures, races. *Everything* at Muraine's beginning.

Voices speak amid the void.

A male voice comes into focus, saying, "Our fathers and mothers, the Ashenawks—and those before them—hath given the Fennukye a duty most heavy. We, those children, shall see it done. I, Neroshen'Nal of the Throne of Ravier, will do my part. But if that part is taken from me by fate, always will there rise another in my stead to do what must be done. This I ask of you, Father Natoreis'Rotasine, make two lesser siblings for me, for I would not wish the burden upon their shoulders. Merely company for when my strength wanes, and when my heart is made sad. Name them after you: RotaSyn and NeiSator. Let them be as the light after storms, and hope after wars. That they, together, be the truth dawn gives of the coming day, and promise dusk proclaims of a pending night. Let few be able to overcome them."

Another masculine voice adds, "I, Dhoshma of the Throne of Ravas, will be with them as well, always a fire to reveal the way."

"And I, Gammidii of the Throne of Rime," speaks a third male voice, "shall be there, patient and at the ready for what is to come next. Never, shall I and those of my line fear the end. Only may my other half be as fire to ice, able to dissuade me from my chosen path."

"May our sisters, three," says Dhoshma, "claim their parts as well. We bid you, Ashenawks, to craft them, make them better, brighter, wiser than even us, brothers, three."

"But the last sister," says Gammidii, "make her Neroshen's other half, for RotaSyn and NeiSator are not enough, not equal, and he will need an equal to summon him from the dark, should he fall. Let it be done."

The word 'done' echoes around. It switches to the voice of Savakaidyn.

Golden fire lights at the bottom of the void.

The end of my journey of falling has come. I fall through the fire. The pain is searing, blinding, unbearable to many. Yet I must go through it. I've no choice. I scream the words to save me again: "Ravieras-Savak-Kavas, come!"

The golden fire transitions to liquid. That liquid shifts into Savakaidyn. As soon as his form is whole, he says in that deep voice, "Once you land, you must stand up. Then you must not take another step. Your feet must remain planted to the spot. I cannot hide you otherwise, you understand?"

I nod through the pain, taking a moment to look down. Hills of gray sand are waiting for me. Fog rises up to swirl over those gray hills. Not too far away from there, a sheer cliff drops down into a land I've no wish to visit. Landscapes of consuming fire, of ice, of famine, endless torture, endless war, endless decay. The sounds and stench reach even the gray sand dunes.

I ready myself to land in the one place untouched by the horrors all around. I splat in the sand, nearly drown in it. I manage to stand up, determined to wait this out. My pain subsides to an ache in my joints.

Should be easy from here, right? I think.

I'm wrong.

The fog shifts into spirits of the dead. They approach where I stand. They touch my face, my arms, my chest, chilling me. I have sensations akin to the moments of Zymarc trying to turn me. It hurts. Yet I must not move.

Soon, Savakaidyn flies lower. He hovers above me, glances down too. He says, "I remind you again, you must not take one step. The dead mean to taunt you. They cannot hurt you. Hold fast. I shall shield you."

He lands, his front paws placed on either side of me. He bends his long neck down. His chin is just a few feet above my head. I'm in his great, cold shadow.

When one persistent ghost claws at my face, about to draw blood, Savakaidyn snaps at him, sets him aflame. The ghost screeches and runs away in pain. He leaps off the cliff. He begins that fall to one of the oceans of death.

My relief is short-lived, for a distant roar pulses through the air. It shakes the ground, rattles my head.

Savakaidyn says, "It won't be long now."

And he's right. Sivondel approaches from east of where I stand, looking over the places of death.

A feminine voice calls out Ryco's name.

My heart leaps within. I start to lift one of my feet. I stop myself, only shifting my weight a little.

Sivondel flies closer, talking to the one upon his back, "This is not where I belong, fair daughter of a dragon. We must retreat once more."

"We're close this time, Sivondel," says Deamond. "Keep going."

She shoots violet fire at Sivondel's wings. The dull metallic purple of them brightens. His wings now shimmer as would polished metal. He's renewed. He starts flying higher, but then his head starts to droop.

"Sivondel!" Dea shouts. "What are you doing? We can't land here. Keep going! We must find Ryco."

Sivondel rumbles a hum, muttering, "I fear, I cannot keep my head up. I . . . am . . . tired? Yes, tired. Must rest . . . must sleep. It's been an age since I've slept. I've forgotten how it feels to sleep. It was at a Kyanite's feet, in a Rubidyn's keep. A Kyanite made me into a spirit. Death. It was long ago that I heard his call." Sivondel tries to shake off the fatigue. But he can't, for Savakaidyn breathes in deep, then lets loose a violet-magenta breath of fire.

Sivondel falls to sleep, midair. With Dea still upon his back, he stops flapping, slows down, floats forward. He's going to land on the gray dunes, if something doesn't nudge him off course.

"Savakaidyn," I beg, "do something. He's going to crush us, if we stay planted here."

Savakaidyn spreads his wings forward, creating a dome around us.

"Sivondel!" Dea shouts in horror. "Wake up!" She pounds her fists on the dragon's neck, to no avail. She takes off, then flaps in place.

Sivondel's now too close for me to see more of Dea. Savakaidyn tightens the dome of his wings. The glow of his green eyes is the only source of light, as Death passes over, literally scraping and sliding across Savakaidyn's wings and back. The Sleeping Dragon's bones creak; the skin of his wings buckles, almost gives way. He grimaces, breathes harder, but holds tight to his task.

I reach up to touch the tip of his nose.

He takes in a renewing breath.

Beyond the dome of wings, Dea's muffled cries echo around, her screams for Sivondel to wake up. He won't. Not until I've gone back.

Savakaidyn slowly draws his wings away, and lifts his head.

Dea's only twenty feet away from us, flapping in place. Tears stream down her dirt-smudged cheeks.

"I've failed," she whispers. "There's no way out of here."

I try calling to Dea. She can't hear me.

Savakaidyn says, "Call to the cousin. Veldakryn. He is near."

I hold out my left hand, and call that blade by his name: "Veldakryn, I'm here. There's someone who needs you."

A cold wind comes from the north, cuts through the heat that's biting at my face. Far in the northern distance, a broken tree floats above a shadowed land. Lightning crashes above black clouds that are gathered there. Red lightning too, like what struck Deezalo's tree. Creatures of flight fly above the black clouds. I can only guess that it is the land where Deezalo was; possibly where Ryco has been, since that fateful day.

As soon as Veldakryn forms in my grasp, I call to Deamond, "I'm here, Dea."

She startles, looks at me. Rather, through me. She's confused. "Tyler? Why—"

I interrupt, to say, "I've not died. Rather, I've brought someone here to help you and Sivondel. I don't have long. Take the blade, Veldakryn. Call to the spirit, Savakaidyn. Summon him with words of: Ravieras-Savak-Kavas. If that doesn't work, try: 'Laevarye, there is a time to die. But, also, is there a time to live. Aevimeis-teras-metsas-sadora-vyn-kryn-din-

Savakaidyn. For now, it does not end with death.' Get ready, Dea. I'm about to throw you the blade."

I toss it high.

It becomes visible to her, and she flies toward me. She catches it in her right hand before it falls to the ground.

Pride blazes in her violet eyes. "Ravier," she cries. "You did it! Truly? You completed the Hexyn?"

With equal pride, I echo, "I completed the Hexyn. As soon as I fade, go to Sivondel. He'll wake up. Fly with him to the north, where that broken tree is. It'll be the fight of your life, once you're closer, but I believe it's where Ryco is. Find him, fly with him, bring him home."

"I will," says Dea. "Take care, Onyx Prince. Or should I say: legend made flesh, before my eyes."

The ghosts get rougher, gripping at my clothes. Snakes come to nip at my boots, and tear at my pants. Swarms of insects hover near, bringing a stench with them. They wait as if eager to feed on my flesh as soon as I've died. That will not be today.

Dea lifts a hand in goodbye. She smiles through tears. "I'll bring the Paradyn home, I promise. We will see each other again, Ravier."

I whisper, "Come what may, Savakaidyn, take me back."

The things of death screech and buzz and hiss around me. In the end, Savakaidyn burns these things with the hot fire of violet-magenta. They must flee, or be reduced to ashes. He gently takes me up in his front paws, to hold me close to his beating heart. He lifts off the ground fast, propelling us up through the void. It all becomes a blur, until reaching the pitch-black. Then only wind tells of the great momentum at which we travel.

A white light comes into view above. It's soon like a whiteout. I must close my eyes. When I open them, a breath is forced into my lungs.

I'm on my hands and knees, gasping for breath. Smoke pours up from the lines of the Pentyn of Magic. Bravely, I lift my gaze to where Zymarc stands.

Striding forward, he grips me by the hair of my head. He forces me to look up at him. "I don't understand. You should have turned. You were right there on the edge." He lets go of me and walks away, angry but unnerved.

I ease up on wobbly legs, to say, "It appears that I've resisted the call and the death. It's time for you to take me home to Paragon. Let us end this War for the Equidyn."

"Fine!" Zymarc spits. "We'll take a dragon there." He storms out of the Interrogation Silo.

Unsteadily, I limp after him. I've been through much, and my legs just won't aid me any longer.

Azabahk is hobbling our way, Caleiso in tow.

She sees us, and quickly closes the distance. "How'd it go with—?"

Zymarc cuts her off. "He's not dead, as you see. Nor is he turned. That's how it went!"

Azabahk has switched to using an intricately carved cane. He toys with its handle. "Well, I do so hate to be the bearer of more bad news, but it seems that, well, someone opened the gate that contained the remaining quarter of the hostages. They are gone."

"Droediin," Zymarc growls. "I knew something wasn't right about him, after last night."

The four of us walk along. Azabahk and I barely keep up.

"There's more," says Caleiso. "I'll let Azabahk tell you."

"Tell me what?" Zymarc's crimson eyes blaze.

"That the Paragonians and their many new allies are on their way," says Arsyn of Jhire, as he strolls out from behind a large, nearby building. "In fact, they're almost here. I'll be taking Ravier with me now, if you're quite finished with that Call of Vitiosus."

Zymarc raises a barrier of magic. He grabs me, drags me along. Azabahk and Caleiso follow in our trail, unsure of what to do except that.

Arsyn attacks the wall of magic.

I Mensa-div to him, *"I know who you are, Arsyn of the Throne of Ravas. You've much to explain."*

Arsyn stops his attacks. He looks to me. A slow smile spreads across his face. He divs back, *"I suppose I do. In fact, we do."*

Zebulon exits the cover of the forest.

Zymarc never once looks back to see if Arsyn will break his barrier. He must be that confident it'll hold.

So the Vitiosyn King doesn't see Arsyn get on the dark horse's back, doesn't hear as he Mensa-divs to me, *"When you're done with this, come find us. We shall wait in Paragon."*

Zebulon strides off with Arsyn.

Meanwhile, I'm dragged through the city of Vaydell by Zymarc, because I can't get my feet under me. Somehow, I don't care that I'm getting scraped up and covered in dirt, along the way. I've already won. There's no greater victory I can have today than what I've already done. To make a spell from my name that makes death pass over me. I now know what it is to die. But also will I know what it truly means to live, for I don't think I've been living this whole time. Simply existing. For now, nothing will deter me, the Sleeping Dragon, from my task. To defeat Vitiosus forever. It is today.

34

Vanquished Desires

In the highest tower that overlooks the city of Vaydell, Zymarc and I wait. He, in front of a tall set of windows, watches the coming armies of Paragon. They've made it to the outer, fortifying walls of the city. Reign leads the Black Dragons in flight. They attack the barrier of magic that's been put in place. It dampens the sounds of war to a low rumble akin to a distant thunderstorm. A few times I, from my place in the center of the room, catch glimpses of Ryco's Sylvadyns far off, shielding Paragonians from spells and arrow-fire. Then I spot Reign and Scepter's cousin, the Vitasadyn returned to his former glory as a proud BlacKaidyn. He joins with Reign in attacking Zymarc's forces. Though a speck smaller in form than Reign, he is the fiercest of the dragons riding with the armies, warring in the air. Mystadyns begin to rise, joining the task of breaking the barrier over Vaydell, only they are within. No longer do they sleep.

Zymarc mutters something under his breath. He lifts a gloved hand to the glass pane as if to claw it. His stance goes rigid.

I grin inside, knowing he must've spotted the Vitasadyn who is a Vitasadyn no more. Either that, or he is livid that the Mystadyns no longer sleep.

Caleiso and Azabahk have left the tower to go get updates. Azabahk is hobbling up the stairs just now. I recognize his rhythm of limping.

Lowering his hand, Zymarc asks, "Did you bring what I asked for?"

Azabahk takes out a metal device. He glances at me, his face draining to a shade of light-gray. "Yes," he says.

Zymarc strides over to him to take the device, proceeding to approach me. He has a rope in his other hand. "Do not fight me, Ravier. I can't have them seeing you from one of these windows." He ties the rope around a pillar at the room's center. Then he attaches the device to the rope. It's an Enigma Star, I realize.

He starts binding my wrists, saying the while, "Caleiso told me of the great difficulty you have in solving these. Whether or not you try to solve it, you'll be depleted of what little magic is reviving within you. Therefore, you'll be unable to escape, unable to Mensa-div, unable to get to your allies. And, best of all, unable to command your Onyx of Malik. They're here too, in case you were wondering."

I put up a pathetic fight, as Zymarc finishes binding me. It's no use. I'm far too weak. Though not weak enough to keep me from spitting in Zymarc's face.

He steps away, wipes the spit off his cheek. A sly grin tugs at his lips. Turning, he goes to look out the window again. "Azabahk, give me updates."

The two converse, as I try to solve the Enigma Star. I know not how long I'm stuck, trying to get it to release me.

Azabahk leaves to go complete his instructions, whatever those are. I've no idea. I'm too preoccupied with other things, like freeing myself.

The rumbling noise increases outside. A crack booms out and shakes the building we're in. I cling to the rope tied round the pillar. Zymarc stumbles, even falls to his knees. He quickly recovers, but he's panicking, his breaths heavy.

I try harder to open the device, even picture when Ben opened it. I wonder, *How'd that one Talok gave me open so easily? I wasn't even trying to open it then.*

It isn't long, before Azabahk comes hobbling up the stairs in haste. He bursts open the door, his eyes wild with fear. "Lord Zymarc, they've broken through the barrier. It can't be refortified."

"What of the reinforcements from the other cities?" Zymarc asks in a calm way.

Forlorn, Azabahk shakes his head. "They'll not arrive, before we are overcome. It is time, my king. Time to flee or make a stand. Our forces can't hold much longer. They need you to make a decision."

The device starts clicking ever so quietly, while Zymarc paces about. I keep at it, rotating the dials. This one has three. I realize, it's sensitive to pressure. *Very* sensitive. It takes a steady hand to make it work, once you've found the right pressure point. After a rotation and soft click, the pressure involved changes. I groan inside. *Come on! I don't have much time. Zymarc means to flee, quickly regrouping with his forces already on their way. He'll be coming right back to reclaim Vaydell. I must not let him leave the city. I must stall him.*

Someone at the base of the tower calls up to Zymarc, a patronizing tone, saying, "Vitiosyn, Vitiosyn, let down your vile ladder, and give us our dear Tyler." It's Eli. The King's Guard have made it in, for I doubt Eli would come on his own.

The strong voice of Talok calls up, "It's over, Zymarc. The city is surrounded. Your forces are barely keeping us and our allies at bay—our allies of the Vons, Darklyres, dragons, and Jokryns. The Amethysts and Onyx of Malik have come to our aid as well. The warriors have come for their prince. I've come for my cousin. The Vons for their equal. And the dragons for their Tamer of Tamers. Others have come for the Legend Made Flesh. We know he's in this tower. Or, rather, that his daggers are. Knowing my cousin, he'd loathe to part with them."

Zymarc yells above the noise, "He's not here. He's been sent to the east, the city of Vitokawr."

I try to shout, but Azabahk silences me with a spell.

Another thunderous boom shakes the tower. Reign has found his voice, and his roar is mighty. Fire is sent on the wind like a wild beast. It attacks Zymarc's forces in the air.

The last dial of the star clicks. It releases its hold, and the ropes loosen.

I take the device in hand, determined to escape this tower. There's a bay window to Zymarc's left. It's not in his view at the moment, because he's looking down at my cousin and the guards, through the tall set of windows. Azabahk is preoccupied with getting up off the floor. His cane has been flung across the room.

I throw the star at the bay window. Glass shatters at the point of contact. The star is gone. I run full speed, and slam myself against the broken window pane. The glass shatters the rest of the way.

Zymarc shouts from inside the tower.

My fall is a long way down. Hundreds of feet. I try to Mensa-div to the dragons of Paragon, to Reign especially. My voice doesn't carry, however, nor does my raspy cry for help. I keep falling, unable to use magic to slow my momentum. A wind rushes up from the ground. I can't think who's helping me. I don't spot a caster of magic anywhere nearby. Even still, I land with a soft thud. Uninjured, I get up. I glance around for my friends. They're not here in the inner court of Vaydell yet. But I see where to let them in. A large gate to the west of me. I start for that direction.

Someone grabs me from behind.

An angry voice rasps in my ear, "You're such an annoying little prick, Tyler." Zymarc pulls me back, drags me toward one of the Vitasadyns, who has landed in the inner court. Many Vitiosyns are piling on the backs of Zymarc's dragons.

I thrash to get away. Zymarc tightens his grip, even backhands me across the face.

Someone Mensa-divs to me, *"Tyler, if you're in there, open the gate."* It's Khyra. *"I've sent you a bit of magic carried on the wind. If you can hear my voice, then you've caught it. Cast a spell to free yourself of your captors."*

I mull over the word for fire. My hands can't cast it, because my wrists are restrained by Zymarc's hold. So I speak, "Oostrinas!" and imagine it as fire sent from my mouth. It burns my tongue and lips. That fire sparks out, to hit Zymarc in the face, as he's preparing to slap me again.

He cries out. Startled, he lets go.

I bolt for the gate. Quickly finding the mechanism to open it, I begin to turn the wheel. My arms shake in effort. I've only gotten the iron gate up a foot, when Zymarc yanks me away.

"Khyra!" I shout.

Zymarc claps a hand over my blistered mouth, and picks me up. He hauls me toward a young, waiting Vitasadyn, then throws me up to Belgorr. "Get going!" Zymarc yells. "I'll stall them. We'll regroup to the east."

"Not Pil'Drouka?" Belgorr queries.

"No," says Zymarc. "Send the severely injured there. I've strong healers waiting."

The Vitasadyn is about to take off.

My heart wants to explode. I worry that I'll be taken from this place, used as leverage to procure Paragon's surrender. In desperation, I think, *This must not happen!*

Branches start growing up from the ground. Zymarc's legs become entangled with them. He falls down, slashes at the tangled mess with a small dagger he quickly pulls from his sleeve. Many Vitasadyns take off. The one I'm on cannot leave because he, like Zymarc, is trapped by the living branches. Soon, the dragon's engulfed by them. Belgorr shoves me off and leaps down.

A branch quickly wraps around my ankle. Swiftly pulling, it drags me away from my captors. I stop at the gate, gasping for breath.

The branch trapping my ankle withers. Khyra helps me to stand. "Tell me of their movements, Tyler, as I get the gate up the rest of the way."

I tell her the direction of our coming attackers, and she manages to cast spells of Gendras to fend off any who approach. Soon, the large gate of the inner court is open.

Warriors pour in. Paragonians on Vonsai; Greyvons in their metal forms; presumably Paydinn's progeny on horseback; and my warriors, clad in the finest garb of the Onyx. The three Amethyst Queens also enter in on foot, with Gyron amidst them.

All sparring ceases, when the Onyx Siveyra speaks out, "Surrender your forces, Zymarc. It's over. You cannot win."

I spot Caleiso nearby, at that moment. Zymarc's about to lash out. I know it. He's the sort of creature you just don't back into a corner, and expect him to comply. We must have a pawn. So I rush for Caleiso, already regretting what I must do. I grab her, slam her against a wall, and bite into her neck. She screams as I drink her magic, her blood. She goes quiet, limp even. I let her fall. She's not dead. But she's been rendered useless.

I wipe her blood from my mouth, wondering if the blood will make me sick. Somehow, I don't think it can hurt me like it can with others of Vaegon descent.

Zymarc yells in a rage. He rushes forward, war hammer raised.

The battle resumes. Chaos entails.

Though I'm revived with magic, and my mouth no longer burns, I've not a clue what to do.

Ben finds me among the fray. He has on the gloves. They're glowing blue. "Quick, Tyler, we need to leave the confined space. Too many in here. We'll be trampled."

He quickly pats Khyra on the arm to get her attention. She rushes away with us. We're just past the other side of the gate.

Talok and the rest of the King's Guard, save for Ryco, are there.

Ben announces, "The Vitiosyn will not surrender."

My cousin's expression darkens. "Nor shall we relent. Belzara, what is the best way?" He turns to Belzara and Ethelvrise.

"He will stall you, as the rest of his fleet goes in retreat," says Belzara.

"He means to regroup in Vitokawr," I add. "Reinforcements are already headed this way."

Alarmed, Belzara states, "We must defeat them now, King Talok. And swiftly."

Giving my agreement, I glance around. "Where's Gemma?"

Musgrae answers, "In Eyo'el, tending to the returned hostages with Krina's help. She didn't want to get in the way, nor be caught again. As for Krina, she is, well . . . Krina."

Kent clarifies, "She doesn't care what the outcome of this war is."

"That's fine." I nod.

Quall proclaims, "We need to draw them out of the courtyard. Khyra, think your Sylvadyns can handle it?"

"They'll do what they can," she says. "Which is much."

"We'd expect nothing less from anything of Ryco's," Kent says. "I'll go in there with them, see if I can't overwhelm the minds of those Vitasadyns."

"I'll shield you," says Warren. "Let's go."

The four Sylvadyns race over the landscape like rivers of branches, coming for us. They take their dragon forms, in Khyra's presence.

"Accompany Warren and Kent into the courtyard. Focus on our enemies' dragons. Do not falter. Go!" Khyra commands.

They race away like slithering branches. They're quickly ahead of Kent and Warren.

Talok glances up at Belzara. "I do believe it's high time to give the Onyx Prince command over his army. Come, Tyler. They are waiting for you."

We navigate through the battlefield. Only straggler groups of Vitiosyns remain outside of the inner court. Talok, Musgrae, and Siege easily cut them down.

Many familiar faces are gathered, getting closer to us. Rozeth and Lemawr; Rorka, Mekka, also Droediin; RayVora, Craesha, with Nebukahn; and King Aygor with Seqwhyett. Even Arkivy Nyrim has come.

But my heart fills with pride at the sight of Smythe, Ghebina, and the countless Onyx Warriors.

Smythe strides forward, giving a quick bow. "We are yours to command, Tyler Ravier. Not just the Onyx of Malik, but all of King ReNovak's army is at your disposal, for he has not yet awakened. And the titled Victor's strength is waning. Only those with your mark could be commanded by your allies. Not the whole of us. Now that you are here, Onyx Prince, what are the orders?"

Tears of joy sting my eyes. I shout the command, "Strike down their king. Defeat Vitiosus. Let us end it forever. It is today."

Those of us lingering outside of the hot battlefield now rush toward it. I take hold of my daggers. Confidence rises. The Vitiosyns have been driven out of the inner court. We meet with them, weapons and magic ready. It is a clash of many weapons, a total bloodbath.

Talok stays planted beside me. Wherever I go, he goes too.

Kent and Warren rejoin the group.

We defend each other.

Zymarc gets a vantage point from a nearby hill. He sends a blast of red fire toward us. Khyra raises her hand to stop it. It explodes overhead. Though she was successful in defusing it, she cries out. Her casting arm has been ripped open. Ben works to heal her.

We huddle around them, blocking much magic. My daggers draw nearby spells into their metal edges. The handles begin to heat up.

Zymarc is coming for us, murder in his gaze. He cuts down many Onyx Warriors, too many to count. No one gathered near us can stop him, when he takes that true form of Vitiosus. He's getting closer still.

"Hurry, Ben," Quall says. "We can't stay here. Got to move."

"Done!" Ben proclaims.

Zymarc's close enough to attack with Deezalo's Hammer. I hope with everything that these King's Guard can withstand him. Musgrae and Siege don't wait for him to strike first. They go at him, push him back, getting us some space from the Vitiosyn King. It's clear that they know a thing or two of how this Vitiosyn King fights.

Talok says, "Eli, Ben, get Khyra out of here. Take her as far as her voice will still reach the Sylvadyns. Go!"

They rush away.

"Nyrim," Talok says, "you're with us."

Nyrim starts casting spells that take the shape of people. They're a great distraction for Vitiosyns. But not for Zymarc, for he must know they aren't truly there. He awakens his fallen Prince-Generals, and they awaken some of the best Vitiosyn Warriors.

We must put them down again.

Not long after the dead have been raised, Musgrae cries out in pain. He's been hit by the blunt end of the hammer. Warren boldly fends off any who would attack his injured comrade, even uses Blue Magic that disorients Zymarc for mere seconds.

Belzara and Ethelvrise take the opening to fight the Vitiosyn King.

The battle goes on for what feels like an entire day, though I later found out it was barely more than three hours from the time I leapt out of the tower to this moment of hearing an anxious woman calling for Zymarc.

The Siveyras in Vaydell found us. They did all they could to restrain Zymarc. But he was unrelenting.

At the woman's call, however, he flinches. The rage about him weakens to dismay.

The dagger handles are hot in my grip. Almost too hot to hold. They are ready to expel the built-up magic in them.

I barely catch Zymarc's whisper of one name: "Neeka."

He turns on his heel and rushes to find her. He even drops the hammer, so he can have more speed to reach her in time.

I aim the dagger tips at Zymarc's retreating figure, and speak, "Oostrinas." It is as a whisper, but the exploding fire from the tips of both daggers is a loud burst. The two beams join into one burst of flame. Unlike the reddish fire of Oostrina, my fire turns to dark-magenta. It hits Zymarc on the back. The enchantment of his coat breaks, the fabric tears.

He does not stop. Only briefly stumbles, as wind sent forth from him pushes many out of his path.

Neeka stands there searching, then she sees Zymarc running toward her. She smiles, holds her hand out to him. She does not see Hydvar, swinging a battleaxe at her neck.

"Get down!" Zymarc yells. He's trying to pull her out of harm's way with magic.

Lemawr shifts to look like Siveyra Dezarin. The Emerald Sorsryn casts a spell of chains that wrap around Zymarc's wrists. RayVora fortifies those chains with fire; they get red-hot. It takes a dozen of the strongest to hold Zymarc in place, to keep him from taking even one step. He watches as Neeka's neck is struck by the axe.

He yells in horrified rage. It's all he can do, as tears stream down his face. His eyes widen in shock.

In the end, Neeka's not beheaded. But nearly so. Her blood splatters all over Hydvar. She falls lifeless to the ground, still in that elegant dress she had on this morning. Not a weapon is on her, not in her hands either.

"Stop," says Zymarc, frantic. "Stay your attacks."

The Vitiosyns cease, and those Vitiosyns brought back to life fall dead once more.

Talok calls for only defensive measures.

There's hardly anyone left for us to fight.

The battle has come to a halt.

"Please," Zymarc begs, "release me, King of Paragon, so that I may bring her back to life. I am able. You have my surrender. My *full* surrender, if you let me do this."

Talok looks to me. "The decision lies with the Onyx Prince, for it is he who has procured this outcome of today."

My heart breaks inside. Zymarc must have consequences. And I will make him feel those sharply.

The dozen restraining Zymarc start to weaken, all except Dezarin.

RayVora says, "Quick, we cannot hold him much longer."

King Aygor comes to give aid with his magic. So do Belzara and Ethelvrise.

Zymarc struggles against the hot, refortified chains.

Approaching, I aim NeiSator at him. I tell Zymarc, "You have had all this time to negotiate terms of truce, of surrender, yet you have been unyielding, Vitiosyn King. Neeka's death is on your hands. You do not get to have her back, when you've taken so much from us."

More tears wet Zymarc's emotionless face. Clenching his jaw tight, he swallows hard. He looks forward with indifference.

I grab hold of his left wrist and slice his forearm open all the way from wrist to elbow.

He cries out, not from pain, but from the loss of Neeka. Her life was in his hands, but now no longer. She is gone.

Both blood and magic bleed from Zymarc's arm. His Vitiosyn form fades. He is made a simple, broken Onyx Sorsryn.

I lower NeiSator. I ask Zymarc's captors to seal up his wound, and release him. "He is no longer a threat. Let him say goodbye to her, for it's what my father, LanSoren, would do."

Once Gyron seals the cut, the chains are removed from Zymarc. The defeated king collapses in weakness. He crawls over to Neeka, and sits beside her. He pulls her onto his lap and cradles her, holds her head against his chest. He whispers, "Why didn't you go north, like I asked? You weren't supposed to be here for the battle." He buries his face in her blood-soaked hair and silently weeps.

Papers rustle behind me. Steady footfalls reach my ears. I know the sound of the person's stride, his rhythm.

A gentle voice says, "She came back for you, Zymarc."

All turn to gaze upon the visitor. Initially, I do not. Rather, I witness the reaction to him. Vitiosyns and Paragonians alike, bow their heads in respect. They sheathe their weapons; they stay their magic.

I turn around. He wears the garb of an Arkivy. Layered robes the colors of Vaegon-eyes: blue, black, and white. Paydinn stands behind him, holding the full-size Watchman's Log open, as his prideful eyes swirl with the colors of fire. I can tell he has long awaited this precise moment to bring the visitor here.

"Neeka had only been in Pil'Drouka for a short while," says my father, LanSoren, "before she came back. She thought she had time to come for you, to ask you to run away with her. To leave all this behind. To let the war fizzle out on its own. To let Vitiosus fade into nothing but a myth."

Though Zymarc was looking up at my father, he now lowers his head in shame. "I've done all that you asked of me, LanSoren."

"Zymarc, we both know that isn't true." My father strolls closer. He passes me along the way to the Vitiosyn. "I never asked you to declare war on the Tamers. There were other ways to honor my requests. They required that you put yourself at risk. To trust others aside from yourself."

Zymarc mutters, "That was an impossible request."

"No," LanSoren argues quietly. "Just a hard one for you to honor."

Zymarc strokes Neeka's pale, blank face. "I have lost everything I have ever loved deeply. I didn't ask to be made into a Vitiosyn, LanSoren. I simply made do with the fate given to me at twenty-two years old."

"Then I shall return to you, one thing. Neeka's life. There is no guarantee, however." LanSoren holds his hand down to Zymarc. "Give her to me."

Zymarc tenderly pushes Neeka off his lap, cradling the back of her head. Then he pulls away and stands up. Dezarin and a dozen others come to bind Zymarc in chains.

LanSoren snaps his fingers. Neeka's body floats up. He's about to start a spell of life-giving force. I go to be by his side.

He side-glances at me. "Shall I give her life, do you think?"

I start to nod. But he says more, "For if I return life to her, I seal my fate of death. There will be no escaping it."

It sickens me to think about it. One life for another. My father's life in place of hers. I have a feeling that this is the right way, though. I say, "I don't believe we were meant to live during the same time, Father. The fate is for one of us to die. We cannot escape it. If it wasn't on that day of my thirteenth birthday, it would've been a different day. Or I would've been the one fate claimed. It's all right. Though I'll never stop looking for the truth of who or what killed you, I can now say goodbye. Neeka doesn't deserve this fate. She's an innocent of this War for the Equidyn, a casualty. I bid you to bring her back."

LanSoren grips my shoulder tight. "You are better, Tyler, than even I. Selfless, while I was selfish. It is why fate has chosen you over me."

I tell him, "I will visit you, through the Books of Time. In the Hearts of the Arkivaras. We'll see each other again. Now tend to Neeka. I don't think she has much time to linger in this place."

LanSoren lets go of me, to begin his work. I haven't the mind to watch. So I withdraw to go search for Khyra and the two with her. They're already coming this way.

Caleiso staggers past the gate of the inner court, in a daze. She's much confused by what's transpiring.

Once Neeka is brought back to life, she goes to Zymarc, still in chains. She caresses his bloodstained face. She kisses him in tenderness, before saying, "Forgive that I did not ask you sooner, my love."

As the two say their goodbyes, for soon we will take Zymarc prisoner, LanSoren studies the many expressions of those gathered. He trails to where Zymarc was first chained, where the Vitiosyn's blood is still pooled on the ground. He dips his right hand in it, then straightens to his full height. He stares at the blood, seeming to contemplate something.

Ben steps forward and offers him a white cloth.

Accepting the cloth, LanSoren smiles in sadness. "Do not blame yourself, Rueisvben'el. You were meant to be made the Eighth Guard, were fated to be given the gloves, were destined to lead all the forces of Paragon to my son. He is saved because of your efforts. You, the youngest of the Sovereignty, are indeed brave and cunning."

My father wipes the blood on the cloth and sets that cloth afire.

Zymarc stops conversing with Neeka. "LanSoren? What are you doing? Have you gone mad?" Zymarc looks around in desperation.

The Vitiosyn reinforcements can be seen in the air, coming from the west.

Paragon and its allies make preparations for another wave of attacks.

LanSoren breathes in the ashes of the blood cloth. He shuts his eyes, as he deepens his inhale. When his eyes open, they are the crimson-red of Vitiosus.

Ben looks down at the ground, his expression guilt-ridden.

I don't know what's happening. I don't know what to do.

LanSoren holds out his right hand, and speaks a word: "Callazentar!"

Deezalo's Hammer comes whirling up from the battleground, to be in LanSoren's grip. Once there, LanSoren forcefully brings the handle of it down over his bent knee. The handle cracks. The hammer shudders as if in pain, as the handle breaks the rest of the way. The voice of Deezalo screeches out from it. Dark storm clouds come over the city to hover directly above us. When LanSoren looks to the looming reinforcements in the sky, those clouds go to them. They send out horizontal rain that turns into thin sheets of sharp glass. The reinforcements fall from the sky. They are no more.

LanSoren tosses the hammer pieces aside, then snaps his fingers. Neeka is drawn into his restraining hold. He shouts, "You must choose, Zymarc! Choose one to remain with you. Neeka or Caleiso? You cannot have them both here with you."

"Neither!" Zymarc shouts back. "I choose you to remain with me."

"That will not be," says my father.

Zymarc argues, "Then tell your nephew who he is, for it won't be me."

"Nor is it for me," LanSoren says forlornly.

"You coward, LanSoren." Zymarc spits on the ground. "You coward! You escape the war, only to come and make me choose between the three things I love most in this world." Zymarc quiets down. He glances to where Caleiso still lies crumpled beside the wall. "Will she be all right, at least?"

"Is she your answer?" queries my father.

There's a moment of silence.

The red in my father's eyes fades. He says, "My son already gave you a promise, regarding her. But you must answer me, Zymarc. Who shall remain with you?"

Neeka speaks up. "It's all right, my love. I shall go. I know what she is to you. Your child. Your everything. You cannot bear to see her go."

LanSoren releases Neeka, and she trails to the towering pages of time, The Watchman's Log. Paydinn assists her in, holding her hand until her body has passed into the book. He lets go, and she fades completely.

My father also trails back to the book. He pauses in front of the pages. He turns around to look at me. "Summon me to the festival, on the second day next year, and I shall come. Above all, Tyler, do not choose the easy way. Nothing is ever easy for a Ravier. We bear the burden, but it will be you to see it through. Now wake that girl up. It's time for her to return to Paragon."

"And Awngeleik?" I ask. "What of her?"

"Your eighteen-year-old self means to return her soon." LanSoren lifts a hand in farewell. "Until the next time," he says, before stepping through the pages of time.

He is gone. And I am empty, sickened as I navigate my way through the crowd to get to Callie. Though I've been weakened by all that's recently transpired, when I pick her up in my arms, my strength is renewed. I recall the times I've had with her of late. I no longer despise this small thirteen-year-old orphan, who's in my arms.

Her eyes flutter open. Her eyes of one blue, and one green. "Tyler," she says weakly. "Is it over?"

I nod, as tears build. "It's over." I begin the walk back to Talok and his guards.

"Where are we going?" she queries.

I'm near Zymarc, when I say, "To Paragon, where I shall make you forget your entire life, all the horrors experienced up to this point. I've a promise to uphold. And I mean to go through with it. You shall be made a daughter of Paragon. You shall no longer hurt us, and we won't have to punish you for what you've done."

Zymarc hangs his head. He refuses to look at anyone.

I stop in front of him. I wait there, until he meets my gaze. When he won't, I say, "Look at me." I wait until he does. "I will keep my end of the bargain, Zymarc. Do we have your full surrender?"

"Yes. But each remaining Vitiosyn must be brought before me. I've not the strength left to give them orders from afar."

"Can you send out letters? Orders of summons, calling them to Paragon?"

He nods.

I ask, "Could you, instead, call for their surrender, if the letters are written by you and a quill of yours?"

"That would work too," says Zymarc quietly.

"Then that is what you shall do, while confined to a prison within the Eye of Paragon."

Zymarc is defeated, and finally looking worn-out. "If I am to be executed for my crimes, might Caleiso be made to forget after my execution? I very much want her to be there with me, when my time has come."

I start to say *no*, when Callie grabs hold of my coat lapels. "Yes," she says. "I very much want that, Tyler. Please, let me be there to say goodbye."

I cannot refuse her request, though I want to. This girl gets what I did not—knowing the cause of a loved one's death, and the chance to be with them in that moment. It isn't fair. But, then, maybe nothing for a Ravier is ever fair.

Still carrying Callie in my arms, I go to Talok and his dragon, Reign. I tell my cousin, "Take us home. Take me to my friend. I need Gemma Galloway."

Talok takes Callie. He hands her up to Siege, who's already prepared to make the flight.

Mystadyns have come to take the survivors and prisoners to Eyo'el. In a short while, I will be home.

* * *

Some hours later . . . we fly over the city gate of Eyo'el. Siege and Eli launch arrows. Those arrows burst with the colors of the Vaegons: blue, black, and white.

Cheers erupt from the surface. Paragonians welcome their victors home.

Once we've landed on the green field of shamrock grass, the King's Guard keep the cheering people from crowding too close.

Behind us, Dezarin and those who helped to restrain Zymarc lead the defeated king through the city.

After a time, we make it to the foot of the castle.

Gemma's already there, sitting on the topmost step, reading a letter. She folds it up, tucks it away. Though she eases up, she waits for me to come to her. And I do, though slowly. I'm too sore to do any more running.

I tell her, "We have Zymarc's full surrender. We've won."

540

She throws her arms about my neck and hugs me tight. But then she pushes away and pounds a fist on my chest. "I won't ever forgive you, Tyler Malik Ravier, for what you did to me yesterday. Making me leave you like that."

I just grip her waist, to pull her in for another hug. "Will you do something for me, Gem?" I rest my forehead on her shoulder.

She hugs me back. Her huffing breaths quiet down. "What, Tyler?"

I pull away. "Will you go with the others, and see that Zymarc sends out letters of summons for his Vitiosyns? He cannot be executed, until each one of his has been commanded to surrender."

"I will, but what do you mean to do while waiting?"

"Shower. Possibly take a nap." I grin. "I'd even eat a full meal, if one was offered to me."

Gemma's mouth drops open in surprise. "Talok," she calls down to him. "Your cousin wishes for a full meal. Can you believe it?"

Teasingly, Talok says, "Where's my cousin? And what have you done with him?"

"He's lost it," Eli proclaims in dramatics. "He was locked away in a tower, like a fair princess. Then he leapt from that tower. He didn't even have enough magic to slow his fall, the lunatic."

Warren suggests, "Yeah, possibly Khyra's insanity has rubbed off on him."

Quall and Ben share a look.

Then Ben flashes a grin at me. "Tyler Ravier will always be brash, for he can't help it."

The others start making their ridiculous suggestions.

Waving them off, I retreat inside.

Everyone within bustles about, too busy to take notice of me.

I trudge up the stairs to the second floor. I go to that room where Gemma and I stayed the first night. It's been made like new. I take a seat on one of the beds and work on getting my filthy boots off. Once they're off, I lie back. I only mean to rest my eyes for a moment. That moment turns into a nap.

Riotous noise outside the castle wakes me up. I go look out the window, even crack it open a little, the same one Callie opened to most likely give Zymarc the evidence that Awngeleik was in Paragon.

Vitiosyn prisoners are on the road, running for the city's exit.

Many are shot down with arrows and magic.

Ethelvrise starts screaming, down on the road. Belzara has been stabbed between her ribs by an enchanted blade. She spots me through the window.

I Mensa-div to the Deathasyn woman, *"Ravieras-Savak-Kavas. Speak it at the moment of your death, Belzara, if you wish to be saved. I have made a way to cheat death."*

"Goodbye, Ravier," she says in div. *"I've lived enough lives. This one the best of them, for I got to see a legend rise at its beginning. Your Ryco still hasn't made it home. I mean to go to The Kievas and help find him, free him. It's the least I can do for you, after all you've done for the peoples of Muraine."*

I shut the window, then withdraw from it.

Ethelvrise cries louder, calls for Belzara not to leave her.

I tear my clothes off, ripping the vest fabric as I yell. I stride for the bathing quarter of the room, and summon a hot spray of water. It beats down on my bare flesh, and burns. It burns for quite a long time. It's not enough. I summon NeiSator into my left grip. I'm about to plunge its tip violently into my forearm. Yet I cannot bring myself to do it. Not after everything I've survived. Gently, instead, I make two cuts on my right forearm. Not to hurt myself, but to proclaim that, twice, I've already died. Once, in the storerooms of the castle with Khyra, and once from the Call of Vitiosus. I'm a survivor, and I proclaim that, with the two marks. They bleed more than I had anticipated.

I drop the dagger. It clatters to the floor. Blood runs down my bare legs. I stand there, broken. More blood drips from my right arm and lands on the tops of my feet. The water spray dilutes it, and it flows on the tile, draining to wherever the water goes in the castle. I press my hands on one of the walls to hold myself up. My body wants to collapse. Though I want the wounds to heal, they don't.

Someone enters the bathing quarter, boots plodding along. Whoever it is, stops.

I rasp out, "Whichever one of you has come to check on me, don't even think about starting a lecture. I only want some quiet for a while."

"Why ever would I lecture you, Ravier?" queries a content, familiar voice. "I'm only happy to be freshly back from the dead; and to see that you've not done anything too stupid, nor have you died, while I was away."

Chills rush over me. I turn around, naked, but hopeful, tormented, unbelieving that it really could be him. "Ryco," I ask, "are you really here?"

That citrine-yellow gaze dances in amusement. "Truly, I am here." He holds up a towel and then covers me, before he brushes his fingers along the wounds of my arm. He is neither sad nor angry. Simply contemplative. "I could heal these for you. I believe, however, you'd rather do it yourself. The right healing spell for it is *Sanabiteis.*" He looks into my eyes. "Speak the word, and heal yourself, Tyler. It's a spell you've known in your heart for a while. You were not ready to remember its sound. To make that which is broken, better. To bind a wound to beauty. It's what you used to heal those EquiNeins in the garden. Now you should use it for yourself."

I speak the word, and the two wounds seal up. They shift to become tiny marks, tattoos, of a howling wolf encircled by a dragon in flight.

So much that hurts in my heart is made whole. The longing for LanSoren's life to return lessens. The confusion that Zymarc could be the father of my mother drops away. How Paragon will ever recover from it all is gone. My worry over Callie becoming a daughter of Paragon and losing her memories disappears too. I only worry over the fate of Zymarc. *Should he be executed,* I wonder, or *should he live out his life, imprisoned? Which holds more justice? Which does he deserve more?*

"Oh no." Ryco groans as he opens a wardrobe. "I know that look. Something's still bothering you. So get dressed, and let's go down to the others. We can discuss it on the way. Also, I've caught wind that there's a certain Vitiosyn scheduled to be executed on Metsa's castle steps within the hour." Ryco tosses me a set of clean clothes.

As I dress, I tell him of my time in Vaydell. The ShenawFayel with Zymarc. All that happened, even the shifts in time, I tell Ryco.

At the end, he asks me, "What are you saying, Tyler? That you don't want Zymarc to be executed because of a few good deeds? Because he helped to stop Deezalo from being resurrected? Surely, that was for self-preservation."

"How can we be sure?"

Ryco sits at the newly fashioned desk, thinking a moment. "There's no sure way to know."

I ask, "There's no spell that can reveal intentions?"

"Hmm." Ryco thinks more. "If Zymarc was still an Onyx Warrior, Gyron could perform such a thing. Perhaps the Jokryn brothers hold the answer. Paydinn and YaeVorkk, specifically. They've dabbled in the most experimental magic. I overheard, however, that they are in Vaydell. Clearing the city of fatalities. Performing last rites and such for those with mortal wounds. They're unlikely to answer quickly enough."

"Vards, Ryke, how long ago did you make it back?"

"Shortly after a certain Deathasyn woman showed up in The Kievas." Ryco smirks. "She means to get her revenge on Deezalo. Deamond and I left through the path Belzara had cleared to get to us."

"Then where's Dea?" I ask.

"Just outside the door, waiting for you to finish getting dressed. You take your sweet time, Sleeping Dragon." Ryco pushes himself out of the desk chair, and knocks thrice on the desktop.

The door bursts open, and Dea rushes in. She wraps me in a crushing embrace. I'm near suffocated by the fluffy part of her wings.

When she steps back, she wiggles her shoulders back and forth. "See, I brought him back. Safe and sound. Possibly he's much improved. He's not said one nasty thing, since I found him."

"For shame, Dea," I say. "That's not an improvement. For who is Ryco of Paragon, if not smug?"

"Urgh!" Dea scoffs. "That little Princess Krina wandering within the city has enough smugness for us all. We'd better go rescue her from

Gemma's wrath. The Witch of Galloway can only keep her temper at bay for so long."

"The Witch of Galloway?" I ask. "Who started calling her that?"

"Skylin," Dea admits. "Spied on her and some others, while we were looking for you. You'll not guess what's happened with Khyra, while you were in here. She finally asked that poor guard on a Dragon Ride. Ben, wasn't it?"

Ryco chuckles. "Don't look so surprised, Ravier. It seems they've accepted I'd never be coming back. And you know how the young are. Not a moment to waste, unless they're you, for you have all the time in the world."

"Is that why you delayed being seen?" I ask, as the three of us head out of the room. "You didn't want Khyra to reclaim you as her life partner?"

"Perhaps," Ryco replies, as he shuts the door behind us. "I've no wish to be partnered with Khyra. Only wanted her to have the protection of the dragons I tamed. I'm quite proud of them. I consider their debt to me repaid. I intend to free them in a few days."

We're soon at the stairs, leading down.

Arguments have started on the first floor.

I glance over the second level's railing.

"Someone go get Talok, and now!" Zepharre shouts. "Tyler as well. We can't finalize Zymarc's sentence without them."

EmiKal says, "Just behead the beast, and be done with it."

Dozens gathered boisterously give their approval.

Zepharre is starting to fiddle with the fabric of his coat. He spots Musgrae and clings to him. "Grae, have you seen them?"

Musgrae answers, "Warren, Siege, and I have been tending to our injured allies. One of the Amethyst Queens has been wounded rather badly, and—"

Ryco started down the stairs, while Zepharre and Musgrae were conversing.

The room grows quiet.

Musgrae looks over Zepharre's shoulder. He takes in a quiet gasp.

"Musgrae," Zepharre scolds him, "I understand that the Three Queens are very strong and beautiful, but even these sorts of things have a lifespan. No one is invulnerable. Losses were to be expected on all sides."

Musgrae rasps out, "Ryke," before he drops the sack of things he was carrying. He pushes past Zepharre. He slowly reaches out. As soon as his hand is pressed to Ryco's chest, Musgrae shakes his head in disbelief. "You devil, you scared us all."

"Where are the others?" Ryco asks.

"Around." Musgrae shrugs. Then he gets suspicious. "How long have you been awake? I swear, I caught a whiff of you and your pinesap, while I was in the kitchen. Thought I was hallucinating."

Ryco replies, "Long enough to know there will be no repayment required for my life. The Black Flame has been most satisfied, of late."

Dea and I come up behind Ryco.

Zepharre suddenly bursts out, "How dare you do that to us, Ryco! Leave without saying goodbye. Without telling us what was going to happen."

"Would you have let me go?" Ryco asks in return.

Zepharre sputters, "I . . . well, I . . . don't know, Ryco. I'll never know. But you can be certain of this, next time you say you're going to go free someone or rescue them, I'll be going with."

Ryco grins in that special way. "So long as Rozeth escorts us. Do you happen to know her whereabouts? Dea and I couldn't find her in her preferred places."

Zepharre flaps his hand. "Getting bedded by some Onyx named Hydvar or other. Something about a delayed Sodon request? I don't know." Zepharre shakes his head. "At any rate, we need to speak with Talok. He's in his quarters, most likely."

Musgrae mutters, "Hopefully not bedding anyone."

"What?" Zepharre raises his voice. "Don't say things like that, Grae. Talok must never know that such things are permitted without long-term commitment, after such a battle as we've had today." Zepharre looks to Ryco again. "Which brings me to another point. Is Khyra your widow or partner? I've not a clue what to tell her, when she gets back. She's gone on a, well . . ." Zepharre trails off.

"An expedition with Ben," Musgrae finishes for the distraught adviser. "To be fair, she didn't think you were coming back, Ryke. And her parents are nowhere to be found. She means to go looking for them, while starting a family."

Zepharre says, "It's a pity she didn't wait just a little longer. I was looking forward to you being the father of her eight children, Ryco."

Ryco sighs. "Your loss is my gain. Come, Tyler. Let's find that cousin of yours. And, Grae? Tell the others? Take Dea, as proof, so they'll believe you."

"Will do."

Musgrae and Dea head off.

Ryco and I make for Talok's quarters. Along the way, Ryco fashions a cloak to hide himself, more importantly, his face.

We further discuss Zymarc's fate.

I ask, "Think you can summon Paydinn and YaeVorkk to Eyo'el? I'd like to know Zymarc's intentions. Also, I'd like to know the truth of what he needed Awngeleik for. He never gave up that truth."

"I'll send an arrow-letter off, after we talk to Talok. Though it will reach them quickly, they may not head for here immediately."

"Be convincing, then."

"I'll try. But the Jokryn brothers tend to do as they please." Ryco comes to a halt just outside of Talok's room. "It should be you to open the door. And, I'll warn you, you may not like what you see."

I'm about to knock on Talok's door. Soft groans beyond the door make me hesitate. Something creaks in the room. Then I hear a slight struggle. I throw open the door, terrified.

Talok sits in a chair, stripped from the waist up.

Ethelvrise straddles his lap. She's hardly clothed at all, as she bites into his neck. She holds tightly to his wrists. He barely fights her. Only tenses with seeming pleasure. His sensual groans confirm his enjoyment.

Ethelvrise gently pulls her fangs from Talok's skin. She spots us and shrieks, leaping off him. She grabs Talok's garb—my father's Waking

Dragon coat—off the floor, and covers herself with it. She wipes the blood off her face with her hands. Ashamed, she won't look at us.

I yell, "Talok, what are you doing?"

He sits, panting, looking from the Deathasyn woman to me then Ryco, concealed in the cloak. Slowly, he eases out of his chair.

Ryco pushes me farther into the room and firmly shuts the door.

Sighing, my cousin explains, "Look, Tyler, Belzara's death created a frenzy. Some Vitiosyn prisoners tried to escape, after one of them stabbed her. The Vonsai caught the slow ones, and *ate* them. Literally. The Vonsai can barely be restrained from eating anything 'Deathasyn' this day. I was hoping that, by her feeding a little on my blood, her scent would be altered to them. As well as bring her some relief from the pain in her heart. She's lost a loved one today. And I feel the pain of my uncle's loss all over again."

Talok begins dressing.

Ethelvrise gawks at the three of us.

I just motion to the clothes still strewn about, asking, "At what point did that *relief* involve you losing half your clothes? And, her, nearly all of hers?"

Talok pauses from buttoning his shirt. "I never intended to bed her, if that's what you're getting at, Cousin. She's too old for me, and I've not permission from the Sovereignty to do such a thing. Besides, she doesn't prefer swords. If you catch my meaning?"

Ethelvrise goes pale in the face, almost white. She pulls the coat's collar higher, to hide as much of herself as she can. She inches her way to the chair Talok was occupying.

Fully dressed, Talok adjusts his clothes to look as smooth as possible. Given the day we've had, many wrinkles, tears, and stains remain. I presume he's about to leave the room with Ryco and me, though he doesn't yet know it's Ryco. But then he starts picking up Ethelvrise's clothes. He folds them, puts them neatly on his bed. Once all are in a pile, he looks to the Deathasyn woman, who's curled up on the chair. Neither her feet nor hands show out from under the coat's fabric. Just her eyes peeking over the collar edge. The hood hides the rest of her head.

Talok bends down to kiss her brow. "I'm deeply sorry for your loss, dear Ethelvrise. Stay in here as long as you wish. I'll not be returning to it for a few days, if ever. I don't know if I can sleep in a room where my cousin caught me in an act he shall not soon be forgetting."

Ryco tugs at my arm, Mensa-divving, *"Cool it, Ty-Ty. I didn't go through all that I did, just so you could strangle your cousin now."*

Talok heads out with us. After cleaning his neck of blood, and healing it some, he says, "She'll be able to visit Eyo'el later. Have Grover extract her favorite memories of Belzara. I want the Arkiveis to figure out a way to make a memorial for Belzara. Ensure that what she and Ethelvrise did for us is never forgotten. We couldn't have infiltrated the city as effectively as we did, without them. I, as well, wish for their side of things to be shown. Do you resent me for that, Tyler?"

"No. Just surprised to find you in there like that. I thought something was restraining you, in the bad sort of way." I contemplate telling him what Zepharre said. I decide against it. Also do I decide against telling him that Sosha was a full-blooded Withrasyn. No need to let more go to my cousin's head, this day.

Talok snickers. "You mean there's a good sort of way to be restrained?"

I pause our walk, to send him a look.

"All right. All right!" He holds up surrendering hands. "So there is a good sort of restraining. But we didn't all get our own Skylin, to ease the burden of the journey, now did we?"

"You jealous?" I ask.

Pinching two fingers together, Talok replies, "Perhaps a bit. But I'll get over it. Or shall I steal her away, while you're gone? Zepharre's already been told to get to work on fixing the portal, or finding someone to repair it. Soon, you'll be back in your nice cozy bed."

I jab right back, "Guess I won't be trying to find out more about Aunt Miriam, then."

Ryco growls. "Are the two of you done comparing your swords?"

Talok stiffens his posture. He strides closer to Ryco, to yank the hood back. He's struck speechless, his mouth gaping open too. He shakes himself out of the surprise. "Back . . . there," he starts to say, but then he trails off.

Ryco says, "Not a word to anyone, ever."

"You are the most loyal of dragons, Ryco. Thank you!"

"Don't mention it."

Talok looks Ryco over thoughtfully. "You know, you look rather fantastic for having just been raised from the dead. Your aura is practically glowing."

"You can see it?" Ryco seems surprised by that.

Talok nods. "Yes, quite of lot of little things have changed about me. It was to be expected. Jasper says it has to do with how long the device was on me. I can see when spirits fade from this world, to go to The Kievas, for example. I'm told that it's a Deathasyn trait. Who knew?"

Ryco shares a look with me, but we change the subject.

"So, Aunt Miriam," I ask, "what's the plan?"

Ryco says, "Try meeting with her if at all possible, these next few months."

Talok adds, "We'll want updates every so often. We'll figure out a way to converse with ease. Don't want to have to open up the portal every single time we need to talk with you, or you us."

"That's fine," I say. "Maybe enchanted quills and paper could work, so long as I keep them near the lake."

"Possibly," says Ryco. "Now to discuss a more pressing matter. The people are calling for Zymarc to lose his head. Tyler seems inclined to interrogate him first, find out all we can."

"What more is there to learn?" queries Talok. "We've already probed him for hours, Warren resetting the time that's passed. He's said all he intends to. He's also signed away his title as the Vitiosyn King to Azabahk, should we need more letters of orders to be written and sent off. If our people wish for a beheading, then that's what he shall get. But an internal beheading. We already know Zymarc's neck can't be severed from the outside."

Ryco asks, "What device do you intend to use on him?"

"A Geldryn one," Talok admits, as we approach the stairs leading to the first floor. "RayVora offered it to us, explained how it works. Zymarc looked not a bit happy to see it."

Turning away from us, Talok announces to the people on the first floor, "Our Ryco has come back to us, and we shall celebrate as we never have before, just as soon as the Vitiosyn King, Zymarc, has met his end. Someone bring him to the castle. Let us wait not a moment more."

A sick feeling creeps up my throat. I don't know what has come over me. I think, *It seems too easy. My dad did say not to pick the easy way. What will come of sparing Zymarc's life now?*

I go line up outside with the King's Guard at the foot of the castle steps. I shuffle through all I know of Zymarc. He's knowledgeable in many things. Even in how to hurt Death. But what good is his knowledge to us, if he never gives it up? Never lets some truth slip out. Could time truly break him, and bring about his confession? And what would that confession be?

I decide that it doesn't matter. This is what the people want. Who am I to stand in the way of a multitude?

35

A Promise, Kept – Part I

The hours of evening aren't far off, as Zymarc is led along the road to the foot of the castle. He's still in the distance, getting closer. Azabahk and a few Prince-Generals survived. They're lined up across from the King's Guard. Talok stands at the top of the castle steps. Gemma has come to be by the guards and me. A little Darklyre girl, one of King Aygor's Wards, refused to be parted from Gemma. Begged to be held. Even did that little girl make her demand of, "Read me a story, Gigi!"

"Why not have Skylin read to you?" Gemma suggests. "She loves—"

"No." The little girl crosses her arms. "She's helping prepare supper. And I'm hungry. She wouldn't give me a morsel."

Deamond offers to take the girl inside, or for a stroll in the groves of fruit trees.

The girl wails, pushes Dea's hands away. "No, Dea! I want Gigi to read me a story!"

Thus, Gemma is forced into compliance. She quietly reads *The Dark Prince* storybook as we wait. It's all we have available to us at the moment.

Retreating to stand behind me, Dea mumbles, "Did they even notice I was gone?"

I whisper to her, "One of the boys did."

When Gemma gets to the ripped pages of the storybook that I stuck

552

back in place, the girl sends me a great scowl. She whispers in spite, "You've ruined it, since Dea read it to us last."

I tell her, "It couldn't be helped."

The girl sticks her tongue out at me. Then she sweetly nuzzles against the nape of Gemma's neck. The little monster.

I shake my head.

Dea scolds the girl in whispering anger, "Do that one more time, and I'll take you inside."

"No you won't," says the girl. "Gigi won't let you, for Gigi told me to do it. To make a face at Tyler Ravier."

Khyra wanders over to us. She's about to say something to Gemma, but she decides against it, for the time has come.

Zymarc is brought forth by Rorka and Mekka, sharing that equal, two-legged stature. Droediin, in Von form, leads at the front. Jasper isn't among the escort of our top prisoner. In fact, the Alpha of the Vons is nowhere to be seen.

The King's Advisers have joined Talok on the castle landing. Zepharre and EmiKal prepare the device. I don't take note of its features, especially from this distance. Truly, I don't wish to know how it works. I want this over with. Yet that sick feeling persists. It might have to do with how badly I want this moment to end. How badly I want the threat of Vitiosus to cease. So many little things hang in the balance, tormenting me.

Ryco, at Gemma's other side, whispers, "Please leave with the girl, before they fasten that on him."

Pausing from reading, Gemma nods. She hesitates to restart. She readjusts her hold on the girl, and drops the book in the process.

Zymarc's passing us at that exact moment. Though he's bound in chains, hands in front, he manages to catch the book before it lands on the ground. He closes it. Straightening his posture, he glances at the cover.

Mekka's about to shove him forward.

Gemma, though startled, reaches for the book.

Zymarc mutters, "Pity you never burned this. The story it could have told, well . . . it doesn't matter, does it, Galloway?"

Gemma accepts the book. A far-off look sinks into her gaze. Tears roll down her cheeks; the Darklyre child wipes them away. Even does the little girl plant a kind kiss on Gemma's cheek.

Zymarc's breaths get shallow. He looks at Gemma in desperation. "Remember what I told you, Galloway."

Gemma's chin quivers. She struggles to hold back more tears. Barely does she keep from sobbing. All gathered grow uneasy, seeing Gemma lose her composure.

I can't help but wonder, *What does he mean by that?*

Talok calls out, "Bring the defeated king forward."

"We are ready for him," Zepharre adds.

Mekka shoves Zymarc forward. Droediin plods out of the way, lets the procession of twenty or so continue on without him.

Zymarc looks over his shoulder at me. For a flash of a moment, it's a different face. Not his. It's younger, more angular-looking, and frightened.

I know I've seen it somewhere else. Possibly, just once.

Gemma gives me the book, before she sets the girl down. "Come," she says, "we shall play hide-and-seek in the city, until the meal is ready."

She rushes for the underpass of the city-in-the-trees. The little girl takes off, flying after her.

Only moments pass, however, when Gemma sobs loudly in the distance.

Musgrae suggests, "Shouldn't one of us go after her? See what's wrong."

Resigned, Ben states, "I'll go." He retreats in a slow stride.

Ryco accompanies Zymarc up the rest of the way to meet with fate.

A crowd has started to congregate tightly together. Paragonians, their allies, and many creatures. Dragons rest on the rooftops of the castle. Reign takes the highest point of it, gazing across the city like a guardian. His cousin flies overhead. He seems to never want to land. Eventually he does, to take the place at the right of Reign.

Zymarc's on the landing, being fitted with the device, when Caleiso is brought out to stand with Azabahk and the Prince-Generals.

His voice thick with emotion, Zymarc says, "Look away, Caleiso, when my time has come."

She ardently shakes her head. Lines of heartbreak crease her face. "I will not. I shall bear witness to the loss of my father, for that is who you are to me. A father to an orphan girl no one wanted. A protector, most severe to those who would hurt his loved ones. You are mighty, in all you doth do, Zymarc'Khran-dei-laashun. That is your full name. The unwanted made wanted. You fought to give a voice to unwanted things. You gave that voice to me and many others. And we thank you. May death be kind to you. Though I shall be made to forget my life spent with you, always will my heart feel the loss of you."

Zymarc looks down in defeat.

Again, his appearance flashes to look like someone else.

I dust off the storybook. About to put it away, I recall Zymarc's great desire to die on other occasions. He now seems unhappy with this fate. *What's changed?* I wonder. Then I remember the face. Prince Setharyn. The Onyx Prince. But how could it be?

I'm tempted to think that Zymarc is using this as one last attempt to be saved. Yet it's not the same as when he took Soren's face or Kaalon's as his own. It's like a trapped soul silently begging for help, by revealing himself to the one who might not ignore it. Oh, but I want to. I can't, when the conversation between Soren and ReNovak fades into memory. Setharyn interrupted them, told his father that ReNovamen wouldn't work to save him. That he would take his own life, in order to not become a pawn of Vitiosus. That the Vardiyas would somehow find a way to bring him back.

I think, *What if he lied? What if Soren assisted him with ReNovamen, and hid the truth from ReNovak? Could the prince in this story be Setharyn? What if Zymarc confessed who he is to Gemma, while she was his captive, and she wanted to believe him? Possibly she even saw Setharyn too, before she went off just now.*

I glance in the direction where she retreated. A breeze rustles the leaves and branches of the giant trees. It's otherwise tranquil, at the city's center.

Droediin, in human form, has taken Gemma's former position at my side. He Mensa-divs, *"Shall we revert time, and burn that book, do you think? For, together, we have that power to turn back the clock."*

He's offering his hand like he did in Vondurheil, when he made us invisible to all.

Zymarc cries out, as the device is made ready upon his neck. He's hyperventilating, shaking. He's terrified. Only the threat of losing Caleiso or Neeka has ever caused his true fear to show through. In a way, he is losing Caleiso. Or, rather, she is losing him.

She does not weep. Her tears are gone. She merely gives him a reassuring smile, as if to say, *It will be okay.*

I rest the back of my wrist in Droediin's palm. He tightens his fingers round it, and speaks words of magic.

All slows to the stillness of undisturbed water.

I set the storybook aflame, and toss it to the path that leads to the castle stairs.

The fire turns vibrant-green. The cover burns to ashes that peel up. A wind swirls near the book. The ashes fade. Glistening wood of the Arkivara is revealed. The pages become as her turquoise-colored leaves. Soon, the altered pages burn up. Rising smoke turns into scenes, which play out before all gathered. Only Droediin and I bear witness to them, however.

It flashes through Setharyn's life, lingering on a speech he gave before a mass gathering of Sorsryns. "May the Light of Vardiyas be with me always, that through me, the Onyx might one day be free of the Laws of Neutrality. I, Setharyn, am the prince, promised to bring goodwill. It is my destiny to set slaves free. It is for me."

The scene shifts to Soren introducing Setharyn to Lady Ashar of the Nyxane, who I know to be Zymarc's mother. She is tall, thin, and dark-haired, elegant in her movements.

"I am honored to be the mother to your ReNovamen, Prince Setharyn. I shall guard my body, so he should be born, renewed. Soren has promised to guard me as well."

Setharyn strolls about, hands in his pockets. Then he covers a painful-sounding cough with his fist. Settling down, he queries, "Are you sure, dear lady, that the process will heal the sickness of Vitiosus? That I will not be reborn as such a vile creature as what was seen in Deezalo?"

Ashar nods. "Yes, fair prince. For that is why ReNovamen was originally created. Should souls be cursed beyond repair, infected with magic deemed incurable, ReNovamen is there to overcome these things through the process of rebirth. It was made by the power of a Tri-Circle. It is tied to three pillars. Our star, our moon, and the combined elements."

Setharyn asks, "What if you die, before he's born?"

"His soul shall wander, searching for a Sorsryn woman with child. He shall replace the unborn one that grows within her."

"Then I beg you, dear Ashar, guard yourself and the unborn one, soon to be with you. For I do not want a mother to be given the Onyx Prince, unknowingly. It hardly seems fair."

Soren inquires, "What of ReNovak?"

"Do not tell him," says Setharyn. "He doesn't deserve to know. But of my ReNovamen. Do tell him one day, Lady Ashar. And I ask that you name him Zymarc'Khran-dei-laashun. The unwanted made wanted. He's not what anyone will want at first. A day will come, however, when many will greatly desire him. It will be as what a phantom has shown me."

They turn to smoke that reforms to show Ashar watching from a distance, as a young boy—perhaps five years old—practices Gendras magic with other children. An Onyx Warrior teaches them the basics. The boy is much smaller than the rest. Teased by the rest. His magic isn't as good as theirs. Barely is he able to create smoke, when the other children hold sparks of fire in their hands. They drench their campfires with enough water to put out the flames. But the boy can only make a few drops of liquid fall from his palms.

Later in the scene, Ashar assures him, "Zymarc, darling, it does not matter. You will get better. Keep practicing. Do not give up, my son."

Tears are in the child Zymarc's eyes, as he asks, "Why am I so far behind the other children? And why will it matter if I get better? So will they get better. In the end, I'll always be one step behind them, Mother. Can't I be a scholar? Why must I be a warrior?"

"Because it is your destiny," says Ashar with conviction. "To make the unwanted things wanted. It's what your father wanted for you. And I must tell you, I was very sick while carrying you. It's why you are smaller than they. In time, you will catch up to them. You can be better than them, in another way, now." She bends down to place her hand on the child Zymarc's chest. "Be mighty and strong, inside. Form a heart, unbreakable. Let nothing ever stop you from what you want in this life, my son."

Quickly, the scene becomes a blur of Zymarc's life before Vitiosus. He is hardly a cruel soul at all. Only good. Only honorable. He once rescued Deathasyn children from the mistreatment of Geldryn teenagers. He met Belzara, formerly called Ethelvrise, shortly after that. They competed to be twin apprentices to Siveyra Dezarin. At eighteen, he leapt off the highest pinnacle in Oniva as a last ritual to be sworn in as an Onyx Warrior. Thereafter, he went on many missions. Sat in on many negotiations. Fought in several battles, to uphold the Laws of Neutrality. Then came an attack of Vitiosus, sometime before he was twenty-four, as he was leaving the land of the Pools of Vosh-Perida. He didn't see his attacker. Everything just went blank for him.

It shows the days following the attack.

While Setharyn dwindled from the initial stages of Vitiosus, Zymarc thrived. He had come a long way with magic, but as Vitiosus changed him, he became stronger, faster, more calculated. Slowly, his honor faded to outbursts and violence. One instance was an encounter with Soren.

The Withrasyn asked him something.

I glance at Droediin. "Did you catch what he said?"

"I did not."

In the scene, Zymarc attacks Soren, bites into his neck. Once releasing the Withrasyn, Zymarc yells in rage, "Get out of my sight, Soren. Don't you ever show your face to me again. You don't have long to wait, either.

For, tomorrow, I shall have a Warrior's End. My life shall be forfeit. Vitiosus will not be resurrected because of me. Now leave."

Droediin holds his free hand out. The scene slows way down. He loosens his grip on my wrist. "I do believe we've seen enough to make a decision, Tyler."

I reply, "To spare Zymarc now, or let it be finished. I can't help but think he still gets something, even in dying."

"I quite agree," says Droediin. "More and more, I'm remembering my time around him, after being turned. Some things aren't adding up."

"Then it's settled," I say. "What about the people? They're not going to like it. They might turn into a mob, and kill Zymarc in his weakened state."

"I shall get Rorka and Mekka to aid in managing the crowd. You focus on keeping Zymarc alive. That device on his neck is ready. It only needs to be activated with a click of a dial. Get ready, Ravier. Time's about to restart."

As soon as things begin moving again, I step out onto the path. "Wait!" I shout.

Talok startles from his conversation with Zepharre. "Cousin, what is wrong? Are you hurt?"

Everyone's looking at me—gawking, more like.

Droediin makes for where his comrades are.

I shake my head. "We can't do this yet, Talok. Shouldn't we gather more evidence that this is the right decision, regarding Zymarc?"

Talok's eyes darken over. "Of course this is the right decision, Tyler. If you can't handle it, go inside till it's over, or go find Gemma and comfort her in whatever distresses her."

Zepharre steps away from Zymarc. "Whenever you are ready, King Talok. The Vitiosyn's life is yours to claim."

Closer, I move toward the foot of the castle. "No, it's not. It's mine to claim. For it's by my efforts, even risking my life, that he was caught. I am the Onyx Prince, Talok, and you are not. Zymarc was Onyx before a Vitiosyn. His life is mine to spare, and I say we spare it for now."

Talok points at me. "If we were in Oniva, I would agree. We are not, however. We're here, where he has killed countless of my people. I cannot forgive him for that. Cannot spare him." Talok gives a curt nod to Zepharre.

EmiKal hangs back, his face damp with sweat.

Zepharre says, "Someone restrain Tyler, until this is over."

The King's Guard, save for Ryco, give me an apologetic look. Jokryns approach. Darklyres too. The people of Paragon get rowdy, shouting in jumbles for the death of Zymarc.

Droediin and the two candidates spring into action, containing the crowd. Dea aids them, convincing her fellow Darklyres to settle down. Or, rather, she convinces Aygor and Seqwhyett to settle their people.

Reign and the dragons take off to fly over the people, intimidating them into dispersing.

I wave my hands out, and push the ones coming for me back with a very strong wind. Only Ryco is unmoved. The rest, to either side of the path, are thrown back.

From his place on the landing, Talok reaches for the device's dial.

Zymarc shuts his eyes. The expression of fear is gone. A smile tugs at the corners of his mouth.

I reach out with my left hand. I'm desperate to stop this.

Talok turns the dial.

I'm dragged toward the stairs. My ribs smack the bottom step. Something cracks. Sharp pain in my side makes it hard to breathe. My left hand is open, but something is trying to close it. I won't let it. Even as the skin of my fingertips burns away, and the flesh disintegrates all the way to the finger bones, revealing veins of magic, I won't let my left hand close.

I cry out like I did that day of dying from the Call of Vitiosus. The pain gets worse and worse. I no longer feel like I'm here in Paragon, but rather on the gray sands of The Kavas, being taunted by ghosts, while looking across the oceans of death.

Someone calls to Talok, tells him to deactivate the device.

Suddenly, the invisible, crushing grip on my hand ceases.

The crowd is louder still. So are the Vons and dragons.

I look up at Talok. His face is ashen-white. "Tyler, why are you doing this?"

Through the pain, I tell him, "Because this is what he wants. He wants to perish."

Zymarc scowls down at me. "You're such an annoying little prick, Tyler. Why can't you just let me die?"

Zepharre hurriedly works to remove the device from Zymarc. EmiKal grabs hold of Zepharre, and throws him aside. He turns the dial.

I hold it from severing Zymarc's neck, even as my finger bones break off at the second knuckle. My magic flows to the ground. I scream. Everything's so loud. So desperate. So dire.

The King's Guard are rushing for the stairs at this point. Ben's not back with Gemma.

Quall tends to me. "Release your hold, Tyler, before you lose your whole arm. Your body can't take much more."

I shake my head. "I won't let go."

"Please!" Quall begs.

The chaos heightens.

I nearly pass out, when EmiKal brandishes a dagger.

Ryco grabs Talok, but he doesn't move him quickly enough. EmiKal stabs my cousin in the side. Zepharre slits EmiKal's throat with a short knife. Though frantic, the head adviser does his best to get EmiKal's body out of the way, so the guards can reach Talok, and tend to him.

Quall shouts at someone on the landing.

Ryco quickly rips the device off Zymarc's neck. And Zymarc is none too pleased about it.

I'm thrown back from the release of pressure. I ease up on my hands and knees.

Ryco commands, "Warren, Siege, take him back to his cell." Then he joins in healing Talok. In fact, many go to aid Talok.

Quall, however, has concerned eyes focused only on me. He's about to help me inside, when someone else picks me up, and hauls me there.

Once inside, Arsyn of Jhire sets me down on a nearby bench.

Talok's asking a blaze of questions, to which a muddle of answers ensue. He curses when the knife is pulled out from his side, and blood spurts from the wound.

My own pain is great. I'm trembling; my left fingertips are still gone.

I don't know where Quall went.

Only Arsyn kneels in front of me and looks the left hand over, contemplating the best course of action. He flashes his gaze up to my face. He puts a finger to his lips. He gives one last look over his shoulder, to see if anyone is watching us. No one is. Then he breathes on my mangled hand. His breath becomes a fire of dark-magenta. The finger bones regrow, and the veins of magic repair themselves. Then the flesh and tendons. The skin and nails too. The Prismatic of Magic lights on that left hand. And Arsyn takes hold of my right, presses the palm of it to my left. The Prismatic bleeds onto that hand too. The pain is gone.

When Arsyn cups his larger hands over mine, his skin becomes stained as well. Its appearance is different, however. Both of his hands and arms seem painted with metal that matches my waking-dagger. Metallic white, copper, and red, with blackened fingernails. Fire wisps off his skin.

He releases his hold on me, and stands up. Both of the changes on us fade, except for my healed hand. It remains that way. I move the fingers of it, making sure it's real and permanent.

Though chaos surrounds us, I ask Arsyn, "Do you know what this is? Why I'm different?"

"I do," he admits. "Let's not talk of it, here."

"Then where?" I ease up off the bench.

"The Pools of Vosh-Perida," he says quietly. "It's where Zebulon and I are headed, after tonight. We've done what we can to fix the portal you broke. It will be ready by morning. You and Galloway must go home to Earth, for a time. The Vardiya there is nearly worn out from her task of keeping time at a standstill for you."

"You seem to know a lot, Arsyn of the Ravas," I state. "So tell me this one thing. Am I Soren, reborn?"

Arsyn looks away in thought.

People bustle about in hysteria. Ryco's eyes are that straw-colored yellow. He's much distracted in healing Talok, in easing his pain, in holding it together after coming back from The Kievas.

Arsyn finally admits in Mensa-div, *"Not exactly. It's a long story. Why do you think your father never told you? Once he accepted that he would die when you are young, he hadn't the time to properly tell you. Hadn't the time to work around all the bindings we are held to."*

I ask in div, *"You mean, what the Ashenawks are bound to?"*

"Not them. The Fennukye. It's what we are."

"But the Phantom of Time," I div, *"he called me the Last of the Ashenawks, and also the first. The in-between. Do you know what he meant? What are the Ashenawks and Fennukye, anyway?"*

Arsyn beckons me to follow him toward a hallway of the castle. And I do.

Once in a place of silence, Arsyn inquires, "You've met the Phantom of Time? When, where? And what did he look like? None of the Fennukye have ever met him."

"Zebulon has. He took Caleiso and me to the Pools of Vosh-Perida, after there was rioting in Vaydell. I met the phantom soon after."

"Weren't you in ShenawFayel with Zymarc? Where was he?"

"Passed responsibility of the agreement to Caleiso for three hours. Had other matters to attend to. Look, Arsyn, I haven't the time to tell all of it. I've asked Ryco to send a letter to Paydinn and YaeVorkk in Vaydell, summoning them back to Paragon. Will you go there? I have a feeling you and Zebulon, together, can travel a lot faster than the rest of us. Ask Paydinn to use his Watchman's Log to speed things along. Make sure they head back, before the people grow so restless that they storm the prison cells. Zymarc cannot die today. Whatever goes down, it must not be that."

"Why, Ravier?" Arsyn studies me. "What does he gain in death?"

"I don't know. And I don't want to find out, by letting it happen. Best to interrogate him, force the truth out of him. It's what I hope Paydinn and YaeVorkk can do."

Arsyn states, "The Paragonians have already done so. Even tortured him some. His determination not to answer remains fixed. It's as if he's been bound not to tell."

"Who could bind Zymarc not to tell?" I ask.

"An equal or superior. That lead Prince-General, Azabahk, for example. He could bind his king not to tell. Has he been interrogated as heavily as the king?"

I reply, "I doubt it."

Arsyn and I stroll farther into the hallway.

He says, "Look at how things have played out. Now that Deathasyn holds the title of Vitiosyn King. Zymarc's revealed who his equal is. Most likely, Azabahk is bound by an equal too. And if his equal is, was, Belzara—his sister, during a different lifetime—now the binding is made unbreakable, for Belzara is gone. She's not there to break the hold on Azabahk. That is, if my musings are correct."

I shake my head. "Unfortunately, Arsyn, I believe you're right. Even so, will you bring the two Jokryn brothers back?"

"Of course. I was headed for the kitchen to collect food for the journey. Then I'll be on my way with Zeb. He and I have much to discuss, along the way."

"I wish you luck, Arsyn of Jhire."

36

A Promise, Kept – Part II

Soon thereafter, Arsyn and I enter the castle's main kitchen that's on the first floor. Not the kitchenette I've been to. Though its ceiling is much lower than any grand hall, it's the size of a large banquet room. The savory scents of freshly baked bread blend with the steam coming off the enormous pots of many different soups and stews. Counters, ovens, and large wash basins line the walls. Countless cookware, cutting boards, food, and utensils are on near every surface.

The people tending to it all bustle about. Keturah has wrangled the assistance of Sonya and the wards old enough to help.

Cringing inside, I whisper to Arsyn, "Let's hope Sonya hasn't been allowed to alter the soups. Best you go for the stews, Arsyn."

He says, "To be safe, I'll take two loaves of bread and an apple spread," as he's already snatching up the loaves, and putting them in a travel sack.

A woman calls out, "And just what do you think you are doing, good sir?" She, in a dress of bright-blue, comes over.

I exclaim, "Zima?" I grin in delight. "You were one of the last held captives? You're all right?"

She glances to where one of her arms should be. She grows sad. "Only missing an arm, dear Prince Tyler. But as you see, I've many helping hands to accommodate for what I lack. Don't you be sorry for me. Nor for the head blacksmith, Yigoshi, neither. He's lost both his legs from the knees down. Yet we are alive. Our fair Paragon lives on. And Vitiosus is at its end."

"Arsyn's going on a journey," I explain. "He needs that bread."

Arsyn adds, "Can't wait around for dinner to be served, you understand."

Zima takes hold of a jar of apple spread that's on a central counter. She gives it to him. "A safe journey to you, then."

After he thanks Zima, Arsyn says, "Tyler, be sure to tell Skylin I'll arrive in time for dessert."

He strides out.

Zima goes back to overseeing the meal preparations.

I scan the people in here, looking for Skylin. I don't see her. I'm about to go ask Keturah where she might be, when Krina enters through one of the kitchen's other doors.

My gut twists into knots. I can't stand the sight of her, especially at present.

I leave before the princess can spot me. I wander the quiet, empty hallways for some time. Then I make for the storerooms below the castle. I need to know they've been restored. And they have. They're fully stocked. No sign of poison anywhere.

As I check each room, taking it all in, I begin to wonder if EmiKal has been serving a common enemy of the Vitiosyns and Paragon. I don't know who that would be. Something underhanded hints to have happened, though. And EmiKal was a part of it. He had to be.

Someone starts talking unexpectedly.

Drawing my daggers, I whirl around.

She says, "Of all the places the Onyx Prince could be right now, he chooses to be down here?" Skylin ambles into the hallway where I am.

"Sky," I whisper. I drop my daggers. I'm overjoyed to see her. I go embrace her, hold her close, as guilt creeps to the surface. I wonder, *Will she understand what I did with Caleiso was simply out of necessity? That it most likely was due to the ShenawFayel's influence? Was that all it was?*

I decide that it is. So I pull away, guilt free, and study her wanting expression. It's electrifying. I cup her face, lean down to kiss her. She tightly grips my coat collar.

I know not how long I explore that mouth, that tongue of hers which never tires of talking. It seems, it never tires of kissing me back either.

I pull away, and let out a soft laugh. "Slow down, Sky. There are some things we should talk about. First, your dad went to go get Paydinn and YaeVorkk. Said he'll be back before dessert. And—"

"Don't want to hear it," she says. "Don't want to think about it. You leaving." She pulls me into the privacy of one of the storerooms and then stands on tiptoe to kiss me more. She wraps her wings about me, digs her fingers along the sides of my neck.

I can't get away. Truthfully, I don't try.

"Eh-hem!" someone says loudly from the doorway.

I glance to the side.

Standing in the doorway, Dea wiggles her shoulders back and forth. "As cute as the two of you are, being sneaky not-so-sneaky, I came to tell you that supper's ready."

Musgrae pokes his head in, to add, "And you're not allowed to go on a full expedition at the moment. Not sixteen yet, you see."

Dea says, "Plus, Arsyn would kill the both of you."

I shrug at that. "Yeah, well, I don't think much could be worse than stopping Deezalo from being resurrected, nor worse than completing the Hexyn, or *dying* from the Call of Vitiosus. Or losing my fingertips, just a short while ago, then having Arsyn use magic to make them regrow." I lift my left hand to wiggle the fingers as proof that they're back.

Musgrae lets out a soft whistle. "What's that, Ravier? Died? You died? Is this a trend you and Ryco are trying to set, to become like the Darklyres?"

"Vards, no!" I laugh, as I go retrieve the daggers I dropped.

"Well, you've got some s'plaining to do," Musgrae says, "regarding the dying part. Ryco mentioned the Deezalo bit already. And given the strength that Arsyn has proven to have, I'm not surprised a bit that he can regrow bones so quickly."

"Tell the lot of you about the dying part, over dinner."

And so we head up for the meal.

Talok is on a platform within the banquet room. He stands, ready to give a toast.

Musgrae joins the seven King's Guard. The eight of them intently watch the crowd, searching for anything out of the ordinary. Who knows if another EmiKal is among us.

Talok begins, as soon as the people have quieted down. "These past three years have been hard for us all. We've lost much. My father, King Sosha. Our dear LanSoren. Many Greyvons of import, a year ago. Thousands of Vons and their Vonsai, this year. Even Merlynite of Vondurheil has been counted among their dead. Countless others have fallen, to give us aid in our War for the Equidyn. But we are still here. Stronger than ever before, with our allies of the Vons, the Darklyres, the Jokryns too. Even do we have allegiance of the Amethysts and Prince Tyler's Onyx of Malik. Together, we have prevailed over Vitiosus. Their king shall pay recompense with his life. He shall die soon."

Thunderous applause erupts from the hundreds gathered in the banquet hall.

Skylin and I go to the Darklyres' table, where SynKievas, Seqwhyett, and the wards have chosen to sit for the meal.

Talok waits for silence, before continuing, "There is one I especially want to honor today. While many of you may be thinking it is my cousin, Tyler Ravier, it is not. There is one who deserves more honor today, than even the Onyx Prince, for his service to Paragon has lasted for longer than I have been alive. My loyal friend. Brother-in-arms. The Paradyn. Our Ryco of Paragon!"

Talok steps down from the platform and goes to the ornate chair at the head of one of the tables. Quall and his triad follow Talok to guard him. They do not sit down. Rather, they draw weapons, save for Quall. He inspects the food served to Talok. The three—Warren, Siege, and Eli—have their backs to Talok's chair, guarding his blind spots.

I catch the Mensa-div between Talok and Ryco, as Ryco divs, *I don't know what to say, Talok.*

"Yes, you do. Say what you've always wanted to say to the people of Paragon."

Ryco approaches the edge of the platform. After clearing his throat, he begins. "I want to thank some of you for giving me the chance to serve on the King's Guard. Also, to thank many of you for defending my position on the Paragonian Sovereignty when it counted."

Ryco makes a point to glance at Zepharre, who just lowers his head. It's hard to tell how Zepharre feels.

"It has been the greatest honor of my life," Ryco says, "to serve you. And you shall never hear such thanks pass over my lips again. You'd do well to remember my words. Donate them to the Arkivara, if you've a mind for future generations to witness the Paradyn give thanks. For I swear by the Vardiyas, it shan't ever be said by me again."

Madeleine calls out from somewhere in the room, "I shall. For who knows when I may lose my memories again. All future generations shall remember the great courage of our Sovereignty. But especially of our Paradyn, who gave his life for his king and then came back from the dead. Many legends are being born before our eyes. How shall we ever bear it?"

Talok raises a glass of Farivoo. Heartily, he says, "By eating, drinking, and engaging in much merriment."

Kent, from his place on the stage, says, "What our dear king means is, by eating such things as the Soup of Ashes *only* when necessary; also, drinking spiked Farivoo *only* to best a king in a bet; and to have much merriment, so long as that merriment doesn't involve feeding on the flesh of our enemies' traitors."

Musgrae adds, "Moreover, soon, the lot of you shall see our memories of Eli of Kirja getting a bite to the neck by he who was a young prince, who became a young king, but is now our mighty king. Talok. Son of Sosha, King of Dragon Tamers."

Those gathered, applaud.

"Ever should you be proud of your king," says Rozeth, as she enters the banquet hall.

Hydvar follows behind her, in confidence. Lemawr, looking like

Dezarin, has entered ahead of them.

The people quiet down.

Walking forward, Rozeth continues, "For he, after losing our Ryco, and only just saved from the clutches of death, himself, did tame a turned dragon. A Vitasadyn in flight. Your mighty king has done what only the Vaegons in myths did doth do. To tame a dragon in the air. But never has a dragon corrupted of Vitiosus been restored, till now. You have seen your people to victory, King Talok. You shall now see them into glory. Legends of the ages." Rozeth accepts a glass of Farivoo, which Hydvar hands her. She raises that glass. "To the Tamers of Dragons, and Keepers of Memories. Forever will the Sorsryns stand in awe of you, whom they once saw as ordinary scholars of magic."

Standing near me, Skylin says, "I'll drink to that."

Rozeth drinks from her glass. Then Talok does. The rest of us join in. Many soon give sounds of cheers and pride for the recent victories. We take to our seats.

Ryco and his three leave the stage to join Talok at his table.

Dezarin quickly makes for his former apprentice. He starts to pass by where I've chosen to sit with Skylin and the Darklyres. He pauses his stride to rest a hand atop my shoulder. "Son of LanSoren? This is not your place, tonight. It is beside the King of Paragon. Both heir to the throne of Pawv'Ragaen and heir to the throne of Nyxane, you are. Come sit with the king and his honored guests."

I'm about to argue, but Skylin sidekicks my leg under the table. "Go," she whispers. "You do *not* refuse such an honor. I mean to find Gemma, just as soon as I've finished eating. No one's seen her for over an hour."

"Thanks, Sky. Tell her I have some questions to ask, if she's up for talking."

"I will," says Skylin, as she shoves me out of my chair.

Thankfully, I was already partway out of it, or I'd have lost my balance. I scowl back at her.

She simply says, "I'm always up for *talking*." She looks at me in an odd way, almost as if I'm her next meal . . . or something.

My face warms to discomfort. I stride for my cousin's table, to escape the desire to be alone with Skylin. I don't know how I'm going to say goodbye to her tomorrow. It hurts to think about.

Ryco slides the chair on Talok's left out. "For you, Onyx Prince."

Once seated, I'm given a plate of food. I dig in, only going slow enough to maintain some semblance of table manners.

Talok busily converses in different languages with the Siveyras, RayVora, Craesha, and other Sorsryns, whom I do not recognize. After a time, King ReNovak trails to our table, looking hardly a king at all. His coat is torn, covered in chew marks, and he smells of dirt and wilted flowers. There's a hint of pond scum about him too. When he sits down, all at the table grow silent. Mostly, we try to ignore the smell.

Craesha's first to say anything to him. "How be your Siveyra Journey, Onyx King? Go all right?"

ReNovak grumbles, "I'm here among the living, aren't I?"

"Took you long enough," says RayVora. "Have you ever truly been with the land of the living, though, my dear? Or were you simply scheming of ways to cheat magic and free the Onyx of the Laws of Neutrality?"

"Please, RayVora." ReNovak grips his head as if it hurts. "Can you save your high-and-mighty lectures for the morrow? Or better. For all the years you have left?"

RayVora swallows a bite of food. "That sounds like a threat."

ReNovak laughs. "Oh, RayVora! That's gold, coming from your lips. Truly, you have done worse than I, over the years."

"And how is it that you would know, ReNovak?" RayVora stares him down. "Where is your proof?"

"Zymarc's allegations against you." ReNovak begins his meal, starting with the meat alternative. He cuts into it.

RayVora scoffs, before dabbing a napkin to a corner of her mouth. "What allegations?"

"It matters not," says ReNovak, only concerned with cutting all food on his plate into bite-sized pieces. "For the evidence Zymarc had against you, was destroyed in Vaydell today. I was not there to save it. And, come tomorrow, the last who knows the truth of what you've done will die. All your dirty little secrets perish with Zymarc. How convenient."

"What secrets?" Craesha poses the question. His air of gaiety is gone.

ReNovak glances at him.

RayVora feels along her forehead, trying to process what's happening. She sets her napkin down.

ReNovak says, "The event happened sometime after your mother's fifth child was born."

"But I only have the four—" RayVora starts to argue.

"Yes, the four sons. We know," says ReNovak. "But also do you have a daughter. Vayohl, wasn't it? Given away to King Guyheiz of the Kyanites, before GrawVadian would know. Before your sons would know. Before *anyone* would know."

RayVora's expression clouds over. "Soren knew."

"Why's that matter?" I ask her.

"Because he let that information slip out around Deezalo. And Deezalo much craved to have a child, born of Vitiosus. I didn't know why, until that night I saw you and Zymarc at the Graveyard of Blackwood Spikes. He meant to have a vessel for transference. My daughter, being half Metimoran, would have been able to survive carrying such a child of power, a future vessel for Deezalo to inhabit. It's how he meant to gain immortality, for being the King of Vitiosus weakened his body over time. I wasn't about to give him such a means to live forever."

"I take it, Vitiosus nullifies the means of rebirth, ReNovamen?" I ask.

Craesha quietly answers, "ReNovamen must be performed within a certain time frame of being mortally wounded or cursed."

Zeekryn comes to the table. "Whatever the lot of you are discussing is unsettling the people. What is wrong?"

Standing up, Craesha comments, "Zymarc has allegations against our mother. Had proof too, of her wrongdoings. Which was destroyed in Vaydell today. Also, Lemawr and that little princess with webbed feet are our nephew and niece. It seems dear brother Paydinn wasn't the only of us five to give grandchildren to our mother."

Craesha turns on his heel, and quickly makes for the banquet room's exit.

Taking his brother's seat, Zeekryn places his elbows on the table. "Five of us?" he asks, after a time.

"You have a sister," RayVora admits.

"Had," Talok corrects. He sets his empty glass down. "Vayohl has been missing for ten years or so, according to King Lemara. Most likely, she is gone. You have my sincerest apologies, Matron RayVora. Whatever these allegations are, surely they can't be worse than what Zymarc is guilty of. At any rate, I've a mind to talk with our prized prisoner down in the cells." Talok eases out of his chair. "Quallendeis, you and yours shall come with."

Ryco inquires, "What of us?"

"Keep Tyler out of trouble."

Nudging Kent's shoulder, Musgrae mutters, "Aye, Kent and Ben, we've been given the impossible task. Best you stick with us, Ryke, for only you can outrun Tyler and his whims."

Talok says, "You may come with me, Tyler, if you wish. I've a feeling, though, you're not of a mind to. Especially after catching me in that act, earlier. Yet, I wonder what you mean to do tonight, before a quick show of celebration for our victory."

"I intend to keep my promise."

"And what would that be?" queries Talok.

Rising from my place, I admit, "To make a certain former apprentice forget all that's happened in her life, so far. To free her to be a daughter of Paragon. Will you accept a renewed Caleiso of Vitiosus? Rename her to Callie of Dysarda, instead? Ensure that she's taken care of?"

Talok glances around, doubt clouding over him. "I don't know who would care for her, Tyler."

Dezarin lifts his hand, gets Talok's attention. "I will attend to that matter of raising the girl as my own."

"Doesn't Leira need to have a say?" queries Ryco.

"I know what she will say," Dezarin says. "And if Lemawr should not like it, he will be made to accept it regardless. He gets his child with Leira, and I get one of my own—this Caleiso, soon to be Callie. Never had children. At least, not children I ever met. There's was a daughter. Just one."

Ryco flaunts an odd look at Dezarin. "So there was someone to inherit your power? Why'd you leave it to Rozeth and me?"

"The daughter's not Sorsryn enough," Dezarin admits.

"But I'm Sorsryn enough?" queries Ryco.

Dezarin smirks. "You're dragon enough. At any rate, I know not of the daughter's capabilities. Simply of her existence. She could very well be dead already. Who's to know?"

"I would know," says Paydinn, suddenly just *there* at our table. He tries not to take notice of me. Yet his eyes keep flaring a different color every few seconds.

Some distance away, YaeVorkk is filling a plate of food, which is already piled high.

Paydinn calls to him, "Brother, we haven't time to share a plate of food, at present."

"This isn't for you," says YaeVorkk. "Get your own plate, Dinn-pay."

"Oh! So we're back to the insults, are we, Vorkk-yae?" Paydinn flashes him an angry look.

When that look is redirected toward him, Zeekryn cringes. "Don't say it, Brother."

"Kryn-zee." Paydinn spits the word out. "What were you thinking, going to Vaydell, when I specifically told you not to? Did it not turn out the way I said it would? That you'd be captured, imprisoned."

"You know," says Zeekryn, "I rather prefer Craesha's. Shawc-rae. Sounds like a curse, doesn't it?"

Paydinn turns contemplative, even nods his agreement. "Yes, that's what I've always thought." He then shakes his head, points a finger at Zeekryn. "Don't change the subject."

"What of Ohl-vay?" Zeekryn goes on.

Paydinn says, "You mean, Vayohl?"

"So you did know that we had a sister?"

"Of course I knew we had a sister. Long after the fact, though. Only met her once. And once was enough. Where do you think that little princess, running about, got her personality? It wasn't from Lemara. That much is certain."

Dezarin sighs deeply. He starts nodding slowly. His appearance changes to that of Lemawr.

Lemawr stops nodding. Looks forward at me. Then he startles as if seeing me for the first time. He blinks rapidly. "This is not where I was," he says, looking about. He groans. "And he had dinner again, without letting me taste a bit of it? That Dezarin is selfish with the food *and* Leira." He looks up at Paydinn. "Did he at least let me take over for dessert? Or did he eat that too?"

Preparing to leave, I state, "You're in luck. We're still waiting for dessert."

"How'd the Hexyn go?" Lemawr queries, leaning forward in his seat. He tries to hold back a grin.

"Beautifully," I admit.

"Water or ice?" he asks.

"Underwater."

"Where?" he probes.

"Vaydell." I grin. "Within a forest not too far from Deezalo's Cathedral."

Lemawr bursts out of his chair, overjoyed. "Tyler! You completed the Hexyn while in ShenawFayel with Zymarc? You devil-born tyke!"

The lot of them—save for ReNovak, only concerned with eating—demand to know the details. I don't tell them what it was actually like using the spell made-of-my-name. Nor do I detail the exact setup of the Hexyn, or the long monologue I spoke to complete it. I figure it's only for me to know. I tell them what weapons and spells I used, as that doesn't necessarily tell them *what* the spell does.

Musgrae sends a knowing glance my way, but he doesn't mention what I said earlier.

Someone rests their hand on the small of my back. Skylin asks, "What's the spell do?"

I turn enough to look at her. Gemma is just behind her, the light in her eyes dim.

I admit, "I don't think any of you would believe me, if I told you. Should you ever need saving from a death beyond a level you can handle, though, speak the words: Ravieras-Savak-Kavas. Say them at the moment of death." I shrug. "See what happens."

"Savak," Lemawr says. "It involves some sleeping of sorts. But what sleeps?"

"The dragon," I say. I tap the table twice.

Paydinn breaks from his stupor. "You had wished to talk with YaeVorkk and me, I do believe, Ravier. Is now a good time?"

"It is." I turn to Gemma. "And you'll come with us, Gem."

She startles. "What do you need me for?"

"You've been with me through all of this. It's only fair that I include you for this last bit."

Gemma's mouth twitches. She tries to look happy. She ends up appearing defeated. Also, when I glimpse Skylin, the lines of her face are drawn taut. She seems hurt that I've not included her this time.

So I grab round her waist, and give her a quick kiss on the mouth. "Save some dessert for me?"

"She will," says Arsyn, taking a seat at the King's Table. He leans back, crosses one leg over the other. His expression for me is one of warning.

Releasing Skylin, I take a step back.

Paydinn practically drags YaeVorkk away from his spot at one of the tables. I do believe they are swearing at each other, in their native tongue.

I walk side by side with Gemma. The four of us leave the banquet hall that's filled with sounds of eating, drinking, and much merriment. Those sounds fade.

Calmer now, Paydinn starts the conversation. "Arsyn's relayed your request to us. That Zymarc not die today. We must know why."

"He gains something in death. Also . . ." I hesitate to say this next part. But, with Gemma at my side, I find the boldness to go on. "I believe Zymarc is Setharyn's ReNovamen. Is there anything you can do to confirm it? Some spell or—"

Paydinn's eyes flicker through several different colors.

YaeVorkk leans away from his brother in disgust. "I did *not* need to see all that went through your mind just now, Brother."

"Shut it!" Paydinn smacks his brother's arm. "Let me think!"

YaeVorkk says, "Does it matter that he might be the ReNovamen of Setharyn? It doesn't make him the foretold Onyx Prince."

Ignoring his brother, Paydinn tells me, "There is a purifying magic I've dabbled in, regarding cursed ones."

"I, as well, have," says YaeVorkk. "It's a variant of your magic, Brother. Its purpose is to eradicate darkness of the soul, leaving purity behind. It works on some curses rather well."

"Yes, yes!" Paydinn exclaims. "But . . ." He trails off.

I ask, "There's a catch, isn't there?"

"There is." Paydinn starts our walk down a hall. "We've tried using it on Vitiosyns we've caught over the years. None have survived it."

YaeVorkk adds, "They either die instantly from the trauma to their Mazhrein, or within two years."

Gemma gives her input. "Even if he was once the promised Onyx Prince? You think he'd die from such a spell being performed on him?"

The two Jokryn brothers take notice of Gemma.

"What are you saying, Miss Galloway?" queries Paydinn.

"Zymarc *is* Setharyn's ReNovamen," Gemma states. "There are some things he told me, while holding me prisoner in Vitokawr, which I cannot repeat. And I saw his underlying appearance, on two occasions. The day Tyler and Siege came for me. And just before Tyler stopped the execution. We've seen what Setharyn looks like, because of a memory sequence LanSoren left behind. There's no doubt in my mind. That is who Zymarc is, under it all. The Onyx Prince, bearing the mark of Vardiyas upon his head. Is there any means you know of, to split Setharyn from Zymarc? Any possibility of reviving the lost Onyx Prince?"

Paydinn and YaeVorkk have come to a standstill.

YaeVorkk breaks the silence first. "That is much to take in."

"Yes," Paydinn agrees. "Much to think about. Much to discuss. To practice."

"Have we permission," queries YaeVorkk, "to test spells on Zymarc?"

Though guilt eats at me, I say, "Do what you must to Zymarc. I'll tell Talok you've agreed to test him further."

"He's in the castle bunkers," says Gemma. "They've been repurposed, made into a prison. He's in the deepest section of cells. No one should be able to hear what you're doing to him. Even so, please use sound-dampening spells."

Paydinn shares a look with his brother.

YaeVorkk asks, "This is the heir of Neftelliim you were telling me of, those centuries ago?"

"The very one," Paydinn says proudly. "Also known as the Witch of Galloway. The Ninth of Enedei. She's the girl Soren broke Laws of Time to go see. On another world, mind you. One day, she will outgrow us all."

"No," YaeVorkk disagrees, while looking at me, "not all." YaeVorkk bows at the waist. "The Father of the Jokryn and I shall see to this task of great import. You have our word, Witch of Galloway. We will do what we can to restore the prophesied one of the Onyx."

Paydinn says, "We'll seek you out, Galloway. Let you know what our findings are."

They leave.

Gemma and I just stand in silence within one of the castle's dimly lit halls.

After a few glances at Gemma, I head for the castle entrance. I go down the thirteen stone steps. Gemma hooks her arm with mine, once we're at the bottom. We go forward on the path, in silence. There isn't much to say for now. Simply do I enjoy the presence of my friend, Galloway.

She's the first to talk, saying, "Can you believe it's nearly over, Tyler? That this very night, the Onyx Prince, Setharyn, could be restored to his people, his father, ReNovak? That, through this prince, the Onyx might one day gain their freedom from neutrality? How are we going to go back home, and pretend as if nothing grand has happened in our lives?"

"I don't know. I just know that we'll never be enemies again. And that's enough for me."

Gemma states, "Jed might have something to say about that."

"He'll have to get over it, then." I grin. "First, we'll get Jaxson on our side. Then ease the two of them into the truth. Bring them here, for the festival next year."

Gemma chuckles. "Are you ready for the havoc they'll bring with them?"

"I doubt they'll top what we've been through, Gem."

"No, Tyler," she says. "A different kind of havoc. Of drama and antics and petty heartbreak. Might even have to cast a spell on Jed, so he can't steal prized weapons or artifacts to take home."

"I hadn't thought of that."

"Of course ya didn't." Gemma laughs. "You've been caught up in being a hero. I'm not going to let you keep that title, though, letting it go to your head. You'll always simply be Tyler Malik Ravier to me. The boy I hurt on the worst day of his life. And who somehow found it in his heart to forgive me. To take me to a place beyond my wildest imagination. A place where I am to play a part. Though I don't know what that part is yet. I don't care. I'm just glad to be here."

"I don't know what to say to that, Gem."

"Then don't say anything. Just walk with me, and enjoy the sight of a rebuilt city we helped to save."

✳ ✳ ✳

Gemma and I walk on in darkness. Moonlight shines bright enough for us to see our surroundings.

Eventually, we head back for the castle, for the banquet hall. The bright lights have been put out. Only dispersed torches on the walls light the room. Near all people have cleared out. My Onyx Warriors guard every entrance.

Talok, the Paragonian Sovereignty, and some other key figures have gathered at a central table.

Warren clears his throat. "Yo, there they are."

Quall beckons us over, and we sit.

Caleiso is seated beside Talok, and Dezarin beside her.

Talok says, "Though there's still much to talk of, we will do that tomorrow. Now that Tyler is here, Caleiso, I do believe it is time for you to say goodbye to your old life. Have you any instructions, anything to say, before he begins?"

She shakes her head.

I ask, "Have you said goodbye to Zymarc and the others?"

"No," she says.

I tell Gyron, from across the table, "Go get him. I'm sure he could use a break from Paydinn and YaeVorkk's further testing of him."

Talok inquires, "What testing?"

I reply, "Just want to be sure there wasn't anything we missed."

"Fine." Talok gestures. "Go get him. Bring the other prisoners who've a mind to bid her farewell too."

Gyron leaves the hall.

I mentally go through the layout of the castle, visualizing the bunkers. I search for a strong aura there. My mind bumps against it, startles its owner, Paydinn. I Mensa-div, *Take a break. Gyron's coming to get Zymarc so Caleiso can say goodbye. Come with them. Give Gemma updates, while I keep my promise to Zymarc.*

Before I'm ready, Gyron, Smythe, and Hydvar are leading Zymarc and seven others into the hall. Azabahk is one of the seven. Zymarc helps him hobble along, as that Prince-General has no staff or cane with him. All prisoners' hands are in cuffed chains. A glowing metal armband is on each prisoner. I can only assume it's used as some draining device for magic to keep them subdued.

"Where is Belgorr?" queries Caleiso. "Did he not survive?"

The Prince-General who cooked up the meal in Vaydell is here, answering her, "He was cursed, me lady, before Vitiosus. Before Zymarc possessed him with that magic. Now that it has been rescinded from us all, save for Azabahk and others yet to answer the summons, Belgorr's strength fades. The curse has taken hold of him again. He shan't last long."

Azabahk says, "But that is as it should be. He shall have an honorable way of death. He will die of wounds, of a curse. Not an execution like us. He'll have the best end, save for you, Princess Caleiso."

"I won't let Ravier take my memories, until I've said goodbye to Belgorr."

Though Paydinn and YaeVorkk are just arriving, they turn back at the beckoning of Dezarin.

Caleiso lingers near Zymarc and the prisoners. They speak in a foreign language. Only Zymarc is silent. Then he snaps his fingers a few times at the others. They stop talking.

Belgorr arrives through the main door to the banquet room. A blindfold covers half his face. He must be led along, for he cannot see.

Caleiso rushes up to him, hugs him though he towers over her. Her head reaches not past his ribs.

"Our Princess Caleiso." He gives a crooked grin, as he hugs her back. "We have done it. We have procured the cure for your curse, little one. Promise us you shall always linger with the Tamers. And be our hope. The hope of Deathasyns that, by your efforts, our clan shall never be slaves to the other Sorsryn Clans again. That the work Zymarc started in them shall be finished because of you."

"I will!" Caleiso cries.

Belgorr forces her to step away. He bends down on one knee, so Caleiso doesn't have to look up at him. "That devil did it. Even in death, LanSoren has procured the answer to our burden. We may die in peace now, knowing you will be taken care of."

Caleiso sniffles loudly.

"No tears," Belgorr tells her. "Though Zymarc will not admit it, I'll admit it for him. All he hath done these past thirteen years, he did for you. For his love for you is a jealous and violent love. No threat against you would he stand for. He cut your enemies down where they stood. But there were things beyond our collective strength as Vitiosyns. Things even Zymarc himself could neither outrun nor outsmart. 'Tis fate, you see."

Caleiso quotes Soren, saying, "Fate is patient, and it keeps track. It never forgets the lives owed to it."

"So do not be sad for us," says Belgorr. "Soon, we'll meet with fate, our journeys complete."

Azabahk says, "Though they be not Siveyra Journeys, they be good journeys."

Caleiso gives her last goodbyes to the eight. She stops at Zymarc's side. "Have you anything to say to me, Zymarc?"

"See you soon," he says. He won't look her in the eye.

Caleiso says, "I love you, Zymarc."

His passive façade falls away. "All who love me die suddenly, without any warning at all. Do not love me. I beg you, look away."

Caleiso cries, "No, for I am not ashamed of you."

"I am," he says, as the façade reappears. "You should be too. Forget me. Yes, that is what is best. Forget, Caleiso, and start anew. Ravier, fulfill your promise to me. Do what must be done. I beg you. No more darkness, no more night. Give her the light."

Instinct seems to take over, for I'm going to Caleiso, and pulling her away from Zymarc.

She screams for him, reaches for him.

"Tell me you love me!" she cries.

"No!" Zymarc shouts back. His hands tremble. His chains rattle. "For that would make a way for you to recall the past, and be reminded of me, and who I was to you. That must not happen. Goodbye, little one."

Caleiso wails, though she no longer fights to get away.

I bite into her neck, and her wails settle to quiet sobs. I gently pull away, wiping the blood from my mouth. I smear the liquid over the mirror-crystal of the watch. As I look at Caleiso, I consider all she'll be forgetting. Thirteen years of life. I wonder, *Can I truly make her forget it all?*

The Count of Despairion echoes around in a ghostly way.

Gemma is looking at me. She stands with YaeVorkk and Paydinn at the room's entrance. *"Thirteen. Done,"* she Mensa-divs. *"De'Eispar-Rione."*

I begin by speaking it: "De'Eispar-Rione." I hold my hands out. Dark-magenta fire forms in my palms, and I start the count. "One. Two. Three. Goes the count."

Three flames flare from me, to land in a semi-circle around Caleiso. They take the shape of three little girls, different ages. One, two, and three years old, most likely. I take out my daggers. I give Caleiso the waking-dagger. I tell her to hold the blade flat between her palms. "Don't let go, until I tell you to."

She nods through the fear.

The three little girls live through some of their memories. When I ready my grip on NeiSator, they turn back into the magenta fire. I cut through those flames, and they explode to become like smoke.

Caleiso falls to her knees.

"Four, five, six," I say.

Caleiso echoes, "It must not stop there."

I ask, "Are you sure that you want to forget it all?"

"I must," she says.

So I cut through the three flames of those years, after they've shown Caleiso learning the basics of magic from Zymarc.

I count more, focusing energy into my hands, my eyes. "Seven, eight, but nine is best."

The flames are hotter this time, and blood-red. Something in Caleiso has changed during one of these three years. At nine years old, she met my father, LanSoren. He didn't have much to say to her. Only, "There's a Deathasyn saying, Little Caleiso. When life grows dim, catch a fire. Chase it, till it is yours. Bottle it up. Store it for when all hope is lost. Then set it free that it may go out into the world and save it."

The memories shift back into the three flames. I cut them down.

"Ten, eleven," I count.

Caleiso says, "I have a confession."

Quickly, it shows Caleiso's time of infiltrating the city of Dysarda, pretending to be one of theirs. Zymarc came for her, when she was eleven.

Grabbing hold of her, he shouted, "Stop fighting me, Caleiso." He shook her. "Do you want to start a war with the Tamers?"

"No," she cried. "I only wish to be with them. Can't you ask for an alliance with them?"

Zymarc laughed in her face. "Don't be a fool. The Tamers and Vitiosyns will never mix. We are considered an abomination to magic, and they are the reflection of the particles. You don't mix what is twisted, with what is right and fair."

The memories fade to fire.

I cut them down too, then say the last part: "Twelve and thirteen. Everything in between."

Caleiso's last two ages rise out of the flames.

It reels through my interactions with her. Then it skips back to that day Zymarc attacked Paragon. He and his forces arrived home. Caleiso was in his quarters, within Vaydell. She was looking for something in one of his desks. She opened that drawer where Zymarc keeps his masks for communicating across distances. She pulled one out, but looked again. Retrieved letters from the drawer. She read them, sat down. Tears rolled down her cheeks.

Zymarc entered the room, surprised to see her there.

She asked him, "Did you ever send these?" She held up the papers.

"It doesn't matter," Zymarc said. "I was about to send one to Paragon, then I caught wind of LanSoren's death. In my sorrow, I delayed sending one. When they refused to return Awngeleik to me, well. You know the rest. What is done is done. It's far too late to form an alliance with them. They would never trust us. Never believe us. So we will drive them from their land, and take it as ours."

Caleiso retired to her room. She burned the letters in a metal bowl and then sobbed herself to sleep.

The last two years fade to flames.

In heartbreak, I force myself to cut through year twelve. But at the last, I speak, "Thirteen. Done. You shall remember no more, your life of before. Caleiso of Vosh-Perida has become Callie of Dysarda. The Apprentice to Vitiosus is now a daughter to Paragon."

The last flame is drawn to Caleiso. It joins with her. Her eyes become that color of crimson-red.

I slowly press the tip of the sleeping-dagger through both of Caleiso's wrists.

She screams, but she does not let go of RotaSyn.

After I've removed NeiSator, I tell Caleiso, "Let go."

She drops the waking-dagger. I drop my dagger too. I catch her up in my arms, as she faints. I lay her on one of the tables. Then I sink into a nearby chair.

The King's Guard come to assess her, also to bind her wounded wrists.

But I just break. I yell as loud as I can. The room rattles, then shakes more. The torches flare with the dark-magenta fire. My whole body heats up as if hot irons are hovering over my flesh, threatening to blister my skin.

Gemma comes to reassure me, calm me, for it is much to bear, making a person forget their whole life lived up to the present.

Zymarc and the others are led out of the room. Zymarc's gaze meets with mine, before he leaves. He Mensa-divs, *"Your promise is fulfilled, and now I may rest easy. For my heart has been made glad. Goodbye, Ravier. See you soon."*

37

He Returns

Hours pass by . . .

Callie rests in Talok's sleeping quarters. Though conscious, she hasn't much to say. Simply does she say her head hurts. Her chest. Her wrists. Her eyes. Dezarin sits in a chair, at her bedside. He prepares potions, salves, and compresses. Rozeth assists him by fetching any ingredients he needs.

Quietly, Talok says, "I've asked that this room be combined with the two adjacent ones, and fashioned like a home. We mean to give it to Lemawr and Leira. Callie too."

"Where will you sleep?" I ask.

"Somewhere," he says. "A different place every night, most likely. All that running about we did makes it hard to stay in one place. I'm sure you'll suffer from the same thing as me. Restlessness."

Quall sets his satchel down on the small table we're at. "That is what herbs are for, dear Talok. I shall make a brew for you."

The lot of us converse in hushed tones, over a cup of brewed herbs. Gemma, Talok, and the guards. I haven't the heart for drinking, however. Neither does Musgrae, it seems. Once giving Ryco the silver cup that was packed away, he tends to weapons.

After a time, I ask, "Shall we go down? Rozeth too. Let Dezarin tend to her in silence?"

Rozeth sets her cup aside. "I need to find Hydvar, first. Meet up with you later. And, Musgrae?"

Musgrae glances up from his task of polishing weapons and leather items.

Rozeth continues, "I daren't ask it here. For it is of a delicate matter. But you, being Ryco's favorite among the King's Guard, well. Since Ryco has humbly refused, I thought you should be next for me to ask a special *favor* of. Will you later, hear me out?"

Curiosity piqued, Musgrae rubs his neck. His hand is covered in shoe polish, and his neck now has some on it. He cringes when he realizes it. He lowers his hand, before asking, "Is it kinky?"

"Define kinky." Rozeth gives a quick grin.

Musgrae laughs. "Yes," he says.

Rozeth tilts her head to the side. "Don't you want to hear the question?"

Musgrae asks in return, "Will I lose any limbs or such?"

"No."

"Hmm," he says. "What about loss of senses? Eyesight, for example."

Rozeth wrinkles her nose. "I'm . . . unsure. It was Hydvar's idea, and he is the one with details. Not I."

"Right!" Musgrae declares, "My answer is still yes." He starts cleaning his neck of the shoe polish.

Ryco opens his mouth to say something to Rozeth, even lifts his index finger to the air. But Rozeth's overjoyed, and already rushing away to find Hydvar. She shuts the door behind her.

Ryco mutters, "You'll regret that, Grae."

"Doubt it," says Musgrae.

"All right." Ryco lifts his shoulders. "Don't believe me, though I've only just come back from the dead today. I will tell you this. Whatever happens, you're not to make it a habit. Understood?"

"Yeah, whatever." Musgrae waves him off. "Did I get all the polish off my neck?"

"Yes," says Ryco, before sipping the last bit of liquid from his silver cup.

Musgrae gripes, "You only looked for a second. Look again, to be sure."

"Your vanity, Grae!" Ryco growls, setting his cup aside. "What do you want me to do? Lick its residue off your neck?"

Quall pours himself another cup of brewed herbs.

From across the room, Eli says, "Yeah, then bite him for me, will ya?"

This erupts into that guard banter, much to do with teasing Musgrae of what the special *favor* could be. Quall's about to pour a third cup of herbs; Siege stops him.

I gesture for Talok to answer my earlier question. But he doesn't answer. Only leaves the room, and the rest of us follow. The banter quiets down along the way.

We head for where the festival's main performances are held.

Preparations for a quick celebration—the chance for Gemma and me to say goodbye—have begun. Upon arriving at the Blackwood Field, we're quickly caught up in the bustle. I lose track of the others, once Gyron plants me with my Onyx Warriors.

"You are to enter with them," says Gyron. "I shall go ahead of you, Smythe and Ghebina behind me. Until then, wait."

I hang back in the waiting area with my Onyx Warriors. We share stories of the battle fought, and war won. The Sodon, and many things. They tease me about Skylin.

One warns me, "Aye, fair prince. That one be mighty fierce."

"And feisty!" says another. "Any occasion spent with her should be a good time."

"Shall ye return to us, fair prince?" Ghebina asks.

"Yes," I reply. "But I need to find out more about my Aunt Miriam, Talok's mother. At least, the one posing as her. She supposedly died when Talok was five. Yet she's still alive, where I'm from."

Smythe says, "If we can be of any assistance, you need only say so."

"I know. And perhaps you *can* help. I need a sure way of communication across a vast distance. Meaning, between where I live on Earth, and here in Paragon."

The warriors think on it, naming off many artifacts. Smythe gives reasons why they won't work. Then he surveys me, and points to my watch. "That timepiece. It's not the same as when we saw it at The Sodon. Did your older self rework it into something new? Could it work for your current purposes?"

"Possibly," I reply. "Wouldn't something have to be here to link up with my watch?"

"Yes," says Hydvar, coming to our group. "Portal waters in a mirror basin should do it. Have Jasper imbue the waters with Crae-Shand Magic."

Rozeth argues, "Crae-Shand doesn't work like that, Hydvar."

Musgrae, at her side, adds, "Its reach is limited."

Rozeth grows contemplative. "Red Magic, however, is hardly limited. Rubidyns could assist. I'm sure of it. Hello, Ravier." She smiles at me. "Came to ensure you were still here, which you are. Talok . . . And Ryco . . . And, well, the lot of them fear you running off for some reason or other, and missing your cue to go out onto the Blackwood Field."

"I won't miss my cue, promise. So long as you find Arsyn, and bring him to me. Want to see what he thinks of the idea of portal waters imbued with Red Magic."

She goes off with Hydvar. Musgrae gives me a wink, before he rejoins them.

The warriors make last-minute preparations. Also do they help me practice how I will walk out onto the field.

When Arsyn shows up, I'm consumed in conversation with him.

I relay the ideas of contact between worlds, and he shakes his head.

"You are making it more complicated than it need be. Adair's paintings are already imbued with Red Magic. The very paint itself is laced with it. That painting of Soren and Adair. Also, that Vision of the Dragon. Both have a pair, here on Muraine. Vision of the Dragon has its partner in Rentwar's Lair: Eye of the Apprentice. As for Soren's, who knows where that one's match is. At any rate, Rentwar gave me the Vision's match. Said to use it how I wish."

"You've thought of everything, haven't you, Arsyn?"

"Many things, yes. But not all."

I ask, "So where is it?"

He clasps his hands behind his back. "With Skylin."

"And where is she? Or am I no longer allowed to see her, because, you know, I'm everyone's toxin?"

Arsyn chuckles low. "Never said toxins were inherently bad. What's a toxin for many, might be a cure for one."

"That aside, will you answer something else for me?"

"Of course."

I state, "Though I'm leaving tomorrow, I want to stay in touch with Sky. Write letters, send them through the painting and such. Visit her, when I come to Muraine. Maybe even one day show her where I'm from. I know our ages won't match forever, but she's become important to me. And I rather like her. I think she feels the same. I want to see where it goes. What do you say, Arsyn? Will you let me date your daughter?"

Arsyn has taken to strolling around me in a wide circle. When he stops, to only stare at me, I gnaw on my lower lip. The anticipation is severe. It's like being choked.

Finally, Arsyn says, "She's in the field of Midnight Anemones. Said something about making a souvenir from the flowers. Tell her what the plan is regarding the painting, and the, uh, well, other matter."

My heart beats wildly. "Is that a yes?"

"How could I say no, to such a request from the Onyx Prince?"

Beside myself, I start to rush away.

Arsyn grabs hold of my arm. "And you should know. I don't think the passing of time will be a problem anymore, so long as a certain something passes through the portal every so often. Two somethings, actually."

"How do you mean?"

Arsyn unclips my daggers from my belt. He presses their pommels together. The daggers become one piece akin to a short, double-bladed staff. Holding it vertical, Arsyn rubs his hands in opposite directions, forward and toward, to get the staff spinning. It hovers. He flicks its top end, and the combined weapon teeters. It spins so fast, a different object is revealed by it. A shape reminiscent to an hourglass.

As soon as I register what I'm looking at, Arsyn snaps his fingers. The staff falls. The weapons come apart at the pommels.

I pick them up, asking, "They sync the portals, make time pass at the same rate between worlds?"

Arsyn nods. "But don't go repeating that knowledge." He snaps his fingers again. "Also, you may want to refrain from mentioning anything about the Phantom of Time, the Ashenawks, and most certainly never mention the term 'Fennukye' to anyone, except your Galloway friend."

"Do I get to know why?"

"Something lingering in the darkness hunts us, Tyler," he replies. "And the greatest of us Fennukye is dead. The second greatest of us fell away to folly, lost all her memories, though we're not quite sure how. We've survived thus far, by guarding our secrets and the truth of what we are. I advise you to do the same."

"I'll try," I reply.

Others around us start moving about. I hadn't even realized that Arsyn slowed time to a complete stop.

"Can't always do that with time," he admits. "When my other half is near, a great deal is made easier. There is more to say to you, Tyler, in the coming months. At present, I'll hold things for you, should your cue come before you're back. Go on, Ravier. Just—"

"Show a little restraint with your daughter, I know. Thanks, Arsyn!"

I dash away, refusing to think on what he has said just now. That sweet, musky scent of Midnight Anemones reaches me; I slow down to a walk. I wade through the tall flowers. Then I trip over something in the dark.

Someone squeals in anger. "No, no! Did you break the box, crush the flowers?" Skylin comes to tower over me with a scowl. Then she takes note that it's me. I wave at her.

"What do you want?" She sulks away.

I get up, confused. I start to talk.

Skylin interrupts. "I told you. I don't want to hear it. Don't want to say goodbye."

"Vards, Sky," I grumble. "Will you let me explain?"

"Explain what, Tyler?" She pouts. "You're leaving Muraine, tomorrow. And I'm leaving Paragon. Who knows when I'll be back. You may never return. And I just wanted to do this one thing of making a fragrance from Midnight Anemones, as a souvenir to remember all that's happened. I've spent all day working on this. See, five boxes. I picked the flowers at different times during the day and night, for they smell a little different depending on how much sunlight or lack of they've received."

I grab hold of Skylin's waist, even as she keeps talking. I inch my face closer to hers. I wait for her to run out of words, then I kiss her. She's stubborn at first. Her lips firm. Her tongue stiff and angry.

I pull away to say, "You found out what I did with Caleiso in Vaydell, didn't you?"

Skylin huffs. "Maybe."

"I'm sorry, all right? Nothing's been easy. The ShenawFayel really got in my head. Made me feel things I didn't want to feel. I felt a love for Caleiso that wasn't my own. Zymarc loves her as his daughter. Since I'm close to her age, that's not what I felt. I felt lust, instead. But I like *you*, Skylin. I choose you. When magic isn't making me lose my head, you're the one I want to be with."

"It can't work, though, Ty." Skylin gets teary-eyed. "We're from two different worlds."

"Sure it can," I reassure her. "We'll figure it out along the way. And we don't have to deal with time passing double on Muraine anymore, compared to Earth. Discovered the solution to that."

Skylin starts to hope; yet she isn't convinced.

So I go on, "And we can write letters to each other, send them through the linked paintings, like that one Arsyn gave you. I can send you new reading material, you can send me food or . . . Farivoo. Just don't spike it, please."

Skylin practically dances in place, her wings quivering excitedly. She grips my arms tight. "Truly! We can do all that? You want me to be yours, for now?"

I grin wickedly. "Sure! Each other's for now. And maybe we can work out a way to use the paintings for portals, should we wish to have a quick visit."

Skylin's expression turns thoughtful. "Oh, but we should start with small living creatures first. Bugs, rodents. That sort of thing."

"Send whatever you want, just nothing that can fly, or is poisonous, nor overly magical-looking. Don't want to raise my mom's suspicions."

"Got it!"

About to say more, I take her hand in mine.

She talks over me, though. "So which of the five Midnight Anemones do you prefer the scent of? Dawn, late morning, afternoon, dusk, or night?"

She opens each box of picked flowers to let me have a whiff. I find I prefer the afternoon and night ones.

"Vards!" she exclaims. "I really liked dawn. But the afternoon's all right. Maybe I'll have Dea assist me with making a blend. Fragrance blends are trickier. Do you know where she is?"

I laugh a little. "You're going to do this now? Don't you want to go with me to the celebration? The farewell meant for me and Gemma?"

"There's no need," says Skylin. "You'll say goodbye to me, in the morning, after I've given Talok that painting. And it isn't *goodbye*, goodbye." She grins. "It's goodbye for now."

"Well then, see you in the morning."

"Um-hmm!" She nods, and her blonde curls bounce. "If you find Dea, send her this way."

"Will do."

And so I leave Skylin in the Field of Midnight Anemones, to go rejoin with the Onyx of Malik. I recall that first night I was here with Callie, and what she did. How she charged that device, got it to latch onto Talok's wrist. It could've killed him. Nearly did. We lost Ryco because of it. Only got him back due to everything working out perfectly in his favor.

I wonder, *Will other things work out in favor of the Onyx Clan? Though I've freed Gyron and a portion to serve me, and I'd never force them to do anything against their will, many are still beholden to ReNovak, now that he's woken up. Does the work that Paydinn and YaeVorkk are performing on Zymarc, even now, hold the answer to freeing the Onyx of the Laws of Neutrality? Could Setharyn be made to replace his ReNovamen, and fulfill the prophesy? Setharyn knew the Vardiyas would find a way to bring him back. What if this is one way they devised? Waiting for a Siveyra or two to become strong and knowledgeable enough to split a ReNovamen from his former self, or make the former replace the present.*

I've rejoined my group of Onyx by now. I push the thoughts aside, as some of my warriors prepare me with what I am to have on.

Dea comes among the group of warriors. Although she's a few yards away, her flirtatious tones reach where I'm standing. She's picked the youngest of my warriors to be her audience, the ones not yet a Sorsryn's Fifty. She says something that makes one of them blush. I don't catch what it is. But when she wiggles her bare shoulders back and forth, a sexy expression on her face, that blushing warrior retreats out of sight. The others nearest them laugh.

Rolling my eyes, I Mensa-div to Dea, *"Stop harassing my warriors, Demon Dea. Go help Skylin with something, instead. She's in the Field of Midnight Anemones near the Arkivara."*

Deamond turns her attention to me. She gives a stately curtsey and then leaves.

The Onyx of Malik settle down.

"Just a few minutes," Smythe tells me. "Make your final adjustments, Onyx Prince."

Smythe's about to walk away, but I ask him, "Do you mind answering something for me, Smythe?"

"Of course not, Prince Tyler." He stands at attention, but not in a beholden way. Only respectful.

I ask, "What does the Onyx Prince mean to all of you? Or, rather, why is he so important to all people of the Onyx Clan?"

"That is a lengthy narrative," Smythe admits. "To put it concisely, however, hold to this. The Onyx King rules the people, who then uphold the Laws of Neutrality. The Onyx Prince corrects the king, should that king deviate in his use of magic. Even from a very young age, this is within the prince's ability."

Ghebina overhears us, and she comes to add her input. "Smythe is forgetting the prince's true worth and inspiration. He is not bound to Laws of Neutrality, the way all other Onyx, even half-Onyx, are. This harkens back to when Nyxane was not a king, but rather, the youngest of three brothers. He was free to choose his path. It is foretold that he was also mediator between Soren and Monel, until, one day, Monel disappeared. Nyxane was soon bound to the laws, the way all other Onyx Sorsryns still are today. But his sons and grandsons—indeed, all eldest male heirs to the Onyx Kings—regain this freedom of choice, freedom to make binding alliances and to break them."

"By the books, Ghebina." Smythe grips his blade's hilt. "How do you know all that? I've never heard the tellings quite like that."

"You recall, Smythe," Ghebina says, "that I'm part Kyanite. And they are the storytellers and illusion makers. A clan powerful enough that the Geldryn never dared to start a war with them."

Gyron calls to all of us, "It's time."

We get into position.

The gathered crowds in the stadiums, and drums and wind instruments playing in the background, create such noise, it's as if the air vibrates.

Gyron and the two are some distance from me. I can't make out what they're saying.

So I focus on what's around me. I take it all in again, except with different eyes. No longer are they of a world and people I never knew existed. I know this world. And I love this place. There is nothing I wouldn't do to protect my people, my warriors, my friends and family. They are my everything.

Siveyra Gyronawv starts the procession of warriors. Smythe and Ghebina are only a couple of steps behind him. They create a triangle formation.

One of the warriors behind says, "Now, Prince Tyler."

I stride forward, glad of the fact that I wear my clean coat of the Sleeping

Dragon, but the black garb of the Onyx underneath. I've extra weapons on me. Not just my daggers. The Blades of Neutrality are on my back, crossed in an *X*, Winter's Vondaen positioned vertically between them.

Smythe told me earlier, *"If you wish to draw that vertical one, you'll need to summon it into your hand with its name."*

The ruby-stone stage is still far ahead of us. I can't see who has gathered on it.

Gyron, Smythe, and Ghebina begin a show of the art of magic and weaponry. They leave it up to me what I wish to do. Simply did they help me know how to enter out on the field. Now that I'm here, I've no idea what to do. My body still hasn't fully recovered from the expended magic of today. Part of me wants my older self to take over, so I can have a break.

I come to a halt, as I was told to do. I'm at the center of the field and the center of the enormous Vardiya emblem etched into that field. I hold my right hand out. I imagine my coat of the Sleeping Dragon being taken off by ghostly hands to place it into my waiting one. I close my eyes briefly. When they open, the coat is in my outstretched hand. I look to the stadiums filled with cheering, chanting, dancing people. Dragons guard the area, and Darklyres rest on the dragons' long necks.

I need only wait a moment for the noise to cease. I call out, "Paragon and her allies have won! Though Gemma Galloway and I must leave you tomorrow, returning after a time, I now summon the one who secured our victory." I toss my coat forward. I quietly speak the words: "Inviteis-Ravieras-Savak." Then I draw the Onyx Blades out and toss them too.

My coat doesn't fall to the ground. It floats, instead. A figure fills it, catches the blades before they can land on the field.

My eighteen-year-old self is here. Summoned by me this time. He walks about in confidence, wearing the Sleeping Dragon. Truthfully, his stride is like an Onyx Warrior. Sure and powerful, but humble. He looks over his shoulder, to me. He bows. He thrusts the Onyx Blades into the ground at a diagonal. He forms that sign of Onyx Neutrality. Green fire wisps off the blade edges.

Cheering rings out.

When he stands to his full height, other figures take shape within the distance separating us. Age fifteen, sixteen, and seventeen. Each one is very different. But recognizably me. Fifteen wears the finest garb of the Onyx Warriors, two simple blades on his back, and the daggers on his belt. He's a little taller. More confident too. He speaks words, aims his right hand to the air, to cast magic. "Oostrinas-delik-kaw!" he shouts, and dark-magenta fire flares from his hand.

It loses its momentum a ways up, and hovers there.

Age sixteen is garbed as an Emerald Sorsryn. He's taller still. All the green cloth seems to make his eyes glow. In fact, his eyes *are* glowing emerald-green. He's the cockiest version of me that's here, covered in near a dozen different weapons or items of various sizes. He rushes the Onyx of Malik, duels them, taunts them, riles them up with magic. He seems very Vonsai in the moment.

I burst with pride for seeing what I become.

Age sixteen lets out a Soren-like laugh, and I shiver. Shiver more, as he lifts his left hand, and speaks out: "Ventus-sev-viiana!" Colored wind the same as what blows over the landscape of Vondurheil is shot up. It loses momentum at the same position as the fire.

Seventeen is stripped of all but his tattered pants. He's even barefoot. Deep scars mar his chest, his arms; even his back, once he has turned away from me, shows deep, scabbed-over cuts. Before turning away, however, he stares at me. His skin is some shades lighter than it should be. He looks much starved of sunlight. It's horrifying to think about what has happened to make my future self look like that. A ghost. A wraith. His fingernails are overgrown, pointed like claws.

The two previous ages go toward him a bit. And he sneers at them like a dog who feels threatened. His canine teeth have grown sharp. His scars start to glow with the dark-magenta color. "Soondasa." He growls out the word, while looking at me. Then he turns to face age eighteen, who waits patiently. Walking forward, he says more, "Krim-dim-drim. You are him. Ravieras-Savak, save me." He rests his right hand on the chest of the oldest of us. Age seventeen starts to weep.

The eldest replies, "You needn't fear, Tyler. I'm right here. I stand as proof that we make it to this age. Eighteen. I'm in the present, looking into the past, and seeing that it is good."

He motions to what's around.

The people. The creatures. The Greyvons. And the leaders on the thrones: Talok, ReNovak, and Rorka. Aygorinaith and two of the three Amethyst Queens are also there. The city has been made better.

The eldest goes on, "Stay strong. Help is coming for you, where you wait. Though our father couldn't plan for all paths, as he was taken before his time, I have finished the work he started, ensuring it all leads to me. And to the phantom. He has been made. But he has yet to draw his first breath. And when he draws that first breath of life, the mighty war all the ages have been channeling into, will come to head in a place you've not been to before. I will be at the center of it, fighting a great evil. An evil that outweighs Vitiosus. I'm not ready yet. Soon, I must be. If I should fail, it will be the death of all things fair and good. The task is heavy upon my shoulders. Yet I am not alone, for there are other Onyx Princes. Three at the end. Are you ready for him. Ready for a restored Onyx Prince?"

The crowd grows uneasy in their chatter. They don't know what he means. But *I* do. I glance in the direction of the castle. I wonder how the Jokryn brothers are faring with their work. Soon, whatever fate has decided will happen.

I draw out my daggers and approach the King's Guard. Ryco is quick to draw weapons. He must see the fear that's come over me.

I don't make it to him.

The ground quakes violently.

Those gathered leap to action, trying to escape the stadiums.

Stumbling, I fall.

The Vardiya emblem of the Blackwood Field cracks at its center. A leafless tree grows up from the scarred field. A screaming figure is chained to it. Zymarc, I realize. He's facing the ruby-stone stage, his hands drawn high over his head, and fastened to the tree.

The Jokryn brothers are nowhere to be seen.

Zymarc's cries of agony cease. A reddish smoke wisps off him. His legs go limp. He passes out, hanging there, hands bound overhead.

The smoke gets thicker, turns to liquid that crawls over Zymarc's slumbering, swaying figure.

Talok reaches me, pulls me up. I'm dragged to safety, amid the chaos.

In div, I tell King Aygor, *"Get Arsyn. Go ensure Skylin and Dea are safe. They're near the Arkivara."*

He flies off.

The quake continues on in violence. Many pile onto dragons and fly to safety. Darklyres simply fly off in the wake of King Aygor.

Ryco makes the ruby stage hover. We go there to wait out the quake.

Gyron and the warriors take to forming sheets of floating ice, which they sit upon. They wait as well.

The eldest of me has stood in the same place, unmoved. He summons the other three to leave, with a wave of his hand. Then he says, "Soondasa-krim-dim-drim. I bid you to come for him." He holds both hands out, relaxed, as if to gently weigh something.

Liquid swirling with the colors of Vaegon-eyes goes forth from him like a snake searching for a victim. It finds its victims of the Winds of Vondurheil and The Kavas Flame. It devours them, then falls from its place in the air. Upon landing, the quake ceases.

Zymarc wakes up. His posture stiffens. He goes into a frenzy, pressing his back against the tree. He watches the liquid crawl on him as if, at any second, it will kill him.

The liquid draws into a puddle on the ground in front of Zymarc. It rises into a figure. That figure becomes the young Setharyn. He's facing the stage, consequently, facing us. Only twenty steps, and he'd be to us.

ReNovak rises off his silver throne. He breathes out the name, "Setharyn? It cannot be."

Weapons in hand, we're ready for anything. Or so we think.

Paydinn and YaeVorkk rush onto the field.

"No, Setharyn!" Paydinn shouts, in breathlessness. "You can't cut him down. You are still tied to him."

YaeVorkk stops in his tracks, and starts having a fit of coughs.

Setharyn looks up at his father, his eyes glowing green. "I'll deal with you later, cheater of magic. First need to rid this world of a Vitiosyn." Setharyn pivots around. He summons the Blades of Neutrality from where they've been placed in the ground.

Fire encircles the two Jokryn brothers, as a barrier is put in place by Setharyn.

"Start digging," says Gyron to the warriors. "Setharyn's barriers were always weakened by the dirt."

Removing some pieces of their armor, the warriors get to work using their metal bracers or pauldrons as shovels.

My eldest self quickly gets in front of Zymarc. He means to defend him. "This one is not yours to claim, Setharyn!"

Setharyn yells back, "He doesn't deserve to live! Step aside, whittler of time. Let me finish him once and for all."

"No," my older self says, hunkering down to an attack position. "His part is not yet made complete. From one Onyx Prince to another, let me warn you. You will not interfere with all my father and I have worked for, by the altering of time. We have not broken Laws of Time, but you will be, should you do this."

Setharyn says, "There can only be one rightful Onyx Prince."

"Then I am him," says my older self. "Stand down, or else. Zymarc shall not be killed this night, for this night he is made a Siveyra—his journey sped up by the magic of two Siveyras, one a Keeper of Time. If the Vardiyas have deemed him worthy of finishing the journey, then he is worthy of living for now."

I Mensa-div to Ryco, *"Give me a bow. Forge an arrow for me."*

He does so, and I take them in hand.

My older self continues, saying, "Let us talk this through. I understand you've been trapped in his mind, since he was called to Vitiosus. Hundreds of years, nigh a thousand, forced to watch what he did. Never free to make your own decisions. Simply to sway Zymarc to be less violent. To assist him in slowing the corruption of Vitiosus. It was a mighty task you were given, Setharyn. And you rose to the occasion. But now you are nearly free of him."

I take aim for Setharyn's left shoulder. Since my left side is stronger, I figure his might be too. I don't care what the consequences are of attacking him. This Onyx Prince will not be allowed to ruin all my future self has worked for. When Gemma comes to press her hand on my back, I release the arrow. It slips through the barrier, continuing on to plunge through Setharyn's shoulder right where I intended it to.

Gemma steps away.

Setharyn cries out, crumpling to the ground.

ReNovak is furious. He strikes me across the face. Takes the bow away, breaks it in half.

Talok draws his long-blade and aims it at ReNovak's throat. "Do that again, and your life is forfeit, Onyx King. You will not ever strike the heir to our thrones again. After this night, you are never to show your face in Paragon. Yet you shall welcome us in Oniva, whenever we should visit, for you are bound to neutrality, and we are not."

ReNovak is pressed down, his face riddled with pain.

Talok releases his invisible hold, and ReNovak gasps for breath while on his knees.

Setharyn yanks the lodged arrow out.

Zymarc shouts in pain. Blood seeps through the fabric of his coat's left shoulder.

Setharyn manages to stand up. He sees the evidence of Zymarc's wound. He shakes his head in fright. "No!" he shouts. "Why must this be? Will I never escape you? Always destined to be tied to such a vile creature?"

Setharyn's barrier is shattered by the Onyx Warriors, who were attacking it, digging under it. The Onyx Prince flees from the scene. Paydinn and YaeVorkk try to cut him off. He is faster. I've never seen anyone run that fast, in fact.

Talok, the guards—all still here—barely register that Setharyn means to escape, as he's already disappearing into darkness.

A familiar screech rings out. Awngeleik rises from the ground where the three cast spells landed. She thinks the prince means to play with her. She chases him, stomps at him. Bites the fabric of his black coat, and whirls him around a bit.

Setharyn doesn't scream. He seems not a bit frightened of her. Only mad. He punches her neck, until she lets go.

My older self calls for her to come. "Let him go, Awngeleik. Let him flee. When he's ready, he'll be back."

Awngeleik turns away from Setharyn, and trots over to my eighteen-year-old self. She waves her head around. Flaps her wings. She gives sounds of delight. She is home. I can't help but wonder where she's been this whole time. I may never know. But I don't care. I go to her. So does Gemma. We pet her, and she calms down to contentedness.

My older self breaks Zymarc's chains. That Vitiosyn must lean on him, or fall, for he is vastly weak.

I neither pity nor hate him. Simply do I accept that he must not be executed yet.

Unsettled by it all, Setharyn flees the city of Eyo'el.

The two Jokryn brothers watch as he goes. They seem torn, but eventually they come over to us.

Paydinn brims with delight, watching us with the Equidyn. "Much that one has endured, in her years of less than three."

Hugging round her scaly neck, I ask anyone who'll answer, "Can I take her home with me?"

Zepharre comes to my side. Gently, he replies, "I'm sure we can figure out a way to make that happen."

Talok adds, "At the very least, you can have her for a few days. I don't foresee any harm in that."

My older self says to Paydinn, "Take Zymarc to his prison cell. Give him food and water. Tend to his wounds. That is all. You needn't say anything to him. He'll have much on his mind. When he's recovered a little, begin the interrogations again. Put him on trial." The eldest glances to Talok, then me. "That is, if King Talok and my former self deem it fair."

Talok sighs raggedly. "We do. Though I don't like it." Talok looks off in the distance. "What of Setharyn? I hardly believe he's been given back to the world, only to flee."

"As I said," says the older me. "When he's ready to come home, and accept whatever fate holds for him, he'll come home. Until then, don't get any gray hairs over it. As for me, I must return to my time."

I make the rope of light appear. I grip it tight, then I sever it, sever my connection to my future self.

"See you in the future," he says, before he's gone.

Many escort the Jokryn brothers, as they haul Zymarc, who's unable to walk on his own, back to the castle. He groans in pain, mumbling words no one can make out. By the time we're to the castle steps, he's unconscious.

Gemma and I are to either side of Awngeleik. She nuzzles against us, demands that she be petted and loved on. Talok and the guards greet her. The lot of us are in the wake of the prisoner and his escort.

Once inside the castle, they go down to the repurposed bunkers, and we go to the infirmary, as it has provisions for EquiNeins. Ben finds her favorite grain. When he gives it to her, she munches heartily on it.

Eli has found the shaving supplies. He insists that Quall teach him how to shave without the use of magic. Since I'm in need of a shave, Quall uses me as the test subject. I get one last look in the mirror, before the stubble is cleared away by Quall's steady hand that holds the razor. I look as if a year has passed. By the end of the shave, my appearance is much the way it was when I left home. Young, just not broken and scared this go-around.

We stay in the infirmary for the rest of the night. Twelve of us. Awngeleik and Talok. The eight guards. Gemma and me. I don't want our time of drinking herbs, sharing stories, nor giving thoughts of what's to come to end. But it does, for we each succumb to the exhaustion of a war well fought. The War for the Equidyn. It is won. The rule of Vitiosus is over. And forever will I guard one of the last things my father left for me. The Walking Demon. The dragon-horse. My vicious but fair Equidyn, Awngeleik. For now, we sleep.

38

Forever Not the Same

Her green wheelie case in hand, and satchel slung over her shoulder, Gemma stands ready near the city gate of the Eye of Paragon. Her eyes are shut, as she faces the morning light of Rentwaramein. A small smile plays across her lips. She wears various garb we've collected along the way, looking *very* fine.

Clearing my throat, I say, "I saw you, Galloway, collecting morsels of food after breakfast. Glad your appetite's back."

She opens her eyes. "Never lost it, Ravier. Just had to go hungry, some of the time."

Talok and the eight meander toward the gate.

Ben has hold of my duffle bag. He hands it to me, saying, "Everything's there. Triple-checked."

Talok states, "Textbooks have been added to your things as well. Grover and Lemawr, and I suppose Dezarin too, have translated our first year's textbooks to English. The material should fill in the gaps of what you don't know about the basics of magic."

Ryco makes a point to stare at me. "We expect you to know it, by the time you come back for your next extended visit."

"I'll make sure he studies," says Gemma.

They each say their goodbyes.

Nearly ready to go, I glance around. "Is Skylin coming, do you think?"

"We're right here," says Dea.

Skylin shyly comes forward, wearing the same dress she had on that night in Grevagg. A pale-yellow, it softly shimmers. Though she didn't that night, she now looks as a Greek goddess to me.

I go to her, hug her, kiss her softly on the cheek, and she blushes. As she steps away, the scent of Midnight Anemones reaches me. It's intoxicating. I almost lose my head over it. It's vastly better than the scent of Anemones at night.

Glancing at Dea, I spot her devilish look.

She inquires, "How do you like the Afternoon Toxin?"

I say, "It's rather nice. Just don't go mixing it with Quall's herbs."

"Yeah," says Warren, "and definitely stay away from the Arkivara Blend, till you're older."

Kent adds, "Don't want another war being started. This time, between young hearts."

Skylin makes a face at him. "No such thing will happen."

Quallendeis holds back laughter. He glances off to the distance. While the restored dragon flies overhead, Reign watches from where he's curled up on the ground and—judging by the sleepy look in his gaze—about ready to take a nap on the hot coals.

Khyra and Madeleine have climbed up onto his back. When Quall lifts a hand in goodbye to them, they wave back.

"See you next year, Tyler!" Khyra calls out. "Madeleine promises to have relearned her skills in stitchery, and to make a whole new wardrobe for you and Gemma. Your friends too, Jed and Jackson, should they wish to come."

Gemma calls out, "Just make his all black, Madeleine! Can't go wrong with that. He'll love it!"

I reach over to pinch Gemma's arm.

She slaps my hand, points an accusing finger at me. "Best we leave, Quallendeis, before a war of young hearts starts."

"Galloway." Ryco moans. "Don't encourage Eli in the rhyming. He doesn't need further help, in that regard."

Talok approaches Skylin, to say, "Your father, Arsyn, said you have something for me, Skylin. Must I guess what it is, before you hand it over?"

Skylin shakes her head. "No. But I already left it with Adviser Zepharre. He hung it next to Khyra's repaired blueprints, in the Advisers' Quarters. A painting that has a match somewhere in Tyler's home. A means of communication between worlds. A painting!" She grins. "Who knew?"

Ben queries, "That dragon painting in LanSoren's study?"

"Yep! Vision of the Dragon." I hug Skylin one more time and tell her, "I'll send you new reading material through it soon."

I step away.

Dea says, "Start with history. She'll love it."

"I will," I say, as I take a last look around. I drink in the sight of a restored city.

"Shall we go?" queries Siege, holding Awngeleik's lead rope. He leads at the front with Ryco, Awngeleik in tow.

Talok, Quall, and Ben take up the back. Kent, Musgrae, and Eli surround Gemma and me, drawing out their weapons. They just can't help falling into the habit their training as guards produced.

Going past the open gate, we head on the path that leads to the portal.

Our time to get there goes too quickly. A sick feeling comes over me. I don't want to leave them. Yet I must. I must go to my other home. The one on Earth. Much has changed in me. I am forever not the same. And that's okay. Truly, I don't want to be the same as I was. The broken boy who just lost his dad. The boy who battled endless sorrow and bitterness for life. That's over.

Anytime I wish to see LanSoren of Trauvo, he's only a visit to the Arkivara away. Or a summons from the past. Never will I forget what he looks like, sounds like. Forever, he will be timeless to me, never aging past when I saw him last.

The streams of portal waters come into view. Someone's already making them gather together into a small body of water.

Rorka finishes making the portal ready. Droediin and Mekka in Von form sit along the bank. Once they see me, they stride over. They say nothing, for equals can understand each other with one glance.

The water is frozen over, and Ben goes to walk upon it. He draws his Katana blade, cuts a symbol in the air. The symbol turns blue.

The portal opens.

Ben steps aside.

"Goodbye for now," I tell all of them. "And see ya 'round, Rorka. Keep the naughty Vonsai in check."

"Droediin and Mekka will," she says. "Gyron and I mean to hunt for Jasper. Lady Ayna as well. Haven't seen them, lately. We'll keep you all apprised of Von matters. But you, Ravier, and only you, will I keep apprised of the *other* matter to do with me. It is for another time. Farewell for now."

I reflect only for a moment on all I've learned of Rorka. She must be the one who has forgotten who she is, what she is. I can only hope that she will remember someday. Perhaps she already has.

Siege hands off Awngeleik's lead rope to me. "Good luck," he says.

"He won't need it," states Ryco, "for no longer is he naïve. Are you, Ravier?"

"I don't know about that," says Gemma. "Take care of Paragon, dear Paradyn. No strangling Eli, before we get back."

"See," Eli says. "Someone here cares about me."

Gemma laughs, before she makes a run for the portal. She manages to keep hold of her wheelie case, and not slip on the ice. She's through the doorway back to Earth, ahead of me.

Awngeleik chases after her. If I had a wish to say anything else to them, that moment is over. So I join her in running forward. We go through together.

* * *

The portal starts closing behind us. We appear below the ice that's remained on Mirror Lake's surface this entire time. The small Vardiya swims along with us. Propelling upward, Gemma and I press our hands on the slick surface. Awngeleik touches her nose to it. It's not until the Vardiya brushes at the ice that it quickly melts away. We burst up, gasping for breath. Awngeleik swims for the shore.

The water's warm again.

Gemma looks at me, and I at her, with that knowing gaze. The one where no words need be spoken, nor thoughts heard in Mensa-div. We simply know how the other is feeling.

Swimming to shore, we crawl onto the rocky bank. The Vardiya washes up on the rocks, and shifts to stone. Gemma tenderly picks it up, before we trudge to my favorite spot of grass and then collapse upon it. We lie there a while, just resting. Just breathing. We made it home. Yet neither of us will ever be the same.

Awngeleik has taken to napping. She's tired too.

Sitting up, Gemma leans over me.

I prop myself up on my elbows, her face close enough that her breath tickles along my chin. I tell her, "Sorry it didn't work out with Ben. I know you were getting attached."

Gemma's lower lip quivers, before she presses both together. Scooting her hips away from me, she gives herself more room to slowly rest her head and one hand on my chest. I embrace her with my right arm, drawing her upper body close against my side.

"It's all right, Ty. Ben's admired Khyra, since he was five. Loved her for at least five years, now. I didn't stand a chance."

"Still." I close my eyes. "It's hard to let go. Hard to process everything that's happened to us, really."

Gemma softly sobs on my chest.

I sit up all the way and pull her onto my lap. We hold each other like that for a while. I wipe her tears away, nuzzling my forehead against the nape of her neck. "I was so scared of losing you, Gem. More afraid of that, than anything else we faced. But, look, we made it back. Hardly any scars to show for it."

She smiles weakly. "At least, not scars we can see."

Sighing, I show her my arm with the wolf surrounded by a dragon. I admit, "Well, I turned some of my scars to this."

She feels along the mark. "How are you going to hide that from your mom?"

"Don't know. I was hoping it'll only show when I'm near a place of magic."

"And if it doesn't fade?" she asks.

I shrug. "I'll wear long sleeves until I figure something else out."

She climbs off my lap to sit, hugging knees to her chest.

I glance at the Vardiya-stone that's resting motionless at our feet.

Gemma asks, "What are we going to do, these next months of Zymarc's interrogation, then trial? How are we going to face the memories of everything he did?"

I give a half-grin. "By remembering that it was you and me, Skylin and Rorka, who were responsible for burying him in the snows of Vondurheil. That was the beginning of his end. The end of Vitiosus."

Gemma adds, "May it stay gone forever."

Now ready to make the walk home, I pat Gemma's arm. "It's time, Gem."

Easing up, she helps me to stand. "Are you ready to go back to a normal existence?"

I snatch up the Vardiya-stone and glance down at it. "Normal? No. I'm just going to be me, absent of magic." I look at her. "But you, it would seem, will always have a spark, Galloway. A way to cheat just a little."

"Well." She twirls her shorter strand of hair. "I am the witch, after all. The Witch of Galloway. And you, the Sleeping Dragon. She, the dragon-horse. All one of a kind."

Gemma and I walk hand in hand, through the forest near my house, wheelie case haphazardly bumping its way across the uneven ground. Awngeleik plods tiredly alongside us. At the forest edge, I stop to take a deep breath.

There's the barn. The workshop. The house's backside. And the expanse of twenty-two steps.

Gemma takes the satchel off her shoulder, and pats it. "Shall we change in the barn?"

I nod.

We go there first. Gemma in the loft, me in the saddle room. Awngeleik concealed in her cloak and partnered with Ginger Snap in his stall.

I slip into my old clothes. They feel odd. So ordinary. Nothing special, until I put one thing in my pants' pocket: my father's enchanted quill, given to me by Grover. Neatly, I fold all garb from Muraine and then wrap them with the Sleeping Dragon coat. I carry it out, then go check on Ginger Snap and Awngeleik. He's lying down for a nap. I assume Awngeleik is too. Not wanting to wake either of them, I steal away quietly.

Gemma's headed down the ladder. "Ready?" she asks all perky-like.

Handing her my coat, stuffed with clothes, I suddenly worry over the tiniest thing. "Gem"—I point to my head then hers—"how are we going to explain the haircuts?"

She grimaces. "Vards! We forgot to have them change it back. I know." She relaxes. "I'll have Kane say he took us for a haircut. It'll only take a phone call to see if he's had a window of time unaccounted for. If that doesn't work, I'll ask one of my Judo class buddies to cover for me. He rarely does anything during the week, except work, workout, shower, then sleep."

I look her up and down, then turn that look to myself. I'm nowhere near as skinny as when I left. "What about the rest of us?" I ask. "I mean, now that I think about it, my clothes fit a little tight. Won't they notice how we've both changed?" I study her.

"I've changed?" Gemma asks, dumbfounded.

"Well, yeah." I look away, feeling guilty though I don't know why. "You're not as scrawny, either."

"Are you hinting that I ate too much while we were gone?"

"No, Gem!" I groan. "I'm just saying that my mom, but definitely your dad, will notice we're different. Less skinny, more muscular, taller too."

Gemma chews on her lower lip, her beautiful brown eyes growing larger by the second. "I don't know, Ty. Maybe there's a spell that'll work."

"How's it going to last, while we're away from the lake?" I ask. "Bottle some up, carry it with us at all times?"

She shrugs, dropping the bundle of clothes. "Why not a feather or two of Awngeleik's? Worth a shot, right?"

"Right! But you don't have to get that from her now," I state, as I exit the barn. "I have a feather of hers and some of her mane in the house. Looks like my mom's car is still gone. Want to come in for a bit?"

Gemma stuffs our clothes and her satchel in my duffle, before handing it to me. "Yes," she says. "I want to delay a Kaida reunion, for as long as possible. The temptation to refrain from using magic on her will be the hardest thing, now that we're home."

We enter through the back door to a clean kitchen.

"Ty?" Gemma asks. "Mind if I shower? I didn't get the chance, before we left. And the air here is so different. Heavy. Muggy. Dirty. It's as if I've just been through a swamp."

"I'm sure we both smell like we've been through one," I tease. "And what do you mean you didn't get the chance? You just didn't want to have a moment's rest, before leaving."

"Neither did you." She pinches my arm.

I roll my eyes. "Fine. Use the one upstairs, in case she gets home soon."

"What are you going to do, while waiting?"

"Write a letter to my Aunt *Miriam*," I state. "Eyo'el suggested that I should. And I've been given the task of finding out if she really is Talok's mom or someone else—a fake."

I lead the way up the stairs of the squeaking-six and silent-seven. Opening the bathroom door, I flip the light on for Gemma. "When you're done, my bedroom door's right there." I point to it.

Gemma gives me a grateful look, then enters the bathroom, pulling her wheelie case behind her.

I retreat to my bedroom. I frown at how dark it is. So much black. I muse, *I must think of a different color to paint it. I'm not going the rest of the summer feeling as if I'm suffocating in ReNovak's enchanted room, nor falling down to the gray sands of The Kavas. Is red too bold? Probably.*

Pushing the thought aside, I drop my duffle on the bed. Once seated at my desk, I search for a blank sheet of paper. No lines. No marks. Simply plain, ready to be filled with quill strokes. I find a few sheets, and take one. Pausing, I'm unsure if I should begin, knowing that, once this letter's sent off, even more could change forever. I recall the courage I found along the way, in Muraine. I put quill to paper, writing:

Dear Aunt Miriam:

I received your birthday card for me, a short while ago. Though my mom didn't ask me to write to you, I know it's what she'd want. For me to meet you. Get to know you. Then, when a close friend told me I really should write to you, I thought, how could I not? You're my only aunt, after all. And who else can tell me certain stories about my dad, and how he was when growing up, better than you?

A lot's happened, this last year without him. But it's getting easier. I'm challenging myself to be better. To do better. And, guess what? I recently made loads of new friends to last a lifetime. Some days will be near unbearable, I know. But I want to share my time with you. Will you come visit my mom and me? There's so much to say. Please come.

Lovingly, your nephew,

Tyler Malik Ravier

After sealing the folded letter in an envelope, I lean back in my chair. I gaze at his quill, resting on the desk. I miss him more than any amount of words could ever convey. One day, I will learn who killed him. And when I do, that soul will bitterly regret ever existing.

A soft knock sounds on my door.

"Come in," I call.

Gemma slinks in, fully dressed. She plops her wheelie case just inside my room, before she towel-dries her short hair. "Showering is so much faster, since the haircut."

I reply, "It looks good on you."

"You finish the letter?" queries Gemma, looking for a place to sit. Her eyes narrow on my duffle bag.

I tap the envelope on my desk. "Right here. Just needs postage and an address. I'll send it off tomorrow."

"Mind if I have a search through your bag for Ben's spell-book? He said he gave it to you."

I motion. "Have at it."

Gemma sits on my bed. "What are your plans for the rest of today?"

I envision it being Skylin sitting on my bed. I swallow down the excitement, forcing myself to glance away. I shrug. "I'll probably write a letter to Skylin. See how long it takes for her to write back."

Amidst her riffling through the things in my bag, Gemma covers a yawn. "If I wasn't so tired, I'd write something to King Aygor's Wards. They've demanded to have new reading materials. More like, stories they'll demand that Dea read to them. Oh, Ty!" She pauses her search. "There are so many people I want to stay in touch with. Talok, the King's Guard. Several Darklyres and Vons. Did Talok mention who's coming to summon us for the trial hearings?" She resumes her hunt.

"Siege and Eli were given that task, over breakfast."

"What if Miriam shows up?" queries Gemma, as she lifts Ben's spell-book out and begins to flip through its pages.

"Then Talok, Ryco, and Eishal will come," I reply. "I told Talok they'd have to sleep in the barn, unless Gemma can work some magic and set them up in the Galloway mansion." I grin wickedly.

Gemma turns serious. "Challenge accepted. I'll figure out a way."

"I know you will."

"Here's some spells to try." She taps a page of the spell-book. "Best chance of success is this beginner Kyanite spell to do with temporarily masking appearance. What we could do is have a full-strength version to start. Go to the lake every day, to cast a lesser version of it, until we no longer need to hide how we've changed. But, as far as the hair goes, if we can easily explain that away, we should. It's one less thing to have the spell mask."

"How long will that take to do?" I ask.

Gemma drops her satchel on the floor, then kicks it under the bed. She continues paging through the spell-book. "Once I have the feather and strands, not long."

I get up to search for them. It doesn't take long. I hand them over to Gemma, before starting the task of unpacking my things. I ensure all things that would make my mother suspicious are hidden in boxes, or in dark corners of my closet. I even tape or tie stuff in place. My daggers, for example, I suspend on string that's tied to some sturdy coat hangers, covered up by hoodies. Throughout my task, I hear Gemma softly speaking some spell word. She keeps grumbling and restarting.

I shut my closet door, finally finished, and turn around.

"Done!" Gemma proclaims.

There she sits, looking the same as when we left for Muraine, except that her hair is short.

"I'll keep the feather," she says. "You keep this in your pocket. Make sure there aren't any *holes* for it to fall through, and get *lost*." She hands me the strands, braided into a circle. That witchy look on her face makes me want to tug on a strand of her hair.

I flip her short, slightly damp hair over her face, instead.

She laughs. Then she sprawls out on my bed in her splat-pose, and groans. "I don't want to go home."

I stuff the braided strand into my pocket, deciding that I should sit at my desk. "Do you want to have an ordinary dinner with me?"

She bolts upright. "Food! You want food? Tyler, are you all right?" She comes to feel my forehead.

I laugh, pulling Gemma onto my lap. "Better than. I just want to do ordinary, for once. Cook an ordinary dinner for my mom, before she gets home. Have an ordinary dinner at the table. An ordinary night's sleep." I pause, before saying, "The extraordinary defeated Zymarc, and just wants a bit of ordinary, before it all starts again."

Gemma squeezes my arm. "Then I shall be your assistant, in the kitchen. But we're not cooking an ordinary meal. For Molly Smith didn't go to culinary school, and share her secrets with me, so that I could cook up ordinary."

"As Madeleine would say," I state.

And Gemma replies, "Not a bit of ordinary." She hugs round my neck, then leans back. "What are you going to tell Jed and Jaxson?"

Moaning, I throw my head back in frustration. I push her off my lap to head downstairs.

Once we're there, I reply, "I'll approach that bridge tomorrow. As for crossing it? I have no idea what I'm going to say to them."

Gemma opens the fridge, eyeing potential ingredients. She bends down, swaying her shoulders side to side. "Beef or lamb?"

"My mom prefers lamb," I reply, going to the spice cabinet. "Maybe I should just show them some spells, while we're at the lake?" I take out my favorite spice of Sumac.

"Get mint, if you have it," says Gemma, as I'm about to close the cabinet.

Finding a jar of dried mint, I give the two spices to Gemma.

The cabinet shuts.

"Or maybe I'll tell Jaxson about Skylin. Slowly unfold the truth from there. It might be easier, once I tell him I like this girl who talks a lot. But there's this problem of her wings smacking me in the head, when we dance. And? Oh yeah. She lives on another planet."

Carrying various vegetables to the counter, Gemma pauses to glance at me. "Jaxson will think you're joking, and Jed will say you're high."

"Probably," I agree, opening the meat package. "How should we do this?"

"Dry rub," says Gemma, opening and closing many cupboards. "That Sumac will do nicely. Brush the lamb with olive oil. Salt and spice. Cover. Set aside."

"Cutting board's up there." I point, before preparing the lamb loin.

Gemma stands on tiptoe, to reach the largest cutting board in the upper cupboard. I can't help myself from glancing at those hips. I know beneath the façade of a spell, she's packed on a lot of lean muscle since we left. Her curves are perfect on her. Hidden for now, only to return in a few months. I look away, sad that she didn't get the guy in the end. *But she certainly stuck it to those Vitiosyns,* I muse. Turning on the faucet, I wash up.

"Heard that!" Gemma whirls around. "I did, didn't I? Serves them right." She plops the board down beside the snap peas and cauliflower.

Drying my hands, I ask, "Want me to sharpen the knife"—I go to slide a chef's knife from the block—"or do you want that honor?"

She takes out the sharpening steel and grips the knife, rhythmically sharpening its edge. It awakens something in me, hearing that sound. Flashes of the battles play out before my eyes. Me, cutting down Vitiosyns in Vaydell. Seeing others cut down. So many horrors of war have I witnessed. The worst were Grawllik's beheading and the night of meeting Deezalo at the graveyard.

Turning away, I'm humbled by the things I've learned of myself. The darkness within. It's there. I feel it. Ryco's seen it. I suppose, Zymarc has too. But only *I* can defeat it. It's my battle, to win or lose, just as it was Talok's war of being a young king, who then became a good king. A merciful one too.

"Tyler?" Gemma's voice quivers. She rubs my back.

I didn't even realize she stopped the sharpening. Didn't hear her footsteps approaching.

"You're safe," she whispers. "We're home."

I turn to face her. "This isn't my home anymore, Gem. But I will try to make it my home again. Will you help me?"

"It's what I'm trying to do now." She purses her lips.

"Then tell me what to do, Galloway. Or keep talking. Don't stop. Don't leave me alone with the quiet, to think."

Gemma sniffles. She wipes away her building tears. She pats my chest. "Talking, I can do. Are you ready for loads of stories from school? The summer camps. The family dinners. Judo class. And? Oh yeah! This other world called Muraine." She grins.

The Barrage of Gemma starts. I smile and laugh and tease her right back, adding sarcasm where I can. We prepare dinner together. Gemma only had to call Kane once, to bring her a special ingredient. I showered, while she kept dinner stirred and simmering on the stove. As the water ran down my back, I played her stories over and over, willing myself to focus on the joy rather than the dark.

Now freshened up, I'm back in the kitchen, and peering into the living room. I Mensa-div to Gemma, *"Your satchel's on the table. I put your suitcase under my bed. We'll get it back to your house another day."*

Gemma opens the front door.

"Tyler Ravier?" Kane calls to me, pointing to his own hairdo. "You're looking good these days. Happy to take the blame for that. And, you, Gemma. Finally got that short hair you've been wanting."

"Is Kaida home?" Gemma asks.

"Mm-hmm." Kane nods tensely. "Got a new boyfriend too. You're not going to like who it is, either."

Gemma clenches the paper bag containing the secret ingredient. "A familiar face?" she asks.

"Yup!" Kane states.

"Great!" Gemma cringes, as she heads back to the kitchen.

Kane asks me, "Should I stick around, until Amira gets home?"

Gemma pops back into the living room. "Just come see that we're actually making dinner." She yanks him by the arm, forcing him to follow. "You witnessing it will be enough for my dad."

Kane whips out his cell phone. "There's this thing on here. What's it called? Yeah, a camera. Smile for a picture. He wants more proof than hearsay."

Gemma's shoulders slump. "I hate having my picture taken, Kane."

I nudge Gemma's shoulder. "Let Kane make the lie believable, Gem." I flip her hair in front of her face, and she bursts out laughing. Then she inhales a strand, and starts coughing. I smile proudly for the picture. And Kane takes it, then shakes his head.

"So," he says, while Gemma fixes her hair. "You ever going to tell me who really took you to town for a cut?"

"Nope!" Gemma proclaims, her hair now out of her face.

"All right," says Kane slowly. "I can only keep covering for you for so long, girl, before the lies give way. If I know the truth, I might be able to keep it from falling down to crush you. Something to think about."

"I'll consider it, big brother."

Kane sighs. "That's all I ask. That, and have a pleasant dinner with Tyler and Amira. Plus, don't do anything stupid."

Gemma motions to her short hair. "Too late for that."

"Yep!" Kane says, "Text me, when you're headed home. I want to see the look of horror on Ginger's face. It'll be one of those moments you never forget. Plus, I need to be there for your safety. Make sure she doesn't attack you on sight."

He leaves.

Soon afterward, dinner's ready.

Gemma keeps things set to warm. The smells swirling around are almost as good as Zima's Kitchen.

Though it opens without a sound, the front door closes firmly.

I hear Mother set her things down on the coffee table, then her shoes being taken off and then dropped.

She takes in a lengthy breath but pauses partway through it.

Gemma and I sit at the dining table, playing a round of Deduce Who, the windmill painting resting peacefully to the right of me, *watching* us. I briefly wonder if it has a partner painting.

Anxiously trying to hold still, Gemma asks, "Does your dude look . . . happy?"

"Gem," I reply flatly. "That's like. *All* of them."

"But I mean like, *really* happy. Like Haru getting praise from my dad, kind of happy."

"I've never seen that," I admit.

Footsteps pad across the kitchen floor. "Did the two of you cook dinner?" Mother's voice holds a pitch I've never heard.

Getting up, Gemma says, "Tyler wanted to cook dinner tonight. I just helped."

I ease my chair out, wanting to run to embrace my mother hard. But that's out of the ordinary for me. I must be calm. Collected. Strong. I can't let on what I've been through. In this moment, I must be ordinary.

"How was work?" I ask her with surprising calm.

"You cooked dinner for us?" My mother asks again, shock in those eyes just like mine. Just like Zymarc's too. It's another mystery to unravel. Is Zymarc truly the father of my mother?

Shrugging, I look away. "Hope you like it."

She strides to the cupboard that keeps the plates. "I could taste it, as soon as I walked in the door. Yet I couldn't believe it. I thought, well . . . no matter what I thought. Let's eat."

I clear the table, Gemma sets it for dinner, and Mother dishes up the food.

As she's doing so, she says, "Kane mentioned the haircut, warned me, actually. Asked that I not overreact. I haven't a clue why he was worried. You've picked a rather stylish look. Those twins might get jealous, and want the same look." Mother sets down one of the serving dishes, before taking her seat. "Was that the point?"

"Nah!" I shake my head. "Just wanted a change."

"Good!" says Mother. "It's time for a change, isn't it?" Not waiting for an answer, she takes a bite of lamb, and a rather pleased expression crosses her face.

"Does it meet with your approval?" Gemma asks my mother.

Mother just nods.

And so the consumption of the delectable meal Gemma and I made commences. The three of us talk about the Jack Wayeland interview. Some of the drama with the Craven twins. And other things. Anytime I start to run out of words to say, Gemma fills in. She always has something to say. And she makes my mother smile, even laugh. Nothing's better than watching the two of them.

That's when I wonder, *Will she like Skylin too? Someday, she'll need to know the truth. But I want to find his killer, first. I want truth and closure to come in the same moment for her.*

After finishing what's on her plate, Mother says, "I could get used to this, Tyler."

"That good, huh?" I ask.

"That good," she agrees. "You're still going to see that therapist I mentioned a few days ago, though. There's no getting out of it. You can argue all you want—"

Grinning, I interrupt. "I'm happy to go."

Mother gawks at me. "You're not going to try to weasel out of it?"

I shake my head. "Nah! But can it be group therapy? I'm tired of one-on-one. I want Gemma to go. Will you go with me?"

Startling, Gemma nods. "Sure. There's got to be something I need therapy for. The bullying. Yeah. I can get help for that. The food addiction too. And, now, cooking addiction. The first day we go, I'll make brownies and ice-cream, and cookies and cake." Pausing, she adds in div, *"And spiked Farivoo."*

I lean back and laugh. "You're going to make us fat, Gem. Then we'll all just be sad and fat and lazy, wallowing in misery together. We'll have to join you in Judo class, to work it off."

Gemma states, "Better to be sad and fat rather than thin and sad, wilting down to nothing. But the Judo. That's a good idea. Now you have to take up Judo. You walked right into it. No walking out." She starts gathering our dirty dishes.

Mother takes them from Gemma, however. "You two cooked. I'll clean. Take the game in the study, and stay a bit longer, Gemma. Unless there was somewhere you needed to be?"

"No, ma'am. Just beating Tyler at Deduce Who."

Mother starts on the dishes, and Gemma grabs the game box.

We head down the hall to my father's study.

I open the double doors, relieved that Soren isn't standing there in greeting. Part of me wonders if he'll always haunt me a little. I close the doors behind Gemma, as she heads for where we played Clue together, weeks ago.

The curtains behind my father's desk sway. Instantly, I'm glancing about the room for anything amiss: open window; dragon painting's slightly crooked on the wall; and my father's desk chair faces the window. Nothing else is different. And I sigh, relaxing some.

Wind blows harder through the open window. I rush to close it, fix the curtains, then turn around.

A man's sitting curled up in my father's desk chair. I startle, almost lunging at him until I realize who it is.

"I was thinking," he says.

Gemma gasps, and drops the game box.

He bounds out of the chair, to collect all the pieces. He sets them on the game table, starting again, "That I might stay here with you, Ravier, for a while. Just until I can forgive my father for not executing Zymarc on the spot, as soon as he and I were separated. He should've at least made an attempt. And, since I'll never forgive him for that, a 'while' actually means 'forever.' This is what I was thinking before coming here. That the *former* Onyx Prince might understand the dilemma the *current* Onyx Prince faces. That he might take me in, and let me stay. What do you say? Can Earth handle two like us?"

"How did you get here?" I ask.

"That doesn't matter." Glancing away, he shakes his head.

"Setharyn," I state. "You *have* to go home."

He motions around. "But I want *this* to be my home."

"My mother doesn't even know about Muraine," I reply, in desperation. "You can't stay here."

"That's a pity she doesn't know." Pacing about, Setharyn clicks his tongue. "It's a wonderful place. At least, it was until a certain psychotic Vitiosyn started running about, ruining it all, while making me watch. So, here's how it is." He stops his pacing. "I either stay here with you, or I go live in the forest. I cannot go back. For, if I go back, I will most definitely assassinate Zymarc. I *hate* him that much."

Wide-eyed, Gemma asks, "Tyler, what do we do?"

Setharyn pouts a little, before saying, "That's obvious. You give the homeless Onyx Prince a new home. Come on! What's the worst that could happen?"

"Quite a lot," I reply.

Setharyn states, "I can teach you loads about magic. And Muraine's history. There's so much I know. Give me a chance."

I stare at his pleading face, recalling that Soren's cheating of magic helped bring about this Onyx Prince, now standing before me. The decision of what to do rests heavy on my shoulders. I cannot believe what I'm about to say.

But, at this point, I muse, *what have I got to fear?*

I tell the Onyx Prince, "You can stay for a while."

Afterword

Dear Reader:

What a ride this has been, writing these three books. I never would have thought, by age 31, I'd have three books to my name. It is a great honor. So many things, really. I hope my characters and the story have won you over. Just know, it's not over yet. I'm just warming up. I can feel it. Tyler demands that more be said. And who am I to stand in the way of an amazing story being told through his eyes? Truly, there are days I simply feel like the characters are writing the story. That I'm their voice. Lol! I feel what they feel. I laugh with them, cry with them, cheer for them. As they grow, I grow. Not the other way around. Being a writer has changed who I am, as a person. I'm better, kinder, stronger.

It was the first week of school, in the Fall of 2005. I had just turned fifteen, that summer. A lot of things happened, prior to the school year starting. I was never the same. This story helped me stay sane, during a time in my life when I was lost and lonely and hurting so, so bad inside. I needed an escape. And I got it, through writing that first ugly, horrible draft in a spiral-bound notebook. The original story started off something like this: What if horses had wings, and could fly? A boy once found this horse, and he named her Angel. He found her in the woods by his home. A boy named, Tyler Craven. This is their story.

Fast-forward fifteen years later . . . Caucasian Tyler Craven became Tyler Malik Ravier, half Caucasian and half Iraqi. Angel was renamed to Awngelic and then finalized as Awngeleik, similar in sound to the name of Angelique. I won't even mention what Gemma Galloway's name used to be. I will say this, however. Tadashi's name was Ted! Amira was Gloria. All the characters were Caucasian. I changed that, in 2013. Started thinking of new things too. New names. New story-lines.

I still have six books planned. Therefore, a lot of brainstorming and writing and agonizing over the story ahead. It'll be a grand time! Please stick with me to the end. I'll do my best to make the wait worthwhile for you.

All the best,
  Julie

Appendix I: Cast of Characters

« »

Earth

« »

The Raviers

Alec Ravier – supposedly Miriam's son. Tyler's eight-year-old cousin he's never met.

Amira Hajjar Ravier – Tyler's mother. Married to Lance for seventeen years. Her family came over from Iraq, in the 1980s.

Lance Oren Ravier – Tyler's father, died one year prior to the start of Volume I: Kings of Muraine.

Miriam Ravier – Tyler's aunt whom he has never met. Lance's little sister. Supposedly lives in London, England.

Tyler Malik Ravier – only child of Lance and Amira. Fourteen years old at the start of Kings of Muraine. Thirteen when his dad died.

Galloway Household

Gemma Elizabeth Galloway – Tyler's classmate and neighbor. The rich girl. Ends up proving to Tyler that she's changed, in Volume I.

Ginger Jones Galloway – Gemma's mother. Lance's girlfriend, during one of his years in college. Jack Wayeland's girlfriend, in high school.

Haru Maki – assists with security at the Galloway mansion and does odd jobs for Tadashi.

626

Kaida Galloway – Gemma's older sister.

Kane Himura – oversees Tadashi's home security. Is also protective of Gemma.

Molly Smith – went to school with Tadashi. Longtime friend of the Galloway family. Now, she's their full-time cook.

Tadashi Galloway – Gemma's father. Met Lance Ravier when they were teenagers.

Other Mentionables

Adair Tomatsu Galloway – Tadashi's grandfather, Gemma's great-grandfather. Apprenticed to Soren of the Monel.

Bruce Parson – founder and CEO of Aviridian Corp, a company dealing mostly in technology.

Ginger Snap – Lance's horse. The only one Tyler convinced his mother not to sell after his dad died.

Goliath & Cosmo – two of the Raviers' horses they sold to Tadashi Galloway.

Hunter Mason – Kaida's former boyfriend. Accused of stealing one of the Galloways' paintings.

Jack Wayeland – friends with both the Galloway family and the Raviers. Allegedly saw the "Bear-Wolf," while out on a hunting trip.

Jed & Jaxson Craven – two of Tyler's closest friends. Jed is the older of the twins and has an attitude. Jaxson is quieter and more easygoing.

The Phantom of Muraine – mysterious being, who wrote notes to Tyler in Volume I. Also protected Tyler and Gemma from the lurking beast, near Mirror Lake.

»–«

Muraine

»–«

Paragonians

Callie of Dysarda – was there in the Eye of Paragon (Eyo'el), for the yearly festival's celebration. Befriended Tyler and Gemma, during her stay.

Castle of Sosha (Metsa) – a sentient castle in the Eye of Paragon. The only structure, aside from the Arkivara, that survived the Vitiosyn's attack in Kings of Muraine.

Eyo'el – The Arkivara of the Eye of Paragon. Eyo'el de Pawv'Ragaen refers to the city. Eyo'el can refer to either the Arkivara or city, depending on the context. Tyler learns more about her, in *The Onyx Prince*. She is the centermost Arkivara of Paragon.

King Kailon (Kailon of Dysarda) – was king during the time of the Withrasyns' curse. Took in the Withrasyn women and gave them a new home.

King Sosha – Talok's father. Brother-in-law to LanSoren. Married LanSoren's little sister, Miriam.

Kristos of Dysarda – younger brother of King Kailon.

LanSoren of Trauvo – Lance Ravier's real name. Full name: LanSoren eldes Trauvo-Rawshuen. Mysterious cause of death. Odd relationship with Zymarc of Vitiosus. No one really knows how well the two knew each other, or the nature of their interactions.

Leira of Dysarda – Kent's mother. Lokasi's wife. After Kent's little sister died, she and Lokasi separated. She has been away from Dysarda for eleven years. In Volume I, Kent mentioned that she's with some Sorsryn bent on exploring Muraine.

Madeleine of Dysarda – a friend to LanSoren. One of Paragon's finest tailors. She and LanSoren designed the Sleeping Dragon coat for Tyler. Knows all of the King's Guard quite well, as she is the one fitting them with new uniforms every year. Lost a third of her memory during the attack on Eyo'el.

Marion of Trauvo – Lance and Miriam's mother.

Miriam of Trauvo – Talok's mother. LanSoren's little sister. Has a different father than LanSoren. Allegedly died when Talok was five.

Yigoshi – one of the top Blacksmiths of Paragon. Well acquainted with many in Paragon's government: the Paragonian Sovereignty.

Zima – owner of and head cook at LanSoren's favorite tavern: Zima's Kitchen. It's where Tyler and Gemma had their first meal in Paragon. It's also where Tyler was served Farivoo for the first time.

Paragonian Sovereignty, in order of rank

King & King's Guard:

King Talok of Paragon (Pawv'Ragaen) – Tyler's cousin. Lance's nephew. Miriam and King Sosha's only child. Age 16. Became the Paragonian King, when he was barely thirteen. His uncle helped to bridge the gap in his nephew's lack of experience and wisdom.

Quall of Trauvo – First of the King's Guard. Age 47. Full name: Quallendeis'el Trauvo-Rawshuen. Grew up with LanSoren, in the Paragonian city of Trauvo.

Ryco of Paragon – Second of the Guard. Age 28. Full name: Ryco'Eldeis de Pawv'Ragaen. Born and raised in the Eye of Paragon, or rather Eyo'el de Pawv'Ragaen. He and Tyler had an instant dislike for one another, in Volume I.

Kent of Dysarda – Third of the Guard. Age 25. Full name: Kentel le Dysarda-Reine. The only King's Guard who is pure Vaegon—a Keeper of Memories.

Musgrae of Bethsaide – Fourth of the Guard. Age 24. Full name: Musgrae'es de Bethsaide-Reine. Has a "pinprick" of Greyvon in his lineage.

Warren of Veldar – Fifth of the Guard. Age 23. Full name: Warren'Eisawv es Veldar-Ruedawn. If Tyler had been born and raised on Muraine, he and Warren would be the same age.

Siege of Gayza – Sixth of the Guard. Age 20. Full name: Siegel le Gayza'Ragaen.

Eli of Kirja – Seventh of the Guard. Age 17. Full name: Eliyek le

Kirja-Ruedawn.

Ben of Yharss – Eighth of the Guard. Age 15.5. Full name: Rueisvben'el Yharss-Rawshuen.

The Arkiveis: Keepers of Memories

Grover of Paragon – was once the Arkivy of Trauvo. When the Arkivy position opened up in Eyo'el, he got it. Now, he's considered the Prime Arkivy.

Eishal of Trauvo – is actually the oldest of the Arkiveis, even though Grover considers himself to be the oldest. Knew LanSoren quite well.

Lokasi of Dysarda – the current Arkivy, for the city of Dysarda. Kent's father. Has tended all active Arkivaras, except for the one in Eyo'el.

Drauggen of Veldar – descendant of the first Arkivy.

Ragaz of Kirja – the Arkivy of Kirja. The shortest and stoutest of the Arkiveis. He's also the Keeper to Gayza. The Arkivara there is thought to be dormant. That's why there are only seven Arkiveis.

Yevolta of Bethsaide – tends the youngest Arkivara. Calmest of the Arkiveis. Well acquainted with Musgrae.

Nyrim of Yharss – the youngest Arkivy. Age 20. He and Ben were raised as brothers, even though they are not blood brothers.

The King's Advisers:

Zepharre of Paragon – head adviser to Talok. Grew up with Ryco and EmiKal, in The Eye of Paragon.

EmiKal of Trauvo – secondary King's Adviser. Though he grew up in Eyo'el, he moved to Trauvo after finishing Guard School.

City Warriors:

Zepharre of Paragon – also the City Warrior of Eyo'el.

Symovi of Yharss – both the Warrior & Medic of Yharss. Raised Nyrim and Ben as his own sons.

City Architects:

Khyra of Paragon – the Head City Architect. Oversees the cities' innovations, primarily in Eyo'el. Once she turns sixteen, she gains her full authority as the Head Architect.

Eva & Dhavin of Paragon – Khyra's parents, who are often traveling. Architects to both Yharss & Dysarda.

Reptestro – Zepharre's great-nephew, one of his oldest brother's grandchildren.

Greyvons, in order of age

Matriarch Shena – deceased. Died in the War of Ichors Von.

Merlynite of Vondurheil – born in the same generation as Jasper. Oldest member of Jasper's personal Von pack of Thedaesiim. Droediin is the last of his living offspring.

Jasper of Vondurheil – the current Alpha of the Greyvons. Was well acquainted with LanSoren.

Mekka of the Vons – one of the last alpha candidates still competing for the title.

Rorka of Pariah – one of the few matriarch candidates to have existed, since the death of Shena. Has her own pack called Theocktras.

Droediin, Son of Merlynite – Mekka's last competitor for the title. Eighth son of an eighth son.

Taeso – one of the newest members of Jasper's Thedaesiim. Gemma's favorite Vonsai.

Dragons (dyns)

BlacKaidyns:

Prelude – deceased. Vaegon Prince Kristos' dragon, in the age of King Kailon's dynasty.

Reign – was the dragon of the former king, Sosha. Now he calls himself Talok's Dragon.

Scepter – Zymarc's head dragon. Also Reign's older brother. Leads the Vitasadyns and their Vitiosyn riders.

Mystadyns:

Claudys – a Mystadyn who frequents Paragon often. Well acquainted with Siege.

Delta – a Mystadyn who often accompanies Claudys.

Echo – often goes wherever Delta decides to go.

Rubidyns:

Matriarch Fayel – deceased. Died in the War of Ichors Von. Farivoo Eldyn was named after her: Fayel's River Food for the Dragons.

Rentwar – King of the Rubidyns.

Rentwar's Recruit – previously under Rentwar's pupilage. Has been promoted for doing Rentwar's bidding.

Other Species:

AshCrawft – ancestor of the GreyLyres, of Grawllik.

Ayzareel – younger brother to AshCrawft. Ancestor of the Darklyres.

Ezareen – Father dragon of AshCrawft & Ayzareel.

Grawllik – a GreyLyre. Technically a distant cousin to the present-day Darklyres.

RaeZorgin – father of Grawllik, a GreyLyre. Set off ten to eleven years ago with Khrendawll, King Aygor's older brother, to hunt down certain items. Aygor hasn't heard from either of them in eight years.

Horses (EquiNeins) & Hybrids

Awngeleik – the dragon-horse (Equidyn). Was given to LanSoren, as a sign of goodwill from Zymarc of Vitiosus. Since LanSoren's death, King Zymarc has been demanding that she be returned to him.

Brash – the horse with broken wings. Was the first of the horses Tyler healed. Ended up being Ben's companion horse, for the journey to Yharss.

Nebukahn – half Greyvon, half nein. Mekka's cousin. Often travels with the youngest Jokryn brother.

Sorsryns

Withrasyns:
Avilon of Paragon – last living Withrasyn. No one's seen her for quite some time.

Awleesia of Waykron – former queen to the Withrasyns. Negotiated with King Kailon, to secure a new home for her women. Knew Gyronawv and King Jzorrdawv. Was also well acquainted with Soren.

Gaula – Withrasyn Ancestor of the Darklyres. Partner to Ayzareel. Considered the first official Dragon's Mistress.

King Morseif – last Withrasyn King. Married to Awleesia of Waykron. Had many children. Only his daughters lived on, to have families in Paragon and elsewhere.

Monel – first Withrasyn King. Brother to Soren and Nyxane.

Soren of the Monel – a Sorsryn of Old (a Sorshrynak). Able to meddle with time. Revealed his identity to Gemma, when she was a little girl. Able to interact with LanSoren. When summoned from the past, he's able to interact with what's around him. Knew Adair Galloway.

Onyx Sorsryns:
Casseil – Setharyn's mother. Died in childbirth. ReNovak's one and only wife.

Ghebina – part Onyx, part Kyanite. A barkeeper at one of the Onyx inns.

Hydvar, Kaalon, & Sawrro – three Onyx Warriors within thirty years or less of reaching their Siveyra Journey.

King ReNovak – current Onyx King, when Tyler and Gemma visit Muraine.

Prince Lemawr – Gyron's nephew. Adopted son of the Laykonian King, Lemara.

Prince Setharyn – King ReNovak's only child. Died from a Vitiosus spell. Had the Vardiya's Mark on his forehead, at birth.

Siveyra Gyronawv (Gyron) – Warrior of the Nyxane. Bound to serve the current Onyx King.

Smythe – an Onyx Warrior. Assigned as a barrack guard, when Tyler meets him.

Zenzar – a young Onyx Warrior.

The House of Dovak: line of succession, ending with ReNovak

Nyxane – first Onyx King.

Dovak – daughter of Nyxane.

Siveyra-lord Novak – only child of Dovak. Father of Divoldane.

Divoldane – daughter to Novak. Mother to RethnoBane.

RethnoBane – second son of Divoldane. Father of Aygawnax.

Aygawnax – only son to RethnoBane. Father of Jzorrdawv and ReNovak. Was the Onyx King, when Gyron became the Warrior of the Nyxane.

Jzorrdawv – ReNovak's older brother. Married to **Ayna**. Never had children. Died on the battlefield. **ReNovak** inherited his throne.

Emerassasyns:

Dezarin of the Aeown – a Siveyra thrice over (Diveyra). Clan: Emerald.

Evie – Rozeth's cousin. Deceased.

Rozeth of the Aeown – a former apprentice of Dezarin's. Was a twin apprentice, partnered with Ryco. Clan: Emerald.

Amethysts:

Queen Kovin – wears a crown of white metal – the White Crown. She is head of the Three Queens.

Queen Arkawna – wears a silver crown – the Silver Circlet. She is tallest of the sister queens.

Queen KaaVus – wears a golden crown – the Golden Diadem. She is the youngest of the triplet sisters.

Deathasyns:

Neeka – a lady Deathasyn Tyler meets in Vaydell.

Viido's Hymn – a young Deathasyn, who asked a Sodon request of King ReNovak.

Vit'Athos – one of Vosh-Vendei's brothers.

Vit'Dod – last Deathasyn King. Knew RayVora and Soren well. Was executed by Zymarc.

Voldrake – one of the rioting Deathasyns, who comes to Vaydell.

Vosh-Vendei – a Sorshrynak. Half-brother to the Geldryn twins: Geldreis and Gendran.

Perida's Kree – one of Vosh-Vendei's brothers.

Other Sorsryns:

Pralueday – an Emerald-Onyx girl, whose name means: the joy that comes before an important event.

Vayohl – Lemawr's mother. Former lover to Gyron's younger brother. Mother of Princess Krina. King Lemara claims that she's been missing for ten years.

Vitiosyns, in order of rank

King Deezalo – deceased. Born as a Geldryn Sorsryn, he became the first Vitiosyn.

King Zymarc of Vitiosus – leads the Vitiosyn Clan. In a former century, he killed King Vit'Dod and the rest of the royal family of Deathasyns. As such, he was able to take over most of the Deathasyn Clan.

Prince-General Azabahk – Zymarc's right-hand man. Underwent ReNovamen. His knowledge spans far back into the past.

Belzara – a Prime-Warrior. Also underwent ReNovamen. In a former life, she served King Deezalo himself. She was once favored by Zymarc.

Something she did turned him against her, but not enough for Zymarc to have her executed.

Caleiso – former Apprentice to Vitiosus. Now promoted to the rank of Prime-Warrior. Perhaps Tyler's most hated enemy.

Belzara's Beloved – a small Vitiosyn woman who was dispatched by the Onyx Warriors under Gyron's command. Rather than leave her in the forest near Eyo'el, Gyron and the warriors take her to the Onyx territory of the Nyxane.

Ahmoset (Squad Leader) – one of Zymarc's Vitiosyn Warriors.

Belgorr of the Moors (Scarred-face) – a Vitiosyn Warrior under the command of Ahmoset.

Jokryns, in order of age – all are Siveyras (older than 1,000 years)

RayVora – Queen Mother to the Jokryns. Was partner to a Metimoran named GrawVadian. She is primarily Amethyst and Deathasyn, but has bits of all the Sorsryn clans in her lineage.

Paydinn – Keeper to the Watchman's Log—a Book of Time. RayVora and GrawVadian's firstborn son. He's considered to be the Father of the Jokryn, for the many children he has helped to produce. His eyes change color with his mood.

YaeVorkk – the second of RayVora's sons. Has taken up the trade of being a mentor. He has had many apprentices over the centuries. Currently, he's under a sleep curse. No one is sure where he is, but it's suspected that he's in a Vitiosyn prison.

Zeekryn – the third of RayVora's sons. He has been a warrior. Now, he's a scholar. Very knowledgeable in many things. But he has no interest in getting involved in the war, and no interest in starting a family like his brother Paydinn. However, he's willing to travel with the Paragonians, and guide them through the Metsundai (Forest Lake).

Craesha – the youngest of RayVora's sons. Very mischievous, but also powerful. Most of his magic is used for toying with those around him, especially his older brothers. Often goes out on adventures with

Nebukahn. Doesn't take much seriously.

Metimoras, in order of age

GrawVadian – former King of the Metimorans. Abdicated the throne, around the time Deezalo's Regime reached its height. Was keeper to the most powerful of the six Books of Time he helped to create: The Grandmaster Journal. No one has seen it, since he died. His family believes that his killer holds that first created Book of Time.

Queen Iissa – current Monarch of the Metimorans. She was blessed by GrawVadian, to lead the Metimoras. She knows the Jokryn family quite well, as they come to pay homage to GrawVadian's former status as king.

Illveidra – Paydinn's first wife, now deceased—rather, in the process of a transformation.

Giveidra – Paydinn's second wife, who's now his first wife.

Laykonians, in order of rank

Liffa-Aroh – Lemara's father. Originally from the world of Jextoran.

King Lemara – Ruler of the Deep. King of the Laykons (Laepurians). Lives in the underwater city of Deivahl. Father of Princess Krina. Married to Vayohl.

Princess Krina – King Lemara's firstborn.

Brinkorr (Brink) – a teacher to the young Laykonians. Was the former bodyguard of Prince Lemawr, before Lemawr left Deivahl. He's also the only one who cooks King Lemara's dinner. When necessary, he's head warrior to the Laykonians.

Broena – in charge of Princess Krina's intellectual education and training in warfare.

Dae'loog Dauger – a Water Dragon (Legharian). The official greeter to those on the surface looking to visit the city of Deivahl. During harvest time, Laykonians do not accept visitors.

LeiHymurs – one of the races that came with Liffa-Aroh from Jextoran. Larger and more animalistic than Laepurians. They visit Deivahl often and are especially fond of playing games with the Laepurians, in the Driv-vell Den.

LeiHymids – mutated LeiHymurs, adapted to live in deeper waters for long periods of time. They never visit the surface. They merely travel up to Deivahl, when necessary. Otherwise, they live deep in Muraine's ocean.

Notes about Laykonians:

Lemara, Krina, Brink, Broena, and other Laykonians like them in appearance are considered to be Laepurians. Legharians are the dragons. LeiHymurs are a six-limbed species adapted to prefer water, even though they can survive on the surface for a time. They are the defense of Deivahl's waters. In times of the harvest, they are the gatherers. LeiHymids are a subspecies of LeiHymurs that evolved over time to be able to live deeper in the ocean. The closest they can get to the surface is the city of Deivahl.

Spirits, Vardiyas, & Such

Spirits:

Aeowneis – Tree Stag. Holds the essence of light, and memories of life.

Sivondel – The Black Flame. Spirit of the Black Dragon. Holds the keys of death. Life essence is given to him, through the flesh and bones of the deceased.

Vardiya(s):

Aysivak – a Vardiya. Able to wield time. Introduced in Chapter 3 of Volume I. Named, in Chapter 2 of Volume II.

Others:

Gatroes (Gatro) – six-limbed, hairless beasts. They prey on Darklyre offspring, primarily. Night creatures (nocturnal). The preferred food source of the Greyvons.

Nerosh of the Mettos – a former master to the twin daggers: RotaSyn & NeiSator.

The Phantom – mentioned by LanSoren, in entry 233 of the English journal. LanSoren felt he had to find the truth of what and whom the phantom is, to escape his fate of death.

Darklyres, in order by clan then rank

Clan Ayzaga (Ayzagauns):

SynKievas of Ayzaga – name means Cheater of Black Heaven, or Marauder of Death (Sylvadyn meaning). He has stolen a whole armory from Arsyn, over the past five years. Also has an obsession over knowing a person's lineage, and the meanings of names.

Clan Jhire (Jhiresons):

Jhire – the firstborn son of Gaula and Ayzareel. Deceased. At some point, he lost one of his wings. He was the founder of a city named in his honor. The term Parasogyn was re-coined to Pairos, by Jhire. A golden likeness of him and his seven siblings reside within the Palace of RawZend.

Arsyn of the Jhire Clan – Leading Sentinel of Jhire. A well sought-after widower, among all Darklyres. Older than he looks. As such, he has a sensitivity to dawn's light that younger, more evolved Darklyres do not.

Skylin of the Jhire Clan – Arsyn's only child. The same age as Tyler and Gemma: 14. Loves history, enchanting weapons, and winning bets. Talks a lot.

Clan RawZend (RawZendians):

Khrendawll – Aygor's older brother, who abdicated the throne. He and Grawllik's father set off ten to eleven years ago to hunt down certain items. Aygor hasn't heard from either of them in eight years.

King Aygorinaith of RawZend (Aygor) – the current King of Clan RawZend. Resides in the city of Grevagg. Is considered the head of the three Darklyrian kings. As such, it is his responsibility to oversee all clan events and various gatherings. Though he is not partnered to anyone, he takes in orphans and troubled children. In Volume II, he has a total of 10 wards. He assigns trainers, to oversee the wards' daily care. Past age 16, they no longer have trainers.

Seqwhyett of RawZend – newest Crown Sentinel. Age 20. Used to be one of the King's Wards. As such, he knows all of them rather well. King Aygor gave him the named blade: Veldakryn.

Deamond of RawZend (Dea) – the oldest of the wards. Age 19. Nicknames include: Demon Dea, the demon, Sentinel's Tease, etc. Is said to be fierce, after waking from death. Highly intelligent and well-read. Also very devious. Aspires to be a Crown Sentinel.

Keturah of RawZend (Ketty) – second oldest ward. Age 13. Constantly disobeying King Aygor. Generally combative with others.

Sonya of RawZend – third oldest ward. Age 12. Easily frightened. More levelheaded than Ketty. Genuinely cares for others, even if she's just met them.

Litreez of Grevagg – Keturah's trainer. Instructs a handful of Darklyre girls, but oversees the education of many residing within the city of Grevagg.

Orteel – Sonya's trainer.

About the Author

J.R. Vaineo is a self-published indie author, residing near Salt Lake City, UT. In 2018, she published her first book: Kings of Muraine. When she's not writing, she and her husband, Jessie, have many adventures together. Mostly in cooking, hiking, photography, analytical talks, and fawning over their three adorable fur-babies.

While J.R. Vaineo writes mostly fantasy fiction—combining elements of epic, portal, paranormal, and dark fantasy—she enjoys reading all genres; except, perhaps, for horror stories. After finishing a creative writing program, through the Institute of Children's Literature, she continued to improve her craft of writing. In 2013, she graduated with her AA degree in psychology. During that time, she expanded on many things, especially focusing on what would prove invaluable for fleshing out characters and plot twists. What started out as a writing prompt, in 2005, has now become a nine book series she is currently working on: The Journals of Ravier. Sometimes, she is quite jealous of the characters' abilities, found within her own writing. If that is a sign of anything, it is this: Obsession.

You can connect with me on:

🌐 https://www.jrvaineo.com

🐦 https://twitter.com/JRVaineo

📘 https://www.facebook.com/j.r.vaineo

🔗 https://www.instagram.com/j.r.vaineo

🔗 https://www.goodreads.com/JRVaineo

🔗 https://www.bookbub.com/authors/j-r-vaineo

Subscribe to my newsletter:

✉️ https://www.jrvaineo.com/newsletter

Also by J.R. Vaineo

The Journals of Ravier books are about finding yourself amidst the losses, victories, and journeys in life. You begin to discover, through personal trials, who you are at your core. Come join Tyler Ravier on his winding path to an important truth: Why did his father have to die?

Kings of Muraine – Special Edition
https://www.jrvaineo.com/where-to-purchase
That night changed my life, forever. I saw them. Two strangers from another world. The one with fangs claimed to be a king. But he was a young king, at best. The King of Paragon. He broke the news to me. My dad wasn't from Earth. Instead, he was from a world filled with magic: Muraine. His other home.

The Special Edition for Volume I has the Murainian Calendar, as well as tables that list off the members of the Paragonian Sovereignty.

Hunt the Dragon Within – Special Edition

https://www.jrvaineo.com/where-to-purchase

I went to Muraine, searching for my father's killer, yet I was greeted by war. I had to do something. And I did. Now, Paragon is broken. And so is their king. Can I save him? Can I also save one of the Sorsryn Clans, from being slaves to the Laws of Neutrality? They are as a weapon, won by the Vitiosyns. Now, it's only a matter of time. Someone's going to die. Will death claim me? Or will it claim Zymarc, Talok, or . . . someone else?

The Special Edition for Volume II has lists of Iconic Weapons, the Ocquilli of Magic, and charts of the 5 particles of magic, as well as some monologues from Soren of the Monel.

www.ingramcontent.com/pod-product-compliance
Lightning Source LLC
Chambersburg PA
CBHW030654190726
48286CB00001B/23